JAGO

RODNEY R. JEFFRIES

INCITARE BOOKS

Published by Incitare Books
P.O. Box 343282
Bartlett, TN 38184-3282

Incitare Books and the colophon of an elephant with its right foot on a
stack of books are trademarks of Incitare Books.

JAGO

ISBN 0-9785494-06

Manufactured in the United States of America

All praise and honor to God for allowing me to realize the dream of authoring a published book. I look to Him always for guidance and inspiration.

This book is dedicated to my lovely wife, Brenda, and to my wonderful son Johnathan. You are my gifts from God, and all that I do is with the hope you will prosper from my efforts.

ACKNOWLEDGMENTS

I would like to express my deepest thanks to my mother, Annie, and my sister, Monica. They are an excellent reading committee. Special thanks to my mother for believing in me and encouraging me every step of the way, I appreciate you for that. I also want to convey an extra special thanks to my friend, business partner and faithful counselor, Brenda, my wife. And in no particular order, many thanks to Tyrone Moore, James Smith, Eric Nason, Lucy Ann Richardson, Earl Wilhite, Ty Jones, and Jean Leasure; all of whom played a part in bringing this book to fruition; I would never have gotten this far without each of you.

To the patrons of my work, thank you so very much for your support. I hope you find this book to be a thoroughly entertaining and thought provoking read.

JAGO

One

The year was eighteen sixty-six. The American Civil War was ended. The great man President Abraham Lincoln was long dead, shot in the back of the head by John Wilkes Booth, a cowardly assassin to those of the North, and a defender of liberty to those of the South. Many restless Negro souls wondered what was to become of them without their benefactor, Abraham Lincoln. Lincoln was a just man, and without his courage, strength, and compassion to lead them, surely, the days ahead would be filled with uncertainty.

It was midst this uncertain time that many newly emancipated blacks left the South in search of a hopeful future they were certain was not to be had in the South. The narrow and busy roads were filled with them, scurrying back and forth with meager possessions in pursuit of a chance at happiness long denied.

All over the war-torn South on every thoroughfare, people would come and they would go. The roadways of Jago Mississippi were no different. Day and night, people came and went. It was six weeks from summer, and an old black man in ragged clothing sat beneath the shade of a willow oak tree watching them come and go. He was thin. This was due to the fact he would rather drink his meals than eat them. His hair was mostly hoary and matted with bits of dried grass stuck in it. His eyes were red and his skin was ashy. He had hardly a tooth in his mouth and his dirty clothing could have used a good washing. Around these parts, he was known as Uncle Whoot, the local drunk. He was alone in the world, and wasn't really anyone's uncle. He was simply called uncle, because white people did not call any black man sir, no matter his age. Rather, if they wanted to show an older-black person a measure of respect, they bestowed the title of uncle or aunt upon the person.

On this day, Uncle Whoot noticed something which struck him as peculiar. In the distance, coming off a fork in the road, he saw a lone weary rider headed towards him. The rider sat tall in the saddle atop a strong-sorrel steed with a flaxen tail and mane. He was a light-skinned Negro, but not so light skinned that he might have been mistaken for white. His hair was wavy and black, combed to the back, and laid down on his head beneath his tan hat. He was a very handsome man, but his face was intense and gruff. His brown eyes were tight with anger. He had the look of one who knew no peace wherever he went. He was probably

1

once a union soldier, as evidenced by the Union Army pants and shoes he was wearing. He probably came from someplace far away, as evidenced by the tan Indian-style top he was wearing, which was not known in these parts. All this Uncle Whoot could tell just by looking at him. However, the one thing Uncle Whoot could not figure out was why, when all the black folks on this road were leaving the area, he seemed to be coming. The rider came closer and closer. Finally, he stopped on the side of the road closer to Uncle Whoot. The rider steadied his horse.

"Good morning, sir," he said, with a very northern tone, like an educated white man, but without the drawl associated with Southerners.

Uncle Whoot had never heard a black man talk like that. He nodded cordially at the man and replied, "Mornin', uh, is ya in da army, calvary?"

"I used to be infantry, but not anymore," the rider answered.

Uncle Whoot smiled. "Well, son, iffen ya ain't army, ya best be takin' off dem Union Army pants befo' dese white folks 'round heah gives ya a Chinaman name like 'He Hung High'."

The rider chuckled and introduced himself. "My name is Micah Gray, I'm looking for my brother. His name is Elijah Wright, and before the war, he was a slave on the Cadence plantation up near Holly Springs."

"Everybody 'round dese parts know Elijah," answered Uncle Whoot, "he a good man."

"Where might I find him?" Micah reiterated.

"Keep dis road bout uh hour," Uncle Whoot explained, "on da right side, sittin' back off da road aways, you gon' see a lit' house wit' a rusty-tin roof, and a lit' garden wit' plenty of young tender corn stalks growing in it. Dat be yo' brother's place."

"Thank you," Micah said, as he spurred his horse onward.

"Ya welcome, 'member what Ah said 'bout dem pants," Uncle Whoot yelled to Micah as he rode away.

Trotting along, Micah thought of how good it would be to see his older brother Elijah. Micah had not seen his brother in ten years. When Micah was fifteen, abolitionist on the underground railroad helped him escape to freedom. During that time, freedom was all that mattered to Micah. He was willing to trade what little family he had in exchange for it. Freedom was everything it seemed, or so he initially thought. Conscience and circumstance had not allowed him to start a family of his own. When he found himself alone, and far from his loved ones, he missed them more than he could have possibly imagined. There were many days, especially in the beginning of his liberty, when he wondered if he had made the right decision. As war between the states progressed, and the opportunity presented itself, Micah joined the Union Army to fight for his brothers still in bondage.

When war was at an end, Micah longed to see the family he had not known in a decade. He wondered what Elijah would look like after all these years. He wondered what Elijah's family might look like, if he had one. Micah wondered how Elijah would feel towards him. Ten years earlier, when Micah knew for certain that he would attempt an escape, he did not tell Elijah or their mother for fear they would try to persuade him to change his mind. Micah simply left in the middle of the night without a goodbye. Would Elijah be angry with him? Would Elijah understand it wouldn't have taken much to harvest the seeds of doubt, which surely would have paralyzed him enough to forfeit his one chance to escape to freedom. Thoughts such as these consumed his mind until there was no more time to wonder. Micah had arrived at the place described to him by Uncle Whoot, and recognized it as the house of his brother Elijah. Micah dismounted his horse. He stooped down and picked up a bit of earth in his hand. He thought to himself, that it was good soil: fertile, rich, and dark brown. Then, he stood and saw a man plowing in the cotton fields. There was twenty acres of cotton growing or being planted. Surely, this is my brother, Micah thought. Micah took the horse's bridle in hand, leading the horse behind him, as he started to walk down the path toward the man in the fields.

The man in the cotton fields watched Micah approaching. It was the heat of the day and unseasonably warm for that time of the year, except at night. The nights were quite chilly. Perhaps, the stranger was one of those passing through on his way North, thought the man in the fields. Maybe, the stranger needed to water his horse, or was down on his luck, and wanted to ask a bite to eat, if it could be spared.

Although, Micah was too far away for the man to make out his features, there was something familiar about Micah to the man. The man could not put his finger on what it was, though. The man stopped plowing just as the sun revealed Micah's face. The man knew this face. Although it was older and hardened, it was the face of his younger brother Micah. Elijah immediately loosened his reigns and ran to his brother. He fell upon his neck and hugged him tightly. Elijah's heart was filled with joy overflowing as he cried and kissed Micah's forehead.

"How is ya, boy?" Elijah greeted. "it good ta see ya!"

Overwhelmed by this strong show of emotion from Elijah, Micah's eyes quickly filled with tears. Tears he could hardly hold back. Temporarily, he was so filled with emotion that he could not speak. It was so good to

Jago

know that after ten years he had been missed as much as he had missed. It was a very tender and touching moment not often shared between men. There were so many questions Micah wanted to ask. So many things he wanted to say. So much, he did not know where to begin.

Across the field stood a little shack of a house, a dogtrot home. The look of it was such that if the elements had half-heartedly challenged it; the house would have offered little resistance before collapsing to the ground. The house, small and unpainted, was made of an aged-gray cedar wood, and it sat several feet off the ground, resting on smooth flat stones. The roof was a rusted-gray tin, with a red-brick chimney spouting out of it.

"Is ya hungry ?" Elijah asked. "Come on ta da house, and we'll habe a little somethin' t'eat."

Micah was still at a loss for words, but Elijah chattered on just as if it were ten years earlier and not a single day had been lost between them. Elijah was twenty-seven, but he did not know the exact date of his birth. Slave owners often kept their slaves in complete ignorance, even as it related to time, neither did they keep good documentation of the birth of slaves. All that Elijah knew of his age was that he was born during the fall twenty-seven years earlier. He was a tall man of six feet. His complexion was very dark, and his features were strong. He was a man of virtue, and he sought the things of God. He walked as if he were a prince; that is, he walked with confidence, as though he were someone in a world that considered him to be nothing. He had a charisma which reached out and embraced your trust. As the two men neared the house, Elijah interrupted his own chatter and called out loudly. "Josephine, Josephine, come on out heah, woman!"

Two women quickly rushed out of the house. The first was an older woman, whose stature was short. Her hair was salt and pepper in color. She was a mulatto woman. Although she was a little on the heavy side, her face was very attractive. She was Josephine's mother, and she was called Mama Julia. The second woman was Elijah's beloved Josephine. She was thin and tall with very compassionate eyes. She stood about five feet and nine inches tall. She, like her mother, was little more than mulatto in skin color. Her beauty was unmatched, almost surreal.

"What all da commotion 'bout out heah, Elijah?" Mama Julia asked.

"My lit' brother, Micah, done come home like da prodigal son," Elijah said excitedly.

"Well then, come on round heah, boy, and let us git a look at ya," Mama Julia said to Micah, as she stepped off the porch to hug him.

4

She was followed closely by Josephine, who also wanted to welcome Micah into the family. Micah's eyes were fixed on Josephine, thinking she was very beautiful, as Elijah ushered them into the house. Micah took a seat at the square-oak table, which seated four. It was at this time that he uttered the first words Elijah had heard him speak in ten years.

"You've done well for yourself, Elijah," Micah complimented.

"Why thank ya, Micah," Elijah said, as Josephine sat two cups of vegetable soup in front of them.

"Where ya been all dese years, Micah?" Mama Julia asked, sort of gleefully.

"New York City, Canada, you name it. I've probably been there, even been as far as Mexico," he answered.

"So, you been ta Mexico, huh?" Josephine asked.

"Yes, I have," replied Micah.

"Ya speak Mex?" Josephine inquired.

"*Un poco*," Micah answered.

"Huh?" Josephine responded, with a puzzled look on her face.

"*Un poco* means 'a little' in Mex, Josephine," Micah explained.

"Oh," Josephine said, as she nodded her head in understanding.

"Ah never knowed dat," interjected Mama Julia, impressed with Micah.

"Why ya move 'round so much?" Elijah asked, curiously.

"There was a law called the Fugitive Slave Law, which read: any run away slave caught shall be returned to slavery. And, since you never knew what sorry soul might be lying in wait to ambush you, and sell you back into slavery for any reward that might be offered, I thought it best to move around every now and then," Micah explained.

"Ah believe Ah done heard 'bout dat law," Elijah replied.

"Well, thank da good Lawd we ain't gotta worry 'bout dat now," Mama Julia said.

"What life like up north?" Josephine asked.

"Ah bet up north was da land of milk and honey, huh?" joyfully, stated Mama Julia.

"Well, I tell you, it was not the peaceful existence that you might expect it to be," answered Micah.

"What cha mean?" Elijah asked.

"I was free, meaning I could come and go as I pleased, but I wasn't truly free," Micah explained, pausing somewhat.

"Go on," Elijah said.

"I wasn't truly free in that white men usually refused to work with blacks, and they wanted to pay us less than they would pay a white man.

Some people wanted to disrespect me as a man, call me boy, or talk down to me. I always stood up for myself, both verbally and physically, if need be. I am not one to back away from a fight. Most of the time, I came out on top, but sometimes I lost. Those were usually the times I was fighting against numbers, though.

"If I went into a restaurant, often they refused to serve me, and for no other reason than I was black. I naturally protested vigorously, as I feel one must do if things are to be made better, but usually it did little good," Micah reflected.

"Dey treated ya dat way up north? Ah thought dey was better 'an dat," Mama Julia said, surprised and somewhat disappointed. "Ah thought da North was da land of milk and honey fuh black folk."

"It was and remains as I have said, even now," Micah affirmed.

"It break my heart ta hear dat," Mama Julia said.

"Mine too, we always heard up north was da place fuh black folk," interjected Josephine.

"And, so it was, it was not a perfect existence, but I was free. 'And, I would rather be free in the worst conditions than to be a slave in the very best of conditions' to quote a very well known abolitionist, Frederick Douglas," Micah explained.

"Ah kin understan' dat," Elijah said agreeably.

"Is ya got somebody special ya need ta be sendin' fuh?" Josephine inquired.

This was Josephine's not so subtle way of asking Micah if he had a wife and children, or at least a woman somewhere. Elijah and Mama Julia were curious to know the answer to the question as well, but Elijah wouldn't have asked. At least not like that, as he felt it lacked propriety to do so before he and Micah had a chance to renew their acquaintance. Mama Julia was going to get around to asking soon, but that shameless Josephine beat her to it. Micah looked at Josephine, and smiled. "No, there is no one special that I need to send for, Josephine."

"Youse a mighty good-lookin' man not ta haves no woman waitin' fuh ya. What's wrong? Ya ain't no suga' breeches is ya?" inquired Josephine shamelessly.

"Josie," Elijah said, looking at Josephine, as if to say behave yourself woman.

Micah laughed and scratched his chin. "It's okay, Elijah. I love women. I love them very much. I just haven't found anyone that I feel that way about as of yet, Josephine."

"Well, it's plenty guls 'round heah. We'll git cha fixed up," Josephine assured.

"Josie, please," Elijah said, embarrassed.

"Well, ya knows Ah is," Josephine said, looking back at her husband unashamed.

Micah's mood changed swiftly to a much more serious one, which left Elijah wondering what was wrong.

"I stopped by the Cadence place looking for you," Micah commented somberly.

"Den, ya seed momma's grave?" Elijah sadly remarked.

"When did she die?" Micah asked.

Elijah took a deep breath and said, "she died five years ago. She got the cancer, and it took her on away from heah. Ya know, Ah really wa'n't spectin' her ta pass when she did. She always got sick a week or two, den sudden like, she would be up again, feelin' like her old self. Da mornin' she died, Ah guess, Ah was spectin' her ta suddenly be up again, smilin' and feelin' like her old self."

In a trance-like state, with tear-filled eyes, Micah sighed and said, "Lord knows, I hate that I missed seeing her one last time. I'd like to have been there with her when she passed. Almost since the day I left, she was on my mind. Sometimes, when I was home sick, I would dream about how she use to rub my head when I was feeling low, and fix me a sweet potato pie. I would always feel better when I woke up. Right now, I regret every second of the past ten years."

Sensing Micah's deep sorrow, Elijah rose from his chair, and placed his hand on his brother's shoulder in a comforting fashion. "Don't regret," he said, "It's true momma use to worry 'bout cha. When ya first left, she was scared dey was gon' brang ya home beat and broke, or dead. When dey didn't, Ah would catch her laughin' ta her self. She laughed, 'cause you outsmarted 'em all, and won ya freedom. She was proud dat you was able to do dat. It made her happy to know yo' chil'ens was gon' grow up free. You wa'n't 'round, but you was always in her heart."

Seeing the mental suffering Micah was going through, the hurt inside Elijah was made fresh and new, but he managed to be a comforter to his little brother. Nevertheless, the hurt was visible on his face. Josephine moved to her man, and wrapped her arms around him. "It's gon' be alright," she said to comfort the comforter.

"Y'all mens gon' haves us all cryin' iffen y'all don't stop," Mama Julia said, as her eyes filled with tears.

It was at this point that Micah realized Josephine was Elijah's strength and glory. Elijah had done well for himself, very well indeed.

"You take all da time ya needs ta git though dis, Micah," Elijah comforted, "And, iffen ya need ta talk or cry. You jes' go right ahead, and know dat O'm heah fuh ya."

"All us is heah fuh ya, Micah," Josephine added.

Just that little bit of encouragement seemed to help. It was enough to help Micah pull himself together. He was not alone anymore. He had family to lean on.

The next morning found Elijah sitting on the front porch of his home, on the top step. He was happier now that Micah had returned than he had been since the passing of their mother. It was a mighty fine morning from his perspective. He thought of the times when all three of them were together, Micah, their mother, and he. It was good to remember, thought Elijah. As long as in your mind you can see and hear those who have returned to the bosom of God, they aren't really dead. They continue to live in you, he thought.

"Elijah," Micah called, standing right next to Elijah.

"Hey, Micah, Ah didn't hear ya come out da house," Elijah replied with a great big smile on his face.

"I could tell as much. Wherever you were, it wasn't here," Micah said.

"Ah was thankin' 'bout when we's all together, momma, you, and me. It was a good place ta be."

"What were you thinking of?"

" Ah kin see her tuckin' us in at night, tellin' us dat we somebody and dat we matter," Elijah said, fondly remembering.

"I remember her saying that to us at bedtime, and telling us to say our prayers. I also remember those stories she use to tell us about a beautiful dream place, with trees that bore fruit of every kind, and we could eat our fill, and sit around all day doing nothing if we wanted. We could go hunting or fishing all day if we wanted, and there would be nothing said about it," Micah said, also caught up in sweet memories.

"It's a shame momma didn't git ta see us live dat dream."

"Huh?"

"We ain't got fruit trees of ever' kind, but we kin lay 'round, and hunt, and fish all day iffen we wont. What you say we go deer huntin', or rabbit huntin', or squirrel huntin'?"

"It's been a while since I have been hunting."

"Dat mean ya wanna go?" Elijah asked, uncertain of what Micah was saying.

"Are you sure that you want to lose a day in the cotton fields?"

Elijah laughed. The statement was truly amusing to him. "Micah, Ah been workin' in da fields my whole life. Now dat Ah's free, Ah thank, Ah kin miss a day in da field. Besides, we still need fresh meat. Lest Ah do, dey's plenty animals 'round heah fit for meat, jes' gotta hunt 'em. Ah figure Ah deserves it afta all dem years of eatin' mostly corn meal and salt pork," Elijah said somewhat bitterly.

"Corn meal. I remember those days. I can even remember being a half-naked little fellow eating corn meal mush from a troth with my bare hands, like swine. Let's go hunting, Elijah. I think we are deserving, just as you have said," Micah said, also bitter, having a moment to reflect back.

"Kin ya really 'member dat far back, Micah. Ya couldn't been no mo' 'an three or four," remarked Elijah, astonished that Micah remembered.

"I remember just the same."

Elijah looked down at the ground. His eyes pooled with water and his lower jaw tightened as he was filled with melancholy remembering such demoralizing events. He looked at Micah. "How ya s'pose dey could habe done us like dat? It wa'n't right."

"They didn't bring us to this country to treat us right, Elijah," Micah answered sternly and soberly.

Out in the wilderness, Elijah and Micah hunted wild game. They were hoping to kill a deer. Elijah was quite fond of deer meat. Neither of them was much of a hunter in times past, but of necessity Elijah had become a very good hunter. He did so several times a week; that is, when he could make time. Micah was also a fair hunter. When out in the field as a soldier, rations often ran low, and the men would hunt to secure a meal. Although Elijah was hoping to have a successful hunt, he had really sought the opportunity to get a chance to be alone with Micah and just catch up on things. They approached an old fallen oak tree in a clearing, and decided to have a sit down for a moment. Elijah pulled out a small leather pouch filled with deer jerky that Josephine had made. He offered Micah some. He accepted, and they snacked a while and talked.

"This is very good jerky," Micah complimented upon tasting it.

"Josephine makes real good jerky. Massa Cadence loved his venison. Josephine used ta be one of da gals dat cooked fuh 'im." Elijah explained.

"Josephine was a slave on the Cadence plantation?" Micah asked, not remembering her.

"Yeah, he bought her and Mama Julia 'bout a year after you left. When Ah first seed her, Ah thought dat da angels had done lit down from heaven. Ah knowed right den dat she was fuh me." Elijah said, happy to recount his first encounter with Josephine.

Micah chuckled. "Did you really now?"

"Ah showly did," Elijah answered, "she wa'n't all high-minded neither. You know some of dem black folks workin' in da big house didn't wanna habe nothin' ta do wit' us workin' in da fields."

"I remember how it was."

"Micah, Ah'm gon' ask ya dis, and iffen ya don't wanna say. You ain't gotta. Why you leave us? Why ya run off and didn't say a word?"

Micah was wondering when Elijah would get around to asking that question. He was surprised it was not asked sooner. "When we were children, I didn't know I was a slave; nor did I have any idea of what it meant. But as I became older and began to understand, I noticed certain things. I noticed that no one ever seemed to smile, never seemed to be happy, except for us children. Not even momma seemed happy. The only two people that I ever remembered seeing truly happy were Carl and his Maggie when the master said they could hop the broom and live together as man and wife. I was less than eleven, but I was so happy that they were happy. I think it did every slave on the plantation a bit of good to take part in their happiness. Everyone seemed a little happier. It was that way for weeks until their wedding. On that night, their wedding night, Master Cadence's eldest son came down to the quarters, and told Carl to wait outside of his cabin. He took Maggie on her wedding night; while her husband was made to listen just outside the door. I never saw Carl or Maggie smile after that. It was then that I first knew I never wanted to be in a situation where someone could just walk into my home, and steal my happiness for no other reason than he could.

"A few years later the strangest thing happened. A few of us kids was playing around the slave quarters, when a bird fell from the sky. It must have flown into the side of the cabin where we were playing around by accident. I remember walking over to it. It was lying on its back, breathing very labored. I could see it was bleeding from it's mouth. I seemed to be the only one concerned about the poor little thing. I knew that it was dying. I picked it up. It did not struggle to break free. I guess it couldn't. I tried to give it water, and it tried to drink. I remember feeling so much compassion for it. It took the bird about twenty minutes to die. I shed a tear for it, and when I looked up from crying. I noticed that nobody, save me, even cared that the poor thing had passed. It struck me then. Would my master even have compassion enough for me to give me a drink of water, or let you and momma care for me should some tragedy befall me. Do you remember Ms. Lizzy?" Micah asked.

"Ah remembers her," Elijah answered.

"Who was she?"

"She was da old woman who use ta watch us lit' on's while our mommas was out doin' their chores."

"What happened to her?"

"Dey sent her away, set her free," Elijah replied.

"What happened to her?"

"She froze ta death when da first good snow came. "

"They sent her off to die. She was too old to be of service to them anymore. She needed someone to help her take care of herself, and they sent her off alone without food, water, or shelter. That's what happened when a slave outlived his usefulness. They take your whole life. When your body bends beneath the weight of care, they tell you when it is time for you to die," Micah said, hoping it was explanation enough for Elijah. What Micah was trying to say was not lost on Elijah. It was a powerful moment for him. "Do you understand what I'm trying to say here, Elijah. I am not good at getting my point across sometimes. I just couldn't let them do that to me? I don't know if a man is entitled to anything on this earth, but I don't believe it is for another to decide that for him."

"Ah understand," Elijah said, feeling empathy for his little brother.

"Do you really, because I have often wondered if you could. It is all the explanation I have to give," Micah said sincerely.

"Da life of a slave is a hard one, and fuh too many of us, too short. Ah don't blame ya fuh wontin' mo' fuh yo' self dan da lot of a slave. Many a times Ah was wontin' ta be wit' cha, but my life is heah. Knowed it fuh sho da day Ah saw Josie. Momma was sick too. Where else could Ah be but heah?"

"It took more courage to stay," Micah earnestly confided, "I just couldn't stand it."

"Oh, Ah chose ta stay, but not as no slave. Ah went ta Massa Cadence, and asked him iffen Ah could work a bit of earth. He said Ah could, and he let me keep a portion of da earnings. Durin' da growin' season, afta we's finished in da cotton fields. Ah'd go ta work on dat bit of earth. Ah'd stay dere late in da night, till da overseer made me go in. Ah needed ta be fresh fuh da field he'd say. Ah'd work ever' day, and momma helped by making pies fuh me ta sell 'fo' she got too sick. It took three years ta do it, but we made five hundred dollars toward buyin' my freedom. A slave in his prime like me went fuh a thousand dollars or more, so Ah still had a long ways ta go, but Ah was sho Ah could git dere," Elijah explained.

"You raised a thousand dollars to purchase yourself?" Micah asked, surprised at his brother's will and determination.

"No, didn't habe ta, Ah guess God knowed what Ah was goin' through. Ah guess he knowed how heavy my sorrow was soon ta be by da passin' of momma. He used a sad day ta make a better one. On her death bed, Massa Cadence came ta see momma. Ah don't know why. Maybe, it was 'cause of all he done ta her. Momma asked him ta sell me my freedom fuh three hundred dollars, and afta she died. Massa Cadence manumitted me. We had saved up six hundred dollars by den. As sad as da day she died was, momma died happy ta know both her chil'ens was free. When she gave up da ghost, Ah felt like we's all free now," lamented Elijah.

Micah thought of his mother for a moment. He believed that he understood why Eli Cadence basically gave Elijah his freedom for their mother's sake. It had to do with the sorted tale of Master Cadence and their mother, Corletta. Corletta had been a slave on the Cadence Plantation her whole life. Eli Cadence took notice of her when she was age fifteen. He had every intention of making her into an odalisque. One more concubine among many slave girls on his plantation. He made advances toward her, offering gifts and special privileges. Yet, she did not warm to his advances, or readily accept his offerings, which only made him desire her above all others.

Corletta's heart belonged to another, a black man. The young man had no last name. He was simply known as Wright. At age sixteen, Corletta became pregnant by Wright, also a slave on the plantation. Eli had told her she was for him, and that she should never know another. The fact that she was in a family way angered him to no limits. She never told Eli who the father of her child was, but he found out anyway, and had Wright whipped and sold. This was why Elijah never knew his father, but he honored him by taking Wright's name as his own when he was freed.

Corletta hoped that because she had been spoiled in Eli's eyes. He would not desire her any longer. Eli's desire; however, did not cool for Corletta. Shortly after giving birth to Elijah and turning seventeen, Eli came to Corletta. He no longer offered gifts. He didn't care anymore if she gave herself freely. He knocked her around, and took by force that which was his possession. Corletta made it known to Eli that she despised him. It mattered not to him. He continued to know her frequently, and eventually, she conceived. A daughter was born to her, but the child was still-born. Eli continued to know Corletta. She conceived again, and bore a son. She called the child Micah, after a prophet in a minor book of the Bible. She did not hate the child, as any woman who had been raped to such an outcome had the right to feel toward such a child. That was simply the villainous nature of slavery, she surmised. She loved Micah without restraint. Her tribulations did not end at being raped at will. For some unknown reason, Eli made Corletta work in the main house as a maid. A curious move considering Corletta was not a light-skinned woman, as was preferable for house servants. It was during this time that Corletta conceived for the fourth and final time by Eli.

It was known to Mrs. Cadence that her husband visited his passions upon Corletta far more frequently than he did upon her. She also knew that Corletta bore him a son. A half-breed white nigger bastard of a son to constantly remind her that her husband preferred the company of a Negress to herself. In her jealousy, she pushed Corletta down a flight of stairs after observing she was suffering from morning sickness, and Corletta lost her un-born child. After she recovered, Mrs. Cadence made Corletta's life an agonizing misery. She started by having Corletta's hair cut very short, a very common practice of white mistresses. Sometimes Corletta came home bleeding from the head or back; where Mrs. Cadence had delivered a jealous blow. Perhaps, this was what Eli Cadence had in mind all along. Perhaps, this was his punishment for Corletta disobeying him by giving herself to another. He genuinely cared for Corletta, and hated himself for it. She was after all just a slave. It was strange to him that he should care so deeply. Love, or something like it, will often drive a rational person to irrational actions. Eli had no true desire to see Corletta hurt as Mrs. Cadence often hurt her, but he wanted Corletta to feel but a measure of the pain, and heartache, he felt at knowing she did not want him.

If this move was meant to break Corletta, it failed. She grew strong in her tribulations. She learned to be as happy as it was possible for a slave to be in spite of her circumstances. After many years, the visits of Eli diminished, and he allowed her to return to the fields. He never stopped caring for her, never stopped wanting emotional reciprocity. And so it was that as Corletta lay on her death bed, he visited her. Even though she was a slave and her opinion was of no value. Her opinion mattered to Eli. He granted Elijah his freedom as a way of asking Corletta to forgive him of his untoward deeds against her. He did not wish for her to go to the grave feeling only contempt for him. This is as it was, and this was the reason Micah believed his biological father and master gave Elijah his freedom.

Perhaps it eased his conscience, eased the burden of knowing that he did Corletta as wrong as wrong could possibly get. It was as if he had grown to be a better man than he was in the past, and remembered that Corletta was a creation of God, a human being with feelings.

As for the relationship between Micah and Eli, they never had much of one, nor would they ever. Eli was killed during the war, not more than two years after Corletta's death. It was no great loss to Micah to learn of his passing. He did not know the man, nor did he want anything from him, not even the name which was rightfully his. Micah took the last name of the man who helped him escape to freedom. The man's name was Brigham Gray.

Elijah and Micah had returned home from hunting. They did not kill a deer as hoped. They did, however, manage to snare a few rabbits. Caleb, Elijah and Josephine's three-year-old son, was very fascinated by the fresh kill. He kept poking at the rabbits, almost expecting them to move.

"Leave dem rabbits 'lone, boy," commanded Josephine.

"What we gon' do wit' dem rabbits?" asked the little one curiously.

"Ah's gon' cook 'em, and we's gon' eat 'em," explained Josephine.

"We gon' eat dem rabbit, mama?" Caleb asked.

"Yes, we is, lit' man."

"Awful 'cited 'bout dem rabbits ain't ya, boy?" interjected Mama Julia, who was helping to prepare dinner.

Caleb laughed, as he ran over and tugged at Mama Julia's skirt tail. She was trying to fix supper, and Caleb was going to make her trip and fall if she was not careful.

"Stop tuggin' at me like dat, boy, befo' you make me fall," Mama Julia laughed, not really wanting him to stop, but to be careful.

"He botherin' ya, Mama?" Josephine asked.

"No, chil', Ah enjoys 'im. Wish dey was mo' of 'em runnin' 'round," Mama Julia hinted.

Josephine caught the remark and smiled. "Well, we is workin' on it, Mama."

"Y'all need ta work a lit' harder. O'm gettin' ta be a old woman; Ah wanna be 'round ta see 'em."

"All thangs in God's good time, Mama." Josephine giggled.

"Mama, Ah wanna eat dem rabbits," said Caleb.

"O'm 'fraid it's gon' be a while, Caleb," Josephine answered.

"Ah bet dem rabbits gon' taste good, ain't dey ?" the boy asked excitedly.

"Ah 'spect dey is," agreed Josephine.

"Why don't ya go play, boy. We gon' call ya when it's ready," Mama Julia said.

"Ah wanna stay wit' y'all," Caleb said.

"Well, sit at da table and stop scootin' 'round," Mama Julia instructed.

"Okay," said the small boy, as he sat at the table.

Caleb took a seat at the table, but was hardly quiet. He seemed to ask as many questions as there are stars in the clear-night sky. So thoughtful and insightful were his questions for a three-year-old, that Josephine and Mama Julia were amazed. Finally, the questions ceased, and the little one dozed off to sleep. Time marched on, and Caleb was awakened by the smell of something good. Excitedly, he ran to Josephine from his bed. Josephine was the only person in the house with him. Elijah, Micah, and Mama Julia were all on the porch engaged in conversation.

"Where dat rabbit, Mama?" asked the little man, as he crawled into his mother's lap.

"Ready fuh dat rabbit is ya?" Josephine asked playfully.

"Ah is, Mama," Caleb assured.

"Well, sit on down ta da table den," Josephine said, putting Caleb on the floor.

Caleb sat in the chair at the table that he could barely see over. "Dat Rabbit taste good don't it, Mama?"

"It's right good iffen Ah say so myself," Josephine answered.

"O'm gon' eat dat rabbit, Mama," exclaimed Caleb so excitedly.

"Yes," Josephine said, as she fixed him a plate of rabbit smothered in gravy, served with a warm   biscuit with homemade butter and covered with wild honey.

Caleb was hungry and dug right in.

"Is it good, Caleb?" Josephine asked.

"Mmmm, Mmmm, Mmmm," is all the boy was heard moaning, enjoying the meal.

Josephine saw that Caleb was pleased. She heard laughter from outside, and decided to join the others on the porch. She left Caleb enjoying his meal. Once outside, she was soon caught up in the entertaining company of the others. She had all but forgotten Caleb. Suddenly, they heard Caleb scream. It scared Josephine badly. She jumped to her feet, and rushed inside. Elijah and the others were also startled. Elijah was second to enter the house. Micah and Mama Julia entered hurriedly behind the concerned parents. Caleb was sitting at the table with his hand over his mouth crying. Everyone was wondering what was going on.

"What's wrong? What's wrong?" Josephine asked with nervous parental concern.

Caleb said nothing. He simply continued to cry, with his hand covering his mouth.

"What's wrong wit' cha, boy?" Elijah said, snatching the boy's hand from his mouth.

Caleb looked at Elijah. Sincerely and innocently he said, "Dat rabbit, done bit my tongue!"

The room erupted into laughter.

"Boy, you done bit yo' own tongue," Mama Julia cried with laughter!

Two

Three weeks had passed since Micah's arrival. It was a breezy night. Something had happened this night; something which was about to change this quiet and peaceful community into one of fear and suspicion. It was late, almost one in the morning. All within Elijah's house were fast asleep. There was a thump. The noise awakened Josephine. The door bumped repeatedly, as if the wind had hold of it. She figured that the wind must have somehow blown it open. It didn't dawn on her that the door could have been opened from the inside. She dragged herself from bed, moving toward the door to lock it, before it awakened others.

Upon reaching the door, she glanced out into the night. She was slightly startled to see someone wondering around outside. It snapped her to her senses. She was just about to call Elijah when she realized that it could be Micah. She looked to where he should be sleeping to make sure. His bed was empty. The night air was slightly chilly, but Micah was standing there with no shoes, and his shirt was wide open. She reasoned that he must have had trouble sleeping due to the news of his mother's death. His mother had been dead a very long time; but for him, she may as well have just passed only a few days earlier. Josephine was concerned for Micah, and decided to go to him. Cool gusty winds blew as Josephine ventured out into the chilly night to comfort Micah. In the moonlight of the starry night, Micah seemed somehow different and strange to Josephine. He seemed to be in deep thought, as if he were bearing a burden too heavy for him.

"Micah," she gently called to him. He did not seem to hear her as she approached from behind. "Micah," Josephine called, close enough to touch him. Yet, Micah did not seem to hear her. She reached out, touching him on his shoulder. Micah sprang around, raising his right hand, swinging violently at her. Josephine, very shocked, jumped back, barely avoiding being struck. She fell backward to the ground. If the blow had connected, it would have knocked her unconscious. As she lay on the ground, her eyes grew wide and her mouth was hanging open. She began to crawl away from Micah. He gnashed his teeth and cocked his big fist as he moved toward her. It was as if she was a stranger to him, a stranger, who had transgressed against him. She feared for her life. She was on the verge of screaming in horror. "Micah!"

Her loud cry seemed to wake him. He shook his head and wobbled slightly, as if dizzy. Josephine looked at him, still very much afraid. She climbed to her feet, putting some distance between herself and Micah, just enough distance to give her the advantage in case she needed to run.

"Josephine, What are you doing out here?"

"What you doin' out heah is da question," she said quivering.

Micah looked around seemingly very confused. "I don't know."

"Micah, was you sleep walkin'?"

Micah didn't know how to answer. He was doing something out there, and he didn't know what. "Sleep walking, I haven't done that since I'm six years old."

"Do ya know what cha jes' done, Micah?"

Micah looked at Josephine, the blank look on his face said it all, he did not know what he tried to do to her.

"You don't remember tryin' ta take my head off, do ya?"

"I tried to hurt you?"

"Ya bout near scared me ta death, and ya don't remember?"

"No, Josephine, I don't."

"Ah ain't never seed nothin' like dat, Micah. What iffen Ah had been Caleb?" she said with a look on her face of concern for the safety of her young child.

"I wouldn't hurt anyone, Josephine."

"How ya know dat? Ya almost hurt me, and ya don't even remember," Josephine pointed out.

Micah was still slightly disoriented, but he knew a critical moment was at hand. He was afraid Josephine would want him out of the house. He made the arduous journey all the way here to find his family. He had nowhere else to go. He didn't want Josephine to be afraid of him. "Easy, Josephine, I won't hurt anybody. I promise you that."

There was something very sincere, and trustworthy in the way Micah said that. Nevertheless, she was worried. "Ah believes, iffen ya at yo'self ya ain't gon' hurt nobody, but what 'bout when ya git like dis. In da mornin' let's tell Elijah 'bout dis, he'll know what ta do."

Micah didn't want that, and he didn't quite know why. He began to move toward Josephine. She stepped back, still afraid. Micah could see this, and stopped advancing toward her. He knew he had to say something to win her trust. "Josephine, I need your help. I need you to trust in me. You, Elijah, Caleb, and Mama Julia are all I have in this world. I need you to search your feelings and know that I would never under any circumstances do anything to harm any one of you. Can you do that for me?" Micah was so sincere in what he is saying, that it caused Josephine to let down her guard, and dismiss her fears. Micah started to move toward her again, she did not move. He raised his hands, touched her shoulders, and looked her directly in the eyes. "Will you trust me? Will you believe in me?" he said, full of faith that she would keep this incident a secret from Elijah and Mama Julia.

"Ah won't tell, fuh now, but iffen it happen again. Ah gotta tell Elijah, ya hear?"

"Fair enough, Josephine."

They returned to the house and crawled into their beds. Elijah slept like a log. He didn't even feel Josephine climb back into bed. Mama Julia, on the other hand, slept lightly. She heard the two when they came back inside. She didn't let them know she was awake. Her mind was troubled. She wondered why Micah and Josephine were outside together, in the middle of the night no less. She hoped they were not up to what she thought they were up too. They all fell asleep, but none of them rested easy. Josephine was afraid of Micah. Micah was wondering what caused him to sleep walk and what he was doing out there. Mama Julia was concerned that Josephine might be cheating on Elijah with his brother.

After breakfast the next morning, Josephine and Mama Julia were alone in the house straightening up. Josephine caught her mother looking at her several times. The first time she thought it was just her imagination, but now she was certain that she was watching her. "Somethin' wrong, mama?" she asked, feeling rather uncomfortable.

"Is it somethin' ya need ta be tellin' me, gul?" Mama Julia said with a serious stern face.

"Somethin' like what?"

"Ah's yo' momma. You kin talk ta me 'bout anythang, and all Ah's gon' do is tell ya what's da right thang ta do," Mama Julia said earnestly, hoping this was hint enough to let Josephine know that she saw her and Micah the night before.

"What cha talkin' 'bout, Mama Julia?" Josephine asked, genuinely in the dark.

"Don't shame me, gul, wit' yo' carryin' on," Mama Julia said, grabbing Josephine by the arm, as so to make her stop cleaning for a moment.

"Carryin' on, what is ya talkin' 'bout?"

"Play dum' wit' me all ya wont, gul, but Ah know what cha up ta. Ah seed it wit' my own two eyes."

"Mama, Ah don't know what cha talkin' 'bout. What cha done seed, or thank ya done seed. Jes' come on out and tell me."

"Ah seed ya last night comin' in wit' Micah, had ta be one or two o'clock. What cha doin' out dere wit' 'im."

"Oh, dat."

"Yeah. Dat. what was ya doin' out dere wit' 'im," Mama Julia scolded.

"Mama, ya oughta be shame thankin' so little of me and Micah."

"What was ya doin' wit 'im, gul?"

"It ain't like ya thank, Mama Julia."

"What was it like, den, Josephine?"

"Micah ain't able ta sleep good lately, news of his momma passin' and all. Ah jes' went outside ta comfort 'im afta Ah woke up and saw 'im out dere."

"Ya jes' woke up, and noticed he was outside, huh?" asked Mama Julia untrusting and very doubtful.

"Yeah."

"Iffen he been havin' trouble sleepin', how come dis da first Ah done heard of it. How come at breakfast y'all ain't said nothin' 'bout he couldn't sleep last night?"

"Fuh what? we ain't chil'ens, you ain't da massa!"

"Cause it look plain bad iffen ya don't say nothin', Josephine. How ya know ya husband ain't wake up when ya got up ta comfort his brother in da middle of da night."

"Dat's how it was," Josephine said with clear resentment.

"Well, iffen he can't sleep again, in da middle of da night, and ya jes' happen ta wake up. Jes' keep on layin' nex' ta ya husband. Dat good man dat done been good ta you and me."

Josephine felt her mother had overstepped her bounds, but did not wish to disrespect her. "Mama," she said, "we ain't gon' talk 'bout dis no mo', befo' Ah say somethin' 'gretful."

Just about that time, Elijah, Micah, and a teenager from up the road known as Hop came into the house. Because of his willingness to lend a helping hand, Elijah was regarded by people in the community as a leader. Solomon Noble, an elder leader in the community, had sent Hop to fetch Elijah at once. Elijah had a troubled look upon his face. Josephine took note of it as soon as he walked through the door. "What's wrong?" She asked, certain that something had happened.

"Dey's been some kinda trouble up near Solomon's way," Elijah answered.

"What kind of trouble?" Mama Julia asked.

"Dis mornin' Collin Bailey's lit' boy, Ken, was found dead over by da creek," Hop answered.

"Dead?" Mama Julia asked, very shocked to hear this.

"Yes, Ma'am," Hop answered.

"What happened?" Josephine asked, shocked by the news as well.

"Dat's what we aims ta find out," Elijah answered.

"He done drowned playin' round dat old creek, huh?" Josephine surmised.

"Maybe," Micah answered.

"Maybe?" Mama Julia said, horrified to think of the alternative.

"We don't know what done happened, Y'all. We's gon' go find out now," Elijah said, trying not to speculate or alarm the women.

"Lawd, Ah hope nobody done hurt dat chil'," Mama Julia said.

None of the men said anything. It was an uncanny silence, inspired by fear and dread.

"Dat boy couldn't a been no older 'an ten," Josephine commented.

"Ah knowed 'im, he round 'bout eight," Hop replied.

"Mama Julia, we better git ready, and gon' over and see iffen da family needin' anythang. Ah know dat Sadie must be catchin' it, loosin' a child," Josephine said, feeling empathy for the boy's mother.

"Yeah, we need ta do dat," Mama Julia agreed.

Elijah, Micah, and Hop arrived at the creek. It was in a wooded area of cedar, pine, and oak; hidden from the view of watchful eyes. The creek was about fifteen feet wide and about six feet deep. When it rained the water had been known to almost reach the top of the bank, but in times like these, when there hadn't been a great deal of rain, a man could easily straddle the flow of water, and never get wet.

Solomon and several other men, Risby Norfolk and Ran Daniels, were already there, standing near the dead child's body beneath dappled sunlight fighting to get through the tree tops. As Elijah approached Solomon and the others, he saw the lifeless body of Ken Bailey lying near the bank of the creek. One of the men took the liberty of covering the boy's face. Solomon had a look of torment upon his face. "Good you could come, Elijah," Solomon said, as he extended his hand to shake Elijah's hand. Just as his name implied, Solomon was very old and very wise. His opinion was revered and highly sought after by the men and women of this community. No important move, it seemed, was made by any of the people there without consulting him first. He was a brave and goodly man. As a slave, he taught himself to read, and later, at great risk to his personal well being if discovered, he taught all who dared learn to read, to do so. He was in his mid to late seventies, some would say seventy-seven, but he did not know his exact age. He stood five feet nine inches with gray hair and beard. His face was dark and wrinkled, reeking of a look of good judgement. His appearance was one of meekness, but there was also a certain undeniable strength. He had a bad right leg and moved about aided by a natural colored oak walking cane. He was both friend and mentor to Elijah. Elijah and he shared many of the same qualities, which was perhaps why he held Elijah in such high esteem. Elijah had youth and prudent judgement, more so than any other young man in this community, which was why Solomon sent for him.

"What happened heah, Solomon," Elijah asked, curious to learn what information they had to go on.

"Well, we can't rightly say. We know he went ta bed last night, everythang was fine. Dis mornin' when his folks woke up, he was gone. They looked for 'im, but couldn't find 'im. About two hours ago, some kids came down heah trying ta catch some crawfish for breakfast and stumbled on 'im. They went and got ole Risby standin' there, and shortly after, he came and got me."

"Anythang else, Risby?" Elijah asked, looking to Risby.

"Dat's it, 'ceptin' his body was already cold," Risby answered. Risby was a dark-skinned man of five feet eleven inches. He had broad shoulders, and a slender waist, and was in his early thirties. He served on the side of the confederate army as a bodyguard to his master and as a fifer. He was reported to have killed two Yankee soldiers in defense of his master. Risby's master promised freedom seven years after the wars conclusion to entice him. His master treated him well, and Risby didn't particularly mind being a slave. After the war, he and his wife settled in Jago. He was at the murder scene, because he was a man of justice, a man that answered the call of responsibility when it went out to him.

"So he has been dead much longer than two hours," Micah concluded.

"Ah thank it's safe to say dat," Solomon answered, "You wanna look at 'im now, Elijah?"

Up until now, Elijah had not really focused on the body of the child lying dead, but it was time to see this treachery up close. Time to know what he, and the good men of this community, were dealing with. "Yeah, Ah reckon so," Elijah answered, not really wanting to, but it had to be done.

Risby moved over and uncovered the body. It was a very saddening thing for Elijah to see the young one lying dead on the ground. The black race had endured a great deal to secure freedom. Two hundred thousand black men, like Micah, fought in the War between the States. Many of them forfeiting their lives in the process. They made this noble sacrifice not so much for themselves. They did it more so to secure a brighter future for their sons and daughters, for all the generations to follow.

Elijah felt great pain throughout the deepest recesses of his soul, seeing the future lying dead. He grew sicker in spirit and body, with each passing second, as he watched so much hope and potential lying wasted on the ground. His stomach felt as if he wanted to throw up, and his body felt weak all over. He sat on the ground next to the body, as it was difficult for him to stand. He clinched his right fist, placing it against his forehead, as he gnashed his teeth.

"Ya okay?" Ran asked. Ran was a stocky man, but looked as if he should stand taller, because he carried himself in a responsible and respectable way that made others look up to him. He was a light-skinned, bald-headed man, with gap teeth, and was thirty years of age. Before the war he was a driver, the equivalent of an overseer, on a plantation in Natchez, Mississippi. Ran's responsible and reliable nature came to the attention of his master, and he made Ran a driver against his will. It was a job Ran despised, because it put him at enmity with his fellow brothers in bondage. When he gained his freedom, he wanted to get as far away from Natchez as he possibly could. He settled in Jago. Where his responsible and reliable nature also came to the attention of Solomon, which was why he was also at the murder scene.

"Yeah, it jes' breakin' my heart ta see such a fine boy like dis," Elijah said, responding to Ran.

"Ah know. Ah know," Ran said, feeling the same sadness.

Elijah composed himself, and climbed to his feet, kneeling beside the body. Ken Bailey was a light-skinned boy. Against his light complexion, the first thing that jumped out at Elijah, and the others, was the discoloration around the boy's neck. It appeared he was strangled with a cord or rope of some kind. "Somebody done choked dis boy ta death," Elijah said, wondering if this was what the others thought.

"He was definitely strangled," Micah concurred.

"We thank dat's what happened," Solomon also assented.

"Y'all moved 'im?" Elijah asked.

"No, we ain't moved 'im. When Ah got heah and saw he was dead. Ah sent one of da kids ta fetch somethin' ta cover 'im wit'." Risby answered.

"Do you see something, Elijah?" Micah asked, wondering why he asked if the body had been moved.

The body was lying face down with the eyes open. The arrangement of it, or lack there of, could only be described as very cold and uncaring.

23

"No, Ah don't thank so," Elijah answered, not sounding sure of himself.

"Gone say what's on ya mind," encouraged Ran.

"It's jes' dat when Solomon told us da boy was fine when he went ta bed last night, and when they woke up dis mornin' he was gone. Da first thang Ah thought was dat one of his folks done done dis to 'im, " Elijah explained.

Truthfully, all of them: Micah, Risby, and even Solomon dared to think the same thing, but would dare not speak it. Only Ran was confident enough not to consider such a thing.

"Showly, ya ain't thought dat," Ran said, somewhat amazed Elijah could fix his lips to say it.

Elijah looked at Ran. "Ah was wrong ta thank it. Least, Ah thank Ah was."

"Why?" Micah asked.

"Yes, tell us why, Elijah," Solomon sad curiously.

"Whoever done dis, hated dis boy. See da way his body layin' heah, so cruel like. Whoever done dis didn't have no feelin' fuh 'im at all, not like family folk who done lived wit' 'im his whole life. Family can't help but care. Ah don't thank dey would've left 'im heah like dis. Least, dat's what Ah thank Ah sees," Elijah explained.

It made sense to them all, but one thing bothered Micah. "Elijah."

"Huh."

"If it didn't happen this way, I mean if one of his family members, one of his parents, didn't bring him out here. How did he get here?"

"What is you sayin'?" Ran lashed out, offended that Micah kept implying that his friend and neighbor Collin Bailey could murder his own child, and go back to his house and sleep. Sleep while his child was lying dead out in the wild, where any wild animal could make a meal of him.

"It's out in the open, let's deal with it," Micah expressed.

"Ya ain't from round heah! Ya don't know us! We don't do dis ta our own!" Ran said with a good deal of rage in his voice.

"Easy, now," Risby said in an attempt to calm Ran.

"He's just tryin' ta help, Ran. We need to consider everythang," Solomon condoned.

"Can't y'all see dis is wrong. Collin Bailey is a good man. He sittin' at home right now grievin' over dis boy. He love all his childrens. It ain't right what y'all standin' heah sayin 'bout 'im," Ran adamantly professed.

"We's jes' tryin' ta git at da truth," Risby proclaimed.

"How is ya'll gittin' at da truth accusin' a good man of murderin' his own child?" Ran said, loyal to his friend Collin Bailey.

"Nobody is accusin' him of anythang," Solomon clarified.

"It sound like it ta me. Ya talkin' like he done it till ya got some reason ta thank otherwise. Sittin' heah jes' like massa, ' slave you done it cause Ah say ya done'. Don't matter ya ain't got no proof," Ran said, disgusted with them.

"It's true, my friend, I'm not one of you anymore, living up north for so long, but I want to be. I don't want to see our children done this way. We have to figure out who did this, and if we can't say who did it. We have to figure out who didn't. Maybe, that will lead us to who did. I hope you understand what I'm saying to you," Micah conveyed.

"Dat's fine, jes' don't turn it into no witch hunt," Ran said, looking Micah squarely in the eyes.

"Dat ain't what we about heah, Ran," Risby admonished.

"It wouldn't be wise to tell Collin what was said heah today, or anybody else for that matter, not until we can find out what happened heah," Solomon said, trying to put things into perspective.

"Ah won't tell 'im. What good it gon' do ta hurt ' im mo' 'an he already hurtin'?" Ran said, knowing all to well Solomon's statement was primarily directed at him.

"Good, then," Micah said.

"How ya thank da boy got out heah, Elijah," Risby asked.

"Ah don't know how he got out heah, could've come on his own," Elijah answered.

"Why would he do that?" Micah asked.

"Ah don't know," Elijah replied.

"No, Ah can't see 'im comin' out heah on his own. He wa'n't no mo' 'an 'bout eight," Risby skeptically said.

"Well, like Ah said, Ah don't know how he got out heah. O'm a guessin'," Elijah said.

Solomon kept his opinion to himself. He was not ruling out anything.

"The question still remains as to how he got out here," Micah reiterated.

To Ran, this implied that they were still vaguely considering Collin or his wife as prime suspects. He didn't like it in the least.

"Look, we ain't da law. We ain't got no 'perience handlin' somethin' like dis. Ah thank one of us oughta ride into Olive Branch and fetch da county sheriff. He'll know what ta do," Ran suggested, somehow certain the sheriff would have better sense than to suspect Collin.

"Now, dat ain't a bad idea," Risby agreed.

"Maybe," Micah said, skeptical of the law in these parts.

"What dat mean, Micah?" Ran asked.

"It means, I don't think the sheriff will really care what went on here," Micah said.

"Why ya sayin' dat," Risby asked.

"I just don't."

"We met da sheriff not too long ago," interjected Elijah.

"And," Solomon said, wanting them to elaborate more.

"I was not left with the feeling, that he felt the law was for us, except if we break it. Then I'm sure he would be quick to enforce it. Especially that fat deputy of his," Micah said.

"Well, he know mo' bout dis kinda thang den we do," Ran said, still willing to move forward on bringing in the sheriff.

"What do you say, Elijah?" Solomon asked.

"Ah thank we oughta try da sheriff, but Ah feel like Micah. Da sheriff ain't have no respect fuh us, and Ah don't thank he gon' try real hard ta git ta da bottom of dis."

"Then, we agree," Solomon said.

"No, but it's the best we can do for now," Micah replied.

"Which one of us gon' ride ta git 'im?" Risby asked.

"I think that it should be one of you," Micah said.

"Why?" Risby asked.

"I don't get on too well with the deputy. I might hurt things more than help."

"Ah will go," Ran volunteered.

"O'm gon' go wit cha," Risby said.

"Good," Solomon said, feeling resolution was shortly coming.

"What we gon' do 'bout da boy?" Risby asked.

"Ah don't thank we oughta move 'im jes' yet," Elijah said.

"You're right, da sheriff might be able to learn more heah," Solomon reasoned.

"Daylight a burnin', Ran. We best git movin'," Risby said.

Ran and Risby departed to bring back the sheriff. Solomon, Elijah, Micah and Hop elected to remain with the body because they didn't want others snooping around until the sheriff had been given an opportunity to investigate, neither did they want wild animals to start devouring it. After a while, Hop left. As Solomon, Elijah, and Micah waited, another of Collin Bailey's children, Norah, came to the scene. Norah was thirteen and was tall for her age. She was slender, but not skinny. Her skin was golden-brown. She had a round face, and today, the saddest brown eyes. As she appeared from behind a tree, Solomon was the first to see her.

"You shouldn't be heah, child," he said, knowing it wasn't a good thing for her to see her younger brother this way.

Norah said nothing. She simply stared at the place where her brother lay. So sad and somber was she. To see her so distraught made the men feel worse. Until now, the dead boy was not as real as he now seemed. Now with someone there who knew and loved him dearly, his short life had a much more profound meaning. Not that they were not sad to begin with, but Norah's emotional connection with her slain brother had drawn them in closer to this sad reality. The distance of not knowing the dead child well did not seem an effective-emotional barrier anymore.

"Norah, child, go home. It ain't good for you ta be heah," Solomon said, concerned for her mental well being.

"Ah'm okay, Mr. Solomon. Ah jes' had ta see wit' my own eyes, else it was jes' gon' keep on seemin' like a bad dream ta me," she said, seemingly calmer now.

"We are truly sorry," Micah said, feeling badly for her.

"When y'all gon' bring 'im home?"

"Soon. Da sheriff on his way now. When he done, we'll git 'im right on home ta ya," Elijah answered.

Norah sadly ambled to the lifeless body and uncovered her brother's face. The men didn't have the heart to stop her. This was one on the very last times she would have an opportunity to look upon his face, except in her mind's eye, where he would forever be young and alive. He almost looked to be in peaceful sleep, but for the frown on his face, and open eyes.

"Why somebody wanna do dis ta ya?" Norah said out loud.

The men didn't have an answer for her. Elijah wished desperately that he had one to give her, if it would have made her burden of the heart lighter.

"We really need ta take 'im home. Momma wouldn't like ta see 'im laying out dis way," Norah said, feeling so sadly for her little brother.

The men could see how much this was hurting Norah to view her brother lying in such a cold manner.

"I know this is hard for you. It might be best if you went on home, and I promise you, we will bring him home shortly," Micah assured.

"Ah don't wanna go home," Norah responded.

"Maybe, home da best place fuh ya," Elijah said, honestly believing home was where she belonged right now. There she would be able to comfort her grief-stricken parents.

"No, it's too many folks comin' 'round, tryin' ta do fuh us. Maybe, we need ta jes' be alone, so we can grieve in peace," Norah lamented.

"Folks mean well, Norah," Solomon said, hoping she would see that.

"Ah know. It's jes' dat it seem like folks too busy comfortin' da livin', instead of rememberin' da dead. My brother ain't even in da ground yet, and folks act like it's a crime ta say his name, like he never was."

The men looked at each other. They didn't know what to say to that. They didn't even know where to begin.

"It ain't jes' dat. Ah can't hardly take seein' my folks da way dey is right now. Momma keeps on cryin', and poppa ain't said nothin' since he first found out Ken dead. He jes' sit 'round kinda dazed like. Then, he'll jes' cry real hard for a minute or two. Then, he'll jes' go back ta staring all dazed like again, not sayin' nothin'. It's so hard fuh 'em, momma and poppa. Ah hate ta see 'em sufferin' so. Ta make thangs worse, my lit' brother and sister keep on runnin' round tryin' ta play. Dey don't even understan' what done happened," Norah continued to say, then she held her brother's hand, and made a vow. "Ah promise ta never forget ya, and whoever done dis ta ya. Ah ain't gon' forget it, and Ah ain't gon' forgive it. Ah promise ya dat."

"It's gonna be alright, child," Solomon said, seeing both anger and renewed sadness in her.

"We really oughta take 'im home. Dat's where he belongs ya know, wit' da folks dat loves 'im," she said somberly, sort of out of the blue.

The things she said, and the way she was acting made an already tough situation all that much more stressful for the men.

"Come on, Norah. I'm going to take you home," Micah said, hoping it was enough to prompt Norah to come with him, as he extended his hand to her.

She looked at him towering over her, as she sat next to her brother. "Ah don't wanna leave 'im."

"I know, but your folks need you more than he does right now. He is in the loving bosom of God, and he is safe there. Your folks need your strength right now to see them through. Go to them, let me take you to them," Micah said.

Norah reflected on what Micah said, and it seemed right to her. Her brother had to be in a far better place than this unforgiving, hate-filled world; where men dared to let breathe such evil thoughts as had taken her brother away from all who loved him. Still, her heart grieved for Ken. Norah would miss him dearly. She did not want to leave him, but felt that she must. Her parents did need her. Norah was strong, and felt within her heart that she had love, and for those who had the strength and courage to use it. Love was enough to hide the faults of this shameful world. The love that they had as a family would see them through this tragedy. For it had to, else life would soon lose its savor, its meaning.

"Ah'll go," Norah said, taking Micah's hand, as he helped her to her feet.

"Like Ah say, we's gon' git 'im home ta ya jes' as soon as da sheriff done, so don't fret," Elijah said, wanting her not to worry for the boy's body.

Norah said nothing more, she simply followed Micah to his horse and allowed him to lift her onto the animal, and they were on their way. They rode for a ways in silence, but that soon changed.

"Mr. Micah."

"Yes, Norah."

"When ya'll find out who done dis, Ah wanna know."

"We will inform your family, but don't get your hopes up that we will find whoever did it."

"Why, Mr. Micah?"

"It was probably some shiftless riff-raff with no place to be and nobody to love. He probably did his dirt, and has moved on through by now."

"Ah hope not, cause Ah wont 'im. He jes' can't git away scott-free without answerin' fuh dis."

"We'll do everything we can to find him, Norah, and justice will be rendered."

"Ah don't wont no justice iffen it mean whoever done dis can live. Ah wonts an eye fuh an eye and a tooth fuh a tooth. Ah wont whoever done dis ta die."

"I think that's just hurt talking, Norah."

"No it ain't, he kilt, and he oughta be kilt."

"Well, I can't tell you not to feel the way you are feeling. If I were in your shoes, maybe, I would want the same thing."

"Iffen ya was me, you would. My lit' brother ain't done nothin' ta nobody. Dey shouldn't oughta done dat to 'im."

"No, they shouldn't have."

"He ain't have nothin' worth stealin'. He ain't owned nothin', but da second hand, hand-me-down cloths on his back. It jes' wa'n't no call fuh killin' 'im."

"No, it wasn't."

Micah started to think about what Norah said about Ken Bailey not having anything of a practical value, and about what Elijah said about whoever did the killing hated the boy. Immediately, he came to the conclusion that someone white did it. If there was no motive other than hate, who but a white person would kill for hate. The white South had lost a great deal as a result of the war: free labor, wealth, property, and an entire way of life. It was enough to drive one of them to this inexcusable madness. It wasn't the strongest of reasoning, but that was how Micah felt.

Norah sensed Micah had wandered off into deep thought. "Mr. Micah, is ya listenin' ta me."

"Sorry, if I seemed to drift, but I had a disturbing thought."

"About my brother, Mr. Micah?"

"Yes."

"Tell me."

"That might not be so wise, Norah."

"Why? Ah wanna help."

"I know, but this thing might turn ugly. It might turn dangerous. I wouldn't want you to be caught up in it."

"Ya thank O'm a child, don't ya?"

"That has nothing to do with it, Norah. It's just better that you don't know everything, just right now anyway."

"But, Ah can help. Ah know Ah can."

"I believe that, Norah" Micah said in a patronizing way.

"Ah ain't no child, Mr. Micah. Don't treat me like one."

Micah smiled at Norah. She believed herself to be a woman, and truthfully many no doubt saw a woman in the flower of her youth, but Micah only saw a child. Yet, he did not want to hurt her feelings. "I'm sorry to have talked down to you, Norah. I assure you that I didn't mean too. It's just, I can't see how you could help."

Norah recognized that there wasn't really much that she could do, and respected Micah for being up front with her. "They's gotta be somethin' Ah can do. Right now, Ah almost feel like Ah did when massa use ta chase me round da plantation. He always use ta give me thangs, always tellin' me how pretty Ah was, always tryin' ta git me alone. Ah knowed what he wonted. Ah didn't wont 'im ta have it, but Ah was helpless ta stop 'im. It's only by da grace of God dat da war ended befo' he had a chance ta have his way wit' me. Dat's how Ah feel right now, Mr. Micah. Helpless."

They arrived at Norah's humble home, a run-down shack. There were a number of people standing around outside, most of them women. All of them trying to be helpful in some way. Micah dismounted his horse and helped Norah down.

"Mr. Micah," she said, looking up into his eyes, "Please, don't shut me out. Whatever Ah can do, O'm willin' ta do. Remember dat, okay."

"I will, Norah."

Micah climbed back onto his horse and rode away. As he journeyed back to the murder scene, he searched for a reason why someone would have killed Ken Bailey. He reflected upon how the black South had gained its freedom, and because of that, much more. A chance to build something for themselves was at hand. Not many in the white South were happy to see this. That had to be the answer, and the answer didn't make for good. It was not likely that the white man's law was going to do much besides give the culprit more than a slap on the wrist, if even that, for what he had done. That changed things for Micah. In his mind, the punishment must fit the crime. That was also a troubling thing, because in his mind, Elijah, the others, and he would have to dispense justice. It might be the only way that it would be dispensed if the murderer was white.

Three

It was early the next morning after the day Micah and Elijah had been reunited. The sun had risen, but had not fully cast its brilliance upon the new day. On this morning, another reunoin was about to take place. Shelby Alexander, a young-white male, stood outside a spacious white, 'T' shaped, wooden middle-class home. He was there long before the sun chose to put in an appearance. Shelby was twenty-eight with jet-black hair and blue eyes. This was his home, and still in his heart. The property was still owned by his family. It was just that he was not welcome there anymore. His father made that clear to him on the day that he left to go fight for the Union Army.

Shelby lacked the courage to knock on the door and make peace with those within. He could have been here long before now, as he was released from active service better than six months earlier, but only now had he found the courage to come this far. He did not expect that peace would come easily, but he was willing to work at it. He really wanted to knock, and see the faces of his parents and his brother. Suddenly the door opened, it was his father, Anias Alexander, and cousin, Justin. The two were discussing all that must be done this day as they stepped through the door, but silence soon filled the air.

"Hello, father... Justin," Shelby said, hoping they would respond favorably.

"Shelby," Justin responded reluctantly.

Anias said nothing. He looked at his estranged son with utter disgust upon his face. He was very head-strong and very unforgiving. He gnashed his teeth, moving toward his son. Shelby stood fast, his hands at his sides.

"You damned Tennessee Tory, get off my land before Ah shoot you where you stand!" Anias said with furious anger.

Shelby braced himself, as Anias raised his hand, striking Shelby across the face. Shelby rolled his head with the blow, but did not yield ground. The blow drew blood from his lips, but Shelby's hands remained disciplined at his sides. The insult of being called a Tennessee Tory, traitors who fought with the federalist against the South, did little to stir him to anger. His father's hand did not have the sting that it once had. Shelby hoped the worst was over.

Anias realized he could do nothing to physically hurt Shelby. He knew that if Shelby chose to fight; he would get the better of him. It frightened Anias a little. He did not let it show.

"Didn't you hear what Ah said, boy. Get off my property this instance," demanded the father of the son. He pushed Shelby who barely gave a step, quickly planting himself again. "God as my witness, Ah will shoot you, boy, if you don't get off my property. Justin, fetch my Henry Rifle from the house."

Justin, seventeen, had had enough loss in his life due to violence. His father and two brothers died in the war. He feared his uncle was about to do something he was sure to regret. Shelby was, after all was said and done, his first born.

"Uncle Anias," Justin said in disagreement.

"Fetch the rifle, boy!" Anias said dogmatically, looking back at Justin.

Justin did not want to get the weapon, but moved to do so, praying for a peaceful outcome.

Shelby and Anias stood there looking each other unflinchingly in the eyes. Shelby knew his father had nerve enough to use the weapon he had sent for and decided to speak. "The war is over, father. Must we go on fighting it," he said boldly.

"How dare you speak that way to me? You fought against everything you know, against me and your brother. Now you have the audacity to waltz back here like it never happened, like it doesn't matter!" Anias said indignantly.

"It only matters if you choose to make it matter, father," Shelby said.

"Don't make me curse the ground you stand upon," Anias said, all the more indignantly.

"I did what I thought right," Shelby explained.

"Right! How was it right to stand against your family, Shelby?"Anias said, confused and acrimoniously.

Justin stepped out of the house holding the Henry Rifle as though it were a plague, but hesitant to give it to his uncle. Anias moved back, snatching the weapon away from Justin. He aimed the rifle at Shelby's chest. The moment of truth was at hand. The moment that Shelby would know if there was room for forgiveness in his father's heart, or if Anias would take his life. Perhaps that was fitting, Shelby felt, since it was Anias who gave him life. Either way, he had decided that he would not leave until he knew. He would know, even if knowing meant being carried away dead.

"Will you kill me, father, for trying to set things right between us?" Shelby said, hoping to provoke love in his father's heart.

"Uncle Anias, please!" Justin beseeched.

"If you ain't got the stomach for this, go in the house, and shut your ears, boy," Anias said, untouched by the words of either of them.

Tension was at a premium. Anias had declared his intentions. The nerves of Shelby and he held steady, but poor Justin was breathy as his abdomen grew cold to the touch. He could feel his stomach turning. He was experiencing something close to an anxiety attack, uncertain of what he should do.

"Uncle Anias, he is your son," Justin said, hoping to awaken some sense of fatherly love in Anias.

"My son is dead. He died a long time ago. This man is as a stranger to me," Anias said coldly.

Suddenly a silver and brown haired woman ran from the house screaming in fear. It was Katherine, mother and wife of the two at odds. She moved between father and son, determined to bring this to a peaceful conclusion.

"Out of the way woman," said the husband to his wife.

"Ah will not move, Anias," she answered.

"Ah am your husband, and Ah am telling you to move away from him and get back to the house," ordered Anias.

"If you mean to kill him, then, you will have to do so in front of me," Katherine said.

"It's okay, mother, go back," Shelby said, pleased to see his mother, but not wanting her to be apart of this happening.

"Ah will not, son. Ah have been married to this man thirty-three years girl and woman, and Ah know what he is capable of. Believe me, he will do you harm," Katherine said, looking into the face of her eldest. "Ah couldn't bear that," she looked to her husband, "Ah have one son up stairs broken in spirit and in body. Do you mean to steal away the only whole son Ah have left?"

"He betrayed us, woman!" Anias said, trying to get her to understand what that meant to him.

"Ah don't care what he did. He is still my son, and Ah still love him in spite of his faults," she said, trying to get Anias to understand a mother's love.

"Woman, you just don't understand," Anias said all so frustrated.

"Oh, but Ah do, husband. Ah haven't been married to you as long as Ah have been to not know you well. And, Ah know how it must sting to a man who values family and loyalty as you do, but Shelby is right. The war is over. We have to put it behind us. Because that's where the past belongs, behind us. We can't carry it with us, because if we do, it will weigh us down. Weigh us down to the point where we can't go on, and we have to go on. We have suffered enough loss. Your brother and his two sons are dead. Our boy, Aubrey, all but destroyed. The fruit of thirty years labor, gone with yesterday. Yes, my husband, Ah understand all to well, but we mustn't let the hurt that we have suffered rob us of our dignity, and of our chance for a happier and brighter tomorrow." Katherine said compassionately as she moved to Anias, rubbing his face tenderly, as he lowered his weapon. Katherine felt every bit of pain that surged through Anias' being. She was in such a precarious emotional position. The only thread which could repair the breach between father and son. Her love knew no bounds. She would fight tirelessly to save what remained of her family. She felt with time, perhaps, Anias would forgive Shelby for standing against them, but that time was not this day. She looked at her son with loving eyes. "Shelby, my son," she called.

"Yes, mother," Shelby answered.

"Do you love me? Do you love us?" she asked.

"Yes, mother, why else would I have come here, but for love?"

"Then this is a good thing, leave us now," Katherine instructed.

"But, mother–"

"Listen," she interrupted, "leave now, and Ah will come to you at a more convenient time, as you can do no good here."

Shelby realized that he had an advocate in his mother, and that there was wisdom in her words. He could see that, through her, peace and unity would be returned to the house of Alexander.

"Very well, mother, I take my leave," Shelby said, as he turned and walked away.

Justin, for one, was very glad to see Shelby leaving. For a moment, he thought there was sure to be blood shed. Katherine was relieved to see this episode at an end as well. She was thankful Anias did no harm to Shelby. The guilt of such an act would surely have destroyed her husband over time, a little each day until there was none of him left. Anias could only feel betrayal. He would have to search his heart most diligently for the answer to the question: could he forgive?

From the window of his second floor bedroom, Shelby's brother Aubrey had been watching. He saw clearly that, with time, Shelby would be forgiven of his deeds. By their mother assuredly, and to an acceptable degree by their father. He, on the other hand, would never forgive Shelby. Not even Katherine would have been able to save Shelby a few moments earlier had he been in Anias' position. Aubrey would have claimed his brother's life to the dismay of their mother. Shelby was very fortunate this day, thought Aubrey. But he always had been lucky. No, Aubrey could not forgive, that would make Shelby's victory complete. He must have some triumph over his traitor of a brother, who was on the winning side in the war. In his mind, Aubrey had paid too high a price to let bygones be bygones. Aubrey was thirty. He once stood six feet tall and weighed a hundred and seventy pounds. He was an out going charismatic individual, who was popular with the ladies. He had his whole life ahead of him, and it was filled with promise, but that was what was, not what is.

In battle, he gave all and lost all. He was in charge of a small munitions storage depot when a surprise Union attack was launched. Aubrey and his men fought valiantly, but to no avail. His face was severely burned on the right side when munitions exploded during the attack. He was missing his right ear, and his right eye was useless, sealed shut by fused skin, which melted like wax in the fire which claimed his face. His right arm had been left a useless, badly burned, deformed, lump of unfeeling flesh. There was a constant ringing in his right ear, like someone had struck a tuning fork and was holding it next to his ear. His weight had dropped to less than a hundred pounds, as he could hardly stomach food. There was such pain in his back that he could hardly stand erect. His out-going nature had been replaced by self-imposed exile. His take on life was now a bleak proposition. He once wanted a wife and children, but what woman would have him now, or so he believed. He had become bitter and mean. Hatred was all he had left now. He often gazed into the mirror, looking at what he had become. What he saw was slowly robbing him of his grip on reality. He was not insane, but he surely stood on the brink. Over and over, he pondered why God just didn't kill him instead of leaving him like this. There were surely more deserving souls of such a fate. Shelby came to mind. Didn't Shelby, who could turn his back on his family, and raise his hand against his brother, deserve this curse more than he? In the mirror on his left side, he saw the man that he was. The man who had the world in the palms of his hands. On the right side, he saw the hopeless monster that he had become, and straight center he saw them both, man and monster. It was utter and complete agony. He would have rather had the one or the other. That way there would be no paradox to poison his mind with reminders of what was with self-pity. It would have been easier to move forward were he a complete monster, better yet, a complete man.

It was approaching ten in the morning and a young-black girl was arriving at the Alexander residence. Her name was Naomi Watts. She was twenty and was without family. Naomi was five feet four inches tall and was of medium skin complexion. Her hair was short, and she wore a red scarf which covered it. She never knew her father. Some said he was a stud hired by her former master from another slave owner to impregnate several women on his plantation. Her mother was sold away when she was but ten years of age. Although she could live any place she chose, she chose to remain in Jago instead of going north with so many others. There was no need for that in her mind, because there was plenty of work to be had right where she was. Life in Jago was what she knew, and she believed in sticking to what she knew. This area, this place, was her family. It was comfortable and familiar to her.

As she arrived to work for Katherine Alexander as a maid, she looked up at the window of Aubrey Alexander. She knew that he sometimes watched her as she came to work. He did not appear to be watching that morning from his window. Naomi was unaware of the small drama that had taken place there just a few hours earlier. As she entered the house, she found Mrs. Alexander about the business of running her household. She was preparing for lunch and dinner. She was in the kitchen, plucking the feathers from two freshly killed chickens. Naomi stood before her with her head slightly lowered and hands crossed in front of her in her grayish home spun fabric dress.

"Good morning, Naomi," Katherine said.

"Mornin' Ma'am," she answered.

"Wish you had gotten here a little earlier today, Naomi. There is so much to do, and Ah'm running behind schedule," Katherine said somewhat frantically.

"Is Ah late Ma'am?" Naomi replied, thinking that she might be late. "Ah thought cha said ta be heah at –"

"Oh no, Naomi, you are on time. The error is mine. Something happened today which has thrown me behind," Katherine explained.

"Yes Ma'am."

"Do you think that you might be able to stay a little longer today?"

"Iffen ya needin' me to, but Ah need ta be leaving in time enough ta git home befo' dark. They's so many strange folks stragglin' through. Ah gotta be careful."

"Ah understand, dear. If we keep you past that time, Ah will have Justin hitch up a team and take you home," Katherine said.

"Yes ma'am."

"Now then, Ah need for you to finish plucking these hens. After that, shell these peas, and get lunch going, and start dinner. There is also some cleaning to be done," Katherine instructed, "Ah think I am going to get started on a cake."

Naomi wondered what in the world was going on. Making a cake was somewhat of an arduous task. Everything had to be mixed by hand. It was a very time consuming and was usually only done on holidays and very special occasions.

"Is it a holiday or somethin' ma'am?" Naomi asked.

"Today is a special day for me, Naomi. Some one very special has returned home. Things are difficult for him right now. Ah just want to give him a touch of home. A little something to remind him that he is still loved," Katherine explained.

This was all the explanation Katherine gave. It wasn't really enough to satisfy Naomi's curiosity, but she was not one to pry. "Yes ma'am."

Naomi went about the business of finishing lunch and was about to start dinner. Katherine, who had been very busy herself, remembered something. "Oh, Naomi, Ah almost forgot. Before you get started on dinner, take this tray up to Aubrey's room. He hasn't been keeping his food down well lately, hopefully some coffee and boiled eggs will settle easy on his stomach."

"Yes Ma'am, Ah'll showly do dat," Naomi answered, "Ah'll knock at da door, and leave da food by it."

"Yes, knock at the door, Naomi. However, if he does not answer, barge right on in and wake him, if he is asleep. Open up the curtain to let in some sunlight. Tell him, Ah said, to try and eat, and to get out of that bed. He will lay there all day turning as white as a ghost if Ah let him," rattled on Katherine.

Katherine's back was to Naomi, and a good thing too, because if she had been face to face with Naomi. She would have seen Naomi looking at her as if she was plum out of her head. Naomi had been working for Katherine close to five months, and had never come face to face with Aubrey. The most she had done was to leave food outside his door. She felt it was not proper to go into Aubrey's room. If he didn't care to come out, she didn't care to go in.

"But, supposin' he ain't dressed proper, ma'am?" Naomi asked in such a way as to display her dismay.

"For heaven's sake, Naomi, he will be under the covers. Besides, you are just going to open the window, call his name to wake him, or gently shake him, and leave the room. There is nothing morally wrong or indecorous about that," Katherine said in such a manner that it made Naomi feel a little ashamed.

"Yes, Ma'am," Naomi said with a still uncomfortable tone.

She took the tray and went up the stairs to Aubrey's room. She knocked at the door. There was no answer. She knocked again. Still, there was no reply. "Mister Aubrey, Ah's got some food fuh ya. Ah'll jes' leave it outside da door heah. If dat's alright wit' cha, jes' say okay."

There was no answer. This made her very uncomfortable. It was starting to look as if she would have to enter the room per Katherine's instructions. She balanced the tray with one hand and reached for the door knob with the other. She was hoping Aubrey had locked the door from the other side. That way she would not have had to enter the room. Unfortunately, the knob turned. She did not want to go in, but told herself the sooner she got it over the better. She used her shoulder to push the door open just enough to peep inside the room. The room was very dark. Aubrey had put a dark cloth over the window, and sunlight was unable to defeat it and the curtain. The room smelled very stale with a hint of urine in the air. The urinating pot needed to be emptied, she thought

"Mister Aubrey," she called, "wake up now, Mister Aubrey. It's gittin' ta be 'bout noon, and yo mama wont cha ta git up."

The light from the open door was enough to allow her to navigate the room. She placed the tray by the bed, but she did not get too close. Aubrey was lying in the bed with his back to her. The covers were pulled up to his shoulders; only the back of his head was showing. Naomi decided she would gently shake Aubrey. She did, but he did not stir. Naomi did not believe he was really asleep. When she shook him, he did not move or make the slightest sound. She believed that if he were truly asleep; he would have done one or the other to some degree. He was simply giving her a hard time in her estimation.

"Mr. Aubrey, wake up now," she said once more.

He answered her not. Naomi was now a hundred percent sure he was faking. She was becoming a little bit frightened of him. She decided to remove the covering from the window and open it, as Katherine had instructed her. Then she would leave regardless of whether Aubrey was awake or not. She quietly moved over to the window, opened the curtain, and took down the covering. She began to open the window.

Aubrey was not asleep, and he did not want her in his space. He was

39

growing angry with her presence. Next to the bed, there was a round metal-white pot, like an average sized pumpkin, with a smooth surface. It was often referred to as a chamber pot, and other less savory names. It was almost filled to the brim with urine. Aubrey quietly took the pot in hand. Naomi was busy trying to get the window open, so she could get out of the room. She had no idea of what was about to happen to her. Aubrey sat up and flung the pot across the room at Naomi. She was startled, and jumped back as the pot struck the wall beside her, splattering urine all over her and the room.

"Get out of here you black wench!" Aubrey cried in such a vile tone, as would frighten the bravest man.

Naomi trembled with fear, afraid to move. It was the first time she had ever seen Aubrey's face. She was terrified of his appearance, not to mention what he had done.

"Are you deaf, ignorant wretch? Out Ah say!" Aubrey demanded.

This took place in but a few seconds. Naomi, in absolute horror, screamed so loud she could be heard from outside of the house. She fled from the room as fast as her legs would carry her.

"He touched in da head! He touched in da head!" Naomi yelled at the top of her lungs, as she ran down the stairs

"Naomi, what is it? What did you do to him?" Katherine asked in a panic, as she met Naomi half-way the stairs.

"Ah ain't done nothin', but what you said," Naomi answered, not stopping to carry on the conversation. She was frantic to get out of the house.

"Naomi!" Katherine called, wanting her to stop and calm herself.

Naomi would not hear of it. She had been scared half to death, humiliated, and was covered with the bodily waste of a madman. All she wanted to do was get out of that house as fast as she could, and never come back.

"Stay out, you hear!" Aubrey yelled from his room.

Katherine was intent upon finding out what had happened. She nervously climbed the stairs, making her way to Aubrey's room.

The room was dimly lit by the sun light provided by the open window. Aubrey was now sitting upright with his feet touching the floor. He had on a pair of long johns. The room wasn't particularly cool, but he always seemed to have a chill.

"What in the name of heaven is going on in here?" Katherine asked.

"That black wench thinks she has the right to enter this room. Ah dare she," Aubrey answered very angrily.

"But, what did she do?" Katherine asked, still trying to figure out what caused him to lose it.

"Her being in here is an offense to me," Aubrey answered.

"Is this her crime, entering your room?"

There was the sound of multiple persons coming up the stairs. Anias and Justin were rushing to see what was going on.

"What tha Sam hell is going on in here? That little gal came screaming and running out of this house like the devil himself was behind her," Anias said, somewhat winded.

Justin was at his side. He said nothing, but was just as curious as Anias.

"Ah think, it was just a miss understanding, Anias," Katherine answered.

"That Negress shouldn't have been in here!" Aubrey yelled.

"She was just doing as I told her to," Katherine said, "Ah think you should apologize to her, if Ah can get her back."

"If you told her to come in here, you apologize to her! Because, you shouldn't have! Ah will not apologize for your mistake!" Aubrey yelled disrespectfully, clearly in opposition to his mother's suggestion.

The general loud disrespectful tone of his son was making Anias angry. He did not talk to Katherine in such a way as this, and he would not tolerate anyone else to. "Watch how you talk to my wife, boy. This is her house, and she has every right to say what goes on in it, do you hear?"

There was a moment of silence. Aubrey realized that he should have not raised his voice to his mother. Nor did he have any wish to anger his father, a man for whom he had the greatest respect. He composed himself. "Ah am sorry for yelling at you, mother, but Ah won't apologize."

Aubrey had suffered much. He had every right to be upset about what happened to him during the war, but Katherine couldn't understand why he chose to display his anger as he had. She was determined to get to the bottom of it. "Ah respect that, but I don't understand Why."

"Because she is a Negress, a year ago she was a slave. It's not right that such an inferior race should walk around free to come and go as they please, and Ah am imprisoned in this body, trapped in this room," Aubrey said with more anger than his mother and father had ever heard in him.

"It is your choice to remain locked away in this room, Aubrey," Anias pointed out.

"Choice? What choice? Ah either stay in this room, or go out to be looked upon like some spectacle at a circus side show," Aubrey said all so bitterly.

"Aubrey, the people living here in our community know you. They have only love, respect, and understanding for the noble sacrifice that you have made. If you only give them the chance, you will find they are willing to embrace you," Katherine said, hoping to help her son find his way.

"Will they, mother? Ah suspect that your estimation of people in general is greatly exaggerated," Aubrey remarked, certain of the true nature of man.

"Sitting around being angry all day won't change anything, son. You can't give up on life, and just sit here dying. There is plenty of living you still have left to do. We are your family, and we are here to help you through this difficult period, just tell us what we can do to help, tell us what you want," sincerely conveyed Anias, who only had love and compassion for his brave son.

"Ah want rest for this weary body of mine. Ah want release from this constant misery, from this hell Ah endure daily. That's what Ah want, father," Aubrey replied, clearly lost in self-pity.

Anias sighed with deep sorrow. He saw with great clarity that there was no way for him to reach his son. Aubrey had given up completely, and it was breaking Anias' heart. Nothing more had he to say. He turned and went back to finish the chores of the day. Justin followed, as he had not the answer either.

Katherine on the other hand would not give up on her son. She remembered the affable young man he was. So kind and optimistic was he. She hardly recognized him now. Katherine feared for him. She was afraid that he would explode, and do harm to himself or to others. She had to reach him, reach him before he crossed the point of no return.

Sometime later that evening, Katherine made her way to her exiled son, Shelby. He was staying in a boarding house ran by a Cherokee-Indian couple. He felt it safer to be there than at the hotel in Olive Branch. There were many who felt as his father did, and might do him harm given the opportunity. His mother was so very pleased to see him. Towering over her, she pulled Shelby's head down to her, that she might kiss his forehead. She looked at him, and rubbed his face.

"How are you, my dear boy?" she asked with compassionate concern.

"I'm fine, mother."

"Your father didn't hurt you, did he?" she asked, placing her right hand upon his chin, gently turning his head side to side that she might see any bruising.

"No, mother, he didn't hurt me."

"What were you thinking. You know how he is. Why did you not send for me first? Perhaps, Ah could have smoothed the way."

"That crossed my mind, but I wasn't sure of how you would feel about me either."

Katherine gently smiled at him "Surely you must know, Ah will always love you no matter what."

"I hoped, but I wasn't sure."

"My dear boy," she said, wondering how he could ever doubt her.

"I'm glad you came, mother."

"So am Ah, Ah've missed you," she said cheerfully, "And, you know what? We will work things out with your father. All it takes is time. Perhaps, you can rent a more permanent place. Your father is stubborn, set in his ways. It will definitely take time, but Ah'm going to work on him."

"Thank you, mother. I truly appreciate that. But, it won't be necessary to rent a place. I'll only be here three months, three months and a half at the very most."

Katherine looked at him very surprised. "You're not staying?"

"No," Shelby said somewhat sadly."

"Your life is here," Katherine said, wanting him to stay, "Why won't you stay?"

"My life use to be here, but it's not anymore. Too much has happened, and people aren't so quick to forgive and forget."

"Ah'm going to work things out with your father. There is no need to leave," Katherine said, trying to convince him that he still belonged there.

"I'm grateful, mother. I want that more than anything, but I feel I've outgrown my life here. I'm someone different now. My hopes and expectations for myself are different than they were before the war began. I feel that I have to go find my place in The world. A place where I can be comfortable with who I am. Comfortable with who I am becoming."

"Where will you go? What will you do?" Katherine sadly asked.

"After I leave here, I'm going to Washington."

"Washington?"

"Yes, mother. Washington."

"Gonna become a politician, are you?" Katherine said somewhat jokingly.

"No," he laughed, "During the war, I did intelligence work for the army. I have a friend with whom I served, that thought this was a skill which might be of some use, and he was able to secure a position for me with a newly formed division of the Treasury Department."

"You're going to work for the government?"

"Yes, I am. I am going to be an agent of the Secret Service. President Lincoln signed the agency into existence on the very same day he was assassinated, as I understand it."

"What does this service do?"

"Counterfeiting of U. S. Currency is becoming something of a problem. Boodlers are becoming far too brazen. We're going to aggressively crack down on them."

"Sounds dangerous, son."

"Possibly, but we want the public to have faith in our government's currency. Those that try to undermine that faith must be challenged."

"And, you are the one to do this?"

"I think so."

"Your family, on both my and your father's side, have been tillers of the soil for generations. It's what we do. It's what you were meant to do."

Shelby began to understand that his mother wanted him nearby. Where she could visit with him and be a part of his life. She couldn't do that if he was living some place other than here in the out lying area of Olive Branch. Traveling great distances was an arduous and often perilous undertaking. She might never see him again on this side of life.

"Mother, did you not know that wherever I go. I take the things that you have taught me with me. I take all the memories, and all the love, that you have shown towards me all the days of my life with me. These are the things that matter. We will always be a family, no matter the distance that separates us."

"Ah don't think you will understand what I'm feeling until the day you have children of your own, and the day comes when they strike out on their own, and go where you can't protect them."

"Mother, I promise to write, and I'll come home as often as I can," Shelby promised.

"How many times will that be, dear boy? Once or twice in the years that Ah have remaining."

"I'll do better than that, mother."

Katherine sat there almost too sad to enjoy the here and now. She surmised that it was true that which is said of children. When they are young, they tug heavily at your skirt tail; and when they are old, they weigh heavily on your heart. What's a loving mother to do?

"Well," Katherine said, "Ah guess Ah"ll be getting along home now. So, Ah can start trying to talk some sense into that stubborn father of yours."

"It was good of you to come, mother. I have enjoyed the visit."

"Enjoy the cake, Ah'll come back to visit as soon as Ah can."

"I look forward to it, mother," Shelby said, wishing she could stay a while longer.

When the next morning came at the Alexander house, the family was seated for breakfast. All but Aubrey that is. The comfortable silence at the table was unusually uncomfortable this morning. They had a problem, and they were unsure of how to deal with it. To speak of it was a major challenge. It was not that Justin was seated at the table. He was a young man that was of age, and was family. Whatever had to be said could be said in front of him. Finally, Katherine could no longer stand the silence, which was only interrupted by the sound of silverware scraping the plate, or the occasional sip. "Well," she said.

"Well what, woman?" Anias answered.

"You know what. Our son is upstairs wasting away. Something has to be done."

"And, what do you propose we do?"

"Ah don't know, but we have to do something." Katherine said determined, but frustrated.

Justin's eyes stayed glued to his plate, as he continued to eat his bacon and scrambled eggs, but his ears were attentive to the conversation at hand. Anias saw the hurt in his loving wife. He saw how much concerned motherly pain she helplessly endured watching her child literally killing himself with regret and remorse. "He is my son too, and Ah love him, Katherine. Ah can't will him to change the path he is on. He has to want to, at least, try to resume his life. Until that happens, we are as helpless as babes in trying to aid him."

"Ah know, but surely there is something that can be done. If only we could get him out of that room, Ah know he would feel better if he just got some fresh air, and felt the sun on his face."

"Katherine, he doesn't want to leave his room," Anias pointed out.

"Well, then, maybe, you and Justin should drag him out."

Anias lowered his coffee cup rather harshly, spilling a bit of the hot-black coffee in it onto the table. He looked at Katherine, not believing she actually said that. At that point, Justin had something to say. "Aunt, Katherine."

"Yes, dear."

"Perhaps, It's not my place to say."

"Yes it is, you are family," Katherine said.

"Ok. Aubrey has been through an awful lot, more than any man should have to bear. He has lost a whole lot. He has lost the use of a limb, and half his face is gone. Ah don't know how much time it takes a man to get over something like that. Maybe, it's longer than you think it should be. Ah know that Aubrey is a strong man. You raised him to be. He will not yield to adversity, not for long. He will fight his way back. Ah believe this as much as Ah believe in anything. It just takes time. Let him sit up there in that room if he wants to. From where Ah am sitting, he's earned the right to be there feeling the way he's feeling."

For a moment, Anias and Katherine were both offended. Even if there was a hint of wisdom in what Justin was saying. Justin, who had no children of his own, couldn't possibly know what misery it was for Katherine to watch her child suffer. It was only a natural desire, a perpetual governing instinct, to help your child in a time of need, Katherine felt.

"Sometimes, my dear boy, that is more easily said than done," Katherine said with a conservative hint of resentment.

Justin said nothing further. For now, the conversation was ended, and silence prevailed once more.

Several weeks had gone by, and it was the morning that Ken Bailey's body had been found. At the Alexander Residence, a curious thing occurred. Katherine made up her mind to enter Aubry's room to air it out. As usual the room was fairly dark, but Katherine knew her way around it. She had a tray of food, which she sat on the stand next to the bed. She doubted Aubrey would eat much of it. She moved toward the window, intent on opening it. As she moved to the window, she stumbled, but did not fall. Aubrey's shoes were sitting near the window. This struck her as somewhat odd, considering his shoes were never there. She opened the window. Sunlight burst in, brightening up the room. No doubt Aubrey would get up and close it again as soon as she left the room, but at least the room would have a chance to air out a little. Katherine bent down to move Aubrey's shoes to the side, when she saw something. Something which made her smile. She looked a bit more closely to be absolutely certain her eyes were not deceiving her. There were strands of dried grass on Aubrey's shoes. She began to rejoice within herself. She quickly exited the room and went outside to where Anias was working. "Anias."

"What is it, woman?" he answered, in no mood for idle conversation.

"Come here for a moment," she said, not wanting Justin to get wind of what she had to say.

Anias walked over to her.

"There is grass on Aubrey's shoes," she whispered in her husband's ear.

"Grass?" He asked, pleased to hear the news, pondering what it meant.

"Grass," she answered, "he must have gone out last night."

"Yeah, Ah suspect so."

"How long do you think he has been doin' that?"

"Ah don't know, but let's hope he continues to go out. Hopefully, the time will come when he feels comfortable enough to move around in the light of day," Anias said.

"For so long Ah thought my prayers were going unanswered," Katherine confessed, on the verge of tears.

Anias stepped in front of Katherine, blocking Justin's view of her, in order to conceal the fact that she looked as if she wanted to cry.

"God always hears the prayers of good descent folk," Anias said, smiling in a comforting kind of way.

"Ah had just about given up on the boy, Anias."

"Ah had given up on him. Ah didn't think he was going to find his way back. Ah was prepared to watch him die."

Katherine was amazed that Anias would admit such a candid thing to her, but she wasn't surprised. Daily as she fought the good fight to reach her son, somewhere deep inside, she was also preparing her heart to let Aubrey go. "Ah think Ah was also seeking the peace within to let go."

"Ah spent many sleepless nights crying for him, praying for him, wishing he could be at peace," Anias admitted.

"Ah never knew. Ah almost felt as if you didn't care what became of him," Katherine said.

"Ah care, woman. He is my son, too."

"Ah didn't mean to imply that you don't love him."

"Ah know, woman. Ah just deal with things differently than you do. Ah know that Ah probably hold too many things inside. That Ah don't always share what Ah'm feeling with you. It's just the way of a man, the way of me."

"Well, neither of us have to worry about him now."

"Looks that way."

"He's going to be all right, isn't he?"

"I hope so, Katherine."

"Should we let on that we know?" Katherine asked.

"So that we can encourage him?" Anias asked.

"Yes."

"No, if he's come this far by himself, maybe, he wants to go the rest of the way by himself."

"Maybe, you're right."

"If he wants our help, Ah believe he will ask for it."

"Ah just don't want him to slip back."

"Ah know. Ah know," Anias said concerned, but also trusting in his son.

"Where do you suppose he goes, Anias."

"A good question, but not an important one. The important thing is that he is getting back into the world."

"Let's keep this between us for now, husband. If he doesn't want us to know he goes out at night, he surely does not want anyone else to know."

Four

It was the third day after Micah's homecoming. Darkness had fallen upon all the land, and another reunion was close. A man with brown hair and distant troubled-brown eyes was returning to his home on foot. He was a tall slender white man. He walked confidently, with his head held high, as though he were a great man. So sure of himself was he, that one might not have noticed the sad frown upon his face. His name was Franklin Wallace. War did not make him as he was. Neither was it loss of material gains, as he had suffered as much material loss as any wealthy southerner. He had made and lost several fortunes, and was confident that he would do so again. No, he was unhappy long before he left his home, or perhaps it is better stated to say his house. For him, it was never a home. It was odd that one who had so much in life, and who still had much, should be so miserable. Nevertheless, misery knew him intimately, and was a constant companion.

The source of his dismay was his wife. He married her with every intention of giving her his very best, which he had done, but she gave him so little in return. He had given her all of his love, holding nothing back from her, seeking only to make her happy. Yet, where he hoped to sow happiness and peace, he only seemed to harvest strife. True devotion without reciprocity had left him bitter. He wished that he had never asked her hand in marriage. He felt strongly that both of them would have been better off had he not.

He moved through the slave quarters void of nostalgia. He once owned better than three hundred slaves. Slave row this place was called. Ninety little white-wooden huts; sixteen by fourteen feet; in several straight lines just out of sight of the Master's mansion. These huts had no floors, just the ground, no doors, just openings. The roofing wasn't very good. Often it seemed to rain more inside than out. These often over-crowded huts weren't good at keeping out the cold either. If one had looked inside, perhaps, traces of what life was like could be seen. One small table with two chairs; one bed if among the fortunate; mattresses on the ground stuffed with grass or shuck. At this time of night, these humble quarters would have teemed with the activity of slaves preparing for the next day's labor, but the quarters were quiet as Franklin moved through them.

He could see his large house in the near distance. A great, reddish-brown, brick home with four large white columns of stone upon its porch, leading to two large hand carved doors of darkly stained maple. The yard was once a great neatly manicured display of wealth, but even in the dark, he could see that it was a den of weeds.

He walked up the steps leading to the front door. He knocked at the great doors, but no one answered right away. The servants were all gone, out enjoying their freedom at his expense, he supposed. Finally, his only son answered the door. It was his twelve-year-old son Jesse, and he was both happy and surprised to see his father. His was so excited that he forgot to speak. He simply ran through the great house yelling. "Father is home. Father is home."

Slowly but surely, all who were in the house started to appear from their resting places. First, his eldest daughter Joselpha, and then the next eldest, Blanch. They were soon followed by his remaining children: Susie, May, and Diane. They all smothered him with hugs and kisses.

He greeted them all in kind. It was one of those rare happy moments for him. At the top of the stairs, looking down on him as she always had, without the faintest hint of a smile was his wife Elizabeth.

"Is there any liquor in the house, brandy perhaps?" Franklin asked sighing, already regretting the first words out of her mouth, which were sure to be unpleasant.

Elizabeth waltzed down the stairs with lady-like airs, a stern face, and superior little attitude.
Franklin kept track of her out of the corner of his eyes as she neared.

"I'm afraid we don't have any brandy, father, but we do have sherry, I believe," answered Joselpha.

"That will be fine, dearest one," Franklin replied.

"I'll get it, Joselpha," Blanch insisted.

Blanch rushed with excitement and gladness to pour her father a glass of wine. Elizabeth made eye contact with Franklin. He could see a hard time was coming by the wrinkled brow on her stern face. Here it comes, he thought to himself, and he was right.

"The war has been over for quite some time, Franklin, where have you been?" Elizabeth asked, waiting like some constable for an answer.

All of the concern and joyful chatter at Franklin's return ceased. Franklin's shoulders slumped as his head wobbled slightly back and forth. His face darkened with anger, resentment, and defensiveness, but he somehow managed a small smile. She doesn't disappoint, Franklin thought, not even a hello. Four years apart and not a single hello. "Hello Elizabeth, it's good to see you, too."

"Here is your glass of sherry, father," Blanch cheerfully said, as she handed the glass to Franklin.

Joselpha was all of nineteen, and was very wise. She could see an argument was coming. She motioned the others into the parlor, and closed the door behind them, as it was considered crass for one to listen to one's parents argue. As the children left, Elizabeth firmly asked again. "Where have you been?"

Franklin looked around, as if looking to see if someone else was present that she might be talking to. Elizabeth's big mouth was the very reason he was not here sooner. He would have liked to have never come back. He could have started over some place new, but this was not the way a good Christian behaved. He would have liked to have struck her, but that would have been unchristian and unmanly. No, he would have never raise his hand to a woman. A white woman that is, he was known to raise it often against slaves.

Whenever he was angry with Elizabeth, he found reason to beat up on some slave. The horses weren't groomed to perfection, the flowers in the garden didn't look pleasing enough, dinner was too hot, or too cold. The slaves which came in contact with him on a regular basis lived a hellish existence. How could one so pious, as he thought himself to be, have treated his slaves so vile. One would think such a religious man would have been compelled to at least treat his slaves better than the infidel. Not so, he viewed the black man as a soulless creature without sense perception; much like a dog or plant. When he stands before the judgement seat of Christ to give an account of himself, he will no doubt declare Elizabeth drove him to commit such atrocities against his fellow man.

Make no mistake about it. Elizabeth was a fine piece of work. She was a cold, lazy, selfish, hellion. Slavery was of itself a brutal, cruel, and demonic institution. Elizabeth thrived in it like a demon in its natural environment. The slaves that waited on her hand and foot would rather have suffered the wrath of Franklin than her, at least he knew when to stop. She kept a supple wooden rod at her side, and used it without sparing across the backs or heads of her maidservants. She was relentless, and the blood of her servants trickled freely, and most often without good cause.

She did not show motherly affection toward her children, as one might expect. It is true that women often do not initially feel a motherly love and bond toward their children at their birth, but from the very first, Elizabeth took it to new heights. She never acted motherly, or even seemed to care about her infants. Once a slave nurse maid moved too slowly to quiet Elizabeth's first born. Instead of coming to see if her child might be ill in some way, she went and got a skillet and struck the slave girl against the head, causing her to loose an eye. She had been awakened from her sleep, and that was not to be tolerated. The very next day, the poor slave girl whose eye had been put out, used her one good eye to witness the sell of her newborn and two-year-old toddler on the auction block. For the little sum of money received for the children, it would have been better to have just given them away, but Elizabeth had a point to make, and she made it loudly and clearly. From that day to this, Elizabeth never lost a night's sleep due to her children crying in the middle of the night, since no slave wanted to witness her child being sold in retaliation. Elizabeth was a cruel woman, but if asked, she would say that she did these things because Franklin treated her as if she did not exist.

Franklin gulped down his wine wishing it would yield its effects swiftly. It was always a little easier for him to suffer Elizabeth when he was somewhat intoxicated.

"Well, I am waiting for an answer, Franklin," she said sternly.

"To whom do you think you are speaking, Elizabeth?" Franklin replied without a smile, filled with stern resentment. "Do you think you run something here? Do you think you run me? Well, let's get one thing straight, you don't. Ah was where Ah was, and that's all the explanation you shall have. Now get out of my presence, and let me enjoy my wine."

Elizabeth's scornful fury was aroused. She would not take that without exception. Loudly and indignantly she said, "You insufferable wretch! How dare you speak to me in that manner?"

"Ah'll speak to you in any manner that pleases me, Elizabeth," Franklin interrupted, coolly and nonchalantly.

Elizabeth looked at him, wanting to strike him. "You could at least have the decency to answer a legitimate question in a civil manner."

Franklin was utterly amazed at Elizabeth, standing there looking at him, as if she had been some how wronged by him, as if he were the one who started this argument. "Ah am astonished at the nerve of you, Elizabeth. You speak to me with contemptible abasement in your voice, as if Ah were a child, and you expect me to respond to you with meekness and humbleness. Tell me, what world do you live in, my dear?" Franklin said callously.

Elizabeth lowered her head. It was not her intention to start a fight. She changed her tone, becoming softer and more gentle. "Ah know that our marriage has become more or less one of tolerance over the years, but Ah do genuinely still love you," she said as suppliantly as she knew how.

Franklin offered up a lightly restrained chuckle to Elizabeth's moment of heart-felt words. "Love, Elizabeth?" Franklin replied, wondering if she even knew the meaning of the word.

"Yes, Franklin," she answered, "Ah still love you. Are cold looks and cruel words all you have left to offer me?"

Franklin laughed and stopped abruptly. "No, Elizabeth, Ah love you. Ah always have. Ah just don't happen to like you anymore."

This hurt Elizabeth badly, but she kept up her great stone face. She prepared herself to offer him a token of reconciliation. She would not have objected to beginning to work out their differences in the bedroom. "Would you like to join me in our bedroom tonight?"

Franklin looked at her coldly. "Ah would sooner know swine than you this night."

Elizabeth turned and walked proudly up the stairs. She did not let Franklin see how badly he had wounded her. The war had most definitely changed Franklin. Although they had never truly seen eye to eye, he always treated her with a measure of respect. In times past, he would have gone out of his way to make peace with her, but he no longer had slaves to buffer his wrath toward Elizabeth. In times past, he would have sought peace. Elizabeth assumed he would do so this time, mistakenly. She had let her guard down for a moment, and Franklin made her pay for it. She would not make that mistake again. Neither would she forget. Franklin was a very moody individual, going through extreme highs, and extreme lows. She intended to wait, and catch him at a low point, and repay him ten fold for his insolence. He said that he loved her still, but she believed it not. If she could not have his love, then she would gladly have his hate.

Several days later, young Jesse Wallace was in the barn with his dog. The bitch had given birth to a small litter of pups, three to be exact. Jesse was thrilled. His father had come home and his dog had given birth to pups. The dog, Jackie, was a Collie, brown with a white ring around her neck, and her pups were a mix of Collie and German Shepard. Jackie gave birth during the night. Her black pups, with wrinkled skin and tight eyes, sucked at her teats. Dogs don't usually let anyone near their vulnerable pups, but Jackie let Jesse near. He had been a good pet owner. Jackie was more than just a dog to Jesse. She was more like family. He talked to her for hours at a time, feeding her from his plate. Wherever he was, the dog was at his side. He loved her more than his sisters. He related to the dog better.

Franklin had missed his son's presence that morning at breakfast, and had come in search of him. He found Jesse in the barn. As he entered the barn, Jackie snarled at him a bit, a warning not to get too close, which Franklin wisely heeded.

"Easy, Jackie, it's just paw," Jesse comforted the animal.

Franklin moved closer, but maintained an appreciable distance, not wanting to make the dog feel as though her pups were being threatened.

"You can move a little closer, paw. She won't bite you," Jesse assured.

"Ah think this is close enough, son," Franklin said, not so sure he shouldn't have been standing a little farther away.

"She had three pups last night, paw," Jesse said somewhat in awe.

"Yes, Ah see," Franklin said, watching them there.

"She did it all by herself. Ah wish Ah could have been here with her."

"Ah'm not so sure she would have wanted you here. Dogs like to do this sort of thing alone."

"Ah bet she would have wanted me here," Jesse remarked, so sure of it.

"Well, maybe," Franklin agreed, knowing better.

Franklin made a visual inspection of the barn. It wasn't really in that bad of shape. It would not take much to get it back into tip-top condition. The Wallace plantation was fairly sizable. Jesse and he would have to work from sun up to sun down just to keep the parts of it that they would use in good order, the house and barn. It would have been easier if he was able to afford to hire help, but that was not doable right then.

Franklin was broke, and not only that, he was in considerable debt. Fortunately, it was manageable debt. He had a plan to get himself, and his family, back to the status which they enjoyed just before the war. He planned to borrow against his property. He wanted to get enough funds to bring in a large crop of tobacco. Smoking seemed to be on the rise, and tobacco had turned into quite a profitable crop. The ridiculous prices that tobacco commanded would surely get him back to financial prominence.

"Paw," Jesse called.

"Yes, son."

"What did you come down here for?"

"Ah need you to help me do a little work around here. Hopefully, you won't have to work very long, just until we get back on our feet," Franklin explained with a sad defensiveness. He hated that Jesse had to work. Franklin felt it was beneath his son to perform Manual labor. His son was meant to command wealth and the respect of the world at large. His place wasn't to have dirt beneath his fingernails.

"Okay, paw," Jesse answered.

"Stop calling me paw. It makes you sound like some common guttersnipe," Franklin insisted.

"Yes, father."

As another day dawned, the Wallace family could all be found gathered at the table for breakfast. Jesse ate his food hurriedly. "May I be excused?" he asked.

"Are you finished?" Elizabeth asked, somewhat surprised.

"Yes, mother, I am."

"Very well, you are excused."

"What are you up to, Jesse?" Blanch asked, by far the nosiest of his sisters.

"Jackie had pups night before last night. Ah just want to check on her, and her pups, before Ah get started with my chores," Jesse answered.

"Don't take too long, we have a lot to do today," Franklin directed.

Jesse went out toward the barn. His dog was barking fiercely. He wondered why she was barking so. There was a sense of urgency in him, as he felt something was wrong. When he opened the barn door, he saw a sight he would not soon forget. He saw his dog, Jackie, courageously dodging in and out of harm's way in an effort to save her pups from a reddish brown copperhead snake. Copperheads are unusual snakes in that they are fearless and will not run from a foe, human or otherwise. They are known to hang around barns in search of small animals such as mice to prey upon. This particular snake intended to make a meal of the defenseless pups. Shock and horror covered Jesse's face, as he witnessed his dog fall prey to the snake's blinding speed. It struck the dog, filling her with venom, which would most certainly claim her life shortly. Jesse let out a yell that was both ferocious and terrifying. He was moved to take up the fight. He picked up a piece of broken plank lying nearby. He engaged the snake, swinging violently at the copperhead, but he was not using a great deal of control. He was both outraged by and afraid of the snake, and missing as he tried to land the fatal blow.

The aggressive copperhead struck at Jesse, who was able to elude it. The boy was screaming and yelling at the top of his voice, determined to kill the snake. The adrenaline was flowing as his body trembled with rage. He would either kill or be killed. It could be no other way. The copperhead lunged at Jesse. It had a strike for sure. It's venom filled fangs were but an inch away from connecting and penetrating the boy's skin, but Franklin intervened, blowing the serpent nearly in two with his .67 caliber, nine-shot, Le Mat revolver. Jesse dropped the plank and fell to his knees at his dogs side. Tears flowed freely, as he watched Jackie begin to fade. Blanch also heard Jesse's cry. She heard it first in fact. It was she who alerted Franklin there was trouble. She stood at her father's side, feeling her younger brother's grief.

"Help her, father," Jesse cried with such a sorrow of voice that Franklin was moved to action on
his behalf.

Franklin ran his fingers through his hair trying to think of what to do. "Do we have any alkaline?"

"Alkaline?" Blanch asked, wondering what good that would do.

"Snake bites are acidic, Blanch. If we get some alkaline into her, maybe, she will stand a chance."

"Ah'll run to the house to see if we have any, father," Blanch said, running for the house.

"Hurry, Blanch!" Jesse cried.

Blanch hastened to the house, searching for alkaline, frantically explaining to her sisters and Elizabeth why it was needed. Sadly, there was no alkaline, poor Jackie was doomed. All of them went out to the barn hurriedly. Meanwhile, poor Jesse was making himself sick with grief. It was almost as if he was dying with the dog. "Do something, father," the boy cried.

"Easy, son, we may be able to save her yet," Franklin tried to comfort the boy.

"Why did this happen?"

"It's just one of those things, son."

The others arrived in the barn.

"Do you have it?" Franklin said, looking at Blanch.

"There isn't any, father," she sadly informed.

Hearing this, Jesse began to cry much harder than before. It was so moving and sad that several of his sisters started to cry. It was all a little bit more than Elizabeth could stand. She moved over to Jesse, and began to lift him by his arm. Jesse expected that she wished to comfort him in some manner. He rose, as he would have very much liked to have been comforted. When he was fully erect, Elizabeth slapped him so hard he was knocked to the ground.

"You little fool, stop crying! It's just a dog! All of you stop that crying this instance, do you hear?" Elizabeth said with merciless tone.

All the children stopped crying instantly. They were both shocked and afraid of their mother. Franklin looked at Elizabeth with contempt, but said nothing.

On the morning Ken Bailey was found dead, Franklin was milking a spotted black and white cow. He was in the middle of letting out a long yawn when Jesse walked up to him. "Have trouble sleeping last night, father?"

"Not really, why do you ask?" Franklin inquired.

"Ah saw you walking around outside last night. Ah thought that might have been because you were having trouble sleeping."

Franklin didn't care to explain why he was out last night, and skirted his son's comment. "You saw me walking about last night? That must've been about one o'clock, son. What were you doing up so late?"

"Ah had a bad dream about Jackie. Ah just had to get up and check on her only surviving pup, make sure he was all right."

Franklin stopped milking the cow for a moment. He saw that his son was still suffering from the loss of his dog. "Are you still keeping the pup in the room with you," he asked, sympathetic to his loss.

"Yeah, Ah have to protect him, you know."

"Ah know, son."

"Ah wouldn't want some serpent to eat him while he can't help himself. Ah hate snakes."

"Ah don't like them, myself, but the snake didn't mean you any harm. It was just trying to survive, like anything or anyone. It's just one of those unfortunate things that happened. Try to put it behind you."

Jesse looked at Franklin, as if Franklin just didn't understand. Parents, it seemed to him, were too busy with life, or just too unconcerned to understand and care about something that was important to someone other than themselves. Jackie was an important part of his life and Franklin was telling him about the accursed snake. Around that time, Elizabeth walked up. "Franklin, Ah need to speak with you privately."

"Now?"

"If it's not too much of an inconvenience," she said with a hint of sarcasm.

Franklin looked at her. He didn't particularly care for her tone, but decided to oblige her. They walked up to the house, not saying a word to each other. Upon entering the house, they went into the parlor. Elizabeth closed the door behind them. She turned and looked at Franklin as if she were a school marm, and he was a disobedient child. Franklin sensed she was about to get it started.

"Franklin, you went out last night," she said, looking at him all so disapprovingly.

"And," Franklin responded defiantly.

"And, respectable gentlemen don't go gallivanting around in the middle of the night."

Franklin gave a smirkish grin. "Ah will do as Ah am so inclined, when Ah'm so inclined."

"My God, you have become such a shameless whoremonger, Franklin," she said quite disgusted with him.

"What!"

"You heard me right. Do you think Ah don't know where you went last night? Well, Ah do, Franklin and Ah'm telling you to stop it!"

"How many times must Ah tell you before you get it though your thick skull, that you don't tell me what to do and when to do it!"

"So you admit it, Franklin?" she said calmly.

"Admit what? There's nothing to admit."

"Admit that you were with your concubine last night."

Franklin looked at her and shook his head, neither admitting or denying the allegation.

"You know who Ah am referring to, that Amanda Hamilton woman.

Franklin continued to look at her, as if she were out of her mind, answering not a single word.

"Tell me, Franklin, is that little bastard clinging to her skirt yours?" Elizabeth said, looking at him, as if she could smack the taste out of his mouth.

"You don' t know what you are talking about, Elizabeth," he answered in a dismissing kind of way.

"Don't patronize me, Franklin," Elizabeth said angrily.

"That's in your mind, Elizabeth," he said, trying to make her feel as if she was imagining the affair.

"Mmm hmm, well, understand this, Franklin. If you have any love to give, then, you give it to me. Ah'm your wife, and it's my wifely duty to fulfill that need, as it is your duty to fulfill my needs. You seem to have forgotten that. There are certain things Ah'll put up with, and there certain things Ah won't. Ah won't stand for your infidelity. You will do well to remember that."

Franklin still did not comment. Why should he? Elizabeth couldn't possibly know where he was the past night. For all she knew, he could have been out committing murder. She was just theorizing, fishing with an educated guess, trying to get him to bite. He wouldn't allow her to bait him into revealing anything. She would have to do better than that. "Ah'll try to bear that in mind," he said, almost as a joke.

Elizabeth knew that he could care less about what she was saying. It was only so much gibberish to him, but he was foolish to think she would allow him to disrespect her. She wasn't the type that would take it lying down. "You had best heed my warning, Franklin Wallace!"

"Is that a threat?"

"Call it what you will."

"Then, I call it nothing."

"This is a serious matter, Franklin."

"Ah gathered as much, but it's not an important matter to me."

"You will not continue to shame me, Franklin."

"The only shame is this lie we're living called a marriage."

"How can you say something like that, Franklin? Our marriage may not be what it was, but it is still a good institution sacred in the eyes of God and the decent people of this community. You just don't appreciate what you have."

"What do Ah have in you, Elizabeth?" Franklin asked, indicating that he had nothing.

"Ah've been a good wife to you. Ah've given you children, helped you to make something of this land, helped to make our name revered. Ah've given you the best years of my life. Ah've given you my very best."

He looked at her for a moment in silence. "Your best isn't good enough, Elizabeth."

"Neither is yours, but Ah have never asked more of you than you were able to give."

"That's a lie, Elizabeth. You've always looked down that pompous nose of yours, demanding more and more, trying to make me into the man you would have me to be."

"Is that why you've taken up with that woman, because she doesn't ask you to live up to your potential?"

Franklin shook his head in utter contempt. "Ah think, Ah've had enough of this conversation."

"An undemanding woman does a good man a disservice by not pushing him to be all that he can be."

"You bore me, Elizabeth," he said, moving toward the door, preparing to leave.

Elizabeth stepped in his path. "Stop the infidelity, Franklin, or a bullet may catch you and your harlot in your sin."

Franklin raised a brow, tempted to do her harm, but restrained himself. He was a southern gentleman, and gentlemen of the south were above such common trifle acts. Elizabeth could tell she had struck a nerve. She was prepared for whatever action Franklin might have been preparing to take against her. Whatever she had coming was worth it in her opinion. She said what she meant, and she meant what she said. Franklin had had enough. He masterfully lowered his shoulder, and bulled his way right past her, bumping her to the side. He slammed the door behind him as he exited the room. He stormed from the house, as he made his way to the stable. He saddled his horse and rode the animal hard and mercilessly, headed where Elizabeth could only imagine.

Elizabeth made her way to the porch in time to see him racing away. Her anger was pushed beyond limits. He was no doubt running to his concubine, she thought. Elizabeth had a surprise for Franklin upon his return. Tonight he would be made to know that she was his wife.

Five

As Solomon and Elijah waited for Risby and Ran to return with the sheriff, a question lingered in Solomon's mind. "Elijah."

"Yassuh."

"You said dat you didn't thank Bailey killed dis boy, but you never said who you thought might have done it."

"Ah don't know. Ah can't know, but..."

"Don't hold back, speak ya mind," Solomon encouraged, sensing Elijah had more to share.

"Well, at first, Ah thought maybe somebody white might've done it. 'Ceptin', Ah can't figure out why a child. Ah mean, besides We's free, ain't too much changed. Dey could've done dis ta a growed colored man, and strung 'im up by his neck from a tree, wouldn't been too much done 'bout it by white folks. Ah wonder iffen it might not been somebody colored done dis."

Solomon arched an eyebrow. "Somebody black?"

"Yeah, Ah mean, Ah thank dat a person who could do somethin' like dis would do it ta da people it's easiest fuh 'im ta git ta. Ain't no white folk ta speak of livin' round heah in Jago. Ain't hardly too many of 'em even passin' through heah exceptin' fuh da chil'ens. Dey come ta play wit' our chil'en, like dey always done. Ah bet cha most people, black or white, ain't never been mo' 'an 'bout fifty miles from where dey live dey whole lives. Ah thank it's easier fuh somebody black ta git in position 'round heah to do dis 'an it is fuh somebody white. Do it make sense what Ah's sayin'?" Solomon nodded his head that it did make sense. Elijah continued, "what iffen some po' soul dat ain't knowed nothin' but hell on some plantation his whole life as a slave done got free, and all dat hurt and wrong dat done been done ta 'im finds its way out of 'im. Maybe, he wanna hurt somebody da way he been hurt."

"Could be, Elijah, but Ah'd hate ta thank dat."

"Iffen it was, it probably somebody dat done moved on by now."

"Yes, why would he stay?"

"He wouldn't stay, would he?"

"No, he would not, unless he plum crazy."

61

The same day that Micah came home, a second homecoming occured. This time between two young lovers. Jasmine had not seen her husband Rory in two years. It was a painful and difficult separation for both of them, particularly for Jasmine. Every since young-black men started running away to fight on the side of the Union Army. Their women had to wait, and wonder if they would ever see them again. It was a terrible thing, not knowing if some one you loved was dead or alive, or if you without them were alone in the world. Jasmine never worried. Rory told her he would be coming back for her, and if Rory said it, then it was as good as gospel to her.

Jasmine was a washerwoman. It was hard work, and she barely made enough to keep fed. Jasmine was hard at work. Her only company as she labored was Caleb, Elijah and Josephine's three-year-old son. As Jasmine tried to work, Caleb often ran up behind her. He would tug at her skirt, and then he would run away laughing. When she could, Jasmine stopped and gave playful chase. On this occasion, Jasmine was stooping down, putting wood on the fire beneath the big-black kettle that she used to boil hot water for washing the clothes. As she was stooping, Caleb ran up behind her and playfully hit her in the back. She turned, laughing at the boy. "Ouch, Ah's gon' get you, Caleb."

Caleb ran away, and Jasmine ran after him. Caleb tripped and bumped his chin on the hard ground. He began to cry. Jasmine snatched the child up from the ground into her arms, comforting him by rubbing his chin. Caleb began to quiet down, and Jasmine carried him inside her home to clean the dust from his face. When she exited the house, still holding Caleb within her arms, sitting on top of a gray mustang was her beloved Rory. A kind of mingled shock and excitement built quickly within her. Her heart fluttered with joy, as light-headedness overtook her. There was an old beaten up oak rocking chair on the porch of her home. Jasmine took a seat in it, for fear that she was going to faint from joy. She sat there for a second, ready to run to Rory, but she didn't. Without a word, she started to rock. Her heart was beating fast, and there was a slight smile on her face that was growing, as Rory gazed upon her.

Rory's weary horse, with head hung low, was just shy of the porch. Jasmine and Rory made eye contact, and Jasmine stopped rocking, as the smile on her face grew to expose her brilliantly white teeth.

"Hey, gal," said Rory in a low sexy kind of way, with a look of great pleasure upon his face.

"Hey? Dat all you got ta say afta two years?" said she, with a voice also dripping with sex appeal.

"Youse beautiful," said he, as he threw his leg over the horse and hopped down, "even mo' beautiful dan da leaves on da trees at autumn time."

"Is Ah now?" replied she, pleased to see Rory had not lost his way with words.

Rory was a man of five feet nine inches, which was an average height for men of the day. He was lean and trim, with smooth-brown skin. His hair was short, kinky, and black. He was dressed in a pair of blue jeans and a blue long-sleeved shirt, with the sleeves rolled up just below the elbows, and black army issue shoes.

Rory made his way to Jasmine gingerly, but with purposeful swagger. He knelt down beside her in the rocking chair. She stopped rocking. Rory looked at her, as men in love often look at the women they love; that is, with eyes filled with joy to see her, and his heart filled with longing and contentment to be near her, wanting just to touch her, wanting to run his fingers across her soft ebony skin.

Jasmine looked away, lowering her head in coy fashion. She quickly moistened her lips with her tongue, and then she looked back at him lovingly. Jasmine was five feet five inches. She had beautiful dark skin. She was a little bit skinny, with unusually long fine-black hair. This was due to the fact that in her nineteen years, it had never been cut, and her father was Negro and Cherokee Indian. She was very pretty, not Josephine pretty, as few women in the world were, but very beautiful just the same.

Rory and Jasmine were very close to sharing a kiss, the first in two years. Their lips pressed tenderly as the blood raced through their veins. Jasmine made soft blissful sounds of delight. It was a beautiful thing. Just when the blood got to racing, almost out of control, Caleb chimed in. "Who dat, Jas'?"

Jasmine was a little embarrassed, and pulled away from Rory, but her lips softly and passionately clung to his lips a moment longer, as if their lips regretted being parted one from another. Jasmine was caught up in the moment, and had forgotten that she was holding the child.

"O'm her Husband, little man, Rory. What yo' name?"

Caleb did not know Rory, and did not answer. He wrapped his arms around Jasmine, and clung to her.

"His name is Caleb, Rory. His momma and her husband been real good ta me. Ah don't thank Ah would have made it iffen it wa'n't fuh dem. Dey been real good ta me," Jasmine said, with sincerity in her voice and a look of appreciation on her face. "Dey sometimes let lit' Caleb heah keep me company, since dey knows how much Ah loves da little on's."

Rory sensed that it had been hard on Jasmine in his absence, and that he owed Elijah and Josephine a great deal of thanks. Jasmine had on a pale dress, which came down to her feet. It was old and very worn, and Rory could tell it had been mended far too many times. He looked down at her beautiful bare feet. The weather was warming, even unseasonably warm, but it was not yet so warm that she should have been without shoes in his opinion.

"Where yo' shoes?" Rory asked.

"Dey's old and da soles is jes' plum wore out; dey barely lasted through winter. Ah thought since it's warm nuff out, Ah'd jes' as soon not wear 'em, cause dey's too small and kinda hurts my feet," answered Jasmine.

"Maybe in da mornin', we can ride inta town, and get you some new shoes and a few new dresses," Rory said cheerfully.

"Dey ain't givin' black folks credit," she informed, "dey ain't hardly givin' nobody credit."

Rory laughed. "Ah gots money. Ah got almost three hundred and ninety United States dollars."

Jasmine looked at him with surprise. "Three hundred ninety dollars? Dat's a lot of money. You ain't made dat in no army."

"Ah Did, kinda. Ah won a good bit of it in a few card games," he explained.

"Card games?"

"Yeah, we had plenty of time fuh dat. We done some fightin', but mostly we's on fatigue duty. Dat is, doin' da hard work da white soldiers wouldn't do," Rory explained, "at night thangs got slow, and we played a lot of cards."

"You showly did iffen ya won three hundred and ninety dollars," exclaimed she jokingly.

"Ah didn't win all of it. Dey paid me thirteen dollars a month da last year or so of da war, and seven dollars a month befo' dat."

Rory and Jasmine conversed for a long while, hours. The time past without notice. Before they realized it, it was getting quite late in the day. Rory wanted to be alone with Jasmine.

"Come on, let's take Caleb home. Where he live?" Rory asked.

"Down, da road a spell dat way, maybe two mile or so," she answered.

"Well, Let's go den."

"Okay," Jasmine said smiling, as she rose from her rocker, with the child on her hip.

She went into the house, and exited with a small cloth filled with biscuits. She gave the child one, which he ate joyfully. She raised the cloth, offering some to Rory. He nodded his head in decline. He hungered, but not for food. He hungered to kiss and love her. Rory, Jasmine, and little Caleb mounted Rory's horse. Rory was very anxious to return the child so that he and his wife might release their passions. It was getting to be the twilight of the day as they arrived at Elijah's home. They knocked at the door, and a voice called telling them to enter. All were seated at the table as Jasmine and Rory entered with Caleb.

"Hi y'all, we's jes' bringing Caleb back. A lit' bit early Ah know, but my Rory done found his way home ta me," Jasmine explained.

"Da Lawd done truly blessed dis day. Elijah's brother done come home too, after ten long years," Mama Julia professed with joy.

Elijah sprang to his feet with a hand extended to greet Rory. He gave him a firm manly handshake. "Good you made it back ta us safe, young fella, God good, ain't he?"

"Yeah, Ah guess he is," Rory answered, not being a very religious man.

Elijah swept his little son into the air, kissing the boy's head. This tickled the child, and he laughed and laughed in his father's loving arms.

"Dis heah is my blessed little Caleb, Micah," Elijah proudly said, walking toward his younger brother.

Micah rose from his seat. He smiled at the happy little one, and held out his arms. Although the child had never seen Micah before, he gladly went to his uncle, and was as comfortable in his arms as he would have been being held by his dad. This pleased all in the room, and no one was more pleased than Micah. He was truly home.

"Two good fightin' men done made it back without hurt nor harm. God is so good," praised Mama Julia.

Micah picked up that Mama Julia said Rory was also a soldier, which he already suspected by the tone of conversation. "Were you calvary or infantry, Rory?" Micah inquired.

"Ah served wid what used ta be da Sixth United States Colored Heavy Artillery," Rory answered.

"The sixth?" Micah asked again, knowing something of the sixth.

"Yeah," Rory answered once more.

"Were you there at Fort Pillow?" Micah asked.

"No, dat was befo' my time?" Rory answered.

Josephine was curious, as to what the men were speaking of, as was every one else in the house. "What's Fort Pillow?" She asked.

"It was a military post located not too far from here over in Tennessee.

One dark day the unthinkable happened there. An overwhelming force of Confederate soldiers overran the fort. After the fighting was done, they slaughtered the captured black soldiers. Most of them unarmed, and some while on their knees begging for mercy, I hear. It was nothing less than savagery. A message to every black soldier of what would happen to them who dared raise their hands against their masters. That didn't work though, it only served to make us fight harder, for we knew that they would grant us no quarter. It became our battle cry, 'remember Fort Pillow'," Micah explained somberly, yet proud of the good men who fell there.

It was a grim moment for the others in the room. They had never really given much thought to what price was paid by black soldiers on the battle field during the American Civil War. Rory and Jasmine stayed with them a while longer conversing, but not much longer. Rory was excited about the prospect of being alone with Jasmine.

Soon, they were alone. Rory had dreamt of this moment so many times that he could not number the dreams if someone asked him to, but he did not have to dream any longer. His dreams were standing before him in the flesh. There was a bed in the corner of this small dwelling, which can only be described as humble at best. Jasmine's home was a little one room house, not much larger than the average slave quarter. Her bed wasn't a real bed. It was a few pieces of unpainted wood fastened together by Elijah so that Jasmine's mattress, stuffed with shuck, would not rest on the cold-wooden floor. There was a simple brown wooden table and chairs, big enough for two, and a black metal wood-burning heater, which resembled a pot-bellied stove, which it also served as a stove. Rory stripped down and climbed into the bed.

Jasmine had longed to make love to him almost as much as he had dreamt of loving her. Jasmine stood before him, afraid to take off her clothing in front of him. She moved over to the kerosene lamp to extinguish its light, but Rory had waited a long time for this. "No, leave it be, Ah wonts ta see you."

"Let me turn it down jes' a lit' bit," she requested.

"Don't. In my dreams, Ah done seed ya taking off your cloths in da light. It kept me goin' many a time when Ah wanted to quit. Please, do dis thang fuh me."

How could Jasmine deny him. All she had ever wanted to do was please him. He was her heart and soul. Her reason for living. She would do as he asked, but she was desperately afraid to take her cloths off in front of him. Their separation was very hard on them both, and Rory was about to find out how hard it was for her.

Jasmine faced Rory, and let down her long hair, which rested well past her shoulders. Jasmine wished it was longer. She wished it came down to her bottom. That way the hair would hide her back. She let her dress fall to the floor and went to him. Even though she tried to conceal it from him, as she laid next to him, he noticed her back. It was scarred, beaten with the whip. Immediately, the desire to make love cooled in Rory, and his anger was kindled.

"Who done dis ta you ?" he asked with anger and sorrow in his voice.

Jasmine had suffered the displaced anger of their former master, Cyrus Drucker. It began shortly after Rory ran away. At first, Drucker used harsh and abusive language toward her. Then, it progressed to having her do demeaning chores. Chores which could only be described as trite and meddlesome. Finally, after receiving word that things were not going well for the Confederacy, Drucker came to her out of the blue, and struck her upside the head so violently that it knocked her unconscious. On another occasion he blackened her eye. After that, she tried to stay clear of him, but he cornered her one afternoon, and said she was looking at him in a manner he didn't like. So, he dragged her to the whipping post, and tied her there, and delivered twenty stripes to her back, only stopping once she had passed out.

Everyone around for miles knew it wasn't really Jasmine that Drucker was whipping. In his mind, Cyrus wanted to punish Rory for betraying him, but Rory was not around to punish. So, he took his vengeance out on the one thing Rory loved in this world, Jasmine.

Jasmine remained silent as Rory angrily waited for an answer. It was over and done. Nothing could change what happened. The pain had long since stopped, and her wounds healed. All that remained to remind her of that dreadful day were her scars. She forgave Drucker in her heart, and now that Rory was home, she was happier then perhaps anyone should have a right to be. She had the man that she loved returned safe to her. She was happy now, and that was all that she wanted, but Rory was furious.

"Did some damn Patty Roller take you fuh a runaway and do dis ta ya?" Rory asked insistently.

Jasmine looked at him, but did not answer. Rory did not even consider that Cyrus Drucker could have done this, and she did not have the heart to tell him otherwise, not knowing how much Drucker meant to him.

"What do it matter now? What's done, done," she replied in low spirits.

"What's done, done. What do it matter? It matters ta me, woman, tell me which one of dem dirty low-down patties done dis thang ta you."

"And, what you gon' do, Rory? You gon' beat 'im up, kill 'im? Ah forgives da man dat done dis ta me. You hear me, Ah forgives! He don't matter! Youse all dat matters ta me. God done brought you home ta me. Ah prayed day and night fuh him ta do dat, and he done done it. Ah don't wanna pray fuh 'im ta keep you out da jail house, or yo' neck out da hangman's noose. As far as Ah's concerned, all dat matters is today and our morrows. We is free now. We can go anywhere you wanna go, do anythang you wanna do. It don't matter what happened in da pas', jes' heah, jes' now, jes' me and you."

Jasmine's words did little to calm Rory's anger. She just didn't understand how much it pained him to see scars on her back. It hurt him even more than if he, himself, had suffered every stripe. He managed to hide his outrage. He gently stroked Jasmine's face with one hand; lightly rubbing her scars with the other; somehow, wishing to remove the scars and the guilt he felt for not being there to protect her. Thinking all was fine, she placed her hand on top of his hand leaning into his strong calloused hand, withdrawing only for a second to kiss his palm. "Make love ta me," she said passionately. Jasmine began to kiss his hand, working up his arm to his hairy chest and neck. Her full open moist lips softly caressed his skin, giving him pleasure nothing short of ecstasy. Then, she reached his lips, kissing him with plenty of probing tongue. Rory's anger genuinely cooled for the moment, as his desire to know his wife, once again, ruled his thinking. He took her in his arms, pulling her close to him, kissing and caressing her hard and wanting. His hands explored every inch of her still exquisite body, and when he could wait no longer. He loved her with the zeal of a bull.   Jasmine had missed the way that Rory made love to her, enjoying it more than she should have. For them both, this encounter was better than their very first coupling. When they made love, became one flesh, for them, it was a joining of souls. A joining which left them lost in each other, and made them complete in each other. When their joining was finished, they lay in the coolness of the night. Their bodies were still hot with passion. Rory clung to his wife, and she to him, resting with his arm around her back upon her hip, and she with a leg over his legs, and head upon his chest. All was right with the world in this fleeting moment, but Rory had to know who dared to hurt her.

"Ah bet Massa Drucker gave dem Patties the devil for hurtin' you like dat," he said to rekindle the subject.

"Baby. Please," she said, as she raised her head looking at him, indicating she wanted him to let it go.

"Ah know you forgive, and if you forgive, Ah forgive, but Ah jes' need ta know." Rory continued to pry.

"If you forgives, why you need ta know?" she said, trying to discourage his interest.

"Because Ah do."

Jasmine sat up. She was deeply disturbed that Rory was holding to this. "Listen ta me. It don't matter. It's in da past."

Rory sat up as well. "It's on my mind, Ah gotta know. Iffen you won't tell me, somebody else 'round heah gotta know. Ah'll just ask 'round."

Jasmine was very disturbed by this. "Rory, Ah don't wont no trouble! Why you spoilin' dis night?"

Rory could see that he was upsetting Jasmine. He smiled at her, trying to melt away her fears. " O'm not tryin' ta, but you gotta understand, Ah needs ta know. Dere won't be no trouble. Ah give ya my word dat, dis night, Ah ain't gon' do nothing ta da man dat done dis ta you."

This was good enough for Jasmine. Her love only knew trust in Rory. At no time had he ever lied to her. He had given her his word that no harm would come to Master Drucker. She believed whole heartedly in Rory and decided to give him what he sought. "'Twas Massa Drucker done dis ta me," Jasmine said lowly and cautiously.

Although she said it in a low voice, Rory heard her clearly, but did not believe his ears. "Cyrus Drucker?"

Jasmine knew this was hard for Rory to believe or accept. She simply nodded her head. Without thinking, Rory confirmed her belief that he would question that Cyrus Drucker would do such a thing. In all the years on Drucker's plantation, Rory thought Drucker was a just man. There were many times that Rory could remember someone being punished in this way, and he couldn't say that these slaves were not deserving, or so he thought at the time. No one should be whipped because he was hungry, and stole bread to sustain himself, but Rory was favored at this time in his life by Master Drucker. He understood, then, that if Master Drucker let even the slightest infraction pass, he ran the risk of igniting a widespread uprising among the slaves. For this cause, Rory always thought Master Drucker's actions just, but what justice was there in beating an innocent woman. "Why he do such a thang?" Rory asked, implying to Jasmine that she must be at fault.

Jasmine expected as much. "It wa'n't what Ah done. 'Twas what you done. Youse like a son ta 'im, and ya run off, and fought fuh da Yankees. Massa Drucker took it out on me, 'cause he knowed dat you loved me."

This wrenched Rory's soul from his very being, and sorrowed him without measure. He would have torn his cloths, and went outside to roll in the dirt to dispel his hurt, were it not a foolish thing to do. No one physically died, but to him Cyrus Drucker might as well have been dead. Rory was sick in his being. If this action was taken to hurt Rory, it surely had, more so than Drucker could ever have imagined. How could Cyrus have done such a cruel thing to his precious Jasmine.

Jasmine saw the deep hurt in Rory's eyes. She clung close to him, hugging him tightly. She was afraid Rory would blame and hate her for what happened, but deep down she knew that he wouldn't. He would have sooner hated the air that he breathed and the life within him. She bite her bottom lip as worry filled her soul. Rory hugged her back so tightly that it should have hurt, but it didn't. It was as though all the love in him had found its way to his arms, and it warmed her spirit, making her feel whole.

"Ah's so sorry," Rory said, filled with more sorrow than his heart could bear.

"Don't be sorry, my love. It's jes' da lot of a slave ta be whipped ever' now and 'gain. Please, jes' hold me, and let us try to get some rest. You gon' feel better in da mornin'," said Jasmine.

Rory held his precious Jasmine close to him. She quickly fell asleep, but not so for him. Rory was having a difficult time letting it go. The hours marched on, and finally slumber granted his weary body rest, but only for a short time. A few hours more passed, and Rory found himself awake again. It is written in the Bible that man is born of woman, and in a few days is filled with troubles. Never were there truer words at that moment for Rory. He felt so much guilt, so much anger, so much hurt for not being there to protect Jasmine, would to God that he could go back and change that horrible day for her. He knew she was not the first slave girl to feel the lash upon her back, and no doubt she was not the last, but that did little to comfort. Making matters worst, it was Cyrus Drucker that did the grievous deed. He taught Rory most of what he knew. All of who he was, was because of Cyrus. The man held a special affection in Rory's heart. He was so much more than a master. He was a mentor, friend, and the closest thing to a father Rory had ever known. This was the chief reason Rory was so hurt. Only with some one that you love can one be so angry. Rory had so much trust and faith in Cyrus Drucker. He supposed now that his faith was misplaced in the man. Rory had forgotten his place, that he was a slave, chattel to be done with as it so pleased the master. He had paid for his forgetfulness dearly, with the skin off the back of his precious, precious, Jasmine. Rory felt that he was little more than a puppy to Master Drucker. A pet to fetch for and amuse Cyrus.

For whatever reason, maybe because it was the topic of conversation, in her slumber, Jasmine raised her hand, begging Master Drucker not to beat her. She began to jerk and moan, as if in great pain. It tore the soul right out of Rory. He did not wake her, but comforted her in her sleep, and she was at peace again. He, however, was a long way from knowing peace. Rory now knew that Jasmine was left with more than just scars on her back. She had been left with scars upon her mind. Seeing men fall in battle did not make such an impact on Rory's mind so dearly as watching his woman beg for mercy in her sleep. He knew Cyrus Drucker had the legal right to do as he saw fit with his own property, even kill her if he so desired. Nevertheless, that didn't make what he did right. What Rory had just witnessed made it impossible for him to ever forget or forgive.

When morning came, Rory took Jasmine into the closest town with a store that had a vast selection of goods. Olive Branch was the name of the town: a biblical reference to the olive leaf that the dove returned to the ark with during the great flood in Noah's day.

Rory had brought Jasmine here in order to purchase her some much needed new clothing. Jasmine's clothes were little more than rags. Rory would not have the ruler of his heart dressed in pitiful rags worthy to be discarded or burned. Upon their arrival into town, they went into Bush's General store. Although they entered the store first, Mrs. Bush elected to help another first; a white man. Rory and Jasmine knew the man. His name was Jerad Wildman, and he walked right past them without bothering to speak.

Rory and Jasmine didn't seem to mind that Mrs. Bush helped Jerad first. It gave them a chance to look around. There were many beautiful dresses, and fabrics fit for making bonnets, dresses, shawls, and all manner of pretty things that women liked to adorn themselves with. Jasmine was very excited. She had never owned a dress that wasn't old and worn before she got it.

As Jasmine looked around Bush's General Store for dresses, Rory found he didn't care for shopping. He walked outside. As he stood outside the store, he saw Uncle Whoot begging for spare change. It pained Rory to see this. Most people just walked by him, as if he were nothing, but Rory had compassion in his heart for the old man. He moved down the street, coming face to face with Uncle Whoot. He handed him money.

"It's a law again' vagrancy, old man," Rory said, "Ah don't wanna see 'im haul ya off ta jail." .

"It don't matter iffen dey do. Ah'll haves a place ta lay my head fuh a spell," Whoot replied.

"Don't beg," Rory said, "It's a shame fuh a black man ta beg."

Uncle Whoot lowered his head in shame. He could see that Rory was a proud young man. "Ah's sorry, young fella. Ah done had ta beg so long, till Ah don't know how not ta." Uncle Whoot said apologetically.

"Is ya hungry? Ah can buy ya a meal."

"Naw, my stomach ain't wontin' no food, probably couldn't even keep dat stuff down."

"Is ya sho? Ya look like ya could use a hot meal," Rory said, hoping Uncle Whoot would accept his offer.

"Ah's sho. What yo' name, young fella?" asked the old man.

"Rory."

"Is you Jasmine's man, dat Rory?"

"O'm her husband," answered Rory, sounding as if Uncle Whoot offended him by calling him Jasmine's man.

"Yeah, dat's what Ah was meaning."

"Ya know my Jasmine?"

"Ah don't know her real good, but Ah knows her. Ah was at Elijah's when he bought her home after dat Drucker almost beat her half ta death," Uncle Whoot said.

Rory was somewhat confused by what Uncle Whoot was saying. It didn't quite make sense to him that Master Drucker would let Elijah take Jasmine off the plantation just to take care of her wounds. Cyrus Drucker owned twenty-eight slaves which could have cared for her wounds right there on the plantation.

"Ya mean she run off after he beat her?" Rory asked, hoping to clarify.

"Naw, she ain't run off. Da war was o'er, and he knowed it too. He was jes' bein' da mean soul dat he is, dat Drucker," Uncle Whoot answered.

Rory started to boil, realizing Uncle Whoot was telling him that the war was over and Jasmine was free when Cyrus Drucker beat her. "Is ya sho 'bout dat, old man?"

"Ah's sho as Ah is 'bout anythang," Uncle Whoot answered.

"When dis happen, old man?"

"Ah don't know no dates, but da war was o'er. Iffen Ah knowed it was o'er, he had ta knowed," Uncle Whoot said, quite sure of himself.

"What Time of Year was it?"

"Ah recollect it was 'round fall, last year," Uncle Whoot answered, wondering why Rory was asking him so many questions about something that he must surely already have known.

"Fall of sixty-five, da war was over a few months by den," Rory said, more to himself than to Uncle Whoot.

Uncle Whoot was a drunken old man. What he remembered, heard, and saw was no doubt often clouded by the hard liquor that was ever present in his system. Rory did not know if he could trust what he was saying, but he believed Uncle Whoot. This put a different spin on things for Rory. Jasmine should have told him this. He felt as if she had lied to him. Not telling everything there was to tell was akin to lying in his opinion. Nevertheless, Uncle Whoot could have been mistaken. Maybe, the war was not over when Cyrus Drucker did what he did to her. Rory was going to find out. After supper that night, he intended to ride over and ask Elijah.

Meanwhile, inside the store, Jasmine quietly and shyly watched Mrs. Bush help Jerad pick out something nice for his new bride. It was her birthday, and he wanted to do something nice for her. Mrs. Bush held up a beautiful light-blue bonnet to go along with a nicely styled light-blue dress that Jerad had chosen. It was very lovely to Jasmine. She wanted a dress and bonnet like that. She had never owned a bonnet before; although she could afford it this day, it was still unlikely that she would own a pretty bonnet like the one Jerad was purchasing for his wife.

Jasmine knew that Mrs. Bush would never sell her the same kind of bonnet that she had sold to a white woman. It simply wasn't done. However, it was possible she might sell her the light blue fabric from which the bonnet was made, thought Jasmine. That is, if Mrs. Bush wasn't paying close attention to what Jasmine had. Jasmine selected two pale-brownish calico dresses, and not the best that Mrs. Bush had either. She knew that Mrs. Bush would not sell her the best she had, even if Jasmine could afford it. She also selected a black pair of female Negro brogans, shoes for colored people. Jasmine also selected several patterns and fabrics, including the lovely blue fabric that she liked.

After Jerad had been served, Jasmine coyly put the items she wanted onto the counter, and requested the fabrics, which Mrs. Bush had to cut for her. Mrs. Bush was a woman in her fifties. She was a thin black-haired woman and stood slightly taller than Jasmine. She also wore dark colored dresses all the time, like she was going to a funeral. Mrs. Bush looked at Jasmine with a loutish grimace, wondering how Jasmine was going to pay for all of this. "Ah hope you aren't wanting to put this on credit, gal."

"No ma'am, Ah gots money," Jasmine said.

"Confederate?" Mrs. Bush asked.

"No, ma'am, Yankee dollars," Jasmine said, putting hard United States currency on the counter.

"Well then," Mrs. Bush said, "Ah suppose we can do business, gal."

Mrs. Bush cut the fabrics for Jasmine. When she got to the lovely light-blue fabric, she paused for a moment. She considered not selling it to Jasmine, but she reconsidered. These were very hard times, and hard cash was scarcer than hen's teeth, she thought.

During the journey home, something was not right in the air. Jasmine sensed something was very troubling in Rory. He seemed far too quiet and distant. He had been lively and very talkative all of the morning. Now, he wasn't saying much of anything. Many people knew of the incident between Drucker and her. Jasmine saw Rory talking to Uncle Whoot. She wondered if Uncle Whoot had stuck his wide nose into business which was not his own. She tried to spark a conversation. "Thank ya fuh da cloths again, Rory. Ah never thought Ah'd own new cloths like dese. Ah never would've thought dat Ah'd ever own mo' 'an one new piece. Dis da firs' time in my whole life Ah done had a pair of shoes dat ain't half wo' out befo' Ah got 'em."

"Da firs', maybe, but not da Las'," assured Rory.

Jasmine was hoping Rory would say more, but he did not. "Ah guess Ah best be enjoyin' dis, probably be a long time befo' Ah can haves it dis good again," Jasmine said, determined to get more than a few words from Rory.

"Even when we's slaves, in my heart, you was always my queen. Ah promise you dat Ah's gon' always work hard ta make sho you and me haves a good life. You gon' haves it bedder 'an a whole lot of white folks. Jes' you be awaitin' and a seein'," assured Rory.

Jasmine looked at her Rory, that was just what she wanted to hear. She believed in him. She trusted in every word he told her. Yet, there was an unsurmountable wall of silence which still prevailed. As comforting as his words were, Jasmine sensed something dangerous up ahead. Something so dangerous that it would assuredly rob them of a happy future. She felt that Rory had learned that Cyrus Drucker had no legal right to beat her as he did. She did not want to have the Drucker argument again. If she said nothing, maybe, Rory's anger would pass. Maybe, everything would be all right in the end, at least, this was what she told herself. Her Rory was such a stiff-necked man. Once he got hold of something, it was hard for him to let it go. That aspect of his personality was most unsettling and troubling to Jasmine. Fear of what he might do compelled her to grab his arm and press her head against it. "Promise me dat we gon' grow old and gray together, Rory," said she, hoping the promise would strike a cord of peace in him.

"What?" Rory replied.

"Jes' promise me, please."

"Ah don't understan'."

"Jes' promise me," beseeched Jasmine, knowing he understood what she was asking.

"How can Ah, only God can number da days of a man. We will be happy as long as we can be happy. Ah can promise dat," assured Rory

This did not sit well with Jasmine. Today may be all the time that they would have to be happy, if anger got the better of Rory. Rory knew fully well that Jasmine wanted him to promise her that he would do nothing which would jeopardize their future together.

Jasmine felt that by not telling Rory all that there was to tell, that he may have considered that grounds to renege on his promise not to go after her attacker, and she was right. Rory was looking for any reason to justify going back on a promise.

Jasmine just wanted to be comforted. It was not enough that he promised, only yesterday, not to take action against the man that hurt her. Although what he meant was he wouldn't take action at that particular time, not that he wouldn't take action at all, which was how Jasmine interpreted what he said. That was what he was telling himself at that moment to justify what he was strongly considering doing.

"Ah loves you wid all Ah got inside me ta love. Ah's gon' stan' by ya come what may, only don't throw us away by gittin' yo' mind clouded wid thangs dat don't matter," Jasmine said earnestly.

This statement was as close as Jasmine wanted to come to mentioning Cyrus Drucker. It was her way of addressing the situation without addressing the situation. Rory understood what was meant and jumped right into it. "You should have told me, Jasmine," he insisted.

"Ah did."

"Naw, ya didn't," he said, all the more adament.

"You knows ever' thang dey's ta know."

"Somebody told me Massa Drucker beat cha afta da war o'er, dat true?"

"Who told ya dat?"

"Dat don't matter, is it true?" Rory said, hoping for a straight answer.

Jasmine was very fearful of telling him yes. In what was surely a mistake, she gave a dishonest answer. "No, he ain't done dat."

"No?" Rory asked again, wanting to give her every opportunity to be straight-forward with him.

"No," Jasmine insisted.

Immediately, she felt badly. Rory had always been honest with her and she with him. The nature of their relationship had always been one of trust, until now. She cursed Drucker in her being for making her lie to Rory. He was not her master anymore, but he was still making her do things she would rather not have done. It was a necessary lie, she told herself. It would keep the peace, she believed. She had done what she believed best, but Rory was not totally trusting.

He heard something in her voice which he found disturbing. He heard untruthfulness. It hurt him. She had never flat out lied to him before. What were things coming to between them, he wondered. Rory strongly felt that she was not being truthful. Yet, he did not challenge her. He felt that he needed to talk to Elijah. Elijah would tell him what he needed to know.

Later that evening, Rory went to Elijah's home. He felt certain that Elijah would be willing to assist him with information about Jasmine's beating at the hands of Cyrus Drucker. He found Elijah and Micah conversing on the porch in the cool of the evening. "Evenin', y'all?" he greeted.

"Evenin', what brangs ya out dis way?" Elijah asked curiously.

"Can Ah talk ta ya fuh a bit, Elijah?" Rory asked.

Elijah did not know what to make of Rory's request. " Sho ya kin, Kin Ah ask why?"

"It's 'bout my Jasmine," Rory answered.

"Ah see," Elijah said.

Micah, who was somewhat curious, listened to Elijah and Rory. If there was a problem, he felt, he might be able to help in some way. Rory did not particularly want him to be a part of the conversation, but did not mind his presence. "Ah wa'n't quite sho who ta ask 'bout dis," Rory said somewhat nervously.

"About what?" Elijah asked, having some inkling of what Rory wanted to know.

"You know Massa Drucker beat my Jasmine real bad," Rory said, knowing that he did.

"Ah remember," Elijah answered.

"You and yo'Missus took care of her, right?" Rory continued.

"Yeah, we did."

"What Ah wanna know, is when dis happen."

Elijah saw that trouble might be brewing. He did not want to unwittingly get in the middle of something between Jasmine and Rory. "What cha wife tell ya?" Elijah asked, trying to proceed cautiously.

The question frustrated Rory. He simply wanted to arrive at the truth, but nobody seemed to want to help him get there. "She ain't told me, dat's why Ah's askin' you," Rory said, not being honest about the matter. Jasmine did tell him. He just didn't believe her.

"Maybe, you oughta ask her again," Elijah said.

"Did he beat her afta da war over?" Rory vehemently asked.

The vehemence in Rory's tone made Elijah all the more certain that he did not want to be in the middle of this. He would have liked to have helped Rory, but did not want to betray Jasmine's confidence. If she felt it was necessary to hold back the timing of the incident from Rory, she must have had her reasons.

"Is dat when he done it, afta da war?" Rory asked again.

Micah saw Elijah did not want to answer. He tried to help his brother out. "Rory, may I say something?"

"Speak ya peace," Rory said, willing to listen.

"I'm sure you are aware that it took some time for word to reach everyone that the war was over. You know for yourself that there were still minor skirmishes going on between troops months after the war was over. If the soldiers actually fighting the war didn't know it was over, it is a reasonable assumption that civilians wouldn't have known either. We use to go around to different plantations, and found that many slave holders still hadn't released their slaves. For some this was deliberate, but for others, they just didn't know the war was over. It's a good year now that the war is over, and I would be willing to wager there are some black people still living in slavery for one reason or another. Word travels slowly sometimes," Micah explained.

"Maybe, is dat how it was fuh Massa Drucker, Elijah?" Rory asked, not willing to let Elijah off the hook.

"Tell me, Rory. What cha gon' do iffen Ah tell ya, and you don't like da answer dat Ah gives?" Elijah asked.

"So, he knowed, huh?" Rory asked.

"Dat ain't what Ah said. Ah's askin' what cha gon' do?" Elijah said in an effort to set Rory's understanding straight.

"Ah don't know, Mr. 'lijah, but Ah need ta know iffen he knowed da war was o'er when he done dat ta her. It's 'bout ta drive me crazy," Rory said with sincere emotion in his voice.

Elijah felt the pain the young man was going through, and was almost persuaded to help him, but the voice of reason told him to proceed with caution. "Ah understan' dis 'portant ta ya, but knowin' how 'portant it is. Why ain't Jasmine told ya?"

Rory wanted to dodge this question, but did not. Rory sighed and chuckled once. "Ah spect cause she thanks Ah's a hothead, but Ah already know. Somebody in town told me Massa Drucker knowed da war was o'er, and you done much as told me by what cha ain't said."

It did not make sense to either Elijah or Micah that he would be here if he already knew the answer to the question.

"Rory, maybe ya oughta go home and jes' talk ta Jasmine, explain ta her how 'portant dis is ta ya. Ah believe y'all kin work it out," Elijah earnestly conveyed.

Rory knew that the confirmation he was seeking would not be given by Elijah. He decided the best thing to do was to return home. He did not harbor any bad feelings toward Elijah. If the situation was reversed, he would not want to get in the middle of this either. He bade Elijah and Micah good night and went home to Jasmine.

She did not ask where he had been. Truthfully, she was glad to see him go out for a while. She was hoping that when he returned the look of restless rage would be gone from his eyes, it wasn't. Rory took a seat at the small, square, white, two-chair table in the room. Jasmine sat across from him, and rested her head in her left hand, smiling at him. "Ya look like da weight of da world is on ya shoulders, let me help ya bear da burden."

"My burden is Ah can't forgive or forget," he said most solemnly.

Jasmine did not really want to go where this conversation was about to lead, but she had to do something before the hatred that was building inside her man destroyed them both. "Do ya know youse my reason fuh livin'? Whether Ah'm wid cha or not, Ah'm always wid cha. Ah thank 'bout cha all day and dream 'bout cha all night. Iffen Ah could, Ah believes, Ah'd crawl up in ya and melt into ya soul, cause Ah can't ever be to close ta ya. Ya my every smile, every thought, Ah don't know who Ah is without cha. Iffen ya loves me only half as much as Ah loves you, let dis go. Let da mistrust and hate Ah see in ya eyes go, let it go fuh loves sake."

"Ah loves ya even mo' 'an Ah loves myself. Ah loves ya so much dat

Ah can't let it go. Youse da air dat Ah breath, da water dat Ah drank, and da food dat Ah eat. Youse every thang ta me, and when somebody hurts ya. It feels like somebody done plucked da life right out of me. As long as Ah live nobody can ever hurt cha, and not answer ta me fuh what dey done," earnestly conveyed Rory.

This saddened Jasmine. It was good to know she was loved, but what of them? Why couldn't Rory see that, even now, white people wouldn't tolerate him harming one of their own. They would kill him for sure, and there would be no them. Why did Rory refuse to see this, she wondered. "Ain't somethin' Ah can say ta help put yo' mind at ease, somethin' Ah can do?" Jasmine asked, lovingly.

"Ain't nothin' ta be said or done. Maybe, Ah could let go iffen it was somebody else done dis ta ya. Ah thank den Ah could let go, Ah don't know. Nobody else would know what cha mean ta me, but Massa Drucker know how much Ah loves ya. He know you in my soul. He shouldn't oughta hurt cha like dat," said Rory, very grievous.

Jasmine looked at him. She did not know how to help Rory. It pained her. "Is it gon' be a us, Rory?"

"Always," answered he.

"Not iffen ya go and do somethin' ta Massa Drucker. Dem white folks gon' kill ya dead iffen ya raise yo' hands against 'im. Don't cha know dat?" Jasmine said, trying to open his eyes to the simple truth.

"Ah don't thank it's gon' come ta dat,"

"Why, Rory?" she asked, wanting him to think about what he was saying, and see the folly of it.

"Cause we ain't slaves no mo'."

"Not ta dem. We gon' always be slaves ta dem," she said, hoping her words would take stronger meaning than just words.

"What cha wont me ta do, Jasmine? Ya wont me ta forget Ah loves ya. Do ya wont me ta turn my back dis time or da time afta dat. Ah's a man, and a man gotta be a man. A man gotta live the way he thanks he oughta, or he ain't really livin'. He can't keep bendin' o'er so somebody can ride his back. He gotta stand up straight and tall. He gotta stand fuh somethin', do ya hear what Ah's sayin'?" asked the man.

Jasmine did not know what to say. She saw there had been growth in Rory while he was away. A growth she did not fully understand. Nevertheless, there was no future for her without him, only love without an outlet. This was why she had to think of something to reach him. "So, pride matters mo' 'an us?" Jasmine asked, not knowing what else to say.

"It ain't pride."

"What is it, but pride?"

"It's me needin' ta be a man. Ya jes' don't understan'."

"Ah thanks Ah do, Ah jes' don't know what ta do 'bout it. Ah was hopin' dat iffen Ah didn't say nothin', dis would pass away. Pass away, and we would be okay, but it ain't goin' away. Ah don't know what ta do. Ah don't wont ta lose ya," Jasmine said sincerely.

"Ya ain't gon' lose me, but cha can't keep lyin' ta me. Dat ain't da woman Ah loves. Da woman Ah loves is gon' always tell me da truth, cause dat's who she is," said Rory.

Jasmine lowered her head in shame. Maybe, had she been more forthcoming from the start, things might be better than they stand right now, she thought. She decided to confess her faults. "Ah's sorry, Ah didn't mean ta lie ta ya. Ah jes' wanna protect what Ah got, what we got," she said, feeling much better now that she no longer had to lie.

"What we got ain't gon' never pass away. Whether Ah's heah or in da grave, Ah's gon' always love ya," assured he.

"But Ah don't wont cha in da grave, Ah won't cha heah wid me."

"It's gon' be alright, Ah promise," assured the young man.

He rose from his chair, moving toward Jasmine. He took her into his arms and carried her to the bed. Jasmine felt much better now. In her mind, Rory had given her assurances that he would not do anything to put their sweet love at risk. They made love: sweet, tender, passionate, joining of the souls, never wanting it to end love. The heat of it was so hot that they were both sweating profusely by the time it was over, but instead of falling away that they might cool from their passion. Rory continued to kiss Jasmine, holding her close to him, as he gently stroked her sweat drenched body, professing his eternal love for her. After a time, they fell fast asleep in deep contentment.

Morning fell, the sun was shining red against a lace of dark clouds. Jasmine reached for the spot where Rory should have been. The fact that he was not lying besides her, caused Jasmine to open her eyes suddenly. She glanced around the room searching for him. She sprang from bed, and dashed through the door out onto the porch in her nakedness. She saw Rory riding off in the direction of the Drucker plantation. She saw that he had his musket with him. It frightened her beyond words. She called to him. Momentarily, he looked back. She saw on his face that a course of action had been decided upon. She knew that he was going to kill Cyrus Drucker. Her heart began to pound so fast that it felt as if it was going to pound out of her chest. "Rory, don't!" she called to no avail.

Rory spurred his horse onward. He had made up his mind.

"Rory, please, we can be happy!" she screamed.

Rory did not look back. Jasmine could see that it was useless to call him. She determined that she must get help. She raced into the house. She was running around with confused energy, like a chicken with its head cut off, trying to get dressed. It took her less than thirty seconds. She did not bother to put on shoes. She raced out of the house at a full run. She had to get to Elijah's house a full two miles away. She gave it everything she had. Her stride widened with each time her feet struck the ground. The ground was wet with the morning dew. The bottom of her dress quickly became wet. Her feet began to stain green as she ran through the grass. Her nostrils flared as wide as possible to take in as much air as she could. Her lungs began to burn, as she dared not lose a step at that pace. The sooner she got to Elijah, the more time he would have to try and overtake Rory. Her leg muscles ached, and the skin on her legs tingled as she approached Elijah's home. She was almost ready to pass out, but she couldn't quit. Her buttocks burned so intensely that she just wanted to fall to the ground, and lay still until the pain passed, but she couldn't stop. As she closed on Elijah's house, it gave her renewed strength. It took her just under thirteen minutes to cover two hard miles.

She was perspiring, copiously, and was so winded that she could hardly knock at the door, but she did with amazing energy. To those inside, it sounded like thunder, like someone was after her. Micah opened the door, and Jasmine collapsed in his arms.

"Lawd, what is dis?" Mama Julia said frightened.

Elijah looked out the door to see if there was someone after Jasmine. Micah carried Jasmine to his bed, and retrieved his pistol, a Remington .44 caliber Army Revolver with a brown wooden handle. He looked outside the door with Elijah, they saw nothing.

"Elijah. Elijah," Jasmine called frantically to him.

"What's wrong, gal?" Elijah inquired.

"Rory, you gotta stop Rory," Jasmine tried to explain.

"Stop 'im?" Elijah asked, wondering what Rory was about to do.

"He gon' kill Massa Drucker. You gotta stop 'im befo' it's too late," Jasmine beseeched.

"Are you sure?" Micah asked.

"He rode out towards Massa Drucker's house, and he had his gun," Jasmine explained.

"Goodness, no," Mama Julia cried.

"How long he been gon'?" Elijah asked, trying to sum up what he was up against.

"Not long, iffen ya hurry, Ah knows ya can catch 'im," Jasmine answered.

Immediately, Elijah headed for the door. "Ah's gon' catch 'im, Jasmine," he said with determination in his voice.

Rory had a head start and was riding a horse. That made Elijah's task all the more difficult, considering all he had to catch up to Rory with was a mule. If he rode hard enough, maybe, he could catch Rory before he got into trouble he couldn't be helped out of.

Micah exited the house shortly after Elijah. "Elijah, take my horse. He's faster than that mule of yours."

Elijah did not waste time thanking his brother. He mounted the horse without taking the time to saddle the animal. He took a bit of the bridle strap and struck the sorrel horse. The animal quickly got up to full run, the dust kicking up behind the strong horse.

Back inside the house, Josephine and Mama Julia tried to calm Jasmine, who was very frantic and upset. "Calm yo' self, gul," Mama Julia said.

"It's gon' be okay, Elijah gon' catch 'im," Josephine assured.

"Da good Lawd will see ta dat," also assured Mama Julia.

"He sho is, don't cha fret none," comforted Josephine.

"Why he wanna hurt Drucker?" Mama Julia asked.

"Fuh what he done ta Jasmine, Mama Julia. He ain't have no right ta beat her like he done," Josephine explained.

Jasmine did not have the breath to engage the ladies in conversation, nor did she want to. She was hot, tired, sweaty. She had literally almost ran herself to death, and was in no mood for talk. She just wanted Rory back safe and sound.

"Ya wont some water, child? Get her some water, Josephine," instructed Mama Julia, fanning Jasmine with her white apron.

"Okay," Josephine said, getting the water.

"She All right?" Micah asked, as he entered the house.

"Don't know, she won't say nothin'," Mama Julia replied.

"She all right, she jes' upset wit' worry. Don't worry none, heah, Elijah gon' brang dat Rory of yours back," Josephine assured.

Jasmine finally had the wherewithal to speak, "Ah's sorry, y'all. Ah jes' didn't know where else ta turn."

"Don't you be worryin' 'bout dat. You like family ta us, and family helps family," Josephine comforted.

"Are you all right, Jasmine," Micah asked, genuinely concerned.

"Ah's fine," she answered.

"Good. Do you need me to ride into town and get the doctor?" Micah asked, wanting to be sure all was well with Jasmine.

"No, Ah's fine. Ah'm jes' worried 'bout Rory," Jasmine explained.

"If you're okay, I'll go see if I can help Elijah with Rory," Micah said.

"Good thankin', Micah," Josephine said, feeling that was the appropriate move.

"Yeah, do dat, Micah," urged Mama Julia.

"Thank ya, Micah, thank ya," Jasmine said gratefully.

Micah saddled Elijah's mule, and lit out after Elijah. The Drucker place was some twelve miles away, in Mt. Pleasant. By the time he reached them, the conflict was sure to be over, Micah thought. He was hoping that Rory wouldn't have the nerve for this business, but somehow he knew better. If he were in Rory's position, he would have responded in the exact same way.

Elijah was riding hard. He hoped to catch Rory before he reached Cyrus Drucker. He was running the risk of riding the horse to death at this pace, but he had to if he was going to make a difference. Unfortunately, Rory was moving at a fast pace as well. Not as fast as Elijah, but he wanted to do this before he had time to talk himself out of what he felt must be done.

This was a strange day for Cyrus Drucker. He was usually up before dawn, but this morning he woke up at three thirty, much earlier than his regular five. He laid there trying to fall back asleep, but he could not. He had the feeling that something of significance was going to happen in his life today. Something not good. He dismissed this feeling, telling himself that it was merely all the stress and strain of his financial burdens eroding his ability to sleep well at night. He was in considerable debt, with no apparent means of keeping his creditors at bay. The war had left him without the slave labor force to plant and harvest his cotton crop. In essence, it had robbed him of his livelihood. This plantation of his had been in his family better than four generations, and it looked as if he was going to be the one to lose it.

He finally dragged himself out of bed, got ready, and made his way downstairs. The house was eerily quiet, as he lived alone. He had no family and there were no servants that lived on the premises. He had a hired woman, who came each morning around seven thirty to prepare meals and clean for him. He went into the kitchen and fried himself two eggs, which he found he did not have an appetite for. It was light out now, and he went outside to take a look around. He really did love this place. It saddened him to think that it would fall into the hands of those who had no dear memories of its grandeur, or an appreciation for its rich history. Seven thirty rolled around. Oddly, his hired woman had not yet arrived. She was usually here before time. He stood there in front of the great white house. It was made of cedar, and was two stories tall, with a balcony all the way around the second floor. The house was built by his great-grandfather. Trying to think of a way to save it, he looked across the distance. He saw a rider galloping onto his land. The rider brought his horse to a stop, then continued on toward him somewhat slowly. Cyrus could tell the man was black, but little else. Cyrus stood there looking at the rider. Suddenly, he knew it was Rory. A wide smile covered his face. He was pleased to see Rory had not been killed during the war. The smile slowly turned to a frown, as he remembered how Rory betrayed him.

Having no living child of his own, as his child died at two years of age on the same night Rory was born, he treated Rory as a son. He gave Rory privileges no other slave on his plantation had. Rory was free to come and go as he pleased after work in the fields was done on any day of the week. Most slaves were only allowed to do this on the weekend. He had planned to give Rory his freedom in time, but not only that. He planned to give him so much more. He planned to give Rory land and Jasmine as well, but Rory betrayed him. After all he had done for him, Rory betrayed him. Maybe, it was his own fault, he should never have allowed Rory the chance to feel like anything more than a slave.

At that moment, Cyrus remembered what he did to Jasmine. He felt the need to arm himself. He ran into the house, and retrieved his firearm, an old 1847 cap-and-ball Walker Colt. He had a certain loyalty to the weapon, as it had saved his life fourteen years earlier, and at the moment, it appeared that it would need to do so again. He went back outside prepared for whatever was about to happen.

Rory dismounted his horse and tied it beneath a Cedar tree about some thirty yards from Drucker. He retrieved his rifle-musket from the horse, and started his walk toward Cyrus. Cyrus Drucker was an older man in his late fifties. He was round in the mid-section, very portly. He stood five feet nine and a half inches. A bow-legged man, more so in his right leg than left, he had a clean shaven face with black and gray hair and blue eyes. Seeing Rory unholster his musket, Cyrus' heart began to race. He started to sweat profusely. "Stop right there, boy!" He commanded, firing a round into the air.

Rory did not stop moving toward the portly man. Army training had taught him to keep his cool in such situations as this. He had been trained to advance close enough to do damage before firing his weapon. Drucker did not want him to come any closer. He too knew the closer Rory got to him. the more likely it was that both of them could be killed, even if he delivered the first shot. "Ah'm prepared to kill you, Rory, if you keep coming!" warned Cyrus aiming at Rory.

Rory continued to advance, uncapping his musket. Cyrus' right leg began to tremble, he was afraid. He did not want to kill Rory, but it seemed that was exactly what he would have to do. He hoped Rory could not see his fear.

"Boy, don't make me kill you!" Cyrus warned one last time.

Rory continued to advance. Cyrus fired a shot, which came so close to Rory's head that he heard the ball whistle past his head. His heart began to race much faster, but he did not flinch. He aimed his musket at Cyrus. They both know someone was about to die. They both had the shot to take the other's life. Yet, Rory hesitated to pull the trigger.

The stress at this moment was more than Cyrus could take. His heart was pounding so hard it seemed he could hear the blood rushing through his veins. He dropped his weapon, clutching his chest. He was having a heart attack. He fell to the ground, flat on his back. He was at Rory's mercy, but that did not matter to him.

Rory realized what was happening. He dropped his musket and rushed to the old man's side. He dropped to his knees, lifting the head of Cyrus. He came there to kill Cyrus, but found out only just then that he couldn't have. He loved Cyrus, who was lying there dying in Rory's arms. If it were in Rory's power, he would change this. None of the bad which happened between them mattered now. There were many good times that they shared, this was all that mattered. "Ah wouldn't 've hurt cha, old man. Ah wouldn't 've," Rory told him.

Cyrus smiled, as if to assure Rory that he knew as much. At this point, both of them knew that all was forgiven between them. Cyrus closed his eyes in death. He laid there, looking as if he were asleep.

Rory wept for him. This was one of the worst days in his life. The only man in his life, who was closer to a father, was dead. He rubbed Cyrus' face. "It shouldn't oughta ended dis way," he said to the man, who could no longer hear him.

Rory heard a horse approaching fast. He looked up to see Elijah riding a horse drenching wet with sweat. He rode right up to Rory and dismounted. "God help us, Rory. What cha done done?" Elijah asked, afraid for Rory and himself.

"Ah ain't killed 'im," Rory made known.

"What happened den?" Asked a doubtful Elijah.

"He done died of a heart attack," Rory answered.

Elijah, who was having trouble believing what Rory was telling him, inspected the body for bullet holes. "Where is Mrs. Waghorn?"

"Who?"

"Da white lady dat cooks and cleans fuh 'im."

"Ah ain't seed her."

"Go check da house fuh her thangs. If she snuck out when dis thang got started, she won't habe took her thangs wit her. She'll be busy tryin' ta git help."

"And, iffen dats how it is?"

"Den, you might habe ta run to save yo' neck."

"Why, Ah ain't killed 'im."

"Iffen Mrs. Waghorn saw you pointin' dat musket at 'im, den you killed 'im, cause dat's how dem white folks gon' see it."

Rory said nothing more, and went to inspect the house to see if there were any indicators Mrs. Waghorn had been there. He returned a short time later. Micah was seen in the distance approaching.

"Ah don't thank she done made it heah yet. They's a plate where somebody been eatin' in da kitchen, but he could've done dat," Rory explained.

"Dat's good, maybe we got a chance. Take dis gun and put it back where you thank it go and reload it iffen ya kin. Den come on back out heah. Meantime, O'm gon' start straightenin' up out heah," Elijah said.

Micah rode up, and was not shocked to see Cyrus lying dead.

"Ah ain't got time ta explain, Micah. Take ya foot, or break off a branch, and start clearin' Rory's foot prints from da house back clean ta his horse," Elijah instructed.

"What good is that gonna do?" Micah asked.

Rory exited the house, running over to Elijah and Micah.

"Nobody can tell ya been in dere, kin dey?" Elijah asked.

"Ah ain't touched nothin', Ah jes' put da gun back," Rory replied.

"Rory git yo' musket, and git on yo' horse, and git out of heah. Travel in da woods, we don't wont nobody ta see ya on da road travelin' away from dis place," Elijah commanded.

"What cha gon' do?" Rory asked.

"Y'all askin' too many questions, jes' work wit' me," Elijah said, trying to save the day.

"What do you have up your sleeve, Elijah?" Micah asked.

"Rory, git movin'," commanded Elijah, "iffen all goes well, Ah'll come see ya at yo' place tonight."

Rory did as he was told. He picked up his weapon, and mounted his horse, heading for the woods. "Micah, Drucker heart done give out on 'im. We kin make dis look like Rory ain't had nothin' ta do wit' it. We kin tell da sheriff dat you is my brother, and Ah brought cha over ta ask iffen he need a hired han', but we can't say dat iffen it look like gun play done went on 'round heah. Rory can't be nowhere 'round heah, and ever'body know Drucker beat Jasmine bloody when he ain't habe no right ta. Drucker got a lady dat keep house fuh 'im. She ain't heah yet, but Ah spect she gon' be heah any minute. Iffen dem tracks ain't clear, dey kin tip da sheriff dat what we tellin' 'im ain't da whole truth," Elijah explained.

"Why not just clear the tracks and leave? They don't have to know we have been here either," rationalized Micah.

"No, we wont ta lead 'im da way we wont 'im thankin'. We don't wont 'im thankin' on his own, which is what he'll do iffen we ain't heah ta guide his thankin'. We don't wont 'im lookin' too hard. He might see somethin' we don't wont 'im to."

This sounded reasonable to Micah, and he began to clear tracks from the house back toward the body. Elijah cleared the tracks from the porch to where Rory had his horse tied, to where the body was. They finished just in time. Mrs. Waghorn and her son could be seen in the distance. A sense of shock overwhelmed the Waghorns, as they saw Cyrus Drucker lying motionless on the ground. There was also fear in Mrs. Waghorn. She was afraid of Elijah and Micah, but not young Waghorn. Elijah and Micah were just blacks to him. Naively, he was of the opinion that any white man was more man than five Negroes, and could set them to flight with but a hard stare. He hurried the horses to get to Cyrus. When he was close enough, he leapt from his rig. "What have you niggers done!?" he asked unafraid, feeling as one having authority in this situation.

Micah was offended by the brashness of young Waghorn, but remained quiet. This was Elijah's play.

"We ain't done nothin', suh," Elijah said, humbling himself to a boy ten years his junior.

"Then what happened, boy?"

"My brother new round heah, he need work. We jes' rode over ta see iffen Massa Drucker might could use a hired han'. We was jes' talkin' ta 'im, when he fell out. We ain't knowed what ta do fuh 'im. My brother was jes' 'bout ta ride ta town ta fetch da sheriff when Y'all showed up," Elijah explained.

"Is that what you were about to do, boy?" Young Waghorn asked, looking at Micah, as he finished checking Cyrus' body to ensure that he was beyond any help that he might be able to give.

"Yes, it is," Micah answered.

"Well, then, get movin', nigger."

Micah was having a very difficult time resisting the urge to snatch this youngster up and whip him all over the premises. Young Waghorn's show of strength went a long way toward helping his mother put away her fears.

Micah rode to Olive Branch, he was uneasy the entire journey. Despite the fact that Elijah explained why they should follow this present course of action, he did not agree. From his view point, it would have been better to have left the Drucker Plantation with Rory. Yes, he would much rather have destroyed any evidence and left with Rory, even if they couldn't destroy it all. Elijah was taking an awful chance with their necks, while Rory went free.

As he rode into the town limits, toward the County Sheriff's Office. He tried to conceal the look of being worried upon his face. He knew such body language might cause the Sheriff to dig deeper into this matter than would be good, and he didn't want that. As he walked into the Sheriff's office, he tried not to look to proud. Pride was a damnable trait in a black man, particularly in the South. A look of grit could land the colored man in jail.

Inside the County Sheriff's Office, he found the deputy, Angus Farley. He was a snuff spitting fat man with a mouth that looked as if he didn't know what a toothbrush was. The fat man looked at Micah oddly. He wondered what possible business Micah could have with the Sheriff's office. It was contemptible to him that Micah had the nerve to be there. Law was for the white man, not this damnable race of former slaves, he thought. "What you want here, boy?" he said in a tone meant to discourage Micah from visiting now and in the future.

Micah's eyes squinted slightly and his face grew stern as an immediate dislike for this man filled him. He was able to sense that if he was in dire need of the services of this office, the good deputy would not be receptive to helping. He might even be a hindrance, as his negative tone implied he would not be willing to stand against the white man on behalf of the black man. "There has been an unfortunate happening at the residence of Cyrus Drucker, he is dead of a heart attack. I have come to inform you so that you might look into the matter." Micah said, unwisely and deliberately speaking with strong verbiage, letting the deputy know that he was better educated and smarter than was he.

The deputy knew Micah was sending him a clear message, and he did not like the confident proud look of Micah or what he was so boldly implying one bit. "Woo-wee, boy. Ah declare Ah ain't never heard no nigger talk like that. Ah bet you one of them swamp-runnin' niggers that made it up north. Yeah, you been livin' there a while. Got yer self a little education while you was up that away too, didn't ya? Probably think you are equal to me, better than me. You don't think you better than me, do you, boy?" Farley said in a strikingly venomous tone.

Micah wanted to tell Deputy Farley that he was smarter and a much better man than he was in every conceivable way, but dared not. He did not want to alienate Farley anymore than he already had. He needed the deputy to perform his duty without bias, which at that point seemed an unlikely possibility. "There is a man lying dead in his front yard. Will you look into this matter, or is it your intent to let his body rot in the sun?" Micah said, unintentionally getting smart with Farley. He just couldn't refrain.

Farley was of the mindset that he was not going to take such impertinence from a black heathen. He was going to have to break Micah down, put him in his place. Angus was seated behind the sheriff's desk with his feet kicked upon it. He stood and started around it, moving toward Micah. This made Micah uneasy. Angus sat on the front of the desk. "Yeah, Ah bet, yer one of them educated niggers that thinks a new world is dawning for tha black race, don't ya? You see brighter days ahead for your people. Well, ain't no new world comin'. It's gonna be tha same old world tomorrow that it was yesterday, and is today. My world, don't forget that, boy. There still plenty of gloomy days ahead for you and your kind." Farley said with a wicked smile upon his face.

Micah started to sweat. The dehumanizing way in which the deputy was speaking to him made Micah feel threatened. He felt as if he needed to defend himself, and the best way for him to do that was to go on the offensive. He was on the threshold of grabbing Angus and going to work on him. Micah was confident that it wouldn't take much pressure to make Angus regress in age and start crying like a little girl. Somewhere down deep inside, Micah found the control to keep from hurting this sorry excuse for a man. Micah wiped his face, with his hand from his forehead to chin.

As the aggression within Micah subsided, the deputy smiled, the sweating led him to believe Micah was afraid of him and frustrated.

Angus hadn't a clue as to whom he was dealing with, but in time he would find out. Just then, the door opened. It was Sheriff Robert Hackman. He was a honorable man, but not one empathetic to the struggle of the black man. He was, however, committed to the execution of the duties of his office. He was an impressive looking man. He was tall, slender, with broad shoulders, and a deep commanding voice. He was surprised to see Micah in the office. "What can we do for you?" the sheriff asked, knowing all to well that his deputy had not been of much help to the man.

"Uh, the boy here says there's been some trouble down Cyrus Drucker's way," interjected Deputy Farley, looking snide and intimidating.

"Trouble?"

"The boy says a heart attack got 'im."

"What were you doing at Cyrus Drucker's place?" Sheriff Hackman asked immediately, suspicious of Micah.

"I'm recently back from up North. I'm living with my brother. He took me over to see Drucker to inquire if he might need a hired hand." Micah explained.

"What's your brother's name?"

"Elijah Wright, sheriff."

"What's your name?" Robert asked, observing Micah's body language, trying to determine how Micah acted when he was telling the truth.

"Micah."

Sheriff Hackman was suspicious of almost everything. He was particularly suspicious of the newly emancipated black race. He had heard that they were thieves, crafty, and not to be trusted. He decided to see what lay beneath the cool facade Micah presented. He pulled out a pencil and some writing paper, with the intention of writing down everything Micah said.

"Why did you say you and your brother went to Drucker?"

"To see if he had work, sheriff."

"Was he alive when you got there?"

"Yes, he came outside and talked to us in front of his home."

"Was anyone else present at the home other than you, your brother, and Mr. Drucker?"

"No one else was present," Micah replied.

"Doesn't he have a woman working for him?" the sheriff asked. "Where was she?"

"She and her son came right after he died."

"What happened after he came out to talk with you?"

"He was just talking, and then he just fell out."

"And, what did you do?"

"What could we do? We didn't know what to do for him, we aren't doctors."

"Smart mouth nigger ain't he?" interjected Deputy Farley, not liking Micah's tone and lack of the word sir at the end of every sentence.

"Go on with your story," Sheriff Hackman said.

"That's about it, except his hired woman pulled up, and I came to fetch you."

The sheriff wrote down everything Micah said. He intended to question Elijah the moment they got out to Drucker's place, question him apart from Micah. If there was any inconsistency in their stories, he would know that they were up to no good.

Once at the Drucker place, the sheriff told Elijah to wait on the porch, and not to speak to his brother while waiting. Sheriff Hackman looked over the body and surrounding area. There was nothing unusual to him. Next, he questioned Elijah. He found no inconsistencies with what Micah told him. He then interviewed the Waghorns. The Sheriff concluded nothing was afoot. "You two, pick up Mr. Drucker's body and carry it inside," instructed the sheriff, looking at Elijah and Micah, "Mrs. Waghorn will you be so kind as to show them where Mr. Drucker's bedroom is. He'll be safe there until the undertaker can be sent for."

This was going just as Elijah hoped it would. Micah and he picked up Drucker's body and carried it inside. They laid him in his bed and left. Mrs. Waghorn started to cry. She would miss Cyrus. Her son stood at her side, as she mourned the passing of a dear friend and employer. She touched Cyrus' face, stroking it down to his neck. Most of his head was now cool to the touch, but his neck and torso were still warm.

"Don't cry, mother. He is gone to a better place," young Waghorn said.

"Ah know," she sighed, "Ah just wish he had some family to mourn his passing. Perhaps, now he will be with his wife and child in heaven's fair."

Micah was glad this was almost over. It looked as if they were going to get out of this mess unscathed. He wished Rory had gone about this business more discreetly. He was glad Rory's neck wouldn't get stretched, but he felt the young man was nothing but trouble, and wanted nothing more to do with him.

Rory had arrived at Elijah's place some time ago. After going to his own home, and finding Jasmine was not there. He figured that she was still at Elijah's home. He was ashamed to go in, but that did not matter.

The women had been waiting and watching. Josephine caught a glimpse of him, and all the women rushed from the house.

"Rory, youse back," Mama Julia exclaimed.

"Where Elijah and Micah?" Josephine asked, worried because she did not see them.

Rory did not answer a word. Jasmine was standing obscurely behind Mama Julia and Josephine, but Rory was all too aware that she was there. The way she looked at him, very disappointed in him, made him feel all the more ashamed. Even more so, he did not want to tell Josephine that Elijah and Micah stayed behind to cover for him.

"Rory, everythang all right?" Josephine asked, becoming more worried with Rory's persistent silence.

"Ah don't know. Elijah and Micah stayed behind ta hide Ah was dere."

"Why?" Josephine asked nervously.

"Because, Massa Drucker dead."

Shock appeared on the faces of all three women.

"Ya killed 'im?" Jasmine asked with a meek, woefully, sorrowful tone. All the women listened eagerly for an answer.

"He died of a heart attack. Ah didn't kill 'im."

"Why Elijah and Micah gotta stay behind den?" Josephine asked, very puzzled.

"Cause Ah was pointin' a musket at 'im when he had his heart attack."

"So ya killed 'im," commented Mama Julia.

"Dat's da way Elijah said white folks gon' see it," Rory said.

"Elijah right, Dat's da way dey gon' see it, Rory," Josephine assured.

She never said it, but there was a definite look of 'what have you done' on Jasmine's face. It was such a sad piercing look that even Josephine could see it beyond her own worry. "Don't fret none, Jasmine, not yet. Iffen Elijah stayed behind, he got a way out dis mess. He a smart man. He gon' fix dis, jes' wait and see," Josephine said with the most remarkable confidence in Elijah.

"Well, no use standin' 'round out heah. Lessgo inside, Ah'll make us up some coffee whiles we wait," Mama Julia said.

Mama Julia and Josephine went inside, but not Jasmine or Rory. Jasmine was furious. It was an anger beyond words. There were tears in her eyes, on the brink of breaking forth. Rory could plainly see that she was hurt, but he did what he felt he had to do. He wanted her to say something. Silence at this juncture could easily rip apart the very fabric of their relationship. "Ah love ya, Jasmine," said he, as if that would make everything all right.

"Do ya?"

"Ah do."

"Is dere gon' be a us, Rory?"

"As long as time goes on."

"Not like dis, even da mightest tree gotta bend a little when a strong wind come along, else it gon' be uprooted."

"Sometimes it's uprooted even if it do bend. So, it's best ta stand as ya gon' stand, come what will."

Jasmine sighed and lowered her head. She turned and went inside, her heart heavy with burden.

Time passed and eventually Elijah and Micah returned. Josephine was so excited to see him that she ran and threw herself on him. All others in the room had a look of impatience on their faces.

"All is well," assured Micah.

Everyone breathed a sigh of relief.

"Ah knowed you was gon' take care of dis, Elijah," Josephine said.

"Da sheriff ain't seem ta find nothin' wrong. So, Ah thank we safe," Elijah said.

"We is, Ah know we is," Mama Julia hoped.

"Y'all, nobody in dis room should ever mention dis again, not even ta each other," Elijah instructed.

"I'm sure you can count on that," Micah said, looking directly at Rory whom he considered an unstable entity.

"You can count on us, Elijah," Rory assured.

With that, as far as Elijah was concerned, the matter was closed.

On the morning that Ken Bailey's body was found, Rory awoke to find that his beloved Jasmine was not lying next to him. He got up, slipped on his cloths, and went outside to look for her. She was nowhere to be found. There had been silence between them for weeks now, not comfortable silence, but distressed silence, the silence of stubborn pride. All sorts of things began to run through Rory's mind. The most troubling thought was that she may have been so upset with him for the Drucker incident that she left him, left him without so much as a goodbye. Suddenly, he felt physically weak. This single thought so troubled his love-struck mind that straightaway he had to take a seat. He felt genuine sorrow and the deepest regret. He did what he felt he had to do in the name of love, and he thought she understood that. He didn't want to lose her. He couldn't even begin to imagine life without her. As he sat in the oak rocking chair in front of their home, he told himself that she would not do such a thing. She wouldn't just leave him. She meant the world to him. She was always with him in heart and mind, surely, she must have known that.

As he sat there with his head hung low and water pooling in his eyes, he looked up to see Jasmine walking across the uneven field directly in front of their home. Against a backdrop of tall-green Cedar trees, she was moving briskly across the field of ankle-high green grass with vibrantly rich yellow, small, rayed like, impatiens like, wildflowers, which had about seven flowers on each stem.

As she moved across the field, the look of her countenance was so sad. Desperately sad one might say. Dandelion, in the showy, white, soft-feathery stage of life, tenderly swayed in the gentle-morning breeze; desiring that its seed be swept up into the wooing wind's loving bosom; as Jasmine's head hung sadly low in deeply perplexed thought. As she crossed the reddish clay dirt road, she adjusted her red shawl, pulling it completely around her, holding it dearly as she folded her arms, as if she were cold and alone. She came to a halt before Rory, standing in a cluster of three-leafed clovers. Upon seeing Jasmine, Rory breathed easier. He didn't really notice how sad she was.

"Where ya been, gal?" Rory asked of her.

"What is life, Rory?" asked Jasmine, standing directly before him with tears in her eyes.

"Huh?"

"What it mean ta be alive?" said she from a place deep inside of her being. A place that she wished Rory could know and comprehend.

"Ah don't understan', Jasmine," said he, not sure what to make of this.

"Ah thank happiness is what it mean ta be alive. Iffen ya ain't got happiness, ya jes' heah, not alive at all."

"What dis 'bout, gal?"

"Last night, fuh da first time in my life, Ah wa'n't happy. It wa'n't dat kinda sad we all get sometimes, but deep-true unhappiness. Ah ain't never felt dat way befo'. It made me feel restless. Ah couldn't sleep. Ah had ta get out and breathe da night air jes' so Ah could know Ah's alive."

"What got ya feelin' dat way?" Rory said, feeling her pain.

"You, Rory," said she sadly, deeply concerned for their love.

"Me?"

"Ever' since ya come back from da war ya been different. It's like ya livin' on borrowed time, like ya wa'n't meant ta come back ta me. Youse my happiness, Rory. It make me sick ta da bone ta thank of livin' without cha. Ah can't live without cha no mo' 'an Ah can separate time and space," said she with a great deal of honest emotion.

"Ah's heah. Ah's gone always be wid cha."

"Ah loves ya, and Ah wont ta have yo' childrens. Ah wont fuh us ta grow ta a ripe old age together. Ah jes' got dis feelin', warnin' in my heart, it ain't gon' be. Ah know ya gotta be a man, Rory. Ah won't ask ya not ta be, but jes' remember dis. Remember dat happiness is life. Remember... you is my happiness. Remember... you is my life."

A single tear trickled from her right eye. Rory moved to her and gently wiped it away, as he pulled her close to him.

"You is every thang good in dis world ta me, Jasmine. Ah can't be happy without cha either. Sometimes, Ah thank Ah can't even breathe without ya. Don't worry, we gon' be together a life time. We gon' live and we gon' love. So happy da whole world gon' be jealous of what we got. Ah promise."

"Ah don't know what Ah'd do without cha," said she, squeezing him tightly, as if to convince herself that he was really there with her, and nothing could ever take him away.

"Dere, dere, now, Ah ain't goin' nowhere, gal," gently comforted he.

"Ah jes' wish Ah could shake dis feelin'.'"

"Don't be sad, Ah can't stand ta see ya sad."

"Ah's sorry," said Jasmine.

"Don't be sorry," said Rory, gently stroking her face, looking into her sad brown eyes, "Let me see dat big bright smile dat warms my soul."

It was enough to compel her to give him exactly what he asked for, a soft tender smile. He had always known how to make her feel very much a loved woman.

"Ah loves ya, Rory."

"No, we loves each other."

"Rory," she smiled.

"Is ya hungry?" asked he.

"Ah guess a lit' bit."

"Come on in, Ah'll fix ya breakfast."

Jasmine smiled that brilliantly white smile of hers, and her inner glow started to shine through. She genuinely loved this man. "Rory you can't cook. Good anyways," said she jokingly.

"But fuh you, precious queen, Ah's gon' try."

Several hours past, and word of what happened had not yet reached Jasmine and Rory, but this was about to change, as Naomi stopped by unannounced. She would often check in on Jasmine while Rory was away fighting in the war. She and Jasmine were good friends. She was greeted with warm smiles as she entered their home.

"Mornin', Naomi," Rory said, still having leftover breakfast, sitting at the small table.

"Come on in, and have a little somethin' ta eat," Jasmine offered hospitably.

"No thank ya. Ah was jes' stoppin' by ta see iffen ya wanted ta come with me over ta Sadie Bailey's place ta see iffen they's somethin' we can do."

Rory stopped eating, sensing something bad had occured. "What done happened?"

"Y'all ain't heard?" Naomi asked, somewhat surprised.

"Heard what?" Jasmine asked, fearing the worst.

"Ya know lit' Ken, don't ya?"

"Dat lit' boy ain't dead is he?" Jasmine asked, kind of shocked like.

Both Rory and Naomi found it rather uncanny that Jasmine would immediately assume death was involved. The boy could've been hurt or sick. Each wondered why she assumed he was dead, but dismissed it as a lucky guess.

"What happened, Naomi?" Rory asked, very curious to know.

"Don't nobody rightly know."

"Don't know?" Rory said, thinking that was very odd.

"Dey don't know what happened. All we know so far is dat he was found dis mornin' 'bout a mile from his house over by da creek."

"Somebody kilt 'im, didn't it?" Jasmine asked, somehow sure that was what happened.

Again, both Rory and Naomi found it strange that Jasmine would guess that young Ken was murdered. He could have died by accidental means, but she seemed to know he was murdered. Again, each dismissed it as a fortuitous guess.

"Dat's what dey sayin'," Naomi replied.

"Lawd, who done done somethin' like dat?" Jasmine said, immediately feeling badly about the situation.

"It's gittin' ta be a mighty sad world, ain't it?" Naomi lamented.

"Dey don't know who done it?" Rory asked.

"So many stragglers on da roads nowadays, could've been anybody," Jasmine interjected.

"Yeah, but some folks sayin'..."

"Sayin' what, Naomi," Rory asked, sensing her hesitation.

"Dey's sayin' Collin done it."

"Collin!" Jasmine said, utterly shocked.

"Yeah, Collin."

"Naw, he ain't done dat," Jasmine declared, as though it were a matter of undisputable fact.

"Ya know somethin' dey don't?" Rory asked.

"Naw, Ah don't," Jasmine said.

"Ah don't thank he done it neither," agreed Naomi.

"He ain't evil like dat, not like some," Jasmine said, certain of the character of Collin Bailey.

"Sound like ya know somebody dat might've done it," Rory said.

"Maybe."

"Who den, Jasmine?" he asked, curious to know.

"Dat ole-crazy Mary Hawkins."

"Yeah, now, she could've done it," Naomi agreed.

The name did not sound familiar to Rory. "Mary Hawkins?"

"She use ta be a slave up near Jackson, Ah hear. She settled down dis way afta da war," explained Naomi.

"Bout three months befo' ya came home, Rory, she hung her four-year-old up from a tree by his arm fuh da better part of a day, we thank, could have been out dere longer fuh all we know. It jes' so happened Elijah went by ta check on her and all dem young on's. Ah guess he was worried 'bout her since she ain't got no man ta speak of. Anyway, he cut da boy down, and took 'im and da rest of dem chil'en ta his house. He took care of 'em fuh two and a half months befo' Mary's brother come long ta claim 'em. He took 'em on up north wid 'im," Jasmine explained.

"Dat Mary a evil one all right, hangin' dat boy up half-naked in da middle of winter. It's a good thang it wa'n't too cold dat day. Ah know all dem kids can git on ya nerves sometimes, but dat ain't no reason ta do what she done," Naomi interjected.

"Dey say she hung da boy up cause he kept on askin' her ta feed 'im. She got five kids, Rory, and didn't need none. She ain't fit ta take care of a ole-mangy dog. Why you reckon God blessed her wid all dem kids, and He leave my womb barren? All Ah wanna do is love 'em," Jasmine said with a bitter tone.

Naomi saw a measure of hurt in her friend. "God gon' bless ya wit' some, just have faith."

Jasmine did not comment on the encouragement from Naomi, neither did Rory, who knew all too well how much she wanted a child. All that Jasmine knew was that she and Rory had been having relations since she was fourteen. Her teen years should have probably been the easiest for her to conceive, but they hadn't been. Jasmine knew that if she was to have children, she should have had them by now. "Ah hear dat ole Mary was all too willin' ta let Elijah take her chil'ens. Ah don't understand dat. When we was slaves, mommas worried everyday iffen da massa was gon' sell off dey kids, cause maybe he had a bad year and was in debt. We had ta worry fuh so long. Now, when we ain't gotta worry, she jes' give 'em away. It don't make sense ta me. Don't seem like nobody oughta have chil'ens iffen Ah can't have none, cause ain't nobody dat can love 'em mo' 'an Ah do."

There was a look of sadness upon Jasmine's face that was so profound that it caused Rory to look down and rub his forehead. It hurt him not to be able to give her a child, and there was something else. He remembered that Jasmine went out the previous night, for how long he couldn't say. That last little part of her statement about nobody having kids if she couldn't. What if it was her? He caught himself. He couldn't think that.

Six

Back at the murder scene, hours had gone by. Micah had returned, and waited with Elijah and Solomon for the others to return with the sheriff. It got to be well past noon... hours past noon.

"They should have been back by now," Micah commented.

"Yeah, dey oughta been back," Elijah agreed.

"Maybe, it was a problem ta find da sheriff," Solomon speculated.

"Maybe," Elijah agreed.

"Ya don't spect nothin' done happened ta 'em, do yeah?" Solomon said, becoming worried.

"Maybe, I should ride on into town, and see what the hold up is," Micah said.

"Ah reckon ya oughta," Elijah concurred.

There was a thicket of trees behind them, beyond which was the dirt road. They heard what sounded like a wagon approaching. It seemed to come to a stop parallel to the general area where they were.

"The sheriff, maybe?" Micah guessed.

"In a wagon?" countered Elijah, very doubtful.

"Most likely, not,"Solomon said.

They continued to listen, as it was apparent that multiple persons were making their way toward them. At least two persons were making their way through the brushwood. The men weren't afraid. It was more likely a friend than a foe. They didn't even believe it was the murderer returning to the scene of his deed. They didn't call out to inquire as to whom it might be. They were content to wait and see. The footsteps seemed to be moving toward, but away from them. That is, they were moving too far to the right of them, past them.

"Solomon, where y' all at over dere," rang out a familiar voice.

It sounded like one of the area ministers, Brother Brownlee. The footsteps changed direction, indicating the men were homing in on the voice of Solomon. After a short time, two persons emerged from the woods into the clearing by the creek where Solomon and the others stood. It was Minister Brownlee and Collin Bailey. Collin had a very sad look upon his face. Elijah, Micah, and Solomon were surprised to see him, but they shouldn't have been. The boy was after all his child.

"Ah come ta fetch my boy home," Collin said.

"Uh, okay, but da sheriff ain't been heah yet," Elijah informed.

"Maybe, but it ain't right fuh my boy ta be layin' out heah like he ain't got nobody dat care fuh 'im," Collin insisted.

"He right y'all," Minister Brownlee agreed.

"It's time fuh me ta take 'im home," Collin reiterated.

"By all means, take him. We just wanted the sheriff to get a look at him first," Micah explained.

"Ah know its hard ta see ya boy like dis, but da sheriff might be able ta see somethin' we don't know ta look fuh. Somethin' dat's gon' help us find whoever done dis," further explained Elijah.

"Their right, Collin," Solomon said, throwing his influence behind Elijah and Micah.

"Jes' a while longer, Collin," Elijah said, hoping he would agree.

"Ran and Risby went ta fetch 'im a good while ago. They oughta be along anytime now," Solomon said, still hoping to convince Collin it was the right thing to do.

"He wanna take da child home," Minister Brownlee said, wanting them to relent in their insistence of keeping the body any longer.

"We're not trying to stop him. We respect his wishes. We just wanted him to know what was going on," Micah said.

Collin wanted to help them, but this was his son. He felt they had the body long enough. He was not angry with them, but definitely felt that he should not have to ask their permission to remove his son. "O'm ready ta take 'im home," he said, more forceful this time.

"Okay, Collin," Elijah said, sensing Collin was not happy with the situation.

"Do you want us to help get him to the wagon?" Micah asked.

"No, Ah thank, Ah can bear his weight. It's probably da last time Ah'll git ta hold 'im in my arms."

Around that time, they heard men approaching on horseback. No doubt that would have been Ran and Risby returning with the sheriff.

"Dat's gon' be da sheriff, y'all. Collin, kin ya jes' give 'im a minute ta look thangs over befo' ya move 'im?" Elijah asked, almost pleadingly.

Collin sighed, and thought on it a second. "Ah guess so."

"Thank ya," Elijah said.

"Ya doin' tha good thang," Solomon assured.

Just as with the minister and Collin, footsteps could be heard coming their way. These steps were sure of their course. However, something was wrong. There were only two people approaching. Everyone present could tell this. Risby and Ran appeared in the clearing. The sheriff wasn't with them.

"Where da sheriff?" Elijah asked, very surprised that he wasn't with them.

"Da sheriff ain't coming," Ran informed them.

"He ain't in town. Takin' some prisoner up ta Louisiana," Risby explained.

"What about the deputy?" Micah asked.

"He says it's a busy day. A lot of white folks needs 'im," Ran explained.

"Did y'all tell 'im a boy been killed?" Solomon said.

"Yeah," Ran answered.

"White folks come first," Risby elaborated.

"Is somebody white dead?" Micah asked, trying to understand.

"He ain't told us what done happened dat was mo' important dan dis," Risby said.

"He said ta take da boy on home. He gon' come and take a look around when he git da time," Ran explained.

"My boy been layin' out heah all day fuh naught?" Collin said, exceedingly bitter.

"Ah's sorry, Collin. Ah thought the sheriff would help," Elijah said.

"Da mo' thangs change da mo' dey stay da same. We's free, and we still ain't nothin' ta 'em. Why dey can't take jes' a lit' time ta help us?" Risby asked, bewildered.

"Well, no use standin' round heah," Minister Brownlee said, "Let's git da boy home."

Collin lifted his son, refusing help. He was hurt, bitter that his child was stolen from him, and the law cared nothing about the matter. Everyone followed him, not saying anything.

As night fell, Elizabeth watched the hours pass. She seemed to grow all the more livid with the passing of each one. Franklin had not returned home. He was the master of the house, and he was not running it as he should. There was plenty of work to be done here, but he was nowhere to be found. All the responsibility seemed to fall on the shoulders of poor Jesse and her. She walked out onto the porch. The wind was picking up, and the smell of rain was in the air. It looked as if the weather would be as foul as her temperament upon Franklin's return, if he returned that night. Elizabeth walked back inside to the polar, where the family was gathered. Jesse was watching his elder sisters play a game of checkers, as the younger sisters sat on the floor with dolls in hand, pretending to host a tea party.

It was a light-enjoyable moment for them. It would make for a very picturesque scene, but for Elizabeth's quiet, constant, thought-filled pacing about the room. The older children knew that she was in a foul mood and pretended not to notice, as they did not wish to draw her attention or wrath, which was surely intended for their father. Each of them took quick secret-uncomfortable peeks, hoping she would take a seat, and rest her weary feet and troubled mind. At any moment, they expected her to let off some steam by debasing their father's image in their eyes. Joselpha had so much compassion for her mother. She desired to say something which might be of comfort to Elizabeth, but her mother was not the type to be comforted by words. When wronged, she wanted revenge. That was her comforter, to repay misery with misery.

The night marched on, and soon it was time for bed. The children all turned in, but the older ones wouldn't sleep comfortably this night. They expected all hell to break loose as soon as Franklin hit the door.

Elizabeth was miserable in her situation. She would have liked to up and left, but divorce was not very common at this time, particularly in the rural south. If she were to have left, she would have basically been on her own. The institutions of court enforced alimony and child support were none existent; and women, who were permitted to work, didn't earn income anything comparable to a man. Women were often driven to prostitution just to support themselves. What was more, women in general did not have many rights. They lacked the right to vote or sit on juries. A man even had the right to appoint someone else as his children's legal guardian in the event of his death, despite having a surviving mentally competent wife. By the end of the American Civil War, only twenty-one states had laws on the books which would allow a woman to hold property without her husband's consent, if she owned it prior to marriage, and fewer still gave her the right to have a say in the guardianship of her children. However, these state laws were at times taken lightly or amended for the worse, because women lacked the vote, and there was no fear of reprisal by them at the ballot box. In a very real sense, the white female was a more oppressed people than the newly emancipated Negro. Without a man, women in America were essentially none citizens.

Elizabeth was all too aware of the situation. Nevertheless, she could not sit idly by while her husband conducted himself in such a despicable manner just because he held all the cards. If she let this go, the next thing you know, Franklin would have his harlot and bastard child in their house, while she and their children were turned out to the streets without lucre or any means of supporting themselves. Before Elizabeth let such a thing happen, she would kill Franklin in his sleep and maintain her possession through Jesse. This she would surely do, if Franklin continued to force her hand.

The weathercock atop the barn was spinning in the strong winds, which seemed to howl in constant misery. The weather had turned foul as signs indicated it would. The rain was falling hard and heavy. Perhaps, this was what prompted Franklin to return home. As if she were a clairvoyant, Elizabeth knew he had returned. Malice had ample time to take strong root in her heart. Tonight was the last time she would wonder where her dear husband had been.

The night seemed darker than usual and quite menacing, a willing ally to the vengeful wrath of a woman scorned. The stairs creaked under weight, as if to confirm what Elizabeth already knew. His footsteps seemed to echo mightily, as if the house wanted Elizabeth to know Franklin's every move, as if it were an instigator, urging her to vengeance. Thunder roared as a lion, willing to hide the inevitable evil of the huntress stalking her prey. Lightning clashed against the night sky, as if taking a quick blissful-anticipatory peek at the madness to come.

Elizabeth gave Franklin time to settle into the guest bedroom in which he had taken up residence. She wanted him to fall asleep. That way, he wouldn't see her coming. Another forty-five minutes past, and all indicators were that Franklin was asleep. The drunken fool, she thought. She could easily enter his room and cut off his manhood before he knew what had happened. His harlot would not want him then, she thought. Elizabeth decided that now was the time to make her move. She climbed out of bed and made her way down the hall. Her steps were soft and quiet, but with purpose. She moved as someone with authority to do what she was about to do. She stood at the bedroom door, and gently opened it, not wanting to wake Franklin from his slumber. She gently closed the door behind her. Franklin was fast asleep. Elizabeth moved over to the bed and stood over his head. She looked down on him with a disapproving frown. Lightening whipped and thunder rolled, as if to urge her to action.

Franklin turned on his side. For a second, Elizabeth thought that he was about to wake, but it was soon apparent that he was not. There was a wooden chair in the corner of the room. She walked over and gently seated herself there. She watched Franklin sleep for the better part of fifteen minutes. Then, sure of what action to take, she rose and briskly moved to the foot of the bed. She slipped off her night gown. Completely naked, she snatched the cover off of Franklin and rolled him onto his back. She began to pull down his longjohns. By now he was awake, not so much afraid, as bewildered. Elizabeth took his manliness in her hand. It was responsive to her touch. She climbed onto the bed in an attempt to mount her husband. Despite his arousal, Franklin was in no mood to bother with Elizabeth. He pushed her off of him before penetration occured. Immediately, she came right back at him. He grabbed her by the shoulders to keep her off of him.

"What's wrong with you woman?" He spewed, as he slung her to the side. Elizabeth lost her balance and fell from the bed. Franklin quickly sat on the side of the bed, checking to see if she was okay. He was just trying to get her off, not hurt her. Elizabeth sprang to her feet, and slapped him across the face. She powered her way onto the bed, pushing him on his back. He grabbed her by the wrists. A slight struggle ensued before he muscled her onto her back.

He had her arms pent to the mattress, his body between her legs, but he did not join with her. She looked up at him with still determined eyes. "Give it to me," she demanded.

"No."

"Yes," she demanded, extending her neck, kissing him on the forearm with an open mouth.

"No, Elizabeth."

"Yes," she said, wiggling her body beneath him in a very sexual way.

This was a side of Elizabeth he hadn't seen or experienced before in the bedroom. He liked it.

Elizabeth was always so conservative in the past, waiting to be asked for her affections. He began to tease her with his manhood, coming close, but not entering.

"Do it," she demanded in a dark sultry kind of way.

He smiled and entered her. The walls of her love were soft and very wet. The inside of her was very hot, hotter than any woman he had ever known. Not even on their wedding night was she such as this. He released her hands. Straightaway, she raised up and began to kiss him with an open mouth on his chest. He wanted more of her, and began to quicken the pace. She laid back and lifted her legs, placing her toes on the wall beyond the headboard, opening wide. She wanted him to know that every inch of him was welcome to every bit of her.

Within her, the ill that he felt toward her started to melt away. Like this, he loved her as much as he did when they were first wed. Elizabeth motioned him to stop for a moment. She laid him on his back and mounted him. She began to ride him like a jockey in the home stretch, headed for the finish line. Franklin's body shivered with pleasure.

Elizabeth was sending him a clear message. What he had at home was better than anything out there in the world. The message wasn't lost on him. His anger towards her was kindled again. Always trying to run something, he thought. He threw her on her back and began to thrust away, ready to end this. Elizabeth sensed he was angry with her again. "Ah love you," she said, hoping to tear down his defenses, hoping he would see her sincerity.

Franklin seemed unmoved by her words. He closed his eyes, so he did not have to look at her.

He was into her body now. In the blink of an eye, she had become just a body to him. A body to pleasure and then put away. This was not what Elizabeth wanted, not what she intended. She was just trying to make things right between them, trying to restore the sanctity of their marriage, to which she was rightfully entitled. If her body was where he was, perhaps she could yet reach him there, with her body. She contracted her love repeatedly, caressing his manliness tightly. It felt very, very, good to Franklin. Once more, anger fled from him, the love he felt for her returned. He opened his eyes. They made eye contact in a very sexy way through the veil of darkness. Elizabeth knew that she had reached him. "Ah love you," she said, hoping he would reciprocate.

Franklin reached his height. It was a strong release. So much so, it left him dizzy and weak.

He withdrew from her, and fell to her side, looking in her direction.

"Ah love you so very much, Franklin," she said, rubbing his arm.

Without thought or hesitation he replied, "Ah love you, too."

This made Elizabeth smile. It was what she wanted to hear, and it was enough for now. She gave him a chance to cool down a bit. Then, they spooned and spent the night in the same bed.

When the next morning came, Elijah and Micah headed out to the cotton field. A full day's work was ahead of them. It was a cool quiet morning. The sun was shining brightly in the sky, pleasantly warming the skin. Serenity seemed to ride the east wind gracefully. Spreading its solace liberally to all who sought it. On such a beautiful majestic day as this. All seemed right with the world. It was easy to forget that just yesterday their yoke was heavy. It was easy to forget, and they wanted to forget what happened the day before. They could not change it. Therefore, it did them no good to linger there. It was a good day to be alive. A good day to be free. They were willing to be content with that. As the men stood ready to begin work, a simple statement was made.

"It's a shame about that boy," Micah lamented.

"Yeah, it is, but he will git ta be wit king Jesus on dat great day when we see God. He ain't got no mo' burdens ta bear."

"I don't envy him that. I would rather have seen him a man, and an old man at that, when he went to meet his maker."
Elijah sighed. "Weren't meant ta be."

"Someone got away with murder," Micah said.

"Sho nuff look like it."

"Well, it's over now."

A chill ran down Elijah's spine. He looked at Micah, wishing he hadn't said that. There was a feeling in his gut. A strange feeling that this was not the end, but the beginning.

Seven

The weather had been good for the past four days after the murder of young Ken Bailey. He rested in the tender care of mother earth now. It was fitting that the child was buried on a sunny day. Rainy days seem to make such somber occasions all the more saddening. All friends and neighbors of the Bailey's had moved forward with their normal everyday lives, but it would be quite some time before everything felt normal for the Bailey's again. Soon though, everyone in this community would be drawn back into the anger and grief that gripped the Bailey family.

It was the end of a long day for Elijah and his brother. They had toiled for long back breaking hours this day, trying to ensure the cotton crop would be ready for the harvest at the appointed time. They were tired, and Micah's feet hurt. They had enjoyed a good meal of stewed venison, and were in the process of preparing for the next workday. It was nine in the evening now. They had started to unwind, ready to take their deserved rest, when there was a knock at the door. Everyone in the small house, save Caleb, looked around at each other. All wondered who was paying them a visit so close to bedtime. Josephine looked in a troubled way at her husband. Elijah rose from the table chair and walked to the door. For a brief moment, he hesitated to open it. He opened the door to find Risby standing there. He was holding a kerosene lamp. Risby had a slight frown upon his face. Elijah knew that his feelings that something wasn't right were well-founded. "What done happened, Risby?"

"It's Ephram and Hattie May Walker. Dey lit' boy missin'."

By now, Micah was staring over his brother's shoulder, and the ears of the women were homed in on the conversation. Even though Risby was trying to be discreet, the women heard every word he said.

"He ain't..." Elijah asked, hesitant to complete the sentence.

"Don't know, jes' can't find 'im," Risby answered, knowing that he was asking if the boy was dead.

"Lawd, Lawd, Lawd," Mama Julia was heard saying in the background.

Josephine quickly snatched little Caleb into her arms, who was sitting on the floor playing by himself. She hugged him tightly, wanting to protect him from an unseen enemy. She did not know if the missing child was dead, or if the person who killed Ken Bailey was involved; nevertheless, she had a feeling, a feeling that the person who killed Ken

Bailey had struck again. She was deeply afraid, not just for her child, but for every child in Jago.

"Lemme git my thangs. Ah'll help look fuh da boy," Elijah said.

"As will I," Micah informed.

"Who all helpin'," Elijah asked.

"Y'all da firs' somebody Ah came ta."

"How long has he been missing?" Micah asked.

"A few hours now, Ah guess," Risby answered.

"Risby, is ya gon' keep on roundin' up folks ta help?" Elijah asked.

"Ah will, Ephram out lookin' fuh 'im now. Ah's gon' see iffen Ran, and some of da others kin help."

"Good then," Micah remarked.

"Ah don't know dese heah folks too good. Dey kinda keeps ta dey self. Dey lives near da woods?" Elijah asked. Really a comment more than a question, but it wasn't perceived as such.

"Dey don't live but 'bout two miles up da road from Collin Bailey, and it's plenty of woods back where dey live," Risby explained.

"Maybe, we oughta start lookin' back in dem woods firs'," Elijah said.

"Yes, I think we should also," Micah agreed.

"Tell everybody dat we gon' scatter out in dem woods nearest where da Walkers live, and tell 'im ta brang some extra oil fuh dey lamps. Ain't no tellin' how long we might be out dere," Elijah instructed Risby.

"Right," Risby said, as he turned on his way to be about this business.

Elijah closed the door and started to gather his things, as did Micah. Josephine gave Caleb to Mama Julia. She moved over to Elijah and hugged him from behind. He stopped his activity and turned to face her. Her brown-compassionate eyes were so sad.

"Everythang gon' be all right, ain't it?" she asked.

He smiled slightly at her. In his heart he believed otherwise, but openly he answered, "It is. It's gon' be alright."

"You ready?" Micah asked.

"Yeah," Elijah answered.

The men exited the house, headed to saddle up the horse and mule. Josephine stood in the door watching until they rode off into the unseen darkness of night. Upon closing the door, Josephine turned to find Mama Julia staring at her.

"You know dat boy dead, don't cha?" Mama Julia said, having no illusions about the matter.

Josephine looked at her in silence for a brief moment. Somewhat somberly she answered, "Yes, Ah know."

On the road to the Walker place, Elijah was reluctant to talk. He had a bad feeling that things were only going to get worse from the very day young Ken Bailey was killed. His worst fears were being realized.

"Do you believe he is dead, Elijah?" Micah asked.

"Yeah."

"Why do you want to search the woods?"

"Same reason you thank we ought."

"Because that's where he left the Bailey boy?"

"Yeah."

"We're about to have a serious problem," Micah said, feeling a murderous rampage was about to get underway.

"We gots a ser'ous problem," Elijah replied, feeling the rampage was already underway.

"We could be wrong."

"Ah don't thank so."

"He could have wondered off, and is just lost, out there waiting for someone to come along and take him home."

Elijah stopped his black mule. Micah stopped along side him. "Ya really thank dat, Micah?"

Micah looked at him for a split second. "No."

The men rode on a bit more, and soon came to where the Walker's lived. There did not appear to be anyone outside. There was candle light burning within the small cabin. They dismounted and knocked on the Door. Hattie May opened it almost immediately.

Elijah took off his worn light-brown hat. "Mrs. Walker?"

"Yes."

"O'm Elijah Wright, dis heah my brother Micah. We heah ta help look fuh ya boy."

She gave them a half-smile frown. The most cordial greeting she could manage at that very moment. "Ah was kinda hopin' y'all might've been somebody brangin' home my boy. Ah been heah waitin', case he come home."

"Have any of the others arrived yet, madam?" Micah inquired.

"No, Y'all da firs'."

"Ah see some woods over yonder. Ya husban' lookin' in dere?" Elijah asked.

"Yeah, he thought lit' Henry might wondered in dere."

"Well, Ah reckon we'll go help 'im look now," Elijah said, hoping this would comfort Mrs. Walker a little.

"How old is Henry, Madam?" Micah asked.

"Gon' be seven dis fall."

"Well, we gon' go on and git started now, Mrs. Walker," Elijah said once more.

"Okay, and thank y'all."

"You're more than welcome, Madam," Micah said, feeling great pity for the woman.

The men headed towards the woods.

"You want to stay together, or split up?" Micah asked.

"We only got da one lamp."

"Not a problem, we can make up a torch. It won't take too long. That way we can cover more ground."

"Well, let's do dat, seemin' ya done already made up ya mind."

"Elijah, look carefully, It's cool tonight. If he is still alive, we don't want the weather to get him."

They made the torch and disappeared into the woods. By midnight more than twenty-five men were aiding in the search for the child. Still by morning, there was no sign of him. Elijah was very tired and decided to head back to the Walker residence. As he emerged form the woods, he saw Solomon sitting on back of a wagon with a descent sized cargo bed. He was too old to get out and physically search for the child, but he was here to show his concern and support. Also, he brought his eighteen-year-old granddaughter, Ethel, along. She had made a fire. There was a pot of hot coffee brewing, and Ethel was cooking fresh eggs for anyone who wanted them. Elijah made his way toward them. Several other men were standing around partaking of the coffee and eggs.

"Mornin' everybody," Elijah greeted.

"Good mornin', Elijah," Solomon reciprocated.

"Mornin', Mista 'lijah," Ethel greeted, "got some good ole eggs and coffee, wont some?"

"Thank ya, 'cause O'm 'bout ta starve. Ya ain't got a few thick slices of bacon ta go long wit' 'em do ya, Ms. Ethel?"

Ethel giggled coyly. "No, 'fraid not, Mista 'lijah." She cracked two eggs, and started to fry them sunny side up.

"How long y'all been heah, Solomon?" Elijah asked.

"Since about four thirty dis mornin'. We got tha word late last night. It took a while to get dese heah vittles together, but we come right on after dat."

"Anybody come back wit' any news?" Elijah asked.

"Not yet," Solomon answered.

"Dat ain't good."

"No, it ain't."

"Iffen he was all right, he'd a answered wit' all dese folks out heah lookin' and callin' fuh 'im iffen he could," Elijah reasoned.

"Don't look on tha bad jes' yet. He all alone out dere. He could jes' be scared to come to folk he don't know, even iffen dey callin' ta 'im by name."

"Solomon, it was nippy out last night. My nose is runnin' now. Iffen he was out dere hongry and cold, scared or not. Ah thank he'd a answered iffen he could."

Those within ear shot of Elijah stopped eating and talking, looking at him. What Elijah said made sense to them. They interpreted what Elijah was saying to mean the child was dead. Everybody knew Elijah. He was a good fellow, and was always willing to do what he could. Naturally, he was one of the first people, that the people of the Jago community came to in troublesome times. The things he said carried weight. He was a man of fine character, and if he were saying a thing. It must be true.

Solomon discreetly shook his head at Elijah, signaling him to watch what he was saying. Not that they would, but he didn't want anybody to go into the Walker's home and tell the Walkers that folks were just outside their door, saying their child was dead, as though it was fact. Solomon raised his wrinkled-dark hand and discreetly motioned for Elijah to move closer. Once Elijah was close enough, Solomon leaned down and whispered in his ear so no one else would hear. "We don't know he's dead until we know he's dead. Let's keep it dat way."

"Youse right, O'm sorry," Elijah said humbly.

Ethel walked up to Elijah and handed him the eggs on a grayish-black-speckled tin plate. "Heah go ya food."

"Thank ya, Ms. Ethel."

Ethel had a look on her face, a troubled and woeful look, that suggested that she had not considered the child might be dead. Her eyes were opened now, and the thought saddened her a little. "Maybe, Ah oughta go in and see iffen Ms. Hattie May need something'."

"Okay," Solomon said, feeling it would not be a bad idea for Ethel to try and comfort Mrs. Walker.

Ethel started to amble toward the house. Solomon called to her. "Ethel."

She turned and looked at him.

"Watch what cha say," Solomon warned.

She nodded her head.

Elijah wolfed down the eggs, and poured himself a cup of black coffee to wash it down.

As he stood there drinking his coffee; he knew, despite Solomon's optimism, the child was dead.

He started to get down on himself. It was not uncommon to see a black man hanging from a tree, as if he were an apple or plum. He had seen young men fifteen years of age and up hanging, but they were always men, or young men close to adulthood, but the killing of little children. Children, who couldn't have possibly said or done anything to offend, were being killed. This type of thing was unheard of. He should have seen this coming, Elijah thought to himself. His gut told him it was going to happen again, and he ignored it. He should have told everyone to guard their young ones well, but he didn't. Now everyone was out looking for another young child. It started to eat at him. He was in a place of deep thought when a voice broke through his wall of concentration.

"Elijah," Solomon called.

"Yassuh."

"Maybe, we lookin' in tha wrong place. Maybe, he ain't in dere. Maybe, we oughta have some men start checkin' elsewhere. He could have fell down a well or something."

"No, Solomon, he in da woods," Elijah said, quite sure of it.

Almost as if by queue, a man came running out of the woods, shouting something. Grover Maddox was his name. "We done fount 'im! We done fount 'im!" Grover headed straight for Solomon and Elijah, continuing to shout out the news as he came. This was what they had been waiting for. Their eyes were glued to Grover as he drew near. "Dey done fount 'im, Mr. Solomon," Grover said, stopping before them somewhat winded.

Solomon leaned forward. "Is he, is he alive?"

"Ah thank so."

A look of happiness and relief overtook Solomon's face. Elijah lowered his head. He was also relieved to hear the boy was alive.

"Where is he," Solomon asked.

"Dey brangin' 'im heah now."

"Where dey find 'im?" Elijah asked.

"Don't rightly know."

"Who found 'im?" Solomon asked.

"Ah thank, Ah heard, somebody say it was yo' brother, Elijah."

"Well, It's good da boy all right," Elijah remarked.

"Ah thank he hurt, Elijah," Grover informed.

"Hurt?" Solomon asked.

"Ole Rail Jacobs came past me on his horse movin' fast. Ah yells to 'im, 'where ya goin' in such a hurry.' He yells, 'ta fetch Doc Mortenson.' So, Ah reckon da boy hurt."

This steals most of the joy and relief the men initially felt when they first heard the news that little Henry had been found and was alive.

"He hurt bad?" Elijah asked.

"Don't know, Ah ain't seed 'im."

Not long after, several men came running out of the woods. Then, they were followed by a crowd of men, fifteen or twenty strong, also moving fast. Ephram Walker was in the midst of them. He was carrying Henry. The small child's body was limp in his arms. An exhausted Ephram fell to one knee. Others tried to help him carry the child, but he did not let them. He climbed to his feet and kept on moving toward his home. One couldn't help but notice the child. Even from a distance, it was visibly clear that the child had been savagely beaten. His cloths were torn and bloody. His face was visibly swollen. Ephram carried the boy right past Solomon and Elijah into the house. The door closed immediately behind him, but for a few who may have been of some use in providing care for the child. Risby, Ran, and Micah were in the crowd of men, and now women, gathered outside the house, waiting for news of the boy's condition. Elijah made his way through the press, and tapped Micah on his shoulder, signaling him to come out of the crowd. He did so.

"Was ya da one fount 'im, Micah," Elijah asked.

Micah shook his head in acknowledgment that he was.

"Where ya find 'im?" Elijah asked.

"Back over close to us. Matter of fact, do you remember that day you and I went hunting a while back, when I first got here?"

"Yeah."

"We stopped and sat on an old tree which had fallen."

"Ah knows it," Elijah said.

"I found him right there, tucked in a crease between the tree and the ground."

"Kin ya show me 'xactly where?"

"Sure."

"Good, come on."

"Why do you want to see?"

"Ah jes' wanna habe a lit' look 'round."

"Okay, then, let's go."

Risby and Ran caught a glimpse of Elijah and Micah leaving. They moved to catch up to them.

"Elijah! Micah!" Risby called.

They stopped and waited for them.

"Where y'all goin'?" Ran asked.

"Back ta where Micah fount da boy."

"Y'all ain't gon' wait ta see how he doin'?" Ran asked.

"No," Elijah answered sadly, feeling somehow responsible for what happened to the child.

"Well, we gon' come wit' y'all," Risby said.

"Suit yo'self," Elijah remarked.

The men journeyed back to where young Henry was found. Elijah started to look around. He was so into it that he didn't seem to notice the others.

"What cha lookin' fuh?" Risby asked.

Elijah did not answer. It was as if he didn't hear him.

"Elijah, what cha lookin' fuh?" Risby asked again.

"Ah don't know. Somethin'. Anythang. Anythang dat kin help me figure out who done dis," Elijah answered.

The others looked at each other, wondering what could possibly be there that would lead them to the person that committed this heinous act.

"Somethin' like what?" Ran asked, wanting to help.

"Ah don't know!" Elijah said frustrated. He calmed himself. "Ah gotta find somethin' ta help us. Else, dis gon' keep on happenin'. Cancha see dat? And, Ah can't habe dat. Ah won't habe dat."

The others saw Elijah's passion and sincerity concerning this. The questions ceased and they all looked for something to help them. They knew not what, but hoped they would recognize it when they saw it. Micah knew that this was probably futile. There must have been half a dozen people who rushed to his aide as soon as he found the boy. All of them contaminating whatever clues that might have been there, but he searched anyway, on the off chance something was there. The effort was in vain. There was no clue to aide them.

Soon they gave it up and returned to their homes. Elijah and Micah were both dead tired. Mama Julia and Josephine watched them as they dragged in. The first thing Micah did upon entering the house was take off his shoes; then, he laid back on his bed. He covered his eyes with his right forearm, and made a long, sleepy, yawn.

"Micah," Mama Julia called to him.

"Just let me rest my eyes for a minute," he said sluggishly.

Not more than a minute later he was fast asleep. Elijah also wanted to take a nap, but he didn't feel that he could. He didn't want Mr. Everett, the man whose property he sharecropped, to happen by and find him asleep in bed. He had no desire to hear Everett gripe about him not being in the field. Elijah decided that he would eat a bit more, enough to fill him this time. Then, he would take to the cotton field. Mama Julia started to fix him something to eat. Josephine sat at the table with Elijah, and started to ask questions about Henry Walker. "Y'all fount 'im?"

"MmmHmm," he acknowledged, too tired to talk.

"He ain't dead?"

"No, he ain't."

"Dat's good. Ah thought sho he was."

"No, he ain't dead, but he pretty hurt," he said, scratching his head, then crossing his arms.

"What happened?" Josephine asked, watching Elijah's head slowly sink into his chest, as he was weary with sleep.

"Elijah," Mama Julia called, trying to wake him.

Elijah's head sprang up, eyes opened wide. His eyes were glassy and red. He rubbed his face with both hands. He smiled at Josephine.

"Why don't cha lay down, baby," Josephine encouraged lovingly.

"Can't, but Ah need ta. My head killin' me."

"Ain't surprised, ya been up all day and all night. It's only so much a body kin take," Mama Julia said.

"No, budda try ta git a lit' work done. Don't wont Mista Everett ta come by and O'm sleep. Don't wanna hear no lip 'bout iffen Ah don't wanna work dis place proper, he'll git somebody in heah who will."

"Huh," Mama Julia laughed, "Youse out doin' a good thang last night, helpin' a neighbor in need. He oughta understan' dat."

"Iffen he don't it's too bad, cause ya ain't no slave no mo' dat gotta jump when he say jump. Long as ya git da job done, he oughta not have nothin' ta say 'bout when ya git it done," Josephine interjected.

Elijah listened to them, too beat out to argue. Despite what they were saying, he knew better. He knew that he had to have a way to put food on the table. A way to keep a roof over their heads. The only skill he had was a knowledge of how to work the land, and since he, a Negro, couldn't own or rent farm land in the state of Mississippi, he was pretty much at Everett's will, which was what the law (black codes, laws that kept the Negro somewhere between slavery and freedom) was meant to do. However, he had to have a little rest. Elijah wouldn't be able to function well with the headache he had. Maybe, when he woke up, the headache would be gone. "Well, O'm gon' habe ta habe a hour or two," he admitted, "Hope, Mista Everett don't come through."

"Ah don't care iffen he do. You comes firs'," Josephine said, angry with Elijah for being so worried about Everett, fearful even.

"Dat's what O'm gon' do, take a lit' nap. Afta dat, Ah'll put in some work. Lit' later, O'm gon' check ta see how lit' Henry doin'."

"Ya gon' eat dis ham and eggs befo' ya go ta sleep, ain't ya?" Mama Julia asked.

"Ah'll git it when Ah wake up."

"Ya gon' be achin' wit' da gas iffen ya eats dis stuff cold," Mama Julia warned.

"Ah'll be all right."

With that he laid down to take a rest.

Back at the Walker home. Many were gathered, waiting for news of the boy's condition. Many of those who searched through the night for the child had gone home to rest, others remained vigilant, waiting for word. There were some twenty people still there. Among them were Solomon and his granddaughter, Ethel. They intended to stay as long as necessary. Solomon looked down the road to see Rail Jacobs coming back alone on his buckskin horse. He made his way to meet Rail, as best he could, dependant upon his walking cane. "Where Doc Mortenson, Rail?" Solomon asked.

"Couldn't find 'im. Word is he out deliverin' a baby. Ah left word fuh 'im ta come as soon as he kin."

"Sho need 'im heah."

About this time, a man exited the house. Jasper Brown, a blacksmith, he also had some knowledge of how to set bone, stitch up wounds, and a general knowledge of useful herbs for minor aches and pains. He was always available to provide limited medical care to colored people, his people. He stood on the porch of the Walker's dogtrot home. He had news of the child, and judging from the look upon his face, a look of lamenting; the news was not good. The crowd went silent without being asked. There was no other way for Jasper to say what he had to say other than to come right out and say it. He looked into the eyes of all those who listened eagerly for news. "Lit' Henry dead y'all, died a few minutes ago."

Immediately through out the crowd, there were sounds of shock. Sounds of weeping and lamenting. Straightaway, Solomon made his way to Jasper. He wanted to ask him a very important question. He was able to get Jasper's attention, and out of respect for Solomon, he came to him.

"Jasper, what did he say?" Solomon asked.

"He didn't say nothin'."

"He didn't say who done 'im like dat?"

"Solomon, he ain't said nothin'. He never come back around."

Immediately, Solomon was perplexed as to what to do next. He, like Elijah, believed this to be the work of the same person that murdered Ken Bailey. He knew that whatever moral consciousness, which might have held this person somewhat in check, was completely overcome now. This person would continue to strike mercilessly at will. He was comfortable with what he was doing. This was evident in the way little Henry was beaten. He was not so brutal with young Bailey. Solomon was counting on Henry to tell them something that would enable them to put an immediate end to this. Such as it was, Solomon and the others would have to wait for another opportunity to learn more. Sadly, that meant someone else would lose a child. Solomon's first thought was to confer with Elijah as to what should be done next. There was a sort of frantic nervousness to Solomon as he and Ethel packed the wagon so that they could leave.

As they were on thier way, Ethel sensed the uneasiness of her grandfather. It made her uneasy as well, but she didn't know why she was uneasy. If Solomon was uneasy, that was good enough reason for her. She had not yet figured out what her grandfather and few others had. That this thing was going to go on. Go on until the killer got tired of doing what he was doing, or they stopped him. And the former didn't seem likely.

Solomon was not of a mind to enlighten her. No need for the minds of women to be so incumbered with such troubles, he thought. Given the choice, Solomon would have rather lived in ignorance of what was now happening.

"What's wrong, ole paw?" Ethel asked of Solomon.

"Nothin' child," he answered.

Ethel knew better, but didn't press the issue. She was the one driving the wagon. She was headed for home, but Solomon had other ideas. "Head on over ta Elijah's place. Ah need ta talk wit' 'im."

Ethel did just as she was instructed. Once there, Solomon noticed Josephine out in the yard playing with Caleb. She was outside, because she wanted to give Elijah and Micah a chance to rest peacefully without Caleb waking them, asking questions, trying to play every few minutes. It was a thoughtful gesture, but this was not a day for Elijah to get much sleep. He had only had an opportunity to get about two hours of it.

"Good mornin," Solomon said.

"Mornin' y'all, good ta see ya," Josephine responded.

"Where dat man of yours?" Solomon asked.

"He sleep."

"Go in dere and tell dat boy ta wake up. Men wit' troubles like we got ain't got time ta be wastin' on sleep."

Josephine was kind of taken aback by this rudeness. Nevertheless, she understood that if Solomon was being so firm, he had reason to be. "Okay," she said, taking Caleb by the hand, leading him inside.

Not long after, Elijah and Micah both exited the house. Elijah's eyes were still extremely red from being tired.

"Ethel, why don't you gone inside, and talk wit' tha women folk fuh a spell?" Solomon said.

Ethel did as her grandfather wished.

"What is it, Solomon?" Micah asked.

"Henry Walker dead."

"Damn," Micah said in a very low voice.

"He able ta say who done 'im like dat?" Elijah asked.

"No, po' thang never did come back 'round."

"He won't be da las'," Elijah predicted.

"Ah know, son," Solomon concurred.

"What cha wanna do?" Elijah asked.

"Dat's why Ah wanted ta talk wit' you. Ah don't wanna scare folks."

"We gotta let 'em know dat it ain't over," Elijah warned.

"Ah know, but we don't wanna just tell 'em. We gotta let 'em know what we gonna do ta deal wit' it, any suggestions?"

"Just warn them to keep a watchful eye on their children. Also, maybe, we can get some of the men together and organize a night watch," Micah suggested.

"Dat sound good ta me," Elijah agreed.

"Okay, we need ta get dis thang together now. We wanna start tonight, if possible," Solomon said, eager to do something to prevent another killing.

"Okay," Elijah agreed.

"Can y'all help me spread the word to meet at my place at about say four?" Solomon asked.

"We will," Micah assured.

By four that evening, a dozen men thought the matter important enough to show for the meeting. They had come out of respect for Solomon and Elijah. They did not fully understand why they were there. Only a select few understood the perceived impending danger, Solomon and Elijah primarily. Solomon, Elijah, Micah, and Solomon's son-in-law, Noah

Jenkins, with whom he lived were standing in the yard together. It was disturbing to Elijah that so few had shown. "Dis all comin' ya thank?" He asked.

"Maybe, it's just taking them a while to get here," Micah responded.

"We best be gettin' started wit' what we got. We got a lot ta work out," Solomon said.

"Gather 'round y'all, gather 'round," Elijah said.

As soon as they came to order, Solomon took over. "We got a big problem y'all, and it's gonna take all us workin' together ta solve it. Most of y'all probably know dat we done lost two children heah over tha past six days. We thank it ain't over yet."

"What dat mean?" Grover Maddox asked.

"We thank da same person kilt both of 'em," Elijah explained.

Solomon continued, "like Elijah is saying, we don't thank he done. He ain't welcome to our children like dat. We want y'all ta spread tha word to watch ya little ones day and night. Next, we wanna set up some sort of patrol at night. We wanna get dat started tonight."

Like with anything, opinions vary. People don't always see things in the same light. And, if this wasn't obstacle enough to overcome. There was always one who had to challenge every action, even when it was wisdom, especially if he had to make sacrifice to participate; today that person was Trents Trudeau. He was a medium complexioned man of mixed heritage, standing about five ten. He was inherently negative about most things, and loved to complain about everything. He was about to become a thorn in Solomon and Elijah's side. "Woe now, Mr. Solomon," Trents interrupted, "ain't we got law in dese heah parts? We need ta let dem handle dis."

"We tried dat already," Elijah interjected.

"Well, y'all need ta try again befo' y'all git us in dis. Ain't dat right y'all?" he asked, turning to the rest of the men present, trying to get them on his side.

Like in any situation, some in the crowd agreed with him immediately.

"Look heah, Trents. Iffen ya don't wont ta habe no part in dis, den don't," Elijah said, somewhat agitated by Trents.

"Woe now, brother Elijah. It ain't dat Ah don't won't no part in dis, but ya gotta understan'; most of us heah got families, and we gotta earn a livin'. We can't be out half da night, den gotta git up da nex' mornin' tryin' ta work all day. Besides dat, y'all don't know it's da same person. Niggas get strung up everyday fuh some reason or another," Trents argued.

"Dis different, cancha see dat," Elijah tried to convince him.

"Ah see ya believe what ya sayin', but dat don't mean what ya believe is right or true, and it don't mean Ah gotta believe jes' cause you do. Ah believe in fact, thangs Ah kin see wit' my own two eyes. And, fact is, Ah ain't seen no proof dat one somebody killin' our lit' on's.

"What do you call two dead babies?" Micah interrupted, finding Trents galling.

Trents looked at Micah very unappreciatively. "Ah's sayin', we all know dat now ain't da easiest time fuh white folks round heah. Dey done los' da war. Every lit' thang any nigga do is gon' be mo' 'an enough ta set 'em off. Dat's all done happened now. Dem lit' niggas jes' said something' ta rile one of 'em is all. Jes' two months ago we fount Junior Gibbins hangin' from a tree. Ya didn't make no fuss den. Why? Cause ya knowed he done forgot his place and said or done something dat landed 'im dere. And, if ya could see dat den, ya oughta be able ta see dat now."

Trents was excusing the behavior and mentality which said it was okay to kill a black man for any ill founded reason. This sounded like utter foolishness to Micah, but he was in the minority here. The Negro had not been emancipated a full year. He had not had time to uproot generations upon generations of teachings to serve and obey the master. That the master was better than he was. That the master was akin to a god. A god who had the power and the right to kill him if he was of a mind to do so. They were poor, uneducated people in large part, who had been trained their entire lives to believe these falsehoods. They had not had the benefit of ten years of freedom, which Micah had, to educate themselves, and to learn to expect more for themselves than to be trampled upon by southern-cultural bias.

Micah failed to take that into account. He was blinded with anger that so many here seemed to be of a single-like mind concerning this issue. He lashed out without thinking. "Have you lost what little bit of brains God gave you? It is all right for them to kill us just because they feel like it? Stop thinking like slaves! You're men dammit, act like it!"

Micah's outburst enraged Trents and many others. Many of them had never even pondered what it meant to be a man. Many of them didn't consider themselves to be men. Their whole existence they had heard themselves referred to as boy, nigger. This was the concept of self for most of them. Nevertheless, they didn't want some educated Negro from up north to call their manhood into question.

"Who ya thank you is ta talk ta me dat away?" Trents rebuked, taking off his jacket, ready to come to blows with Micah.

"Woe, now! Wait a minute!" Solomon said trying to regain control.

"He ain't meant no harm, Trents," Elijah interceded.

"Don't apologize for me, Elijah!" Micah corrected his brother.

"Calm down everybody! Calm down!" Solomon commanded.

Micah had had enough of this slave mentality. He turned to Elijah and Solomon. "Whatever you decide to do, I'm with you," he said, as he stormed to his horse, and raced away.

"Dat nigga too bold," Trents slightingly remarked, watching Micah race away.

Tempers were flaring, and Elijah had also had enough of Trents. He counted Micah and himself as men. Not as some Spanish word (Negro) meaning black that mass uneducated whites couldn't pronounce well, because they didn't understand the phonetics of the Spanish language. Elijah did not define himself as a nigger. "Ah done had about enough of you, Trents."

Trents and Elijah made abrasive eye contact. Solomon stepped between them, fearing physical conflict. Everyone seemed heated, and things were out of control. Solomon couldn't understand why that was. "Wait a minute, y'all. Let's not forget why we heah," he said, trying to get everyone refocused, "We still need ta work out our night watch."

"Solomon, ain't cha been listenin'?" Trents exploded. "We got law. Let dem handle it!"

Solomon was old and hadn't the energy to deal with such temperaments, such foolishness. He had wisdom in great abundance, but wisdom is of no use to those who will not let it guide them.

"You da one dat ain't listenin', Trents," Elijah defended, "Ah told ya we already went ta 'em 'bout da Bailey boy! Dey ain't showed up ta do nothin' yet!"

"Maybe, dat's cause dey know what ya oughta know," Trents fired back, "We jes' niggas! Da white folks is da ones wit' all da land, all da money, all da law! We nex' ta nothin', got nex' ta nothin', but our freedom! We gots ta spect ta lose a few of us, and spect nothin' gon' be done 'bout it."

Elijah realized that he wouldn't get anywhere with Trents, who was gaining support with many of those present, by letting anger prevail. He calmed himself. He rubbed his temple, feeling a tension headache coming on. "Trents," he said calmly, "Youse right, we gotta stomach a lot being black, but Ah can't stomach dis. Ah knows O'm right 'bout dis. Ah ain't sayin' ya wrong, but it da same man doin' dese killin's. We gots ta protect our chil'ens. We gots ta do somethin' so he won't feel he kin jes' do what he doin'. Please. Please. Help us stop 'im."

Calmly Trents responded, "Elijah, thangs is jes' da way thangs is. It gon' work out better in da end iffen we jes let thangs be."

Elijah was deeply saddened to hear the man say this. He did not fault him however. Something within him agreed that it would be better to wink at what was happening, better to turn a blind eye. Yet, Elijah couldn't bring himself to yield to such thinking. This person, whether white or black, had to be stopped. "If dat da way ya feel 'bout it, Trents," Elijah said, "gone and leave, and ain't no hard feelings 'bout it."

Trents looked at him for a moment. He picked up his dusty jacket off the ground, and without another word turned and walked away.

"Anybody else dat feel like dey don't won't no part of dis, go. Like Ah say, it won't be no hard feelings," Elijah continued. With that, he watched the majority of the men walk away. In time, they would come to see that Elijah was right. This was not the end, but the beginning of their woes as a community. When they came to that realization, they would be eager to help. At that moment, however, only four men remained: Risby, Noah, Solomon, and Elijah.

Solomon, however, was too old to be of much help on a nightly patrol. His movement was too restricted to get to a crisis in a hurry, and without a firearm to aid him, he was as much at risk as the very children he was trying to protect.

"Ah guess it's jes' us y'all." Noah said, not really wanting to be a part of it if this was all of the community participation they would have. Noah was a tall man with very dark skin. He was thirty-nine years old. He was lean and powerful looking. He had straight white teeth, and smiled a lot. He had big bright eyes, and talking with him, one could easily get the sense that he was dull of mind.

"Ran couldn't be heah, but he said he would help," Risby informed.

"It's a lot of woods out dere. How we gon' git dis done wit jes' five folks?" Elijah said, feeling overwhelmed.

"Somethin' is better dan nothin', Elijah," Solomon remarked.

"Da night ten hours long. Ah was countin' on mo' folks ta help," Elijah said, still feeling overwhelmed.

"Yeah, we still gotta work our places," Risby said, also feeling overwhelmed.

"Five enough ta start wit'," Solomon assured, "in da mornin', Ah'll go 'round and start talkin' ta everybody one-on-one. Dey all good folk, and Ah believe we'll get some mo' help."

"Ah hopes ya right, cause iffen ya ain't. It's gon' be a hard row ta hoe," Noah said.

"How we gon' do dis? Maybe, three hour a turn?" Risby suggested.

"One person at a time gon' be like nobody out dere wit' all we gotta cover," Elijah said.

"It's something'," Risby pointed out.

"But, it ain't enough," Elijah reiterated, feeling defeated before he even started.

"What cha wanna do, den?" Risby asked.

"All us need ta be out dere all night long."

"We can't do dat, Elijah," Risby argued.

"Sho can't," Noah said, siding with Risby.

"Ah know," conceded Elijah, "but, it's what we need ta do."

"We ain't gon' worry about what we can't do, or what we need ta do. We jes' gon' do what we can. Three hours a piece fine fuh tonight. We'll do better tomorrow," Solomon encouraged.

"Who wanna do what?" Elijah asked.

"Ah'll take firs' watch," Noah said, quick to get his preference.

"Ah'll go nex'," Risby said.

"Micah and me will take it from midnight ta three, and Ah guess Ran got it till day break," Elijah surmised.

"Dat's dat, y'all gone home and take ya rest," Solomon said.

"Ya got Ran, Risby?" Elijah asked.

"Ah's gon' let 'im know," Risby assured.

Risby and Elijah left. Nobody was particularly pleased with what had been put together so far, but it was the best that they could do for the moment. When Elijah got home, he found Micah waiting for him outside. "How did it go?"

"Not too good, we got all of five folks ta try ta cover all da woods 'round heah," Elijah explained.

"Five?"

"Ah know, ain't hardly enough," Elijah said, his head hurting from a tension headache

"I can't understand why more people didn't show up."

"Dey can't see dis thang got us all. Dey ain't lost nothin', and iffen it ain't botherin' 'em. Dey ain't got time ta waste on worryin' 'bout it."

"Yeah," Micah agreed.

"Well' Ah guess we best try ta git some rest. It's gon' be our turn fuh ya know it."

They went inside, trying to rest.

At the Wallace plantation, Franklin was standing on his porch. His left shoulder was leaning against one of the great white columns. He was watching the sun set in deep thought. Elizabeth found her way out onto the porch, and rested her back against the column directly opposite him, looking at him with a smile on her face.

"What, Elizabeth?" he asked, curious as to why she was looking at him so.

"You seem distant. What's on your mind?"

"Nothing that you can help me with, my dear."

"You never know, Ah might."

Franklin simply smiled at her. Among men, it was an unspoken rule to shield their women from their troubles, unless it was absolutely necessary. Before the war, when he had no real need of a loan, bankers were eager to do business with him. Now, at this particular juncture in his life, when funds were needed most, many of those same bankers were not so eager as they once were to lend him capital. Even though he still had land and property to put up as collateral, it was still a difficult proposition. Land was not what it was. So many former plantation owners had sought to rebuild, but had been unable to make a successful go of it. To make matters worse, many of them found their land confiscated by the government, and had to endure certain legal difficulties to regain it. Furthermore, cotton was no longer king. It would never again hold so large a share of the European market as it had prior to the war, it was believed. Banking institutions, to say the least, were uneasy about lending at that time. As far as Franklin was concerned, only one banking institution in Memphis was willing to make him a loan. However, it was at an outrageous profit for the bank. So much so that it gave Franklin an unescapable feeling of being financially raped. There was no need to trouble Elizabeth at this time, so he wouldn't. "It's nothing of great importance."

Elizabeth was content to leave it at that. She moved over to him and took his hand in one of her hands, rubbing it lovingly with the other. Softly she said, "thank you."

"For what?" He asked, confused as to why she would be thanking him.

She lowered her head. "Last night, Ah woke up, and you weren't lying next to me. Ah became livid. My first thought was that you had abandoned our bed for that woman. Ah checked the guest bedroom where you had been sleeping. You weren't there. Ah was boiling by this point. Ah heard a noise in Jesse's room. He was sitting on the floor playing with that dog of his. Ah took my anger out on him, telling him to get back to bed in the most cruelest of ways. Ah was wrong for that. Ah'll have to apologize to him. Ah Checked the rest of the house looking for you. You were nowhere to be found. Ah was so upset, that Ah couldn't see straight. Ah thought to look outside. You were sitting on the porch, deep in thought, just as you were just now. Ah felt a sense of relief. Ah knew you hadn't returned to her. Ah thank you for that."

Franklin looked at her in silence. He didn't know what to say, really. He thought it was somewhat naive of her to assume that he had given up anything. Naive of her to think that just because he was here when she saw him, that he had been there the whole time.

"You were out here on the porch all of the time, weren't you, Franklin?"

"He looked at her briefly. "Sure, Ah was." The way he said it was not very reassuring to Elizabeth

At the Alexander home, Anias and Katherine were very happy. There were signs that Aubrey was continuing to venture out at night. He was out this past night in fact. They didn't care where he went in the middle of the night. They only cared that his little outings seemed to make him better in spirit. He was talking to them more, and sometimes seemed almost cheerful. It was good to see such improvement in him. Anias and Katherine delighted in discussing his progress, now. Yet, there was another matter that they didn't discuss. A matter that still caused friction between them every time the subject was mentioned. The subject was their son Shelby. Katherine so desperately wanted there to be a reconciliation between Anias and Shelby. Anias, however, would have no part in that. He was a stubborn, stubborn, stubborn man. Katherine had her work cut out for her, and time was running short. Shelby would be heading to Washington not so very long from now. Katherine and Anias were sitting on the porch in a white swing chair, enjoying the night air.

"Anias, Ah went to see Shelby again today. He asked about you," Katherine said, trying to get him to take some interest in Shelby."

Anias cut his eyes at her, but did not respond verbally, as Katherine had hoped he would.

"He isn't here to stay," she informed, "He'll be leaving soon."

"The sooner the better," Anias said bitterly.

"Are you so old and stubborn that you will punish the boy forever? Make peace with your son."

"Ah'm not the one who broke the peace, woman! Why do you expect me to make all the concessions?"

"That's not what Ah'm asking. Ah'm asking you to meet Shelby halfway, to forgive and forget."

"Oh, Ah forgive him, but Ah suspect it will be a very long time before Ah forget."

"Forgiving without forgetting isn't forgiving at all. Anias, your son is going to leave here. He's going to make a life for himself far away from here. He is going to make a life far away from us. We'll be blessed if we see him once every ten years. Maybe, we won't see him that often if he feels there is no point in coming back. Don't waste all your time hating the boy, because you won't get that time back. And, as a family, we won't always have each other. Don't take your hate to the grave with you."

"Woman, don't you understand? Why must Ah meet him halfway? Ah never moved. It was he that walked away from me. It was he that turned from our family."

"Well, now he has come back to it, let him."

Anias sighed and shook his head from side to side in frustration. He had made up in his mind that he was not going to go out of his way to make amends with Shelby. What's more, he was tired of this conversation.

"Just let him come by for a visit, for dinner. That's not too much to ask is it, Anias? Will you let him visit for my sake?" Katherine implored.

"Ah don't want him here," Anias said point blank.

"Ah love my son, Anias. Ah want to see him as often as Ah can, while Ah can."

"Ah'm not keeping you from seeing him. Just keep seeing him wherever it is you go to see him."

"Ah'm going to ask him to come for supper."

"Woman, don't make me talk badly to you! Ah told you he's not welcome here, and that's that."

"But–"

But, nothing! Ah don't want him here," Anias said, dead set against having it any other way.

Katherine did not care for Anias' tone, but she knew it would not be easy. Presently, it seemed almost impossible. She would drop the matter, for now.

At the home of Rory and Jasmine. Rory was sitting on the porch in the rocking chair, also enjoying what remained of the sunset. Jasmine stepped out onto the porch. Rory extended his hand to her. She took his hand, and he pulled her onto his lap. She rested her legs over the arm rest, draping her arms around his neck. She kissed him on his neck. She felt very good, like the feeling one has when day dreaming. "Ah loves you," whispered she in his ear.

"Oh, my queen, not half so much as Ah loves you. Everywhere Ah go. Everythang Ah do. You wit' me. When Ah was in da war, Ah seed thangs no man ought see. Thangs dat can change a man, make 'im touched in da head. Ah made it through 'cause of you."

"Cause of me?" she asked, wondering how.

"In da worst of times, Ah could hear yo' sweet voice tellin' me ta stay strong, tellin' me ta keep goin', ta come back ta ya. Ya saved my life, 'cause Ah knowed Ah had ta see you again. Ah remember da promise Ah made ta ya da day Ah left. Ah promised, Ah was gon' make it back ta ya. While Ah was away, Ah promised ya over and over again in my mind, Ah was gon' come back ta ya. Ah made up in my mind dat's what Ah was gon' do. Ah had ta come back ta ya. Ah'd gladly give my life fuh ya. Yet, Ah knows Ah can't never live without cha. You so much of my heart and soul until Ah don't feel like O'm alive unlessen O'm wit' ya."

Jasmine smiled with a joy of soul which is not possible to put into words. It was good to know that she was his heart. The very pulse of his being. She looked deep into his eyes, pleased just to be close to him. She stroked his face with gentle passion. In every sense, but the physical, they were truly one soul. Theirs was a simple existence, full and rich in love. If the world were to take notice of them for just a second, it would despise them for having something so pure and good. The bliss they shared was the pursuit of happiness obtained that the forefathers of the constitution wrote. Strange that happiness should cling to them, when so many others with so much more of everything this world had to offer could not find it.

"Love me," she whispered.

"Now?"

"Yes. Ah wonts yo' seed in me. Ah wonts it ta take root in me, ta grow in me. Ah wonts ta brang forth good fruit. The best of you and me. When you touch me, Ah'll be prayin' dat cha leave me wid a baby."

Anytime that Jasmine wanted to be touched, Rory was more than happy to accommodate her. As a matter of fact, if she wanted to be held, touched, or just simply made to feel loved. He would be there to provide for the need. Whatever he could do to make her life a happy one, he was willing. They rose from the chair. He picked her up, and carried her inside, sharing soft kisses along the way.

On the end of Jago nearest Mt. Pleasant, there was a very old graveyard.

There were graves more than a century old. It was roughly ten square acres is size. To the left of it, there was a dirt road of red clay, and a white wooden fence covered with red dust, which bordered the road. To the most rear of it, there were thickets of bushes and Magnolia trees, to the most right of it, a clearing of open field. This cemetery was for blacks only. Freemen and slaves both rested there. Many of the graves were marked. For all those that had a marker, there were more that were unmarked. Most of the markers had a single name and the year of passing. There was nothing else to tell a person who they were, or what they wanted out of life. Although the cemetery was old, it was not neglected. It was well cared for and still in use. Ken Bailey was buried there, and this day, so too would Henry Walker take rest there. At the front of the graveyard, there stood a small white church house made of cedarwood. The front of the building faced the road. It was not a very large structure. On a Sunday morning, there was standing room only, and so it was this day. The church was erected there shortly after the Negro emancipation. Building it was one of the very first things that the people who decided to stay here did. No one could truly say why they elected to build it there. Perhaps, it was so they would not forget those who came before them and died slaves, never knowing the freedom that they now enjoyed. Perhaps, this was their way of not leaving them behind.

The funeral of young Walker was a sad thing. One of the saddest things a person could see. After Minister Brownlee had delivered the eulogy, they carried the small wooden box with the child's body out to the burial ground. Ephram lead the way behind those carrying his son. Hattie May, however, couldn't stop sobbing. Josephine, Mama Julia, and some of the other ladies stayed behind to comfort her.

"Whew, It's hot in heah," Mama Julia said, fanning Hattie May, but sweating and feeling faint herself, "Kin somebody git her some water?"

Ethel Jenkins grabbed a silver dipper hanging on the wall and ran outside to the water barrel to get some water. Josephine saw the way Mama Julia was sweating. She was soaking wet with sweat. She was overweight and was breathing heavily. Josephine was concerned for her. "Mama, sit down befo' you fall down," she warned.

No sooner than Josephine said it. Mama Julia felt light-headed and slipped to one knee. Ethel returned with the dipper of water, and saw the other two women present trying to help Mama Julia to her feet.

"Lawd, is she gon' be alright?" Ethel asked, handing Mama Julia the water intended for Hattie May. "Let's help her outside y'all. Da air a lit' bit cooler out yonder."

The ladies all began to help Mama Julia get outside including Josephine.

"Stay wit Hattie May, Ethel," Josephine instructed, "We kin handle dis."

Poor Hattie May, Ethel had almost forgotten the poor grieving woman. She sat next to Hattie May, and took her hand. The tears were still flowing heavily from her eyes.

"Ah know it's hard, Ms. Hattie May, but maybe you'll feel better if ya go outside."

"Ah can't do dat. Ah can't watch 'em put 'im in da ground."

"Ya can't?" Ethel asked, not understanding why she wouldn't want to take this last opportunity to say goodbye.

"Ah can't go ta 'im, knowing he can't come ta me," Hattie May wept.

"Oh, Ms. Hattie May, but he goin' ta a better place. He goin' home ta God."

"God," she whispered in a single-sad chuckle, "God punishin' me."

"No, he ain't Ms. Hattie May. Ah know it might feel like dat right now, but he ain't."

"Yes, he is. He know what Ah done, and he punishin' me fuh it."

"No matter what cha done. God gon' always forgive ya."

"Is he?"

"Yes, he is."

"You don't know what Ah done."

"Whatever it is, God will forgive if ya ask 'im ta," Ethel assured.

"Ah killed my babies," Hattie May revealed.

"What?" Ethel said quite shocked, releasing Hattie May's hand, withdrawing from her. What did she mean? Was she the one committing the killings? These were the thoughts that quickly ran through Ethel's mind.

"When Ah was a slave girl no mo' 'an sixteen, da massa made me take up wit' a buck on da plantation. He wonted us ta haves childrens. Didn't matter dat Ah didn't love 'im. Didn't matter how Ah felt. All dat mattered was increasin' massa's slave stock. When Ah was pregnant dat firs' time, Ah got ta thankin' 'bout what kinda life my childrens gon' haves. How if it's a girl, she gon' be made ta give herself ta somebody she don't love jes' so da massa kin haves mo' slaves. How her childrens might be sold off from her. How dat'll break her heart. Ah got ta thankin' how iffen it was a boy. How he was gon' git da lash across his back jes' cause massa wanna whip on somebody. How he wa'n't gon' let 'im have pride in his self. Ah knowed Ah didn't wont dat fuh my childrens. So, Ah took duh root, and Ah los' dat child. Ah got pregnant again, and Ah took da root again. Twice Ah killed my babies whiles dey was still in my womb. Den, ole massa sold me off. Cause a slave gal dat can't haves no childrens ain't worth da salt in her bread. Da nex' massa Ah got had da same ideas as da firs'. Ah got pregnant two mo' times, and two mo' times Ah kilt 'em in my womb. Dat massa figured Ah couldn't have no childrens either. So, he sold me off on da nex' massa. Ah was hurtin' in my soul by den, but Ah'd rather be hurtin' in my soul dan brang childrens into dis sad world. Jes' den, when my soul was so sick Ah didn't wanna go on, Ephram came into my life. And, Ah loved 'im almost from the minute Ah seed 'im. He changed me. Changed da way Ah seed dis world. He wonted childrens, and Ah wonted to give 'im childrens. Fuh da firs' time in my life, Ah wonted ta have childrens. Not long after, Henry was born ta us. Den, da war come and freed us. Ah thought we'd be happy forever heah. Ah forgot all about what Ah done. Da lit' innocent lives Ah took. Ah forgot, but God didn't forget. Ah didn't wont da babies he gave me. So he took da one Ephram gave me."

Ethel didn't know what to say to this revelation. She did not approve personally of what Hattie May did, but neither did she condemn her actions. Slavery was in many ways a far more difficult thing to endure for women than for men. Slave women had to suffer the lustful eye of the master. The envious hate-filled heart of his wife, who knew her husband's heat for the slave quarters, and not for her.

Slave women were forced to breed babies with partners they didn't particularly care for, and many times had to watch their families sold apart. That was a hard thing for any parent to suffer, but how much more difficult it must be for a mother. A mother who carried a child inside of her for nine months, and loved the child unconditionally after birth. What heart could suffer such miseries as those slavery had to offer. Hattie May wasn't the first to spare her unborn children the misery of slavery, and no doubt she wasn't the last.

Ethel did not in any part approve of what Hattie May did. It was wrong. She did not judge, but felt she must defend the honor of God. God didn't tell her to do what she did, and he certainly didn't punish her, as Hattie May contended.

"Ms. Hattie May, God loves us. God is good, and he is mercy and love. He wouldn't punish ya like dat. Don't never let yo' heart doubt 'im. Believe in 'im, and trust in 'im. He'll see ya through what ya goin' through right now, and in a better time, you'll know he loves ya. You'll know dat he done always loved ya."

Hattie May could not appreciate what Ethel was saying to her at that time. All she could see was the grief of the situation that she had to endure. She loved her child, loved him dearly, and he wasn't with her anymore. A more mournful thing than Ethel could begin to understand, not being a mother.

She took Hattie May's hand again, and pulled her head onto her shoulder. As for the child Hattie May had lost, he was interred in the ground, and for a second time everyone went on about their business. They were content to put this sad day into forgotten memory. It would have been wisdom, had they not forgotten recent events. Yet, they did forget, and because of it, grief would have them yet again.

As promised, Solomon went about trying to get others to patrol the woods at night. He feared there was little time remaining before the predator struck again. His efforts thus far had been semi fruitful. He soon found himself at Rory's home. It was Jasmine that answered the door and invited him in.

"Rory, Mr. Solomon heah ta see ya."

"Who?"

"Oh, ya don't knows 'im, do ya?"

Rory shook his head, acknowledging that he did not know Solomon. At the same time, he felt some shame because he didn't. It made him feel like a stranger in a place he grew up in to some degree. "How ya doin', suh?"

"Oh, O'm tolerable. Ah hate Ah ain't had a chance ta meet cha befo' now, and Ah hate ta be meetin' ya dis way. It's a bad time right now, and da folks around heah need young mens like you ta help us make it through."

"How, suh?"

"You might know dat we done lost two little boys, murdered dey was."

"Yes, we heard."

"Some of us believe it was tha work of da same person."

"Really."

"Yes, and we don't thank he done yet."

Rory was shocked to hear Solomon say this and it showed on Rory's face. Straightaway, Rory noticed something that bothered him. Jasmine didn't seem shocked. Solomon didn't notice this because his back was to her. "Is ya sho'?" Rory asked.

"Pretty much."

"What cha need me ta do?" Rory inquired.

"Well, they's plenty woods 'round heah. Both dese childrens was found in da woods. We thank dat what happened ta 'em, happened at night. We trying ta get as many men out at night as we can ta patrol da woods. Dat way, maybe, he'll move on and spare us da loss of any mo' of our young." Solomon answered.

"Ah see."

"Can ya help us?"

"Yeah, Ah'll be glad ta help," Rory responded.

"Good."

"When do ya need me ta start?"

"As soon as ya can, tonight if ya can."

"What time?" Rory asked.

"We most worried about midnight to four," Solomon informed him.

"Okay, what do ya wont me ta do?"

"Anybody dat cha see out in da middle of da night, approach 'im, see who he is. If ya don't know where he live, ask 'im. Ask 'im why he out in da dead of night. See 'im home if ya feel uneasy bout what he tellin' ya. And, no matter what cha do, don't let ya guard down. Dis somebody we lookin' fuh is dangerous. Don't do none of what Ah jes' told ya if you feel like you bout ta walk into something ya might not be able ta walk out of. Ya understand what O'm sayin'?" Solomon asked.

"Yeah."

"Who ever ya see. Whatever ya see. Report dat back ta me da nex' day. We'll see ta it from dere."

"Okay, but how Ah know who s'pose ta be out and who ain't?"

"Ain't nobody black suppose ta be out afta curfew, not even us, but we gonna do what we gotta. We jes' askin' dat cha patrol da woods sort of round tha area ya live in. It's another fella, Marshal Burke, dat gon' patrol around heah too. You'll know 'im. He a tall skinny dark-skinned fella, and he ride an ole-black mule bare backed all da time. Ya can't miss 'im. Right now, y'all da only two workin' dis area. Anybody else ya see ain't got no good business out dat time of night. Ah'll let cha know if dat change."

"Ah know Marshal," Rory said.

"Good."

They exchanged a few more details and pleasantries, and then Solomon left. Rory saw him off and returned to the house. Jasmine was sitting on the bed. He walked over and sat beside her. It was still bothering him that she didn't seem the least bit shocked by the fact that Solomon believed the murders to be the work of one person. He wanted to ask her why, but he didn't really know how to breach the subject. That didn't stop him though. "Jasmine, can ya believe dat?"

"What? Dat one somebody doin' dis?"

"Uh huh."

"Yeah," she said, "Ah believe it."

"Don't it kinda shock ya."

"Ah s'pose it oughta, but it don't. Ah kinda thought dat all along."

It surprised Rory to hear this coming from her. "Ah ain't never heard of such a thang as dis in my whole life. How could you thought it?"

"Ah don't know. Dat firs' time Naomi told us 'bout Ken Bailey. Ah knowed it ain't over."

"How?"

"Ah jes' did."

"Ya jes' felt it gon' happen again?"

"Yeah."

Some of the things Jasmine had said in the past, and what she was saying now, just didn't sit well with Rory. He knew that others no doubt saw matters as she did, and this was not a crime. However, Jasmine was such a caring and compassionate soul. Her love of children was so strong. She loved to be around them, and was very good with them. She prayed often to have children of her own. What had happened didn't seem to shake her enough to Rory. That is, knowing her as he did, it bothered him that she was so accepting and seemingly so much more undisturbed by this; not as he felt she should be. He wondered if she knew more than she was telling, but he was afraid to ask her more. He was afraid that she might have something to do with the murders. He didn't want to know that, not right now anyway. He loved her so, and he couldn't bring himself to question her character as he was tempted to do. He thought of the time he was away from her. He thought of all that she had gone through, and wondered if it changed her. His countenance fell. He appeared deeply saddened to Jasmine.

"What's wrong?" she asked.

"Nothin'."

"Don't look like nothin'."

"Ah loves ya," said he.

"And, dat made ya sad?" said she jokingly.

"Don't never doubt my love fuh ya," he said quite seriously.

"Ah knows ya love me. Ah jes' wonderin' why ya got all sad like, all sudden like."

"Ta know somebody hurtin' babies, don't dat make ya sad?"

Jasmine reflected on his explanation for a moment. "Yeah, Ah reckon it do."

Sadness blanketed her face also. It was as if all that was needed to awaken the expected compassion within her was the reminder that innocent little lives were unjustly taken from them. Rory was relieved to see the sadness in her. It fully restored his faith in her, and doubt of her was vanquished.

Eight

Twelve days passed uneventfully. Many of the impatient, including Rory, were of the mind that Solomon and Elijah were wrong. They chose to believe this. Instead of believing that what they were doing was making it difficult for the killer to move unabated. They were losing sleep, and would much rather have been in their warm beds next to their women. Not out on a cool night with a chill in their bones. Rory was riding along the outskirts of the wooded area not more than a mile from his home. He heard the sound of a horse moving toward him. Even though the night was well lit by the moon. It was still difficult for him to make out who was approaching. He wasn't nervous or afraid. He assumed it was someone who was supposed to be out. His assumptions were correct. As the person moving toward him drew nearer, it become apparent that it was Marshal Burke. The men stopped their animals along side each other.

"Seed anythang?" Marshal asked.

"Nothin'," Rory responded.

"Ah tell ya O'm gettin' right tired of dis."

"Ah feels da same way, but we doin' da right thang, ain't we?"

"Ah reckon, but O'm jes' gettin' tired is all. O'm gon' talk wit' Solomon on da morrow and see how long he thank we gon' have ta do dis."

"He ain't gon' know dat," Rory said.

"Well maybe, he kin work something' out so we don't have ta be out every night. Maybe, we kin do it every other night or something'."

"Look, Ah feel da same way, but jes' hang in dere, okay. If we save a life, Dat's worth missin' a lit' sleep over."

"Ah reckon."

"Good man."

"Well, O'm gon' ride on up heah a ways. As sleepy as Ah is, Ah hope, Ah don't mess around and fall off my mule," Marshal joked.

"Well, dat gon' wake ya up," Rory kidded.

Marshal chuckled and rode off into the night. As for Rory, he continued his ride in the opposite direction. Not long into the ride, he heard a sound in the woods parallel to him. It shocked him. He looked suddenly in that direction, stopping his horse. It sounded like something large was moving through the brush. He listened very attentively. He heard nothing and began to doubt himself. He started to ride. Again, he heard a noise coming from the woods. He stopped, this time, and he did not doubt that he heard something. His heart started to race. He was feeling spooked, but not only him. His horse also seemed spooked. "Easy now, gal," he said, trying to hold the animal steady. He heard the sound again. He was confident that it wasn't an animal. An animal would most likely keep moving. It wouldn't want to make contact with him, or so he rationalized. It wouldn't stalk him, so he thought. Whatever was out there was definitely stalking him, and given the reason he was out there, he believed it to be a human being. His heart seemed to race faster, but he was not about to panic. He had his musket with him. He pulled up on it, ready to do work. "Whoever ya is! Ya better come up out dem woods!" There was an almost eerie silence. "Ah know ya dere, and ya budda know Ah means business," he said in a forceful tone, aiming his musket in the general direction in which he heard the sound. There was a considerable amount of movement coming from the area in which he heard the noise.

As a figure emerged from the woods, there was loud laughter. It was Jasmine. "Boy, you know you done tickled me."

"Jasmine," he said surprised, "What cha doin' out heah in da middle of da night?"

"Ya better come up out dem woods," she laughed, mocking him in her deepest voice, "You should've heard yo'self."

"Don't be out heah in da middle of da night playing', Jasmine! Dat's a good way ta get a ass full of buck and ball," he said, indicating she almost got shot with three buck shots and one bullet. "What cha doin' out heah anyway?" he asked angrily, as he dismounted.

"Don't be mad at me."

"Why ya out heah?"

"Cause."

"Cause what?"

"Cause Ah missed ya."

This broke his angry tough demeanor all the way down. "Ya missed me?"

"Ah was lonely fuh ya. Ah wonted ta be near ya."

"It could be somebody dangerous out heah, baby. Ah don't wont cha out heah."

"Don't worry, Ah can take care of myself."

"Dat ain't da point."

"Don't be mad, Rory. Ah jes' wonted ta be near ya. It make me happy ta have ya close ta me. Ah can't sleep a lot of times. Ah watch cha when ya sleep sometimes, and it comforts me ta be near ya. Ah woke up tonight, and Ah wonted ta be comforted by yo' sweet face. Ah jes' loves ya is all."

"Jasmine, the things ya say. What O'm gon' do wid cha?"

"Love me ya whole life," answered she.

"And, Ah will," assured he, tenderly stroking her face, "Come on, let me take ya home."

"Ah wanna stay wid you."

It touched Rory's heart to hear Jasmine say such things, but this was out of the question. "Ah don't wanna deny ya, but Ah gotta. It's dangerous out heah."

"Den, let me brave da danger wid cha."

"Jasmine," said he, wanting her to see how impractical such a move was.

"Ah don't wanna be without cha."

"Don't make no fuss now. O'm gon' take ya home, and Ah wont cha ta try ta get some rest. When O'm done heah, O'm gon' come ta ya. O'm gon' always come ta ya "

Reluctantly, she relented, yielding to his wishes without further argument. Rory returned Jasmine to their home, and was off again. The remainder of his assigned time that night passed excruciatingly slow. His heart was with Jasmine, and he longed to be with her. He wondered if she was still awake. What she might be doing. What she might be thinking. He would be all too happy when this thing was over and life returned to normal. He had no desire to be apart from Jasmine, not for one minute. His place is with her during the night. Not out here in the wilderness. When his watch for that night was done, he returned to her. Jasmine was asleep, but tossed and turned restlessly. He undressed and eased into bed next to her. At once, she clung to him and was at peace.

When the light of day had come, a gruesome discovery was made. This time by a young woman and her two sons taking a short cut through the woods to her brother's house. Another child had been murdered. This time it was a young girl. Immediately, Solomon and Elijah were summoned. It was just after eight in the morning now. Solomon arrived before Elijah, who was accompanied by Micah. As Elijah approached, he noticed that Solomon looked weary, troubled, and obviously disappointed. The stress of this situation was starting to take its toll on the old man. Elijah was concerned for his friend and mentor. "Ya all right, Solomon?"

"Dis shouldn't have happened," Solomon replied with overtones of anger, "We doin' everythang we can do, and he still got another one."

"Nobody saw anything I take it?" Micah asked.

"Nobody ain't reported nothin' ta me," Solomon answered, "we must have had fifteen or twenty men out last night, and he still was able ta do dis right under our noses."

"Why did he take such a risk with so many people out last night? He could have easily been seen or caught," Micah commented.

"Maybe, he can't help his self," Elijah hypothesized.

"What?" Solomon said, not really understanding what Elijah was getting at.

"S'pose it's somethin' pushin' 'im ta da point he feel like he gotta do it," Elijah explained.

"It's more likely that he is just bold, and has no respect for us," Micah surmised.

"Let 'im keep thankin' dat, we'll git 'im," Elijah assured.

"We better, O'm gettin' tired of buryin' lit' children," Solomon exclaimed.

"We gon' git 'im. Ah ain't gon' rest till we do," Elijah vowed.

"Maybe, we need to re-think this and try something else in addition to the watch," Micah suggested.

"Well," Elijah sighed, regretting what must be done next, " let's take a look at her."

"What's her name?" Micah asked, as they walked toward the child. Her portly body was lying face down.

"Arnzie, Arnzie Williams, she lived about three miles north of here. She ain't but bout ten years old," Solomon apprised.

"Ah know her," Elijah said.

One of the first things that everyone noticed was that one of the child's shoes was lying a few steps away from her body. Micah wondered why that was. The first thought that ran through his mind was that she might have been raped before dying. Elijah, on the other hand, saw a different reason the girl's shoe wasn't on her foot.

"Has anyone checked to see if he had his way with her?" Micah asked.

"No, Ah don't believe so," Solomon answered.

Micah gently turned the child's body face up and raised her skirt. He began to visually examine her vaginal region for a back flow of semen. There were two more men there in addition to Solomon and Elijah. Risby and a man named Vance Baker, the men were shocked that Micah would do such a thing right out in the open. It was shameful and disrespectful.

"What cha doin'?" Vance asked quite loudly, indicating Micah should desist promptly.

"I'm checking her to see if she was raped."

"Well, maybe we could've got one of the women folk fuh ta do dat," Vance replied, very disapprovingly.

Micah looked around, everyone, even Elijah was looking at him as if it was not the most prudent thing to do. "I'm sorry, I was just trying to help."

"We know," Solomon said, in a move to show support for Micah, "Was she raped?"

Vance backed off, dismissing what Micah did as a necessary evil.

"Doesn't look like it," Micah answered.

"Ah don't thank dat's why her shoe off, iffen dat why ya thank she might've been raped," Elijah commented.

Micah and the others looked at Elijah, waiting for further explanation.

"He dragged her heah," Elijah expounded.

"How ya know dat?" Vance asked.

Elijah picked up the shoe and moved over to a spot on the ground in front of the body. He kneeled down and placed the heel of the shoe at a forty-five degree angle on the ground. "See heah."

The others gathered around and took a closer look. Sure enough, there were faint disturbances in the ground consistent with marks that could have been made by the heel of the girl's shoe being dragged along. The marks were very light, but definite and conclusive.

"Ah thank ya right, Elijah," Risby concurred.

"And, fuh da firs' time, he done told us something'," Elijah concluded.

The others looked at him wondering what it was that they should now know, which wasn't so apparent to them, but was to Elijah. He saw the blank expressions upon their faces. He began to help them see what he saw. Arnzie Williams was a short-portly girl, weighing better than a hundred pounds.

"Dem firs' two lit' on's, he carried 'em to where he left them. We know dat fuh sho' 'bout lit' Henry Walker, cause of da way his body was kinda hid like. Why he didn't do dat heah?" Elijah asked them.

Micah got it. "Cause he couldn't. She was too heavy for him to carry. He is physically weak. We are looking for a man of small stature."

"Or else a woman," Vance interjected.

It wasn't a possibility they had considered; that is, that a woman might be doing this, but they were thinking it now.

"Well, dat's a lit' help, but not much," Solomon said.

"So, now, what do we do?" Micah asked.

"We don't tell what we done fount out heah," Elijah insisted.

"Why?" Micah asked.

"He startin' ta make mistakes. We start lettin' it git out what we know. He might tighten up again. We don't wanna do nothin' ta let 'im know he helpin' us git a bead on 'im," Elijah explained.

"Are you sure we don't want to share the information?" Micah openly disagreed. "This may be just the information someone needs to help us catch him. I mean, someone may know something that they don't realize they know, and this information could help."

Micah was correct, but then again so was Elijah. Thinking the matter through, as to which course of action would be more advantageous, Solomon weighed in. "Ah thank Elijah got it right. We keep dis quiet."

Everyone there trusted in Solomon's judgement concerning this, except for Micah, but he too trusted in Solomon's leadership. They all vowed to keep what they had learned among them.

"What cha wont us ta do now, Solomon?" Risby asked.

"Elijah, Ah wont you and Micah ta take dis child's body home ta her folks. Risby Ah need ya ta come wit' me. Ah wanna talk wit' everybody we had on watch last night in dis area ta see if
they saw or heard anythang."

"Of course," agreed Micah, "has anyone informed the child's family?"

"Don't know, but it's da third hour of da day. Ah reckon dey know she missin' by now," Elijah said.

"Elijah, if dey up to it, ask 'em anythang ya can thank of dat might help us," Solomon instructed.

"Yassuh," Elijah answered.

With this, they dispersed. Elijah picked the dead girl up. He noted that her body was completely cold. She had been dead for quite some time. This re-affirmed to him that the murder took place during the night. Elijah was anxious to talk with the Williams family to see if they had any idea how she ended up away from them and dead.

As they took the child home on the back of a wagon borrowed from Risby, they were, to put it mildly, not looking forward to it. This would be the first time that they would actually have to inform a family that their child was dead. Elijah wondered how one did such a thing. Was there some compassionate protocol which should have been exercised, or did they simply bring the body forth and let it speak for itself. He was not certain of how to do this. It didn't feel right to him, that he should simply go in carrying their dead child. It would be best to go in and break the news to them as gently as possible. It wouldn't be easy anyway he sliced it. And to make things worse, the family would want answers, and unfortunately, Elijah didn't have any to give them. His head was starting to hurt again. It seemed to ache constantly of late. He looked at Micah, who rode alongside him on his horse. Micah seemed to shake, as if he were cold, and he was sweaty. Strange, considering it was mild and pleasant out that day. Elijah figured he was also having trouble with what must be done, but he was wrong. Micah had been having trouble falling a sleep and trouble staying asleep. He seemed to keep looking over his shoulder, as if danger was near. Elijah noticed this in Micah, but he assumed it was being triggered by the extreme stress they were under, particularly at this moment. He also thought he might simply be sick or getting sick. "Micah, everythang all right, ya ain't ill is ya?"

"I'm fine," he answered, pulling himself together.

"We gon' be dere in a minute. Ah was thankin' dat Ah could go up, and break da news to 'em easy like befo' we let 'em see da child. Will ya wait wit' da body, tills Ah calls fuh ya?"

"Sounds fine."

As they got close to the William's residence, Arnzie's's father, Varner Williams, was out working the cotton field. What's more there were several of his younger children playing about. Seeing this, Elijah stopped the wagon a good distance away. "Ah thank O'm gon' walk da rest of da way."

Elijah hopped off of the wagon and started to walk toward Varner Williams. Varner was some fifty yards away, but to Elijah it was not nearly a long enough distance. His head was pounding, and to make matters worse, there was a sickly feeling in his stomach. Not the normal sickly feeling, but a feeling more like that experienced when traveling over the apex of a steep hill at a great speed.

Varner saw Elijah coming. He was aware of the goings on in the community, but it didn't dawn on him that Elijah's visit may have pertained to that. For some reason, he simply chalked it up to a neighborly visit. Varner was a dark-skinned tall muscular man. He had a narrow face with large flaring nostrils and graying hair on the sides. He was a simple man leading a simple life. He was just trying to make it the best he could. Each day before he worked the cotton fields. He worked his garden, which was the way he got the majority of the food on the table. He was busy trying to provide for his family of seven. Perhaps then, it was not a wonderment that he seemed unaware that one of his children was unaccounted for. Not one to waste time, he worked up to the last possible second before Elijah was upon him. At which point, he stopped to greet Elijah. "Good Mornin', Elijah. What bring ya out my way?" he asked unsuspectingly.

"Uh, Varner, we need ta talk. Yo' wife about?" Elijah said with an uncomfortable tone of voice.

"No, her and my eldest boy Otis is out lookin' fuh one of my gals. She done snuck off dis mornin' befo' day. She done earned herself a good whippin', and O'm gon' see she get it. Ah tell ya childrens mo' trouble dan they's worth sometime."

Elijah looked at Varner, bewildered, not knowing what to say. His headache rose in intensity, as a very sharp pain rushed through his right temple. He frowned from the pain, and rubbed his temple. "Varner, maybe we oughta go inside fuh a minute. Ah got something' Ah needs ta tell ya."

At this point, Varner became troubled. He looked at Elijah, who looked very uncomfortable, and then to Micah holding a stand offish position down the road. "Who dat wit' cha, Elijah?"

"Dat's my brother Micah."

"Why he waitin' back dere?" emotion swelled in Varner; he got a lump in his throat, as he noticed there was something on back of the wagon. "What in dat wagon?"

This didn't seem the proper setting to Elijah to tell Varner about Arnzie. "Maybe, we need to go inside, Varner."

At that point, Varner knew what was in the wagon. He started to tremble slightly, and his eyes swelled with tears, which he held in check.

"What in dat wagon?" he asked again, wanting Elijah to confirm his beliefs.

The little ones ran about oblivious to the sad reality taking shape there. There was a fullness in Elijah's chest, which felt as if his heart was about to burst. He wanted to just come out with it, but he was having difficulty.

"It's my baby gal, ain't it?" Varner spared him having to say it.

It took all the courage Elijah could muster to utter one little word of confirmation. "Yes."

Varner hands trembled mightily, as he let out a loud cry, falling to his knees, too weak to stand. This scared his little ones. They had never seen their father cry before. They stopped playing and the two of them clung to each other, and began to cry also. The situation felt overwhelming to Elijah. He didn't quite know how to handle it. Micah knew that the sad task of informing the family of Arnzie's passing was done. He dismounted his horse, and tied it to the back of the wagon. He got on the wagon. It was time to take Arnzie home to those who loved her.

Nine

As in past times, the people of Jago found themselves preparing to bury another young child, Arnzie Williams. The people of the community had been slow to see, and even slower to react, but now they had finally gotten it, and were all too ready to help. A meeting had been called at Solomon's home for a second time. A confluence that Solomon did not call. A wide-spread sense of outrage and fear gripped the people. They demanded of Solomon that he do something more than he was currently doing.

It was amazing to Solomon that they should now look to him. He had practically begged them to help before a third child was lost.

They were collectively applying pressure to him as if he were the law. Unfortunately, he did not know what to do. At that time, there were no procedures in place to deal with this sort of thing. No agencies with people of expertise in handling such perverse unspeakable iniquity. There wasn't even a name for this kind of crime yet. And, even if this sin had a name, and aide was available, it was certainly not available to them. The newly emancipated man of color with no legal rights to stand upon.

It was the night of the same day young Arnzie Williams was murdered. Now, Solomon was an old man. As he stood before the multitude of seemingly everyone in the community for miles around. The stressful weight of this matter rested heavily upon his gray-troubled brow. The people seemed an angry vengeful mob to him. He listened to them murmur against him, as if he were somehow at fault. He would not face them given the choice, but he dared not run from this calling. He called them to order with zeal in his voice of a man half his age. He would not appear weak and feeble before them. "Silence," he said as one having authority, "SILENCE!"

They became still and quiet as obedient children. It was an uncanny silence.

"We doin' everythang dat can be done. If you mens wanna help, come see me in da mornin'. Ah'll get cha on patrol, but other than dat. Da bes' thang y'all can do is go home and watch over ya children. Explain ta 'im how thangs is, and tell 'em not ta be trustin' strangers," Solomon told them.

The silence remained, but for a brief second. There was a voiceful thorn in the midst of the people. An adversary which seemed to be on the

144

opposite side of every endeavor. Trents was among them. "Solomon, y'all go ta da law like Ah said ya ought?" his voice rang out.

Solomon visually searched him out of the crowd. "No, we didn't."

Immediately, there was widespread murmuring and criticizing of Solomon's handling of this whole matter throughout the crowd.

"Ya should've done dat, why ain't cha?" Trents criticized.

Solomon was standing on his porch, which was a good foot off of the ground, overlooking the people. Standing with him to his right were his son-in-law Noah, Elijah, and Micah, and to his left Risby and Ran. Micah had no love lost for Trents, and was offended that he even had the nerve to open his wretched mouth.

"You lean back on the elbows of do nothing, and you have the gumption to tell somebody what they should've done?" Micah said angrily.

Without conscious thought, Elijah subtly and quickly touched Micah, signaling him to halt. He remembered what happened on the last occasion they met, and didn't want a repeat. Micah got the hint and held his tongue.

"What you say?" Trents responded loudly.

It took everything Micah had not to jump all over Trents, but he was not going to allow Trents to escalate this situation anymore than he already had. Solomon breathed a little easier that Micah didn't come back at Trents. It would make it much easier to handle this large gathering.

Calmly, Solomon said, "It was explained ta ya dat we went ta da law, and dey ain't concerned about what's happenin' heah. But, we is gon' go back ta 'em, and ask 'em ta help us again, and we gon' keep doin' it till dey is."

This seemed to steal Trents thunder for a moment, but only a moment. "Well, ya should've been doin' dat all da time."

The people agreed almost as one with Trents.

"Well, Trents, it's always easier ta see thangs a lit' clearer on da back end. And, since ya see thangs so clear. Maybe, ya can come back in da mornin' and sign up ta patrol at night. And, when we meet ta see what mo' we can do, maybe, you can come, and share some ideas. And, if what we do still ain't enough ta stop da killings, maybe, you can stand up heah befo' dis press of people, and explain why what we doin' ain't workin' so far. We welcome any help dat cha can give," Solomon politely said, putting Trents under pressure to do or shut up.

Trents realized Solomon was putting him in his place, and everyone else did, also. Trents, like most people around the area, was a sharecropper. In addition to that, he, like everyone else, had to hunt for meat, and work a garden for vegetables. It was a full-time job just to survive. It took great sacrifice to find time to patrol at night, and still do what was expected as sharecropper, and as the head of a household. It took sacrifice to organize and plan, since all of this took away from the time a body had to make a living. Trents realized that he had stepped out there, and was standing in the spotlight. "Now, Solomon, Ah ain't sayin' y'all ain't doin' a good job. O'm jes' sayin' a lit' mo' need ta be done," Trents said, trying to stand down.

"And, O'm invitin' ya ta step up and help us do it," Solomon politely reiterated.

Trents had a family of eight children and a wife. Most of his kids were too young to be of much real help to him in his daily rigors. At the end of a long back-breaking workday, he was a very exhausted soul, and he just wanted to rest. He didn't want to contribute in the manner Solomon was suggesting. He wanted others to do the work, and he would throw his two cents in on a sort of advisory level. "Alright then, Solomon, Ah'll do what Ah kin," he said, trying to save face, not intending to do very much.

"Ah know y'all upset, and scared too, Ah suspect. Everythang we can thank to do is bein' done. And, Ah know it don't seem hardly enough. Ah can't blame ya fuh feelin' dat way. If anymo' of you mens wanna volunteer to patrol at night, we welcome ya. Da mo' mens we got out, da harder it's gon' be fuh 'im ta do his dirt," Solomon said.

There was still much murmuring and discontent among the people, but they didn't know what to do either. They were forced to put their trust in Solomon. They gradually dispersed and returned to their homes. When the last of the crowd had left, Solomon and those standing with him remained.

"What are we to do?" Micah asked, sensing the growing dismay of the community.

"Ah don't know, but da people deserve better dan we givin' 'em," Solomon said wearily.

"They's gotta be somethin' else we can do," Risby said, feeling puzzled.

"We gon' go back ta da law, and demand dey do somethin'," Solomon insisted.

"And, if they don't?" Micah asked.

"Ain't no if dey don't, we gon' keep pressin' 'em till dey do," Solomon contended, "maybe, dey'll get tired of us askin' everyday and do somethin'."

"Ah hate ta put all my eggs in dat basket," Elijah said.

"What else can we do?" Risby asked. "Ah mean, if da law don't help, we gotta do somethin'."

"They's a fort in Memphis," Ran pointed out, "maybe, dem federal boys can help us."

"Fort Pickering? Ah don't know 'bout dat," Noah said.

"It's worth a shot, Ah reckon," Elijah said optimistically.

"Yes, it is," Solomon agreed, "what else can we do?"

"Back when we was slaves. On Sundays, Massa let us go to church. There was dis circuit preacher dat use ta come through. Ah don't know how many y'all knows Reverend Kyle. He a good white man, and he live in Mt. Pleasant. Iffen da sheriff don't pay us no heed, Ah thank we oughta go see Reverend Kyle. Maybe, we can get 'im ta go ta da sheriff fuh us," Risby suggested.

"Now, dat's good thankin'. Dey bound ta respect him," Noah said, agreeing with Risby.

"Anythang else?" Solomon inquired.

"Maybe," Micah answered.

"What? Speak up," Solomon said, interested in what Micah had to say.

"When I was up North, I had occasion to meet a certain man. A black man, an abolitionist by the name of Houston Thurgood. It was noised about that he was a man of some weight. I understand that he is living up around Washington D.C. I could write him. I don't know if he would remember me, but he might. He might be able to use his influence on our behalf somehow."

"He way up in Washington and we down south. How he gon' help us? He a world away," Noah contended.

"Can't hurt," Elijah said, encouraging Micah to move forward with writing the letter.

"Get cha letter together, Micah," Solomon instructed, "if da law don't help, like Elijah say, it can't hurt. Anythang else anybody can thank of?"

"I still say that we should let it be known in the community that the person we are looking for is probably a man of small stature, or maybe even a women," Micah re-asserted, "You never know. It may help."

Solomon began to ponder the matter again.

"I don't know, Micah," Elijah disagreed, "Ah don't thank we wont nobody ta know what we know about whoever doin' dis."

"How does it hurt us?" Micah contended. "And, more importantly, how does what we know help us?"

"Dere ya habe it. If we don't know how it help us, how it gon' help somebody else. The only person dat it might help is da lost soul doin' it," Elijah argued.

"That's how it might help us. The news may reach him of what we know. If he believes we are getting close to him, it might scare him off," Micah argued.

"We don't wanna scare 'im off. He'll jes' move to another place, and keep on doin' what he doin'," Elijah argued.

"Another community ain't our community," Ran interjected, "Ah stand wit' Micah. Put what we know out dere."

"Dat's wrong, Ran," Risby contended, "another community won't know what we know, and might not even put it together. You wont dat on ya conscience?"

"Ah wont da killin' ta stop," Ran answered.

"Stop. Not move," Risby countered.

Solomon had been listening. There were good points on both sides of this argument, making it all the more difficult to render a prudent decision. He looked to Noah, as a sort of tie breaker. "What you say about it?" Solomon asked Noah.

"Ah don't rightly know what ta do ta tell ya da truth," he answered.

"We can't do it, Solomon," Elijah argued, "Risby is right. We don't wanna send dis problem nowhere else. And if it don't scare 'im off, da only thang we got workin' fuh us is gone. He gon' start bein' mo' careful."

"Even if it doesn't scare him off, it may help somebody who doesn't yet realize they have some information that may be of use to us," countered Micah.

"How?" Elijah asked.

"I don't know, but it might," Micah replied.

Solomon rubbed his eyes with the lower palms of his hands, as if something might be in them, and there was in a manner of speaking, confusion. He felt that Elijah was the most steady person there, a true thinker. What little information they had was because of his ability to see what they could not. He deferred to Elijah's judgement. "We gon' keep what we know to ourselves, and try to find another way to use it. We can't tip our hand."

Micah breathed a sigh of deep frustration. He felt that they were making a big mistake, but did not argue the point anymore.

"Is there anything else we can do?" Solomon asked.

No one had anymore suggestions to offer. It had been a long day, and was going to be an even longer night.

"Let's gon' home and get some rest den," Risby said, "it's gon' be time ta go on watch in a lit' while."

They all dispersed. Each of them having feelings of dejection and helplessness. The night passed without incident. When Elijah and Micah returned home, after their watch, they didn't try to sleep for the few hours until the sun came up. They probably couldn't sleep if they tried. Micah was frustrated that Elijah wasn't trying harder to see his point of view on certain things. Yet, he didn't let it come between them. They quietly sat around drinking coffee until daybreak. At which time, they went outside and started doing some chores. Micah milked the cow and Elijah began to chop wood. There was enough wood in the house for Josephine to use in the stove for breakfast, but she would certainly need more. Micah took the milk inside and came back out and started to gather up the wood Elijah had chopped. He picked up a good bit, and Elijah moved over to Micah. He started to load Micah's arms with wood so he wouldn't have to make too many trips. A look of pain came upon Micah's face, and he dropped the wood. He began to rub his right shoulder, which was hurting him badly. Elijah didn't think he was putting more on Micah than he was able to bear. He should have been able to carry the wood quite easily.

"What's wrong, Micah?"

"I was chopping wood the other day, and somehow I hurt my shoulder."

"How long ago?"

"Two days ago."

"Hmm, ya should've told me," Elijah said.

"It's nothing," Micah replied.

For a moment Elijah's mind raced, They were looking for someone who would have problems lifting around a hundred pounds. They assumed it would have most likely been a man of small stature or a women, but Elijah realized that it could also have been a man who had sustained an injury. He looked upon Micah with suspicion, but quickly placed it in the back of his mind as not likely. Yet, he did not forget. "Well, let's finish dis. We got a lot ta do befo' we ride into town ta see da sheriff."

Ten

Later Elijah and Micah rode into Olive Branch. Solomon had his granddaughter, Ethel, drive him into town. Risby and Ran also made the trek. Olive Branch was a very small town, with not very much in it, but more than many other small towns like it. It had one main thoroughfare of about a hundred and fifty yards with a number of businesses tightly nestled together on either side. It had a telegraph office, a freight and postal service, several stores, a saloon, one hotel, a bank, a doctor's office, a dentist office, and a stable which was on a side street apart from the businesses on the main street. There were several restaurants, a funeral home, and of course, the county sheriff's office. Despite its small size. It was quite a busy little town. They all met up at Sam Bush's General Store.

"Okay, Y'all, we ready?" Solomon asked.

Everyone was quite nervous about this venture, but they all expressed readiness. All except for Micah. "Solomon," he said, "I'm going to wait out here if you don't mind."

"Ya rode all dis way not ta go in and see da sheriff?" Elijah asked, somewhat surprised.

"Why Micah?" Solomon asked.

"I know me. You know me, and we all know my temperament can get the better of me sometimes. I'm not one to bite my tongue. I've been in the sheriff's office before, and I can tell you. It's gonna be best if I stay out here," Micah explained.

"If you think dat's best, Micah," Solomon conceded.

"Oh, I do. It's gonna take someone far more tempered than I am to deal with what that fat bastard Farley is gonna dish out. Excuse my language, Ms. Ethel. I don't wanna hurt what we are trying to do."

"Elijah sighed. "Well, let's go y'all."

"Ethel, wait out heah wit Micah," Solomon directed.

"Yes, ole paw," she answered.

Micah and Ethel watched as Solomon bravely led the others down, and across the street into the sheriff's office. He had a feeling things weren't going to turn out as they had hoped.

"Ya thank dey gon' help us, Mista Micah?" Ethel asked.

"I hope so, Ms. Ethel. What say you and I go into the store here, and buy us up a little treat while we wait?"

"Ah ain't got no money," she informed.

"But, I do. It would be my honor to treat you."

They went inside the store, and began to look at a large assortment of candies on the main counter. Mrs. Bush was helping a female customer with some fabrics, and Mr. Bush was busy stocking a shelf. "Be right with you folks," he said in a friendly manner, moving behind the counter to service them. "Now, what can I do for you?"

"We wont some candy," Ethel said excitedly.

Mr. Bush began to explain what he had, pointing to the large jars on the counter. "Here you have your hard candies, your soft candies, some licorice, and my personal favorite peppermint sticks."

"Ah don't know what to get," Ethel said, "what Ah oughta get, Micah?"

Micah noticed some boxes and bars of chocolate candies on the shelf behind Mr. Bush. "What are those candies behind you?"

Mr. Bush was surprised at how good Micah's diction was. "You aren't from around here, are you?"

"I was born not too far from here, but I haven't lived around here for quite some time," Micah answered.

"I can tell," Bush commented, "these are chocolates from Europe, Switzerland mostly. The bars will cost you four dollars, and the boxes will run you up to ten. Before the war, these candies use to be very popular among the plantation owners around here, but they move slow nowadays."

The prices were outrageous to Micah. He knew for a fact that a person could purchase a steak dinner with all the trimmings in some of the finest restaurants in New York City for just under five dollars. "I think we had best get the peppermint, Ms Ethel."

"Excellent choice, I have a special on. You can purchase any seven pieces of any candy on the counter here for five cents," Mr. Bush said.

"How much for a single piece?" Micah asked.

"Run you a penny a piece. So, you see, you are getting a deal for five cents," Bush insisted.

"We'll take seven pieces. Pick out what you want, Ms. Ethel."

"Ah don't thank Ah can eat dat much candy."

"Don't worry, Ms. Ethel. When the others are done with their business, they'll need something sweet after the bitterness they will have swallowed," Micah assured.

Now, it just so happened that inside the sheriff's office, Deputy Farley was on duty. Another deputy sheriff was also there. A young man by the name of Abner Lewis. Abner was twenty-four. He was quite a dashing and good looking fellow. He stood five feet eleven inches, with sandy brown hair, and was slender with a pleasant smile.

Deputy Farley was sitting at the sheriff's desk looking over some flyers, and Abner was standing at his side, looking also. When Solomon and the others entered, Farley went out of his way to be rude. "Where did all you niggers come from?" He vilely insulted. "Is it some kind of nigger holiday that I ain't aware of ?"

"What can we do for y'all?" Abner asked courteously.

"We like ta see da sheriff," Solomon spoke up.

"Nigger what business do you think you got with tha sheriff?" Deputy Farley asked, still quite vile in his tone.

"He's not here. Can we help?" Abner asked, ever courteously.

Solomon didn't feel comfortable in this setting, which was what Farley intended. Abner seemed quite friendly enough, but Solomon didn't care to have this conversation with Deputy Farley in the room. Yet, there was nothing he could do about it.

"Do ya know where da sheriff is? We really wont ta talk ta him," Solomon said.

"Stupid nigger, didn't you hear tha deputy here tell you he wasn't here?" Deputy Farley insulted. "If you got business with this office, state it, or be on your way!"

Solomon, Elijah, Risby, and Ran could all see why Micah elected to stay outside, and having had the pleasure of Deputy Farley's company for this short period of time, they wished they had done the same. They were use to being talked down to by white people. It was their way of reminding the black man who had the upper hand, but Farley was far too blatant and superfluous in his cruelty; particularly, for a man who was suppose to represent law and order.

As Ethel and Micah waited for the others to come out of the sheriff's office, they sat on the porch in front of the store enjoying peppermint sticks. Around this time, a fancy coach pulled up driven by a hired black man, Henry Tuggle. In the coach sat a beautiful white female, Abigail Covington. Her five-year-old daughter, Hannah, was with her. Abigail was slender and young, twenty-five years of age. She was an English woman with blonde hair, and fair skin, but not freckled. Her husband, Merriwhether Covington, brought her to America some seven years earlier from England. He was an older man in his fifties, and a widower ten years before introducing his young bride to the ways of the South.

With all of his children from his previous marriage grown, he decided to visit Europe. Upon seeing Abigail, he knew he had to have her in his life, and arranged her hand in marriage.

Abigail was arrayed in fine apparel, a lavender dress with gray-laced trim, and a yellow bonnet. Henry opened the coach door for her and the child. Abigail exited the coach, moving with airs of sophistication and grace. She went into Bush's General Store, taking a brief moment to smile and nod at Ethel. She did this mostly because of good up bringing. Being one not born and raised in the midst of slavery, it was difficult for her not to be courteous, even to black people.

Not more than two steps behind Abigail was little Hannah. Hannah was a beautiful bright-eyed child. She had a cute little round face with blonde hair. Upon seeing the candy, Hannah stopped and stared at Ethel and Micah. Henry, who was walking behind the child, stopped as well. He wanted to keep a watchful eye on the child.

Ethel saw that the child wanted some candy. She broke the child off a small piece, without the child having to ask for it. Hannah was all smiles. She had a beautiful smile. She tore into the candy with abandonment. Henry, standing behind Hannah dressed in black servant's suit, smiled at Ethel's kind gesture.

"Ya wont some candy, suh?" Ethel offered Henry.

"Thank ya," he said, taking the candy, "Ah ain't never had none befo'."

"Me neither, dis my firs' time eatin' some, too," Ethel informed.

"Micah was surprised to hear this. "You've never had candy before?"

"No, we ain't got money ta spend on dat kinda thang," she answered.

"Right sweet, ain't it? Kinda like a sugar cane stalk," Henry commented.

"Ah reckon," Ethel answered.

"It's good, ain't it?" Hannah said.

"Yes, it is, little one," Micah answered.

"Henry," Abigail called from inside the store.

"Comin', Ma'am," Henry responded, as he took Hannah by the hand. "Come on child."

Hannah pulled away from him. She wanted to stay with the candy, seeing Ethel had plenty more. Henry perceived there would be no harm in allowing Hannah to stay with Ethel and Micah. He left her there, and went in the store to Mrs. Covington.

"What's your name?" Hannah asked Ethel.

"Ethel."

"And, I'm Micah."

"Well, my name is Hannah. And, I like that candy. You s'pose I can have some more." The child said with disarming bubbling charm.

"Well, Ah reckon ya can, Hannah," Ethel consented, giving her a little more peppermint.

"Can you read?" Hannah asked Micah.

"Yes, I can."

"I'm smart, and I can read too."

"You can?" Ethel said, quite taken with the little lady.

"You know why I'm so smart?" Hannah said quite congenially, like an adult trapped inside a child's body. "Cause my momma teaches me. I can read, and I can count to fifty, too."

"Can you, now?" Micah said, taken with the child's charm.

"I can. You wanna hear?" At once, without waiting for an answer, Hannah began to spout out numbers.

Sitting there listening to the child, Micah experienced a good feeling. He was pleased that little Hannah was so accepting of them. It left him feeling that there was hope for the future. That prejudice and hate's days were numbered. Around this time, Abigail noticed Hannah wasn't in the store, and stepped to the door to see where she was. She saw Hannah standing there conversing with Ethel and Micah.

"You count very well there, Hannah," Micah complimented.

"I know," she said full of innocence.

"Hannah," Abigail called.

"Yes, momma," she answered.

"What are you doing there?"

"I'm just talking to the niggers," she answered innocently.

Micah and Ethel both looked at Abigail. They were surprised, for some inexplicable reason, by what Hannah had said. Ethel quickly realized that she was looking Abigail in the eye, fearing this might offend Abigail. She looked down at the ground, not wanting trouble. Micah, however, continued to look her squarely in the eyes. Abigail, who wasn't originally from the South, and didn't have the ways of the South deeply ingrained within her being, felt shame. Shame that she was allowing the hate-filled legacy of the South to be instilled within her daughter. Ensuring that hate would endure long after it should have faded into desolate forgotten memory. Yet, it would remain. The enemy of hope, justice, and peace. The enemy of the black man, who simply wanted the right to exist on an equal ground. The joy and hope which Micah felt quickly fled from him. Abigail was truly sorrowful that things were as they were, but they were this way long before she arrived. Who was she to change it. "Come inside with me, dear," she said to Hannah, taking her hand, leading her inside.

Ethel looked sadly at Micah, and in a low discouraged voice said, "Ah guess we gon' always be nothin' but niggers."

Micah looked at her, and was at a loss for words. He looked to the sheriff's office, waiting for the others to exit.

Inside the sheriff's office, things weren't proceeding as Solomon and the others had hoped. Deputy Farley was constantly attacking them verbally. Making them feel inferior, as if they were out of order to even dare stand there.

"Suh," Solomon said, "somebody killin' our children. We need y'all help ta stop it."

Farley chuckled several times. "They can kill up a hundred little niggers for all I care. Serves you right for runnin' off to those damn Yankees, wanting to be free. Now look at you, runnin' back to us. Y'all are like little children that can't take care of yourselves. Freedom ain't what you thought it would be, now is it?"

Solomon didn't care for all the cheap rhetoric coming out of Farley's disgusting looking foul mouth, with brown teeth stained by snuff. What Farley was saying didn't wash with Solomon. He knew that he was asking no more than what was reasonable, because help was exactly what the white community would demand of the law if faced with the same situation. Solomon kept his cool, but Elijah had a look of contempt upon his face for Farley. He wasn't even aware that he was allowing it to show. It didn't go without notice from Deputy Farley, however. "What the hell are you lookin' at like that, boy," he said angrily.

Elijah realized Farley was talking to him, but was slow to react.

"Ah ain't gonna tell you again! You get that damn look off your face right now, before Ah knock it off!" Deputy Farley barked.

Elijah humbled himself in the most docile way. He cleared his face of emotion as best he could, and lowered his head and shoulders, looking to the floor.

Farley rushed over to Elijah. He stood in his face. His breath as foul as feces fresh from the anus. "Don't you ever presume to walk into this office and look at me like that ever again, do you understand?"

Elijah nodded his head submissively. His dignity as a man debased.

"We'll jes' go outside and wait fuh da sheriff," Solomon said.

"Not around here you won't!" Farley barked. "Around here that's called vagrancy, and vagrancy is against the law. So, if you don't wanna get locked up, you best get on back to your work places. That's where yer suppose to be anyway."

Abner stood there looking in silence while all of this was occurring. He didn't feel it was required, but neither did he object. He wouldn't have said it quite so abrasively, but he also felt that blacks were as children, and simply weren't ready to be free. He felt that the Negro race was in their present unstable condition solely as a result of greedy,wealthy, northerners looking to exploit the riches of the south for their own financial gains. If the North was truly interested in freeing the black race, why then had they to this point left them so ill prepared to be free. Why else would they have left them so thoroughly at the mercy of their former masters by not granting them any rights, not even the right to vote. This was Abner's thinking, and it was well-founded upon solid reasoning in his opinion. Solomon and the others left the office, and Farley followed them out. "Y'all get on back to where you belong, ya hear?" he said. "Ah'm gonna walk the town in fifteen minutes, and if Ah catch any of you around. Yer goin' to jail for vagrancy."

Abner stepped out of the sheriff's office, and stood next to Farley giggling. "You think you were hard enough on 'em, Angus?"

"Ah think, Ah wasn't hard enough. We have enough to do without trying to help them figure out how to be free," he said, as he went inside, and kicked his feet upon the sheriff's desk.

Solomon and the others walked back up to Bush's General store feeling quite dejected, having suffered Deputy Farley's vituperation. As they approached, Micah saw by the look upon their faces that it went just as he suspected it would. He stood and walked to meet them. "How did it go?"

"Ya don't wanna know," Risby answered.

"So, I take it we are in no better shape than when we came?" Micah concluded.

"Dem people ain't right. Why won't dey do better by us?" Elijah vented.

"How many times I gotta tell you, Elijah," Micah said, "they didn't bring us here to treat us right."

"What we gon' do now?" Ran asked.

"Let's get out of heah before dat deputy comes out, and throws us all in jail," Risby said.

"If ya ain't already, get cha letter together and send it off to dat Houston Thurgood fella ya know up near Washington, Micah," Solomon directed, sounding and looking very weak and feeble.

"I'll start it as soon as we get back," Micah assured.

"We best get goin'," Risby reiterated, "he'll lock us up fuh sho."

The others looked at Risby, wishing he would be quiet about that. They were aware that they needed to get out of town, and do so quickly, but they were also aware that they still had a little time.

"Solomon, is you alright?" Ran asked. "Ya ain't lookin' so good."

"O'm fine."

"Y'all, we best get goin'," Risby said again, "ain't none us got no money ta get out of jail."

They heeded Risby's warning this time, and made haste to get out of town. Once outside the town limits, Solomon had Ethel to stop the wagon. Risby and Ran pulled up alongside them in Risby's rig. Elijah and Micah also stopped alongside Solomon's wagon on the opposite side, Micah on his horse, and Elijah on his mule.

"Risby," Solomon called.

"Yeah, Solomon," he answered.

"Will you ride on over and see Reverend Kyle when ya get a chance. Maybe, he'll help us."

"Me and Ran will ride on over to Mt. Pleasant and see 'im on da way back home."

"We gon' come back tomorrow, Solomon?" Elijah asked.

"No," he answered, "Ah thank dat'll be foolish. Dem people ain't likely ta help us. Ah see dat now."

"Dey'll help us fuh Reverend Kyle sake, won't dey?" Ran asked.

Solomon looked at Ran, feeling not so confident of that. "We can hope."

No one said it, but they all sensed strength and hope failing in Solomon. He was their leader. They relied heavily upon his wisdom. Elijah began to feel that perhaps the strain and burden of this situation was too much for one so old to bear. Out of concern for his friend and mentor, who was beginning to look poorly, Elijah determined that from now on, he would step up and take the lead on this. He would rely on Solomon in a consultant capacity, so that Solomon did not have to play such an active role in this sad affair. He decided that he would go to Solomon privately and inform him that this was what he would like to do.

"Well, we gon' git along over ta da reverend's house," Ran said.

"Okay, let me know how it went as soon as ya can," Solomon requested.

"Ah'll stop by on da way in," he replied, and was off.

"Solomon, O'm gon' stop by and see ya a lit' later on, maybe even in da morning," Elijah said.

"Okay," Solomon responded with a weary voice, and with that, they all departed one from another.

Sometime later, Ran and Risby arrived at the home of Reverend Aniston Kyle, a white man. It was a nice square shaped, single floor, white, wooden, colonial house, not of any notable size, but quite picturesque. It had lovely impatiens still in bloom, magenta and white in color. It had a lovely quaint swing chair on the porch. A white picket fence surrounded the house. From the outside, it appeared to be all that a man could want, but beyond its inner doors there was unrest. Reverend Kyle was dealing with the loss of his youngest son.

Although the war had officially ended in April of sixty-five, fighting was still occurring in mid May. As fate would have it, just before the start of war, the Reverend's youngest son went to live with his eldest son for a time in Texas. When fighting erupted, the boy joined confederate forces there. On May 13th of 1865, during a skirmish near a hill called Palmito on the Rio Grande, His son was killed. He was nineteen years of age at the time of his death. According to the accounts of his elder brother, who was there when he fell, he died at the hands of a black soldier. Word of his son's death reached the reverend in June, around the same time that most blacks were being released from the vestige of slavery.

Reverend Kyle loved his son dearly, and had struggled with grief these many months over his loss. Not that he held the black man in any high esteem, but since the death of his boy, he had come to despise the black race as a whole. Unfortunately, Ran and Risby were unaware of the reverend's loss. The kind descent man that Risby knew as a slave was no more. He now had a reprobate mind, unable to forgive, loathing the black race.

Ran waited on the wagon while Risby walked up and knocked on the door. Reverend Kyle answered the door. Risby smiled, pleased to see the man well after so long a time. The reverend did not smile back. He looked at Risby with a stare of hate. Straightaway, Risby sensed that the man was not himself. It made him feel uncomfortable. He was surprised to see such a look upon the reverend's face. There was no mistaking the hate in the reverend's eye. As a black man, he was well-versed in the look of hatred. "How ya doin', suh?" he asked, certain this was not the time to ask for help. "Ah came ta see ya, but looks like now might be a bad time. Maybe, Ah kin come back later."

"Don't bother coming back," Reverend Kyle said, almost as one drunken with spirits.

"Ever'thang all right, suh?" Risby asked, wondering if there was something he could do to help the reverend, who seemed in pain.

"You killed my son."

"Huh?"

"You murdering black devils killed my son."

"Ah ain't kilt nobody, suh."

"You killed my son!"

"No suh, ain't no man's blood on my han's."

Ran, who waited on the wagon, saw what was happening. "Risby, let's go."

Risby decided that Ran was correct in his assumption that now was an excellent time to leave. He didn't truly understand what was happening, but he figured that he did not need to understand. He began to walk away. Reverend Kyle exited the house behind him. "Damn all you black heathens to hell!"

"Let's go, Risby!" Ran said, quite nervous about the situation.

Risby did not run to the wagon, but neither did he move gingerly. The reverend followed right behind him.

"That's right you black devils, get off my property. If Ah could, Ah'd wipe everyone of you off the face of the earth," Reverend Kyle yelled.

Ran wasted no time getting away from there, after Risby climbed aboard. He was anxious to get back home. He had had enough of white people for one day.

"What ya reckon done happened ta 'im?" Ran asked, not knowing what to make of what just occurred.

"Don't know, act like he touched in da head."

"Ah jes' knowed he was gone help us, Risby."

"Don't look like it."

As they journeyed back home, they just wanted to get the day behind them. It had been a very long day, a very unnerving day. They didn't even consider what their next move was. They just wanted to take a rest from the mental beating they had suffered.

"Ya wanna stop by Solomon's place," Risby asked.

"No, Ah know Ah said Ah would, but Ah jes' wanna go home. Ah kin let 'im know tomorrow."

When the morning came, Elijah and Micah tried to make up on some of the chores which they had fallen behind on over the past several days. They had to put in a good six hours of work, and it was now noon. Were it not for the efforts of Josephine and Mama Julia to take up some of the slack, they would have been in far worse shape.

Elijah decided to ride over to see Solomon. It wouldn't take too long. At least, as he saw it at that point. Once there, Solomon was sitting on the porch of his home in a fairly nice dark-stained rocking chair. Elijah dismounted his mule, and sat on the steps of the porch at Solomon's feet.

"How is ya, Solomon?" He asked.

"Oh, tolerable, Ah guess. Ah remember better days, but every day dat cha alive is a good day. Ah reckon."

"Yeah, Ah reckon it is."

"Ran came by dis mornin'."

"Good news?"

"No," Solomon said, his brow wrinkled with bewilderment and worry.

Elijah sighed, "Well, what cha wanna do now?"

"Ah don't know. Let me thank on it a spell."

"Solomon," Elijah said reluctantly, "Ah been kinda worried fuh ya. Ya ain't been lookin' too good lately. Ah ain't never knowed my own daddy. He was sold off befo' Ah was born. Ah cares fuh ya dat a way. Ya da closes thang Ah done ever had ta one. Ah don't wanna see no harm befall ya. By dat Ah mean, this thang we dealin' wit' kin run a body right down ta da ground. Ah don't wont dat fuh ya. Let me take over da worries of dis thang. Cause, Ah kin see it ain't good fuh ya no mo' ta carry it on yo' shoulders."

Solomon smiled at the young man, touched by the sentiment. "Don't worry fuh me. If it was mo' 'an Ah could bear, Ah'd tell ya so."

"Ah don't know iffen you see it though, Solomon."

"Listen ta me, O'm too old ta be of much use ta Noah in da fields, but Ah can do dis. Youse a young man, and ya gotta keep yo' house goin'. Ah know dat gotta be hard enough wit' what cha do now. Ya done stepped up mo' 'an most da mens 'round heah. You can't do it all. In a few days, it's gon' be June. It's gon' be time to start choppin' cotton, and in a few mo' months it's gon' be time to pick it. If ya fall behind on ya work, Mista Everett ain't gon' wanna hear why ya ain't got it done like ya ought. He gon' come down hard on ya. He might throw ya off ya place. Worse, he might throw ya off ya place and have ya throwed in jail, sayin' ya agreed ta work da place, and ya ain't done it proper. Ya know da law gon' side wit' 'im. Please, young friend, let me take tha lead on dis. Let me do da work. Ya gotta earn a livin', stay home and do dat. When Ah need ya, O'm gon' call."

What Solomon was saying sounded wise to Elijah. It was about to be the hottest time of the year, and the work load was about to pick up. Making matters worse, although they were free, they still lived under the black codes; despicable laws designed to keep blacks lingering between freedom and slavery. One such code allowed for the land-owner to enter into an agreement with a black to work a property for one full year, beginning in January. These verbal or written agreements gave the landowner the right to take legal action against the Negro working the property, should he not perform his work in a satisfactory manner. There was no being fired or quitting. It pretty much gave the landowner an unfair advantage. It may have seemed a reasonable gesture to some, but white men were not asked to enter into agreements in this way for doing the same work. Nor did vagrancy laws apply to them, as they do to blacks. Landowner agreements, curfew laws, and vagrancy laws worked hand in hand to restrict the movement of the Negro, and to contain him in his work environment. Very much the same way movement was policed during slavery.

During this time of year, when the call of the cotton fields was not at its height, the whites were very relaxed with these laws. During the busy season, the laws were sure to be more heavily enforced, and Mister Everett was sure to come around more often. So far there had not been an issue, but if Everett should happen by and Elijah was behind in his work. Everett could, and most likely would, have the law apply pressure to make Elijah conform, or face prison. Elijah realized that it would be best if he was to focus more on honoring his agreement with Mister Everett, and less time trying to solve the murders so actively. "All right, Solomon," he agreed. "but, you need ta take it easy, don't let dis thang burden ya ta da point yo' health start goin' down."

"Don't worry, O'm gon' be all right."

Elijah returned home.

Eleven

A solid week passed uneventfully, and the month of June was upon them. Elijah was uneasy. He knew that sometime soon it was going to happen again. Another child was going to be killed. Images of death ran through his mind. He could graphically see all of the children killed so far. He could see all of the blood so vividly. The brutality of their horrible violent deaths plagued his mind relentlessly. He could imagine the terrible suffering. He couldn't sit around and wait for death to scourge them again. As he sat at the breakfast table, he didn't seem to hunger. The others seemed to enjoy the breakfast of eggs and hashed potatoes, but for him the smell of food in his nostrils left a sickening feeling in his stomach. Caleb was sitting in his lap, and Elijah looked at his innocent son sitting there, and was filled with emotion. He kissed the boy in the top of his head. He came to a decision. "O'm goin' back into town, and O'm gon' ask da sheriff ta help us again," he proclaimed.

Micah stopped eating, but still held his fork. "I don't think that's prudent."

"What else is we ta do? Wait?" Elijah asked, resolved to this purpose.

Josephine kept her mouth shut, but inwardly, she felt that it was a thing which must be done. Mama Julia, on the other hand, spoke her mind. "Elijah, y'all already went ta 'em, didn't ya?" She said. "And, didn't dey tell ya dey wa'n't gon' help. Ya needs ta stay away from 'em"

"Mama, bide yo' tongue," Josephine countered, "Dis mens talk."

"I don't think it's a good idea," Micah reiterated.

"What else is we ta do?" Elijah asked, searching for an alternative.

Micah hadn't an answer for him.

Josephine weighed in. "Ah don't wanna git twixt y'all on dis, but cha gotta do what cha thank is right, Elijah."

This was all the encouragement Elijah needed. He rose from the table. "O'm goin'."

"Now?" Micah asked.

"Yeah, now."

"Hold on a minute, I'll come with you," Micah said.

"It's gettin' ta be da busy time of year. Jes' stay 'round heah and keep workin'. Dat's probably gon' be da best thang," Elijah said.

"You're sure?" Micah asked.

"Yeah."

"Be careful now, ya hear?" Josephine said, as she walked over and kissed Elijah on the cheek.

With that, Elijah headed into town. He was alone, and was nervous about the whole thing. If asked, he would dare say that he was afraid to do this. Yet, it seemed to him that he must. A lack of courage was not a good enough reason for him not to continue to ask the law for help. Not when the lives of the very young were at risk. That may not have meant much to Deputy Farley, but it meant a great deal to him. Upon Elijah's arrival at the sheriff's office, he noticed that his palms were sweaty. There was a feeling of unease so strong in him that he almost turned back. Yet, he bravely walked into the office. It would be his bad fortune that Deputy Farley was on duty. Young Abner was there also, but not the sheriff. Farley looked at Elijah and immediately became angry.

Abner smiled, impressed with Elijah's courage and persistence. "Let me guess. You wanna see the sheriff?"

"Nigger, shouldn't you be in a field somewhere choppin' cotton?" Farley said angrily.

"Somebody killin' our lit' on's, suh. Ah come ta ask y'all ta help us stop it," Elijah stated.

Farley had no patience for this. He moved over to Elijah, and back-handed him so hard it split his lip. "You black, what did Ah tell you about that?"

Elijah looked him boldly in the eye, determined not to be brushed off. Calmly he besought them. "Somebody killin' our childrens. Please, help us stop it."

Deputy Farley lit him up again, striking him harder across the cheek. "Get your black carcase out of here, and back to tha fields, boy!" Farley grabbed Elijah by the collar and turned him around. He shoved him toward the door.

Elijah turned to face him. His hands remained controlled at his sides. He was determined that he was not going to be ignored or dismissed. He would have an acceptable answer. He looked Deputy Farley in the eyes once more. "Please, help us stop da killin' of our chil'ens," he said assertively.

Deputy Farley did not like the way Elijah had stood up to him. He was to be obeyed, and he was not going to tolerate Elijah's disobedience. He grabbed Elijah by the collar and thrust him violently to the floor. He began to stomp and kick Elijah without mercy. Elijah did not try to defend himself by fighting back. That would only encourage Abner to help Farley beat him even harder. He tightened himself into a ball, and tried to defend himself that way. Deputy Farley kicked him harder and harder, until finally Abner pulled him off. "Let the man be, Farley," he insisted, having respect for Elijah in the way he had conducted himself.

Farley stopped his attack and looked at Abner. "Man? Don't you know a boy when you see one?"

"Man, boy, whatever, let him be," Abner insisted.

"You better watch yourself, Abner," Deputy Farley said very winded, "Yer gonna mess around and get a reputation as a nigger lover."

Abner was offended by this. It sounded as if Deputy Farley was threatening to make it known in the white community that Abner was sympathetic to the Negro race. That he was willing to side with them against his own kind. Many of them would distance themselves from him for being perceived in such a way. Abner got the message and backed off. "Do with 'im what you want, Angus."

Elijah was on the floor. No bones were broken, but he was hurting. Farley kicked him again, and then he pulled him to his feet. He roughed Elijah to the jail cell, and banged his head against the iron bars three times. "You uppity nigger," he said, as he opened the cell door and shoved Elijah into it. "Ah'll show you what happens when you get out of line around here."

Elijah was beaten, but he was not broken. "Our chil'ens dyin' without call. You kin help us stop it. Ah demand dat cha do."

Farley looked at Elijah with a stare of hate so intense that if it could be seen, it would have been likened to a ten foot evil monster of rage and unspeakable form. With a cold venomous tone he said, "You black som bitch. You got too much grit in ya, but Ah can help you fix that."

There was an ax in the corner of the Sheriff's office, which belonged to Deputy Farley. The head of it had slipped off. He had been of a mind to fix it. He took the ax handle in hand. It was a good three feet long. Farley went into the cell and began to beat Elijah like a dog. Abner could have stopped it, but he chose to wink at it. He put on his hat, and went out to patrol the town.

It was getting to be late in the day. Only an hour or so of sunlight remained. Mama Julia, Micah, and especially Josephine were all beginning to worry about Elijah. Josephine wanted Elijah to speak up for the people of their community. They needed help, and someone had to boldly step up and demand it. It was in Elijah to do, and she wanted him to do it, but she didn't think through the consequences. The boldness of a black man to speak up for himself was surely not to go unnoticed by the whites. In these parts, it was not uncommon for such black men to be found hanging from a tree. Even worse, it is not uncommon for such black men to turn up missing, never to be seen or heard from again. Micah and the ladies were all sitting around the table, waiting for Elijah to return. Micah made up his mind to go look for his brother. He rose, headed for the door.

"Micah, where ya goin'?" Josephine asked.

"He's been gone far too long. I'm gonna ride into Olive Branch to look for him."

"Micah," Josephine called, "don't go by yo' self."

"I'll stop by Risby's place. Maybe, he will go with me."

Just as Micah said he would, he stopped by and solicited Risby's company. They rode to town, and there was no sign of Elijah along the way. Shortly before they arrived, Sheriff Hackman had returned. He was surprised that they had a prisoner. "What's he in there for, Angus?"

"He was disturbing tha peace, Robert," Deputy Farley answered.

The sheriff could see Elijah had been beaten badly. "You do that to him?"

"He got out of line with me, and Ah had ta teach 'im some manners," Deputy Farley explained.

Sheriff Hackman let it go at that. Although, he was all to aware that Deputy Farley was a cruel and heartless man by nature, and probably used far more force than was necessary. Around this time, Micah and Risby pulled up on Risby's wagon.

"Dis time, Ah thank O'm gon' be da one ta stay out heah, Micah," Risby joked.

Micah smiled slightly at him. He turned and boldly walked into the sheriff's office. Sheriff Hackman was sitting behind his desk, trying to catch up on some reading. "What is it?" he said sort of un-welcoming.

"My brother came into town to see you today."

"I remember you," Sheriff Hackman said, thinking of the Cyrus Drucker incident. "Your brother is in back. Perhaps he had intentions of seeing me, but he managed to get himself arrested before that."

"Arrested!? For what!?"

"Disturbing the peace!" Farley barked, sitting in a chair against the wall. "And, if you don't lower your voice. Yer gonna end up in there with 'im. Ah don't know who you niggers think that you are, that you think you can talk to a white man anyway you want."

Micah ignored Deputy Farley, and the deputy was aware that Micah was purposely ignoring him.

"How much to get him out, sheriff?" Micah said confidently.

"That oughta be about twenty dollars, wouldn't you say, Robert?" Farley said, trying to influence the sheriff's decision. Also, he was sure Micah wouldn't have that kind of money.

"Well?" Micah said defiantly, looking at Sheriff Hackman, still ignoring Deputy Farley.

The sheriff looked at Micah, and like Farley, he didn't care for Micah's attitude. "Ah would have let him out for five, but now twenty seems appropriate. What's more, if you open your mouth again with the same disrespectful tone you've just displayed, Ah'm gonna lock you up and charge you thirty to get out. Do you understand?" Sheriff Hackman said dogmatically.

Sheriff Hackman didn't take this stance simply because Micah was a black man, but because Micah came across as disrespectful. He wouldn't see his office disrespected by any man, white, black, or otherwise, he thought.

"There you go, Robert," Deputy Farley said, happy to see Robert taking such a stern stance.

Micah said nothing. He reached into his pocket and counted out twenty dollars, placing it respectfully on the sheriff' desk. However, that was not good enough.

"Ah asked you a question. You will acknowledge that you understood me in a respectful manner, or you will go to jail, understand?" Sheriff Hackman asserted himself.

Deputy Farley was loving it. That foul grin of his was wide enough to expose all of his ugly brown teeth.

Micah yielded for the sake of his brother. "Yes, sir, I understand."

Deputy Farley started to laugh, a dirty-little snicker. Sheriff Hackman got up, and went to the back to release Elijah. When he returned with Elijah, Elijah was walking as if he were a drunken man. He took a hard blow to the back of the head during his encounter with Farley. The blow was to the lower-back portion of his skull. The area of the brain where sight takes place. Elijah could see, but his vision was blurred, coming in and out of focus. What was more, his balance seemed to be off. Upon seeing his brother in such a state, Micah gnashed his teeth angrily. Yet, he couldn't say anything. He knew that they did this, and it would be counter productive to complain. He helped Elijah out to the Wagon.

"Lawd have mercy," Risby said, as he rallied to help Micah with Elijah.

"He's in bad shape, Risby. Let's get him home quickly."

"Why dey do 'im like dat?" Risby asked, knowing Elijah wouldn't have done anything to provoke such treatment.

Micah didn't have an answer for him. "Let's get him home, Risby."

They got Elijah home as quickly as possible. Josephine was waiting impatiently for Micah's return. She had been ever watchful, almost since the very time Micah left. When she saw Risby's wagon with Elijah's mule, and Micah's horse tied to the back of it, she became very fearful. On the verge of tears, she ran out to meet Risby. His rig was a small two seater with not a lot of cargo space. Elijah was on back of the wagon seated upright with his back resting against the backboard of the seat. Micah was seated next to Elijah, holding him steady.

As soon as Josephine saw them, she lit out to meet the wagon. Mama Julia followed right behind her. Caleb was asleep, which was a good thing. It would not have been good for him to see his father in such a bad way with everyone else so emotional, especially Josephine. At that point, Josephine didn't know if Elijah was alive or dead. She raced toward the wagon that she might know. She ran into the path of the horse.

"Woe!" Risby said to his ole nag, as the animal came to a stop.

Josephine moved around that she might see her husband, and was immediately grieved. "What happened?"

"He all right, Josephine," Risby tried to comfort.

"All right!" she said, in a state of shock. "Look at him!"

"He's gonna make it, Josephine," Micah comforted, "Let us get him to the house."

Risby popped the reigns, and the horse continued onward. Josephine walked alongside the wagon, holding Elijah's hand. All the while regretting having advised Elijah to go into town. Risby stopped his rig directly in front of the house. Then, he proceeded to help Micah get Elijah inside. Josephine was trying to help bear his weight, but was mostly in the way. The men didn't tell her to let them handle it. They understood what she was feeling. They took Elijah to his bed. "I'm gonna go get some help," Micah informed.

"No, Micah. Yo' place heah wit' yo' family. Ah'll go git help," Risby insisted.

"Fine, but don't try to get that white doctor. See if Jasper Brown is available, okay. He is more likely to come," Micah said.

Risby shook his head in agreement. He did not concede that Doc Mortenson would not do everything within his power to help, but feelings in terms of black and white at this moment were heated and untrusting.

Josephine and Mama Julia scurried about trying to do everything that they knew to do to help Elijah. He was completely out of it. Josephine was very much afraid that Elijah was going to die. After she had done all for him that she could, she sat next to him, holding his hand without ceasing, going to God in prayer.

Risby finally returned with Jasper after an hour and a half. Jasper did all that he knew to do for Elijah, and he prayed that it was enough. He stayed there most of the night, mostly watching to make sure Elijah's condition did not change for the worst. He left when the morning came, but returned several times to check on Elijah over the next five days. During that time, Elijah experienced short intervals of consciousness. During those times, Josephine forced water into him. Also, she gave him a tea made from tree bark and leaves of a gum tree, as instructed to do by Jasper. It was a remedy he learned from his mother.

Most of what Jasper knew of medicine, he learned from her. She was something of a doctor as a slave. A necessity, since a slave had to be near death before the average slave owner would spend money to bring in a doctor. An Indian taught her about the tree bark. Indians had long known that tree bark had a property in it good for treating headaches, colds, menstrual cramps, and even fever.

Now, on the fifth day, when morning had come, about the fourth hour of the day. Elijah came to himself and was in good spirits. He was hungry. Josephine fixed him something to eat, and served it to him in bed. Everyone was glad to see him in such good spirits, and apparently doing well.

"How long Ah been down?" he asked.

"Five days now," Micah informed.

"Lawd help me, Ah gotta git out in da fields. Ah don't wanna fall too far behind," Elijah said, trying to get out of bed.

"Woe, Elijah," Micah said, physically holding him down, "I've been making sure the work gets done. Don't worry about that now. I want you to just concentrate on getting better, okay."

"Yeah, baby, don't worry 'bout da work 'round heah. You what matter now," Josephine said lovingly.

"Listen ta ya woman, boy," Mama Julia urged.

Elijah relaxed for a moment, but almost immediately his mind was troubled again. "Ain't no mo' chil'ens been kilt yet, is it?"

"No, not yet," Micah answered, "did one or all of them do this to you?"

"No, it wa'n't all of 'em, jes' Farley," Elijah said, sort of ashamed of what happened.

168

Josephine knew her husband well, and recognized the shame in his voice. "Don't you feel no shame. Ya ain't got nothin' ta feel dat way 'bout."

"Ah gotta go back," Elijah said, trying to rise from the bed again.

"What?" Micah asked, wanting to believe his ears were deceiving him.

"Ah gotta go back. Ah gotta git 'em ta help us befo' we lose mo' chil'ens."

The first time Elijah insisted he had to go back, Josephine became afraid for her him, but at the same time, she felt more proud of him than she had ever been before. She was not willing that he should go. She did not want him dead. "Ah don't wont cha ta go. Youse a better man dan any dem ya tryin' ta get ta help us. Youse a good man, and Ah need ya. Me and yo' son, we need ya, don't go."

Micah was also very proud of his brother for not being afraid to take a stand. Such courage was the mark of a true man. But like Josephine, he was afraid they would kill him next time. "Listen to her, Elijah. You can't go back."

"Y'all," Elijah said, looking at both of them with stern compassionate conviction, "Our chil'ens is da mos' precious thang we got. Dey gifts from da good Lawd above. It's our job ta watch over 'em and protect 'em. Ah can't thank of no creature on God's blessed earth dat's gon' turn its back on its young on's when danger near. Its gon' do what it gotta do, and O'm gon' do what Ah gotta do. If dey wanna take my life fuh tryin' ta save da chil'ens, dey welcome to it."

"No, dey ain't!" Josephine said, becoming livid with Elijah's insistence on this matter. "Ah done told ya dat ya got me and Caleb ta thank about. We need ya, don't you forget dat."

Mama Julia said nothing concerning this. She agreed with the others that he should not go, but she had a new-found respect for her son-in-law. Sometimes, you have to stand in order to be heard. She understood this. If he desired to do this, she would not raise her voice against it.

Elijah was very weak, and probably couldn't stand. Yet, Micah saw that he was determined. Such determination was inspiring. "You aren't going anywhere, Elijah, but if it makes you happy. I will go."

"Micah, dat's six in one han' and half a dozen in da other," Josephine said in disagreement, not wanting anyone to go.

"Ya ain't gotta fight my battle," Elijah said.

"No, it's not your battle, Elijah. It's our battle," Micah insisted.

"Is y'all crazy?" Josephine asked angrily. "Ain't nobody gotta go. It's another answer, we gotta find it is all. Y'all hear me?"

"Somebody gotta stand up fuh da chil'ens sake, Josephine," Elijah insisted.

"It ain't gotta be y'all," she said vehemently.

"If not us, then who?" Micah asked.

"Micah, don't go. It ain't da good thang ta do. Ah see dat now. White folks is crazy. Da war done changed everythang, and dey hate us fuh it. If ya had asked me six days ago, Ah would've said go. Cause Ah thought it was some decency in 'em, but decent folk wouldn't have done dis ta my man jes' fuh askin' fuh help. Ah know somethan' gotta be done, but askin' da folks in town ain't it. Ah done heard y'all talkin' 'bout ridin' ta Memphis, up ta da fort. Ah thank you stand a better chance wit' dem federalists dan ya do wit' da white folks 'round heah. Go ta da Yankees, not da evil folks in Olive Branch," Josephine said vehemently.

"I think it will eventually come to that, but as for right now. I think that I have to go into Olive Branch," Micah said adamantly.

"Why?" Josephine responded furiously. "Ain't nothin' but heart ache in dat place. Ah know it now, and you knowed it befo' Elijah went."

"Josephine, it gon' probably take two or three days ta git ta Memphis and back. Ah know in my heart another lit' on' gon' be dead befo' den. We gotta try and stop dat iffen we kin," Elijah insisted.

"Mama Julia, dey ain't listenin' ta me. Help me talk some sense into dey thick skulls," Josephine petitioned.

Mama Julia looked at her daughter, and then looked down, unable to side with her.

"Mama, not you too," Josephine said very frustrated.

"I'm going, Josephine. And don't you worry. It's gonna be okay," Micah said.

Josephine looked at Micah as one not ignorant or deceived. " Six days ago, Ah would've believed ya, but not now."

Micah had a Remington .44 caliber Army Revolver, which he purchased used at the close of the the war for $10 from the Union Army. It was a surplus item. He had it locked away in an old-brown chest in which he kept his things. He strolled over to the chest and unpacked it.

"Ya can't take dat wit'cha, Micah," Mama Julia said.

"She's right," Elijah pointed out, "it's a law against a black man carryin' a gun. If ya take it wit' cha, ya jes' askin' fuh trouble. Besides, ya don't need it. Ya goin' in peace, ain't cha?"

"Ya ain't gotta go, Micah," Josephine reiterated.

"Yes, I do."

"But, not wit' dat," Elijah insisted.

Micah felt as if his hands were somehow tied behind his back, but he knew that Elijah was right. He couldn't take the pistol with him, and for more reasons than one. He seriously wanted to put a bullet in Deputy Farley, and his temperament was such that if Deputy Farley crossed him wrong, he would not have hesitated to kill him. That would surely bring the wrath of the white community down of every black person around for miles. It was better not to allow himself to be so tempted.

"Micah, get Risby dem ta go wit cha," Josephine insisted, as a sense of fear for Micah gripped her.

Micah looked at her, as if it was not even a consideration. "No, not this time."

"Micah," Mama Julia called, as he headed for the door, "God bless ya."

He smiled at her, and looked at Elijah. Elijah nodded at him, as if to encourage him. Micah nodded back at him in understanding. He exited the house and headed for town. Now, Micah was no Elijah. His philosophy was entirely different. Elijah believed fervently in peaceful obtainment. Even if those from whom he hoped to obtain responded violently to him. Not that Micah was a warmonger. He also believed in peace, but neither was he one to offer the other cheek when violent transgression was upon him. He believed that if a man strikes you, you beat that man to the ground. If a man kills one, then you kill two. He made no apologies for his beliefs. He did not think of himself as Christ-like. For him, it was not natural to let someone strike him without returning the favor. This was the fundamental difference between Elijah and he. Anytime trouble wanted to stare him in the eye, it would find Micah staring back. And speaking of trouble, Micah hoped Farley was on duty. He wanted Farley to start something with him. He wished for it. Farley may have started it, but he was certain that he would be the one to finish it.

As Micah rode into town, he developed a sort of tunnel vision. He did not see anything or anybody. His attention was solely on the door of the sheriff's office. He was almost at the sheriff's office before he snapped out of it. He and his sorrel horse had a long hot ride into town. Around the corner was the town stable, which had a water troth outside of it. He rode there, and allowed his horse to get a drink of water. He took out a handkerchief, wet it, and wiped his face. He tied his horse next to the troth, and decided to be about his business. He walked back to the sheriff's office and went in. To his surprise, the office was empty. It made him kind of angry. Any other time Farley would have been there doing a whole lot of nothing, he thought. Now, when he came looking for him specifically, he was nowhere to be found. As he stood there cursing Farley in his mind, Farley walked through the door. He was alone. Micah was worked up mentally, angry even, but as Farley walked in, his anger left him quickly. It was almost as if the very sight of Farley frightened it out of him. Micah was ready for confrontation, but now that it was upon him. He was not so sure that he wanted it.

Deputy Farley was sweaty, hot, and in a broody mood. He was not of a mind to be bothered with niggers. His anger was kindled against Micah. "What do you want, boy?" He asked in a hot dismissing tone, walking past Micah, taking no thought to look at him.

"There is a madman going about killing black children. I want you to help us find him, and bring him to justice," Micah said, sounding superior, and looking at him in a way Deputy Farley didn't like.

"You damned-nigger cocksucker you! O'm your better, don't you look at me like that."

"Like what?" Micah said, his heart quickly filling with contempt for Farley.

"Ah said don't look at me that away! You better wipe that god-damned look off your face, boy!"

"And, if I don't?"

In disbelief, Farley stuck out his chest like an angry cock. "What did you just say?"

"I said, I don't believe that I'll be talked to any kinda way by you today. And, you best show some got-damn respect before I do to you what you did to my brother!"

Deputy Farley was taken aback by such boldness on Micah's part. He was wearing a side arm, a Griswold and Gunnison .36 caliber Colt Navy-Type Revolver with a brass frame and round Dragoon-style barrels. His first thought was to drop Micah where he stood. Micah could see that Farley was seriously contemplating shooting him dead. Farley flinched, as if to draw his weapon.

"Do it! Slap that iron and make it smoke! I see you're hankering to! But you better know that by the time you pull up on it, I'm gonna be on you, and God help you then."

Their eyes locked, and Farley thought it over. He was certain that he could get his weapon out. He may have even gotten off a shot, but maybe not. He considered things carefully. He knew himself to be a fairly slow draw. He had to also consider certain other things. There wasn't a lot of space between them, maybe four steps. If he were to get his weapon out, and if Micah were to reach him at that point, a struggle over a loaded weapon would have ensued. Deputy Farley didn't want that, as it could have gone either way. Farley concluded that it was best to leave the pistol in its holster. Yet, he felt something had to be done. He was not going to take such bold and aggressive action from a nigger. He was tempted to move over and fight Micah. He quickly decided against that. Micah may have still gotten the pistol somehow.

"Yer a mighty bold nigger, ain't cha?" Deputy Farley spouted, itching to go for his weapon, but careful not to do so.

Micah saw that his act of intimidation had worked. "Shut your fat-gutless mouth."

Farley wanted to give Micah a good ole country cussin' to say the least, but he was afraid to utter another word. Micah made his move. He boldly walked over to Farley, and lifted the pistol out of Farley's holster. Deputy Farley's knees started to shake, and he could feel sweat running down his leg. He couldn't believe that he had just let Micah strut over and take his weapon. Micah unloaded the weapon, and removed the bullets from Farley's holster. He laid the unloaded weapon on the sheriff's desk. "You are a cowardly dog, Farley," Micah snarled, daring Farley to make a move. "I'll be going now, and I'll just take your bullets with me. I wouldn't want you to take your courage in hand and shoot me with it while my back is to you." He walked out of the sheriff's office, regretting having let his anger get the better of him. There was certain to be repercussions for such an act of none temperance on his behalf. He moved briskly toward the stable to get his horse, and get out of town, and rightly so.

Deputy Farley wasn't about to let this go. He shook with anger. He started to ramble through the sheriff's desk, looking for loose ammunition. He had made up his mind to kill Micah, today. There were two rounds in the desk. He quickly loaded his pistol, and stepped out of the sheriff's office looking for Micah. He saw Micah rounding the corner headed for the stable. His initial thought was to get a couple of good-ole boys to help him put Micah down, but he decided against that. Micah had debased him, and if he were to get some of the men to help him kill Micah. Micah would still have stolen his manhood, and there would be no way to retrieve it from him. Farley had to have his manhood back, and by his reckoning. The only way to get it was to face Micah alone, and make him grovel before his death. Farley was not slack in getting around the corner to face Micah. Micah had mounted his horse, and was ready to move out, but he wouldn't get the chance.

"Nigger, get down off that horse!" Farley barked, his weapon aimed at Micah.

"I see you found a little courage," Micah coolly cut, as he dismounted. "Now, you know O'm gon' kill you, don't you?"

"Then get busy doin' it, and stop running your foul smelling, cowardly, mouth," Micah insulted, continuing to wound Farley's already battered pride.

Farley cocked the hammer of his weapon, ready to let it drop. "Keep pushin' me, boy. And, yer gonna get to hell more sooner than later."

Micah wasn't afraid of death. As a soldier, death came for him once, but he saw it coming and put up one tough bout of a fight. Death turned from him on that day. "That's okay, Farley. I'm a man, and you can only kill a man once, but how many times will a cowardly dog like you die in your life time?"

"O'm gonna bust a cap in you, boy. But first, you gonna get on your knees, and beg me for your life."

"I don't think so, deputy," Micah bravely spouted, "as I said before, I am no coward. I'll die here only once."

Farley was so angry that he hardly knew what to do. "O'm gon' break you before you die, boy!"

Micah looked at him very defiantly. "Cowards can't break men."

That did it. Micah's words were cutting deep into Farley's pride. He was determined to see Micah on his knees groveling, and it had to be immediate. Deputy Farley had every advantage in this situation. There were no innocent by-standers around to be accidentally shot. There was distance between Micah and himself. He had his weapon drawn, aimed, and cocked. He could have killed Micah right then, and it would have been over. No one would have questioned his motives. If he was of a mind to, he could have even ordered Micah back to the jail. Where he could beat him until he broke, but he had allowed Micah to get inside his head. Allowed mere words to compromise his ability to be sensible. He was allowing Micah to bluff him into throwing away every advantage.

Farley's anger made him feel as though he were as strong as an ox. In his mind, Micah was just a nigger, and any white man was more than any ten niggers. Micah's bold antics just caught him off guard was what Farley told himself. Feeling strong and confident, he rushed to engage Micah. He would pistol whip Micah into submission, make him grovel in the dirt. This was Farley's thinking.

Micah was hoping that he would react foolishly, and Farley had. Farley rushed Micah, intent on striking him across the head with the butt of his pistol. Although Micah was slender and lean, he was pure muscle. He muscled Farley's gun hand into the air, rendering the weapon useless for now. He used his tremendous leg strength to force Farley hard into the side wall of the stable. Farley felt that he had to bring the pistol into play. He made a fist with his free hand, striking Micah violently between the neck and shoulder. Micah grabbed his hand, and muscled it into the air. He was afraid Farley would pull the trigger, which was sure to bring others running. He had to get the pistol away from Farley. He lowered his forehead and rammed it brutally into Farley's face repeatedly. The deputy's face turned flush with pain. Micah took his knee, and began to pound it mercilessly into Farley's side. Farley was mostly flab, and was clearly out of shape. Micah was hurting him, but he didn't think to pull the trigger. Fearing Farley would eventually pull the trigger, Micah decided to take a chance. He released Farley's hand without the gun, quickly stepped back from him slightly, and fired into Farley with a wickedly, punishing, and vicious uppercut. Farley's head snapped violently backwards. He fell to his knees so dazed that he dropped his pistol, but before Micah could get it. Farley recovered his senses enough to make a desperate tackling launch at Micah, forcing him to the ground. Both men were off of their feet, but Farley was closer to the weapon. He made it to one knee, trying to scramble for the pistol. Micah wasn't going to let him. He hustled quickly, and wrestled Farley into the stable. The pistol was of no use to either of them in there. Fortunately for Micah, the stable owner wasn't there. He would have surely helped Deputy Farley.

Now that they didn't have to worry about the pistol, Farley felt confident that he could take Micah. He battled Micah with a surprisingly quick hand flurry for such a heavy man, and he was landing blows with good accuracy. However, Micah was not to be outdone. He flurried fiercely back at Farley. There were three horses in the stable, two in pens, and one tied to a post. The violent heated nature of things had them kicking up a fuss. Farley caught Micah with a hard blow to the jaw. It knocked him backward. He came dangerously close to the horse tied to the post, and the animal kicked its hind legs at him, scarcely missing him. Micah had had enough of this. Just as Farley was sure that he could take Micah, Micah was equally certain that he could take Farley. Instead of going to Farley's hard head, he punished his soft gut. Hard thunderous blows stole all the fight out of the heavy brutish man. Micah knew he had him, and went back up top. He lit Farley up with a fiery right cross to the chin that ended the fight, landing Farley on the ground. Half-dazed and trembling, as he unsuccessfully struggled to get up, Farley knew that he was beaten. He was afraid of what Micah would do to him next, and cried out loudly that he might be heard, hoping to bring someone to his aide. Micah wasn't having that. He pinned Farley down, and began to pound his gut brutally. "Shut up you evil bastard!" Micah commanded dogmatically.

"Please stop, mister!"

"Oh, I'm mister now, am I?" Micah said sarcastically, pounding Farley's gut several times more before stopping. "Don't make another sound."

Farley complied quickly, becoming very quiet. Micah released him and stood upright. Farley was in pain. He grabbed his stomach, and rolled over onto his side. His eyes began to become very watery. He was on the verge of crying, like a little girl.

Micah became very frightened, realizing what he had done. He was of a mind to flee for his life. Farley was sure to get some others and kill him for sure. As frightening as this certainty should have been, it wasn't what frightened Micah. What frightened him was that they may kill Elijah and his family as well. He couldn't run from this. He began to visually search the stable for something that he could use to take Farley's life. He spotted a pitchfork sitting near the door of the stable. It would be a quiet and effective tool with which to kill. Just then, Micah experienced a moment of clarity. There was a more palatable way out of this, as it would not have been wise to kill Deputy Farley. Surely someone must have seen him go into the sheriff's office, and no doubt saw him come out, shortly followed by Deputy Farley with a gun in hand. The sheriff would implicate him quickly. Given this consideration, it wasn't profitable to kill Farley. To Micah's knowledge, nobody saw Farley and he struggling, which left an open door.

"I know what you're thinking, Farley. You're thinking that you're gonna get the sheriff, that other deputy, and maybe a few others, and kill me before the sun sets on this day. Am I right?"

Farley, being so humbled, answered not a word. Yet, his humiliated eyes confirmed everything Micah said would shortly come to pass. He would surely see Micah dead before the sun sat on that day.

"Yeah, I thought so," Micah said confidently, "Deputy Sheriff, now that's a position of respect.

I mean the people around here must admire and respect you for the safety and security you provide them on a daily basis. I lived out west for a while. Believe me when I say that some of the towns out there are wide open. You're taking a serious chance just crossing the street in some of the towns out west. There is gun play all over the place, but not here. You and the others are to be commended for that. You keep the peace, and you make it possible for good people to live quiet peaceful lives."

Farley looked at Micah wondering where he was going with what seemed to be babbling. He knew that Micah must have surely been aware that for all his flattering talk. It was a vain gesture. Surely, Micah must have known that by days end, he would rest with his forefathers in the grave.

"The people respect you, Farley. They appreciate you, and they have faith in your ability as a lawman. It makes a man feel good and proud to know that he is appreciated and respected, doesn't it? You can walk around with your head held high, and the people look at you with admiration and say. ' there goes Deputy Farley. He's a fine lawman. A valued member of this town.' And, you feel worth in yourself, because you are somebody, and you are recognized as such. I have a question for you, Farley," Micah stooped down close to Farley's ears, "how long will they continue to have faith in you once they get wind of this? How long will they continue to respect you once word gets around that you weren't able to subdue a single unarmed darky? How long will they continue to look up to you once they learn that I bested you, had you almost crying, calling me mister? Mighty and respectable you, calling me mister. Me, the son of a slave. Can you image what they will think of you? I'll bet, you can almost hear them right now whispering, laughing, behind your back. How long before they start to challenge you every single time you try to do your job? You know I'm not lying, Farley. They'll figure if you couldn't handle one lowly coon. You certainly can't handle them. Once that happens, how much longer do you think that you'll get to keep your nice respectable job? Where you get to sit around all day with your feet kicked up. The way I see it. You have a decision to make. You have to decide whether it is more important to see me dead, or to maintain your respect, authority, and livelihood in this community. It's not the easiest of times that we live in. People, white and black, are close to starving. They've got next to nothing, but you've got it real good. I would think on that if I were you. We both know that if you tell them I put up a ruckus. They will help you kill me on principle alone, but you had best know that before I die. They will know the why of it. They will know everything that happened here today. You'll be a nobody then, because you couldn't take care of less-than-a-man by yourself. Can you stand to be a nobody, Farley? Can you stand to be looked down upon, like so much trash. Respect is a funny thing. When you have it, you don't give it much thought. But when you don't, you crave it like you crave food, drink, and air to breathe. You'll be willing to fight for it, die for it. Because every time you don't fight, you die a little anyway. You're letting somebody take away your ability to see yourself in a positive way, and that's slow death. You can take my word for that. Being a black man, I know something about it. If you wanna walk in my shoes, open your mouth concerning what happened here. I will be dead true enough, but you will feel as if you are too. The choice is yours, Farley." Micah stood and walked out of the stable to retrieve Farley's pistol, a Griswold and Gunnison confederate knock-off of a Colt Navy Revolver. Not a soul was in sight. Micah picked up the pistol and unloaded it. He walked back into the stable, and helped Deputy Farley to his feet. He presented the weapon to Farley. The deputy took and holstered it. Micah's damp handkerchief was still in his jacket pocket. He took it out and began to wipe Farley's face, to help refresh him. Farley was too weak in spirit and body to object. The two men exited the stable. Deputy Farley was walking limply, rubbing his stomach in a soothing manner. The town blacksmith, the owner operator of the stable, was returning. As he rounded the corner headed for the stable, something seemed not right with Farley.

"You okay, Angus?" he asked, looking at them strangely.

Now was Farley's time to revenge against Micah. The two of them could surely take him, but he remembered all that Micah said to him. "I was walking over to the stable to see you, and Ah took to feelin' not so well, is all."

"About what?"

"We'll talk about it later, when O'm feeling a little better."

"Who are you, boy?" the blacksmith asked of Micah.

"This here fella got a horse that's more wild than tamed, it got away from 'im, and he was running after it this way when Ah took sick. Ah told 'im to give me a hand." Farley looked at Micah. "You go catch that horse now. Ah reckon that Ah can make it the rest of the way."

"Angus, you sure you don't want me to send this boy to find Doc Mortenson, you don't look so good," the blacksmith said.

"No, Ah'm fine," Farley assured, "O'm just gettin' on in years Ah guess."

"Well, boy, you get on like tha deputy here says."

Micah was reluctant to turn his back on Farley, but he had no choice. Maybe, things were all right for now. Yet, he knew that Farley would seek occasion to kill him. It was just a matter of time. Micah went about his business to round up his horse and get back home. He looked back at

Farley, who limped back toward the sheriff's office like a wounded animal. Micah wondered when he would come for him.

After catching his horse, he went straight home. Elijah did not expect that Micah would yield any better results than he did, but his plan was that they would continue to annoy the sheriff's office so much that they would eventually help. He had no idea that Micah had in all probability fastened that door shut. When Elijah saw Micah, appearing to be well. He was of good spirits, hopeful he had a measure of success. Elijah was still in bed, feeling better than he did that morning.

"How it go?" he asked hopeful.

Micah was slow to answer. He moved closer to Elijah, so the others would not hear. He whispered to Elijah what he had done.

"Why you do dat?" Elijah said, with an angry scowl on his face.

"Keep quiet," Micah said defensively, "You can't tell anybody."

Josephine looked over at them. She decided that maybe they needed a little privacy. She grabbed Caleb and headed outside to help Mama Julia with some chores. "We'll be back in a lit' bit, y'all."

"We better get you out of heah, dey gon' kill ya fuh sho," Elijah insisted.

"I don't think so, at least not for a while. Nobody saw the fight. I told Farley that if he kept quiet about it. I would too," Micah explained, "so, you see. I'm safe for a while."

"Ya thank dat'll work."

"I do. No white man wants it known that a black man was able to best him, but I do think that he'll try to get me at some point down the road."

"Lawd, Micah, What O'm gon' do wit' cha?"

"I will not let white folk walk all over me just because they think they have a right to."

Elijah wished that Micah would not be so hotheaded. From that day forth, he would worry about Micah more than he should have. Right now, however, he pondered their next move. "As soon as O'm able, we gon' ride to Fort Pickering in Memphis. We ain't got much mo' time befo' another lit' on' is gon' git kilt."

Twelve

The night passed slowly. Elijah wasn't resting comfortably. He couldn't help but think about the children. He desperately wanted to save them from anymore harm. Everyone else was asleep, or so Elijah believed. Micah was not resting well either, but unlike Elijah. He got up and gently tipped outside. He did not realize Elijah was awake and watching him. Elijah didn't give it much thought. He felt Micah was probably just restless. They were all restless, he thought. Elijah dozed off and woke up several times through out the night. Each time he awoke, he did not think to take note of whether Micah had returned to bed or not. Night passed into morning, and trouble was at the door step.

It was about the second hour of the work day. Solomon and Risby had come to pay Elijah a visit. Micah was already outside busy with his chores. Upon seeing Risby and Solomon, he somehow knew that another child had been killed. He stopped working and began to move toward Risby's wagon. Once the wagon came to a stop, they did not even bother to greet.

Micah sighed. "Not another one?"

"Afraid so," Solomon confirmed regrettably, "Ah come to see Elijah."

"He's inside," Micah answered.

"Still bedridden?" Risby asked.

"Yeah, he wants to get up, but Josephine won't let him," Micah confided.

"Well, Ah'd still like ta see 'im for a spell," Solomon said.

"Given the circumstances, I suspect he'd appreciate you keeping him informed. Let me see if he is up to company," Micah said.

Micah went into the house and advised Elijah, and the others, of what had happened. Against Josephine's wishes, Elijah dressed and went out to talk with Solomon and Risby. He informed them that he wanted to accompany them to the murder scene. Solomon advised him that they could handle this, but Elijah insisted. Micah saddled his horse and Elijah's mule. Risby rode the mule and graciously let Elijah ride the wagon with Solomon. Ran had been careful not to let anyone near the child's body, as Solomon and Elijah suggested they do some time ago. They began to examine the body, a young boy.

"Who is this child?" Micah asked.

Elijah simply looked at the boy's body.

"His name's Josiah. Don't know his last name. Him and his folks was jes' passin' through on dey way up north," Ran informed.

"How ya know all dat?" Risby asked.

His folks been lookin' fuh 'im since around ten last night. Dey jes' happened ta talk ta ole Whoot. He sont 'em ta me," Ran explained.

"Who found him," Solomon asked.

"Polk Macray."

"How long ago?" Risby asked.

"Since a little after sun up."

As they continued to talk and ask questions of Ran, Elijah looked at the boy's battered bloody, body more closely. He suspected the child was no more than eight. He was a dark-skinned child. As with most of the victims, he had been badly beaten. Elijah noticed that his clothing was torn in places, particularly around the collar of his shirt. He also noticed that his knuckles were bruised. Elijah's mind started to work feverishly. He experienced a frightening enlightened moment. "No," he said.

The others stopped talking and looked at him.

"What is it, Elijah?" Micah asked.

"Look at 'im," Elijah responded.

"What?" Solomon asked.

"Da one we lookin' fuh ain't no stranger. It's somebody from around heah," Elijah said with certainty.

Everyone seemed surprised by this statement.

"What makes you think that?" Micah asked.

"Cancha see plainly dis heah child fought wit' everythang he had in 'im ta save his life?"

"Yeah, we see dat," Ran agreed.

"Don't it jes' jump out at cha?" Elijah asked.

The others looked at the child. They only see the obvious, the boy struggled.

"What?" Risby asked.

"Da others, dey ain't put up no fight. They all lived 'round heah. Dis boy and his family was passin' through on dey way up north."

"Yeah," Solomon said, wanting Elijah to get to his point.

"He fought hard not to die heah. Why he fight, and dey didn't?" Elijah asked.

Like with a lamp placed atop a hill in the darkest night. Understanding was illuminated. All those present there began to see as plainly as Elijah.

Solomon was the first to vocalize it. "Cause dey knowed him, and dis boy didn't."

"They trusted him enough to let him get close enough to do them harm without much effort. This child didn't trust him," Micah added.

This was frightening to every one of them. It was one thing for a complete stranger to kill, but how could someone they knew have possibly done this. It could have been someone that had eaten at any of their tables. Someone that they spoke with daily. There was a familiar insidious evil at work. One that hid behind a deceitful smile.

"That settles it, we've got to get the word out that one of our own is doing this. That it is someone physically weak. Possibly a man of small stature, or a woman," Micah insisted.

This time there was absolutely no resistance to Micah's suggestion. They were all scared to death. It was easier to guard against a stranger, but how did they guard against someone who was suppose to be around.

"Ah reckon you right," Risby conceded.

Elijah was still unsure, but he couldn't find it in his heart to challenge the wisdom of sharing what they knew about the killer with the community.

"Elijah?" Solomon called, wanting his opinion.

"Ah don't know. Ah reckon it's da right thang ta do," he answered.

"Dat's what we'll do," Solomon decreed.

"What we gon' do next?" Risby asked.

"Take dis child home ta his folks. We can't do much mo' 'an dat. In a few days, when O'm feelin' a lit' better, me and Micah gon' ride ta Memphis. We'll see iffen we kin get some help from da soldiers at da Fort," Elijah said.

"Dat sounds fine, Elijah," Solomon said, "Ah jes' don't know how much time we got befo' he kill again."

"Kin anybody go sooner?" Elijah asked.

It was the busy season. Risby and Ran didn't want to fall too far behind on their workload. Solomon was too old for such a journey. So nobody stepped up.

"Well, if nobody else can go any earlier," Micah said, " we'll have to hope nothing happens before then."

Risby and Ran returned the body this time, and over the next few days. The community of Jago helped the parents bury the boy. Then, the parents of the dead child continued their journey north, grieved to have ever passed this way. Four days had now passed since the burial, and Elijah and Micah made good on their promise to ride into Memphis to solicit help from the soldiers at Fort Pickering. Risby loaned them his wagon to make the journey. It took them better than a day to reach

Memphis. They tried to meet with the Fort's ranking officer right away, but he was unable to meet with them right away.

After waiting most of their second day there, Elijah and Micah finally obtained an audience with the ranking officer of Fort Pickering, Major Thaddeus Anderson. Anderson was a tall-slender man thirty-eight years of age. His face was clean shaven, and the black hair on his head was neatly combed in place. He wore his uniform with stately pride. He was an impressive figure, and looked like a leader of men. He was a rising star in the military. He was born a man of wealth and privilege. After military service, he had ambitions in the world of politics. His father and he both felt that a distinguished stint in the military would prove a valuable stepping stone. Military service had always been a useful tool in the climb to power. The major was courteous enough to shake hands. Almost as if he were a seasoned politician working his constituents at some grand event during an election year. Major Anderson sat comfortably behind his desk. He was right at home in a position of authority. He was bred for it. "What can I do for you gentlemen?" He asked in such a way as to make Elijah and Micah feel as if they had come to the right place. He was energetic and attentive, as he leaned forward in his burgundy leather high-backed chair.

"We need your help," Micah informed.

"Help," Anderson interrupted, trying to be helpful, "have you tried the Freedmen's Bureau. It's an organization which was set up during the war years to help good people such as yourselves transition from slavery to freedom. It is still around you know. I have it on good authority that Congress it working to extend its life for a time. Perhaps, they would be better able to assist you in your transition."

"We know what the Freedmen's Bureau is," Micah countered.

"We don't need dat kinda help, suh," Elijah responded.

"We think military assistance is what we need," Micah explained.

"I see, go on," Anderson replied.

"Somebody killin' our chil'ens," Elijah informed him, "we don't know what ta do 'bout it."

Major Anderson leaned back in his chair, and began to think on the matter for a moment. This was a more serious matter than he anticipated. It was certainly not a matter he was anxious to dive into. He sighed and leaned forward again. "Give me a little more detail, please."

"Somebody is killing our children. We've lost four in a little over a month," Micah. explained.

"Some of 'em not much older dan lit' lap babies," Elijah added.

"We think it's the work of the same individual. They have all been strangled, all found in the same five mile area, all with no witnesses. We're stumped, we need your help," Micah explained.

"What has the law in your area done about this?" Anderson asked.

Elijah let go of a single constrained chuckle. "Nothin'."

"That about sums it up. I don't think the sheriff and his deputies view us as citizens," commented Micah.

Major Anderson did not comment on this. He understood the politics of the matter. A civil rights bill had been passed by Congress, just this past April, after a bitter fight with President Andrew Johnson, who vetoed the measure. But up to this time no Southern states recognized or had complied with the law. It was a tough and sticky situation.

"They adamantly refused to help?" the major asked.

"Dat's right, major," Elijah confirmed.

"What action do you wish me to take on your behalf, gentlemen?" .

"Don't rightly know. What kin ya do?" Elijah asked.

Major Anderson sighed, and interlocked his fingers, resting his elbows on his desk. He began to twiddle his thumbs, uncomfortable with the question. Candidly, he answered, "Unfortunately, not very much."

The countenance of both Elijah and Micah fell. They were of the opinion that military intervention was their last best hope.

"Why can't you help, Major?" Micah asked, very frustrated.

"The political climate is such, right now, that I simply can't."

"What does politics have do with our situation?" Micah shouted angrily.

Anderson was tempted to come back at Micah hard, but he didn't. He remained cool and rational. He understood the considerable strain Micah must have been under having to deal with so complicated an issue as serial killings, although they were not called such at that time. He wanted them to have a feel for the climate at that time. Hopefully, it would help them to understand that his hands were tied. "Please, calm yourself," he said.

"I'm about as calm as I can be under the circumstances," Micah said with definite frustration.

"I want you gentlemen to understand what's going on. There is a great deal of fighting in Washington between President Andrew Johnson and Congress, right now, as to what should be done with the South. As to what should be done with you, the Negro people," Anderson paused for a moment, not quite sure of what to say next. "Did you know that after General Lee surrendered at Appomattox, the very next day he rode home free as a bird to resume his life. He wasn't charged with treason, or with conspiring to rip this country apart. Only Confederate President Jefferson Davis and a few insignificant others were detained, and if I am not mistaken, most of them have now been released. As someone who served during the war, and watched many a good man lose his life for the cause, that in my opinion, is a complete and utter slap in the face of the union soldier. We should have our foot on their rebel necks. Instead, all the average reb has to do, and this will make you laugh, is take an oath of allegiance to the United States to have his civil rights and property restored. That has to be the absolute most lenient punishment in history for such a damnable offense. I said all that to say this. President Johnson, who quite frankly is no Abraham Lincoln, is shielding the South from what it is due. I hear he actually spends most of his days greeting Southern delegations, issuing pardons to the very upper crust, who in all liklihood caused the South to move toward secession. Some say that he is merely trying to carry out the plans of President Lincoln. Others say that he is afraid the South will renew the fight if he is too hard on them. There may be some credence to that. There have been reports that many riots are occurring throughout the south.

"Most of them small and primarily against the Negro people. The burning of school houses and church buildings, that sort of thing. There was even a very sizable riot here in Memphis just this past May. Gangs of white citizens, aided by the law, for some reason found it necessary to go into a nearby Negro shanty town here in Memphis, beating and confiscating guns from the Negro men and destroying property. There were a good number of Negro deaths, close to fifty as I understand it, and five Negro women were reported raped in this incident. One can only speculate as to why it happened. I personally believe that when liquor and harsh feelings get together, trouble won't be too far behind. Liquor has the power to make otherwise decent men into little more than wild animals. So, you see, matters have the potential to escalate and get out of hand rather quickly in this intense environment. Since the vast majority of these riots and attacks, are being directed toward your race. Washington feels that if the military were to step in on your behalf, and pray tell some white southern lives were lost in the process, it might be just the kindling southern agitators need to compel their bitter brethren to renew the fight. I personally don't believe there is much threat of this happening. The support elements to mount such an effort aren't in place. Nevertheless, our president believes it to be possible, and in all fairness to the man, it is a reasonably valid concern. Orders to us here in the field are clear. Take no actions which might compromise our position in the south. I don't agree with it. Nevertheless, I don't make policy. President Johnson is calling the shots, and it seems, he is committed to preserving the peace at all cost. I hope the things that I've said here today have opened your eyes to the greater view."

"But, showly you kin do somethin'," Elijah said, in an almost dazed state of disbelief, his stoic nature failing him.

"I know this is not what you want to hear. It is downright galling in fact, and by my own admission, certainly not the most equitable way to treat the Negro people, who have been and remain loyal to the Union."

"This can't be. You've got it wrong," Micah said, not wanting to believe there was nowhere for them to turn.

"No, I am not wrong," Major Anderson said, " Federalist forces here in the South are thin at best, and there is talk President Johnson wants to pull us out all together. That sends a very clear message to me, does it not to you?"

"Dey's gotta be somethin' ya kin do," Elijah almost begged.

"My hands are tied. Please, try to understand that."

"Elijah, he won't help us," Micah said, trying to get Elijah to see it was useless to persist.

"Not won't. Can't," the major said.

"Ain't no difference to me, Major," Micah said with a dismissible tone.

"Iffen you can't help us, what we gon' do?" Elijah asked.

"Sadly, I don't know," Anderson compassionately answered.

"Come on Elijah, our business is done here," Micah said.

Elijah who was holding his dusty light-brown hat in his hands, lowered his head, and sadly put it on. Micah and he rose and left the office without a goodbye. Outside of the Fort, they were at a loss as to what to do next. They felt deserted and forgotten by their liberators.

"What we gon' do, Micah?"

"I don't know. I just don't know."

"We all alone," Elijah said, feeling lost.

"Looks like it," Micah answered.

"Worst thang is we gotta go back home wit' no answers fuh all dem folks dependin' on us."

"Let's go to the Freedmen's Bureau."

"Why? Dey can't help us. Ya know ain't nothin' dey kin do, and ya said dat back at da Fort."

"I know, but maybe I'm wrong. Maybe, they can help. Let's exhaust our options before we declare them pointless."

They made their way down by the riverside of the Mississippi where there was an office operated by the Freedmen's Bureau. It was crowded there in the dark-red bricked two story building.

Some of the functions of the bureau were to provide supplies, medical services, and food to the newly emancipated blacks, but not to blacks alone. These were very lean-austere times. Everyone was suffering, including whites. Many of them were also in need of help. Many of them received food and supplies from the Freedmen's Bureau.

As Elijah and Micah waited, there was a sense in them that this was a waste of time. They waited there hours before an agent of the bureau could see them. It was a black man. They were surprised, but pleased, to see him. His name was Hilkiah Mifflin. He was a prosperous looking dark-skinned man, with an afro parted on the left side. He was tall and slim and was dressed in a black suit. His facial features were such that he reminded them of a younger, black, Abraham Lincoln. At least Micah thought so; having seen a likeness of the man in a painting once. Hilkiah seemed friendly and familiar to them. Elijah and Micah both felt that he would at least listen and do his best to help.

"How may I be of service to you?" Hilkiah asked, sounding like an educated man, but tired. His workday had been very long.

"Ah's not sho ya kin help us," Elijah said.

"Try me," Mifflin said.

"There have been a number of murders in our neck of the woods. Someone has been killing our children, and we haven't been able to stop him. The law refuses to assist us, and we've just came from the Fort. The commanding officer there said that the army can't help us. Our backs are against the wall, and we have nowhere else to turn. Are you able to help us?" Micah asked

"We could if we had a little more to work with. We could intercede with the courts on your behalf. We could help you get the justice of which you are deserving. However, you don't know who is behind the source of your woes, which ties our hands. We have to have someone to go after."

This was disappointing news, but Elijah felt a sense of optimism, because Hilkiah was at least willing to aide them. "Mista Mifflin, youse willin' ta help us, and dat mean a lot ta us, tell us. What kin we do ta git y'all in dis."

"As I said, We need someone to go after."

"We don't know who is doing it. That's why we are here," Micah said, "we need someone to help us track this person down."

"That is not us, sir," Hilkiah responded, "we help establish schools for colored people. We supervise contracts between freedmen and their employers. We provide supplies, and medical help to those who need it, but we aren't an investigative agency. We don't have people dedicated to that purpose. I'm sorry."

"Can you pressure the law to help us?" Micah asked.

"We could, but it is doubtful that they would truly help you. This is the kind of thing that takes time. They could stall us from now until dooms day, insisting that they are doing every reasonable thing to resolve this, and unfortunately, we couldn't dispute that they weren't." Mifflin said.

"Showly dey's somethin' mo' ya kin do ta help," Elijah said.

"Unfortunately not, but I would make this recommendation to you. There are men who specialize in investigation. They work for fee. I would recommend that you employ such a man."

"There are no pinkerton men around these parts," Micah said.

"Perhaps, you might inquire to see if one is willing to travel," Hilkiah suggested.

"Even iffen one would, Mista Mifflin, money is tight. We's po' black peoples. We ain't hardly got nothin'. How we gon' pay somebody ta come all da way down heah from New York, or Boston, or some place like dat? Where we gon' git da money?" Elijah asked.

"Perhaps, if everyone within your community pooled their resources, you might have enough to hire someone," Hilkiah recommended.

"Dey ain't hardly a cent ta be had amongst da whole of da folks in Jago. We barter twixt one another fuh most of what we needs. Ah don't thank we kin come up wit' da kinda money it gon' take ta git somebody down heah, but we'll try," Elijah said, trying to remain positive.

"I am sorry that I can't be of more help to you. I will discuss your problem with my colleagues to see if there is some other option open to us that I may have overlooked. If there is something more that can be done, rest assured that I will see that it is done," Hilkiah assured.

Elijah and Micah left the Freedmen's Bureau feeling it was another dead end. It was too late to head back for Jago. They elected to get a room in the Negro part of town. There was still a lot of visible damage from the riot that happened there during May, but they managed to find a hot meal and a bed. When morning came, they prepared to leave. After climbing onto their borrowed wagon for the return trip home, Micah sensed the feeling of defeat in Elijah. He was in a trance-like state, pausing for seconds at a time. He was silent and distant, staring into space, not really seeing anything. His demeanor was one of hopelessness. The people of Jago had so much faith in him. They expected him to figure out this riddle, to put an end to it. It was a tremendous source of stress and burden. The very hairs upon Elijah's head seem to gray before Micah's eyes. He was starting to look ten years older than he really was. The weight of this thing was too much for him to bear. Elijah hadn't slept well since the second murder, nor had he eaten well. Elijah was on the verge of giving up. Micah saw this clearly. "What are you thinking, Elijah?"

"O'm thankin' Ah don't know what ta do next."

"You're not alone. We'll get through this."

"How, Micah?"

"I don't know, but we will."

"Ah feel like jes' breakin' down and cryin'."

Micah sighed and looked at Elijah with very empathetic eyes. "If you gotta to keep goin', do it."

Elijah lifted his hat, and with a single stroke, rubbed from his forehead to the back of his neck. He twisted his neck from side to side, trying to release some of the tension. He looked to the sky.

"God, don't forget me. Don't forget me."

Micah looked down for a moment, feeling as though he were invading Elijah's private moment, a vulnerable moment that he should not have seen.

Elijah noticed that this was an uncomfortable gesture for Micah. "God is all we really got in dis worl', Micah. We need ta depend on 'im, and trust in 'im. When he ready, he gon' see us through dis, Ah reckon, O'm hopin'. Maybe, God jes' won't us ta leave."

Micah did not comment on the statement.

"Maybe, when we git back home, we ought jes' tell everybody ta pack up, and head up north, jes' leave this mess behind us," Elijah said, really asking Micah's opinion if he thought it was a good idea.

"You know I ain't much on the South. I think every black man should pack up and leave this God forsaken land. If you want to go, go, but don't do it because you're trying to run away from your problems. There gonna be troubles wherever you go. You can't run from them."

"Ah can't get from under dis problem, Micah. I can't fix it."

"You mind if I tell you a little story? It helped me once when I was really scared of what lay ahead."

"O'm listenin'."

"When I was in the army, just before our first battle as a colored unit. Our commander, a young white lieutenant about the same age as me, talked with us. I guess he could sense how afraid many of us were. He talked about the importance of individual courage. He told us of a battle which took place hundreds of years before Christ. There was this king of a land called Persia. Darius was his name. The king's empire was threatened by a young conqueror called Alexander the Great. Alexander had an army of about fifty thousand men. To meet this threat, the Persian king assembled an army of about three hundred and fifty thousand men. The Persian king was confident that victory would be his. After all, the odds were heavily in his favor. So confident was he, that rather than let his generals lead the attack. He decided to do so himself. There was no way he could lose, right?" When the battle began, seeing that the tide was against him, Alexander did a surprising thing. He turned all of his troops in the direction of the Persian king. The king, sensing his life was in danger, turned and fled from the battlefield. When his soldiers saw this. They no longer felt obligated to risk their lives in battle, and stopped fighting. Because of the lack of courage of one man, the entire Persian empire fell and was plundered. I learned two important things from this story. One, Alexander taught me, that when everything is against you. You must still hold fast to heart and courage. If you do, things will usually work out in the end for you. The second thing, which I learned from the Persian King, is if you do not cling to courage and run when you should stand your ground. You leave an opportunity for others to take advantage of you, and believe me, they will. Do you understand what I'm trying to tell you, Elijah? The people of Jago need leaders who are going to stand their ground. They don't need someone who is gonna teach them to run when the going gets tough. If you tell them to pack up, and run from this, you have taught them not to be men, but rather dogs to be kicked about and whipped, as it pleasures whoever has the will to do so. That's no way to live. They have turned to you to lead them, and whether you want the job or not it's yours. To have hope is to trust in. You trust in God, and the people of Jago trust in you. What will you now do?"

"Micah, Ah got a family. Ah gotta do what's best fuh 'em."

"I understand, Elijah. You have a wife and a child, and that's something. It's good to have people in the world who love you, and you don't have to worry about them being sold off. That's more than I may ever have, but you have to teach them what it means to be free, especially your boy. You have to teach him to be responsible for himself. This world is a hard place, especially for us. Don't teach your son to bend his back so somebody can ride it."

"Ah jes' wanna live a quiet peaceable life."

"After the storm, the sun generally shines again. This is your storm, brave it. Better times await on the other side of this trouble."

"Ah don't know how ta brave it."

"Like I said before, you aren't in this alone. You've got me and the others. We'll figure this out, just don't run, or everyone will."

Maybe, youse right."

"I don't know if I'm right, but it's what we must do."

"God help us."

Thirteen

While Elijah and Micah were away trying to solicit help in Memphis. Solomon, Ran, and Risby had been spreading the word, that they were most likely looking for a physically weak male of small stature, or possibly a woman. They had begun by informing all of the men who worked patrols at night, getting them to help spread the word. Ran stopped by Rory and Jasmine's home to inform Rory. He knocked at the door. Jasmine answered.

"Good mornin', Miss Jasmine."

"Good Mornin', Mr. Ran. How ya doin'?"

"Oh, Ah don't reckon Ah can complain. Wouldn't do me no good no way," he joked.

"No, Ah don't reckon it would," Jasmine smiled.

"Where dat young man of yours?"

"He in heah tryin' ta get some sleep."

"O'm sorry dat Ah didn't git no chance ta talk wit' 'im last night, but Ah got somethin' important ta tell 'im."

"Okay. Ah'll get 'im up."

Not long after, Rory stepped out to speak with Ran. He had no idea what horror was about to be unleashed in his mind. Jasmine waited inside, wanting to give them privacy.

"Sorry ta be wakin' ya when ya tryin' ta be gettin' some sleep, but we thank dis heah important," Ran conveyed.

"Dat's okay, Ran. What is it?"

"We kinda got a idea who we lookin' fuh."

"Y'all know who it is?" Rory asked, both surprised and excited.

"No, but we got some information dat might help us."

"What is it?"

"Well, fuh one thang, we thank it's a kinda small man. He weak like, can't lift nothin' too heavy."

"Hmm," Rory chuckled, surprised that they knew that much about the killer.

"Somethin' else too."

"What's dat?"

"It might be a woman, and mo' 'an dat. We thank it's somebody dat live 'round heah. It ain't one of dems jes' passin' through like we firs' thought."

192

Rory didn't say a word. His heart seemed to drop down into his stomach. He was troubled that they suspected it could also be a female, someone who lived in the community. He thought of how Jasmine loved children, and how she knew most of the children in Jago. He thought of all the times Jasmine was out late in the night, claiming she had difficulty sleeping. Claiming, she just had to get out, and go for a walk, to help calm her so she could fall asleep.

"Anyway, dat's what we thankin'," Ran confided.

"How y'all know it's somebody from 'round heah?"

"Solomon don't wont us ta say jes' yet."

"Dat sit right hard on da mind, don't it?"

"Yeah, it do, Rory. Could be somebody we see most everyday. Maybe, somebody ya laugh wit' and shake dey han'. All da while dey doin' dirt. Somebody you wouldn't never thank would do such a thang."

"A woman?" Rory said, regretfully thinking it was possible.

"Yeah, could be," Ran confirmed once more.

"Y'all sho?" Rory asked, his mind deeply troubled.

"Like Ah say, it could be," Ran reiterated, noticing a strange look on Rory's face. His eyes were growing wide, and he looked shocked and bewildered. "Ya know somebody we ought be takin' a look at?"

Rory realized that he might have been acting in a way that made Ran suspect that he might know something. He had to control his body language, because he was not about to tell Ran that Jasmine went out sometimes late at night. That he didn't know where she went or what she did, but he had to tell Ran something. "Ah was jes' thankin' about some ole gal Jasmine and Naomi Watts heard 'bout named Mary Hawkins. Y'all might need ta take a look at her," he said, hoping Ran didn't suspect Jasmine.

"Ah know her. She don't live 'round heah no mo'."

"So, y'all don't thank it's her?"

"No, can't say dat Ah do," Ran admitted, "she moved a good while ago. She was a real sad soul, Rory."

"But, she hurt her childrens, right?"

"Yeah, she did."

"Den, she might be round heah somewhere doin' dis."

"Don't think so. Some say she moved down N'awlins way. Some say she went north. Ah don't know where she went, but Ah do know dis. Dat lit' gal had a hard time all her life. Slavery was hard on us all, but it was harder 'an most on her. See, when she was eleven, twelve, years old, there was dis overseer on her plantation. He was a evil man. On Saturday nights, after he done got good and liquored up, he'd call dat lit' gal to his cabin. He would tell her dat she was seed doin' somethin' dat she ought not been doin'. Lies mostly. He'd tell her she had a whippin' comin'. He'd make dat child get naked, make her get down on her knees with her bottom in the air. He would take dis big cedar paddle, and beat dat child till she started to cry like a baby. He wouldn't stop neither till her brown bottom was fire red. With tears still runnin' down her face, he would order her to his bed. All her childrens is his childrens.

"Thinkin' back on slavery, O'm glad Ah's a man. What our women folks had to put up wit' is a shame. Most of 'em got through it all right, Ah guess. Some didn't mind, got what they could out of it. Most jes' accepted it as the way thangs is, and moved on. But fuh some, it left scars on the mind as real as dem left by the lash at da whippin' post.

"Every time Mary hurt her chil'ens, she was really trying to hurt da man dat done her like dat. She knowed why she was doin' what she was doin', too. She knowed she wa'n't right in da head, and she done somethin' 'bout it. She asked Elijah to take her chil'ens, and to get hold her brother to come get 'em. She loved her chil'ens enough to give 'em up befo' she did 'em real harm. Dat's why me and most other peoples round heah don't believe she would be killin' now," Ran recounted.

Upon hearing this tale, Rory inwardly agreed with Ran that Mary Hawkins was not guilty of murdering Jago's children. Yet, he was grieved. In his mind, Jasmine was looking more like a strong suspect. "Well, Dat's dat."

"Spread da word, Rory. We don't wanna lose no mo' chilrens. Somebody gotta know somethin'. Like Micah say, dis bit of information might help somebody dat don't know dey know somethin'."

"Ah'll pass it on, Ran."

"Good, O'm gon' be on my way," Ran said, "Ah got plenty mo' folks ta see."

Ran got on his mule, and rode out of sight. Rory watched him as he did so. He stood there long after Ran had disappeared from sight. Rory was afraid to go inside and look into Jasmine's eyes. He was afraid that he would see guilt there.

Jasmine looked out of the door and realized Ran had left. She stepped out onto the porch and stood next to Rory. "What he wont?" She asked.

Rory didn't look at her. "He jes' come ta tell me dat dey got some news 'bout da killah."

"What he say?" She excitedly inquired.

"Dey thank it's a man, a small sort of weak man."

"Why dey thank dat?"

"Didn't say."

"Dat can be jes' 'bout anybody."

"Maybe."

Jasmine noticed Rory wasn't looking at her. "What's wrong?"

"Nothin'."

"Why you ain't lookin' at me den? " She asked.

"Ah jes' got a lot on my mind," he said, still not looking at her.

"What else Mista Ran say?"

"What Ah told ya is what he said," Rory answered in a tone which was not rude, but disturbing to Jasmine just the same.

"Look at me," said she, taking his hand, holding it gently.

Rory turned and looked at her. He looked upon her full luscious lips, her wonderfully beautiful nose, and the graceful symmetry of her pleasing face. He could not, however, bring himself to look into her warm, trusting, brown, doe-like eyes.

"You lookin' at me, but cha don't see me," said she, "tell me what's wrong. Together, Ah knows we can fix it."

Her voice tenderly called to a place deep in his heart, touching the very core of his spirit. Even though he was afraid of what he may have found there, he was compelled to look into her eyes. Within them, he saw past the flesh, past the soul. He saw an all-giving eternal love for him, which knew no limits.

Just looking into her eyes, love possessed him, ensnaring every fiber of his being through and through, pulling him into the center of the storm which was her love. It was likened to being naked in the midst of turbulent, blistering, tempest tossed waters during a raging hurricane upon all the oceans of the world. Frightening to most, yet, he would not escape it. He embraced it fully, desiring to be nowhere else.

One capable of such boundless, all encompassing, powerful love could not be a murderer of small innocent children, his heart told him. Yet, he loved her so much that he dared not trust what his heart told him. He feared that his love for her was so overwhelmingly blinding that he might not be able to see the truth, even if he desperately wanted to. He took her in his arms. "You my whole world," said he, perplexed beyond reason.

Jasmine sensed some relief in his voice, but she knew something was still eating at him. The wisdom within told her not to pursue the matter further. She kissed the palms of his hands. There was an enchanting way about her.

"My heart, my mind, my soul, and body is all yours," said she, enticingly.

"Really," Rory answered smiling, knowing what was coming.

"What cha gon' do wid all dat, Rory," said she, tempting him.

"Da heart and soul, Ah'll keep close ta me, and give ya mine. Wid da mind, Ah'll hold it dear and respect it. And wid da body, O'm gon' love it all da days dat Ah walk da earth."

"What cha gon' do wid my body right now?" asked she, softly kissing his lips.

"Oh, Ah don't know."

"Ya don't?" said she, kissing him still.

"Well, Ah can thank of a few thangs," said he, becoming excited by her passions.

"Ya can?" said she, kissing his neck.

"Mmm Hmm."

"A few thangs like what?"

"Oh, jes' a few thangs."

"Come on, tell me," said she, touching him in discreet places.

"Well, Ah thank Ah can show ya better 'an Ah can tell ya."

"Yeah, show me."

The one thing Rory never tired of was becoming one with Jasmine. He took her inside and allowed passion to consume them. Yet, in the back of his mind, one lone disparaging thought held fast to the forefront of his consciousness, and it would not yield. Was it Jasmine?

Some hours later, as it would happen, word was about to reach Naomi of what kind of person might be the killer through, of all people, Jasmine. As she was often known to do, Naomi stopped by on her way home from work to chat with Jasmine for a while. Rory was asleep inside as they sat out on the porch conversing.

"Have ya heard about da killa?" Jasmine asked.

"Heard what?" Naomi answered.

"Dey know somethin' 'bout 'im."

"Yeah, what dey know?"

"He a kinda lit' weak man."

"A lit' weak man, dat ain't nothin', it's a whole lot of men's 'round heah like dat Ah spect."

"Dat's what Ah told Rory, but he say it's a help."

"Don't see how."

"Dey say it's somebody from 'round heah, too."

Naomi looked at Jasmine quite surprised. "Somebody from 'round heah? How dey know?"

"Ah don't know. Dat's what Rory say Mista Ran told 'im."

"Lawd, Jasmine, da next thang y'all gon' be tellin' me is President Lincoln ain't dead."

"Ah don't know 'bout dat, but dey's sayin' it's somebody from 'round heah."

"Ah can't hardly believe dat, Jasmine."

"Ah never thought it would be one of us."

"Ah lit' weak man," Naomi thought out loud.

"Rory say, he might be hurt some sort a way or somethin'.'"

"What you say?" Naomi asked, as a chill ran down her spine.

"What? Rory say, he might got some kinda injury?"

Naomi started to shake with fear and excitement. "Ah thank Ah know who dey lookin' fuh."

This commanded Jasmines attention, and she was all ears. "Who?"

"Da white folks Ah work fuh," Naomi answered.

"Da Alexanders?" Jasmine asked.

"Mmm hmm, Dey got a ole crazy son dat stay locked up in his room. Jasmine, he hate black folks."

"Dat don't mean nothin'. It's a lot of white folks dat hate us. Dey ain't never thought dat dey was gon' lose da war. Dey never thought we was gon' be free."

"Listen ta me, Jasmine. Ah ain't never seed 'im but once. He look like somethin' dat chases ya in ya dreams. He got a face dat'll scare lit' chil'ens."

Jasmine laughed.

"O'm serious, Jasmine. He got his self all burned up during da war. One of his han's ain't nothin' but a nub," Naomi frowned, "most of his skin all mangled like. One of his ears ain't nothin' but a hole. He ain't got no hair on most of his head. It'll make yo' skin crawl wit' fear just ta look at 'im. He stay up dere in dat room all day, wastin' down ta nothin'. Ah bet he ain't no bigger 'an a twig."

Jasmine started to look upon what Naomi was saying with more and more credibility. She started to bite at the fingernail on her right thumb. "What iffen it's him, Naomi?"

"Ya know, now dat Ah thank about it. Da Alexanders been actin' mighty strange heah of late.
Dey seem mo' happy. Dey be whisperin' a lot, and dey be talkin' in a way dey don't thank Ah understan'. Somethin' about mo' grass on his shoes.

And, dey don't never do it when Justin around. Ah thank dat son dat stays locked away been goin' out. Ah bet he do it at night, cause he don't wanna be seed during da light of day."

Jasmine shared a revelation. "All dem chil'ens been kilt at night."

"It's him, Jasmine!"

"Lawd, Lawd, Lawd."

"It's Him, Ah should've knowed it all along," Naomi said, pacing the porch with nervous energy.

"What we gon' do?"

"What cha mean what we gon' do? We gon' tell Solomon dem."

"He a white man, Naomi."

"So!"

"What can dey do 'gainst a white man?"

Naomi stopped pacing. She knew as well as Jasmine did that the law would not be with them. A black person couldn't even testify against a white man in the South. "Ah don't know what dey kin do, but we gotta tell 'em."

"Den what?"

"Ah don't know. We'll let Solomon dem handle dat."

"O'm gon' git Rory."

"Fuh what?"

"So, he can take ya ta see Mista Solomon."

Jasmine rushed in and woke Rory. She excitedly explained everything to him. It sounded like a promising lead to Rory. One that he was overwhelmingly happy to hear, because it meant Jasmine was not the killer. He dressed hurriedly and saddled his horse. He rode Naomi over to see Solomon. Upon arriving at Solomon's home, Rory helped Naomi off the horse. He brought her face to face with Solomon.

"Tell 'im what y'all told me, Naomi," Rory directed.

"Well, Mr. Solomon, Ah work fuh da Alexanders. Dey got dis son, most folks don't even know he back home. Da war didn't leave 'im whole. He jes' what y'all lookin' fuh. He sickly, ain't no bigger 'an a stick. So, he can't be too strong. He live around heah, right on da outskirts of Jago. He hate black folks, too."

Solomon rubbed his gray beard, intrigued by what Naomi was saying. "How you know dat he hate us enough ta kill lit' children?"

Naomi lowered her head. She was somewhat ashamed to answer, because it was a difficult thing for her to recount. She managed to be straightforward. "He threw his piss pot on me, and called me out my name fuh no reason. He done it cause O'm colored."

Solomon's forehead became wrinkled with doubt. "Just 'cause he–"

"He doin' it Mr. Solomon," Naomi interrupted, seeing doubt on Solomon's face, "Ah knows it sho as Ah knows night follows day."

Solomon didn't know what to think. Not that he believed Naomi was lying, but her judgement may have been lacking. She may simply have been angry with the man, because he disrespected her. Being disrespectful doesn't make one a murderer. He couldn't dismiss it either. Aubrey Alexander fit very neatly into what they believed themselves to be looking for.

Rory, standing right next to Naomi, wondered why there was this sense of hesitancy on Solomon's part. He wanted Solomon to act decisively in dealing with this man. He wanted it to be Aubrey. It had to be him, because he couldn't bear for it to be Jasmine.

"Mista Solomon," Rory said, "ya gonna do somethin' 'bout what Naomi done told ya, ain't cha?"

"He doin' it, Mista Solomon. Ah knows he is," Naomi reiterated.

"Ah ain't doubtin' ya, Naomi," Solomon assured, "we just gotta be real careful about dis thang is all O'm gettin' at."

"Jes' cause dey white, Dey can't get away wit' killin' us, not no mo'. We ain't slaves no mo' dat dey kin do us like dat," Naomi argued.

"We gonna do somethin', ain't we?" Rory asked.

"We is, but y'all young folk gotta be patient. We can't jes' run ta da sheriff accusing a white man of murderin' our children. We gotta have somethin' stronger 'an our word. Our suspicion ain't gonna do. Even if ya seen 'im in da middle of killin' one our childrens, it ain't good enough. We gotta have proof dat dey can't deny," Solomon professed.

"Well, what we gonna do?" Rory asked.

"Don't know yet. We gonna have ta get together and talk 'bout it," Solomon explained.

"Y'all ain't never thought it might be somebody white, did ya?" Naomi asked.

"Fuh all we know it might not be, we gotta wait and see," Solomon said.

"How? By lettin' 'im kill another lit' chap?" Naomi stated boldly.

Solomon thought that the young lady had quite a mouth on her. "No, Naomi. We ain't gonna let nobody hurt our children, not if we can help it."

"Y'all ain't gonna back down from 'im jes' cause he white, is ya?" Naomi asked.

"No, we gonna find out what we dealin' wit' and go from dere."

"Don't back down from 'im, Mista Solomon," Naomi encouraged, afraid nothing would be done.

Solomon simply looked at Naomi, not knowing what more could be said to assure her that they would do the right thing, the wise thing.

"Solomon and Elijah, dey gonna handle it, Naomi. Ah got faith in dat. We jes' gotta give 'em a chance ta thank on it, like Mista Solomon say," Rory assured.

Naomi looked at Rory, and then at Solomon again. Solomon shook his head up and down with a smile on his face, reinforcing what Rory had said.

"Come on, Naomi, Let me get cha on home," Rory said.

Rory got Naomi home safely, and returned to his own. Naomi paced her room all evening long, thinking about Aubrey. When it was time for bed. She had trouble sleeping. She hardly got any. She felt that she knew something that nobody else was taking seriously. At least, this was the feeling she had. She was convinced that Aubrey Alexander was the killer.

When morning came, Naomi went to work at the Alexander home. There was an unshakable nervousness about her. The very thought that a murderer was just upstairs made her flustered. She tried to conceal it, but Katherine took note of her odd behavior. "Naomi," she said, "what's the matter with you?"

"Huh?" Naomi answered, nervous like.

"What's wrong with you?"

"Nothin'."

"I beg to differ. You are as jittery as a turkey on Thanksgivings eve."

Naomi looked at Katherine. She was so nervous that she could have just about have jumped out of her skin. She had to work hard to get control of herself. She wanted to prove to Solomon and the others that Aubrey was guilty. She decided to try and obtain information. "Is everythang okay wit' Mista Aubrey?"

Katherine found this a curious question. "Why. Yes. He's just fine."

"He been goin' out at night, late night?"

The question caught Katherine off guard. "Why do you ask, Naomi?"

"It's jes' da thangs Ah been hearin' you and Mista Alexander say."

"And, what have you heard us say?"

"It's jes' y'all seem happy when y'all talk 'bout 'im now, not sad like before. Ah was jes' wonderin' iffen he doin' better."

Naomi's seemingly genuine concern disarmed Katherine. "You are a very observant girl, Naomi."

"Is he better, Miss Katherine?"

"Yes, he is."

" He goin' out at night?"

"Yes, he is," Katherine readily admitted, not seeing the harm in answering Naomi, "Anias and I are so pleased."

"How long he been doin' dat, Miss Katherine?"

"Can't say really, at least a month we suspect."

This news made Naomi's heart beat faster. She was more certain now than she ever was that Aubrey was the killer. "Dat's good ta hear, Miss Katherine."

"Thank you, Naomi. We've prayed so long that he would find his way back."

"Well, dat's good ta hear, Miss Katherine."

"You have no idea, Naomi. You suffer with your children when they are in pain. You can't help it. It's just a mother's lot Ah suppose."

"Ah kin imagine ma'am."

"We've not said anything of this, because we only discovered it by chance. We feel that when Aubrey is ready to resume his place in the world, he will. We don't want to push him any faster than he is willing to go."

"Yes, ma'am."

Katherine noticed Naomi had a peculiar look upon her face, not as at first. She looked as if she knew something that she was not suppose to know, something that Katherine didn't know. It was a puzzling look to her, but she thought nothing of it. "Ah guess that Ah seem the chattering fool to you."

"No, ma'am."

"Well, you must forgive me if Ah do. It's just that Ah've had this secret bottled up in me. And, now that you know. It's just all flowing out of me. Ah've wanted to share this good news about Aubrey with someone for weeks now."

"Miss Katherine," Naomi said, with a certain meekness, "where he go when he go out? What he do?"

"We don't know, Naomi. Right now, it is enough that he is getting out."

"Yes, ma'am," she answered, feeling sure that the Alexanders didn't know what Aubrey was up to.

"He probably just goes for a walk, to get out of that stuffy room, to give his legs a stretch."

"Yes, ma'am."

Inwardly, Naomi's mind was flaming with condemning thoughts. She couldn't wait for the work day to be over with so that she could run to Solomon. Her tongue was burning to tell him all that Katherine had told her. Surely, this would be enough to convince him that Aubrey was their man.

Later that evening, on her way home from work, Naomi went two miles out of her way to stop by Solomon's home. Once there, she told Solomon everything that Katherine had said. Solomon assured her that everything was being taken into consideration. He assured her that everything was being discussed, and would be acted upon. It was not enough for her, too much talk, not enough action. Also, she felt that she was being ignored. She decided that she would take it upon herself to spread what she knew about Aubrey. Surely, someone would give an attentive ear to what she had to tell them. One person she told was Trents. He listened to every word that she had to tell him with particular interest. He decided that he would get some of the others together and would pressure Solomon and Elijah to take action.

Fourteen

Later that night, Elijah and Micah returned home. It was a long and disappointing trip. When morning came, Elijah rode over to inform Solomon of what happened in Memphis. Sitting on the porch, he prepared to apprise Solomon of their standing.

"How did it go at da fort?" Solomon asked somewhat anxious to hear.

Elijah took a deep breath. "Not too good."

"What dey say?"

"Dat dey can't help us."

"Why?"

"Some foolishness 'bout dey don't wanna touch off another war wit' da South," Elijah explained.

"What?" Solomon asked, finding it hard to believe what Elijah was saying.

"Dey don't wanna help us, cause white southerners might git mad, and start trouble."

"Dat don't make sense."

"Ah know, but dat's what dey said."

"So, we ain't no better off dan we was?"

"Dat's da way it lookin', Solomon," Elijah said very frustrated, "we went ta da Freedmen's Bureau, too. Dey can't help us neither. They said we oughta get together and hire some northern folks dat kin hunt da killa down."

"Hire 'im wit' what?"

"Dat's what Ah said."

"Maybe, it won't be no need in dat. We might've got a break, but Ah was countin' on help from dem federal boys ta help make it come ta some good."

"What cha mean?"

"We thank we got somebody dat might be doin' all dis killin'."

"What," Elijah said, so surprised that he had to stand.

"We might got our killah."

"Who is it?"

"Well, ya know Naomi Watts, right?"

"Ya thank Naomi doin' dis?"

"No, Elijah, she works fuh da Alexanders, ya know 'em?"

"Yeah, Ah knows 'em."

"Dey had two boys off fightin' in da war."

"Shelby and Aubrey."

"Well, Aubrey back home. Naomi say he been home fuh some months now, did ya know dat?"

"No, Ah ain't knowed it."

"Naomi say, he got hurt bad in da war. A fire done stole most of what he was. Don't look da same, and ain't da same. He real sick like, and he don't weigh hardly nothin' no mo'. He got a lot of hate in his heart fuh what done happened to 'im, hate fuh us."

"He sickly, and done lost a lot of weight. He probably can't lift nothin' too heavy. " Elijah began to reason out loud.

"And, he don't live too far from heah. So, da children might know 'im," Solomon pointed out.

"Yeah, but if a fire done got hold of 'im, da lit' on's probably be scared of 'im, wouldn't dey?"

"Maybe, maybe not."

"Ya got somebody watchin' 'im, Solomon?"

"Not yet, Ah wanted ta talk wit' cha and da others firs' before Ah did anythang. He white, and dat's gonna be a problem. Specially now dat we ain't got nobody ta help us."

"Yeah."

"Now y'all back, Ah figure we can meet tonight and work out what we gonna do."

"Ah guess dat's da best thang," Elijah said, "ya thank we need ta habe somebody watch 'im though?"

"Not till we figure out what we gonna do," Solomon answered.

"Ah don't know 'bout dat, Solomon," Elijah said, feeling strongly that Aubrey should be watched.

"If he da one doin' dis, and whoever we put on 'im is forced ta kill 'im. You know white folks, dey liable ta kill every colored 'round heah. We don't wont dat."

"Ya right, dey killed up forty-six colored folks in a riot in Memphis last month fuh doin' less 'an dat. But, Ah still feel like we gotta do somethin'."

"We will, Elijah, but we gotta work out what we gon' do."

"Dat seem right, but it seem wrong too. What iffen he kill again while we decidin' what ta do?"

"Ah know it leave a bitter taste in ya mouth, but if we don't handle dis thang right. It could be even mo' of us dead 'round heah dan it was in Memphis."

"Dis thang kin drive a body mad."

Solomon smiled. "Well, it ain't no easy thang to deal wit', dat's fuh sho."

Elijah returned home to work in the fields. There was no shortage of work to be done. He and Micah needed to catch up on chopping cotton, a process of manually removing the weeds which spring up with the crop by chopping it away with a hoe. They had twenty acres to cover. They wanted to finish this before July hit. It would become extremely hot then.

After the workday was done, Micah and Elijah rode over to Solomon's home to discuss options. Upon arrival, Risby, Ran, Noah, and Solomon were waiting for them on the porch. They began their meeting.

"Okay, y'all know what we up against. What we gonna do?" Solomon asked, hoping someone had a workable suggestion.

There was not an immediate answer from anyone. They all had to think the matter over. Finally, Elijah made a suggestion. "First thang we gotta do is watch 'im. If he doin' dis, we stop 'im from killin'. Den, we take 'im back ta his folks, and let 'em know what he been up ta. Maybe, dey'll be decent and have 'im committed."

Every one of them thought that Elijah was being naive about the matter, but nobody laughed.

"So, ya sayin' wait fuh 'im ta move on one of our lit' chaps?" Ran asked.

"How else we gon' know?" Risby interjected.

"Even if we do, it's not realistic to think these people are going to turn their backs on family and have him committed. They're not gonna do that for us," Micah reasoned.

"Ah know 'em y'all. Dey decent folk," Elijah explained.

"Not that decent," Micah remarked.

"What else we gon' do?" Elijah asked.

"Kill him," Micah answered.

Noah laughed, finding the remark absurd. It may have been an unthinkable amusing suggestion to him, but nobody else was laughing. It took Noah a second to realize that.

"We willin' ta go dat far?" Solomon asked.

"O'm tryin' ta walk wit' God. Killin' 'im, dat ain't da right thang ta do," Elijah said.

"Leave God out of this. He has no place in this business," Micah said.

"No matter what happenin', Ah gotta try ta be Christ like, even now," Elijah calmly rebutted.

"We can't keep on lettin' 'im kill our lit' chaps. Da law ain't gonna help us. Ain't nobody 'round heah gon' help us, but us. Ah ain't fuh killin' neither, but what other choice we got," Ran said, in favor of the act.

"How ya gonna do dat?" Risby asked.

"In front of some po' chil'?" Elijah asked.

"We don't have to do it like that. We can take him out of the presence of the child, even pretend to let him go. Then, we can kill him and bury him in the woods. His people will never know what happened to him. He'll just disappear one night, never to be seen or heard from again," Micah conspired.

"Can we keep a thang like dat hid? If two people know a secret, dat's one too many," Solomon said.

There was silence for a moment. Everyone had to think over if they were going to move forward with this. Each of them had to decide if they were willing to place their lives in each others hands. Because, that was what it boiled down to in the end. If anyone of them was to let it slip, even to a family member or a trusted friend, their lives would surely be at risk. Noah wasn't comfortable with this kind of talk. "Y'all can't kill no white folks," he insisted, "dey bound ta find out. Den, where y'all gon' be."

"The fact that he is white has nothing to do with it. He is a murderer. A murderer that has killed time and time again. To kill him is not a wrong," Micah justified.

"But, he white," Noah contended.

"Do ya stand wit' us?" Ran asked.

"Ah, Ah don't know," Noah said, fearful and wanting no part in this.

"What cha mean, you don't know?" Risby asked.

"What iffen y'all get fount out?" Noah asked.

"We won't be, not iffen everybody heah keep dey mouth shut," Ran assured, "And, why you keep sayin' y'all? Ain't cha got no part in dis?"

Noah didn't answer, but everyone there was aware at that point that he was a weak link. He held the white man in very high reverence. A reverence which would not allow them to trust him with their lives. Elijah did not want to kill Aubrey, but it was not because he was afraid, which was why Noah was reluctant to kill. Elijah simply thought that killing was wrong; therefore, he couldn't be party to it. Solomon was ashamed of Noah. He couldn't even bring himself to look at him.

"Maybe, we better thank of somethin' else," Elijah advised.

"Maybe, we ought," Solomon concurred.

"Well, if anyone has any ideas, I'm listening," Micah said.

"We gotta watch 'im fuh sho," Elijah insisted.

"Is that all we're gonna do, watch him? What happens when he kills? Are we gonna wink at it, and do nothing because he's white? There is no way I'm gonna sit back and watch that happen!" Micah vowed.

"Ah jes' don't see what else we kin do other dan wait fuh 'im ta make a move," Risby said.

"The question remains. What happens then? What are you prepared to do?" Micah asked.

"Maybe, we'll try it Elijah's way," Solomon said.

"Restrain him, and tell his family he's crazy, and hope they'll put him away?" Micah asked, feeling such thinking was madness.

"It's what we kin live wit'," Noah said.

Micah looked at Noah, losing all respect for him. "That's not going to be enough, because they're not going to commit him."

"Maybe, dey'll keep 'im from killin' any mo' even if dey don't lock 'im away. Dat's what we wont, ain't it? We jes' wont 'im ta stop killin'?" Risby said.

"So, you're willing to just let this pass, if they'll just keep him from killing again," Micah said, finding the thought hard to swallow. "You're willing to just let him go about his life without answering for what he's done?"

Everyone of them lowered their heads in shame as Micah looked at them. All of them but Noah that is, he saw absolutely nothing wrong with letting the murderer go unpunished. The others knew that it wasn't right, but it was the best that could be hoped for they felt. They had too long been slaves, and their minds just wouldn't allow them to consider being much more, Micah concluded. He was trying to be patient with them, but it was hard for him not to be angry with them. What was to become of the black race if they were willing to stand by and let something like this go unpunished, thought Micah. Why were they willing to be disenfranchised second-class citizens, he asked himself.

"It's da best we kin do, Micah," Elijah said, feeling small.

"Is it?" Micah answered.

"Who do we wanna put on 'im?" Solomon asked.

"I'll take him," Micah volunteered.

"Uh, no, Ah don't thank dat's a good idea," Elijah said.

"Ah thank O'm wit' cha dere, Elijah," Risby said, "you ain't da one fuh dis job, Micah."

"I'll abide by what we have agreed upon, gentlemen," Micah said, feeling his integrity was being questioned.

"Ah know, jes' don't wanna tempt cha," Elijah explained.

"Yeah, no sense in dat," Risby agreed."

"Ah'll start watchin' 'im tonight," Elijah offered.

"Who else ya won't wit' cha?" Solomon asked.

"O'm gon' go wit' 'im, Solomon," Risby volunteered.

"Ya need another body ?" Solomon asked.

"Don't wont too many, me and Risby will be enough," Elijah said.

Micah did not protest. He didn't take offense that Elijah did not want him anywhere near Aubrey Alexander. Micah was fairly hotheaded and he was aware of this shortcoming. After the meeting was over, they dispersed.

Elijah and Risby met up around ten at night, prepared to watch the Alexander house all night. They took up a position about fifty yards from the house, in a wooded area. They sat beneath a pine tree, watching. It was about 11:15 P.M. The moon was shining brightly. They would be able to see with ease. There was a lamp still burning down stairs in the Alexander home, and one upstairs. Risby had a small white clothe bag. It contained food.

"Ah got some deer meat dat my missus cooked, haves some?" he offered.

"Thank ya, Risby."

They sit there eating and conversing. At eleven thirty, the light down stairs went out, and not five minutes later. The lamp upstairs went out.

"Okay, Risby, it's time to go to work. Can't really see round back from heah."

"One of us gon' haves ta move round," Risby concluded.

"You wanna go, or me?" Elijah asked.

"Ah got it."

"Okay, iffen he move, hoot like a owl three times in a row. Ah'll make my way ta ya."

"Ya don't thank he'll catch dat?"

"Don't see why he would, plenty owls 'round heah."

"Ah reckon."

"And, Risby."

"Huh."

"Go easy on dat food. Dis time of night, all dat eatin' a put cha right on ta sleep."

"Don't ya be worrin' 'bout dat."

Risby worked his way around to the back of the house, and took up position alongside the barn. He could see everything that Elijah could not from there.

The night went by slowly, and around three o'clock. It became very difficult for Elijah to stay awake. He caught himself dozing, and decided to stand up and walk around for a bit. He hoped it would revive him enough to get through the rest of the night. After walking around for five minutes, he made the mistake of sitting down, as his body was physically tired from working all day. Slumber took hold quickly; he struggled to stay awake. He rubbed his face, and concluded that he needed to stand. Just then, someone tapped him on the shoulder. It startled him, and he jumped.

"You're not asleep over here, are you?" Micah asked.

"Must be, cause Ah sho ain't heard ya."

"Don't let that bother you. If there is one thing fighting in a war will teach you, it's how to move through the woods quietly when it counts," Micah assured.

"Ah hope Ah didn't fall asleep."

"It's hard trying to work all day, and stay up all night, isn't it?" Micah joked.

"Ah guess it is," Elijah laughed.

"Well, he hasn't moved in at least an hour. I've been around here looking for you all that long."

"Good."

"Where's Risby?"

"He made his way back over yonder somewhere, trying ta make sho he could see da back of da place."

"Hope he's not sleepy."

"Ah hope not either. Ya couldn't stay away, huh?"

"No, I couldn't, Elijah," Micah readily admitted.

"Ah don't thank nothin' gon' happen tonight. If he ain't done it by now, he ain't."

"Well, the night isn't over with until it's over."

"What time is it?"

"Around three thirty."

Micah sat there with Elijah for the rest of the night. Around five-forty-five, Risby made his way back to where they were. He was surprised to see Micah.

"What cha doin' heah?" he asked.

"Couldn't stay away, Risby," Micah answered.

"So, he ain't moved all night?" Elijah asked.

"Not from where Ah was," Risby answered.

"Ya habe trouble stayin' woke?"

"Ah tell ya, it got awful rough round two," Risby confessed.

"We gon' work in two man teams tonight," Elijah said, "one body can't do dis. We'll be done knocked off and be done let 'im slipped by.

"Let's get out of here, it's starting to get light out. We don't want to run the risk of being spotted," Micah said.

They returned to their homes. Micah and Elijah had breakfast and were about to get a few hours of sleep before working in the cotton fields. There was a knock at the door. It was Ran with Risby. Upon seeing their troubled faces, Elijah was in a state of disbelief.

"No," Micah said, with a disbelieving tone.

"He got another on'," Ran apprised them.

Josephine and Mama Julia started to listen attentively. Elijah wanted to shield them from this. Micah and he stepped outside, and all of them stepped a short distance from the house.

"Dat can't be, Alexander ain't moved las' night," Elijah stated.

"Well, somebody did," Ran asserted.

"It can't be Alexander, Elijah. We watchin' da wrong man," Risby conceded.

"Maybe, he got by y'all somehow las' night," Ran suggested.

"No, he ain't done dat. We would've seed 'im," Risby assured.

Elijah started to feel badly. "Ah can't say fuh sho, Risby. Ah couldn't hardly keep my eyes open las' night. Ah was fightin' 'gainst it hard, but Ah might habe fell asleep."

"Ya took sleep?" Ran asked.

"Ah don't thank Ah did, but Micah walked right up on me. Ah ain't seed or heard 'im till he touched me," Elijah shamefully admitted.

"He didn't get by. I had a good view of the front of the house, no one left," Micah assured.

"Ya sho?" Ran asked.

"I'm sure," Micah confidently answered.

"He ain't da one killin'," Risby concluded.

"Where was the child murdered?" Micah asked.

"About a mile up da road from Solomon dem," Ran informed.

"Solomon dere already?" Elijah asked.

"He dere. He waitin' on us," Ran said.

The four of them made their way to the scene of the murder. Noah, Rail, and Solomon were there. They had not allowed anyone to get near the body. Solomon was sitting on his wagon, holding his head. He had a very bad headache, but he wasn't complaining. Nevertheless, his look of pain did not go without notice.

"Ya okay, Solomon?" Elijah asked.

" fine."

"Ya don't look fine," Risby stated.

"Ya ain't gon' look fine neither once you see dat boy over dere," Rail said.

This got the attention of the new arrivals. They ventured slowly into the woods to have a look at the body. It was just as Rail said. It was a very sickening sight. The child's body was lying face down near a tall oak tree. This child's body was in far worse condition than any of the victims before him. He had been beaten to a point that he didn't even look human. Risby became so disturbed by the sight that he turned and vomited. Micah's eyes watered. Silent anger overwhelmed him, as tears began to flow from his eyes down his angry face. Ran turned his head, refusing to look directly at the child. Elijah looked at the body; his eyes became fixed on the child. It saddened him to a point that he couldn't even speak. He walked over to the child, kneeling down besides him. He took hold of the child, pulling his body close to his chest. He mourned the child with tender regretful tears.

"This has to stop," Micah said somberly.

Elijah said nothing. He continued to grieve for the child. To see so much death, as they had seen of late, was burdensome to the soul. Yet, there was nowhere for them to turn. There was no way for them to stop it.

Solomon, who had seen much during his life, was being crushed by the weight of this thing. The others looked to him to lead them, but he was all but spent. He was bewildered, and did not know in which direction to turn. Everything and everyone was against them it seemed. Solomon stood and walked into the woods over to Elijah, placing his hand upon his shoulder.

"Elijah," Solomon gently called, "pull yo'self together, we need cha."

Solomon looked around at those about him. He saw that hope was fading from them. Perhaps, it was better to say that it had passed from them. The seeds of despair had taken hold, and its roots began to sprout.

"Good mens, Ah am heah, hear me," Solomon said, as they looked to him, "dey's some thangs men ought not see, but we see 'em. Dey's some burdens dat men ought not have ta bear, but we bear 'em. Ah know we done seed da worse kind of death dey is heah. Innocent blood been spilled wit' no purpose. Ah know ta look at it, it seem like mo' 'an plain mens can bear. Even so, Ah jes' want y'all ta remember dat dere is a God, and he won't allow no mo' ta be put on us than we is able to bear. We can bear dis. So, don't give up hope. Ah know y'all lookin' 'round and it seem like hope ain't nowhere ta be found, but dat's when ya cling ta it most, by keepin' it in yo' hearts. Keep it in yo' heart, cause dat's where it's gon' do da most good."

All of them heard Solomon, and drew strength from his words. Yet, it was Elijah that Solomon, above all, wanted to inspire. He knew that Elijah had the inner fortitude to see this thing through to its end. Solomon had come to realize that this sad burdensome chore was a job for young men.

"Ah will cling ta hope," Ran said.

Solomon looked at Risby. Risby said, "Me too."

Noah and Rail both shook their heads, agreeing to hold fast to hope.

"I won't give up, Solomon. I won't lose sight of hope," Micah assured openly, but inwardly found it a difficult thing to do.

Solomon looked down at Elijah; his hand still upon his shoulder. Elijah did not answer. He stood, holding the child's body. "Who is dis child?"

"Judgin' from da shirt he wearin', Ah thank it's Ezra Joel," Rail answered.

"How old he is?" Elijah asked.

"Nine," Rail answered.

"O'm gon' take 'im on home ta his folks," Elijah said in a sad disheartening way.

As Elijah walked away, carrying the child, his head was hanging low. Solomon called to him. "Will you keep hope alive?"

Elijah looked at him, feeling so much grief over what was happening, feeling so responsible for his inability to stop the murders. "Ah don't thank dat Ah know what dat is no mo', Solomon."

The others watched him gently lay the child's body over his saddle, and mount his mule. He took the child's body in his arms, holding him as if he were asleep. He started to ride away.

"Ah worry about Elijah," Risby said to Solomon, "he take a thang, and hold it too close to his heart. It ain't his fault what's happenin', but Ah don't know iffen he understan' dat."

"Don't worry about 'im. Ah know Elijah. He's real strong, stronger 'an he know," Solomon confidently attested.

Elijah rode to the boy's home to return his badly abused body. He tried to console the family as best he could. It was not an easy thing to do, not this time, or the times before.

Later, Elijah returned to his home. Before going inside, he took a moment to kneel down and pray to God, believing God would make a way for him. After finishing his prayer, he felt much better, strengthened, having left his petition for help before his Master.

He went inside. Risby was there. He was concerned for Elijah, but Micah was the one for whom concern should have be shown. He was extremely angry over the killings. Elijah walked in to find Josephine, Mama Julia, Micah, and Risby sitting at the table discussing the murder of Ezra Joel. That is to say Risby and the women. Micah sat there in a quiet rage.

"What goin' on heah?" Elijah asked.

"Ya took dat boy's dyin' real hard today. Ah was kinda worried about cha," Risby explained.

"Ah don't know if Ah wont ta talk about dat 'round my family," Elijah said.

"Everybody knows what's goin' on ' round heah, not talkin' 'bout it ain't gonna make it go away," Josephine said.

"Step back from it some, Elijah. Don't keep it so close ta ya. It'll eat cha up inside," Risby warned.

"Fuh some reason, Ah thought it would get easier ta see 'im. Ah thought somethin' inside of me would toughen, and it wouldn't hurt so much ta see death so close, but, it ain't gettin' no better. It hurt mo' today dan it did dat firs' time, when Ken Bailey was kilt," Elijah confessed.

"Death a hard thang, Ah don't know if it's s'pose ta get easier ta be around it," Risby said.

"It don't get no easier ta see death, not iffen ya got a heart," Josephine said.

All this time, Micah had sat there quietly simmering and listening. The state of things seemed very dark and bleak to him. He was trying to find hope, but he couldn't. Increasingly, with each passing day, he felt lost. His anger was growing, and he felt helpless, because he wanted to fight back, but he didn't know who to fight. He got up from the table and walked over to the east wall. Without warning, Micah began to strike the wall hard and repeatedly with his right fist. "I'm so damned tired of this," he shouted.

This behavior startled everyone, particularly, Josephine; she hadn't felt at real ease with Micah around since the night he took a swing at her. As everyone watched Micah lose control, Josephine rose from her chair, and moved behind Elijah. She felt safer behind him. Caleb, who was being held by Mama Julia, started to cry. Micah was scaring him.

"Micah!" Elijah called to him, realizing he was scaring just about everyone.

Micah continued to hit the wall with increasing energy and forcefulness. Risby wondered what was going on with him. "Stop dat, Micah."

"Micah!" Elijah called once more.

"Micah, ya scaring da baby," Mama Julia said, thinking that the murders were getting to him and he just had to let off some steam.

Suddenly, Micah stopped hitting the wall. The walls were made of wood, and he hit them with everything that he had. His hand was bleeding. He was breathing hard, and didn't really feel the pain.

"Boy, what's wrong wit' cha? Yo' han' ain't broke, is it?" Mama Julia asked.

Micah felt light headed. "I'm sorry."

"Ah know dat dis is gettin' ta us all, but don't let it make ya do dat ta yo'self," Elijah said.

Josephine did not like what she had just witnessed. Micah's display had only served to heighten her insecurities about him. She really wanted Micah out of the house, but he was Elijah's brother. Elijah was sure to frown upon such a request from her. Elijah would say that this thing was a heavy burden, she believed. He would say it was just a way for Micah to relieve some of the pressure, and dismiss it. But Josephine knew better. A voice within told her that something was not right with Micah.

Josephine briskly walked over to Mama Julia, and took Caleb from her arms. She began to quiet the child by singing a hymn: Amazing Grace. The sweet soft melody of her voice quickly calmed Caleb. He loved to hear his mother sing. The words of the song also called out to Micah, comforting him. He looked at Josephine and knew that he had frightened her more than anyone else. He understood why, and it concerned him. "I'm sorry, Josephine," he said.

Josephine kept right on singing to Caleb, answering not a word to Micah.

"Ah don't guess it's nothin' ta be sorry fuh," Elijah said, answering for Josephine, "Ah wanna hit somethin' too sometimes."

"But, you don't," Josephine said, sending a clear message.

"I'm sorry, Josephine. Really, I am," Micah said, feeling badly about the situation.

Josephine did not respond to Micah's request to forgive his behavior.

"It's all right, Micah," Elijah said, expressing forgiveness for Josephine.

"Well, O'm gon' git on home now," Risby said, "and Micah, what Ah was sayin' go fuh you too. Don't hold dis thang so close ta ya dat it eat cha up inside."

Mama Julia got up, and grabbed Micah's hand, looking at it. "Yo' han' gon' be swoll' up somethin' fierce in a lit' while."

"I'll be fine, Mama Julia," Micah replied.

"Probably better boil some water fuh ya ta soak dis han' in. Hot water will keep da swellin' down a lit' bit, and draw some of da soreness out, keep it from painin' ya so bad," Mama Julia said, concerned for Micah.

"Ah'll go fetch some water," Elijah said.

As Elijah walked Risby out, Josephine stood there inwardly debating whether or not to tell Elijah that Micah was a sleepwalker, and he became violent when he was in such a state. Given Micah's recent behavior, it seemed right to her to inform Elijah of this.

Fifteen

At Noah Jenkin's home, Noah and Solomon, his father-in-law, were seated at the table having dinner. Solomon was not very hungry. He did not look well either. A very spry gentleman for his age. He had been feeling the years catching up to him of late. That evening, he looked particularly old. He felt particularly tired, particularly feeble. He also looked very sad. He looked as if some one very close to him had passed. He sat there in deep quiet thought. So much death about him here of late. He wondered why this test. There was no comfort of mind to be had. No peace for the weary of heart. No rest from this burden of deep perverse hatred, which claimed the lives of those so young. Where were they to go from here, he wondered. How were they to put an end to this madness, which haunted the souls of men of good conscience.

"Ole paw, is ya alright?" Ethel asked, seated in a chair across the room.

"Ah reckon so, just got a bad headache is all," Solomon said, "It feel like da worse headache Ah done ever had in my whole life, but Ah know it's probably just what we's all goin' through right now."

"It been hurtin' long?" Ethel asked.

"A few hours Ah guess, it'll pass," Solomon responded.

"Maybe, ya oughta lay down and take a nap. Dat might help it some," Hazel, Solomon's daughter, said to him. She was also seated at the table with Solomon and Noah

"Ah might need a little sleep. My arm feelin' kinda tingly numb like," Solomon said.

"Dat kinda numb like when ya leg go ta sleep on ya, Ole paw?" Ethel asked.

"Kinda, Ah guess," Solomon answered, not quite sure how to describe it.

"My leg go ta sleep all da time, real bad too, when Ah sit too long; but Ah can't recall a time dat my arm done went ta sleep," Hazel recounted.

"Well, Ah guess it start ta happen when ya get ta be my age," Solomon surmised.

"Maybe, it's time fuh us ta step back from dis heah trouble, Solomon," Noah said.

"Step back?" Solomon asked, wondering how it was that Noah felt that they could step back, even if they wanted to step back.

216

"Yeah, step back, dat's gonna be good fuh you and me. Ah don't see nothin' but trouble fuh us if we keep pushin' dis thang," Noah said.

"Trouble?" Solomon asked.

"Yeah, trouble," Noah reiterated.

"And, what trouble might dat be?" Solomon asked, sensing where Noah was going.

"Ah thank ya know what O'm talkin' 'bout, Solomon."

"Why don't cha spell it out fuh me?" Solomon asked.

"Okay, Elijah and dem others ain't nothin' but trouble. Ya heard da way dey was talkin' da other night. White folks ain't nothin' to play wit'."

Solomon looked at Noah, very disappointed in him as a man. "Dey ain't just talkin', Noah. Dey da only mens 'round heah tryin' ta step up and stop what's goin' on. If it wa'n't fuh Elijah and dem others, as ya say, wouldn't nothin' be gettin' done 'bout all dis. What cha wanna do, let whoever killin' just keep on doin' it?"

There was a noticeable bit of hostility in Solomon's voice. Everyone there heard it clearly. Hazel, realized that Solomon disapproved of her husband. Noah was a good man and she loved him. She felt a need to defend him from her father's disapproving eye.

"Ole paw," Hazel said, "Noah mean good. It's a way dat can seem right ta a man, but sometimes dat way ain't always right. Ah know ya believe in Elijah and dem others. Noah heah, he my husband and yo' son-in-law, can't ya trust his judgement? Can't cha trust dat he tryin' ta do what's right by ya? Ya all caught up in dis thang. Ya ain't sleepin' good, got cha head hurtin'. Ya ain't eatin' good. All dat work bad on yo' body. Maybe, Noah can see thangs a lit' mo' clear dan you can."

Solomon looked at his daughter's round pretty face, into her trusting hazel eyes, hence her name. He knew fully well that Noah was wrong. "Ah don't mean no harm, but Ah don't thank he see nothin' at all. It's somebody out dere killin' young on's, our young on's. Little black children dat ain't even had a chance ta start livin' yet. Tha white folks 'round heah too busy bein' mad about losin' tha war ta care what's happenin' ta us. If us black folks won't stand up, and do whatever it takes ta stop dis, it won't get stopped. Dat's what we all need ta see."

"They's talkin' 'bout killin' white folks, Solomon," Noah argued, "ya know ain't nothin' good gonna come behind dat."

"Ya scared of 'em, Noah?" Solomon asked.

"What?" Noah responded, somewhat shocked by the question.

"White folks, is ya scared of 'em?" Solomon asked.

"Huh?" Noah replied, not really knowing what to say.

"Is ya scared, cause if ya is, dat's alright. Dey been had dey foots on our necks fuh so long dat it's hard not ta be scared of 'em, but don't be so scared dat ya won't let men who ain't scared stand up and be men," Solomon stated.

"Solomon, Ah ain't scared of nobody," Noah said, offended and angry, "Ah takes care of yo' daughter and you! Ah works da fields everyday, all day long, so you kin eat! So, ya kin keep a roof over yo' head! Ah ain't gotta do dat, not fuh you! Youse a man like Ah is, and ya kin take care of yo'self. Ya need ta show me some respect! Ah do all Ah kin fuh ya, and sound like ya don't 'preciate it! Don't talk ta me like O'm some chil', like O'm some kind of coward, cause Ah ain't no coward," Noah said, spitting out words so fast that he almost stumbled over them.

"Ah appreciate everythang dat ya do fuh me, but dat don't change nothin'. If ya scared den ya scared, ain't no harm in dat," Solomon said.

"He ain't meant no harm, baby," Hazel said, afraid Noah would kick her elderly father out of their home.

"You ain't gotta speak up fuh me, Hazel," Solomon fired back, "O'm a near eighty year old man, and Ah know how ta say what Ah wanna say."

"Ya sayin' Ah ain't no man, Solomon? Is dat what you's sayin'?" Noah said very defensively.

"Maybe, ya feel dat way 'bout yo'self, but dat ain't what Ah said. Ah told ya dat Ah know how ta say what Ah wanna say. Ah said, it's alright ta be scared, and it is. Ain't a man dat done ever lived dat ain't been scared of somethin' at some time. You can be scared, as long as ya stand up ta what scares ya. And, if ya can't do dat, don't look down on dem dat can."

"Ah done told ya dat Ah ain't scared of nobody!" Noah said, deepening his voice.

Hazel rushed to her husband's side, putting her hand on his shoulder to cool his temper. "He ain't sayin' youse scared, baby. He ain't sayin' dat."

Ethel was sitting in the corner wondering if she should say, or do, something to try to halt this argument, which had everyone acting like people she didn't know. Yet, she did not want to appear to be taking sides. She said nothing.

"You need ta respect me, Solomon! In my house, you needs ta respect me!" Noah said.

"Ah ain't disrespectin' ya, Noah. Ya gon' see dat later on. Still, we can't keep lettin' whoever killin' our young on's keep on doin' it. We gotta be prepared ta do whatever we gotta do. Dat Alexander boy ain't da one dat been killin', but if he was. We couldn't turn our backs ta it jes' cause he white."

"Ya can't go round killin' white folks neither," Noah argued, "we might be free, but dey still got da upper han'. We don't need ta do nothin' dat's gon' git dey attention, git dey wrath. Don't tell me dat cha so old, and yo' mind so gone, dat cha can't see dat."

Solomon's head started to hurt considerably more, as he listened to Noah. "Ah reckon O'm gonna go outside fuh a spell."

"Yeah, do dat. O'm tired of lookin' at cha," Noah said.

Solomon took his oak cane in hand, leaning upon it to stand. He walked outside onto the porch. He looked up into the night sky. The stars and moon were shining brightly in the heavens. It was so very peaceful and serene. One would not have guessed that such troubles as Jago saw could possibly have abounded.

Hazel stepped out onto the porch with Solomon. She looked at her father, not the least bit pleased with what happened between her husband and him. "Ya hurt his pride, Ole paw," Hazel said, wanting Solomon to go inside and apologize to Noah.

"Bigger thangs round heah ta worry 'bout dan a man's wounded pride. Children is dyin' and we can't stop it. Dat's what we need ta worry 'bout right now," Solomon answered.

"Noah worried 'bout dat too. He jes' know dat we gotta live wit' white folks."

"Let 'em try livin' wit' us fuh a change. We ain't gotta be da ones ta always bend."

"You hear yo'self, Ole paw. Dat ain't you talkin'."

"How come it ain't? Do ya thank dat we's nothin'? Do ya thank our children don't matter? Dey matter, and we matter. Our childrens is dyin', and we ain't got time ta waste worryin' 'bout white folks. We jes' don't," Solomon argued.

"Ole paw, Ah ain't sayin' dat our childrens don't matter. Ah ain't sayin' we don't matter. O'm jes' sayin' dat Noah understands dat white folks kin be our enemies, or dey kin be our friends. Right now, folks in Jago needs all da friends we kin git."

"Ah don't see what nothin' you sayin' got ta do wit' our problem."

"Ole paw, what you thank gonna happen, if jes' da talk dat a black man thankin' 'bout killin' a white man git back ta da whites in Olive Branch or Mt Pleasant? We gotta be careful is all, and ya gotta thank 'bout da company ya keep."

"Ya worried 'bout Elijah, Micah, Risby, Ran? Ya scared dey don't know how ta keep dey mouths shut. Well, you wouldn't know what cha know if Noah didn't open his mouth."

Hazel didn't have anything to say about that. "If Elijah and da others wanna kill white folks and git dey selves kilt doin' it, dat's fine by me. But, you my daddy, and Ah don't wont cha caught up in nothin' dat's gonna cost us you."

"Ya worried 'bout da wrong thang, Hazel. We gotta find out who doin' da killin' first of all. If dey's black we'll deal wit' it, and if dey's white, we gonna deal wit' it."

"Dat's what scarein' me."

"Look, nobody wants ta kill nobody. We sho don't wanna kill no white folks, but if somebody white is doin' dis. Who is we gonna turn to? White folks? We can't even get 'em ta look inta dis. Ah don't thank dat dey gonna do nothin' ta 'im, if he turn out ta be white. It come a time, ya gotta decide what yo' life is worth. It come a time, ya gotta decide what cha willin' ta give yo' life fuh. Ah been in dis world a long time, Hazel. Ah been a slave, and Ah been free. Ah know in my heart dat no man ought let another man come into his home, and steal everythang dat matters ta 'im. Our children is everythang dat matters, and every black man around heah, every man, ought thank dat's worth dyin' fuh, or killin' fuh."

"Everybody don't see thangs yo' way, Ole paw," Hazel said.

"Do you?" Solomon asked of his daughter.

"Twixt you and Noah, Ah don't know what ta thank. Ah see what both of y'all sayin', and both y'all makin' good sense."

"But, do ya believe dat dey's some thangs worth dyin' fuh, worth killin' fuh?"

"Ah don't know."

Solomon looked at Hazel with all the love of a parent in his eyes. "Life is a short thang, Hazel. Every man dat's livin' know a day comin' dat he gotta die. We don't say too much about it. We try not ta thank too much about it. And, it seems ta us dat we ought do everythang we can do ta live for as long as we can. We say yassuh, and no suh wit' our heads hung low. We let everythang dat can be taken from us be taken. Some can even stand by and let dey children be killed, hopin' death won't knock at dey door. All in tha name of jes' livin' a little longer. Dat ain't no way ta live."

"Why all dis talk about death?"

"Ah jes' want cha ta see dat death comes ta us all. Don't be scared of dyin' so much dat cha scared ta live. Ah'd rather live one hour, and do somethin' dat matters, dan live a hundred years and ain't done nothin'."

"Not everybody got dat much courage, Ole paw."

"Ah don't know 'bout dat, Hazel. Ah thank we all got courage. We jes' scared ta use it sometimes."

Hazel stood there trying to make sense out of what Solomon was saying. It seemed so profound to her in a way. Yet, she didn't fully grasp what he was trying to convey.

"Don't worry fuh me," Solomon said, "Ah done tallied up dis life of mine. Ah see what it's worth, and Ah know what O'm willin' ta give in exchange fuh it."

"So, you gonna walk wit' Elijah dem, even if it cost ya yo' life?"

"It might not come ta dat."

"O'm scared it will."

"Don't fear," Solomon said bravely.

"Ah wish dat Ah could be as strong as you is about dis, but Ah can't," Hazel admitted.

Solomon grabbed his forehead with his left hand. A painful frown covered his face. He wobbled slightly, as if he was about to fall.

"What's wrong, Ole paw? Is ya alright?" Hazel asked, becoming very concerned, grabbing Solomon to steady his balance.

"It's my head."

"Yo' headache makin' ya dizzy?"

"My head hurtin' somethin' terrible, and Ah got dis loud roarin' noise in it."

"Come on, Ole paw. Let's git on inside," Hazel said, bearing most of Solomon's weight as they went inside.

"What's goin' heah?" Noah asked, as Solomon and Hazel entered the house.

"Help me wit' 'im," Hazel said.

"What's wrong?" Noah asked, as he helped.

"Ole paw, what's wrong?" Ethel asked.

"Sit 'im down heah in da chair," Noah said, as he and Hazel sat Solomon in a table chair.

"Ole paw, what's wrong?" Ethel asked again.

Solomon had broken into a sweat. It scared Hazel to see Solomon like this. She didn't know what was wrong with him. She began to fan Solomon with her hands. It didn't seem to help, as Solomon started to look much worse. His face started to droop on one side.

"Git 'im some water, Ethel," Noah said.

"My head," Solomon said, his speech slurring.

"What's wrong wit' yo' head?" Noah asked.

"He say his head hurtin' somethin' fierce, and he hear a loud noise in it," Hazel explained.

"A loud noise in his head?" Noah asked.

"Drink dis, Ole paw," Ethel said, as she tried to help Solomon drink the water by holding the cup to his mouth.

Solomon never drank the water. He grabbed his right arm, almost as if slapping a biting mosquito. He trembled slightly, and began to fall out of the chair. Hazel screamed, afraid that her father was dying right before her very eyes. Noah did not let him fall. He picked Solomon up and gently placed him in his bed.

"What's wrong wit' 'im?" Hazel cried.

"Ah thank he might be havin' a heart attack," Noah said.

"Lawd, no," Hazel cried.

"O'm gonna go git Jasper," Ethel cried.

"No ya ain't," Noah said, "It's dark out, and it's too dangerous round heah nowadays fuh jes' about anybody ta be out after dark. Ah'll git Jasper."

Hazel was crying, inconsolably. For as long as she could remember, Solomon had been the rock of their family, and a cornerstone of the community. He had always been a vibrant part of her life. It pained her to think that he wouldn't always be around.

"It's gonna be alright, momma," Ethel said, trying to console her mother.

"Ah'll be back wit' Jasper as soon as Ah kin," Noah said, as he ran out the door.

"Hurry," Hazel cried.

It took a while for Jasper to arrive. He informed them that Solomon had suffered a severe stroke. The stroke had left Solomon without motor function. There was little that Jasper could do for Solomon, but did what he could. He stayed with Solomon for the better part of the night. Jasper, having done all that he could, left with the coming of dawn. He dropped by Elijah's home to give him the news on Solomon. Elijah and his house were having breakfast. The knock at the door was cause for alarm. Elijah and everyone else wondered if another child had been killed. Elijah got up and opened the door. "Jasper," he said, surprised to see him.

"Mornin' everybody," Jasper greeted.

"Come on in, and put a little somethin' on ya stomach," Elijah said.

"No thanx. Uh, can Ah see ya outside fuh a minute?" Jasper asked.

"Sho ya kin," Elijah agreed, fearing another child had been killed.

"What is it?" Micah asked.

"Ain't no other baby been hurt is it?" Mama Julia asked.

"No, thank God," Jasper answered.

They were all relieved to hear this, especially Elijah. Elijah stepped outside to hear what Jasper had to tell him. He closed the door behind him.

"Elijah," Jasper said, "Ah hate ta be da one ta tell ya dis. Solomon had a stroke last night."

"A stroke?" he said, not really knowing what it was, only that it was something bad.

"It was a pretty bad one."

"Mmm, mmm, mmm, Ah sho hate ta hear dat," Elijah said, feeling badly for Solomon.

"Da stroke left him bedridden. He can't move, talk, or nothin'."

"Look like everywhere Ah turn ain't nothin' but bad happenin'."

"Ah know how ya feel."

"Solomon been a rock around heah. Ya kin always turn to 'im fuh help and advise. If dey is anythang he kin do fuh ya, you kin count on 'im ta do it."

"Yeah, you could count on 'im."

"Ah count on 'im Jasper. Ah been knowin' 'im a long time. He been a pappy ta me. He been teachin' me ta read. He ain't never steered me wrong."

"Ah reckon a lot of folks around heah feels dat way about 'im."

"Next ta my momma, most of who Ah am is owed ta 'im. He taught me a lot."

"Well, Ah knowed ya is close ta 'im. Dat's why Ah wanted ya ta be one of da first ta know."

"Ah sho 'nough 'preciate it, Jasper."

"Thank nothin' of it. Well, it's been a long night. Ah reckon dat O'm gonna get on home."

Jasper mounted his horse and rode away. Elijah watched him ride away. Elijah was in very low spirits. His heart went out to Solomon and his family. Like anyone, Elijah hated to see bad things happen to good people. Unfortunately, Elijah had had to endure much in the way of unpleasant events lately. Also adding to Elijah's sorrows, was the fact that he relied heavily on Solomon's leadership and good judgement.

Elijah never really felt comfortable with Solomon taking so active a lead in their endeavors to solve the murders. He encouraged Solomon not to, feeling this was work fit for younger men. Elijah felt that he should have taken the lead. Nevertheless, Elijah always believed that he would have Solomon's guidance to fall back on. Inwardly, Elijah knew that the others would soon look to him solely to be the leader that Solomon was.

It is a responsibility that he was not sure he was ready to assume. It scared him to think that the weight of this matter now rested squarely upon his shoulders. For a brief moment, Elijah wished that this responsibility, this burden, was not his to bear. He inwardly questioned why the fate of so many now rested with him. He took a deep breath and gathered his courage. If the fate of this matter was now in his hands, he would not lay down his burden.

Elijah walked inside. His face looked very sad and troubled. At once, Josephine noticed his sad countenance. They all noticed his sad disposition.

"What's wrong?" Josephine asked.

"Solomon had a real bad stroke last night," Elijah candidly answered.

"Lawd," Mama Julia said, shaking her head grievously, "don't look like nothin' but misery ta be found in Jago nowadays."

"He die?" Josephine asked

"No, but he can't talk or move on his own," Elijah answered.

Micah sat quietly. Emotional turmoil still raged within him. He struggled with his unrest. Although, he was concerned for Solomon. He simply wanted a moment of peace from the troubles of Jago, which plagued them.

"Ah wish happier times was on us," Mama Julia said.

All of them looked at Mama Julia. Like her, all of them desired better days.

"Ah thank O'm gonna ride over ta check on Solomon," Elijah said, "Micah, ya wanna ride wit' me?"

"Yeah, it might do me some good to get out," Micah answered.

Micah and Elijah saddled up and headed for Solomon's home. Most of the trip, there was silence between the two brothers. Micah seemed so out of it. He was in no mood for friendly conversation. As they arrived at Solomon's home, Noah was working in his garden. Upon seeing Micah and Elijah, Noah stopped working, and began to walk toward them. Micah and Elijah stopped their animals directly in front of Noah. Noah was blocking their path to the house. They thought nothing of it. Elijah offered up a friendly sympathetic smile. However, Noah was feeling very aloof. "What y'all wont?" he said rudely.

Micah and Elijah sensed Noah's hostility toward them. The smile slowly disappeared from Elijah's face. "We come ta see about Solomon," he answered, "Kin we go in and check on 'im?"

"Ah don't wont y'all round heah."

"Ah don't understan'," Elijah said, "Why ain't we welcome heah no mo'? What done brought dis on?"

"Look, Ah jes don't wont y'all comin' round heah is all," Noah said.

"Why?" Micah asked.

"Cause Ah don't."

"Noah, if Ah done said or done somethin' dat Ah ought not, Ah wanna say O'm sorry fuh it," Elijah professed.

"Ya bein' sorry don't do no good," Noah said with anger.

These were very stressful times for them all. Elijah attributed Noah's behavior to the pressure and stress. He was simply interested in Solomon's well-being. If Noah did not want them there, Elijah would respect his wishes. "Ah guess now ain't da best time ta visit Solomon."

"No it ain't," Noah said bitterly.

"We'll leave now," Elijah said.

"Do dat."

"Befo' we go, tell me, how is he?" Elijah asked.

"He jes' had a stroke. How ya thank he is?" Noah said, in a very ugly way.

"We gonna go now," Elijah said, not wanting this to get out of hand, "we'll come back at a better time."

"Y'all ain't gotta show yo' faces round heah no mo'. So, don't come back, cause Ah don't wont cha round."

"Noah, Ah don't know what da problem is betwixt you and me, but Solomon mean a good bit ta me," Elijah said.

"He mean somethin' ta ya," Noah angrily spouted, "how he mean somethin' ta ya, when it's cause of y'all dat he where he is?"

"What?" Micah said, becoming angry with Noah for his accusation.

"Our fault, Noah?" Elijah asked.

"Yeah, it's y'all fault. Y'all two niggas and dem others, ain't nothin' but trouble. Ah tried ta tell Solomon dat, but he wouldn't listen ta me. Now, look at where he at. Y'all round heah talkin' 'bout killin' white folks, puttin' all dat pressure on dat old man. It's trouble makin' niggas like y'all dat make it hard fuh good niggas like me dat's jes' tryin' ta get along."

Micah had gone from being mildly angry to a livid boil. "Hear this then, good nigger."

"Micah!" Elijah said, trying to impede Micah's anger, trying to maintain this fragile uneasy peace. "If dat's how you see it, dat's yo' business, Noah."

"Let's go, Elijah," Micah said, hot with anger, "cause, this good nigger is about to bite off more than he can chew."

"Nigga, you ain't nobody," Noah spouted angrily, offended by Micah's insult.

"Your grace period is over, Noah. Open your mouth one more time, and I'm going to get off this horse and smarten you up," Micah threatened.

"Who you thank you is?" Noah began to say.

Micah, being more bite than bark, hopped off his horse. Elijah knew a fight was in the making. He hopped off his mule, and stepped between Micah and Noah before Micah could reach Noah. Noah threw his fist up, but didn't make any forward progress toward Micah.

"We ain't fixin' ta do dis," Elijah asserted, "we ain't gonna fight amongst ourselves. Micah, git back on ya horse, and let's go. And, Noah, don't cha say another word."

Micah looked at Noah, ready to trounce him. Noah heeded Elijah's advise and didn't say a word. Truthfully, Noah's heart was pounding. He didn't really want to fight Micah, but he wasn't gonna let Micah intimidate him either.

"Please, Micah, let's go," Elijah said.

"You are right, Elijah. He's not worth my time," Micah said, as he turned and mounted his horse.

Elijah also mounted his mule. He didn't say goodbye or anything to Noah. He was afraid that anything he might have said would only serve as a catalyst to touch off a fight. He struck his animal with his bridal strap, and quietly rode off.

Micah looked at Noah, wanting him to mouth off. Noah said nothing. Micah followed Elijah. Elijah was feeling worse than he did before he came there. He was letting what Noah said get to him. Maybe, what happened to Solomon was his fault, at least to some degree. Elijah told Solomon to take it easy, to let him take the lead. Solomon didn't really listen, and Elijah didn't insist. Now, Solomon had suffered a debilitating stroke. Elijah wondered had he been more insistent, would Solomon have been spared the stroke. It was impossible to know, but it bothered him just the same.

"What a foolish man that Noah is," Micah said, riding up alongside Elijah.

"Thangs is gettin' crazy 'round heah, Micah," Elijah said, "Ah done ate at Noah's table, called him friend. Now, he don't wanna habe nothin' ta do wit' me. Now, he say, O'm a trouble maker, and da cause of what happened ta Solomon."

"He's foolish, don't listen to him. You may have thought of him as a friend, but he was never your friend, not if he can turn his back on you. And, what happened to Solomon is just one of those things. It's not anybody's fault."

"Ah know, but look like ever'thang gettin' all cloudy. It's gettin' hard ta figure what Ah should do, or who Ah kin count on."

"You can count on me, and we'll figure out what should be done together."

"O'm glad ya come back when ya did, Micah. Ah hate ta thank where Ah'd be right now without cha. O'm gonna see dis thang through to da end. Ah'd hate ta habe ta do it alone. Ah believe Ran and Risby gonna be there, but Ah ain't sho. Ah would've thought Solomon and Noah would always be heah wit' me, but it ain't so. Ah believe you gonna see dis through wit' me even if nobody else do, Micah."

"Your belief is right," Micah assured.

"Ah hope so, Micah, it's so few of us now."

"Sometimes, it only takes a few. It's better to have a few men of quality than many who aren't committed."

Sixteen

Later that Evening, Elijah and Micah met up with Ran and Risby at Risby's home. Solomon's loss was a huge blow. They had come together to decide what should be done next. Risby's home was very nice. It was small, but comfortable. Risby and his wife had put a lot of work into it, not that the furniture was any better than anyone else's in Jago. It was just that there were curtains, which Mrs. Risby had made. There was also a painting, which depicted life on the busy streets of Chicago. This was interesting, because most black families didn't have any art work hanging on the wall.

They sat at Risby's round cedar table, with a brown finish. His wife and two small daughters were in the backroom, leaving the men to discuss business. Participation in the nightly patrols had fallen off. Many of the men felt that it wasn't doing any good, and felt that it would be wise to stay at home to protect their families.

As they sat discussing matters, there was a knock at the door. It was Trents. Risby made the mistake of letting him in. Trents had been of a mind to catch up with them for a few days, every since his visit from Naomi. He had intended to get some of the others to make this visit with him. However, he spent most of his day working, and hadn't made time.

Risby welcomed him in, pleased to see that he had taken an interest in attending this meeting. Beyond those present, not many of the men of Jago made time to attend these meetings.

"Come on in Trents," Risby said, "it's good ta haves ya."

Trents entered, but did not take a seat, even though one was available. He kept looking at Micah. Micah observed this, but did not question it.

"We was jes' talkin' over what we oughta do next, Trents," Ran said, trying to bring him up to speed.

"Ah heard it was another murder yesterday," Trents said, "y'all been watchin' Alexander?"

"Yeah, it ain't him," Ran answered.

"Ah don't thank it's no white man no way," Trents said.

"Maybe, it ain't, Trents. We don't know," Elijah said.

"Ah thank it's somebody black," Trents said, looking at Micah, "What 'bout dat brother of yours. Maybe, he doin' dis."

Micah stared at Trents, anger building in his eyes.

228

"My bother ain't no killah," Elijah quickly defended, "What cause he got?"

"Look at 'im," Trents said, staring back at Micah, "he know how ta read, write, and cipher. He talk as good as a white man, better 'an some. My woman talks ta yo' woman, Elijah. Josephine told her all about how up north he stood up fuh his self, sassin' and fightin' white folks when he felt like dey wronged 'im. How ya know dat when he look at us. He don't see nothin' but a bunch of no count niggas dat's too scared ta even look at a white man, let lone tryin' ta stand up fuh ourselves. How ya know dat he don't hate us fuh not bein' like him, and takin' it out on our childrens. Thank about it, ain't none of dis started till he come heah. Didn't he find Henry Walker? Dat's kinda strange ta me, ain't it strange ta y'all? We got patrols out every night, but childrens still gettin' kilt. How ya figure dat's happenin'? How wit' all dem eyes out dere, ain't nobody seein' nothin'? Ah'll tell ya how. Y'all lookin' fuh somebody dat ain't suppose ta be out, but what about dems dat is. What about dem dat's on patrol, like Micah heah. Micah heah, he been on patrol every time some child done been kilt. Dat's kinda strange ta me, ain't it strange ta y'all?"

"No, it ain't, Trents, Ran counters, "It's a whole lot of us dat's been out on patrol when childrens was kilt, and Micah wa'n't on patrol every time a lit' chap got kilt."

"Maybe he wa'n't, but all dis Killin' ain't started till after Micah come heah," Trents countered.

"So, I'm the murderer, Trents?" Micah asked, getting very angry with Trents.

"Ah thank ya is," Trents slyly answered.

"Well, I think you need to get the hell out of here," Micah said, ready to pounce on Trents.

"Why, because da truth gettin' to ya?" Trents said.

"No, because you are a fool, out right, and I'm tired of listening to your foolishness."

"You da fool, if ya thank Ah can't see ya fuh what cha is, a cold-blooded killah."

"Leave now, Trents," Micah said, warning Trents.

Trents moved closer to Micah, and stood close to the wall nearest Micah. Micah didn't know what Trents thought he was doing by moving closer to him. Trents did not realize it, but he was close to touching Micah off. There was a lot of anger in Micah, and he was not above taking his anger out on Trents.

"Dis ain't yo' house, Micah, it's Risby's. When he say leave, Ah'll leave," Trents boldly said.

"You ain't doin' no good heah, Trents," Ran weighed in, "why don't cha gone and leave, like Micah say."

"Like Ah say, Ah'll leave when Risby say," Trents reiterated.

Micah stood up from the table. A move which made Elijah nervous. Risby was just about to tell Trents that he should go, and Elijah was about to ask Micah to sit back down. Neither of them got the chance to speak their peace. Micah walked right up to Trents, standing in his face.

"Git out my face, nigga," Trents warned.

Micah quickly grabbed Trent's face in the palm of his big right hand, and shoved Trent's head into the wall behind him. It shocked everyone, especially Trents. He didn't believe Micah would move on him. Trents tried to fight back, but Micah was bigger and stronger. He grabbed Trents by the collar, and literally lifted him off the ground, pinning him to the wall.

"If I wanna kill somebody, Trents. I'll start with a loud mouth like you, not a child," Micah said.

Risby did not appreciate the way they were disrespecting his home. "Y'all gotta take that outside!"

"Let 'im go, Micah," Elijah demanded.

"Micah, let go," Ran also said.

Micah was about to let Trents go, but he wasn't moving fast enough for Elijah. Elijah moved over and laid hands on Micah to make him release Trents. Anger had Micah, and without thought, he released Trents, and swung at Elijah. Elijah was ready. He got an arm up, blocking Micah's blow. Elijah was as strong as a team of oxen. He wrapped his arms around Micah, restraining him. Try as he might, Micah couldn't escape Elijah's powerful grip. Trents tried to take a cheap shot at Micah, but Ran stopped him.

"Open dat door," Elijah said to Risby, struggling with Micah.

Risby opened the door, and Elijah muscled Micah out of the house. Risby closed the door behind them. Once outside, Elijah released Micah, and quickly backed off. "Easy now," Elijah said, "calm down now."

"That pile of horse manure had that coming, and you know he did," Micah said angrily.

"Ah ain't arguin' again' dat, but ya still gotta respect Risby."

"I ain't gonna tolerate that from the likes of him, Elijah!"

"What's wrong, Micah?"

Micah cooled a bit, and it dawned on him that he shouldn't have gone off like that. He didn't understand, himself, why he was so angry all the time. "I don't know what's wrong, Elijah. I don't know," Micah candidly admitted.

"Ah know you ain't da killah, Micah, but Trents is right. It could be somebody colored."

"No black man or woman is doing this, Elijah. I know it," Micah confidently said.

"Ya can't know dat," Elijah said.

"But, I do. During the war, not far from Petersburg, Virginia. I took part in a battle. I'll never forget it. It was the summer of sixty-four, July 30th. There was this rebel strong point, Elliott's Salient. If we could take it, our cannons could pound Petersburg. It was a tactical advantage that we had to have.

"There were these miners among us. Somebody got the bright idea to dig a tunnel right under the enemy, and set off an explosion. Our command liked the idea and we did. The commander of our corps, General Ambrose Burnside, decided the colored troops would lead the attack. We were excited, ready to take the fight to the rebs. We drilled for weeks preparing to take Elliot's Salient, right up until the time the tunnel was ready.

"It was around three in the morning on that hot July summer night. We were fired up and ready for battle. We were all formed up, and set to go, literally waiting for them to sound the charge. We wouldn't get our chance to lead the assault. Word came down that the white soldiers were gonna lead the attack. That was a mistake, they always doubted our courage, and ability to soldier. We, black soldiers, were ready in heart and mind to take the fight right to the enemy's door step. The white soldiers, they were battle tired. Their morale was low. They had been holding the lines there since mid-June. Their hearts weren't in what was being asked of them.

"When the explosion went off, soon after, the white soldiers rushed the enemy position, and our big guns were set loose. The ground shook as if mighty giants roamed about. War is the purest form of hell men upon the earth can know. The big guns roar, and you feel your bones tremble. Bullets whistle about you, seeking your life. Smoke fills the air, and steals the very breath from your lungs. Men cry out, terror stricken, as their lives are forfeited to this madness. Simple rational thought becomes a weight of unmeasurable burden. satan stood up within the hearts of men in that place. We forgot mercy, compassion, and how to stay our hands from spilling our brothers blood. We lowered ourselves, and became something fit for the destroyer to rule over. I fully expected to look around and see satan sitting upon his throne in this hell, taking pleasure in his reign.

"By the time we, black soldiers, were called into the fight, the battle was all but lost. There was panic, men fleeing from battle trying to save their lives. Confusion and chaos was rampant. Our command structure in the trenches just seemed to break down. Many of us found ourselves pinned down in the very crater of our making by the explosion. It was a giant cavity about two hundred feet long, sixty feet wide, and about thirty feet deep. It provided us a measure of safety for a time, but then the cannon and mortar fire started to find us. Men were set to flight, their bodies tossed high in the air. When they found earth again, they were missing an arm, a leg, or a head. It is the most horrifying thing you could ever see. You wanna fall to the ground and try to bury yourself in the dirt until it is all over, but you can't. You have to be a man about it, even though your senses tell you to flee. We were pinned down. Death fell from the sky, and if you dared to show your head. A reb was sure to shoot it off. We couldn't go forward. We couldn't stay. Nor could we go back. Death was lurking all about, claiming those around me.

"I was with a young fellow that I had known for a year. Porter was his name. Like so many of us, he didn't know his true age, thought he was twenty-two. I had been teaching him to read. He was doing real fine. He was standing right next to me, then he fell. At first, I thought a reb bullet had caught him, but as he fell to the ground. I saw one of our own, a white soldier, had bayoneted him in the back. We all knew the day was lost. Turns out the white soldiers were moving down the line killing colored soldiers where we stood. They figured the rebs would go easier on them if they weren't caught fighting besides niggers.

"I knew death meant to have me, but I wasn't about to go gently. Porter hadn't hit the ground good before that white boy was trying to bayonet me in the gut. I managed to grab the blade, and get it turned enough so that it only caught me in the side. He withdrew it, and tried to have another stab at me. I still had hold of the blade and forced it up. Everything was happening so fast. Somehow, we got to wrestling over that musket. I managed to kick him in his gut, and he went down. I stabbed him with his own bayonet. Then, I took the blade from his musket in hand and slit his throat. Before, I could even catch my breath, or even think about what had just happened. Another white soldier was coming, he had his musket aimed at me. I thought I was dead. He pulled the trigger just as I dived out of his path. I was certain that he had caught me, but he had missed. On my back, I looked at him. Foolishly, he was trying to reload. I quickly climbed to my feet, ran right up, and gutted him with my blade.

"I didn't know what was happening. I looked around, and there were three of them coming. One was approaching from my left and two from my right. I knew that I had to get out of there. I had to make it back to the union lines. I ran up the crater, and dived out, certain some reb's buck and ball was gonna find me. I was amazed that I was still alive. Keeping my face low to the ground, I started to crawl back. I had been stabbed in the side, and I was bleeding. Men were running over me, trampling me. I was afraid, and I thought that I was going to die. I crawled over countless wounded and dead. All the while, I was worried some reb sharp shooter was gonna get a bead on me, or some white union soldier was going to finish me. I crawled two hundred and fifty yards back to the union lines. And, once I made it back. I wasn't sure that I was in any better shape than I was in the crater. I was trying to get help, but nobody seemed to take notice of me.

"I passed out, and woke up several days later in a field hospital. They said that I was very fortunate to have been stabbed where I had been. It missed all of my innards, they said. I didn't think it so fortunate. I should never have been stabbed, not by another union soldier. The white man is not to be trusted, Elijah. He is a selfish treacherous animal, an evil beast without conscious. No black man or woman is killing our children. I know that, even if you don't."

Micah had broken into a sweat. The perspiration fell from his face like large drops of rain. His shirt was literally soaked. Elijah could easily tell that Micah was reliving the events of that forsaken July day of 1864. Elijah visually saw him shake, and he seemed to have some shortness of breath. He appeared both angry and afraid at the same time. Watching this, Elijah was moved to something beyond compassion for his younger brother.

"Micah, I don't know what to say," Elijah conveyed with great empathy, finding it difficult to grasp what Micah must have gone through.

"Ain't nothing to be said."

"But, still."

"You save that pity that I see in your eyes, Elijah. Cause, I'm still standing."

"It ain't pity."

"Pity, compassion, they are the same thing."

"It ain't pity."

"Well, whatever it is, save it for someone in need."

"Micah, youse my brother. It pain me ta know ya suffered like dat, still sufferin' from da looks of it. What you sees in my eyes is pride in ya, and respect fuh what cha done, not pity. It took grit ta fight in the war, and ya hated on both sides."

Inside of Risby's home, Risby and Ran kept Trents inside.

"Y'all see how he is," Trents said, referring to Micah, "He y'all killah."

"Trents, jes' shut up," Risby said.

"He violent, and Ah bet he da one doin' dese killin's.Y'all needs ta listen ta me now. He jes' showed y'all who he is, and y'all sho need ta see it."

"Trents, ya come up in heah talkin' all crazy ta da man, callin' 'im a killah. If Ah was him, Ah probably would have done worse ta ya," Ran said.

Elijah came back inside. He looked at Trents, but said nothing to him. "We gonna go now. Jes' came back ta git our hats."

"Micah all right?" Ran asked.

"Yeah," Elijah answered.

"We'll finish our meetin' tomorrow," Risby said.

"Sorry thangs got out of hand, Risby," Elijah said.

Upon arriving home, Elijah recounted what happened at Risby's home. Mama Julia and Josephine listened, attentively. Mama Julia found the tale entertaining, as she was firmly in Micah's corner. However, Josephine was not on Micah's side. Unknown to Elijah, Josephine agreed with Trents. She strongly believed that Micah could be the murderer. It didn't help to hear what Micah did to Trents either. He had no right to touch the man, she thought. She did not say it, but by bed time, her nerves were frazzled, and she was afraid to sleep with Micah in the house. She asked that Elijah step outside with her. She had to get this off of her chest. She had to act before it was too late.

With the others in bed, Elijah and Josephine stepped outside, as Josephine requested. They began to walk toward the road. Josephine didn't want to take any possible chance that what she was about to say would be heard by anyone other than Elijah. She was nervous and was really uncomfortable with saying what she felt she must say to Elijah. However, she came right out with it. "Elijah, Ah wont cha ta ask Micah ta leave heah."

Elijah was surprised by this. "Why?"

"Cause O'm scared of 'im."

"Why?"

"Cause Ah's scared Trents might be right. Ah should have told ya dis when it firs' happen, but Ah let Micah talk me out of it. Micah sleepwalk, and he git violent when he do it. Ah followed 'im out heah one night, cause Ah thought he was sad over losin' y'all Momma. Ah thought he was gon' kill me. He dangerous, Elijah. And, it look like he gettin' a lit' worse everyday. You done seed dat wit' yo' own eyes. Ah fears fuh us. He might kill us all over in da night. Ah wonts 'im ta go."

Elijah didn't know how to respond to this. His immediate impulse was to defend Micah. "He done been though a lot, Josephine. He ain't no killah. He ain't gon' hurt nobody."

"Somethin' ain't right about dat boy, Elijah. Ah's scared of 'im. Ah wonts 'im ta go."

This displeased Elijah. He knew how tough Micah had it. He empathized with Micah, knowing the things Micah suffered during the war, knowing how alone he had been. "Ah can't turn 'im out. He done been through too much, and Ah jes' can't do it."

"You puttin' him befo' yo' family, befo' me. Ah's yo' wife. O'm s'pose ta come befo' yo' brother. Don't tear us apart over dis.

"Ah ain't puttin' 'im befo' ya, but he family too, and Ah ain't gon' turn my back on 'im. We gon' habe ta work dis out.

Josephine began to grow angry. "Ah wonts 'im out, Elijah."

Elijah looked right at her, and put his foot down. "No."

"Youse puttin' 'im befo' me. Dat ain't right, Elijah."

"Ah ain't gon' put 'im out."

"You wrong."

"You wrong, Josephine. How you gon' tell me ta put my brother out. How you gon' tell me dat Ah need ta choose twixt him and you. You ain't got no call ta be callin' 'im a killah. My Momma ain't raised no killahs. Micah might be a little high strung, but he ain't hurt no chil'en, and he ain't gon' hurt us. We all a lit' high strung wit' all dis madness goin' on. Ah don't see how we can't help but be. Ah ain't gon' toss 'im out, and dat's dat."

Josephine was angry with Elijah, but she let it go, having respect for Elijah's God-given authority as the head of their household. However, she was done talking to Elijah, period, for that night, and the next several days, also.

Seventeen

Rory woke up to find himself alone. It was getting to be quite a habit. One he didn't like. He wondered where his beloved had gone. He was troubled, because doubt of her haunted him. Children were dying, and the looming thought that she may have been responsible grew in him. It was torment to think such thoughts of his beloved. He asked himself what he would do if he should know for certain that she was the plague which stole life from the children of Jago. He would have to act. He would have to gently take her life, and his own along with hers. He could never live without her. Just then, the door opened, and Rory's beloved Jasmine stepped softly inside, believing him to be still asleep. Seeing he was not, she smiled at him, and with gentle voice said to him, "You up already?"

"Where ya been?" Rory asked, upset with her.

"Jes' out walkin'."

"How many times Ah gotta tells ya dat Ah don't wonts ya out dere at night. It's dangerous."

"Don't worry, Rory. Da night my friend."

"Don't go out dere like dat, ya hear?" Rory said, his voice rising, becoming all the more angry with her.

"Don't be mad at me, Rory. Ah toss and turn, can't get no sleep, and look like da night call ta me. It wanna comfort me. Ah likes da night. It seem like da world what God intended fuh it ta be at night. A quiet peaceful paradise where ole sin-sick man can't do me no harm."

"It's dangerous out dere, Jasmine."

"Da night ain't gon' let nothin' happen ta me. Da night my friend. It'll hide me befo' it let somethin' hurt me."

Rory looked at her very lovingly. "Don't go out dere. Iffen somebody took ya from me, Ah wouldn't wanna go on. Ah wouldn't wont nobody ta hurt cha like dey hurtin' dem chaps."

Jasmine smiled at him, knowing that he loved her dearly. "Because ya loves me so, Ah wont go out at night no mo'. Ah'll jes' toss and turn."

"Thank ya. Da world jes' so crazy now."

"Ah know. Part of da reason dat Ah wanna be out dere some nights is, because Ah feels like iffen Ah's out dere den, maybe Ah can stop da killah from killin'. Ah feels like Ah know when he gon' kill, but Ah can't never be dere ta stop 'im. Las' night, Ah know he kilt, but what could Ah do?"

Rory looked at her, wondering if Jasmine was furtively trying to tell him that she was the murderer and was unable to stop herself. "Ya know he kilt somebody last night?"

"Ah don't know, but Ah feels like it. It's jes' a feelin'. Ah hopes Ah's wrong."

Rory wondered what she was trying to tell him. "Ya always seem ta know, Jasmine, and ya be right too. Ah wonders about dat. You ain't–"

"Rory," she laughed disingenuously, knowing what he was about to suggest, shocked that he would dare think that of her. "Naw, boy, you knows Ah wouldn't hurt no lit' chaps. Ah feels like Ah was put on dis heah earth ta love 'em and teach 'em what Ah can. Ah couldn't never hurt one 'em. Ah loves da childrens. Ah'd give my life ta save 'em iffen Ah could. Ya know dat, don't cha?"

Rory really believed her, but once again, he had to ask himself if that was because he genuinely believed in her innocence, or was it simply his great love for her blinding him to the truth in order to spare his devoted heart the misery of knowing that she was a murderer.

As much as he wanted to believe what his heart told him, he knew not to trust it. "Ah believe in ya. My heart tell me ya wouldn't never hurt nobody."

Jasmine ambled to the bed. "Listen ta ya heart." She kissed her man, finding no fault with him, forgiving him for daring to think that she could be the murderer of small children. As for Rory, he decided that from that day forth. He would stay close to Elijah and the others.

As Jasmine guessed, another child was murdered during the night. A boy named Seth Kennedy. He was seven years old at the time of his death. His body was discovered, in the woods, shortly after dawn. Elijah had been summoned. As he went to the murder scene, the things that Josephine said to him concerning Micah assaulted his mind. He refused to believe that Micah could be the murderer, but it was hard for Elijah to kick against a certain fact. He couldn't escape the fact that none of this started until Micah's arrival. Was that just coincidence? Elijah could only wonder.

The murder scene was just as all the others. The child was lying face down on the ground, and he had been strangled and left in the woods. Elijah looked at the boy's body quickly, not wanting to focus on it. It hurt him to see this. He chose to focus on the area around the murder scene. The ground was very moist and soft, as it rained several days earlier.

Within the deep, dark, bare, soil, Elijah noticed something–several footprints.

"How many folks done been near dis boy?" Elijah asked Ran, who was there with Risby as well.

"Us, and dems dat fount 'im, Ah reckon," Ran answered.

"Da ones dat fount 'im, where is dey?" Elijah asked.

"We sont 'em on dey way," Risby replied.

Around this time Micah arrived, he was on patrol last night in another area apart from Elijah. Micah walked up. He came as soon as he was summoned. He looked upon the child's dead body, very displeased with what he saw, but said nothing.

"Who was it fount 'im, Risby?" Elijah asked.

"Da Butler boys, Henry and Walt."

"Kin ya git 'em back heah?" Elijah asked.

"Ah don't know. Dey was on dey way ta work, over in Mt Pleasant, for Mister Watkins's. Dey done hired dey selves out ta 'im as tanners."

"Will one of y'all ride over dere, and see iffen y'all kin get 'em back heah?"

"Ya wanna ask 'em some questions?" Ran inquired.

"Somethin' like dat." Elijah answered.

"Ah'll fetch 'em iffen Ah can," Ran said, moving to do so.

"Micah," Elijah called, "will ya ride home, and ask Josephine ta send her tape for measurin', like what tailors use."

"What have you found?" Micah asked.

"Footprint," Elijah replied.

"The murderer's print?" Micah asked.

"Don't know, O'm tryin' ta see."

Both Risby and Micah moved closer to have a look at the print.

"Let's see that," Micah said.

"Why ya thank it's him?" Risby asked.

"Ah jes' do," Elijah answered, "Look heah at da print. It's a good shoe. Da heel ain't all wo' down."

"Dat don't mean it's his," Risby said.

"Ah know, and dat's why Ah sent fuh Walt and Henry. We gon' find out," Elijah said.

They stood there looking at the print for several more seconds, and then Micah left to get the tailor's measuring tape. No sooner than Micah's back was to Elijah. Elijah looked down at the ground where Micah was standing. Micah's prints were left in the soft ground. Elijah was very inconspicuous in the way that he looked at Micah's prints. He didn't want

Risby to know that he was comparing Micah's prints with the print that he believed to belong to the murderer. Micah's footprints were much larger than that of the murderer's footprint. Elijah breathed an inner sigh of relief. If this was the murderer's footprint, then Micah couldn't possibly be the murderer.

Sometime passed, and Micah returned with the instrument of measurement. The print was a size eight. Ran returned a short while after this. The Butler brothers were not with him. They could not leave the leather maker's shop, but promised to come and see them as soon as their work day was done. Elijah couldn't wait that long. He had to know now if the print that was on the ground next to the boy's body belonged to one of them. He had made several conclusions, and believed that the print was not made by one of them.

"Take dis boy's body on home," he said to Risby and Micah, "Me and Ran gon' gone back over heah and see Walt and Henry."

Micah and Risby did as they were instructed by Elijah, but something troubled Micah about this. What troubled Micah was that this almost seemed routine, like it was no big deal. It all seemed so casual to him. Nobody's face seemed to display the proper grief for this poor child. No one had shed a tear. It seemed to Micah, as though they had hardened their hearts, and become immune to this. He did not speak what he was feeling. He just felt it. They all went about their appointed tasks with a lack of condolence, or so it seemed to Micah.

Elijah and Ran visited Henry and Walt Butler in the tannery of a leather shop owned by their employer. Elijah explained to them that he believed a footprint at the murder scene belonged to the murderer. The brothers were both tall and lanky, and their feet were both bigger than the print found at the murder scene, and the heels of their shoes were worn. This sealed it for Elijah. He concluded that the print had to belong to the murderer. It must, or whoever made the print would have reported the dead body to them, which no one else did, save the Butlers. Elijah found he had gained something very important. He had gained the knowledge that his brother was not the killer, nor was it a woman. He now believed that they were looking for a man, a white man. A white man who was doing well enough to afford a new pair of shoes. He believed this because the heel of the shoe of the footprint was not worn badly. These were hard times. He knew that most black people were just getting by. The vast majority of them couldn't afford new shoes.

Several more days went by, and life went on uneventfully. Elijah and his household were having breakfast. Elijah was thinking of how difficult it was to get the community's cooperation. He and the others (Risby and Ran) had been trying to raise enough money to hire a private detective from up north. It was proving very difficult. They had pledges totaling three hundred dollars. This would not be enough to entice someone to travel there and stay for an unspecified length of time. Elijah figured that they would need five to eight times as much as they had. He contemplated asking everyone in the community to grow extra crop and donate them. They could then sell the crop and apply the earnings to what was pledged to get someone there to help them. However, this would take time and everyone's cooperation in the community.

Josephine served her husband, as he sat there intensely weighing his options. As she did, there was a certain unpleasant smell that invaded her nostrils every time she came near Elijah. It was not a smell of being unwashed. It was a smell that she did not know. It was a thick loud smell. So thick that it seemed she could taste it. So thick that it seemed as if she were to rub her tongue, and examine her finger, the smell would be visible on her finger. The smell caused her to feel a faint nauseousness in her stomach. She leaned down and sniffed Elijah's shirt. Elijah, Micah, and Mama Julia all looked at her, wondering what that was all about. Josephine looked at them. "Y'all don't smell dat?"

"Smell what?" Elijah asked, unable to smell it.

"Dat smell," Josephine said.

Mama Julia sniffed the air. "Ah smells it, but Ah don't know what it is."

Josephine sniffed Elijah's skirt again. "It comin' from you, Elijah."

Micah looked at Josephine, but said nothing, because he knew what it was that Josephine smelled.

"It's dis shirt ya got on," Josephine said, "Ah washed it two days ago. It ought not be smellin' like dat. What cha done got inta, Elijah?"

Elijah sniffed the shirt sleeve. He barely smelled what Josephine smelled, as this smell was always with him, to his reckoning. "Ah ain't had dis heah shirt on since ya washed it."

"It must've got sour or somethin'," Josephine said, "stand up, and go take it off, so Ah kin wash it again. Dat smell makin' me sick."

Elijah stood, preparing to do as Josephine directed, as she began to help him take it off. At that point, Micah spoke. "You can't wash out that smell, Josephine."

"How come Ah can't?" she asked.

"You'll have to burn that skirt to be rid of that smell, or bury it at the very least," Micah said.

"What is you talkin' bout?" Mama Julia asked, thinking Micah was talking crazy talk.

Chillingly, Micah looked at Elijah and Josephine. "I know that scent. I've smelled it on the battlefield where the blood of fallen soldiers had been spilled, and their corpses lay rotting in the hot sun. It is the smell of death."

"Death?" Josephine said, snatching her hands away from Elijah's shirt.

"If you stay around it long enough, the scent of death will get into your clothing, and try as you may, it can't be washed away," Micah said in a lamenting tone.

In Memphis, during his lunch hour, Hilkiah Mifflin took a moment to reflect on the problem which was brought to him by Elijah and Micah. As he sat alone at a table in a small Negro restaurant overlooking the Mississippi River, eating a meal of boiled potato and buffalo tongue, he gave great thought to their problem. Elijah and Micah had ridden all the way there from Mississippi, hoping that he would be able to help them. He felt that he had let them down. It was unacceptable to him that they should be left alone at such a dire time to fend for themselves against such evil as one who would dare murder children.

As he sat there watching the steamboats go up and down the river, Hilkiah considered diligently what might be done to assist Elijah and Micah. After much careful thought, Hilkiah felt that the best option would be to draft an urgent letter to his superiors in Washington, at the Freedmen's Bureau headquarters, and strongly urge that they contract an investigator from the private sector to help the citizens of Jago resolve this crisis with which they were faced. Hilkiah realized that it was a long shot that they would agree.

The Freedmen's Bureau was very unpopular in the north. Northern citizens collectively felt that the bureau was very expensive to maintain, particularly as a peace time institution. There was a great deal of northern public outcry to dismantle the agency, as they viewed the bureau as an agency that benefited the South. Many hard feelings still lingered from the war. A war which had only ended a year earlier.

As the bureau primarily benefited the newly emancipated Negro, it was allowed to continue, as there was a genuine need at that time to help blacks adjust to freedom. The bureau was unpopular with northern constituents, and the Congress was controlled by northern politicians, who were ever mindful of their constituents' concerns. Spending of the Freedmen's Bureau was always under great scrutiny. This was why Hilkiah felt it was a longshot. He was afraid that his superiors, with Washington bureaucrats breathing down their necks about spending, would be reluctant to justify the money to hire an investigator as a warranted measure. Nevertheless, Hilkiah felt that he must try. Whether lives would be saved or lost may very well have rested with this decision.

After finishing his meal, Hilkiah returned to his work. At the end of his workday, he drafted a letter asking for help on the part of the citizens of Jago and sent it by mail. He hoped that the letter to his superiors would do some good. Unknown to him at that time, it would prove a faithful measure.

On the outskirts of Washington D.C., a tall handsome man of color was visiting the construction sight of his new home. He was a man in his forties, and his name was Houston Thurgood. He was an abolitionist of some renown. Now that freedom had been won, he had transitioned to advocating the obtainment of equality for his people and women.

As he stood there watching the construction of his house, which sat on a hill, he was visited by his wife. She was a white woman of similar age to his own, and was an attractive brunette. Her name was Lydia. Houston loved Lydia, but love was not the sole reason that he took her to wife. Houston strongly desired equality for himself and his people. In part, this was his way of striving for equality. A zealot for equality, he felt that by taking a white wife. He would procure equality by exposing white America to the mixing of the races. He felt that once white Americans were exposed to this, and became use to it mentally, it would help them to accept the black man as an equal.

Lydia also loved Houston, and shared deeply in his political convictions, especially for women. It didn't hurt either that Houston rose to a measure of affluence because of his many paid speaking engagements as an abolitionist. The house they were building cost eight thousand dollars to construct, which was a good sum for the day.

Lydia had a letter in her possession. A letter that she opened by mistake, but upon reading its contents, she was compelled to hurry to the construction site to present the letter to Houston. The letter was from Micah Gray. Houston opened the letter, and this was as it read:

Mister Houston Thurgood
Salutations
Friend, I hope this letter finds you well. I hope it is not too

presumptuous of me to think of you as a friend. We had occasion to briefly meet once. It left quite an impression upon me, and I feel that I know you so much better than I actually do. I admire the courage that you showed in going around the North, speaking publicly of the plight of our people, while we were yet in bondage. I believe that it was through the efforts of countless good people like yourself that the savage institution of slavery was brought to an end. You pricked the hearts of those in the North, and because of it, we are a free people today. However, the fight to be truly free is still very much a work in progress. I live in a place known as Jago, Mississippi. The most vile and unthinkable thing is happening here. We are faced with the crisis of someone killing our children. We, ourselves, have not been able to put an end to this evil. We have gone to the law, but to be black in the South is to be unseen, unheard, and ignored. We have no champion to hear our cry. There is no one to help us put an end to this wretched madness. You are a good man, concerned for our people. I petition you, that if there is anything you are able to do to help us, I beseech you do as much. I bestow upon you many thanks in advance.
Your friend.
Micah Gray

Having read this, Houston was moved to compassion for his people. He stood ready to take up the fight on the behalf of the citizens of Jago. Houston's work to obtain equality for his people brought him into contact with many politicians on a daily basis. He asked several of them to help the people of Jago, who were beset by tragedy. Houston's petition, as well as the petition of several other abolitionist working along with him, and the letter from Hilkiah Mifflin all worked together, proving fruitful.

All that was being done, in Washington D.C. on behalf of the citizens of Jago, because of the efforts of Micah and Elijah primarily was unknown to Micah and Elijah. Elijah was in a very low state of mind. He prayed to God both day and night to deliver him from this crisis. This crisis which weighed so heavily upon his conscience. It was about to drive him mad. Elijah was only twenty-seven years old, but the murders had such a tight grip on him that he seemed much older. Everyday, his face grew all the more haggard. Everyday, there were more and more gray hairs crowning his troubled head. Everyday, he became a little more withdrawn, like an old man who felt his best days were behind him and had grown ill content with the life left ahead of him.

Eighteen

It was early in the morning, and Elijah wasn't even done with his breakfast, when there was a knock at his door. Seated at his table, he looked at the door, as did Micah, and everyone else at the table. Elijah just stared at the door, dreading the very prospect of answering it. Micah looked at Elijah and saw the burden upon his brother's brow. Micah stood from the table and walked to the door, but he also dreaded the prospect of opening it. Nevertheless, he did. For if they would not answer the call to stop the child murders, who would? Most of the men who were willing to help them consistently in the beginning had all but deserted them and helped very sparingly. This thing had gone on far too long. Making matters worse, it was the middle of the busy season, when the call of the cotton fields was at its height.

Despite the community's tribulations, everyone still had to earn a living. It was a very demanding time, and most could not afford to stay up most of the night, and try to work all day. They wouldn't do it, even on alternating nights. So, the work of this burden was left to the very few. Elijah, Micah, Ran, Risby, young Rory, and several others were all that was left to contend with the murders on a consistent basis.

Upon opening the door, Micah found Ran and Rory standing there. They also had the look upon their faces of men who had been burdened to a point of almost breaking.

"Another one?" Micah asked.

Ran sighed sadly. "Yeah."

Elijah began to sink to an even lower emotional depth than he was feeling just a moment earlier. He took a deep breath of frustration. He gathered his strength and stood from the table. He seemed so down. Josephine wished there was something she could say or do to lift him from the deep depths of despair. Elijah got his hat, and walked out the door. "Let's go," he said.

Soon they came to the place, and just as all times before. It was in the woods. Risby was there already, watching over the body to ensure that not too many people walked around the body, contaminating the scene.

The morning sun was shining down through the oak, cedar, and pine trees. It was slightly breezy, and an otherwise pleasant morning, but for this. Lying dead on the ground was another young black boy. Lester Green was his name. He was all of eight years old. Elijah stood there looking down at the boy's dead body, his heart breaking for the child. When he could take no more, Elijah began to look around, determined that this time he would find something to help bring this curse to an end. He looked and looked. They all looked, but found nothing. Finally, Elijah moved back to the boy's dead body, and turned him face up.

One of the first things that he noticed was the smell of vomit. Often times, when people are strangled to death, a gag reflect is triggered, and regurgitation occurs. There were traces of vomit on the boy's cloths, and on the tip of his black shoes. On the ground around the boy's body were small traces of previously digested food. There were small green pieces of pole beans, and small pieces of chicken. All of these things Elijah was able to recognize, but there were tiny pieces of something there that he didn't immediately know what it was.

"Looks like he threw up," Micah said.

Elijah didn't answer. He was busy trying to figure out what he was looking at: small, oddly shaped, white pieces of something in the dried vomit on the toe of the boy's shoe. It was bothering Elijah that he didn't know what it was.

"Strangled to death, just like the rest of them," Micah said.

"How many mo' times is we gon' have ta do dis," Ran said, disturbed by the cruel violence of it all.

Micah said nothing, he was wondering what Elijah was looking at with such an intense puzzled look upon his haggard face. Elijah took his hand and took hold of the small piece of matter stuck on the tip of the boy's shoe. The substance was hard to the touch, and the surface of it was smooth and sharp at the edges. He took a good sniff at it, trying to determine what it smelled like, but it was difficult to get a smell from it.

"What dis is?" Elijah asked, holding out his index finger. So they could see the small speck of matter barely the size of the head of a writing pen.

They all looked at it, but none of them knew what it was that they were looking at.

"Hmm, don't know," Ran said, "somethin' he ate Ah guess."

They all looked at him, as if to say, we know that much.

"Ah can't rightly say what it is, Elijah," Risby said.

"Let me see that," Micah said.

He took the small matter from Elijah. He rubbed it between his thumb and index finger for a moment, and then to everyone's surprise, put it into his mouth. They all looked at him with amazement.

"What it taste like?" Elijah asked.

"It's sweet," Micah answered.

"Sweet?" Rory said.

"It's candy, peppermint candy," Micah concluded.

"You sho?" Elijah asked.

Micah didn't immediately answer. He took his hands, and opened the boy's mouth. He ran his index finger along the chewing surface of the boy's upper teeth. On one of the boy's molars, Micah found what he was looking for. With the nail of his index finger, Micah gently scratched away a small amount of what he felt on the tooth. Sure enough, it was more of the white stuff Elijah found on the boy's shoe.

"I am sure that it is peppermint candy. I had some a while back. It got stuck between my teeth," Micah explained with every confidence in his reply.

"Is ya thankin' what O'm thankin'?" Elijah said.

"Yes, I am," Micah answered.

"What?" Rory asked.

"You might be livin' alright, Rory, but most peoples around heah is jes' half-way gettin' by. You gotta work hard jes' ta keep food on da table. Ya gotta work dem fields all day long under da hot sun ta make 'em yield somethin'. Mo' times 'an not, you doin' dat on a egg or two fuh breakfast, and a bowl of vegetable soup fuh supper. Ain't too many po' folks walkin' around on a full stomach. It's a whole lot of folks goin' ta bed hungry most nights. We can't hardly catch enough or grow enough ta keep good and fed. What lit' bit of money we gets our han's on, we ain't usin' it ta buy candy," Ran explained.

"We usin' it ta buy what we need ta stay alive," Risby added.

"Whoever is doing this, Rory, is probably using candy to lure the children out here," Micah, also, added.

"He done made a mistake," Elijah said.

They all looked at Elijah, not seeing how the candy helped them. The only way they saw this as being useful was that it told them how the killer had been luring the children out into the woods where he could prey on them.

"How?" Rory asked.

"Ah thank we got 'im," Elijah said.

"How we got 'im?" Ran asked.

"Hold up now," Elijah said, not wanting to get too far ahead of himself, "we gon' make sho he ain't got dis from his folks befo' we run off half-cocked."

"Ah don't see where ya goin' wit' dis," Risby said to Elijah.

"Let's take the boy home to his folks," Micah said, trusting that Elijah knew what he was talking about.

As always in these instances, there was much bitter wailing and expressions of grief by the family that had lost a child. Elijah was deeply moved by the Green family's loss, but he didn't feel as badly as he had at other times. There may have been some hope now. There may have been a chance for them to catch the killer. A way for them to be proactive instead of sitting around waiting for this villain to strike again. It all hinged on whether or not the Greens gave their son peppermint candy or not.

There was a growing impatience in Micah. He wanted very much to pull Lovey Green, the dead boy's father, to the side, and ask him if he gave Lester the candy. Nevertheless, he took his lead from Elijah, and Elijah was of a mind to give the Greens a moment to grieve. Elijah was there with the Green family for hours before he felt comfortable asking about the candy. Finally, after he had given them a chance to get in a good cry, he pulled Lovey aside.

"Ah knowed it was a killah on da loose, but Ah never thought he'd kill one of mine," Lovey said all so sadly, "Ah should've tried ta help y'all catch 'im a lit' mo' than Ah did. Maybe, we might've caught 'im befo' he kilt my boy."

Elijah felt such sympathy for Lovey. If he could help it, this would be the last time that a child of Jago's was killed. It all came down to the question he had to ask Lovey. Yet, in a strange way, he was almost afraid to ask Lovey if he or someone he knew gave the boy candy. Elijah was afraid he would say 'yes', and they would have nothing again. At that moment, Elijah felt hope, and it was keeping him from hurting so badly over the murders. Once you have a little hope, it is hard to see it snatched away. Yet, Elijah had to know if the hope that he felt was real or imagined.

"Is ya gave yo' chil'ens candy, peppermint candy?" Elijah asked, almost in a soft murmur.

"Naw, Ah ain't give 'em no candy. Ah's barely makin' it. Ah ain't got no money fuh dat," Lovey answered.

A sort of joy erupted in Elijah's heart, but he didn't let it show. "Is it anybody you know of dat's been givin' yo' chil'ens candy?"

"Naw, ain't nobody been givin' 'em candy. Don't hardly nobody come 'round 'ceptin' other young on's, and most of dey folks is as hard up as Ah is. Dey ain't givin' out candy. Why ya wanna know?"

"Yo' boy had been eatin' candy. Ah was jes' wonderin' where he got it from."

"Ah don't know where he got dat from," Lovey responded.

Soon after this conversation with Lovey, Elijah and the others left. They went to Risby's house to discuss what came next. They were absolutely confident that it was the person who murdered Lester Green that gave him the candy. It was the break that they had been waiting for, and to think that they almost let it slip by them, but for Elijah's keen sense of observation. He never quit searching for a way to end this, and he never gave up. Now he stood at the payoff for these savage months of suffering. "We gonna git 'im y'all," Elijah said, with an inspiring confidence.

"How, Elijah?" Micah asked. "All we know is that he is using candy to lure them to him."

"Dese is hard times. We all knows dat. Ran, it's like you and Risby said, 'Folks is half-way starving. What lit' money we git our han's on, we ain't using ta buy candy. We using it ta try ta live.' He got money ta spend on candy, y'all," Elijah said excitedly.

"So, all that tells us is that he is doing a little better than most," Micah pointed out.

"Yeah, and we oughta praise God he is," Elijah said.

"Where ya headed wit' dis," Risby said, "Ah can't see it like you can."

"Da candy, all we gotta do is find out where he got da candy," Elijah said.

"What?" Risby laughed.

"Ah said dat wrong," Elijah admitted, "what O'm tryin' ta say is all we gotta do is find out who been buyin' candy."

"For a minute, I thought you had something," Micah said, looking earnestly at Elijah, feeling they were still at a dead end, "He could have gotten that candy from anywhere: Olive Branch, Mt. Pleasant, Byhalia, Holly Springs, even Memphis, or a half-dozen places in between here and Memphis."

"Ah don't thank so," Elijah said, "remember, most all dem young on's knowed who kilt 'em. We knows dat, cause ain't but one of 'em so far put up a fight, and he was passin' through wit' his family on dey way up north. He didn't know 'im good enough ta trust 'im. Dat's why whoever kilt 'im couldn't take 'im by surprise. Iffen it's somebody dat dey knowed, it's somebody dat live 'round heah. Let me ask y'all somethin'. Iffen ya needs somethin' sto' bought, do ya go ta da farthest place from ya, or do ya go ta da closest place dat cha kin git what cha afta? Ya go ta da closest don't cha? Iffen he ain't goin' too far ta git da chil'ens he killin', what make ya thank he gon' go half-way round da worl' ta buy candy. He ain't. He gon' git it right round heah. Ain't but two places round heah dat he kin go, and dat's ta Mt. Pleasant and Olive Branch, and dat sto' in Mt. Pleasant ain't got all dem different types of candy like Mista Bush keep at his sto', and dat's where we gon' start."

"Okay," Micah said smiling, "You may have something. I'll give you that, but there could be tens, even hundreds, of people that have purchased candy from Bush."

"Maybe, but Ah thank he buy it pretty regular like. Ah bet cha ain't too many folks buyin' it regular like."

"He could've bought a bunch of it at one time," Ran said.

"We gon' ask 'im dat, and who buy it regular," Elijah said.

"What iffen Mista Bush don't remember everybody he done sold candy too, or what kind of candy he done sold 'em?" Rory asked.

"We gon' ask 'im anyway," Elijah said, "we gon' ask Mista Raleigh over in Mt Pleasant, too."

According to plan, they divided into teams. Micah and Rory paired up, and proceeded to Mt Pleasant. Elijah, Ran, and Risby headed to Olive branch. When all was said and done, they had the names of twenty individuals who had purchased peppermint candy regularly, or in bulk, over the last four months. Having obtained this vital information, they came together again to plot out their course at Risby's house.

"Did you all have any problems getting your list?" Micah asked.

"Naw, Mista Bush was right helpful. He like ta talk anyway," Risby replied.

"Y'all?" Ran asked.

"At first Raleigh wanted to give us a hard time, but Rory bought a little something from him and he cooperated with us," Micah said.

They began to examine the names that they had, twenty in all. Seventeen of the people on their lists were white. One of the persons was a very prominent white man; Franklin Wallace. The names of so many white people on the list was cause for concern among them, as it would be difficult to secure justice against a white, and particularly a white person of means, such as Franklin Wallace.

"How do you want to play this?" Micah asked Elijah.

"Twenty folks is a whole lot of folks ta try and be watchin'," Rory said.

"Ah say we starts watchin' dems dat lives closest ta us," Elijah said.

"We ain't gon' watch 'em all?" Ran asked.

"Ah knows most da folks we got heah," Elijah said, referring to the names they had collected, "some of 'em live better 'an twenty miles from

Jago. Twenty miles ain't no long, long, way from heah, but it ain't no hop, skip, and jump neither. Ah say we look at dems dat lives five ta ten miles from heah."

"Dat'll knock off nine folks," Risby said.

"We budda watch 'em all," Rory said, "we don't wanna get some chap kilt cause we wa'n't watchin' somebody."

Elijah agreed with Rory, but manpower was limited. So, they commited to watching those living in a five to ten mile radius. When surveillance began, Rory and Micah were paired together. Their assignment was to watch Franklin Wallace. Elijah deliberately gave this assignment to Micah. He was concerned about Micah's short temper. Elijah didn't want to run the risk that Micah would come face to face with the killer, not given Micah's temperament. Micah's temper was too unpredictable. Elijah was concerned that he would do something rash, which would create an even bigger problem than the one they were dealing with, should the murderer be white. Elijah believed that Micah would have a difficult time keeping himself from killing the murderer, should he catch the murderer in the middle of trying to kill some poor helpless child. Elijah felt that Franklin Wallace, above all others on their list, was least likely to be a cold-blooded murderer. Had Elijah had any idea of what would happen at the Wallace plantation, he would not have sent Micah.

Rory and Micah watched Franklin for the better part of two weeks. In that time, Franklin had gone out late night twice now. On one occasion, it was in order to drink and gamble with friends. On the second occasion, he went to seek the company of his mistress.

On this night, Franklin was preparing to go out again. It was well after midnight, and Rory and Micah were tired of watching Franklin's exploits. Although it was a mild and pleasant summer night, with a balmy breeze blowing occasionally, they would rather not have been there, lurking behind trees in the darkness of night, spying on this man, whom they were fairly certain was not the one they sought. They were restless, as mosquitos harassed them. Rory would have much rather been home with Jasmine, holding her within his arms, and Micah just wanted to be home asleep in a comfortable bed.

They watched Franklin wonder into the barn, and shortly thereafter gingerly gallop from the barn on his brown horse with black tail and mane. Feeling it was safe to do so, Micah moved to get his horse, which he had tied to a tree a short but discreet distance away.

Rory was about to do the same, when in his peripheral vision, he saw movement to the right of him. He jerked his head around quickly. The stealthy movement sort of scared him, and he was trying to see what it was that he thought he saw. He stood perfectly still, looking, listening, hoping to catch a glimpse of the figure once more. He saw nothing. Suddenly, he felt a tap from behind on his left shoulder. It was Micah.

"We don't wanna let him get too far ahead," Micah whispered.

"Thought Ah saw somethin'," Rory quietly responded.

"What was it?"

"It looked like a flash of white."

"An animal?"

"Seem like it was standin' upright."

"Which way did it go?" Micah asked, ready to check it out.

"There," Rory pointed in the direction of the deserted slave quarters, more than a hundred and fifty feet away from them.

"Let's go," Micah said, headed toward the slave quarters.

"What about Mista Wallace?" Rory asked, not willing to lose Franklin chasing a phantom, which he may or may not have seen.

"Did you see something?"

Rory had to think for a moment. If he said 'yes', Micah was going to pursue what he thought he saw, which left Franklin Wallace out there unwatched. If Franklin happened to have been the killer, that could cost them the life of a child. Rory wasn't sure that he wanted to take that risk

"Ah thank Ah did," Rory said.

"Yes or no?" Micah asked.

Rory thought it over, and he was sure that he saw something resembling a human being. "Yeah, Ah seed somethin'."

"Then, let's go," Micah said, confident that they were doing the right thing.

They ventured down to the slave quarters, which was beyond the line of sight of the Wallace house. The farthest most slave quarters were adjacent to the woods. Rory heard faint distant movement coming from the woods. "Ya hear dat?" he whispered.

"I heard it."

They followed the sound into the woods. They followed the sound with uncanny quietness. They wondered around in the woods for one hour and a half, following faint brisk sounds of movement. They must have walked five or six miles, when it dawned on them that they were in Jago. Then, there was still silence. They had lost the sounds, which they were following. They heard faint sounds of two or more people talking. They begin to journey toward the faint sounds. They heard laughter. It was still faint laughter, but it was getting closer. Then, they heard nothing at all. It was dead silence. Micah and Rory listened, knowing they were close, but were still unable to locate exactly where it was that the voices were coming from. They heard a cry, a loud almost pleading cry. It was a child, and Micah and Rory knew it. The child cried out louder than before. Micah and Rory understood that a child was being murdered. They threw stealth aside, and noisily raced in the direction of the crying child. The cry was constant as they draw near. Suddenly, the cries stopped. It scared them, because they knew that it meant the child was dead or was dying. Then Micah saw it. He saw a male Negro child on his knees with someone standing over him with his hands wrapped around the child's neck, strangling him to death. Micah rushed to the child's rescue. He laid hands on the person strangling the boy. His first thought was to kill this ruthless son-of-a-bitch. Micah spun the killer around, and was shocked to see Jesse Wallace. Jesse was only a child himself, twelve years old. Micah did not kill Jesse, but he had very little pity on him. Micah grabbed Jesse by the collar and slapped him four rapid times. Jesse's lower lip began to bleed. Jesse feared for his life. Micah was an imposing figure, and he slapped Jesse very hard. Jesse's first impulse was to cry out, but he was afraid of Micah, and found that he couldn't.

"You little bastard," Micah said, shoving Jesse to the ground.

Rory knew the child that Jesse was trying to strangle to death. The boy's name was Ezekiel Bowden. The boy was nine years old, and was very frightened at the moment. His face was bruised. His lip was bleeding, and his right eye was beginning to swell shut.

"Is ya okay, boy?" Rory asked of the child.

The boy did not answer, but began to cry.

"It's going to be okay, son," Micah assured Ezekiel.

"We got 'im, Micah," Rory said, "We done caught da killah."

"Just in the nick of time," Micah added.

The way Micah looked at Jesse was not comforting to Jesse. He didn't know what was about to happen next.

"Why was ya doin' dis, Mista Jesse?" Rory asked.

Jesse did not answer. He was very afraid of Micah. He felt like a small mouse that had been cornered by a large venomous snake. It was a paralyzing fear.

"Go get Elijah, Rory," Micah said in a demanding way.

"Maybe, we oughta take 'em to Mista Elijah and da others," Rory said.

"No," Micah insisted, "We don't wanna move them just yet. Everyone should come here, then we'll decide what to do."

Micah had assumed a very commanding tone. Rory felt compelled to do as Micah said without challenging it.

"Okay," Rory answered.

"Please. Don't go, mister," Jesse said, deathly afraid of what Micah would do to him once Rory left.

A strange sort of sorrow was kindled in Rory's heart for Jesse. Rory couldn't explain why he felt this compassion for Jesse. There was simply something sad about him to Rory. Rory wasn't afraid to leave Jesse alone with Micah. Rory knew Micah would not do anything to Jesse in the presence of young Ezekiel.

"Everythang gonna be okay until Ah get back, Mista Jesse," Rory assured.

Micah said nothing to confirm what Rory had said. He just stood there, looking down on Jesse with contempt. Ezekiel sat there on the ground sobbing loudly. Jesse wished he would stop crying. He didn't want the crying to upset Micah to a point that Micah took violent action toward him for making Ezekiel cry.

"Don't cry, boy," Micah said to Ezekiel, "Everything is just fine."

Rory disappeared, and after a long while returned with Elijah. Jesse was glad not to be alone with Micah anymore, but he also worried about what they planned to do with him. Elijah was surprised to see that the killer was Jesse Wallace. He could hardly bring himself to believe that a child could have committed so many cold heartless murders.

"Y'all sho it's him been killin'?" Elijah asked, looking at Jesse's shoes. They were about the same size as the footprint that they found near Seth Kennedy's body, and the heels were in good condition, just like the murderers shoes. Even so, it was hard for Elijah to believe this evil of the boy.

"We caught him in the middle of strangling this child to death," Micah said.

"It's him all right, Mista Elijah," Rory said.

"Why ya do dis, boy?" Elijah asked.

Jesse said nothing.

"Was ya da one kilt all dem young on's?" Elijah asked.

Jesse sat quietly, answering not a word.

"Answer him!" Micah snapped meanly.

"Yes, sir, Ah killed them," Jesse answered, afraid of Micah.

"Why?" Elijah asked.

"Ah don't know," Jesse answered.

"Ya don't know?" Elijah said, finding Jesse's answer difficult to comprehend.

"Watch him for a moment, Rory," Micah said.

Micah and Elijah walked away a short distance from Rory, Ezekiel, and Jesse. They had to discuss what should be done.

"What are we going to do?" Micah asked.

"Ah don't know. He jes' a chil'," Elijah responded, "Ah thought when we caught up ta 'im he'd be a growed man. Ah wa'n't spectin' dis. O'm gon' habe ta thank on it fuh a spell."

"I say we get Rory to take Ezekiel home. Then, I say we let that Wallace boy go," Micah said.

"What?" Elijah said, very surprised Micah would suggest such a thing, "Why we gon' do dat?"

"Right now only you, me, and Rory know about this, save Ezekiel. We should keep it that way. I say we let Wallace go. He won't tell anybody about this. He can't. In a day or two, I'll slip into his house late one night, and slit the throats of he and his whole family while they sleep. Our problem will be solved, and any problem the elder Wallace will present will also be solved." Micah said quite seriously, earnestly looking at Elijah.

A spine tingling chill surged through Elijah's being. It was such a sinister thing Micah was suggesting. For a split second, Elijah was afraid of Micah. Elijah quickly dismissed his fear. This was a very candid time, and required very candid discussion. Micah's suggestion, as sinister as it sounded, was a plan which warranted consideration. It was sad to say, but the justice system in Mississippi was not going to seriously consider imprisoning a white man for killing a Negro. Micah's suggestion may have been the only way to secure justice in this matter. Even so, Elijah did not consent to this course of action. He did not wish to be an offense toward God, and what Micah was suggesting was surely such an offense.

"He jes' a chil', Micah," Elijah said.

"You know what we are up against, Elijah. This is the only sure way to put an end to what this boy is doing."

"Ah know, but everybody needs ta be in on dis decision."

"It would be better if we kept it among the three of us, and that's two too many."

"Ah know, but maybe we kin thank of somethin' else. Iffen it's some mo' ideas out dere, Ah wanna hear 'em."

"It's your play, but you had better get about the business of making your decision. There aren't a whole lot of hours left before sun-up. If

Wallace is not home before his family wakes, they will come looking for him, and that's trouble."

"Da way Ah sees it, dey's gon' be trouble heah on out any which way we go."

Elijah and Micah walked back over to Rory and the children. Rory looked to Elijah to make the decision as to what should be done. Rory had a solid belief in Elijah as a leader. He waited to hear what Elijah wanted done.

"Rory, please, go back and try to run down Ran and Risby. Dey's watchin' da Nelson place. We need 'em heah."

"Okay, what 'bout Ezekiel? Wont me ta take 'im on home?" Rory asked.

"Ah reckon not," Elijah said, " His folks is bound ta be sleep. Da boy is safe. Besides, we don't wont word ta git out jes' yet about Jesse heah."

"Alright, Ah'll see iffen Ah can find Mista Risby and Ran."

"Rory, be quick about it. There is a time concern.," Micah said.

"Right," Rory said, as he headed off to find Ran and Risby.

Shortly after Rory left, Elijah moved over, and knelt down next to Ezekiel. Elijah was curious to know how Ezekiel was enticed out in the dead of night to a secluded spot where Jesse Wallace came close to killing him.

"Can Ah go home now?" Ezekiel asked.

"In a lit' bit," Elijah answered.

"Momma gon' be worried iffen Ah ain't dere when she get up."

"Don't worry about that. We will explain to your folks what happened," Micah said.

"Why is ya heah?" Elijah asked Ezekiel.

"Ah come ta play wid Jesse," Ezekiel said.

"In da middle of da night?" Elijah asked.

"He gimme some candy yesterday, and he let me play wid his pup. He say, if Ah meet 'im ta night, he gon' gimme some mo' candy, and he say he gon' gimme a pup. He say not ta tell nobody else, cause he ain't got enough candy fuh everybody. He say he jes' got enough fuh him and me." Ezekiel explained.

"So, ya snuck on out heah by ya self ta meet 'im?" Elijah added.

Micah, who was standing near Jesse, looked down at Jesse. A scowling look covered Micah's face. It was a look that made Jesse's heart race with fear.

"We thought you were using candy to get them to come to you," Micah remarked to Jesse.

Jesse didn't say a word. He looked down at the ground, trying not to make eye contact with Micah.

"Let dis be a lesson ta ya," Elijah said to Ezekiel, "don't never go out, and not tell yo' folks where ya goin'. It's all kinds of evil in da worl'. Yo' folks can't protect ya from it iffen ya don't trust 'em enough ta tell 'em everythang. Da worl' too dangerous fuh ya ta hide stuff from yo' folks. Ya understand?"

"Yassuh," Ezekiel said.

Hours went by before Rory returned with Risby and Ran. There was just under an hour before sun-up. There was much to discuss, much to consider. Rory was left to guard Jesse. Elijah, Micah, Risby, and Ran went off into the distance to discuss Jesse's fate. Micah wasted no time making his feelings known as to what he felt should be done.

"I vote we let Wallace go. A few days from now, I will see to it that he never harms another soul," Micah said.

"So, you wanna kill him?" Risby asked, "Well, what about his pappy? He a powerful man round dese parts. He won't rest until he finds out whoever kilt his boy."

"No man can plunder a strong man's home, except he first kill the strong man," Micah said.

"Ah don't wanna go dat route," Elijah said, "it done already been enough killin'. It ain't right ta kill a man and his whole house fuh what his son done. What else kin we do? "

"Ah don't know," Ran said, "we can't go ta da law. A black man ain't got no part in da law, not again no white man. Da law ain't gon' help us."

"It's gotta be somethin' we kin do dat's better 'an mo' killin'," Elijah said.

"We ain't gotta kill da whole family. We can jes' kill da boy. He snuck out his house. His folks ain't gotta never know what happened to 'im," Ran said.

"He a chil', y'all," Elijah argued, "Ah ain't fuh killin' chil'ens."

"Elijah," Micah said, "During the war, toward the end of it, we came upon a town with old men and young boys left to defend it. Boys around Jesse Wallace's age or younger fired on us. It is impossible for me to know if I killed one of them during the fighting, but one thing is certain. They fired on us, and we fired back. I didn't care to fight old men and young boys. I signed on to kill men who fought for the rebs, not boys. I had to ask myself this one question: was I going to be any less dead because a child fired the shot that killed me? The answer was 'no'. There are things you are asked to do during a war. Things that will surely turn your stomach, but at the end of the day. You have got to do what you've got to do in order to survive. Make no mistake about it. This is a war, and we've got to do what we've got to do."

"He's right, Elijah," Ran agreed.

"Ain't no cause, never, ta kill a chil'," Elijah scolded.

"Well, what do you want to do? Let him go free, and not be punished for what he did?" Micah asked in a somewhat angry manner.

"Maybe, dat's what we oughta do. Don't y'all see where dis thang goin'. It's trouble. White folks is hell, and Ah jes' as soon not deal wit' 'em," Risby said.

"How we know he ain't gon' kill again iffen we let 'im go?" Ran asked.

"Risby, we gotta make a stand heah," Elijah said, "We can't let 'im go, and we can't kill 'im."

"Well den, what we gon' do?" Risby asked.

"O'm fuh takin' 'im home ta his folks, and lettin' 'em know what he been doin'," Elijah said.

Micah laughed mockingly. "And, what's dat suppose to do? Do you think that boy's father is going to side with us, a bunch of niggers, against his own son. I tell you nay. It ain't gonna happen. We should put an end to this here and now."

"We can't kill 'im. He jes' a chil'," Elijah insisted.

"A cold-blooded nasty little bastard is what he is, and given the chance, he will kill again. It is our responsibility to stop him. It is to our advantage to do it now," Micah insisted.

"Ah won't kill 'im," Elijah stated firmly, "Ah wanna take da boy home ta his folks, and give 'em a chance ta do da right thang."

"Elijah, if I'm that boy's father, the right thing for me to do is protect him at all costs. Rest assured that is what he is going to do. We are an insipid race to whites. They don't see us as worthy of their respect or consideration. That boy could kill a hundred of our children, and I doubt his father would do much to stop him," Micah argued.

"Ah don't believe dat. Ah believe every man got good in 'im, and he oughta git da chance ta do da good and right thang," Elijah said, believing this fully.

"Will somebody talk to him," Micah said, very frustrated with Elijah.

"Ran, what cha thank we ought do?" Elijah asked.

"Ah don't know. At first, Ah say kill 'im, but now Ah jes' don't know. Dis a hard row ta hoe. Ah'll go along wid what y'all decide," he said, perplexed by the matter.

"Risby?" Elijah said, inquiring as to what he thought should be done.

Risby took a deep uncertain breath. "Ah reckon O'm gon' side wid you, Elijah. We can't kill 'im, and we can't let 'im go free."

"It's settled, O'm gon' take da boy home ta his folks, and O'm gon' ask 'em ta lock 'im in da asylum," Elijah decided.

"You are all making a mistake," Micah warned.

"Maybe, but it's da right thang ta do," Elijah said.

The debate was over, and the decision had been made, as to what to do with Jesse Wallace. The four men returned to where Rory and the children were. Rory was wondering what came now. Not only Rory, but Jesse as well. Jesse knew that they had been debating whether to kill him or not. His heart was racing.

"Get up, Mista Jesse," Elijah said.

"What are y'all going to do with me?" Jesse asked, afraid they were planning to kill him.

"You wont us ta come wid cha ta do dis?" Risby asked.

"What are y'all gonna do to me?" Jesse asked again, not liking the most obvious possibility.

"Ah reckon not," Elijah answered Risby, "Y'all see Ezekiel on home."

"I am going with you," Micah informed Elijah.

From Jesse's point of view, Micah was a threat to his life. He was very displeased and frightened to hear Micah was coming along. Along to do what? Was what he asked himself.

"Stand up, Mista Jesse," Elijah said.

"What's going on? What's about to happen?" Jesse asked.

"We are going to take you home to your parents," Micah answered.

"You're going to take me home?" Jesse asked, not really trusting what he was hearing.

Jesse was expecting Elijah and Micah to kill him. He believed they were lying to him just so he would cooperate. He stood, and his legs began to shake. He thought of running, but his legs felt sluggish from all the sitting he had done while waiting for his captors to assemble and decide his fate.

"Why would you let me live?" Jesse asked, believing they meant to kill him.

"See, he knows what he is deserving of," Micah said to Elijah.

"Why should we kill you, Mista Jesse?" Elijah said, "Youse sick, a sick soul need ta be helped, not kilt. We gon' take ya to yo' folks. So, dey kin git ya some help."

Jesse had never seen himself as suffering from a sickness. He did not understand why Elijah saw him that way. It was not the way of the world to want to help someone, who had fallen in such a manner as Jesse had. The way of the world was an eye for an eye. Even so, Jesse believed Elijah. There was something in Elijah that was trustworthy. He began not to fear that he would be killed by Elijah and Micah.

Nineteen

At the Wallace home, breakfast was being served. Everyone was present at the table except for Jesse.

"Jesse still asleep?" Franklin asked.

"He isn't in his room," Blanch answered.

"He probably got up early, and is out with that dog of his," Joselpha said.

"If he would rather play with that ole mutt of a dog than eat breakfast, it is fine by me," Blanch remarked.

"He needs to eat," Franklin said, "we've got plenty of work to do around here. He needs to keep up his strength. I'm going to go fetch him."

Franklin was outside, preparing to look in the barn to see if Jesse was inside playing with his dog. Before he could do so, he saw Jesse coming across the front lawn in the company of two blacks, Elijah and Micah. Franklin wondered what business Jesse had with these men. Perhaps, they were interested in working for him. Franklin stood there on the porch, waiting for them to draw closer. When they were close enough to have a conversation, Jesse looked down at the ground. This body language told Franklin that Jesse had done something that he didn't have any business doing, and was ashamed to look him in the eyes.

"Has my son gotten himself into trouble?" Franklin asked, believing nothing very serious had happened, unprepared for what was ahead of him.

"Yassuh," Elijah answered, "he done done somethin'. We thought we oughta brang 'im on home to ya."

"What have you done, son?" Franklin asked, expecting some light infraction.

Jesse still could not bring himself to look at Franklin, and could not bring himself to utter a word.

"Yo' boy is sick, Mista Wallace," Elijah said, "he mighty sick, and we wont cha ta git 'im some help."

"Are you not feeling well, Jesse?" Franklin asked. "Come here so Ah can feel your forehead to see if you are warm to the touch."

Jesse tried to move to Franklin. Micah put a hand on Jesse's shoulder, and Jesse did not move. The fact that Micah would dare put his hand on Jesse made Franklin sizzle.

"It ain't dat kinda sick, Mista Wallace," Elijah informed, "ain't too many white folks around dese parts know about dis, but somebody been killin' black young on's, Mista Wallace."

"What does that have to do with my son?" Franklin asked.

It became difficult for Elijah to be candid about this. It was almost as difficult for Elijah to come out with it, as it was for Jesse to look at Franklin.

"Your son is the one that has been committing the murders," Micah said frankly.

"Surely, you jest, boy," Franklin replied, "it's not amusing."

Micah was nobody's boy, and didn't care for Franklin calling him one.

"It's da truth, Mista Wallace," Elijah exclaimed.

"My son is no murderer, and Ah dare you black devils come onto my property making such bold accusations. You overstep your bounds," Franklin said, becoming furious.

"Told you," Micah said to Elijah, about ready to snatch Franklin off of the porch for his insolent retort.

"We ain't heah ta make ya mad, Mista Wallace. We jes' gotta deal wit' dis heah problem," Elijah said.

"Jesse, come here," Franklin commanded, feeling as if he needed to defend his son.

Jesse moved onto the porch behind Franklin. He did not say a word.

"You two get off of my property," Franklin commanded Elijah and Micah.

"Mista Wallace–" Elijah said.

"No lip, boy," Franklin interrupted, "just get off my property."

"Mista Wallace, we gotta talk about dis," Elijah tried to reason.

"Didn't you hear me say to get? You have become a disobedient race in your freedom. In the days of old, Ah would have you flogged to within an inch of your very lives for your back-talk and vicious lies," Franklin raved.

"Those days are gone, and you had best, get that through your head," Micah said boldly.

"What did you say?" Franklin asked, ready to knock Micah to the ground.

"Calm down now, Mista Franklin, we gotta talk about dis. Mista Jesse sick, and ya gotta git 'im some help," Elijah said, trying to be the voice of reason.

"You don't tell me how to deal with my own son, boy! Ah tell you, and Ah will deal with this. Now get off of my property."

"We wont cha ta put 'im in a asylum, Mista Wallace. His sickness can't hurt nobody else dere," Elijah said.

"Who do you presume yourself to be, that you think you can make demands of me?" Franklin barked.

"Mista Wallace, Ah's tryin' ta work dis out wit' cha.You gotta calm down, and jes' hear me out," Elijah said, "please, suh, jes' listen."

Elijah was very cool and controlled in his tone. His voice was very calm and respectful. The anger in Franklin started to decrease. He was starting to get into a mood to listen. Micah kept quiet, not desiring to be a disruptive force.

Elijah said nothing for a moment. He was trying to give Franklin time to compose himself. When Elijah felt Franklin was emotionally poised, he continued. "Mista Wallace, Ah knows dis hard ta hear, but Mista Jesse got caught tryin' ta choke a lit' boy ta death las' night. Ah wish Ah could jes' turn 'im over ta ya and be done wit' it, but Ah can't. Ah gotta know he won't never again spill innocent blood. Please suh, try to understand dat."

"My son is not a murderer. He wouldn't do that. He is not capable of murder," Franklin contended. He looked at Jesse. "Jesse, tell them there has been some kind of mistake. Tell them you would never kill. Tell them."

Jesse wanted to say something, but the words got in the way. He had murdered, and the look of impenitent guilt upon his face wouldn't allow him to hide the evil deeds of his hands. Jesse's silence and the transparent guilt upon his face told Franklin that he was guilty of all Elijah and Micah had said. It was a crushing realization for Franklin.

As a father, he had always tried to do the best by his children he could. He had taught Jesse right from wrong–to be God fearing. He had tried to teach him how to conduct his life in a manner in which he could hold his head up without shame. Yet, despite all of Franklin's good intentions, despite all he had tried to teach his son, it had not been enough. Franklin felt an absolute failure as a father at that very moment. There was a deep sadness in Franklin. It was such an intense hurt that Franklin was confused.

"Ah'll send him away. Ah'll send him to an eastern school for boys," Franklin said regretfully, "He can do your people no harm there."

Elijah saw that Franklin was hurting. He felt compassion for him, but what Franklin was suggesting was not good enough.

"Suh, dat sound fine. It will take care of our problems round heah, but what of dems dat don't know about da sickness inside 'im wherever it is you gon' send 'im. He might kill again. We can't jes' push 'im off on nobody else like dat," Elijah said.

"He won't kill anyone else! Ah'll see to it," Franklin shouted, "besides, what does it matter to you what he does someplace else? All that should matter to you is that he isn't harming your kind. He is no longer your concern. He is my concern, and Ah will handle it from here."

"Youse wrong about dat, suh. He my concern, and you gotta put 'im where his sickness can't hurt nobody else. It gotta be done," Elijah said sternly.

"Ah will not commit my son to an asylum. That is out of the question," Franklin insisted.

"Ya gotta put 'im somewhere where dey know what he done done. Ya gotta put 'im where dey kin keep a eye on 'im. Dat's da way it gotta be, suh," Elijah demanded.

"Watch your step, boy. It sounds like you are telling me, and Ah won't be told by the likes of you, what to do with my own son," Franklin made clear.

"Ah don't mean no harm, suh, but Ah is tellin' ya," Elijah said point blank.

"And, what will you do if Ah refuse to lock my boy away, go to the sheriff?" Franklin said, not caring for Elijah's boldness, trying to feel out Elijah's intentions.

"No suh, you and me both know dey ain't gon' do nothin'. So, Ah can't turn ta dem," Elijah said.

"Then, what will you do?" Franklin asked, curious to know how Elijah planned to enforce his edict of having Jesse committed.

"O'm gon' go ta da Freedmen's Bureau. Dey couldn't help us when we didn't know who was killin', but dey kin help us now. Dey helped a black man up in Chattanooga get justice against a white man fuh beatin' 'im fuh no call. Ah's sho dey kin help us handle dis, but Ah don't wanna do it like dat. Ah wanna spare ya da open shame of havin' everybody knowin' what Mista Jesse done. Ah wanna give ya da chance ta do da right thang," Elijah said.

Franklin became very concerned by Elijah's declaration that he intended to involve the Freedmen's Bureau. He now had no choice but to recognize Elijah's demands, and reconcile to the fact that he had to act.

"Go inside, Jesse," Franklin instructed.

Franklin said nothing more until Jesse was inside the house. Elijah and Micah looked at Franklin with quiet very serious resolve.

"Ah shall consider your demands," Franklin said, "only, Ah will need some time. My wife and Jesse's sisters will need time to digest all of this. Surely, you understand."

"Ah do, suh. Ah understands dis a hard thang ta wrap yo'self around," Elijah answered, "how much time ya thank you gon' need?"

"A few days at most," Franklin answered.

"All right den, Mista Wallace, take a few days to git yo' family ready fuh dis," Elijah said.

Micah stood there observing Franklin. He did not trust Franklin. There was something about the angry look in Franklin's eyes, and his agreeable demeanor and words. They were not congruent. This told Micah that Franklin honored them with his lips, but betrayal lurked in his heart. Micah heard a canard behind Franklin's soothing words and saw treachery was forthcoming.

"Thank you for bringing him home to us and not taking matters into your own hands. Ah will deal fairly with you," Franklin promised.

Elijah and Micah left. Neither of them had any illusions, they knew assuredly a fight was coming, but Elijah was hopeful that Franklin would do the right thing. He wanted to give Franklin a chance to do the good and profitable thing.

Franklin watched them leave. He would not be dictated to by former slaves. They were less than men in his opinion and were not worthy to make any demands of him. Yet, he couldn't ignore them. Elijah had threatened to involve the Freedmen's Bureau. The bureau would no doubt come to the aide of the Negroes. Although the Freedmen's Bureau had no legal jurisdiction in such matters, the bureau's very interest in the matter would put considerable pressure on the powers that be. Southern authorities wouldn't have the spine to stand up to the Yankee protagonists. They would bow to Yankee demands. Once that happened, the regular court system would be with the Negroes, Franklin feared. Jesse would be lost if that happened. Franklin simply couldn't allow that to take place. He had to curtail this thing before outside forces exerted their influence. Franklin went inside. Jesse was now seated at the breakfast table, but wasn't eating. He could hardly look at his father. Franklin didn't say anything to him.

"Elizabeth, may Ah speak with you for a moment," Franklin said.

"What is it, dear," Elizabeth responded, not yet done eating.

"It is a private matter, my dear."

Elizabeth looked at Franklin. There was a degree of none cooperation in her eyes, but she saw distress in Franklin's eyes. Distress so powerful that she became agreeable. She stood from the table, and they walked into the parlor. Franklin closed the door behind them.

"What is it?" Elizabeth asked.

"Ah don't want to alarm you, but Ah feel you need to know. Jesse has some problems. Problems which Ah am now forced to deal with," Franklin said.

"What are you talking about?" Elizabeth asked.

"Jesse has been killing Negro children. He was found out last night."

Elizabeth laughed faintly, thinking Franklin was joking. She soon realized Franklin was serious. "Ah don't believe it."

"Ah didn't want to believe it either, but it is true," Franklin assured.

"Who told you this preposterous lie?" Elizabeth said. "And, why do you believe it?"

"Jesse wasn't at breakfast this morning, because he wasn't home last night. He was out trying to kill a Negro child. The Negroes caught him in the act. They returned him home to us this morning," Franklin explained.

"How can you believe the coloreds over your own son?"

"Ah didn't believe them. Ah believed Jesse. He didn't deny their accusation."

"Jesse wouldn't kill anyone, not even a nigger. Ah will prove it. We will call him in here. He will tell you the truth," Elizabeth said, not wanting to believe this obscenity of her son.

Elizabeth headed for the door. Franklin grabbed her by the arm and looked her in the eyes.

"There is more, Elizabeth," Franklin said, with a look of deep concern, "the Negroes want us to have Jesse committed, and they are threatening to bring in Yankee government officials to force us into compliance."

This shook Elizabeth. She clung to Franklin. "No. You mustn't let that happen."

"Ah won't, Elizabeth. Ah promise you that Ah will handle this," Franklin assured.

There were certain men that Franklin knew. He often drank with them. He was certain that they would be willing to help him deal with this unsavory business. It was early yet. Many of these men wouldn't be available to him at this time of day, but it would take some time to reach Olive Branch. By then, some of them would be at the town saloon. Franklin left the house without a goodbye. He mounted up and headed for town.

Elizabeth returned to the breakfast table. A strange mix of sadness, doubt, and fear began to overwhelm her. She looked at Jesse, and he knew that she was aware of what he had been doing. There was nothing Jesse could say. He looked down at his plate, as a defensive frown formed upon his face. It was a very uncomfortable breakfast for them both.

Now as it would happen, several of the men that Franklin had in mind were waiting outside Bush's General Store. It was not that they intended to purchase anything from Bush. They were simply waiting for the saloon to open at noon, and it seemed more becoming to them to wait in front of the general store instead of the saloon. It didn't bother them that there was a law against vagrancy. That law was more for lazy coloreds. The men were Elam Webster, Asa Saunders, Zechariah Barnes, and Benjamin Klein.

Elam was a man around five feet ten inches in height. He was a slender, but solid looking man. He had a broad, round, face with a steady chin, and grave blue eyes. His hair was black, and he had a tapered beard which covered his face. He also had a mustache. He was a farmer, and a man of unforgiving qualities.

Asa Saunders was five feet nine inches in height. He was a very thin man. He had a round slender face with deep seated gray eyes. He had a wide mouth with very thin lips. His face was clean shaven. His hair was brown and tapered, with a part on the left side. His ears weren't big, but they had a flaring quality. Asa was a bit of a redneck and a dependable sort.

Benjamin Klein was just over six feet. He was also a slender man, but heavier than Asa, and not quite as unshakable looking in his build as Elam. He had critical brown eyes. His hair was brown, and was combed to the back with a part down the center. His hair was fairly long and straight, and curled at the ends just below his ears. He had no mustache, and the sides of his face were clean shaven with a brown goatee on his chin that hung two inches. He had a stern face, which looked as if it had forgotten how to smile. He was very analytical, very given to reason.

The last of them was Zechariah Barnes. He was the most gifted of them intellectually, but wasted his gift on useless endeavors. He was a professional gambler, and was very skilled at his trade. Zechariah was six feet even. He was an intelligent looking man, who was quite good looking. He had tapered black hair with a large bushy mustache above his lips, and a small, slender, goatee.

Asa and Elam were engaged in conversation sitting on the porch in front of the store. Benjamin and Zechariah were busy reading old newspapers from up North, the New York Tribune to be exact. Zechariah was seated in a chair, and Benjamin was standing, braced against a pole. Benjamin made several noticeable, displeased, and very disagreeable sounds as he read. He took the paper, almost daring to rip it in two.

"These Yankees are a wretched lot," Benjamin said unwaveringly.

267

"How so?" Zechariah asked, as he stopped reading the paper to look at Benjamin.

"They refer to the war in this paper as the 'war between the states'. Why can't they just call it what it was. It was the war of southern independence," Benjamin professed, "You know in a generation or so, they will have it completely wrong if the Yankees keep perverting the truth the way that they are.

"The way this Yankee paper reads, you would think the South fought to preserve slavery. Damn few southerners owned slaves. Ah would venture to say that more than ninety percent of southerners didn't own slaves. To read this paper, you would think slaves were as common a commodity as was cotton before the war, and every southerner owned one. That is a deceitful lie. We fought for our independence, not slavery. They paint us the villain."

"To the victor goes the spoils of war, Benjamin," Zechariah said, "Surely, you didn't expect the North to publicize that the North and South had become two uniquely different economic and social cultures that clashed. Surely, you didn't expect them to admit that we had every right under the constitution to break away. You couldn't have expected them to admit that the North invaded the South unprovoked, because it feared countries, such as England and France, would recognize the Confederacy as a sovereign state, separate and apart, from the North. You couldn't have expected the North to release the South, who paid a disproportionate amount of taxes for benefits received. You didn't expect them to go broke while the South prospered by attracting foreign trade with our lower tariff. All these things would have meant the slow demise of the North. The whole war was about lucre, and nothing more. Surely, you can't expect the North to admit that, not when a lie will do."

Elam and Asa had stopped talking to listen in on Benjamin and Zechariah's conversation, which seemed more interesting.

"Ah know, but the whole perception of the South in northern papers is a nagging thorn in my side,"Benjamin said.

"The whole war was Abraham Lincoln's fault, anyway," Asa said.

"Yes, and Booth did him no disservice when he put a bullet in the back of his skull," Elam added.

"Lincoln was a lying hypocrite," Benjamin said.

"Sure was. Not only Lincoln, but Ulysses S. Grant, too," Asa added, "General Lee never owned slaves, but Grant did."

"Not that Ah disagree, Benjamin, but how was Lincoln a lying hypocrite?" Zechariah asked.

"Lincoln had the nerve to declare all slaves held within the Confederacy free. He didn't have the right to do that, but there were six parishes in Louisiana, and forty-eight counties in Virginia that remained loyal to the union. It was legally within his power to free slaves held within those counties and parishes, but he didn't. That makes him a lying hypocrite in my estimation," Benjamin said.

"Ah hate to play devil's advocate, but during the war it was Lincoln's, so called, responsibility to prevent any further rift in his country. It wouldn't have been wise of the man to alienate his allies with such a move as freeing their slaves."

Benjamin looked oddly and quite disapprovingly at Zechariah. "You know for a Southerner. Sometimes, you sound just like a damn Yankee."

"Ah suppose you think the darkies deserve to be free," Elam said to Zechariah, "Well, Ah don't. It's hard enough for the average white man to make a living for himself and his family without having to compete with some darky, who is willing to work for half of what a white man would. He will work for less, because he needs less. The nigger is just a little higher than a dog. He is use to living like an animal. He has no pride, no ambition, or any concept of what it is to be human. Now Ah ask you. How can the white man compete with something like that? We can't, and shouldn't have to. If niggers aren't here as slaves, they need to go back to Africa."

"Lincoln wanted to send them to Haiti and Liberia," Benjamin added.

"Too much expense in that, Ah'm afraid we are stuck with them," Zechariah laughed.

"You won't find it so funny when your daughter brings home some sex-crazed, thick-lipped, nigger, who spills his seed in her day and night, spewing forth little mongrel babies," Asa cut.

"Easy there, Asa," Zechariah said, "Ah merely think that a conversation is more interesting when an opposing narrative is presented. One should not take that to mean that Ah am siding with the North or niggers. On the contrary, like you, Ah believe that this is our country. White men made it what it is today. If anyone should have the upper-hand in it, Ah am of the opinion that it should be us. As for my daughter bedding niggers, if Ah had one, Ah would kill her before Ah would let her marry a black."

"Spare your daughter, kill the nigger," Asa said jokingly.

"Ah suspect we shall shortly have bigger problems to contend with than niggers sleeping with our women. Ah hear that the Yankee legislature in

Washington is trying to enfranchise the Negro. There is serious talk, that they are trying to give them the same rights as white men." Benjamin said.

"The vengeance of their spiteful northern hearts," Asa said.

"Don't they understand that blacks don't have the mental capacity to endure such responsibilities as come with being a fully enfranchised citizen. Hell, they don't even understand what it is to be free yet. They are ignorant wretches. How can you entrust them with the vote?" Elam asked.

"Well, the North means to give it to them," Benjamin said.

"Ah'd feel more comfortable giving women the right to vote," Elam said.

"Would you really?" Zechariah asked.

"No. That's six in one hand and half a dozen in the other," Elam answered laughing.

"Even if the North does try to give niggers the same rights as whites. It's one thing for niggers to have rights and another thing for them to use 'em. Do you boys know of Bedford Forrest?" Asa asked.

"General Nathan Forrest's kin?" Zechariah asked.

"Bedford's got some definite ideas about how to deal with this growing nigger problem," Asa informed, "he's sure niggers can be persuaded not to exercise their impending new found rights. He is sure they can be persuaded not to unleash their nigger passions, so that they don't soil the virtue and integrity of white women. He is sure they can be persuaded to keep their place, if you understand my meaning."

What Asa was suggesting was a very old paradigm, even at this point in history. The use of violence to advance a said group's social and/or political agenda has a name. It is called terrorism. Beginning at this point in American history, hate was starting to take a physical form in the United Stated. Over time, it would take many names, the white line of Mississippi, the pale faces, the constitutional union guard, the knights of the white camellia, and of course Bedford Forrest's ku klux klan.

These terrorist groups had but one purpose in mind, to prevent the black race from gaining a significant social, financial, and political foothold in the cultural landscape of the United States. Not only the Negro was at risk, but anyone who would help the Negro better himself. Through these terrorist organizations, the South was hoping to ensure an opportunity to regain power and momentum in Washington. This without having to compete with the Negro politically as they struggled to do so. Thus, preserving the white race's dominant role in the South, and more importantly the country.

As the men sat there, Franklin rode up. They were quite surprised to see him in the middle of the day.

"What brings you out this early in the day, Franklin?" Zechariah asked. "Don't tell me that you couldn't wait to lose money to me in a card game."

Franklin climbed from his horse and took a seat next to his consorts on the porch.

"Something the matter?" Elam asked.

"Ah have a thing which is difficult to solve," Franklin answered.

"You have a problem," Zechariah simplified.

"What is it? Perhaps, we can help you," Benjamin said.

"There is this colored boy. He is causing me some distress," Franklin admitted.

All of the men laughed. Franklin wondered what was so funny.

"We were just talking about the nigger problem, Franklin," Elam said.

"You know they are getting a little too drunken with their freedom if they distress a man like you," Benjamin said.

"We know what to do for that nigger to teach him some manners, Franklin," Asa said.

"What is he doing that he has no business, Franklin?" Elam asked.

Franklin did not really care to say, and the men saw as much on his face.

"That doesn't matter, Elam. Our friend has come to us with a problem. A problem that we can help him solve. It does not matter what the boy is doing to cause the problem. It only matters that he is a problem," Zechariah said.

The others understood not to press Franklin for more information as to what the problem was.

"Who is this crazed nigger that is troubling you?" Asa asked.

"His name is Elijah," Franklin answered.

"Elijah Wright?" Asa asked.

"The very same," Franklin answered, "You know him then?"

"Ah know of him," Asa replied.

"Ah would like to pay him a visit tonight," Franklin said, "would that be a problem for you, Asa?"

"Ah said that Ah know of the boy. Not that Ah like him, or care what happens to him," Asa made clear.

"Should we bring a rope, or do you just want him knocked around for a bit?" Benjamin asked.

Franklin had not given much thought to that. He didn't want to kill Elijah, but he felt that he really did not have a choice. It was a possibility that beating Elijah badly would not deter him from involving the Freedmen's Bureau. Killing Elijah would stop him from involving the Freedmen's Bureau, and was also sure to deter anyone who might consider rising in Elijah's stead.

"Ah think he has to die," Franklin answered.

All of them wondered what Elijah did that was so wrong that Franklin wanted to kill him for it. Asa couldn't resist trying to find out why he wanted Elijah dead. "Did that nigger try to force himself on one of your daughters?"

"Ah suppose you have a right to know why Ah'm asking you to kill," Franklin allowed.

"Perhaps, but if you don't feel comfortable sharing that with us. Ah don't want you to feel obligated to say. You were an officer in the confederate army, and you are a man of importance in this community. If this Elijah got out of line with you, Ah'm sure you are justified in killing him," Zechariah said.

"Niggers gotta be made to learn that they still have to respect us, free or not," Asa said, still fishing for a motive.

"That they must," Elam agreed.

"Tell you what, Franklin," Benjamin said, "The saloon is about to open. Why don't you buy us a few drinks. Then, we will get a few more of the boys together and around dusk we will ride on over to niggerville and pay this boy a visit."

This sounded good to Franklin. It was better to be a little bit drunk when you killed a man. It tended to help dull the guilt of what you had done. They headed for the saloon, and waited for darkness to fall.

Twenty

At Elijah's place, Elijah and Micah had been at odds as to how matters should have been handled concerning Jesse Wallace. At the moment, there was a very uncomfortable silence between Elijah and Micah, as they sat at the table. Elijah was in deep thought, telling himself that he did the right thing. Micah looked at him wondering how Elijah planned to deal with what is surely coming.

"What are you gonna do?" Micah asked.

"Huh?" Elijah said.

"What are you planning to do?" Micah asked. "You know as well as I do that while we are sitting here doing nothing. Franklin Wallace is no doubt getting a few of his rowdy friends together. They are gonna ride through here sounding like thunder, and they are going to strike hard. They are gonna burn down your whole world before your eyes, and then they will kill you. You know that I'm right. What are you going to do about it?"

"What cha wont me ta do, Micah? Ah's tryin' ta do da right thang, and dat's givin' da man a chance ta do right by us."

"Listen to yourself, Elijah. You need to ask yourself when has the white man ever done right by us. They didn't bring us to this country to treat us right. How many times do I have to tell you that before you understand? They are treacherous bastards, and they are going to kill you if you don't take measures to stop them. Trust me, I know. White men that fought alongside me in the same uniform during the war, tried to take my life. If they could do that to me, who fought alongside them, imagine what they are gonna do to you for standing against them."

"Ah ain't scared of 'em, Micah, and Ah ain't gon' run from 'em. Ah's a man jes' like dey is. Iffen dey kills me, dat's dey sin. Dey da ones dat's gon' habe ta stand befo' da judgement seat of Christ, and give a account fuh what dey done. God gon' give 'em dey just reward. And, killin' me still ain't gon' do 'em no good, cause you gon' stand in my place, and see dat justice git done."

To Micah, Elijah was talking like a madman. Josephine and Mama Julia thought so as well, as they listened from the next room. Micah was frustrated by Elijah. Elijah may have been willing to die, but Micah wasn't willing to let him die without a fight.

"I understand that you are not afraid to die. I understand that's something every man has to do, but there are people depending on you. Your wife and child need you. Mama Julia and I need you. You just can't let these men take your life, because they want to take it. You oughta know that I won't stand by and let it happen. So, I ask again. What are you planning to do to stop Franklin Wallace from killing you and me?"

"And, Ah ask again. What kin Ah do? Runnin' is da only thang Ah kin see ta do, and Ah ain't gon' do dat. So you tell me, what is Ah ta do?"

"We have to fight," Micah insisted.

"A blood-thirsty man only lives half his days, Micah. Violence ain't da way. It ain't never been da way," Elijah said.

Once again, Micah looked at Elijah as though he were insane. He didn't understand Elijah nor Elijah's way. Elijah was not a coward. He had proven that time and again. Yet, he wouldn't kill men who sought to kill him unjustly. Seeing Elijah would not condone violence, Micah began to think of other ways to deal with the impending danger.

"Okay, Elijah, if that's the way you want it. Let's try it this way. We will call a meeting this evening. We will ask everyone to stand with us when they come for you. Wallace probably won't have anymore than ten or fifteen men with him. If thirty or forty of us are here waiting for them. They won't try to kill you for fear of forfeiting their own lives in the process. This is the way to go. It's a preventive measure, and it is peaceful. Does that satisfy you?"

"Ah reckon," Elijah said with a look of not being totally sure upon his face.

"Then let's see to this. Daylight is burning, as Risby says," Micah said, feeling pressed for time.

Micah and Elijah went about the business of trying to get everyone together to organize a peaceful resistance. They visited Risby and Ran first, and then they all split to get the word out to meet at Risby's place by five.

By five, they had a very good turnout. At least forty-five men were there. Micah didn't waste time calling everyone to order. "Thank all of you for turning out for this meeting," he said, "as many of you may have heard, We caught the person responsible for murdering our children. Unfortunately, it was the son of a prominent white man, Franklin Wallace. Jesse Wallace is the one who has been killing Jago's children. We went to Franklin Wallace, and asked him to have his son committed."

Immediately, murmuring began among the men. They all knew that this spelled big trouble. Trouble they didn't want.

"As a result of this, I believe that Wallace is going to try to kill my brother tonight. That is where you men come in. If we all stand together at my brother's home, Franklin Wallace and those with him will not make trouble," Micah said confidently.

There was greater murmuring from the men. There was congruent discontent among them with what Micah was asking them to do. Fear grew among them. The cool response of complaining from the men gathered there was disheartening, and was cause for concern from Elijah.

"Da battle is almost won y'all," Elijah assured, "iffen you jes' stan' wit' me, no mo' blood will be shed."

Trents was among the crowd of men. He didn't want to risk his life, nor did anyone else there.

"Elijah," Trents said, "why when y'all found out who was doin' da killin'. Why y'all didn't turn it over ta da sheriff?"

"You know why," Risby interjected, "because he ain't been no help ta us in da pas'."

"Still you should've tried," someone in the crowd said.

"Iffen we come ta ya house, and stand wit' cha, what you spect gon' happen when Franklin Wallace and da rest of dem white mens come," Trents asked.

"Nothing," Micah assured, "they won't start trouble, but that's only if everyone here stands together."

"Ah don't know," someone else in the crowd said, "what if dey get ta shootin'?"

"They won't," Micah said, "their lives are precious to them. They won't risk their lives if they are out numbered."

"What iffen dey leave dere, but pays each and every man who was wit' cha a visit later on. When we ain't all together," Trents asked?

"There is some risk to us all. I won't stand here and tell you differently, but in my opinion, it is worth the risk to secure the safety of our children," Micah said.

"We ain't asked y'all ta do dat," still another voice cried out from the crowd, "we can keep our own chil'un safe, and our own necks too. Y'all shouldn't have stepped out dere like dat. Y'all forcin' da whites ta come in heah and kill you, and y'all want us ta stand wit' cha so we can get killed too. Well, Ah can't do dat."

"My friend," Elijah said, "Ah ain't askin' ya ta die. Ah's askin' ya ta live. Ah's askin' ya ta live like a man. We's men now, every last one of us is mens now, and one man ought not fear another man. Only da God dat made us is worthy of our fear, and him alone. What good is yo' life iffen ya gots ta live it in fear. It's wrong for Jesse Wallace ta kill our chil'ens. It's even greater sin fuh us ta abide in fear, and not demand dat he stop it."

"Elijah," Trents said, "why y'all demand dat Mista Wallace lock his son away? Y'all could've jes' told 'im what his boy was doin' and let it at dat. Maybe, Mista Wallace would've stopped 'im from killin'. Y'all shouldn't have backed 'im inta a corner like dat."

"And, what iffen he didn't?" Risby asked. "Dat boy seems ta like killin'. He like it so much dat Ah don't thank he'd stop on his own."

"Well, y'all should habe gabe 'im da chance," someone from the crowd yelled.

Micah had learned from times past not to say too much at these meetings. Nevertheless, it was hard for him to stand by and listen to them. Micah believed that a man had to be a man, and he was proud to hear Elijah say as much. The others there, however, almost made his stomach turn with their docile weakness.

"Y'all hold a meetin' fuh every thang else. How come y'all ain't hold no meetin' when y'all found out dat Jesse Wallace was doin' da killin'. We should've all been had a chance ta have our say about da decision of what ta do. Dat was da time y'all should've been callin' a meetin'. Not now, when y'all done stirred up all dis heah trouble," Trents said.

"It wa'n't no time fuh dat. A decision had ta be made, and Ah made it," Elijah explained.

"You made da decision, but we gotta suffer wit' cha iffen it's a bad decision. Ah say iffen you bake yo' pie, you oughta eat it. And Ah say you oughta not ask nobody else ta help you eat yo' bad pie," still another person from among them said.

Elijah did not care for all the grief he was receiving for the decision to spare Jesse Wallace's life, and insist that the boy be committed to an insane asylum. It was the right decision from Elijah's perspective. It would have been wrong to kill Jesse, and it would have been equally irresponsible to leave him in an environment which would still allow him to kill. Yet, no one seemed to see this. Elijah stood behind his decision. Even if he had to stand behind it alone. "Ah did da only decent thang dat could be done at da time," he said, void of anger or contempt for his brethren as they ridiculed him. "Any of y'all dat don't wanna walk wit' me, don't feel like ya gotta. Do what each of ya feel it is good ta do. Ah won't ask no mo' of ya dan dat."

Immediately, they forsook him. Micah saw them walking away, and was deeply offended by them. "What the hell is wrong with you people?" He lashed out. "A monster has been killing your children, and you wanna look the other way. God help us as a people if you cowardly fools are the best we've got."

"Micah," Elijah said, "let 'em go."

"Where is the man in them?" Micah asked.

"Da only somebody in dis worl' you got control over, is you. You can't force nobody else ta see thangs yo' way, and it don't do ya no good ta git mad about it cause dey don't see thangs yo' way," Elijah said, trying to enlighten his brother.

"We don't stand a chance against Wallace and those with him when they come for you if our own won't stand with us," Micah argued.

"Ah'm wit' y'all," Risby said.

"Ah's wit cha, too," Ran vowed.

"Me too," Rory said.

"Rory, you don't even have any children. You have no reason to risk your neck. I am thankful to you," Micah said, impressed by Rory's loyalty and courage.

"Y'all standin' fuh right, Mista Micah. Ah'll stan' wid any man dat stan' fuh right," Rory said.

After all was said and done, only the five of them remained. Sadly, Elijah realized that five men weren't enough to deal peacefully with Franklin Wallace and the men that would be riding with him. Elijah didn't want these four brave souls to get killed. "Ah thank each and everyone of ya fuh bein' willin' ta walk dis road wit' me, but Ah can't ask ya ta. We is too few, and dat mean fightin'. Ah don't wont cha women and chil'ens ta habe ta bury none of ya. Ah'll walk dis road alone."

"Are you crazy? You are my brother, and I'm going to stand with you," Micah declared.

"Ah ain't scared ta fight, Mista 'lijah. Ah ain't scared ta die. O'm gon' stan' wid cha, and don't you worry bout me," Rory said.

"We in dis thang together," Ran said, not willing to forsake Elijah.

"Sho is," Risby concurred.

"Listen ta me, y'all," Elijah said, "Da five of us is all we got wit' courage enough ta see dis thang ta da end. If all of us is in da same place, and if all of us happen ta git kilt tonight, or which ever night dey come. Who gon' see dat justice git done? Who gonna see dat da killin' of our chil'ens stop. We is precious few, and we gotta go about dis thang wise like. We can't afford dat we should all be lost. Do y'all understand? If Ah fall, it's up ta y'all ta keep up da fight."

"No. We will not desert you," Micah said, "We stand together."

"Micah," Elijah said, placing his hand on Micah's shoulder, "Iffen somethin' happen ta me, Ah need you ta look afta Josie, Caleb, and Mama Julia. Kin Ah depend on you fuh dat?"

"You should have listened to me, and let me kill Jesse Wallace," Micah said, very displeased with this situation.

"Will you take care of my family?" Elijah asked.

"You know that I will," Micah answered.

"It'll be dark soon," Elijah said, "we best git on home."

"You go ahead. I'll be along shortly," Micah said.

"Don't try nothin', Micah. It's better dat one falls dan all of us," Elijah said, knowing Micah.

"Ah won't try anything," Micah assured.

"Okay," Elijah said, "Ah'll be seein' y'all. If not on earth, den when we all git ta heaven."

They all said sad goodbyes, realizing they may never see him again after that night. Elijah made his way home. He expected Micah to come through the door at any moment, but Micah didn't show.

Soon night came, it was a quiet and peaceful night. Elijah sat at his table nervously rubbing his sweaty palms on his legs. He wished Micah was there with him. Could Micah not watch and wait with him for these last few hours, he thought, understanding the misery that Christ must have felt in the garden of Gethsemane. Elijah felt very much alone in the trial to come. Josephine was also very nervous. She understood that Franklin Wallace would seek to take Elijah's life. If not that night, sometime very soon, Franklin would come for him. Mama Julia was also upset. The only one resting easily was Caleb, and he was too young to understand.

Not long into the night, Elijah, and his house, heard many horses circling in front of their home. Elijah knew that there were at least eight men outside waiting for him.

"Come on out here, boy!" Franklin Wallace called to Elijah.

Josephine became sorely afraid of losing her man, morose that Elijah did not flee when he had to chance to escape. Elijah, however, seemed amazingly calm. His character was such that he would not go into hiding to save his life. All men die, as he saw it. If this was his time, then it was his time. He walked toward the door.

"You can't go out dere," Josephine said, grabbing Elijah by the arm, trying to stop him.

"Stay in heah, boy," Mama Julia pleaded.

"Iffen Ah don't go out, dey gon' come in heah," Elijah said, removing Josephine's hand from his arm, tenderly touching her face, "iffen dey means ta kill me, Ah wonts dey do it out dere, and not in front of my wife and chil'."

Elijah headed for the door once more. Josephine felt as if she could pass out. She didn't want Elijah to go outside.

"Wait, Elijah," Mama Julia said, as she ran to get Elijah's rifle, a .36 caliber Sharp's 'slant breech' Sporting Rifle, trying to hand it to him.

Elijah smiled. "Dat will only make thangs worse. Besides, dems dat live by da sword dies by it."

Elijah stepped through the door and out to face danger. An intimidating sight was before him. Nine men on horseback with white sackcloth covering their faces. Five of the men were holding flaming torches. Two holes were cut into the sackcloth that the men might see. The light from the torches seemed to make the eyes of the men flame, as if they were demons from hell. They meant to kill Elijah. One of them had a rope in hand, and another had a bottle filled with oil. Elijah understood that they meant to hang him and set him ablaze. Yet, Elijah did not fear. "What y'all mens wont heah?"

They laughed.

"Surely you can't be that stupid," Franklin cut.

"Ah ain't done ya no wrong, Mista Wallace. So, Ah ain't got no call ta thank you heah ta do me harm. So, What y'all wont heah?"

Again, they laughed, mocking him.

"Are you really that stupid?" Franklin asked, almost hating to kill Elijah, because he seemed such a harmless soul, not at all the lion he seemed when demanding Jesse be locked away.

"Ah don't think it's a stupid question!" Micah said, emerging from the night, as if he were a ghost to the right of the hooded men, with a Spencer Repeating Rifle pointed at them. "What the fuck do you cowards want here?"

The men's horses moved with startled fear. One of the men to the far left of Micah eased for his pistol.

"Get yo' han' way from dat!" Rory said, emerging from the left of the men, with a white handkerchief covering his face, with his .58 caliber rifle-musket pointed at the man.

The man Rory was talking to was Jerad Wildman. Jerad turned to see him, but wasn't foolish enough to draw his .44 caliber Third Model Colt Dragoon.

"Woe Now," Elam Webster said, who was also in Rory's line of fire, throwing up a hand, not wanting to provoke Rory, "take your hand off the gun, fool."

Jerad thought about trying Rory, but he didn't want to set off a gun fight. Nevertheless, he tried to stare Rory down with his hand still poised upon his Dragoon pistol.

"Take yo' han' off dat," Rory warned, "Ah ain't gon' tell ya again!"

Jerad slowly moved his hand away from the Dragoon.

"Listen up you cowardly sons-of-bitches! I will paint the ground red with the blood of every last one of you yella dogs if any of you move just one more time! If you think I'm playing, try me," Micah said with great authority and commitment to purpose. "Wallace, answer the got-damn question! What do you want here?! And, I better like your answer!"

Franklin knew he was at a disadvantage and was reluctant to say anything, but Asa Saunders, who was right next to Franklin, felt a need to mouth off. "Y'all boys can't think that tha two of you can take all of us alone."

"Dey ain't alone," Ran cried out from behind the rabble, unseen in the darkness.

"Naw, dey ain't," Risby also cried, hidden in the darkness somewhere behind the lynch mob.

Hearing Risby and Ran call out from the darkness of night, was unnerving to the masked riders. They couldn't determine how many men were with Micah and Rory.

"If trouble breaks out, I'm gonna shoot you first," Micah coldly assured Asa.

Asa became as a wise man, shutting his face, as Micah had a Spencer Repeating Rifle aimed in his direction. Jerad Wildman, on the other hand, felt contempt for Rory, who had his rifle-musket aimed at Jerad's head. "What you got there, boy?" Jerad challenged.

"Buck and ball," Rory coolly answered, letting Jerad know that he had three buckshot and one bullet for him.

"What you gonna do with it, boy?" Jerad said defiantly.

"Keep jawin' and you gon' find out," Rory answered Jerad's challenge, moving so close to Jerad that the tip of his 40 inch musket barrel was only inches from Jerad's face.

"Shut up," Elam said to Jerad, wanting Jerad to stop escalating matters.

What Elam didn't realize was that Jerad had a reason for what he was doing. Although Rory had his face covered, there was something about him that was familiar to Jerad. He was trying to keep Rory talking long enough to figure out who he was. Jerad didn't say anymore. Although he wasn't afraid to, Jerad knew that Micah didn't want to risk a gun fight here, despite the tough talk. Nevertheless, Micah had Elam and the others spooked. In his mind, Jerad was working out Rory's identity. Although he didn't have it yet, it was right on the edge of his consciousness. Rory backed off.

"Why ya heah, Mista Wallace?" Elijah asked once more.

Franklin had better sense than to admit that he was here to lynch Elijah with Micah pointing a repeating Spencer at him. He said nothing.

"Ah thank Ah know, Mista Wallace," Elijah said forgivingly, "Ah understands dat Ah done asked ya ta do a hard thang, a bitter thang, but Ah ain't asked ya ta do no mo' 'an what's right. You and dese mens gone about yo' way in peace, and far as our problem go—he sick, Mista Wallace, put 'im where his sickness can't hurt nobody else. Ah can't back away from insistin' on dat."

Franklin knew Elijah was right, but Jesse was his son. Franklin couldn't bring himself to lock away his only son in a mental institution. At this time, asylums, particularly in the rural south, were filthy dumping grounds for the mentally disturbed. They offered no real treatment for those entrusted to their care. This was before the time of Freudian theories of psychoanalysis. Franklin would not see his son essentially imprisoned in such conditions.

"My brother wants you to go home, Wallace, and do the right thing. You best go home and do it. Listen up the rest of you vermin, when you ride out of here, you had best let what happened here tonight go! You had best swallow your pride, and stay on your side of the world, but I know you ignorant, redneck sons-of-bitches! Some of you are gonna want to try me! I'm not as forgiving as my brother! If I catch any pale-faced cracker around here with a gun, I will assume you are here to throw down, and I'm gonna kill you! If any of you dogs start trouble, I am going to finish it! That goes for now or later! Now, if any of you wanna take exception to anything I've said, step up! Other wise, get the hell off this property, and don't stop until you get to Olive Branch," Micah roared.

The masked riders began to ride off, but Jerad stayed put for a moment, sullenly looking at Rory. He had figured out who Rory was. "Ah know who you are, boy," he hissed, "Ah'll be seeing you."

"Ah know who you is, boy," Rory countered, "and you budda hope you never see me."

Jerad rode off with his hooded friends into the night. Jerad and Rory did know each other. They had a history. After the men left, Ran and Risby made their way into the light.

"Y'all didn't listen ta me," Elijah said.

"No, we didn't," Micah answered.

281

"O'm gon' follow 'em ta make sho dey don't double back tryin ta catch us off guard," Ran said, moving to do so.

Micah walked over near Rory. "What did that one say to you?"

"It ain't nothin'," Rory assured, "jes' some cracker talkin' noise."

"Micah, you was talkin' pretty rough to 'em," Risby said, laughing.

"I would have liked to have done more than talk to them," Micah replied.

"You tryin' ta make 'em git cha, ain't cha, Micah?" Elijah asked.

"Dey ain't gon' come round heah like dat no mo', Mista 'lijah," Rory said, "we scared 'em."

Josephine stepped out onto the porch holding Elijah's octagon barreled sporting rifle as if she were prepared to use it. Micah and Rory chuckled at her.

"Why ya got dat?" Elijah asked.

"You knows Ah wa'n't gon' let 'em take ya," Josephine answered.

Even Risby had to laugh at that. Elijah sighed and his shoulders slumped. He was humbled by the fact that his wife was prepared to defend him. They all went back inside, relieved the events of this night ended peacefully. Inside, Mama Julia had fresh coffee brewing. Everyone sat there happily chatting about the evening. Then, there was a knock at the door. Elijah got up to answer it, thinking that was Ran. He opened the door to find a white face staring back at him. It shocked Elijah. He believed that one of the white men that tried to lynch him had come back to shoot him. Micah thought the same thing. Everyone did. Micah quickly stood, drawing his Remington Army Revolver, ready to fire. He didn't have the shot; Elijah was in the way.

It was a good thing Micah couldn't fire without hitting Elijah. He would have been firing on an advocate. The man was Shelby Alexander. His presence there was the fruit of their labors, through Hilkiah Mifflin, Houston Thurgood, and many others. Shelby was there to help.

"I'm looking for Elijah Wright," Shelby said, unaware Micah was prepared to take a shot at him.

Elijah quickly gathered himself, realizing Shelby was not a threat. "Ah's him."

"I'm Shelby Alexander. I'm with the United States government," Shelby informed, "I've been asked to look into some trouble you've been having here."

Everyone breathed a little easier.

"Come on in, suh," Elijah said happy to see Shelby.

Micah put away his weapon, as he and Risby moved to greet Shelby.

"We sho nuff glad ta see ya," Risby said.

"Yeah, we didn't think we were going to get any help," Micah said.

"Can Ah offer ya some coffee?" Josephine asked.

"No thank you," Shelby answered.

They began to explain all to Shelby, even the very events of that night. They begin to feel comforted, feeling a savior had come to deliver them, save Micah. He didn't trust any white man, too many bad experiences with them in times past to ever trust them. Nevertheless, he was hopeful that Shelby's arrival would signal a turning point for the better in their tribulations.

Later on in the night, after Franklin and his stunned friends separated, Franklin returned to his home. He went into the parlor and poured himself a tall glass of whiskey. He underestimated Elijah and Micah. Franklin fully expected to ride into Jago and lynch Elijah with no opposition. He didn't expect such a bold and courageous stand on their part. This concerned Franklin. He realized that he was dealing with men, crafty ones at that. He had to up the level of his game. He couldn't afford to misjudge the courage and intellect of his Negro foes. He had to come at them in a different, less overt way.

Twenty-One

When morning came, Shelby Alexander went to the sheriff's office bright and early. The sheriff, Robert Hackman, was about to make his rounds of the town. He and Deputy Farley that is. Shelby walked into the Sheriff's office, and found himself face to face with Sheriff Hackman and Deputy Farley.

"Well, if it ain't the southerner turned Yankee," Deputy Farley said, and spat a mouth full of snuff onto Shelby's boot.

Shelby looked at Farley and smiled. "That's a very filthy habit, but you appear to be a filthy man. So, I suppose that I can't expect much more out of you."

Deputy Farley didn't like Shelby's mouth. "Yankee government boys been known to disappear around here, Yankee government boy."

"Angus." Sheriff Hackman said, wanting Deputy Farley to stand down. "What can we do for you, Mister Alexander?"

"You boys seem to know who I am. That leaves me at a slight disadvantage," Shelby said.

"Ah'm sorry. Ah am Sheriff Robert Hackman and this is my deputy, Angus Farley. We've been expecting you. The telegraph operator took the liberty of informing us that you received an official government communication. Please forgive him for that, but he felt that Ah needed to know, since the telegraph directed you to investigate a Negro complaint in my county. Are you with the Freedmen's Bureau?"

"No, I am with a newly formed agency of the government," Shelby responded.

"What agency might that be?" Sheriff Hackman asked.

"Forgive me for declining to answer that. I would like to get to the business at hand," Shelby said.

"By all means," Sheriff Hackman replied.

"The Negroes in Jago have been plagued with a series of murders against their children," Shelby said.

"We know about that," Farley said.

"Then why haven't you done anything about it?" Shelby snapped.

Farley didn't immediately have a good answer for Shelby, but that didn't keep him from answering. "We can't run way out there to nigger town every time some colored gets himself killed. The niggers are a

284

violent race. They are no longer slaves, and they seem to be killing themselves off without the firm hand of the white race to guide 'em."

Shelby looked at Sheriff Hackman. "Where did you find this simpleton?"

"What did you call me?" Farley asked.

"Since your deputy is an obvious cretin, I will put the question to you, sheriff. Why haven't you done anything about the Negroes' complaints of murder?" Shelby sternly asked.

"We did look into it, but not extensively," Sheriff Hackman revealed, "You have to remember that the blacks don't have any real legal standings as citizens. They are free, but they don't have any rights. Ah have two deputies and a whole county to cover. It is a demanding task. Ah can't very well devote very limited manpower to solving the problems of those who have no rights above the concerns of fully enfranchised citizens, who have every right to expect that Ah'll address their concerns promptly."

What the sheriff was saying sounded reasonable, and the sheriff sounded as if he actually believed in what he was saying. However, it was not acceptable to Shelby. If for no other reason than simple decency, the sheriff should have given a higher level of priority to stopping the murders.

"Sheriff, if a Negro broke one of your laws, tell me, would you arrest him?" Shelby asked.

"What kind of question is that?" Sheriff Hackman replied.

"Ah thought it was pretty straightforward," Shelby said.

"Of course we would arrest 'em," Deputy Farley answered.

"I find it odd that you can find time to arrest them, if they are breaking the law, but you can't find time to help them stop one of the greatest violations of our laws. Murder is unlawful," Shelby said, accepting no excuses.

"It is all in how you see it," Sheriff Hackman said.

"It doesn't matter how I see anything at this point. The coloreds have caught the person responsible for the murders," Shelby informed.

"They have?" Sheriff Hackman asked.

"A nigger?" Farley asked.

"No. It is the son of Franklin Wallace. The boy's name is Jesse," Shelby informed.

"Not likely," Sheriff Hackman said.

"You believe a bunch of niggers?" Farley added.

"They caught him in the act of trying to kill. I am told he confessed," Shelby states.

"What proof do they have?" Sheriff Hackman asked.

"I told you they caught the boy trying to murder, and he confessed to them. That should be enough to move forward," Shelby said.

"So, all you have is the account of several blacks?" Sheriff Hackman asked. "That won't get it done. In the state of Mississippi blacks aren't allowed to testify against whites. A man as seemingly well versed in the law as you should know that."

"He's a Yankee now, sheriff. He wouldn't know," Deputy Farley said.

"That law is unconstitutional, and you know it. The coloreds are entitled to more consideration than you are giving them. Congress is already moving to enfranchise them. It's only a matter of time before Congress outlaws these outrageous laws you have, which only apply to blacks. They will be allowed to testify," Shelby said.

"Not around here," Farley said.

"Even if Ah wanted to let them," Sheriff Hackman said, "Franklin Wallace is a very powerful man. He is not going to let you sidestep the law, not when his son's freedom is on the line, and it surely is. Maybe, Congress will overturn this law, but right now the law stands."

"Ah am sure an exception can be made given the circumstances," Shelby countered.

"Ah wouldn't count on it," Sheriff Hackman said.

"We will see about that," Shelby said.

From that point on Farley remained quiet, he saw an opportunity to make some money.

"Will you arrest Jesse Wallace?" Shelby asked.

"Ah will not. If all you have are black witnesses, Ah can't arrest Jesse Wallace. Ah will not go up against one of the riches men in the state, not unless Ah am absolutely sure of the outcome. As the law now stands, a black cannot testify against a white. You have nothing," Sheriff Hackman responded.

Shelby realized that it was a waste of time trying to convince Sheriff Hackman to arrest Jesse Wallace. Perhaps he would have better luck with the town mayor, Shelby thought. "Thank you for your time, sheriff." He turned to leave.

"Shelby," Sheriff Hackman called, "let me give you a bit of advice. Remember where you are, and when you are. You are in the heart of Dixie, not long removed from a bitter war against Yankee oppressors. Don't waste your time going to the town leaders. You won't be able to compel them to side with you against one of the most renowned sons of the South. Ah can assure you that they will laugh you to scorn if you try."

Sheriff Hackman was right, and Shelby knew that he was right. Shelby didn't expect this to be easy, but it was certain that he did not expect it to be this difficult, not when the killer had already been identified. There was no cause for alarm, however. There was more than one way to deal with this calamity. There must surely be other tangible pieces of evidence out there that could be used, he thought. He would collect it, and bring forth charges against Jesse Wallace; and if the South did not yield to what was right, he was going to ensure that federal pressure was applied to get the desired results. Those willing to let Jesse Wallace go free wouldn't be able to dance their way around the law after he did that.

Shelby decided to ride out to see Elijah. He was not the only one on the move. Deputy Farley was also taking a little ride. He rode out to see Franklin Wallace. Not long after, he found himself sitting face to face with the man, in his parlor, having a glass of Franklin's best sherry.

"This is mighty fine wine," Farley said, sipping joyfully.

"Get to it, Angus," Franklin said.

"Okay, Ah hear you have been having a problem with the niggers over in Jago. Ah am here to tell you that your problems have just gotten worse. The niggers have went out and got the Yankees involved. A government man was in our office this morning. He asked the sheriff to arrest your son for the murder of all them black children that your son supposedly killed. The sheriff refused, said the law was on your side, but that ain't gonna slow that Yankee boy down. Ah'll give you odds that he is out doing a little investigating, trying to link your boy to those murders. Ah just thought that you should know. For a price, Ah can keep an eye on him, let you know what he is up to."

Franklin became exceedingly nervous upon hearing news that a government official was there investigating the murders. He knew what Deputy Farley was up to also. Franklin was willing to play his game. "Okay, Angus, consider it a deal."

Shelby finally arrived at Elijah's place. He found Elijah and Micah working in the fields. Elijah was very happy to see Shelby. He was sure that Shelby had good news.

"How are you men doing?" Shelby asked, as he dismounted.

"Right tolerable," Elijah answered.

Micah said nothing, nodding slightly at Shelby. Micah had on a side arm; it drew Shelby's attention. Shelby thought it a bit unusual for Micah to work the cotton fields armed. He failed to take into account that Micah had stood up to the men that tried to kill Elijah.

"Expecting trouble?" Shelby asked Micah.

"Maybe, maybe not, it's better to have and not need than to need and not have," Micah responded.

"I suppose that it is true," Shelby replied.

"What brang ya heah, Mista Shelby?" Elijah asked.

"I am having some trouble with the local sheriff. He refuses to arrest Jesse Wallace on the strength of your testimony alone. We will need more evidence than we currently have. I was wondering if you might be able to point me in the right direction."

"We caught 'im tryin' ta kill, and he told us from his own lips dat he kilt all dem young on's . Three of us, not includin' da boy he tried ta kill, heard 'im admit it. Ain't dat good enough?" Elijah asked.

"Here's our problem. There is apparently some law on the books which forbids any black to testify against a white. I will try, but I do not believe that we are going to be able to move them on this point," Shelby explained.

"I'm sure they would move on it if the shoe was on the other foot," Micah said.

"I am sure they would, but that is a point which is neither here nor there. If they want to play games, let them. We are going to take what they give us, and beat them at their own game," Shelby contended.

"What kind of evidence is ya talkin' about?" Elijah asked.

"Anything that I can take into a court of law and physically connect Jesse Wallace to these murders," Shelby stated.

"Ah don't rightly know what dat could be," Elijah said, pondering the matter.

"Well, let's start with what lead you to Wallace. There may be something there that we can use," Shelby said.

"Like we told ya befo', da boy's las' kill throwed up while he was bein' choked. We seed candy in his vomit, and in twixt his teeth. His folks ain't give 'im dat candy. So, we thought whoever kilt 'im did. We asked Mista Bush over at da sto' who been buyin' dat kinda candy, and dat's how we caught up ta 'im," Elijah explained.

"I don't see how we can use that," Shelby stated.

"Well, that's all that we have," Micah said.

"Surely, there must be something else," Shelby said.

"Something else like what?" Elijah asked.

"Sounds as if you will not be happy unless you, yourself, actually see the boy committing the murders," Micah said to Shelby.

"Truthfully, that is almost what it is going to take," Shelby responded.

"There will be no more murders, not if we can help it, and we can," Micah assured.

Twenty-Two

At the end of the American Civil War wealthy southerners; that is, those whose lands was not confiscated by the United States government, were left with plenty of land, but no one to work it for them. The free slave labor that they depended upon was no longer. They had a problem. The solution, in the state of Mississippi, was not to allow blacks to own farmland. Most blacks knew how to work the land. It was their one area of expertise, but they were denied the freedom to own their own lands. Seeing the opportunity to nurture a mutually beneficial relationship, or so it seemed to blacks, the coloreds would enter into covenants in January of each year with white landowners to cultivate the land in exchange for a share of the crop yield. The landowner would advance them enough cash to live on during the year, which the blacks would repay out of their portion of the harvest. The practice was known as sharecropping. It was not an equitable system, as the landowners reserved most of the rights, and the system was designed to keep the sharecropper indebted to the landowner.

Elijah sharecropped on the property of one Ian Everett. Mister Everett was a good friend to Franklin Wallace. Ian was on his way out to see Elijah, and he was not in a good mood at all. It was a long ride from where Everett lived in relation to Elijah. He did not venture this way unless it was planned, and he had no such plans. It was a trip he would rather not be making. When he reached Elijah's place. He called out in a very hostile way. "Elijah, Elijah Wright, Come on out here, boy!"

Elijah could have easily guessed that this was Franklin Wallace's next move. With great humility and obedience, as if he were no more than a dog, Elijah prepared to go outside to speak with Mr. Everett. Micah was inclined to go with him.

"No, Micah," Elijah said, "Wait fuh me in heah, please."

"Are you sure?" Micah asked.

Elijah nodded his head, indicating that he wanted Micah to remain inside. Elijah walked outside to find Ian waiting for him, as if he were an unruly child standing before an angry parent. Everett was mounted on a tall white horse. He was wearing expensive black boots, which came up to his calves. He was wearing gray pants with a white shirt. There was a stern angry look upon Ian's face. His piercing emerald eyes looked down upon Elijah with great dismay. He was a man use to having his way, and he had come to hand down his edict to Elijah. "Elijah, word has reached me that you are causing trouble. If there is one thing that Ah will not abide, it's my Negras causing trouble. It reflects poorly upon me, embarrasses me. Ah will not tolerate that. Do you understand?"

Elijah looked at Everett, unsure of what to say. He wanted to remind Ian that he was no longer a slave, no longer property. However, tact needed to be exercised. Elijah lived on Ian's property.

"Well, don't stand there like some dullard, speak up," Ian demanded.

"Ah understands, suh."

"Good. Ah hear that your brother is living here with you."

"Yassuh, he live wit' me."

"You should have made it your business to let me know that he was staying with you. Ah did not give my approval for him to move onto this property. He is a troublemaker. Ah want you to turn him out. He is a bad influence on you. Furthermore, any white man that you come into contact with should be shown the same respect that you show me. Show him the same obedience that you show me. Do you understand?"

"Ah hear ya."

"You hear me?" Ian angrily spouted. "You show me the proper respect. 'Ah hear you, sir.' Anything you say to me should have a sir at the end of it. Do you understand?"

"Yassuh."

"That's better. Now, concerning this trouble that you've been causing. Ah want you to go to that Yankee, that Tennessee Tory, Shelby Alexander. You tell him that you don't require his help anymore, and that he can go on back to wherever he came from. Do you understand?"

Elijah looked at Ian, having no intentions of complying with anything he said.

"Ah hear ya, suh."

"You see to everything that I have told you. Do it today."

"Yassuh."

Ian rode off without a word more. He was highly confident that Elijah would do as he instructed him to do. Elijah walked back into the house. There was a noticeable angry look upon Micah's face.

"What?" Elijah asked.

"Why did you let him talk to you like that?" Micah asked, feeling Elijah should have put Ian in his place.

"Ta buy time," Elijah explained, "Ah ain't backin' down, and Mista Everett is gon' kick me off this place iffen Ah don't. If Ah had spoke up, he was gon' see ta it today. Dis way, Ah got a day or two ta find some place else ta live."

"Where we gon' go?" Josephine asked.

"We'll find some place," Mama Julia said, letting Elijah know that she stood with him.

"Wallace put him up to this," Micah said.

"Sho he did, but it don't matter," Elijah said, "We got 'im on da run, and we gon' keep it dat way."

"Dis lit' hole ain't much, but it's our home," Josephine said, sad to know she would soon be leaving it.

"We'll find another house," Elijah assured, "it's our family dat makes it a home."

"Ain't no mo' white folks 'round heah gonna let ya work dey land, Elijah, not afta dis," Mama Julia pointed out.

"Then, we'll leave here," Micah said, "I have some money. We'll go some place that will let us own farmland."

"But not befo' dis is done," Elijah said, "Ah ain't leavin' heah till dat Wallace boy done been put in da crazy house. We might habe ta sleep under da stars till dat's done, Josephine."

Josephine looked at Elijah. She was not particularly happy to hear Elijah say this, but she understood.

"Lawd, it's fixin' ta git rough," Mama Julia said.

"That it is," Micah agreed.

"Dey might try ta kill ya again," Josephine said, quite concerned for Elijah.

"Ah don't thank so. Iffen dat's what dey was plannin', dey wouldn't never sont Mista Everett. Shelby Alexander got 'em scared. Dey gonna wait till he gone befo' dey try somethin'," Elijah reasoned.

"You hope so, anyway," Micah said, expecting the whites would do more than send Everett.

Micah's instincts served him well in expecting a violent reprisal. Even as Ian Everett was riding out to Elijah's home to pressure him. The men who attempted to lynch Elijah, with the exception of Franklin, were busy planning Micah's demise. Asa Saunders, Elam Webster, Zechariah Barnes, Benjamin Klein, Jerad Wildman, and several others were assembled together.

"What are we going to do about that boy?" Asa asked.

"That boy has the head of a lion upon him," Benjamin said.

"He's stout-hearted alright," Elam agreed. "and Ah'll tell you something else. If we take him on straight ahead, that nigger is gonna take some of us with him."

"They's more than one way to skin a cat, Elam," Asa said, "one of us can lay in wait for him. Benjamin is right handy with a rifle. Ah bet he could pick that boy off a hundred yards out."

"Ah sure could," Benjamin said gloating.

"See," Asa said, "all Benjamin has to do is wait back off in them woods round where those niggers live. Benjamin may have to wait a while, but sooner or later that uppity nigger is gonna give him a chance to put a bullet in him."

Most of the men there laughed in agreement with Asa, but not Zechariah Barnes. Zechariah by far was the most intelligent one among them. He had listened in silence up to that point. "Now why do you suppose Franklin Wallace isn't here at this meeting, gentlemen? You don't suppose that it might be because he understands that we can't touch Elijah or his brother right now, do you?" Zechariah said, getting them to think. "True enough that boy, Micah, has to be punished for what he did, but we can't do it, not with that federalist running around on the coloreds' side. We are asking for trouble if we touch him now," Zechariah contended.

"What are you suggesting we do?" Jerad Wildman asked.

"We can kill that Yankee, too," Asa said.

"Use your head, Asa. We don't do anything," Zechariah countered, "We do nothing at all. Killing the Yankee would only bring others, which would only make our yoke heavier. We don't kill that crazed nigger either. We do nothing at all, but Ah'm sure we can promise some nigger a hog, and he will do the job for us. That way we don't cause ourselves any troubles with that federalist that's snooping around, and we still get that colored boy dead."

"A hog is an awful lot to pay just to rid ourselves of a nigger. Let's offer one of them a ham, and that's too much. Particularly when a few cents spent on a bullet or two will be just as effective," Jerad said.

"That nigger is gonna be a hand full. Believe me, whoever does this is gonna want the whole pig. Ah have a sow that gave birth to a litter. Ah would be willing to part with one out of the litter to get rid of this boy," Benjamin said.

"You miss the point, Jerad. This negra won't cower before us. That makes him dangerous. As Elam pointed out, a Negra like that will kill one or more of us if we try to take him. If he does that, pretty soon, Negras will be standing up like men all over the place, and we can't have that. This is our country, and we will rule in it. The way to handle this situation is to have a Negra kill him. He will be looking for one of us, but that black scoundrel will never suspect one of his own. Furthermore, and most importantly, none of us will be put at risk, and that boy will be just as dead than just as if one of us had personally killed him," Zechariah plotted. "After Alexander has gone, we will make it clear to the Negras that we were responsible for this Micah's death, and we will leave a few more of them dead. That should quiet any courage building in them."

"What about the others who were with him?" Jerad asked. "You planning to deal with them now? We don't know who they are, and they are just as deserving of death as the loud-mouthed nigger."

"Presently, they don't hold the same priority as this Micah. He is a threat which must be put down immediately. We will deal with the others at a more convenient time. A time when Shelby Alexander isn't around," Zechariah conspired.

"What if Elijah suspects we put a nigger up to killing his brother? He may get Alexander to escort him out of our reach before we can get to him, before we can force him to tell us who the others were with them that night," Asa said.

"That's a chance Ah'm willing to take," Zechariah said.

"Ah'm not willing that any of those coons should get away," Elam said.

"Neither am Ah," Jerad said.

"Zechariah is right," Benjamin said, "We can't go on a killing rampage. We can get that Micah now without causing much alarm in Jago. Chances are, Elijah will still be there when the dust settles."

"What if he is not," Elam said, "what if he leaves?"

"Then he leaves," Zechariah said, "quite frankly, so long as we get this Micah, Ah don't care as much about the others."

"Well, Ah do," Elam said, not willing that any who supported Elijah and Micah should be spared the penalty of death.

"What if all those involved leave once we've gotten rid of Micah, fearing for their own lives?" Jerad asked. "We will never get them then."

"They wouldn't do that, because they think that we don't know who they are," Benjamin said.

"We don't know who they are," Elam said, "and we can't assume they won't think that we don't know who they are."

"They will scatter," Jerad contended.

"Maybe, but it is not so bad a thing. This Micah will be dead. He is the courage among them. Kill the courage, and the remaining Negras will be easy enough to control. It is a bonus if the Negras infected by him voluntarily amputate themselves from the docile coloreds," Zechariah explained.

"Ah see your point," Elam said, finally in accord with Zechariah.

Jerad was now the lone voice of dissent. He felt that they should not let a single one of the blacks involved escape punishment for their complicity in challenging them when they came for Elijah.

"We should not let any of them get away with what they've done. Those black bastards shoved guns in our faces. How do we, as men, turn our backs on that?" Jerad said with a vengeful heart. "We should find out who they are, and kill every last one of them. That will teach every nigger to fear us."

"Killing one will be as effective as killing the lot," Zechariah countered.

"Yes, Jerad, Zechariah's plan is the better scheme," Elam said.

"You mean the safest," Jerad scorned.

Elam looked at Jerad quite offended, feeling Jerad was looking down on him. "That too."

"Jerad, Ah understand your dismay, but why should we place ourselves in harm's way when we don't have to. We should do it Zechariah's way," Benjamin said.

"Benjamin's right," Asa agreed.

"Listen to me," Jerad said, "Ah think Ah recognized one of those boys. We can take him now."

"You think you recognize?" Elam spouted.

"You wanna just kill up some darky, because you think you recognize him?" Benjamin asked.

"Ah'm sure it's him," Jerad said.

"You didn't sound like it," Elam said, denying Jerad an opportunity to build support, wanting to get back at Jerad for implying he was a coward.

"Jerad, Ah think that Ah speak for everyone when Ah say we'll handle this as agreed upon," Zechariah said, ending the discussion.

Jerad quietly stepped back, realizing he couldn't change their minds.

"Ah guess the next question is who do we get to kill that nigger," Benjamin said.

"Leave that to me. They's an ole boy in Jago that Ah know, who can't stand this Micah. Ah bet he'll be more than happy to kill him," Asa said.

"Are you sure this boy is up to it," Zechariah asked, "this Negra won't be taken easily."

"He can take 'im," Asa said.

Jerad stood there listening. He looked down on everyone in the room, especially Zechariah. He saw Zechariah as too smart, and not as the bravest of men. Jerad didn't waste anymore time trying to convince them to approach this matter head on. He would leave them to their own devices.

At Franklin's home, he sat in the parlor. He was carefully considering his options. He knew that Jesse's life was now in his hands. He knew that Shelby Alexander would come after Jesse fiercely.
Franklin needed to find a way to discourage him. He considered trying to bribe Shelby, but if Shelby was an honest man, a bribe was as much an admission of guilt as a confession. He didn't want to run the risk of giving Shelby something to lock his jaws around. He couldn't go after Elijah and Micah, not with Shelby around and nor did he want to, considering Micah was likely to kill him if he tried. Franklin asked himself, if those options were closed to him then, what options were open to him? After much thought, he had an answer.

The very next day, Asa Saunders made good on his promise to enlist an assassin to kill Micah. He found his way to Trents home. He knocked at Trents door, and Trents came out to speak with him.
"Walk with me," Asa said to Trents.
"Ah ain't seed ya in a good while. Where ya been?" Trents asked, as he walked along with Asa.
"Well, me and my little black beauty had a fallin' out of sorts, Trents. Ah'll ride out all this way for a twist, but not just to be neighborly."
"Then, why is ya heah now?"
"Ah'm here on business. Elijah Wright's brother, Ah hear you can't stand him."
"Well, ain't no love lost twixt us, iffen dat's what cha wanna know."
"You hate him?"
"Ah reckon dat's a good word fuh what Ah feels fuh 'im."
"How much do ya hate him, Trents, enough to kill him?"Asa asked brazenly.
"Enough ta kill im? What dis about, boss?" Trents said, stunned by what was being suggested.
"Ah wanna make you a little offer, Trents," Asa said, "Ah want you ta kill that boy. Ah got a litter of pigs. Ah'll let you have one, if you take care of that boy for me."
At first, Trents didn't know what to say; he was not an assassin, but he could definitely use a hog. It took an awful lot of time to hunt fresh meat

for his family, having a hog would help ease his burden of having to make time to hunt and set traps so much.

"A sow?" Trents asked.

"Ah see, you wanna mate her so you can always have meat, huh?" Asa laughed. "Yeah, we will make it a sow. Yer a clever nigger, Trents. That's why yer right for tha job."

"Alright then, Ah'll kill dat nigga fuh ya, boss."

"You want the pig first?"

"Ah'll wait till it's done. Ah trust ya ta do like ya say."

"Okay, then, Ah'll get that pig to ya as soon as you've killed that boy."

"Ah jes' wanna know. What cha wont 'im dead fuh?"

"For the same reason yer willin' to kill 'im, he is a nuisance. There is a harmony between my world and your world. Everybody understands his place, and we get along because of it. Our worlds will be better off without him around upsetting the order of things. How long will it take you to get him?"

"Ah can't make ya no promises dere, boss. When Ah gets my chance, Ah'll take it."

"Ah don't suppose that Ah can ask anymore than that."

So with that, this detestable conspiracy to take a man's life was set into motion.

Some days later, Elijah was tending his garden. He was in the midst of the corn stalks, gathering some of the corn for dinner, and some other vegetables for Josephine and Mama Julia to can for winter .

Suddenly, he heard brisk footsteps in the garden with him. At first he believed it to be Micah, but it was a bad assumption on his part. Elijah was so confident that it was Micah, Josephine, or Mama Julia that he didn't bother to look around immediately. When he did look around, it was Ian Everett, and he was right upon Elijah. Everett took his fist and clobbered Elijah right on the jaw. It was a hard blow, and Elijah went down. On his back, Elijah looked up to see Ian standing over him. An angry scowl was upon Ian's face. He was holding a whip, which he let unwind to the ground. His intentions were very clear to Elijah. Elijah had disobeyed Ian and that would not be tolerated.

"Didn't Ah tell you to get your black carcass into town and tell that Yankee that you didn't need him here anymore?" Everett yelled.

Elijah should have been ready for something like this, but he was completely unprepared. For a moment, he felt as if he was still a slave. A fear of Ian hit him, and he responded as he had been trained to respond. "Yassuh."

"Then why haven't you done it?" Ian yelled, looking as if at any moment he was going to unleash the sting of the whip.

"Because–"

"Because what?" Ian yelled, letting the whip fly with all of his might. "When Ah tell you to do something, then god-dammit, Ah expect you to do it!"

Elijah's first impulse was to cover up, as the whip struck him. Everett drew back his hand again, and the whip whooshed over his head, ready to strike again. Just then, it occurred to Elijah that he wasn't a slave anymore, and he didn't have to take this. As the second lash struck, Elijah raised his arm trying to grab it, but the whip was like a rattle snake: quick, alive, and full of bitter bite. He couldn't take hold.

"That unruly brother of yours is still here Ah'm told! Ah'll see to him next," Ian raged, as he lashed out at Elijah once more with the whip.

The whip struck and wrapped around Elijah's forearm, breaking the skin, but he was able to grab hold of it. Swiftly, Elijah got to his feet. The beating was over... for him. Elijah was a very reserved fellow. He was always in control. He never let his emotions get the better of him. But on those rare occasions when he got angry. It is better to say that he got mad, because he became something of an fierce lunatic.

"Let it go, boy," Ian yelled, not yet realizing that he had trouble on his hands.

"Come heah," Elijah said with a cool frightening anger, slowly reeling Ian in to him.

"Let it go damn you," Ian spouted, trying to resist Elijah's pull, "you're only making it worse on yourself."

It was a tug of war between them over the whip. Elijah was winning the battle. Elijah wasn't talking at all, but the unrestrained look of anger in his eyes, coupled with the defiant act of resisting, was speaking volumes to Everett. For the first time in his life, Ian Everett was actually afraid of a black. It was obvious to Ian that he could not overpower Elijah. An impulse hit him to release the whip and run away, but he was afraid to release the whip. He was afraid that Elijah would take the whip and beat him with it. He had never been beaten with a whip before. Instead of releasing, Ian held fast, moving backward as best he could.

Elijah continued to reel him in, getting closer and closer. Elijah was close enough to reach out and touch Ian, and he did. With a raging right hand of power, Elijah wrapped his long-dark fingers around Ian's thick soft neck and began to squeeze. It was as if everything Elijah had suffered as a slave, during the whole murder ordeal, and every bit of repressed anger he had ever felt in his entire life was manifesting itself in the form of furious power in Elijah's right hand. His grip was relentless and merciless around Ian's thick neck.

At first, Ian elected to use both of his hands to keep the whip at bay, but he began to feel as if he were some small, helpless, animal ensnared within Elijah's powerful grip, which was able to determine life or death for him. Ian's eyes began to water as panic filled them. His skin turned a bright red, as he let go of the whip, trying to pry Elijah's powerful hand from his throat. Ian believed he was going to die if he didn't do something quickly to force Elijah to let him go. He tried to knee Elijah in the testicles, but Elijah was awkwardly positioned. So, Ian's effort was in vain. He hit Elijah on the side of the head. Elijah's grip seemed to tighten. It scared Ian even more, because absolutely no air was getting in. All the more panicky, Ian tried with both hands to pry Elijah from his throat. He began to struggle violently. Suddenly, Ian's legs forsook him, and he found himself on his knees. Looking up at Elijah, Ian's eyes begged for mercy, as his tongue began to protrude from his mouth.

Around this time, Josephine wondered from the house. She looked out toward the garden. There in the garden, she saw her husband taking Ian's life. It shocked her so badly, she was momentarily paralyzed. She couldn't even find the will to scream.

Elijah's eyes drifted up and he happened to see his wife standing there terrified. What Elijah was doing to Ian seemed somehow surreal to him. Seeing Josephine standing there so afraid was very sobering to Elijah. He loosened his grip and was ashamed of himself. "Lawd, forgive me. What is Ah done done?" He asked himself, feeling sorry in the most profound of ways for this wrong. "Forgive me, Mista Everett, Ah's so sorry."

Ian looked at him with eyes of disbelief that Elijah would dare do something like this to him.

"Let me help ya up, suh," Elijah said, holding out his hand to Ian.

Ian didn't say anything. He smacked Elijah's hand away from him. On his knees, feeling as if he could throw up, he inched away from Elijah. Ian thought Elijah was apologizing to him because he was white; because he was somebody and Elijah was nothing; because there was a line that a black man did not cross in the white-dominated South. He thought that because he was white and Elijah was a former slave, he had the right to treat Elijah as he did. He thought that Elijah understood this and acknowledged it. Why else would Elijah have relented? Ian was wrong in his thinking.

Elijah apologized because there is a way that a man who follows after God carries himself. It is a way that is long suffering of the short comings of others. A way that does not seek an eye for an eye. It is a way that leads a man to strive to live in peace with all, but Ian did not understand this.

When his lungs were filled with air, and his throat didn't hurt as much, Ian was back to feeling like his old self. Rubbing his throat, he stood. Feeling that Elijah had remembered his place, anger started to swell in Ian. He forgot that Elijah could have easily killed him. Ian reasoned that since Elijah relented in his efforts to harm him, that Elijah wouldn't raise his hand against him again.

"Micah," Josephine screamed, getting over the shock of what she had just witnessed, "Micah!"

"You filthy nigger, Ah dare you put your hands on me," Ian said, as he struck Elijah on the left cheek with the palm of his hand, "who in hell do you think you are?"

One blow delivered from Elijah could have rendered Ian unconscious on the ground in his weakened state, but Elijah stayed his hand. This was exactly as Ian expected him to do. What Elijah did next deeply bewildered Ian. Without uttering a word, Elijah offered Ian his right cheek. It took Ian a moment to figure out what was happening. It offended him, because he realized what Elijah was doing. Ian considered himself to be a God-loving man. Elijah had reminded him that it is one thing to believe in God, and quite another to live a Godly life. He felt that Elijah had bested him twice, and his anger sweltered to an even greater degree. He raised his hand to strike Elijah again, but he didn't get the chance.

Micah was there. He grabbed Ian and slung him violently to the ground. Micah fastened his fist, ready to go to work on Ian. He moved in to do just that. Ian threw up his right arm to guard his face from blows. He was very afraid of Micah, and rightly so. There was a look of hatred in Micah's eyes. Hatred which would show no mercy. Micah drew back his big fist to deliver punishment.

All that Ian could see was Micah's large fist about to bear down on him, promising to instruct, correct, him in the adage that it is always prudent to show respect for a man, lest his wrath be kindled against you. Ian gnashed his teeth, anticipating a hard painful blow.

"Micah," Elijah yelled, "Let 'im up!"

"What? Why? He needs to be taught a lesson," Micah said, filled with contempt for Ian.

"Let 'im up."

"No!"

"What cause ya got ta beat 'im? He ain't done nothin' ta ya. He ain't even said a word ta ya. How ya gon' beat a man dat ain't never said nothin' ta ya or lifted a finger ta ya?"

"This bastard hit you!"

"Dat's right, he hit me. Dis a problem twixt him and me, and Ah ain't got no problem. Iffen he wanna hate by his self, dat's his problem. Now let 'im up."

Micah released Ian, and looked at Elijah with amazement, trying to figure him out. "I don't understand you."

Elijah moved to Ian and offered his hand once more to help him up. Ian became all the more wildly livid, he didn't want Elijah to treat him kindly. Elijah's kindness was seen by him as a feeble attempt to get out of the reckoning that he believed Elijah and Micah were due. Ian was not going to forgive or forget this. He climbed to his feet without help from Elijah.

"Animals. Animals. That's what you are, and Ah am going to see that you are put down like the rabid dogs you are," Ian cried.

"Get your ass out of here," Micah said loudly, as he pushed Everett down and began to drag him by the arm towards his horse, with Everett struggling to keep his legs under him.

"Micah," Elijah yelled to no avail.

Micah harshly helped Ian onto his horse.

"You get the hell off of my property and take this mad dog brother of yours with you," Ian barked.

"Iffen dat's da way you wont it, Mista Everett." Elijah calmly said.

"That is the way Ah want it! You get off of my property today! If you don't, Ah'll come back with a gun," Ian roared.

"You do, and I'll kill you," Micah boldly assured.

"We'll be gone by da end of da week," Elijah said, "ain't no need fuh trouble."

"Ah said today," Ian screamed with a hoarse voice.

"And, he said by the end of the week," Micah countered, raising his voice.

"The end of da week is soon as Ah kin git out, Mista Everett," Elijah calmly said.

"Ah want you gone today, and Ah will be back with the sheriff to see to it," Ian angrily growled.

"Bring him," Micah shouted, "we've been trying to catch up to him anyway!"

"You damned smart-mouthed nigger," Ian yelled.

Micah was fed up with Ian. "I've never busted a cap in an unarmed man before, but you are about five seconds away from having to dig a rusty bullet out of your pale ass, if you don't get the hell out of here now."

Ian began to rapidly spit out obscenities at Micah and Elijah, but he did so on the move, as he hastily rode away. Ian Everett had never been so insulted in his life. He rode straight for the sheriff's office in Olive Branch.

Micah turned and looked at Elijah, as Josephine rushed to her husband. Micah thought that Elijah was a very peculiar man. He didn't understand him.

"Lawd knows Ah's scared O'm gon' lose you, Elijah," Josephine said, wrapping her arms around his neck, pressing her face against his. She was very shaken by this incident.

"Ya ain't gon' lose me, stop worryin' like dat," Elijah said.

"Da good Lawd knows Ah can't help worryin' about cha. Let's leave heah now. Let's strike out walkin' iffen we gotta. Ah don't care iffen we leaves wit' nothin' but da cloths on our backs. Dat's enough as long as Ah gots you alive."

"We ain't gotta do dat, Josephine," Elijah said.

"Ah's scared of dat man, Elijah. Ah's scared of all dem white folks. God only knows what dey gon' do. Ah don't wont 'em ta kill ya. Let's leave, please, let's leave."

All Micah could do was stand there and watch, as Josephine begged Elijah to leave. He wanted Elijah to stay and fight, but Elijah had much to lose. Elijah had a family that needed him. Micah would understand if Elijah left, as Josephine wanted. It seemed the wise thing to do.

"Ah can't," Elijah said, "everythang we got in dis worl' is in dat house, and Ah ain't gon' leave without it. We'll git off Mista Everett's land, but Ah need time ta buy another mule and a wagon ta pack our belongings in. When dat's done, we'll get off his property, but not before. And, we ain't gon' leave Jago until Jesse Wallace been locked away."

Ian Everett wasted no time getting to the Sheriff's office. He made everything known to Sheriff Hackman. He wanted the sheriff to ride out and kick Elijah off of his property. The sheriff had heard of Micah's exploits. Specifically, the incident in which Franklin and others tried to lynch Elijah. He did not know about the planned attack in advance, nor did he condone it. As for Micah, the sheriff didn't want any part of him, at least not yet. Not with Shelby Alexander around, who was sure to back Elijah's and Micah's play.

"You have a contract with the boy to work that property for the year, don't you?" Sheriff Hackman asked, as he sat behind his desk.

"You know that Ah do," Ian said.

"Has the boy broken anything in the contract?"

"No," Ian answered.

"Then on what grounds do you wish to involve me in this matter? It sounds to me as if you have crawled into bed with Franklin Wallace, and gotten a little bit more than you bargained for."

"Those niggers have guns, which is unlawful. And, make no mention of the fact that they put their filthy hands on me. As the law, you need to do something about them."

"Ah'll do nothing. You shouldn't have gone out there throwing your weight around on behalf of Wallace. Stupid moves like that are exactly the reason we have a federalist agent here now breathing down my neck. Ah am not going to go out there and tangle with those boys over this. The boy said that they would be off of your property by the end of the week. My advice to you is to give him to the end of the week. And, here is a little more advice, let Franklin Wallace fight his own battles. You do not want to stick your nose in the middle of this."

"Ah didn't realize that we had a coward for a sheriff," Ian said, angry that Sheriff Hackman wouldn't help him.

Sheriff Hackman smiled deceptively at him. "Have a nice day, Mister Everett."

That ended Everett's encounter with the sheriff. He went to his friends to enlist their help in dealing with Micah and Elijah, but found a cool reception when it came to taking Micah on. There were no takers. Taking Micah on would be best handled as an exercise in subterfuge.

Trents had been carefully assessing the best way to carry out the task of dealing with Micah. Micah was a man of action and was use to the heat of battle. He would react quickly and rationally to an attack, which meant he would not be taken easily. There were only two advantages that Trents reasoned that he had against Micah. One, Micah did not know that he had been enlisted to kill him. Two, Micah's temperament was a strong liability. He was a hothead, and surely that could be used against him. But how? There was also another problem. Micah was almost always in the company of Elijah. Elijah was always a cool thinker, which off-set Micah's hotheaded disposition. Also, Trents knew that Elijah wasn't going to stand idly by and let him do away with Micah. It would be idiocy to think that he would. Trents reasoned that he would have to separate Elijah from Micah and strike quickly before Micah had a chance to react. Then, he would have to kill Elijah, too. There was no way around it. Unless, he could manage to dispose of Micah in such a way that would look accidental. Trents tossed and turned all night thinking about this. Just before dawn, he figured out the best way to deal with the situation.

Shortly after breakfast, Trents rode over to Elijah's house. He found Elijah and Micah out back of the house chopping wood. There was an old tree stump which Elijah used as a chopping block. Elijah took a small round piece of wood and stood it on end on the stomp. With one powerful swing of the ax, Elijah split the wood in two. Micah was standing nearby talking to Elijah. About what, Trents did not know. Micah stopped talking as soon as he saw Trents. Elijah looked around to see Trents and was surprised to see him.

"Mornin', Trents, what brang ya out heah?" he asked.

"Ah got a lit' news Ah thought y'all might wanna hear," Trents said.

Elijah and Micah looked at each wondering what news would be so important that it would bring Trents over to pay a visit, given his dislike for Micah.

"What is it?" Micah asked.

"White folks, word out of town is, dey's gunnin' fuh ya, Micah," Trents responded.

"That is old news Trents, but we thank you for it," Micah responded.

"Ah knows y'all mean good, but watch what cha doin'. We don't wont white folks ta come down heah in a mob goin' from house ta house killin' cause dey mad at y'all," Trents said.

"Ain't no need ta worry 'bout dat, Trents," Elijah said, "Iffen dey was gon' do dat, it would've been right afta our lit' run in wit' Franklin Wallace and his lynch mob. We got us a government man down heah now. Ah don't thank dey wanna do nothin' wit' him around."

"Don't be so sho," Trents said.

"If you are here to criticize us, turn on around and head on back to wherever you came from, because we don't need that," Micah said.

Trents really didn't like Micah's mouth.

"Ah understands, Trents," Elijah said, "Ah don't wanna cause da folks livin' round heah no harm in no way, but we is where we is wit' dis. It ain't no turnin' back now. All we kin do is hope da whites come afta me and nobody else."

Trents picked up a piece of wood and placed it on the chopping block.

"Youse a brave nigga, Ah gives ya dat."

Elijah drew back the ax, and split the wood. "It ain't about bein' brave, Trents. It's about standin' fuh what's right."

Trent's picked up another piece of wood, preparing to place it on the chopping block, but Elijah put the ax down and started to gather wood he had chopped so far.

"Is ya done had yo' breakfast yet, Trent's?" Elijah asked, still gathering wood. "We probably got a lit' left over iffen ya wont it."

"Ah done ate," Trents said, looking at Micah.

"All right." Elijah said as he began to walk toward the house with his arms full of wood. He intended to come back and gather some more wood.

Micah started to gather up wood, and Trents put the piece of wood he was holding onto the chopping block. He took hold of the ax. Micah saw him, but assumed that Trents was simply trying to help. He committed the cardinal sin of turning his back to Trents as he gathered wood. When he saw this, Trents could hardly believe his eyes. He was alone with Micah, and Micah's back was to him, when he was holding a sharp ax in his hands. Micah was wearing his Remington Army Revolver, which was giving him a very false sense of security. He didn't suspect Trents.

"Ya need ta be careful, Micah," Trents said.

Micah looked back at him. "Huh?"

"Ya need ta be mo' careful," Trents said, as he split the wood.

Micah wondered why Trents said that to him and began to feel uneasy. "I know that I need to be careful, but why do you say it?"

"White folks is out ta get cha. You don't never know how dey gon' come at cha."

At that point, Micah realized that he was vulnerable. Trents could have been on him before he had a chance to drop the wood and draw his weapon. Trents could plant that ax right in his skull before the wood finished hitting the ground. Trents stood there looking at Micah with the ax in hand. Micah was wondering what his intentions were. "Are they going to come at me through you?"

"They wont me ta kill ya. Willin' ta give me a sow ta do it."

Fear and anger hit Micah at the same time. "So, you are here to kill me?"

"Ah told 'em Ah would," Trents admitted.

Micah reasoned that his best way out of this was to drop the wood and try to put enough distance between himself and Trents to give himself enough time to get out his gun and blow Trents head off. Death was staring Micah in the face, and he was ready for it. "Come and get me then."

"Woe," Trents said, dropping the ax and putting up his hands, "Ah told 'em Ah was gonna kill ya, cause Ah don't wont 'em ta go out and get somebody else ta do it, ya understand? Somebody you don't know and ain't ready fuh. Ah ain't heah ta do ya no harm. Ah's heah cause Ah wanna give ya a chance ta get out of heah. Leave Jago, Ah'll tell 'em dat Ah jes' couldn't get ta ya. Dat way ya get out of dis wit' yo' life, and yo' blood ain't on my han's."

Micah dropped the wood, ready to draw his weapon. "Are you sure that's the way it is?"

"Dat's da way it is. Ah ain't tryin' ta hurt cha, else Ah would of done kilt cha when yo' back was ta me. You wouldn't even knowed you was dead until dat great gettin' up mornin' when we all gotta stand befo' da judgement seat of Christ," Trents said.

Soon, Elijah returned and had to wonder what was going on. Micah had his hand on his revolver, and Trents still had his hands in the air.

"What's dis?" Elijah asked.

"The whites have sent Trents to kill me," Micah said.

"Ah ain't come ta kill 'im. Ah's heah tryin' ta save his life," Trents countered.

"Dey sont cha ta kill 'im?" Elijah asked.

"Asa Saunders came out ta see me, said they wonted 'im dead, and dey wont me ta do it. Ah ain't never kilt nobody, and Ah ain't gonna start now. Dey's promising a pig ta kill 'im. You know how tight thangs is. Dat's a lot ta some folks. Ah ain't wont 'em ta go out and get somebody a lit' mo' hard up 'an me. Somebody who won't thank twice about killin' 'im."

Elijah perceived that Trents was being truthful. "Take ya han' off dat twist shooter, Micah. Trents tellin' ya da gospel."

"Ah wouldn't take too long about clearin' out of heah, Micah," Trents said, "O'm jes' hopin' dey ain't got nobody else, and dat Ah's da only one dey done sont ta kill ya. Ah can't be sho. Da mo' time go by. Da less faith dey's gonna have in me ta do dis. Dey gon' get somebody else."

"I will not run. Let them get someone else to kill me. I know to watch for one of my own now, and I will," Micah assured.

"Thank of me and mine too, now will you," Trents said, "Ah's takin' a big chance comin' heah ta warn ya. Da whites might get smart and figure out what Ah done done, and ya know what dey gon' do ta me fuh dat."

"We all have our portion of risk to bear," Micah said.

"Well, Ah'll be damned," Trents said full of resentment, "Nigga, Ah's tryin' ta help ya stay alive, and you don't care iffen dem crackers come down heah and string me up."

"He ain't mean it like dat, Trents," Elijah tried to amend.

"Ya can't prove it by me. Elijah, what's wrong wit' dis nigga? He gonna mess around, and get me and him killed. Y'all need ta leave Jago."

"Trents, I don't mean you any harm. I'm grateful to you for what you are trying to do, but you made a choice to be a man today. In the South, especially, that is not an easy decision to make," Micah said.

"What is you talkin' about?" Trents sneered.

"He mean dat by not doing what da whites wont, you is standin' manfully," Elijah tried to explain.

Twenty-Three

Franklin had given serious thought as to how he should proceed. He had a plan to get Shelby Alexander to leave and forget what he was summoned to Jago to do. Several days preparation had gone into Franklin's next move.

Early in the morning, he headed for town and marched into the sheriff's office. He found Shelby Alexander, Sheriff Hackman and his two deputies Angus and Abner waiting for him. Franklin sent word that Shelby should meet him there, which Shelby was all to eager to do. Franklin entered the Sheriff's office as though he owned the world and all in it. There was a lack of politeness in him, as he walked up to Shelby with his high-minded ego visibly on his shoulders, like a chip. He got right down to it. "Alexander, you have come here, and moved about this town helping to fuel the lies, which are spreading like wild fire. Because of your very presence here, people are assuming the lies that they hear are true. They are calling my son a murderer, and a hundred other vicious names no doubt. You are hurting my standing, and the standing of my family, in this community. It has to end. It has to end today. What evidence do you have that anything those illegally freed slaves have told you is true? Let's see it. I want to hold it in my hand. If you don't have evidence, leave this town. There is no need for you to be here."

Franklin's approach was upsetting and quite offensive to Shelby, but he kept his calm. "It is unfortunate that your reputation has been damaged, but I am here to do a job, and if your reputation is damaged in the process, so be it."

"Your job is to determine the truth, and if you were doing your job, you would know that these accusations are untrue," Franklin said, "have you talked to the families of these so-called victims? What evidence do you have? Ah want to know what you've got that justifies this Yankee harassment."

"No, I haven't talked to the families of the victims, and I don't have any physical evidence, yet," Shelby answered.

"It is amazing that you Yankees won the war, given your lack of thoroughness in the most simple of things. Every time the coloreds yell wolf, you Yankees, self proclaimed protectors of the coloreds, come running. The truth be damned if it gets in the way. What would it have hurt you to talk with the families of these so-called victims. Well, your lack of thoroughness ends today. Ah am going to help you do the job properly that you were sent here to do. Let's go talk to my son's accusers. Let's go talk to the parents of the victims. Let's see your evidence so we can put an end to this utter foolishness that you Yankees seem to revel in at the coloreds' call. As a former southerner, you should be aware that coloreds are known to stretch the truth with an uncanny frequency, but Ah don't suppose that would matter to you foolish Yankees."

"Why would you want to waste time like that, when you know that any testimony the coloreds might give is inadmissable in Mississippi courts?" Shelby asked.

"You do it, because then you would know that you are being taken for a fool. You will not find any coloreds who have lost children, certainly not by my son's hands."

Straightaway, Shelby began to suspect treachery was afoot. Franklin was calling Shelby's hand. A very risky and bold maneuver at this juncture. He wouldn't do that, not unless the deck was stacked in his favor. Shelby felt that he had no choice but to play along. "Okay, let's ride."

Accompanied by the sheriff and Shelby, Franklin headed for Jago. Their first stop was at Elijah's house. As they sit on the porch, Elijah and Micah were very surprised to see Franklin and the sheriff as they approached.

"Maybe, you oughta take off dat gun," Elijah advised Micah.

"I don't think so," Micah replied.

"Dat's da sheriff wit' Mista Shelby and Franklin Wallace. He don't need ta see ya wit' dat gun on. Listen to me now. No need ta invite trouble ta sit at yo' table, not when you ain't gotta."

"I'm not taking it off, but I will step inside while they are here."

Micah stepped inside, but stood close to the door, so he might hear what was being said. Shelby, Franklin, and the sheriff rode up, stopping before Elijah.

"Hello, Elijah," Shelby said, "We need to talk with you. Please, tell the sheriff, and Franklin Wallace what happened the night you caught Jesse Wallace trying to commit the murder of one of your children."

"Ah resent that," Franklin protested.

Shelby didn't bother to respond to Franklin. "Tell them what happened, Elijah."

"We caught 'im about six miles from–"

"Who is we?" Franklin interrupted.

"My brother and some others," Elijah answered.

"What others?" Franklin tried to intimidate.

"Let him talk," Shelby said.

"We caught 'im tryin' ta kill a young boy by the name of Ezekiel Bowden. He was tryin' ta choke 'im ta death," Elijah explained.

"You saw this?" Franklin asked in a hostile tone.

"Well, naw, Ah ain't seed it, but–"

"Didn't you just say 'we caught him'? Correct me if Ah'm wrong, but doesn't 'we' mean inclusive of you?" Franklin said, trying to trip Elijah up. "Are you listening to him, gentlemen. His story is changing. Had you taken time to do your job properly, Shelby Alexander, you would have seen that this boy is lying."

"Ah ain't lyin', Mista Wallace."

"Ah say that you are. Ah say that my son never tried to kill anyone, and Ah say that you are fabricating this whole thing. Where is this child that my son supposedly tried to murder? Let's go talk to him?"

"My brother dem caught 'im tryin' ta kill dat boy, Mista Wallace, and dat be da truth."

"It is an out and out lie! My son never left our home. He was in bed asleep when this supposedly happened. Ah know, because Ah looked in on him."

"Dat ain't da truth, Mista Wallace. We brought 'im home ta ya da nex' mornin'."

"Are you calling me a liar, boy?" Franklin said, raising up in the saddle, as if he was about to come off of his horse and attack Elijah.

Elijah did not answer. Franklin Wallace was looking him directly in the eyes. Elijah looked away, down at the ground. Years upon years of servitude had conditioned him to respond in this way.

"Do you see this?" Franklin said. "The boy can't even look me in the eyes. That is the true mark of a liar. A liar will never look you in the eye for shameful fear his lies will be seen by you. Ah told you they were an imaginative people when it comes to telling lies."

"Ah ain't lyin'," Elijah responded, still looking down.

From within the house, Micah was becoming angry. Yet, he dared not step outside to help Elijah. Micah was not going to take off his weapon. If he stepped outside wearing the gun, he might have to kill the sheriff, who was sure to want to seize the weapon. If he took off his revolver, Franklin Wallace may have taken advantage of the opportunity, and killed him while he was unarmed. Micah didn't put it past him.

"You are lying, and Ah am going to prove it," Franklin vowed, "Let's go see this child you say my son tried to kill."

Elijah didn't know what to make of this. It didn't make sense to him that Franklin would want to have the child's account of the night Jesse Wallace tried to kill him on record with Shelby and the sheriff. Nevertheless, Elijah thought that it was to his advantage to go along with this. He felt that Franklin could call him a liar, but it would soon become apparent who was lying once all of the black families that lost children had their say. Elijah felt this could only help their case. Humbly, he looked at Franklin. "All right, suh."

Micah wanted to come out to ride along for this, but he would not do so unarmed. Elijah was on his own for now. Elijah mounted his mule, and the four men rode off to the Bowden farm. Once there, they saw Lee Bowden, Ezekiel's father, working in the cotton fields. They rode up to him, and climbed down from their horses. It had been a long ride, and they wanted to stretch.

"Lee, dis heah is Mista Shelby Alexander. He da government man dey sont heah ta help us. Dis da sheriff, and dat's Mista Wallace. Tell 'em about da other mornin' when we brought Ezekiel home ta y'all, afta Jesse Wallace tried ta choke 'im ta death."

Lee looked at Franklin with a quick frightened glance. "What you talkin' 'bout, Elijah?"

Elijah caught the glance toward Franklin, as did Shelby. Shelby realized that Franklin had been hard at work stacking the deck in his favor. Shelby tried to instill the confidence in Lee to speak up. "Don't be afraid Lee. I am here to help. Just tell me what happened."

"Ain't nothin' happened, suh. Ah don't know what y'all talkin' 'bout," Lee insisted.

"Lee, he heah ta help us," Elijah assured, "ya gotta tell 'em what happened."

"By all means, speak up, Lee, but be careful not to lie. God in heaven will have no mercy upon your black soul if you do that," Franklin said harmlessly enough.

"Ah don't know what Elijah talkin' 'bout. Ain't nobody brung my boy home, and ain't nobody tried ta kill 'im. Now dat's da truth," Lee swore.

"Lee," Elijah said with disappointment.

"Ah's jes' tryin' ta do da right thang, Elijah," Lee said.

"Sure you are, and Ah appreciate it. You could side with this liar, and make trouble for me, but you are an honest colored," Franklin said, "Where is your boy? Let's put the question to him. So, there will be no doubt that this liar is indeed a liar."

"Go get your son," Sheriff Hackman directed.

Lee, went into his home and came back with Ezekiel. Ezekiel was afraid of the white men. He moved in closer to his father, grabbing him by his arm. Everyone could sense that the child was afraid. Elijah and Shelby wondered why.

"Ezekiel," Elijah said in a very friendly way, "will ya tell us about da other night, when you and Jesse Wallace got together in da woods so he could give ya some candy?"

"Jesse Who?" Ezekiel responded.

"Do you know my son Jesse, Ezekiel?" Franklin asked.

"Naw suh."

"Did someone try to hurt you in the woods the other night, Ezekiel?" Shelby asked.

"Naw suh."

"Are you certain?" Shelby asked, sensing the boy was not being truthful.

Ezekiel looked up at his father, as if he needed permission from Lee to say what was actually in his heart. The look upon Lee's face, squinting eyes, tightly pressed lips, and jaws which grew sterner by the second, was one that almost threatened the boy. Ezekiel looked at Shelby. "Yassuh."

"Who owns this property that you work, Lee?" Shelby inquired.

"Mista Ian Everett," Lee answered.

"Have you seen him lately?" Shelby asked.

"What are you fishing for, Alexander?" Franklin asked abrasively. "This boy was not coerced in anyway by me or any one associated with me. Ah know that is difficult for your Yankee heart to believe, but it is true. It is sad that you would believe, of your own accord, that Ah have forced this boy to be less than forthcoming with you. Dismiss your personal prejudice against the ways of the South, and look soberly at the facts that are before you. Allow yourself to consider that Ah am being truthful, and Elijah is not. "

Shelby knew that Franklin had gotten to Lee. He knew it as sure as he knew his own name. Yet, it mattered not. Franklin was playing his hand close to perfection. At a glance, it certainly looked as if Elijah had gotten government help there under false pretenses. The most damning thing, however, was that he had an alleged victim on record as saying that what Elijah claimed, did not happen. Elijah realized that he had to stand up. Franklin was having his way with him. He couldn't sit idly by and let it happen this way.

"Ah ain't lyin'," Elijah said, "you da only liar heah, Wallace. What happen ta all dat talk about dealin' fairly wit' us, Wallace? It wa'n't nothin' but a lot of empty talk, but Ah reckon dat's all a liar good fuh, empty—vain talk."

That cut Franklin deeply. He stood up tall and erect, and stuck out his chest, like he was going to strike Elijah. "Ah dare you talk so boldly and familiar to me, boy. Ah am Mister to you."

"What you is ta me is a liar dat don't know how ta brang up his murderin' chil'ens," Elijah fired back.

Franklin's temperament rose from a slow simmer to a violently bubbling boil. "You insolent–"

"Da truth stang, don't it?" Elijah said, sounding more like Micah than himself. "Ah reckon da fruit don't fall too far from da tree. You was gon' kill me da other night when you and dem mens come ta my house tryin' ta protect ya son.

"Yes, And Ah should have killed you," Franklin lashed out in anger.

At that moment, Franklin caught himself. He realized that he had allowed Elijah to goad him into confessing, in front of a government official sent to investigate the matter, that he came to Elijah's house to kill Elijah in order to protect Jesse. Something there would be no need to do, if Elijah was lying, which was now apparent to all that he was not.

Franklin cooled his temper, realizing that he needed his wits about him, as Elijah was very clever. This was the second time that he had underestimated Elijah. Franklin vowed inwardly that it would never happen again.

Franklin looked at Shelby and the sheriff. He wounded himself in their eyes with this outburst, but he hadn't killed himself. However, the door was open, and Shelby walked right through it. "So, you were at his house with a lynch mob? I find that a strange action to be taken in order to protect someone who is innocent."

Franklin was under attack, but he was not going to fight Elijah's fight. He had been knocked down, but he stood right back up and stuck to his fight plan. He went right back to the attack, jabbing at Elijah's claims with the facts. "Lee, did Ah understand you to say that what Elijah says concerning your son, never happened?"

"It ain't happened, suh," Lee said.

"Your boy was in bed asleep, was he not?"

"Yassuh."

"Ezekiel, you don't know my son, Jesse, do you?"

"Naw suh," Ezekiel coyly responded.

"He never tried to hurt you in any way, did he?"

"Naw suh."

Sheriff, Alexander, Ah think the facts speak clearly for themselves. Unless either of you have any more applicable questions, Ah suggest we move on to the next family that has supposedly lost a child at my son's hands," Franklin said.

Shelby was not content to let Franklin escape so easily. "Why did you and others go to Elijah's house with rope in hand to lynch him?"

Franklin stuck to his strategy. "Alexander, correct me if Ah am wrong, but Ah thought you were here to investigate the supposed murder of black children, as charged by Elijah Wright. You have heard Wright's claims soundly refuted by the supposed victim and his father. What more do you want? Ah, like you, want to get to the bottom of this. So, please, do your job without bias. Stop trying to nail me to the crucifix for your own personal gain."

"Mista Shelby, maybe, ya oughta talk wit' my brother and some of da others dat was dere dat night," Elijah contended, ready to fight Franklin all the way.

"Why?" Franklin said, "he could get a hundred coloreds to side with him. Let's talk to the ones that count. Let's talk to the families of these supposed victims."

"He done got ta 'em all, Mista Shelby," Elijah contended, "Ya needs ta talk ta Jesse, Mista Shelby, talk ta 'im, jes' you, him, and da sheriff."

"Ah won't submit my son to that," Franklin countered, "why should he, and the rest of my family, be troubled with this foolishness. This matter can be resolved by simply talking to the families of these so-called victims, and Ah haven't tampered with them either. He is just saying that to confuse the issue, because he is afraid that you will learn what Ah already know. My son is no murderer."

"Yo' son kilt dem chil'ens, and ya knows it," Elijah contended, looking Franklin in his eyes.

"Alexander, you tell this deceitful bastard not to say another word to me. You get him under control, or you send him home," Franklin barked, not liking that Elijah would dare look him in his eyes.

"You is da one cloudin' da truth," Elijah said, "Youse a liar, and ta hide yo' sins ya causin' others ta lie."

"Shut him up, Alexander," Franklin barked.

Franklin seemed heated to everyone, but he was purposefully projecting this persona. He was simply trying to draw Elijah in, hoping Elijah would make a mistake that he could capitalize on. However, Elijah was very crafty. He was far more crafty than people gave him credit for being. Already, Elijah saw that Franklin had this game all but won. However, there was one move that Elijah was counting on that he was sure Franklin had overlooked. Elijah would go along with this charade of visiting the families of the murdered children. He had to on the off chance that one of them would come forward with the truth. Elijah wasn't counting on that however. His eye was looking toward the end game. Where he was certain that he could steal the game away from Franklin, and prove once and for all that Franklin was a liar, and Jesse was a murderer.

They decided to question Collin Bailey's family next. His son, Ken, was the first child to be killed. The next round of this game was played within the confines of Collin's home. Elijah felt that Collin was the best bet to speak the truth. "Collin, tell Mista Shelby heah about yo' boy Ken."

Collin looked at Elijah with very emotional eyes, as if it hurt to think of his son. This was a most promising sign to Elijah. It signaled to Elijah that the memory of Collin's lost son would compel him to tell the truth. Elijah was hoping many moving words would come from Collin, but Collin said something that was expected. It was just that he said it in a very unexpected and troubling way. "Ah ain't never had no boy named Ken."

Elijah looked at Collin with stunned disbelief. He couldn't believe that Collin would deny even fathering the boy. "You gon' deny yo' own flesh and blood."

"Ah ain't got no young on' named Ken," Collin denied again.

All Elijah could do was look at Collin. Collin looked away from him in shame. Elijah saw that it was tearing Collin apart to speak such a profane obscenity. It was also plainly visible to Shelby that this act of denial was a mean pang to Collin. Collin's wife Sadie, and their daughter Norah, were also in the house. Elijah looked to them. Shame also blanketed Sadie's face. Elijah knew that she would stand by her husband. Norah, however, looked angry, as if she was ready to burst out in truth.

Elijah did not wish to exact a more cumbersome burden upon this family, but if Norah was willing to cooperate, Elijah felt that he had to try. "Norah, did ya habe a brother named Ken?"

Norah looked to Collin and then to her mother. Sadness covered Norah's face, deep sadness. "No suh, Ah ain't had no brother named Ken."

"There, you see?" Franklin said, looking at Shelby. "They have never had a child named Ken. How could my boy have killed someone who does not exist? Elijah made the whole thing up."

"Is there anything you need to ask them, Shelby?" Sheriff Hackman said.

Shelby felt that he should say something, but he didn't know what. Nor did he wish to put this family through anymore pain. "No."

"Are you starting to see the truth of the matter?" Franklin said in a confident, almost snide, way.

"I see what's going on," Shelby answered, aware that Franklin had stacked the deck mightily.

"Let us not tarry. There are many more families to visit. We need to see them all today," Franklin said with a commanding tone.

"Well, let us be going," Sheriff Hackman replied.

The men left the Bailey home. No sooner than the door closed behind Elijah and the others. Norah was pricked in her heart, and she could not hold her peace. "Poppa, We shouldn't oughta done dat. We shouldn't oughta denied my brother. We come in dis world wid nothin', and dat da way we leave it. Da only thang left afta us, so dat anybody can ever know we was, is da life we done lived. My brother lived a good life. He ain't never done nobody wrong. So, how we gon' deny his good life, and let da one dat kilt 'im go free."

"Hush yo' mouth, gul. Hush yo' mouth," Sadie said sadly, deeply pained that she was prepared in her heart to deny her son if asked.

"Ah's gon' go tell 'im da truth," Norah said, moving toward the door.

Collin denied Ken, and it pained him more than Sadie and Norah could ever understand. Yet, he did what he thought best. As Norah reached the door, Collin grabbed her by the arm and slung her to the floor, but not in anger. "Sit yo' lit' ass down, gal. Ain't da father mo' 'an a sista? Ah loved Ken too, mo' 'an you loved 'im. Ah brought 'im into dis worl', but he gon'. We can't bring 'im back. All we got is our family, and we gotta hold on ta what we got. We done lost enough, and Ah won't lose no mo'."

Lying on the floor looking up at Collin, Norah was moved to compassion for her father. Franklin threatened their family. He and four others came into their home in the middle of the night, threatening to kill Collin and rape Norah and Sadie, while the younger children would be made to watch. It was Franklin's way of letting Collin know that he could take all that Collin had anytime he wanted. This was why Collin lied. He was just trying to protect his family in the only way he knew how, by compromising, cooperating with the enemy.

Norah understood, but she didn't agree with Collin's choice. Yet, what could she do, or even Collin for that matter. The world is one of compromise, willingly or unwillingly.

As for Elijah, Shelby, Sheriff Hackman, and Franklin, they spent the better part of the day visiting every family that lost a child, except for the family headed North. Sadly, every single family, in one way or another, that lost a child denied having done so. Most said they never had children, denying them altogether. One family said they had a child, but that the boy died of pneumonia in early winter. Elijah expected as much from each of them.

Franklin made his move to end the game. "This should satisfy you, Alexander. It should be obvious to you that there is no mischief here. All that remains for you to do is report to your superiors that this was a wild goose chase. There is no need for you to be here, go about your business."

"He ain't done yet," Elijah said.

"Ah beg to differ," Franklin replied, knowing he had Elijah and Shelby right where he wanted them. "What more is there for him to do here? You seem a fair man, Shelby. Surely, you can take no pleasure in debasing my family name with your presence here. Your investigation is done, leave here. If you don't, Ah'll be forced to contact both of the United States Senators from Mississippi. Their voices still carry weight in Washington. Ah know one of them personally, and Ah'm sure that once Ah petition them, they will see to it that you cease harassment of my family for unfounded reasons."

"I don't respond well to threats," Shelby said.

"Ah assure you it is not a threat. Ah am merely apprising you of my intent should you continue to persist in doing injury to my name with your presence here," Franklin said.

"He ain't done heah yet," Elijah insisted.

"Yes, he is," Franklin assured, knowing he could now force Shelby to leave through political means.

"No, he ain't," Elijah reiterated, "we got six mo' folks ta see, and Ah know dey gon' tell us da truth."

"We have been to see all of the families, as Ah understood it," Sheriff Hackman said, confused by Elijah's statement.

"Ain't no mo' families ta see, but it's six dead chil'ens dat ain't told dey story. It's five lit' boys and one lit' gal, and dey still habe a say in dis. If dey's sleepin' in da grave, dat oughta be reason enough fuh ya stay, Mista Shelby."

"Yes it is, Elijah," Shelby answered.

"What kind of a madman are you?" Franklin asked.

"Ah ain't crazy," Elijah asked.

"Desecration of a grave just to prove or disprove a moot point is utter madness to me," Franklin said, "you are not going to let them do this are you, Sheriff Hackman?"

"Shelby, it does seem a bit excessive," Sheriff Hackman said.

"Mister Wallace accused me of not being thorough with my investigation. Well, I am trying to correct that shortcoming. Mister Wallace above all others should be pleased that I am being so thorough."

"You have heard family after family tell you that they haven't lost any children to murder. Why can't you simply accept that and be done with this matter," Franklin said to Shelby.

"To be quite frank with you, Mister Wallace, I believe that you corrupted those people. I am not quite sure how, with threat of violence, I suspect," Shelby said.

"Why is it so difficult for you to believe that My son was not involved in any murders? Why is it so difficult for you to accept that there have been no murders? Why is it so difficult for you to let this thing go? No matter how much searching you do invariably the truth remains the truth. You were once a proud southerner.

"Ah don't know what turned you to self-loathing, turned you to the mistrust of your fellow southerners. All Ah know is that it is hurting your ability to be rational. Ah would recommend that you sit down and examine your motives for your relentless pressing of this matter. The facts are before you, and the facts confirm my sons innocence. Relent your folly, and let it give way to rational behavior based on sound logic and not personal bias," Franklin preached.

"I am always rational, Mister Wallace, I am not given to folly or personal bias. We are going to open those graves," Shelby replied.

Franklin shook his head in dismay at Shelby. "If you insist on going through with this invidious act then be my guest, as Ah can say no more."

"You are being unreasonable, Shelby," Sheriff Hackman said.

"We are going to do it, anyway," Shelby replied.

By the time they reached the church grave yard and were well underway unearthing a body; the evening sun had begun to sink low. Elijah and Shelby labored tirelessly to unearth the body of Lester Green, the last child murdered. As they got close to the child's wooden coffin, Shelby stopped for a moment to look up at the sheriff and Franklin. The sheriff was looking back at him as though he were completely mad. Franklin seemed to fluster about. Finally, they reached the coffin.

"We don't have to do this," Franklin said.

"Why not? We've gone through the trouble of digging him up," Shelby said, certain that Elijah and he were about to be proven right.

They pried the coffin open, and to their consternation, an elderly woman's body was in the coffin. An elderly black woman that Elijah had never seen before. He didn't even have the slightest idea of who she could be. The foul stench of decaying death overwhelmed their sense of smell, as they began to feel like fools with Franklin and Sheriff Hackman looking down on them.

"Are you sure this is the right grave?" Shelby asked.

"Ah thought it was," Elijah answered, as he looked around trying to get his bearings. He looked and looked, feeling more the fool with each second. He was certain that this was the right grave. "Dis it."

"Apparently not, Elijah," Shelby said, feeling very much the fool. His voice rising with anger toward Elijah.

Elijah looked at Franklin, "He moved 'im."

Franklin shook his head in dismay at them both, and with bruising confidence said, "Invariably, the truth is the truth no matter how you try to twist it. This would be laughable were it not such a sad spectacle, and Ah hope that it snaps you to your senses, Shelby. An educated white man should know better than to go around trusting in the ravings of an ignorant nigger. Do not shame yourself any further. Let your superiors know that there is no great conspiracy going on here against the poor helpless coloreds, as you perceive them to be. Be truthful with your superiors, and then leave."

There was nothing Shelby could say. For the first time, he was really doubting himself. Maybe, Franklin was right. Maybe, there was some self-loathing which he had allowed to cloud his judgement. Why was he willing to desecrate someone's grave, when he had all of the evidence that he needed to make an informed decision without going this far. Maybe, there was some personal bias that he harbored against white people of the South. Shelby felt that he had to take a good hard look at that.

"Ah'm going home now," Franklin said, "Ah'll leave you two to contemplate the error of your ways."

"You two need to put that poor woman back in her grave," Sheriff Hackman said, as he mounted up to ride off with Franklin.

After Sheriff Hackman and Franklin had left, Elijah and Shelby began to cover the grave. They didn't talk to each other. Shelby was tempted to ride off and leave Elijah to this hideous task. Shelby felt shame. Shame that not even the pitch black of darkest night could hide. When they were almost done, Elijah dared to speak. "He moved da body, Mista Shelby."

Shelby just looked at Elijah. "Sure he did. He went through the trouble of moving six bodies. He went through the trouble of threatening all those people to the point they would deny ever having children. Do you really believe he would do all of that? I am sure you are familiar with the saying that you know a tree by the fruit it bears."

"And, what cha mean by dat?" Elijah asked.

"In this case, that the man insists that his son never killed anyone, and he is bringing forth good fruit to support his claims. You, on the other hand, can only seem to manage rotten fruit."

"Dat boy done kilt, Mista Shelby. Everybody colored around heah know it."

"What you know and what you can prove are two entirely different things, and in case you missed it. Wallace just proved his son's innocence in convincing fashion."

"So, what is you gon' do? Is ya gon' run off and leave us ta handle dis?"

"What more do you want me to do? Cause, I have to tell you that I'm having doubts about the validity of your claims."

"Ah wont cha ta finish it."

"Elijah–"

"Thank about dis, Mista Shelby, Elijah interrupted. Today, when we was at Lee Bowden's place, Franklin Wallace told you dat he came ta my house ta kill me to protect his son, didn't he do it? He let dat slip cause he was mad, and it da only bad move he done made today. He done showed ya everythang he wonted ya see, but don't forget what he showed ya dat he didn't wont cha see. You asked 'im flat out why he came ta see me wit' a lynch mob, and he wouldn't answer. Why? Cause he wont cha ta forget dat so he can blind ya wit' lies that look like truth. Everybody dat ya talked wit' today was scared of dat man, and Ah know you seed dat. It wa'n't yo' 'magination. Dem folks was scared of 'im. Franklin Wallace is a rich man. He got money enough, and courage enough, to do whatever it take ta save his boy. Ya asked me iffen he went to all da trouble of threatenin' folks to lie. Ah say he did. Ya ask me iffen he moved all dem bodies. Ah say he did. You got eyes ta see. Ears ta hear, and a mind ta thank. Use 'em so you can know what's goin' on heah. Don't forget da fear dat ya heard in dem folks voices. Don't forget da fear ya seed in dey faces. Don't set aside what cha mind tellin' ya it all mean. Youse da las' smidgen of hope we got. Don't give up. Keep pushin' till you git at da truth."

Shelby knew that Elijah was right. There was no doubt in his mind that Franklin forced the families of the dead children to say the things that they said, and he understood that he couldn't walk out on Elijah. "I'll do what I can, but the clock is ticking. Wallace is going to force me out. It's just a matter of time. We can only hope something good happens before he does."

"Ah got faith in da good Lawd dat it will."

Twenty-Four

At Jasmine and Rory's home, the sun was rising, and it was more than just a new day. It was really a new beginning. The murders were over, and Rory was so thankful that the murderer wasn't Jasmine. Rory was lying in bed with Jasmine in his arms. He wondered how he could ever have doubted her, vowing in his heart to never doubt her again. Jasmine was still asleep, as he looked at her, gently stroking her hair. She was the most beautiful thing he had ever seen, more beautiful than she had ever been. He wondered how that was possible. There was a joyous excitement within Rory. A joy likened to that which a child might feel on Christmas morning. He was just very happy. Jasmine opened her eyes and kissed his chest.

"Mornin', my queen, my lady," said he.

Jasmine liked the way Rory welcomed her into the world. Lady was not a word often used to describe black women at this time. In many songs of the day, and in the thinking of white America at this time, the black woman was considered anything, but a lady.

"What ya smilin' bout all early in da mornin'?" asked she playfully.

"O'm smilin', cause O'm heah wit' cha. You make me happy."

"Mmm Hmm, jes' tell me anythang, cause ya knows Ah believe ya, don't cha?" said she, playing with him, never doubting that she made him happy.

"It's true, Ah feels good about cha."

"And, Ah feels good about cha too."

"Let's get up, and enjoy dis heah day. It's real pretty out."

"Ya wanna go down ta da pond fuh a swim?"

"Dat sound good. When ya wanna go?"

"How bout now, right afta breakfast dat is."

"So early in da mornin'?" said he.

"Yeah, da water will be cool and won't be nobody round. Ya never can tell what a man and a woman might get inta in a quiet, out da way, spot like dat."

Rory laughed. "Yeah, Ah guess we could get inta somethin' good."

"Mmm Hmm, real good," said she, raising up to kiss Rory's lips.

They got up and had breakfast: peaches, black berries, and plums. Soon, they were standing at a large quiet pond in the middle of the woods. They undressed, and Jasmine went into the water. "Come on," said she.

"Ain't cha scared a snake or somethin' gonna bite cha in dere?"

"Ah come heah most every night and ain't nothin' bit me yet. Come on in, Ah got somethin' good and hot fuh ya."

"Oh yeah, what cha got? Soup?"

"Ha ha, come on in heah and find out."

Rory stepped in. "It's cold in heah."

"Don't worry, O'm fixin' ta warm ya up."

Jasmine swam to Rory. She clung to him, wrapping her legs around him. She began to kiss him passionately. Rory was loving it. They made love in the pond. It was a wonderful experience for the both of them. They were in complete undefiled bliss. They were young, and so very much in love. Jasmine was only nineteen and Rory was but twenty.

They stayed in the water loving each other, just enjoying the moment and each others company. When you are young, and in love such as were they, every kiss has such an unbelievably sweet and pleasant taste. Every touch is a tender and soulful sensation, time loses its meaning, and everything around you slows. A state-of-mind flourishes where even the faults and transgressions of your true love against you are easily forgiven and forgotten. The only thing that matters in this perfect world made by young lovers is the one that you love. For it is your whole desire to be with your first and one-true love, and nowhere else.

This is as it was for Rory and Jasmine. The bond between them was strong, so very strong. Two hours went by without notice, and they finally decided it was time to get out. They came out of the water and begin to dress. Jasmine's body was wet and beautiful, glistening in the sun. Rory looked at her naked pleasing form with a deep loving gaze. Jasmine caught him staring.

"Why ya lookin' at me like dat?" said she, with a smile. "It ain't nothin' ya ain't seed befo'."

"What you and spring got in common?"

"Huh?"

"Ya know, da season of da year."

"Ah don't know. What cha figure me and spring got in common?"

"Ya both warm, beautiful, and full of life," said he in a very inspired, serious, loving way. "Ya surround who Ah is, like a cool breeze about my skin on a hot day."

What Rory said caught Jasmine off guard. She stopped dressing for a moment and looked at him, finding the things he said pleasing to the ear and heart, loving him a little more than she did just a moment earlier.

"Ah love ya, Jasmine. Ah love ya. Ah love ya. Ah love ya. Ah could say it without ceasing from now until heaven, and earth, all time passed away. It still ain't gon' be enough ta match what Ah feels in my heart fuh ya. Ya fill me wit' somethin' Ah can't get enough of. Somethin' Ah can't hardly put inta words. It's like, Ah kin pluck a apple from a tree. It's gon' taste sweeter cause of you. Ah ain't jes' sayin' dat cha make thangs better dan dey is. It's a whole heap mo' 'an dat. Ah can be talkin' ta somebody, and Ah'll say somethin'. Ah'll catch my self, and Ah knows dat ain't me talkin', but you in me. You da life in me, like da blood flowin' through my veins. Ah once heard a preacher man say dat man don't live by bread alone. Ah believe dat's true, at least fuh me. Ah lives by da love of you."

"Oh, Rory," said she, with a tear in her eye, very touched by his sentiment.

"Ah jes' wonted cha ta know what's in my heart."

Jasmine gracefully moved to him and gently kissed his lips. She held him so very tightly. He took her into his arms, brushing his lips across her soft face, clinging to her.

"Ah loves ya too, Rory," said she, "Ah can't say it da beautiful way you can, but Ah's do. Ah loves ya wid every bit of me, through and through."

"When O'm wid cha, Ah feels like dat fella in da Bible."

"Fella in da Bible?"

"Ya know, da first man."

"Adam?"

"Yeah, him, Ah feels like O'm in paradise and da whole world mine. O'm happy, mo' happier 'an Ah feel like Ah gots a right ta be."

"Oh, ya got a right ta be dis happy. We got a right ta be. It's so good and so right fuh us ta be together and happy."

Suddenly, Rory started to look around. "Come on, Jasmine, let's get on home."

"Somethin' wrong?" Jasmine asked.

"No, Ah don't reckon so."

"Ya see somethin'?"

"No, jes' got a feelin' like somebody watchin' us."

Jasmine smiled, not really believing anyone was there. "Well, if it is, dey sho done got a eye full den, ain't dey?"

Jasmine's smile helped Rory to relax a little, and he dismissed what instinct was telling him. "It ain't nothin', Ah don't guess."

"Let's go on home, like ya say, and work on dat baby some mo'."

Rory looked around once more. The woods were quiet, but for the sounds of crickets, birds, and the like, singing their timeless songs of summer, which was as it should have been. Rory took Jasmine by the hand, leading her to his horse. He mounted the animal and pulled Jasmine up behind him. The feeling that they were being watched took hold in him again. He looked around. Rory had his musket with him. It comforted him a little. Jasmine didn't sense anything wrong. She was caught up in the blissful joy of being there with her beloved Rory.

As they journeyed toward the road along this path, uneasiness began to grow in Rory. It wasn't much further until they would be out on the road. A much safer place, he felt. Rory believed that he heard something. He stopped the horse and listened.

"What? Ya hear somethin'?" Jasmine asked.

"Ah thought dat Ah did."

"Probably some of dese ole kids 'round heah playin'."

"Hmm, maybe," Rory said, quite uneasy, which unnerved Jasmine.

"Y'all lit' chaps git on home," she yelled.

"Ah don't thank it's no childrens playin'."

Rory lightly tapped his horse with the straps of his bridal. The gray mare started to move again. They finally reached the road. They were out in the open, and this made Rory feel a whole lot better.

"See, it weren't nothin'," Jasmine said, sensing Rory's uneasiness passing.

"No, Ah don't reckon it was," Rory said, feeling much better, "let's ride inta Olive Branch, and see if we can buy us a pie. Ah sho nuff wont a piece of apple pie."

"Dat's a mighty long way ta go fuh jes' some pie. Go on home, Ah'll make ya some fried apple pies. They taste jes' as good, and ya ain't gotta ride so far ta get one."

"Now, dat's when a man know a woman love 'im. When she willin' ta go through da extra trouble of makin' 'im a apple pie jes' cause he wont some."

"You knows dat Ah loves ya, and dat Ah'll do anythang in da world dat Ah can fuh ya."

"Ah knows it now," joked he.

"She hit him in the side playfully. "Ya been knowin' it all yo' life."

Jasmine saw something in the woods to the right of them, and it stole her joy. Rory saw it also, white men. They were shadowing them. Two of them Jasmine had seen, but didn't really know them. They were Byron James and Luke Gallager. James was a man five feet eight and three quarters inches tall with sandy brown hair and light blue eyes. Gallager was five eleven with slender built. His hair was blonde and he had blue eyes. Gallager's demeanor lacked the arrogant swagger of the other two.

He almost seemed timid. The third man, and the most dangerous, was Jerad Wildman. He stood six feet tall. He was a powerful man, but not in a lean muscular way. He was big and brutish, boorish even. He had brown hair with fiery brown eyes. He was abrasively confident. Both Jasmine and Rory knew him, and well at that.

Jerad's father was the overseer on the Drucker plantation for several years when they were growing up. There was no love lost between them. Jerad always despised Rory, because of the way Cyrus Drucker treated him like a son. Drucker even went so far as to give Rory a spotted Shetland Pony once, which he use to ride Jasmine around on as small children. Jerad, a child himself at the time and not much older than Rory, always felt that Jasmine and Rory should have been in the fields working, instead of enjoying pony rides.

Rory named the pony "Moon-Eyed Joe". The animal turned up dead just a month or so after being given to Rory. The animal had been poisoned, and Rory knew by whom. Jerad did it, and now he was here again to make trouble. Rory brought his horse to a stop. The men also stopped.

"Told you, Ah knew who you was, boy," Jerad said, referring to the night that Franklin Wallace and he tried to lynch Elijah, "told you, Ah was gonna be seein' you."

"What y'all wont?" Jasmine asked, afraid there was going to be trouble.

"Rory knows what this is about, don't you, boy?" Jerad said in a menacing tone.

Rory didn't answer. He was busy trying to figure out what he should do. The fight had come to him, and he was by no means ready for it. He was very worried that Jasmine would be hurt.

"We don't wont no trouble," Jasmine said, fearing just that.

"Too late for that, that dere nigger of yours stuck his musket in my face. Ah ain't one to let something like that go," Jerad proclaimed.

Jasmine wished Rory had killed Jerad when he had him in the sight of his musket. She realized that someone was about to die and the odds were against Rory and her.

"Let her leave heah," Rory petitioned.

"Ah ain't leavin' ya," she said.

"Shut up, Jasmine," Rory spouted, his first time ever really raising his voice to her, "she don't need ta be part of dis."

"Why should we do that?" Jerad taunted.

"Yeah, why should we do that. She's a right pretty gal," Byron James said with a despicable evil smile upon his face.

"Yes, she is," Jerad taunted, "Ah believe that when O'm done with you.

Ah'll have her spread her legs and do for me what she does for you."

"She got a right pretty mouth. Ah think Ah'd like some of that," James said, looking lustfully at Jasmine.

A chill ran down Jasmine's spine, troubling her, frightening her. Pure anger boiled in Rory.

"Ah'll be dead first," he said.

"Well, that's tha general idea," Jerad mocked.

Byron and Luke laughed.

Jasmine was more afraid than she had ever been in her life. "Don't do dis, y'all."

"O'm takin' some of y'all wid me," Rory vowed, making sure to put that thought on their minds, hoping they would stand down.

"Boy, all you gon' do is die," Jerad assured, reaching for his Colt Dragoon Revolver, almost gingerly.

As Jerad went for his weapon, Rory kicked his own horse hard in the sides. The animal took off. Jerad got off a shot, but missed. He and his companions laughed, as though this were a game. They gave chase.

Rory's horse was small and fast. It could easily out run his pursuers if he were alone, but he was not alone. With so much weight on its back, the mare was sure to tire soon. When that happened, Jerad and the others would overtake them. Jerad and Byron continued to shoot at them. Rory knew it was hard to hit a moving target, particularly when the shooter was also moving. Yet, he was afraid they would hit Jasmine. He wasn't willing to gamble with her life.

Faced with few options, Rory ducked into the woods. Jerad and the others wouldn't be able to get a clear shot at them there. Rory also hoped that the woods would provide an opportunity to slip past them. Jerad and his pals followed, hot on Rory's tail. Rory was able to put a little distance between them. Enough distance so that he could not see them in the dense woods. It didn't matter, however. The horse's hooves striking the ground was making a considerable amount of noise, which was all Jerad and the others would need to follow.

Rory stopped his mare and quickly pulled out his musket. He fired in the general direction of the sound of their pursuers. The men halted their pursuit, realizing Rory was shooting back at them. Rory realized that the men had halted, but he also realized it was only a temporary yield. He quickly dismounted and snatched Jasmine down from the horse. Rory smacked the horse on it's rear, and the animal took off to the right. Rory and Jasmine went left. The running horse was making the greater noise, enough to mask Jasmine's and Rory's movement. Rory hoped Jerad and the others would follow the horse.

Rory and Jasmine ducked behind a large oak tree and tried to be as quiet as possible. Rory's musket was a single shot weapon and had to be reloaded after each firing. Rory quietly began to do so. Jerad and the others had dismounted and taken cover, reluctant to ride into gun fire.

"That nigger is shootin' at us," Byron said in disbelief, looking around trying to search out Rory.

"Maybe, we oughta just let 'em be. We don't wanna get shot by some scared nigger," Luke advised.

"Like hell," Byron said, wanting Rory badly.

"Shut up," Jerad commanded, "We're gonna get that boy."

"But, he's shooting at us," Luke pointed out.

"Did you think that he was just gonna stand still while we hung 'im?" Jerad asked.

"You really gonna kill 'im," Luke asked, believing Jerad meant to scare Rory, to rough him up a little.

"As sure as he's black and O'm white," Jerad said.

"He might kill one of us. Niggers ain't suppose to have guns," Luke said.

"Well, he does. Now, shut up and stop cryin' about it," Byron said.

"Ah don't know about this," Luke said, not wanting to go forward.

"Shut up, and do what Ah tell ya," Jerad said with a commanding vigor.

"Ah don't wanna get killed out here," Luke said adamantly.

"You won't," Jerad assured.

"They are probably long gone. Ah heard 'em ride off right after he took a shot at us," Luke said.

"Ah ain't fallin' for that. They're still in here," Jerad assured.

"How can you be certain?" Luke asked.

"Cause, it's what Ah would have done," Jerad assured.

"Ah think yer right. They're still in here," Byron agreed.

"And, we're gonna get 'em. Fan out, keep yer eyes open and heads low. Ah wouldn't want that nigger to shoot it off," Jerad said.

Jasmine and Rory remained quietly behind the oak tree, hoping Jerad and the others would follow the horse, giving them a chance to slip out of this mess. Rory soon gave up hope of that happening. The very fact that Rory did not hear them told him that they had dismounted and were hunting Jasmine and him. Rory reasoned that they couldn't stay where they were any longer. He reached for Jasmine's hand and she took it. Jasmine's safety was the most important thing to Rory. He had to get her out of this. They moved as quietly as possible. Rory's plan was to stay ahead of, and out of the sight of, their pursuers. If they could just do that, he was sure that they could slip away at some point. There was only one problem. Rory kept hearing faint sounds directly behind, to the left, and right of him. Sounds which could have been mistaken for small animals making their way through the brush, but Rory knew better. They had him out flanked, driving Jasmine and him, like hounds driving the prey to the hunters. Rory kept looking around, expecting to see one of his pursuers at any moment. Yet, he did not. Chances were, if he didn't see them, they didn't see him. At least, this was what Rory hoped.

Rory's heart was pounding very hard. It seemed he could hear it. He fought hard to maintain a cool head. A cool head was one of only a few things, the most important thing, that he had working for him at that moment. He couldn't give that away. Even as they evaded danger, Rory was trying to think of a viable plan.

They soon came upon a small-hilly formation of rocks covered with grass and moss. As they went around it, Rory spotted a small cave in the rock formation. It was not even a cave really. It was a small hole, just big enough for one small person. Up to now, Rory had done just as his pursuers expected him to do, run. Upon seeing the hole, Rory had come up with a plan.

"Hide heah," he whispered.

Jasmine did as he told her.

"O'm gon' lead 'em away from heah," he whispered, "when ya thank it's safe, get out of heah. Get somewhere safe and bring back help if ya can."

Jasmine had a bad feeling about this. "Hide heah wid me."

"Can't," he whispered, "dey sho ta find us."

"Promise me dat you'll come back ta me," Jasmine whispered.

Rory looked at her with troubled eyes. "Ah love ya."

"Promise me," she said, finding Rory's evasion of her request disconcerting.

"O'm gon' lead O'm away, and den O'm gon' try ta slip past 'em when Ah can," he whispered.

This seemed to satisfy Jasmine. Rory quickly took some shrubbery and covered the hole. He moved away from Jasmine's hiding place quietly. Once far enough away, he made plenty of deliberate, but not suspicious noise. He stopped and listened. Sure enough, he heard three distinct faint noises headed toward him. Now, the smart play would have been for Rory to do just as he told Jasmine he would. He had given Jasmine a chance to escape, and now, he should try to out maneuver Jerad and the others and escape.

However, Rory was not of a mind to do this. Jerad had made it clear that he intended to kill Rory. Even if Rory was to elude him now, Jerad would still be out there, and would no doubt come for Rory at some other unexpected time. Rory was not of a mind to have it that way. Besides that, and most importantly, Jerad threatened to do Jasmine harm. No man could ever do her harm, not while Rory had breath in him.

He decided to double back and pinpoint his pursuers positions. Once he had done this, he intended to pick one of them off. Once one of them went down, the confident rational thought of the other two was sure to be greatly diminished. That would be all the advantage Rory felt that he needed.

Rory had already sized them up. He wanted Jerad, because he was the head, the strength behind this present danger. But he would also take Byron James. Byron also had strength, and Jerad wouldn't be so anxious to take Rory on once Byron was dead. It had to be one of these two. If he killed Luke, Jerad and Byron would still have the will and mindset to hunt him. Rory knew what he had to do, and moved to do it, confident that he could.

Jerad started to worry, because he heard absolutely nothing of Rory. Jerad and the others were moving clumsily. They were unintentionally making just enough noise so that a skilled hunter could pinpoint them. Up to that point Jerad hadn't worried about the noise, because he knew that he had the numbers, and that Rory was traveling with Jasmine. He was certain that Rory would want to protect her, and do so by continuing to run. It was too quiet for Jerad, and he began to suspect that Rory had hidden Jasmine and was cunningly hunting them. Jerad stopped moving. Not hearing him, Byron and Luke also stopped moving. Jerad cautiously made his way to Byron, keeping his head as low to the ground as he possible could.

"Ah think that nigger is huntin' us," Jerad whispered.

"He wouldn't do that. He's got tha gal with 'im," Byron reasoned.

"Listen, he was makin' a little noise. Now, he ain't makin' none. He's huntin' us," Jerad assured.

"He could've slipped us."

"Nope, he's huntin' us."

The hairs on the back of Byron's stiff rebellious neck started to stand up, as he started to become afraid that death was lurking about, ready to devour him. "Well, what are we gonna do about it?" he whispered, looking around in fear.

"See that sort of clearing over there?" Jerad pointed to the clearing. "O'm gonna go over dere. He oughta be able to spot me. He's gonna try to get close enough to shoot me. You and Luke oughta be able to spot 'im then."

"That's awful dangerous, Jerad."

"It's even more dangerous playin' this his way," Jerad said, "make yer way to Luke, let 'im know what's goin' on. Y'all fan out and get him. Don't mess this up, my neck is on the line."

Jerad gave Byron a little time to get to Luke and explain. Then, Jerad started to make his way to the small clearing. Once he reached the clearing, Jerad took cover behind a tall skinny pine tree. Although the tree was tall, it didn't have much width, not for a wide man like Jerad. Jerad felt that Rory would be able to spot him easily.

Just as Jerad was hoping, Rory spotted him. Rory spotted a large limb, which had fallen from a tree. If he could make his way to it, he had a clear shot at Jerad. Rory laid prone and quietly started to crawl toward the limb. Once there, he took a peek to see if Jerad was still there. To Rory's surprise, Jerad was exactly where he saw him last. Rory started to wonder why that was, and he also wondered why Jerad would linger in an area which really didn't provide adequate cover.

Rory reasoned that they were on to him. They were trying to set him up. Rory moved away from his position, hoping he hadn't been seen. He moved to a denser population of trees, and started to visually search out Byron and Luke. He heard a barely audible noise to the left of him, like a breaking twig. It was Byron James. Rory was of a mind to take him, but he didn't have a good shot. He continued to look around, and soon spotted a human form hiding behind a bush to Byron's left. Spotty lighting and the thick greenery of the bush where the figure was made it difficult to see. He couldn't make out any physical features, but it was definitely a man. Rory assumed it was Luke. Rory had a good shot at him, but Luke wasn't one of those that he needed to kill, not first anyway. He thought about trying to work his way to where he would have a good shot at Byron, but decided against it, because the only place he could do it left him vulnerable to immediate attack from Luke.

Knowing where Byron and Luke were, Rory felt that he could now move on Jerad, who Rory felt was the best target. He quietly and sedulously moved to a position behind a tree where he had a good shot at Jerad, but could also keep an eye on Byron and Luke. He was confident

that Byron and Luke had not seen him. If they had, they would not have allowed him to take up a position where he could have a good shot at Jerad, and still be able to evade them once he had made his shot. Rory made sure that Luke and Byron were still in place. They had not made a significant move.

From the kneeling position, Rory took aim at Jerad. He held his breath for the split second it would take to make the shot, but he didn't shoot. Jerad was white, and Rory was reluctant to kill a white man. Nevertheless, Rory realized that Jerad had left him no choice. He would kill all three of them and bury them there in the woods. The white folk around these parts would never know what became of them. He checked on Byron and Luke once more. They were still out of play. Rory aimed at Jerad once more, and this time he would not hesitate.

As he prepared to pull the trigger, he had made a mistake. A mistake which would cost him dearly. The person he assumed was Luke, was not. Luke spotted Rory earlier, but didn't have the heart to shoot him. He was not a murderer, but he couldn't let Rory kill his friend either. He was almost right on top of Rory. Realizing that Rory was about to make his shot, Luke dashed toward Rory. He sprinted hard. Rory heard him and was shocked. Rory quickly turned to shoot Luke, but it was too late.

Luke tackled him, and Rory's musket discharged into the air. They started to wrestle. Rory was on his back with Luke over him. Luke hit Rory in the jaw. Rory hit him in his. Luke backed off, and they both climbed to their feet. Luke lunged at Rory. Rory lit him up with both hands. Luke fell down to his knees, but Rory had lost. Byron arrived, running like an antelope. He hit Rory across the forehead with the butt of his pistol. Rory was stunned, but did not go down. He struck Byron in the jaw very hard, but Byron still managed to grab hold of Rory.

"Take yo' got damn hands off me," Rory yelled, as he hit Byron again.

By this time Jerad had arrived, and they wrestled Rory to the ground, pinning him down. From that point on, Rory's time on this earth was drawing to a close.

"Got you, now! You little-nigger bastard," Jerad spouted.

"You go ta hell," Rory barked.

"Ah'll send you first, coon," Jerad spouted, as he struck Rory across the face.

"Good work, Luke," Byron said.

"O'm gonna teach you to never point a gun at a white man, boy," Jerad vowed with violent excitement.

With Rory struggling, they dragged him to the clearing. It was the one spot where the sun shined brightly through the canopy of trees. Luke held Rory's hands behind his back. Byron got low and held Rory's legs. Rory knew that he was done for. In the back of his mind, he wondered how he made such a mistake as letting Luke get the drop on him. Rory was certain that Luke was out of play, his position accounted for.

Now, the pain began. Jerad picked up two small, round, brownish, palm-sized rocks and closed them in his large fists. With all of his might, Jerad hit Rory in the gut. It knocked the wind out of him. Before Rory could even think about catching his breath, Jerad struck him with an even more vicious blow to the mid-section. If Rory had not been held, he would have fallen to his knees and curled over. Jerad delivered another merciless blow to the gut. He saw a look of great pain in Rory's eyes. Knowing Rory was suffering, was very exciting to Jerad. He mustered even more strength, and brutally bashed Rory's mid-section.

Around this time, Uncle Whoot emerged from the woods. It was he that Rory mistook for Luke. Uncle Whoot had no real home. He often made himself a bed of leaves and grass, and slept in the woods. He was awakened by gun fire and got up to investigate. Uncle Whoot had witnessed everything that had gone on. Remembering Rory's kindness toward him, he had stepped forward to try and help. "What y'all doin' dere?" He asked. "Leave dat boy lone, he ain't done nothin' ta nobody."

Byron knew Uncle Whoot and sprung up to deal with him. He grabbed Uncle Whoot by the arm, slinging him to the ground. "Get yer wrinkled ass over here, and sit down!"

"Dat boy ain't done nothin' ta nobody," Uncle Whoot said, wanting them to stop beating Rory.

Byron kicked Uncle Whoot over and put his foot on his chest. "Finish it, Jerad! Whoot here ain't gonna be no problem."

With unbridled vengeance, Jerad punished Rory with another heavy-handed blow to the gut. This time, one of Rory's ribs broke. Rory was hurting, but it didn't hurt as badly as the pain he felt in his heart when he saw Jasmine standing behind an oak tree in the woods watching this. He wondered why she hadn't gotten herself to safety. Now was the time that she should be making her escape. Jerad and the others had not spotted her.

Thinking on it, Rory knew why Jasmine hadn't left. It was her love for him that compelled her to stay. Rory knew that Jasmine wanted to come to him. He shook his head, telling her to stay put.

Jerad interpreted Rory's head shake as a defiant gesture and hit him harder. With beastly rage, Jerad hit Rory in the Jaw. Rory felt several of his upper teeth loosen, as excruciating pain rippled through his jaw. Jerad fired into Rory's jaw again, dislodging several teeth. The great force of this blow caused those teeth to come flying from Rory's mouth. With a heavy, pitiless, bruising right hand, Jerad delivered another punishing blow to the gut. Another one of Rory's ribs broke.

"Stop!" Rory cried.

Like a mad bull, Jerad savagely pounded Rory's gut again, and again, and again, and again, and again, and again, and again, and again, and again, and again. He hit Rory so many times that it seemed unimaginable that a human body could take such abuse. Almost every rib on the left side of Rory's body was now broken, and two on his right. Rory trembled with pain. He couldn't take it anymore. Jerad hit him again. The pain was unbearable. Rory cried out with a blood curdling scream. Jerad and Byron took no pity on Rory. They laughed, taking no thought for what they did. Luke wished that he were somewhere else, not a party to this accursed thing.

"Please, stop," Uncle Whoot beseeched, "y'all killin' im!"

"Shut up!" Byron said.

Uncle Whoot's plea for mercy fell upon deaf ears. Jerad viciously struck Rory in the left eye. The eye immediately turned upward in Rory's head, as sight in that eye grew dark. Seemingly instantly, it swelled shut. Still, no mercy was rendered. Jerad struck Rory on the left side of his head, and Rory's ear started to ring.

Tired and ashamed of holding Rory, Luke let him fall to the ground. Rory had all but passed out from the inhuman pain. His senses had deserted him. Instinctively, not by conscious thought, Rory realized that he was free. He tried to climb to his feet to run away. Rory's body was so numb with pain. He did not realize Jerad and Byron were kicking and stomping him. By the time they stopped, Rory's spleen was ruptured. Ten inches of his large intestine was damaged and had blood pooling in it. One of his kidneys was failing and the other was severely bruised. His right arm was broken. Three of the fingers on his right hand were also broken.

"Get a rope," Jerad commanded Luke.

Luke looked at Jerad, not wanting to comply. From the woods, Jasmine had suffered every brutal blow with Rory. Knowing they were about to lynch him, she could no longer stay hidden. She knew that Rory would disapprove of what she was about to do, but she could not help herself, not even if she wanted. Rory was her heart, her soul, her reason for living. It was impossible for her to look away, to say nothing, to do nothing, as

Jerad prepared to lynch Rory. She had to come forth. Even if all it meant was that she would die with Rory. She boldly left her hiding place and walked toward them. Byron's penis started to swell in his pants. What they would do to her body, concerned her not. Even if they killed her, it mattered not. All that mattered was that she was near her blessed Rory.

"Don't take 'im from me," she said with dire sadness, drawing as close to Rory as she could before stopping, "he all Ah got."

The very fact that Jasmine left her hiding place and came to Rory, pricked Luke in his heart. Jasmine must surely have known what they would do to her. Luke understood that Jasmine dearly loved Rory. It surprised him. All of Luke's life, he thought that black people were just promiscuous sex-crazed heathens with no real understanding of what love truly was. Most people would have forsaken a lover in order to save their own lives, but Jasmine was right there, knowing what they would do to her. Luke didn't think that black people could love. He knew better now.

Jerad had just beaten a man close to death, and wasn't in a mood for rape. "How 'bout Ah just send you with 'im, wench," he said, pulling out his Dragoon pistol, taking aim at Jasmine's head.

"Lawd, Lawd, Lawd, please, don't do dat, Mista," Uncle Whoot begged.

Jasmine uttered not a single word, nor did she show any signs of fear. Jerad and the others were amazed by this. Rory, who was in no condition to do anything, heard Jasmine's voice. It had a sobering effect on him. He feared for her and from some place deep inside. He found the strength to begin climbing to his feet. He had to protect Jasmine. Jerad, Byron, and Luke couldn't believe what they were witnessing.

"Will you look at that," Luke marveled.

Rory hadn't made it to his knees yet, and it is very doubtful that he could have made it to his feet. Even if he could, he wouldn't have posed a threat. Byron kicked him viciously on the left side of the head. Rory fell back to the ground, and straightaway a thick yellowish substance started to ooze from Rory's left ear.

Jasmine raised her clinched fists above her head, gnashing her teeth, deeply sorrowed to see them hurt Rory anymore. "Please, stop," she cried, trying to go to Rory.

Byron saw that she wanted to go to Rory. He wouldn't give her the pleasure. He stopped her before she could reach Rory. He grabbed her and pushed her away, groping her breast in the process. Jasmine didn't care, she just wanted to go to Rory. Byron walked to her, circling her. He grabbed her buttocks, squeezing them hard. Jasmine didn't care. She was in a surreal place. All that her sad eyes could see was her precious Rory dying and she longed to go to him.

Byron took out his penis and raised the back of Jasmine's dress. He rubbed the stiff head between the cheeks of her exposed bottom. All the while, Jasmine stood perfectly still, feeling Byron was a vile, despicable, little, worm-infested rodent. Her skin crawled from his touch.

"You want some of that, gal?" Byron lewdly hissed.

"If you wont my body," she said sadly, but defiantly unafraid, "take it, and leave us be."

Byron was of a mind to have her. From behind Jasmine, Byron groped her breast and slipped two fingers past the lips of her vagina. One lone angry tear rolled down Jasmine's cheek, not for herself, but for Rory.

"Don't do dat ta her, Mista Byron," Uncle Whoot beseeched.

Luke knew that what Byron was doing was wrong and was angered by it. He was ashamed and appalled to be apart of this. In Luke's opinion, white men were the highest and most moral form of life on the planet. What Byron was doing was beneath white men, he thought. "Leave her be."

"You wanna go first, Luke?" Byron asked, continuing to grope Jasmine.

"Take your god-damned hands off her!" Luke warned, putting his hand on his .44 caliber double action Star Revolver. "Ah won't tell you again."

"What in hell is wrong with you, Luke?" Byron asked, stepping away from Jasmine, putting his penis back into his pants.

"We're not animals," Luke proclaimed.

"She's just a nigger gal. She's use to havin' plenty of men in her," Byron insulted, "what do you wanna do with her anyway?"

"We're gonna kill her," Jerad said, taking aim at Jasmine's head once more, "we're gonna kill all three of 'em."

"Lawd, Lawd, Lawd. Don't kill us, please, suh," Uncle Whoot begged on his knees, "don't kill us, suh. Don't kill us, suh."

"Go right ahead," Jasmine said, as she looked at Rory, "iffen ya done kilt him, you done kilt me."

"Tha one we came for is on tha ground dying, ain't but a few hours of life left in 'im, if that. You have your revenge. There is no need for anymore killing," Luke said.

Jerad looked at Luke acrimoniously. "Ah'll be tha judge of that."

"Ah ain't for killin' women, Jerad. Even if she is a nigger," Luke professed.

"That is a waste of a good hump," Byron agreed.

Jerad looked at Jasmine again. He saw that she was suffering to see

Rory the way he was. He was a bloody broken pulp, and he would be dead soon. Jerad felt that having to watch Rory die was punishment enough for Jasmine.

"We forgot to find out who those others were with 'im tha other night," Byron said.

"He won't be telling us now," Luke said.

"Let's go," Jerad commanded.

Luke and Byron followed without argument.

Byron looked back at Jasmine, with a depraved smile. "O'm gonna come see you sometime. So, you can thank me for saving your life."

The evil doers disappeared into the woods, headed for the road. Jasmine rushed to Rory's side. It was as Luke said. Rory didn't have much longer. He was unconscious, and did not respond to Jasmine's attempts to wake him. Jasmine, however, could not bring herself to see the simple truth.

"He gonna make it," she said, clinging to fading hope.

"O'm gon' try ta get help," Uncle Whoot said, knowing Rory would not make it.

Forty-five minutes went by. It seemed an eternity to Jasmine. She talked to Rory, but he did not answer. She told him how much she needed and loved him. She recounted memories during their childhood; things that he said to her just a short time earlier, down at the pond. She told him of the things that she wanted for their future. Finally, she heard a voice calling from afar.

"Jasmine," the voice called, "Jasmine!"

"Heah we is," she answered, "heah we is!"

Soon, Micah appeared. "Help is on the way."

"White folks done 'im like dis, Micah," she said as she broke down, crying inconsolably.

"Hold on, Jasmine, Elijah went to get Risby and his wagon. Help is on the way."

Micah lifted Rory over his shoulder and began to carry him toward the road. It would be easier for Elijah and any others to spot them there.

Jasmine followed close behind, tears flowing from her eyes like rain. Not long after, they reached the road. Elijah and Risby arrived, and they loaded Rory on back of the wagon. They took Rory to his home and placed him in his bed.

"Did somebody get Jasper?" Micah asked.

"Ah sent Uncle Whoot fuh 'im," Elijah replied.

"He better get heah soon," Risby said, "cause he ain't gonna last much longer."

Micah and Elijah looked at him, as if he shouldn't have said that. Jasmine also looked at him, very displeased. "He gon' make it," she said, "Ah know he is."

"O'm sorry, Jasmine. Ah ought not said dat," Risby apologized.

Jasmine said nothing. She continued to tenderly stroke Rory's battered face while holding his hand. Thirty more minutes went by before Jasper Brown arrived. He was stunned to see just how badly Rory had been beaten.

"You can make my Rory all right," Jasmine said, really telling Jasper, not asking.

"O'm gon' do my best," Jasper assured.

"He gonna make it. Ah know he is," Jasmine said.

"Step back, and let 'im work," Elijah said to Jasmine, pulling her away.

She moved away, but refused to be more than a step or two from Rory's side. Micah grabbed Uncle Whoot by the arm, and asked him to step outside.

"What happened?" Micah asked.

"Lawd, it was terrible," Uncle Whoot said.

"What happened?" Micah asked again.

"White folks beat 'im jes about ta death."

"Who beat him? What are their names?"

"Byron James. Ah don't know da other two, but Byron called one of 'em Luke. And, dat Luke fella called da last one Jerad."

"Where can I find this Byron?"

"Ah sees 'im in Olive Branch all da time. Ah thank he live in town."

"Not for long," Micah said in a very low devout voice.

"Dey jes' kept on beatin' dat boy. Ah told 'em dat he ain't never done nothin' ta hurt nobody, and he ain't. He ain't done nothin', but try ta help folks. Dey wouldn't listen ta me though. Da one called Jerad told Rory dat he was gonna teach 'im not ta never point a gun at a white man."

Right then and there, Micah realized what Rory's beating was all about. His countenance fell, and he became deeply grieved. Rory prevented one of the masked men with Franklin from taking a shot at Micah, and it had gotten Rory beaten almost to a point of death. Micah hated this. Rory was a good man in Micah's estimation, and one of only a few real men in Jago. Micah told Franklin and those with him what he would do should they spill Negro blood, and he was of a mind to do as he promised. Unless they got him first, he was going to kill Jerad, Byron, and Luke. As Micah stood there with Uncle Whoot, boiling with anger, Naomi walked up. Word had reached her of what had happened to Rory. She was there to do what she could. "Rory in dere?" she asked.

"Yeah," Uncle Whoot replied with a sad look upon his face.

"He ain't dead, is he?" she asked.

"No, he is not, but it's not looking good," Micah lamented.

"Jasmine wit' 'im?" Naomi asked.

"Mmm Hmm," Uncle Whoot responded.

"Ah better gone in dere den, cause she gon' need somebody."

Naomi went inside followed by Uncle Whoot. Shortly after, Elijah exited the house, feeling the small home was becoming too congested.

"It was those low-down bastards from the other night," Micah said angrily, looking at Elijah.

Elijah rubbed his head. "When will dis thang end."

"Soon, because I'm going to kill every last one of them."

"No."

"Oh yes," Micah assured.

"Violence begets mo' violence," Elijah said.

"Looks like peace does too," Micah argued, feeling that being peaceful was emboldening their enemies to feel as if they could kill them and not incur an equal response.

Elijah let Micah's remark pass. "Vioence, dat's not da way, Micah, not now. We got a government man down heah, and we gettin' somewhere. We gettin' justice, but we won't get nothin' but death if ya do dis. We gonna go ta da sheriff, and we gonna force 'im ta arrest dem dat done dis ta Rory."

"Wake up, Elijah! They haven't done a damn thing about the Wallace boy, and they aren't going to. That's just the simple truth of the matter."

"Dey is goin' to give us justice. We jes' gotta give it time is all, jes' give it time."

"Elijah, you are a good man, but a foolish one."

Elijah got angry, and almost said something wicked to Micah, but caught himself. "We's free today, because good men saw dat slavery was wrong, and did somethin' about it. We can't overlook dat. A man is heah now, because dese killin's is wrong, and he tryin' ta do somethin' about it. Justice might be slow in comin', but please give it time."

"We're free, because the North wanted to spite the South for rebelling, and you are right. Justice is slow in coming, but I'm not going to wait too much longer for it. I'm going to go out and get it."

"Ya can't take da law inta ya own han's. Ya jes' can't."

"But, they can?"

"Dey's wrong ta do it."

"Then, we will all be wrong."

"For blessed sake, Micah!"

"There is a man in there dying! He's dying for you, and for me," Micah said angrily, pointing at Rory's home. "All he did was stand up and be a man, and they cut him down for it. He didn't have to stand with us the other night. He doesn't have any children, and he didn't have anything to gain by standing with us. Only two men with children, among all the sorry sons-of-bitches around here with children, stood with us. Rory didn't have to stand with us, but he did. He did it to help a friend, because it was right, and I'm not forgetting that."

"Ah ain't forgettin' it either."

"Then, act like it!"

"Micah, when the soldier fightin' next to ya falls on the battlefield. You don't stop fightin' da battle ta kill da man dat shot 'im. Ya fight on, cause da battle still gotta be fought."

This angered Micah all the more. "Don't speak to me about something of which you know nothing. War is about taking lives, taking away your enemy's ability to resist. So, you can impose your will upon him. Right now, they're taking lives. So, they can impose their will on us. So, we will do what they want us to do. They're all about taking lives, and from now on. I'm all about taking lives."

"Ya can't do dat, Micah. Cancha see ya can't?" Elijah said, trying to dissuade his younger brother.

"Can't you see they'll keep right on pushing you, until you push them back?"

"Don't do it."

"I can't walk with you on this anymore. I'm going to handle this my way."

"You listen ta me, and you listen good!" Elijah said, pointing a finger at Micah. "Da government man is tryin' ta get us justice, and we gonna let 'im get it! You ain't da only somebody livin' round heah! Don't go off half-cocked, and mess dis up fuh everybody! Ya too hotheaded, Micah!"

"Sorry to hear you feel that way, Elijah."

"And, O'm sorry you feels da way you do."

Around this time Ran could be seen headed their way. Micah and Elijah ceased their arguing. Upon arriving, Ran could tell that the brothers were at odds. He elected not to get in the middle of it.

"Ah came as soon as Ah heard," Ran said, "Rory gonna be all right?"

"No, Ah don't thank he is," Elijah answered.

Just then, the door of the house opened. Jasper stepped out holding his black bag. They looked at him, wondering if Rory had passed.

"Is he?" Micah asked.

"No, he hangin' on," Jasper answered, "Ah don't know how, but he is."

"Why ya leavin'?" Ran asked.

"Ah can't do nothin' fuh 'im," Jasper replied, "O'm gonna let 'im die in peace."

"Ya can't do nothin' fuh 'im?" Elijah asked.

"No, he bleedin' on da inside. Ah can't do nothin' bout dat. Ah ain't got da skill," Jasper admitted.

"Kin Doc Mortenson help 'im?" Ran asked.

"Maybe, but Ah don't thank so. To fix Rory, he'll have ta be cut open. He's already weak, and jes' barely hangin' on as is. Cuttin' on 'im gon' probably jes' speed up his death."

"Ya thank he sufferin' real bad, Jasper?" Ran asked.

"Ah done seen a man trampled by a team of horses, and he wa'n't in worse shape 'an Rory is. Ah spect he hurtin' pretty bad. It's a good thang he ain't conscious. Hopefully, he'll pass on dat way."

"Ah guess all we can do fuh 'im now is pray," Ran lamented.

"Dat's about it," Jasper replied.

"This is not right," Micah said.

Although unconscious, Rory heard Jasmine's sweet distressed voice calling to him. He felt her tender sad tears falling upon his skin. He had to say goodbye to her. Through sheer will of heart, he fought his way to consciousness. He opened his good eye, and saw the most beautiful sight in this world, his Jasmine. He gently smiled at her.

"Ah knowed you was gonna make it," Jasmine said, smiling back at him.

Rory was close to death, and he knew it. Strange that he made it through a war unharmed, and fell victim to hate even though the war had ended.

"Ah knowed you was gonna make it back ta me," Jasmine said, softly kissing his swollen lips.

"Ah's sorry," Rory said, softly touching Jasmine's face.

"Ain't nothin' ta be sorry fuh," said she.

"It is," said he, regretting having to leave Jasmine, "Ah wonted ta give ya childrens. Ah wonted ta make ya happy all da days of ya life."

"You still can," said she, the smile slowly fading from her face.

"Ah wish dat Ah could."

His eye swelled with water, ready to spill. He would not cry for himself, but for his one and only great love. He thought that they would always be together, through countless ages.

"Rory," said she, knowing they would soon be parted on this side of life, "don't leave me."

"Ah's sorry. Ah wanna stay, but every man gotta walk dis road, It's my time."

"No. Don't say dat."

"Ah wont cha ta go on wid cha life. Ah wont cha ta live a long happy life. Be happy, do dat fuh me."

"Rory. No."

"Do ya love me?"

"Mo' 'an Ah loves myself."

"Den live a happy life fuh me. Promise me ya gon' live a long happy life."

Jasmine's one constant desire in life had always been to please Rory. With great reluctancy, she sadly assented to his final request. "Ah promise."

"When ya old and gray, and God calls ya home. Ah'll be waitin' fuh ya. Waitin', where da soul never dies. Waitin', where we can always be together."

"No, stay wid me," begged she of her most cherished Rory.

Rory wanted to say more to comfort her, but his life was done. With his last breath, he proclaimed one last precious time. The thing she had always known. "Ah loves ya."

It was over now. He yielded up the ghost. He had gone to a place that Jasmine did not know. A place, she could not follow. It started to rain, and it seemed to Jasmine that it was raining all over the whole world. For it had to be, the world was surely mourning the lost of one so precious and dear as Rory. Jasmine started to tremble with grief. Low panting breaths passed through her tear drenched quivering lips as it sank in that Rory was no longer with her. "No. No. No," she cried.

Naomi rushed to Jasmine, rubbing her shoulders in a comforting way. "It's gonna be all right."

"Why," Jasmine cried.

Risby wished that he knew some words which would ease Jasmine's pain. Uncle Whoot began to cry quietly. He wished that he had done more to help Rory. Jasmine's loud cry summoned the others from outside. Ran moved to Jasmine, and like Naomi, tried to comfort her. Jasper checked Rory's body to see if he was indeed dead.

Elijah reflected upon all the mayhem and suffering that these young lovers had endured. He thought of young Rory's belief in him, that he would bring the murderous calamity in their community to an end. Yet, people were still dying. Elijah was deeply grieved for Jasmine's loss. Rory and she should have had far more time in his estimation.

Micah looked upon Rory, and at his suffering widow. He started to cry, silently, angrily. It should not have come to this, he thought. "They've got to pay," Micah said in a whisper of anger, in the midst of all this confusion. Nobody really heard him, except Elijah, and he didn't hear him clearly.

"What?" Elijah asked, also reeling with sadness over Rory's death.

"They've gotta pay," Micah reiterated, louder this time.

"Micah," Elijah said, grieving himself, and in no mood to deal with Micah.

"They're gonna pay," Micah vowed.

"Micah, let's not do dis now," Elijah said.

"I'm not gonna let this go."

"Let cha head cool, Micah," Elijah said.

"It's cool enough."

"Let's talk about it later," Elijah said.

"Too much death has been visiting us lately. It's time for them to taste a little of it," Micah said.

"Let's talk it over later."

"I'm done talking," Micah said as he turned, headed out the door.

Fearing what Micah might do, Elijah followed him out. "Don't do nothin' stupid."

Micah looked back at Elijah with fury in his eyes. "You keep on sitting around here waiting for some white man to solve your problems for you if that's what you want to do. As for me, I'm not going to wait. Nobody can solve our problems like we can, remember that."

"Where ya goin'?"

"To solve our problems."

With this, Micah turned his back to Elijah. He got on his sorrel horse and rode off. Seeing Rory die had taken a great deal of strength out of Elijah. Otherwise, he would have stopped Micah. He just didn't have the strength to deal with him at that moment. He could only hope that Micah did not get himself killed. Ran and Risby exited the house.

"Where Micah go?" Risby asked.

"He rode off dat way. Ah don't know where he goin'," Elijah answered.

"Ah heard 'im tell ya that he was gon' make 'em pay. Dat ain't what he gone ta do, is it?" Risby asked.

"Maybe he is. Ah don't know," Elijah answered.

"Why ya ain't stop 'im?" Ran asked.

"He grown, Ah can't make 'im do nothin'," Elijah said, "All Ah kin do is hope he don't get his self dead befo' he calm down."

"Calm his self. Dat boy got a bad temper. You oughta stopped 'im," Risby said, "you know how thangs is in da South right now. We don't wont Micah doin' somethin' dat's gon' have white folks round heah doin' ta us what dey did ta dem in Memphis."

"Micah won't do nothin' ta cause dat," Elijah said, not completely sure.

"He got a bad temperament," Risby reiterated.

"Dat he do," Elijah admitted.

"Ya should've stopped 'im, Elijah," Ran said.

"O'm gonna see if Ah can catch 'im," Risby said.

"O'm gon' come wit cha," Ran said.

"Feelin's got hold of 'im right now is all. When he calm down, he gon' be all right," Elijah said.

Risby and Ran didn't listen to Elijah. They mounted up and headed out after Micah. It was raining out, and this was just a sad day. Elijah stood there on the porch watching Ran and Risby ride off to look for Micah. He wondered if he did the right thing to let Micah go. He was tired of having so much weight on his shoulders.

Risby and Ran tried, but never caught up to Micah. They worried about what he might do. After it had grown dark, Ran checked back by Elijah's house to see if Micah had come home. He had not. They wondered where he was, and more importantly, what he was doing.

Twenty-five

As midnight rolled around, Elijah lay in the dark, hoping Micah would walk through the door. He was very worried for Micah, and even more worried about what Micah was planning.

Dawn rolled around, still there was no sign of Micah. Elijah and his house got ready, and attended yet another funeral. Not that of a child, but of someone very young just the same. Elijah expected to see Micah there at Rory's funeral, but there was no sign of him.

Collin Bailey was there. As they committed Rory's body to the ground, Collin kept looking at Elijah. There was a good bit of shame visible on his face. Yet, he continued to look at Elijah. As they began to fill Rory's grave with dirt, Collin made his way to Elijah.

"O'm sorry, Elijah," Collin said openly, his head hung low.

Elijah just looked at him, but not in an angry way.

"That man say he kill me, and have Mista Everett kick my family off his land, iffen Ah don't lie fuh 'im. Ah had ta do it. Ah knows ya thank Ah ain't nothin', dat Ah ain't no man, but Ah had ta do what Ah done."

Elijah looked at the man with a degree of empathy, and placed his hand on Collin's shoulder. "Ah don't judge ya, neighbor, and Ah don't condemn ya neither. Be on ya way, and don't trouble ya mind dat Ah holds somethin' again' ya, cause Ah don't."

"Thank ya. Thank ya," Collin said in a relieved and grateful kind of way.

Elijah patted him on the shoulder several times in comforting fashion, and gave him a brief gentle smile. Then, Elijah began to walk away.

"My daughter Norah," Collin called to Elijah, "She done run off. She shame of me Ah guess. Iffen she come ta ya, tell her how thangs is. Make her understand dat Ah did what Ah had ta. Will ya do dat, Elijah?"

Elijah nodded his head in affirmation to Collin's request.

After the burial, many people came by Jasmine's home, to leave food, to speak a kind word of her beloved Rory. Jasmine appreciated it. He was all that she wanted to speak of. All that she wanted to think of. After a time, everyone left. All but Naomi that is, she would not see her friend left alone at such a time as this. Naomi watched her dear friend sitting there, looking as if she no longer enjoyed life. It was normal after the loss of a loved one to feel this way, Naomi supposed. Nevertheless, it was very painful to watch Jasmine in such misery, as they sat at the little two-chair table where Jasmine and Rory enjoyed so many intimate meals.

"Naomi, dey took my Rory from me, and dey done killed us both when dey done it."

"Ya still alive, Jasmine," Naomi answered compassionately.

"Naw Ah ain't. Da world use ta be paradise. Now, it's a sad, lonely, place dat don't make no sense. Ah feels like O'm dead. Everyday a burden Ah gotta suffer through."

"Jasmine, stop doin' dat to yo' self."

"How? Rory my life, and now my life is gone. Ah use ta be scared of dying, of death. Ah don't fear death no mo'. Now, death seem like a trusted friend. A good friend who will come to take me to dat secret place, to him. So, we can be together always."

"What dat mean, Jasmine?" Naomi asked, becoming concerned for Jasmine's fragile state of mind, and where it might lead her. "Stop talkin' like dat, now. Ya scarin' me. Rory told ya to live a long and happy life, and ya gotta do dat fuh 'im. Ya hear me? Ya gotta do dat fuh 'im."

Jasmine looked at Naomi, with eyes weary of life. "Don't cha understan'? He was my happiness, da song upon my lips, da smile on my face, da joy in my heart. He da thoughts in my mind, and da thangs dat Ah feel. He da sun dat warms my soul. Rory is all of me. What right dey have ta take so much from me?"

"Dey was wrong ta kill 'im. Dey was, but cha still gotta keep on keepin' on. Ya gotta let go of yo' pain. Da days might be a struggle now, but just give it time. Time will heal ya," Naomi tried to comfort.

"Heal me. Ah don't wanna be healed, not by time. Ah don't wont time ta steal no part of 'im from me, not da sound of his voice, not da way he looked at me wid love in his eyes. Ah wont 'im ta live in my mind day and night. Ah won't let time make me let go of 'im. Ah don't wont a single memory ta fade. My memories all Ah have left of 'im, now."

"Don't be scared of dat, Jasmine. Ah know how much you was ta 'im, and Ah know how much he is ta you. When ya love somebody like dat, time can't steal yo' memories away."

"It ain't right, Naomi! Ah had a life time of love ta give 'im, mo' 'an a life time."

"Ah know it, and Ah wish Ah could do mo' ta comfort ya."

"Yesterday, Ah had 'im close ta me, had his arms about me. Our morrows looked so bright ahead, and we took no thought fuh da thangs of yesterday. We had all da time in da world befo' us. Now, time smites me. Now, dere ain't no happiness ahead of me, only behind. Yesterday is all

Ah wont. How did it come ta dis? How did all my morrows get lost in yesterday?"

Naomi moved her chair closer, sitting next to Jasmine. Jasmine leaned her head over, and cried upon Naomi's shoulder. It was such a sad thing to witness that Naomi soon shed a mournful empathetic tear.

"Ah loves 'im, Naomi. Wid all Ah am, Ah loves 'im."

"Ah know ya did."

"Ah wanna hear his voice, and see his face. Ah wanna tell 'im dat Ah loves 'im, and keep 'im close ta me always."

"Ah know."

"Ah'd give all Ah have ta have 'im back wid me again."

"Ah know."

"He my life, how O'm gonna make it without 'im?"

"By da grace of God."

"God," she said. Angry with God for taking her Rory. "Why God take 'im from me?"

"Ah know death is hard, but it's fair," Naomi tried to comfort.

"Is it? It's so many folks in da world dat ain't got nobody ta love 'em. Uncle Whoot, he ain't got nobody, and don't nobody love 'im. Ain't nobody gon' miss 'im. Why not take him? Why God couldn't leave me my Rory?"

"Jasmine, ya don't mean dat. Ah know ya don't. You don't wish no ill on nobody."

Jasmine felt sorrow for having said what she had about Uncle Whoot, but she didn't apologize. She simply offered an excuse. "Ah miss my Rory, and look like everythang remind my po' heart of 'im."

"It's gonna be dat way fuh a while, but it'll get better."

The rest of this sad day passed slowly and quietly. Countless tears fell from Jasmine's eyes, as Naomi tried to comfort her. It was late in the night now, and Naomi was fast asleep. It had been a long tiring day. Daylight was but an hour away.

Jasmine could not sleep. She longed for her precious Rory. She quietly slipped out, leaving Naomi in peaceful slumber. She walked to the graveyard. She stood there in the twilight, as night gave way to dawn. A soft, peaceful, orange hue gently took hold of the new day, caressing the sky.

Jasmine sat beside the bit of cool moist earth where her dearest love was at rest. She frowned, as if she was about to cry, but did not. She took a deep memory-filled breath. Bitter sweet memories overwhelmed her, as both joy and pain echoed through her, consuming her. She lay softly, tenderly, upon Rory's grave. Her face touching the damp ground. She grasped the moist brown soil in her hands. "Oh, Rory, sweet gentle love, where ya gone? O'm so lost without cha," she began to cry, "Ah prays ta heaven, hopin' God will see how lost Ah is without cha, and have pity on me. Pity me enough ta let cha come ta me fuh jes' a little while. Ah miss ya so much. Iffen ya in da presence of God, fall down at his feet, and beg him to let cha come ta me. Ah need ta see ya. Do ya hear me, my love? Ah need ta see ya."

Jasmine's body was so very tired. For two days now, she had gotten next to no sleep. There, upon Rory's grave, a certain peace filled her, and granted her a moment of serenity. She found much needed rest, falling asleep.

Back at Jasmine's home, Naomi awoke. She was very alarmed when she didn't see Jasmine. Jasmine had been so distraught, and the way she spoke so kindly of death had Naomi very worried. She began to look for Jasmine. The first place that she looked was at Rory's grave. Naomi was relieved to find Jasmine there, and more importantly, alive. Naomi went to her friend. Jasmine was still asleep. Poor Jasmine has had such a rough time these past few days, Naomi thought. She sat next to Jasmine. She was reluctant to wake Her. She wondered how it was that Jasmine could fall asleep on the hard cold ground. Naomi didn't fret over it. If the only place that Jasmine could find rest was there, close to Rory, then, this was okay. Naomi watched over Jasmine like a doting parent. "Po' love-sick soul," Naomi gently whispered, "take yo' rest."

Jasmine had lost her love, but back in Olive Branch much later that day. Jerad was preparing to do something special for his love. Her name was Eula. She was twenty-three years old. Jerad wanted to do something nice for her. So, he visited Bush's General Store, and purchased her a just-because gift. A lovely-gray frock that Eula had had her eye on. It set him back a pretty penny, but it was well worth it. And, he wasn't done yet either, he had plans to take Eula out to dinner. Eula was an attractive woman, not pretty, but attractive. She stood five feet and six and a half inches tall. She had fair skin with freckles, and long red hair. She had a cute figure. She was a lady of great quality. She was a true southern belle if ever there was one. She had a very big outgoing personality. It was her charm above all else that caused Jerad to be smitten with her. Eula and Jerad were married six months earlier. As Jerad walked into their home holding the gift which he had purchased for her, Eula was pleased to see him.

"Whatsoever do you have there, Jerad?" Eula asked with excited, almost dancing like, southern charm.

"You mean the gift?" Jerad joked. "Well, Ah hear that dere is this beautiful young southern flower who is just so very loved by her husband that he just had to do something to show her his love. Tha gift is for her."

"Woo, Ah like that. What is this beautiful young flower's name?"

"Her name is passion, grace, and elegance."

"My, My, My, such sweet words upon your lips. Well, give me that gift so Ah can open it."

"Oh, this ain't for you. It's for Luke's wife. He asked me to hold it for him."

Eula looked at Jerad, not the least bit amused, well, slightly amused. "If you desire to remain in my good graces, and to continuing having three meals each day prepared by my hand, I suggest strongly that you not toy with my affections."

Jerad let out a big happy laugh. "O'm not playin' with your affections, Eula."

"Yes, you are Jerad Wildman."

Jerad sat in a big, brown, high-backed, leather chair and pulled Eula onto his lap. Eula pretended to put up a fight, enjoying every moment of it. Jerad tried to kiss her. She turned her head and leaned away from him. Jerad pulled her back toward him, and tried to kiss her again. Once more, Eula leaned away from him.

"Eula, Ah wanna be nice to you. Ah was just funnin' with you. Ah bought you this gift, and Ah wanna take you out to dinner. Ah wanna do that for you. It's my pleasure to do for you, and all that O'm askin' in return is a kiss."

"Well, since you put it that way," she said as she re-positioned herself and kissed him.

"The stuff of my dreams," he joked, "get up and open that gift."

Spryly, Eula got up and began to open her gift. She was all smiles upon seeing her beautiful new frock. She held it up to her bosom and danced around with it, very pleased. Jerad delighted in Eula's pleasure. Eula could not have been any happier. "It's lovely," she said, full of gayness.

"You like it?" Jerad asked.

"Ah love it," Eula said, so very happily.

"Good. Nothing pleases me more than to see you happy," Jerad sincerely conveyed. Eula was so gay and vibrant. Jerad wished that he had more gifts to give, if for no other reason than to simply watch her open them. It filled his heart with the deepest joy to see his wife so very happy.

"It's not over," Jerad said, "We've still got to go into town for supper. A nice supper with cake for dessert."

"Ah love you, Jerad. This is truly one of the most joyous days of my life, and it still isn't over yet."

"No, it is not. You go ahead and put that new frock on, and we will be on our way."

Jerad was so very gentle and loving with Eula. He had a surprising depth of love in him. It was particularly surprising, because just two days earlier, he killed a young man. He killed him with no more thought than he would have given to swatting a fly. He took Eula out to dinner, and they had a very enjoyable evening.

At Elijah's home, Elijah had trouble sleeping these past few nights. He worried about Micah. Micah was so temperamental, and no one had seen him since the day Rory was killed. Elijah hoped that Micah hadn't gotten himself into trouble. He hoped all was well with him. Elijah was nothing, if not consistent. He tried to do as a man should. He tried to be as he felt he should be, as outlined to him in the Bible.

He believed that there was a place for the black man in America. He believed that the black man was not a second-class citizen, and that the laws of the land could and would work for them. So, Elijah remained vigilant and persistent in working toward Justice and equality for his kind, even if it meant he was to be kicked out of his home, and would not have a place to lay his head. As Elijah sat at the table, Josephine saw the burden on his shoulders.

"Don't worry," she said, "we may not have a home soon, but God will provide. Rely on 'im, cause he didn't bring us dis fuh ta leave us."

"Ah ain't worried 'bout habin' a home. Ah know God will see ta dat," Elijah said.

"Ya worried 'bout Micah?"

"Yeah, he been gone ten years, and now dat he back. Ah wanna know 'im, but he done changed so. He ain't dat lit' fella dat use ta follow me 'round, and get on my nerves so bad dat Ah wonted ta push 'im down. It don't help none either dat all dis trouble been goin' on. We ain't had a chance ta know each other again. Ah jes' don't wanna lose 'im all over again. Ah don't know what he out dere doin', and iffen Ah don't know where he at, Ah can't help 'im."

"Ah don't mean no harm, but he got along ten years without cha."

"Ah know, and Ah wonder how sometimes."

"Ah thank Micah gon' be all right."

"Ah thank so too, but Ah know momma would wont me ta watch out fuh 'im."

"She would, but one thang Ah done learned 'bout Micah is dat he his own man."

"So, ya sayin' dat Ah can't look afta 'im?"

"Ah thank he feel like he need ta be watchin' out fuh you."

"Ya know, Ah thank youse right."

"Y'all different, but y'all da same. Ya both see wrong, and wanna right it. Ain't neither one of ya afraid ta stand up. It's jes' y'all go bout it in different ways. It's a whole lot of mens round heah dat saw what was goin' on, but you and Micah some of da only few dat stood up ta do somethin' bout it."

"Dat might be, but still, Ah worries 'bout 'im. Ah don't know 'im no mo'."

"Dis mess gonna be over soon. Den, maybe, y'all kin get ta know each other again. "

"He was real mad da last time dat Ah saw 'im. Ah don't know what he might do."

"Keep believein' in 'im, like ya always have."

"Ah believe in 'im, but he was a different kind of mad da other night. A kind of mad that Ah ain't seed in 'im befo'. O'm scared of what he might do. O'm scared he might put us all in harms way."

"Ah was wrong about 'im, Elijah. Ah felt like he was tha one doin' da killin's, but Ah was wrong. Ah was wrong, and O'm glad Ah was wrong. Ah misjudged 'im. Don't make my mistake of judgin' wrong. O'm sho he won't do nothin' dat's gonna get none of us hurt."

Elijah wanted to believe that, but the look that he saw in Micah's eyes the day Rory was killed left him doubtful. The night went by, and Micah still did not come home.

The very next morning, Shelby Alexander stopped by to visit Elijah. Elijah was very glad to see him. He hoped that Shelby had some good news for him. As they stood outside near the garden, Shelby was about to give Elijah the truth of the matter.

"How thangs goin'?" Elijah asked.

"That's why I'm here, Elijah. I'm trying to talk to people, but nobody is willing to talk. I can't find one bit of evidence to support what you say happened here," he explained.

"So, what cha sayin'?"

"I'm saying that I can't keep up the investigation much longer."

"But, dat Wallace boy is da one been killin'. We caught 'im in da middle of tryin' ta kill a chil', don't dat mean something?"

"It should, but this is the South. The way our opponents are using fear to keep people from cooperating with me, pretty much ties my hands."

"So, what is ya gonna do?"

"That's what I'm trying to tell you, Elijah. There isn't much that I can do."

"Youse not gonna leave us, is ya?"

Shelby took a deep breath. "I'm afraid that I'm not left with much choice. I'm not doing any good here, and there is an assignment waiting for me in Washington."

"Listen ta me, you is da only card dat we's holdin' dat dey fear. If ya walk out on us now, what's gonna happen ta us?"

"Well, what do you want me to do, Elijah?"

"Ah wont cha ta keep pushin' dis."

"For how long? Wallace is applying pressure, and my superiors will soon have me removed from this investigation."

"Ah know, but cha gotta stay till we get justice. Look, in a few days, me and my family won't habe a roof over our heads. Mista Everett kickin' me off dis place, cause Ah won't back down, cause Ah got you heah, and it's scarin' 'em."

"That may be, but it doesn't change the fact that we aren't getting anywhere," Shelby said.

"We will, iffen ya keep pressin'," Elijah assured.

"I can't stay here forever."

"O'm not askin' ya stay heah forever, but cha gotta stay long a nuff," Elijah argued, "dat boy a killah, and ya know it."

It was hard for Shelby to say no to someone who was as persistent and passionate as Elijah was about this issue. Yet, Shelby did not know what more he could possibly bring to the table to help the situation. There was no easy resolution. There was no foreseeable end in sight to this thing. Shelby wished there was more that he could do. He just didn't know what that was.

"Elijah, I will stay around for a while longer, a week at most. I will wire my superiors to that effect, but after that time. I will be leaving."

"It might take longer 'an week."

"That's all the time that I'm willing to invest in this. My superiors have asked me to pull out already. I told them that I would like to stay a while longer, but that won't buy much more time. My superiors are getting pressure from politicians empathetic to Franklin Wallace in Washington. Unless, I get something to go on, I am going to have to bow to their demands "

Elijah felt that Shelby was rushing this. He wanted Shelby to take his time, and see this thing through to its end. Elijah was afraid that there would be no justice if Shelby left before ensuring that Jesse Wallace was committed to a mental institution. Another thing which also had to be considered was that the white men who tried to lynch him before, would probably find Elijah, and finish what they were of a mind to do.

"Okay, a week," Elijah said.

"Then we are agreed?" Shelby said.

"No, we ain't, but thangs is da way dey is."

"I wish that I could do more, Elijah."

"Okay."

"You don't understand, do you?"

"No, Ah don't. Ah believe dat da law kin work fuh colored folks. Ah believe dat da law gotta look at dese murders, and see 'em as wrong. It look like ta me dat cha ain't too worried about justice fuh us, but tell me dis. If justice ain't gave by dem dat's meant ta give it, how will justice be done? When it come time fuh da law ta give you justice, do ya wont it ta look swiftly, and be on it's way without givin' ya justice. Cause, dem dat is da law got plans elsewhere, and in a hurry ta get to it."

"It's not that way."

"Ain't it, cause dat's what Ah see."

"Then, you don't see. I just fought in a war. I am a southerner, and I stood against my family, and the things that the South stands for. I did this not because I hate the South, but because I firmly believe in the principles upon which this country was founded. I believe that all men are created equal, and that slavery is contrary to that principle. I believe in justice for all, but I also believe in the principle of innocent until proven guilty. The burden of proof lies with us, and there is no proof that Jesse Wallace murdered anyone. I could stay here another year, if they would let me, and never find anything to say otherwise. Without proof, Jesse Wallace is an innocent."

"He ain't innocent."

"In the eyes of the law, he is."

"Ya know dat we ain't lyin'. Dat boy is a cold-blooded killah, and it sound like he gon' go free."

"I believe he has killed, and is likely to do so again. Without proof, what can we do?"

"So, O'm standin' out heah alone."

"I'm with you."

"Fuh one mo' week."

Shelby looked at Elijah feeling there was nothing more he could do. There was a moment of awkward silence. Elijah wondered if he should mention what happened to Rory. He was hoping that through Shelby he would be able to bring those responsible for Rory's death to justice. That seemed impossible now, and Elijah didn't bother to mention Rory's death, as he felt it would do no good.

Twenty-Six

At the Wallace home, the Wallace family was seated for breakfast. Franklin was worried. Shelby Alexander had nothing, but Shelby was not standing down. He kept searching for proof that would validate Elijah's claims. Franklin and Elizabeth were both doing everything that they possibly could to ensure that Jesse remained free. May and Diane, the youngest siblings, were not at the breakfast table.

"Jesse, Ah want you to stay close to the house today," Franklin commanded.

"Again," Jesse responded, as Franklin had not allowed him to venture out since Shelby's arrival.

"Yes, again," Franklin said looking at Jesse sternly, "That Yankee is still snooping around. Ah don't want you getting into trouble."

"Yes, dear, It is best that you stay close to home," Elizabeth reinforced.

"So, no chores then?" Jesse asked.

"No, not today," Franklin said.

"Well, what am Ah to do?"

"Play with your pup," Franklin suggested.

"You might also try reading a book," Elizabeth added.

"Read," Jesse said, disagreeably.

"If you think about it, Ah'm sure you can find plenty to do," Elizabeth said.

"Don't worry, Jesse. Ah can beat you at chess or checkers a few times," Susie said, "that's sure to make the time go by quickly."

Jesse looked at Susie, thinking that wouldn't be much fun. "Ah can hardly wait."

Joselpha laughed, catching Jesse's sarcasm.

However, Joselpha was the only one that could find reason to laugh. Franklin played it cool for the sake of his family, but his nerves were on end. Already, his family name had been dragged through the mud concerning this. Granted, no whites in the South would be terribly offended that Jesse had killed blacks. Many of the upper crust, however, would take occasion to look down upon his family. An alliance through marriage, for Jesse, with some of the finer families in the area was possibly no longer likely. As no man of means would be willing to trust his daughter to one with such murderous tendencies as those displayed in

Jesse. Franklin was determined that no further hurt be done to the family's honor.

After breakfast, Franklin decided to ride into Olive Branch to check with his spy, Deputy Angus Farley, to see what Shelby had been up too. Jesse, just as he had been told, stayed close to home. He played several games of checkers with Susie. He even managed to win a game, much to Susie's dismay. As the day went by, Jesse became very bored with staying around the house. He was bored with checkers. He was bored with reading. He was bored with staying in the company of women, his mother and sisters. He wanted to go outside for a while. The only problem was that his father told him to stay close to home. Jesse understood that to mean that he should stay in the house. However, as time went by, and boredom took more of a toll on him. He started to long for a little adventure, a little excitement outdoors. He began to twist the directive from his father. He told himself that anywhere on their property was close to home.

Around noon, Jesse found occasion to separate himself from the women of his family. He told them that he was going upstairs to his room, but he actually darted out of the back door. So that he would not be seen, he decided that he would play around the slave quarters. No one would see him there. The slave quarters were several lines of small white huts where the Wallace slaves lived before their emancipation. It was quiet and deserted now. It was a private spot for Jesse to play without having to worry about being seen.

Once there, Jesse gathered up a hand full of small stones. He began to throw them at the huts in the slave quarters. He took no great pleasure in this. It was simply something to do. Something to help him pass the time. As he moved about the slave quarters tossing stones at the walls, he was unaware that he was being watched. He felt a sharp pain in his lower back. Someone hit him with something. At first, Jesse thought that it was one of his sisters. He spun around ready to tell one of them off. He found someone standing there that he did not expect. Norah Bailey was standing not more than twenty feet from him. She threw a stone at his head, but Jesse ducked.

"You know who Ah is?" Norah asked.

"Some crazy gal that had better stop throwin' at me if she knows what's good for her."

"O'm Norah."

"So," Jesse said, not caring who she was.

"You knowed my brother," Norah informed Jesse.

"Oh... your brother?" Jesse said, knowing where she was going with this.

"Yeah, you kilt 'im," Norah said, throwing another stone at Jesse. Again, he ducked, and the stone missed him.

"Ah've killed lots of little niggers."

"Ah know," Norah said, throwing a stone very hard at Jesse, catching him in the shoulder as he tried to avoid the throw.

"Ah told you to stop throwing at me," Jesse said, moving closer to Norah.

"Yeah, ya did," Norah said calmly, throwing another stone, which missed Jesse.

"You alone?" Jesse asked, calmly moving closer to Norah.

"Yeah, Ah's alone," Norah said, fresh out of stones, moving to meet Jesse.

"What was your brother's name?"

"Ken Bailey."

"Ah remember him."

"He was a good kind soul."

"O'm sure he was."

"You gotta answer fuh what cha done."

"To whom?"

"Ta me."

"Aren't you afraid of me?"

"Ain't you scared of me?

"No."

"You oughta be," Norah said quite earnestly.

Jesse laughed. He was not afraid of any girl. The two were within close range of each other. They could reach out and touch each other. They calmly circled each other, sizing each other up.

Jesse understood that Norah came there to do him harm, to fight him, kill him. He did not know which. He felt, however, that it was a mistake for her to have come there alone. She was not alone, but he would never know this. Killing for Jesse was like an addiction, like drugs, alcohol, or gambling. He had no intentions of killing that day, but Norah had come to him so willingly. It was difficult for him to resist thoughts of killing her. He could overpower her and take his time with her. There was nothing she could do to stop him, he thought. If he was but a few years older, this would be true. However, they were about the same height, and about the same weight, and about the same age. Jesse was twelve, and Norah was thirteen. The advantage that being a mature male would have over almost any female simply wasn't there. In a few years, Norah would not be a match for Jesse. At that moment, however, this thing was a closer contest than Jesse might have imagined. The way that they circled each other reminded Jesse of dance.

"You come to dance?" he joked, not really grasping the seriousness of this moment, confident of his ability to take Norah.

"No," Norah answered calmly.

"What are you here to do?"

"Whop yo' ass," Norah said, quickly firing a hard right into Jesse's jaw, and then rapidly backing off.

Jesse grabbed his jaw, surprised at Norah's quickness. He didn't realize that she was ready to get it started. She wobbled him a bit. His confidence level wasn't shaken, however, not in the least. He felt that Norah caught him with a surprise punch. Jesse raised his fist to make sure that she wouldn't catch him again.

Norah stood slightly hunched, shaking her fist up and down, much like a prize fighter ready to earn his prize. She had a serious determined look on her face. She fired a hard wide right, which overpowered Jesse's attempt to block, connecting with his chin. It didn't hurt him. His block took most of the sting out of it, but he understood that she meant business. Norah stayed light on her feet, moving about, so that Jesse had to work to bring the fight to her.

"You're pretty strong for a gal," Jesse said.

Norah said nothing. She focused on recognizing her opportunities to land blows. She saw an opening, and sent one right down the center, bloodying Jesse's nose. Jesse quickly wiped away the blood with his right sleeve. He was good and mad now, and he had just about all of this that he was going to take. He began to flurry blows on Norah, backing her up, connecting several blows to the side of her head. He was overwhelming her, but Norah didn't back down. She stopped yielding ground, and began to flurry right with Jesse. Both of them held their heads back as their fists flew, trying to connect. Norah pulled out suddenly, stepped right, and landed a strong wide right to Jesse's jaw. He backed off, giving her room.

"Come on," Norah yelled.

"O'm coming!"

Jesse stepped to her, swinging wide, trying to land the power blow. Norah backed off, trying to circle him in order to land a wide shot of her own.

"O'm gonna get you," Jesse yelled.

"Get me, then!"

Norah remained light on her feet. She was an elusive target. Jesse moved in, trying to cut her off. So, that he could go to work on her.

"Yeah, O'm gonna get you," Jesse spouted.

"Heah Ah is," Norah said.

Norah was pretty much having her way with Jesse. She was connecting frequent blows, mostly to the side of Jesse's head. She was frustrating him, making him angry. She was picking him apart, almost at will.

Jesse decided that he would try a different strategy, realizing that what he was doing allowed Norah to use her quick speed. He had to neutralize that. He figured that once he got his hands on Norah, it was all over with. He rushed Norah, taking a few head shots in the process, but he accomplished his goal. He had her in his grip. He forced her hard into the side of one of the huts. He slammed her into it repeatedly, and hit her in the stomach several times, but they were not clean shots, as she had grabbed his wrist to keep him from hitting her with all of his strength. He grabbed her by the collar of her dress, and slung her to the ground. He believed that he had her. He rushed toward her, planning to pin her to the ground, and beat her half to death.

Norah got a foot up, and Jesse ran right into it. It caught him in the stomach. He bent over, holding his stomach. Norah quickly leaped to her feet, almost like a frog, and pulled Jesse's shirt over his head, tearing it in the process. She began to hit Jesse with everything she had, mostly blows to the sides of his head. She caught him in the nose again, and it felt as if it was broken, as blood seemed to gush from it like a fountain. Jesse was bleeding all over his shirt. He started to swing blindly, and caught Norah in her side. It was a punishing blow. She grabbed her side in pain, relenting in her attack. Jesse managed to get his shirt down, but before he could make a move on Norah, she moved on him. She grabbed him by his bright red hair, forcing his head downward. Jesse swung at her, catching her on the arms, and in the sides. The blows hurt her. She began to move backward, still pulling down on Jesse's head. He was losing his balance, falling to his knees. As he fell, Norah pulled out two hands full of his hair. Jesse climbed to his feet, and they looked at each other. Jesse wiped his bloody nose, and started to move toward Norah again. There was serious rage in his eyes. He was of a mind to kill her. Norah was starting to tire, and Jesse seemed to be getting stronger. Norah felt that momentum was now with Jesse. She backed away from him, keeping distance between them. She raised her left arm, pointing an angry finger at him. "You gonna pay fuh what cha done!"

"So, come make me pay," Jesse yelled back at her.

"Ah'll be seein' ya!"

Norah turned and ran away into the nearby woods. Jesse didn't care to follow her. He had certainly had enough of her, but he was very angry with her. After all of this was over (Shelby's investigation that is) Jesse had plans for Norah to come up missing. So, she was right. They would be seeing each other again, he thought.

Jesse wiped his bleeding nose again with his sleeve, and held his head back to stop the bleeding. There was a trembling anger that roared through him as he began to walk back to his home. He was so caught up in anger, getting even with Norah, that it didn't dawn on him that he was walking where his mother, or one of his sisters, might see him. As he got close to the house, he remembered that he was not suppose to be outside.

With great effort to keep from being seen, he made his way to the cedar tree adjacent to the house. He climbed the tree, and hopped off onto the roof. He carefully made his way to the second floor hall balcony, and lowered himself onto the balcony. The balcony doors were open, as it was the heat of the day, the doors were left open to let in a cool breeze.

Jesse went inside, quietly walked into his room, and shut the door behind him. He took off his torn bloody shirt, and tossed it into his closet. He took a pitcher of water, and poured it into a white, yellow-floral pattern, wash basin. He cleaned himself up a bit. He looked into the mirror, and wondered if anyone would be able to tell that he had been in a fight. He didn't have a black eye, busted lip, or anything. He just had a bright red nose. They would not be able to tell, he thought. He put on another shirt, and laid across his bed. He wanted a little adventure today, and he got it to be sure. As he rested upon his bed, there was a knock at his door. Elizabeth peeked her head into his room.

"May Ah come in?" she asked, moving into the room before Jesse answered.

Jesse looked at his mother as if he didn't want to be bothered by her, wondering what she wanted. He sat up on his bed to talk with her.

As Elizabeth came into the room, she noticed the wash basin full of bloody water. Before she could ask the question, Jesse answered her. "Ah have a sore in my nose," Jesse explained, "Ah was picking at it, and it started to bleed. Ah got it stopped."

Elizabeth had no reason to doubt him, and said nothing more concerning it. "Jesse," she said, "why don't you come back down stairs with us. It would probably be better for you than moping around in here all alone."

"What do you care if Ah mope?" Jesse asked, doubting his mothers concern.

"What did you say?" Elizabeth replied, not being one to tolerate insolence from children.

"You don't care about me. You don't love me. Ah know that. So, you don't have to pretend that you care about me moping around up here."

At this point, Elizabeth's initial anger passed. She realized that what she said next had to be void of anger. "Why do you feel that way?" she meekly asked.

"Because, you don't. You never talk to me. You never say anything to me, not unless you want me to do something. Ah can't remember a time that you have ever said that you loved me. Father loves me. Ah've heard him say it, and everyday he shows me. But you, if you didn't want me, if you can't love me, you should have left me where Ah was, cause Ah didn't ask to be here."

Jesse had just been in a fight, and his emotions were charged. Were it not for this, he would never have spoken to his mother this way, but it was good that he did. Elizabeth had lost touch with her son, but now she knew what was going on inside of him. Elizabeth didn't know what to say to the things Jesse had revealed to her. It was true that she was not the most affectionate of women. She grew up in a household where her father nor mother told her that she was loved. They never told her, but she understood that they did. Elizabeth just assumed that Jesse, and her other children, knew that she loved them. It came as a shock to her that Jesse didn't. Elizabeth recognized her shortcomings as a mother. She was moved to compassion for her son. She sat on the bed next to Jesse. She reached for his hand, but Jesse pulled away from her. His withdrawal hurt Elizabeth. She did not try to touch him again.

"Ah do love you, Jesse," Elizabeth said with sincerity and humility, "Ah have always loved you. Ah just made the mistake of assuming that you knew. Ah am sorry for that. Ah wish there was some way to go back to the times that Ah should have told you that Ah loved you, and say as much. Sadly, there is no way back. There is no way for me to go back, and be the mother that Ah should have been up to this point. Ah hope that you can forgive me, and from now on. Ah will take the time to tell, and show you, just how much Ah really do love you."

Elizabeth stood and took a deep breath. She looked at Jesse with a warm smile, but he did not look at her. Elizabeth walked out of the room. A great swell of emotion overwhelmed her.

Her eyes began to water, but she did not cry. She stood there in the hall feeling badly. She wondered if it was because she failed to show Jesse love that he killed. She wondered how long he had felt that way, if she could reach him, and how she would set things right between them. She thought of Proverbs 31:10-31, the description of a virtuous woman, and measured herself against it. She walked somberly down the stairs, and into the parlor. All of her daughters were gathered there. She looked lovingly at all of them, realizing how precious each of them were. Diane and May, the youngest girls, ran around the room playing. Blanch and Susie sat on a light green couch talking. Joselpha sat in a dark stained chair with light-green cushions. It was she who looked up to see Elizabeth staring at them somewhat somberly.

"Mother," Joselpha said, "is everything well?"

"Ah love you," Elizabeth said quite emotionally, "Ah love each and everyone of you."

Joselpha and the older girls looked at Elizabeth strangely. They had never heard her tell them that she loved them. It took them unawares. Blanch looked curiously at Joselpha, wondering if Joselpha knew what was going on with Elizabeth.

"Ah love you all," Elizabeth proclaimed once more, "did you know that?"

Diane, who was the youngest child, walked to Elizabeth. Diane was six years old. "Ah love you too, mommy," she said with a big bright smile.

Elizabeth swooped Diane up into her arms, and hugged the child tightly. Elizabeth began to cry. Joselpha closed her book and stood. She did not know what to make of this. Neither did Blanch nor Susie know what to make of Elizabeth's behavior. Joselpha knew that something was wrong. She walked over to comfort her mother, rubbing Elizabeth on her back. Elizabeth wrapped an arm around Joselpha's shoulders, pulling Joselpha close to her. She kissed Joselpha on the forehead. "Ah love you, Joselpha," she proclaimed, with tears running down her cheeks, "did you know that?"

"Ah knew," Joselpha answered, smiling.

Susie moved in, and was also greeted with a warm kiss upon the forehead from Elizabeth. "Ah love you, Susie," she said, "you do know that, right?"

"Yes, mother, Ah know," Susie answered.

Blanch was not use to seeing her mother so emotional. She didn't know how to handle it. She was reluctant to join in this rare display of love from her mother, but Elizabeth hadn't forgotten her. "Blanch," she said, holding out a hand to Blanch, "Ah love you. Ah want you to know that."

Blanch went to Elizabeth, taking her hand. The lot of them stood there very emotional and teary eyed.

"May, my dearest," Elizabeth said, "Ah love you also."

"Ah know that," May said, laughing.

Upstairs in his room, Jesse sat thinking of Elizabeth. It was difficult for him to hear that she loved him. All this time he had hated her for not loving him. Faced with the knowledge that she did love him, he had a decision to make. He had to decide whether he would forgive his mother, or whether he would go on hating her.

He exited his room, and walked down the stairs. There Elizabeth stood in the parlor surrounded by her daughters. Upon seeing Jesse, Elizabeth put Diane down. She held her arms out to Jesse. At first, he looked at her, not sure that she could be trusted with his love. He forgave his mother, and the burden of hating her was lifted from his soul. He went to her. Elizabeth hugged him tightly. Something that Jesse did not completely understand was happening. Something that he didn't expect. It hurt no more. He hurt no more.

Twenty-Seven

At Jasmine's home, Naomi and Jasmine had just finished dinner. That is to say Naomi had dinner. Jasmine hardly touched the food on her plate. Naomi was concerned. She was afraid that Jasmine would become faint with hunger at some point. However, Naomi realized that she couldn't force Jasmine to eat. Jasmine was so very quiet of late. Naomi often chattered on, trying to get Jasmine to talk, trying to take her mind off of her troubles. This tactic rarely worked with Jasmine anymore, however. Even now, as Naomi tried to talk with Jasmine, Jasmine seemed far far away.

"Jasmine," Naomi called, "Jasmine."

With big beautiful sad eyes, Jasmine finally looked at her. It was almost as if she were awakening from a sleep.

"Where was ya?" Naomi asked.

"With Rory."

"Ah know dis hard on ya, but cha need ta eat somethin'."

"Ah ain't hungry."

"You might not feel hungry, but cha gotta be. Ah ain't seed ya eat enough da past few days ta keep a bug goin'."

"Ah jes' ain't hungry."

"Why don't cha just eat it anyway," Naomi urged.

"Cause, Ah don't wont it," Jasmine replied.

"Well, then, why don't cha try ta get some rest?"

"Ah ain't sleepy."

"But cha tired though, if ya lay down, Ah bet cha go right on ta sleep."

"Ah don't feel tired."

"But cha is, gotta be. You ain't hardly been gittin' no rest."

"Ah ain't sleepy."

"Just lay down fuh a spell."

"No."

Naomi was becoming very frustrated with Jasmine, and the frustrated look upon Naomi's face said as much to Jasmine. Jasmine was acting like a spoiled child to Naomi. Naomi was but a hair away from using abrasive language toward Jasmine. Nevertheless, she tried to understand what Jasmine was going through, and controlled her tongue. "Well, O'm gonna wash dese heah dishes," Naomi said.

She got up from the table, and cleared the dishes from the table. She prepared the water, and started to wash the few dishes. Meanwhile, Jasmine rested her head on the table. She felt herself dozing off. As soon as she fell asleep, Naomi touched her on her shoulder, shaking her. Jasmine was a little bit angry about that. "Ya told me ta get some sleep," she said, "what cha wakin' me up fuh?"

"Get up, gul. Elijah done went and fount 'im," Naomi said.

"Huh?"

"He heah."

"What?" Jasmine said, wondering what was going on.

"Look," Naomi said, pointing to the others.

Standing near the door, which was open, were many of Jasmine's friends. Elijah, Micah, and Josephine looked at her with smiles upon their faces. Risby, and Ran, and Jasper, and Mama Julia, and a host of others were all crowded around someone, talking to the person. Everyone was blocking Jasmine's view. She could not see who they were speaking with. She could not tell who they were so glad to see.

"Get up, gul. Go on over dere," Naomi said.

"What's dis? What's goin' on?" Jasmine asked, feeling confused.

Naomi took Jasmine by the hand, and pulled her to her feet. Naomi began to push Jasmine toward all the people. Everyone stepped aside to let her through. As the last few people stepped aside, Jasmine saw Rory standing there. He looked at her, smiling a great big smile. Jasmine's mouth fell open, and tears of joy fell from her eyes. Rory held out his arms to her. Jasmine rushed to him. She embraced him so hard that it seemed she was going to break his ribs. Everyone smiled and laughed, happy to see them together again.

"See, Jasmine," Naomi said, "God sent 'im back ta ya, just like you prayed he would."

"Ah done missed ya so much," Jasmine said, still hugging and kissing Rory.

"He home now," Naomi said.

"Ah had da wors' dream, Rory. Da wors' dream Ah done ever had in my whole life," Jasmine said, kissing Rory's hands, looking upon his handsome face. "Ah dreamed dat cha died, and left me, Rory. It was jes' a bad dream, jes' a bad dream."

As Jasmine looked happily into Rory's eyes, his eyes became the saddest that they had ever been. Straightaway, Jasmine realized that Rory's death was not a dream. She realized that she was dreaming. She looked around, and everyone was gone, save Rory.

"No, Rory, stay wid me," she pled, realizing that he would soon be gone.

Rory looked upon her. A sorrowful smile blanketed his face. He gently stroked her cheek.

"Ah don't wont cha ta go," Jasmine said, all so lovingly and sadly, "Wearisome nights been 'pointed ta me ever' since ya left. My soul hates my life without cha."

Jasmine clung to him; for she was flesh of his flesh and bone of his bone. She was one with him forever and nothing could change that for her, not even his death. She held tightly to him, as if she could have kept him there by holding on to him. Rory held her lovingly within his arms, gently swaying her. She was comforted. After a time, Rory took Jasmine's arms from around him. He tenderly kissed her hands.

"Cancha stay a while longer?" asked she.

Rory looked behind him to the open door, as if someone were there. Rory gently touched his head to Jasmine's head. He looked upon her face once more. He looked behind him again, as if someone were calling to him. Holding Jasmine's hands, he gently released. He turned and walked out the open door. Jasmine wanted to follow. She tried to follow, but her legs would not move. "Wait, Rory, Ah wanna come wid cha," said she, "wait, Ah wanna come."

Just like that, he was gone. Jasmine woke up. Her head sprang up quickly from the table.

It scared Naomi, who was resting on Jasmine's bed.

"What?" Naomi said, wondering if Jasmine heard something.

Jasmine jumped to her feet, and rushed to the door. She ran outside, looking around. Naomi followed, wondering why Jasmine ran outside.

"What is it?" Naomi asked.

"Ah thought Rory was out heah. Ah thought that if Ah hurried. Ah could see which way he went. Ah wonted ta go wid 'im," Jasmine tried to explain.

"Ya fell asleep, and ya was dreamin'. Ya jes' woke up sleep crazy is all. Come on back inside, ain't nothin' out heah."

Jasmine continued to look around, certain that if she looked hard enough. She would see Rory. As the sleepy daze that had hold of her subsided, she realized that Naomi was right. It was just a dream. "It seemed so real," she said.

"Dreams is like dat," Naomi replied.

"Ah was sho dat if Ah looked around. Ah'd see 'im."

"It was jes' a dream, sweetie. Come on back inside," Naomi said, taking Jasmine by the shoulders, leading her inside.

As they went inside, Jasmine felt a bit of ease, having seen Rory, even if only in her dreams.

Twenty-Eight

It was close to midnight. There was a hard rapid knock at Elijah's door. Elijah thought that it might be Micah. Maybe, Micah had gotten himself into trouble, and had come home for help. Elijah rose from bed.

"Don't answer, Elijah," Josephine said fearfully, "might be white folks come ta kill ya."

"No, dey wouldn't be knockin'," Elijah reasoned.

Elijah slipped on his pants and shirt, and walked to the door. "Who is it?"

"It is I, Shelby Alexander. I need to speak with you."

Elijah opened the door and stepped outside to speak with Shelby. Surely, it must have been something very important. Why else would Shelby be here so late in the night?

"Did you have anything to do with this?" Shelby asked. "If you did, I need to know now."

"Anythang ta do wit' what?" Elijah asked.

"A child is missing. Did you have anything to do with it? You're not helping our cause going about it this way."

"You thank Ah done kilt one of our chil'ens jes' so we kin keeps ya heah. Naw, Mista Shelby, dat ain't my way."

"It's not a black child, Elijah. A little white girl is missing."

This took Elijah by surprise. "A white chil'?"

"A white child, Elijah. Her name is Hannah Covington. Are you sure that you didn't have anything to do with this?"

"Hannah Covington?" Elijah asked, very surprised. "Merriwhether Covington's lit' gal?"

"The very same. So, if you had anything to do with this, you need to tell me."

"Mista Shelby, Ah ain't had nothin' ta do wit' it. Ah pray her all right."

"Elijah, Merriwhether Covington is a very powerful man. If you or one of your people did this, Covington will see to it that every colored man, woman, and child around here for miles is butchered. There probably won't be much that I will be able to do to stop it."

"Don't cha thank Ah know dat?" Elijah said. "Ah wont justice, but not at da cost of mo' lives."

"If you did this, tell me. I may be able to get some soldiers in here to keep the peace. That's the only way to ensure innocent-black lives will be spared, but I have to send for the soldiers now. Tell me if you or your people were involved. Turn those individuals over to me. They will die to be sure, but that is how it has to be. That's the only thing that will save colored lives."

"Ah know dis ser'ous, but Ah done told ya. We ain't had nothin' ta do wit' dat lit' gal missin'. Habe y'all been ta find out where dat Wallace boy was when she come up missin'? He where ya oughta be lookin'.."

"I just don't see Franklin Wallace making the mistake of letting the boy kill a white child. He has to know what that means. But if it is Jesse Wallace, justice will rule the day."

Inwardly, Elijah was offended. Shelby didn't think that Franklin was careless enough to make such a mistake, but black people were. Elijah looked somewhat acrimoniously at Shelby Alexander. It bothered him that Shelby was making such a big deal out of one white child missing. One white child that they didn't know for sure was dead.

Here Shelby was, late in the night, trying to get to the bottom of it. If Shelby had put this much effort into addressing the murder of black children, Jesse Wallace would have been committed the day after Shelby got here. Elijah did not fret over it, however. He knew that they were sure to get some action now.

"Dey searchin' fuh her, Mista Shelby?" Elijah asked.

"They have been looking for her since six this evening."

"Dey sho she ain't jes' wondered off?"

"It is difficult to say, but it doesn't appear to me that the child just wondered off. I'm going to head back into town now. I've gotta keep on top of this. "

"Ya mind iffen Ah comes wit' cha?"

"No, I don't. As a matter of fact, it may be good if you did come with me. You've seen Jesse Wallace's work. That may be useful to us in the search for the girl."

"Ah was thankin' da same thang. Ah wanna help y'all find her."

"What do you recommend?"

"He like ta leave 'em hid in da woods. Dat's where y'all oughta be lookin' first."

"Okay, I'll pass it on. Is there anything else?"

"How long did ya say she been missin'?"

"Since around six, I'm told."

"It's goin' on six hours. Iffen he done had her dat long, she gon' be dead when y'all find her.

He don't waste time doin' his dirt. If she still alive, she ain't got long."

Shelby looked at Elijah very distressed. "I hope you are wrong."

"Ah hopes so too, but Ah know how he work."

"Well, let's get a move on. We wanna be there when she is found."

"Okay, let me 'plain ta my Missus what's goin' on."

Elijah went inside. Josephine was standing just inside the door. She and Mama Julia had been listening to Elijah and Shelby talk. Elijah knew that they had been listening as soon as walked through the door. "Y'all heard?"

"We heard," Mama Julia answered.

"O'm gon' ride inta town wit' Mista Shelby. Maybe, Ah kin help 'em find da chil'," Elijah said.

"Ah don't know iffen Ah wont cha ta do dat. Some of dem dat wonted ta hang ya. Dey might see dey chance, and try ta lay hands on ya. Ah don't wont cha goin' inta town by ya self," Josephine said, concerned for Elijah's safety.

"Ah won't be by my self. Mista Shelby gon' be wit' me. Ah'll stick close ta 'im. Dey won't try nothin' round 'im," Elijah assured, trying to comfort Josephine.

"Ah don't wont cha ta take da chance," Josephine argued.

"She right, Elijah," Mama Julia agreed, "iffen dey wont cha bad enough, dey'll git cha and him too."

"Ah gotta go. Mista Shelby thought we had somethin' ta do wit' dis. Ah bet cha dat he ain't by his self in his thankin'. One of us budda be dere ta put 'em on da right track. Ah don't wont us gittin' blamed fuh somethin' some white done done."

Josephine and Mama Julia couldn't argue with Elijah's logic. They didn't want Elijah to go, but it was definitely in the best interest of every black person in Jago that he did.

"Why it always gotta be you?" Josephine asked, fearing for Elijah.

"Ah don't wont 'im ta go neither, Josie," Mama Julia said, "he right though. Dey will blame us iffen dey kin, and come down heah killin'."

"Don't you worry. O'm gon' be all right," Elijah comforted, "let me put on my shoes. So, me and Mista Shelby kin git on inta town."

Elijah put on his shoes, and grabbed his hat. He went outside, and hastened to saddle his mule. Josephine peeped through the door as Shelby and Elijah rode off into the night. She wished that she had given Elijah a kiss.

Around this same time, Deputy Farley showed up at the Wallace plantation. He had come to inform Franklin of what was happening in town concerning Hannah Covington. Franklin was in the parlor having a glass of Cognac. Franklin had been worried the entire day. He had a feeling that something bad was going to happen. This uneasy feeling was the very reason that he wasn't in bed already. Farley knocked at the door. Franklin was in deep thought. So deep was his thought that he doubted if he really heard the knock. Franklin should have heard the knock if no one else did. The parlor was the second room to the left downstairs. Everyone else was upstairs where all of the bedrooms were located. Farley knocked again, harder this time. Franklin snapped out of his trance. He wondered why someone was knocking at his door so late in the night. He answered the door, and was surprised to see Farley standing there. Right away Franklin knew that something big had happened. "What is it, Farley?"

"Ah came ta tell ya that you may have a problem."

"Come in, and tell me."

Farley walked inside to the parlor. He didn't take a seat. "Hannah Covington is missing."

A soul-stirring chill ran down Franklin's spine. Merriwhether Covington was one of the most powerful men in the state of Mississippi. He was the most powerful man in this area. Franklin ran a distant second. With his resources so greatly diminished, Franklin would be hard pressed to stop Covington from having Jesse locked away for the rest of his natural life.

"When you say missing, what exactly are you saying?" Franklin asked, wanting to clearly grasp the situation.

"Ah don't understand."

"Is she missing, as in she wondered off, and they are unable to find her? Is she missing, as in they believe that she met with foul play?"

"Ah don't know. Hannah's mother, Abigail Covington, left the child outside under a tree playing with her doll while she went inside for a bit. When she got back, Hannah was missing. Her doll was still under the tree. One of the nigra women workin' for the Covingtons, the cook, saw the child from a window sitting under the tree while Mrs. Covington was inside. She said that the child was just playing under the tree, and then she wasn't. She didn't think anything of it. She just figured the child went to play somewhere else. She was the last person to see the child."

Franklin didn't know what to make of this, but he reasoned that the child wouldn't just wonder off and leave her doll behind. "Wait here, Farley."

Franklin exited the parlor, and rushed upstairs to Jesse's room. He opened the door to find Jesse playing on the floor with his puppy. He appeared very angry to Jesse.

"Ah know it's late. Ah was just about to go to bed," Jesse explained.

"Did you leave this house today?" Franklin asked in a very voiceful frightening tone.

A blank look covered Jesse's face. Franklin's angry tone was scaring him. Jesse wasn't about to admit that he willingly disobeyed his father. He was not about to tell him that he was outside that day, and that he got into a fight with Norah Bailey. If Franklin learned that he disobeyed him, Jesse was afraid of what Franklin would do to him.

"Ah asked you a question, Jesse! Answer me!"

Jesse had no idea what this was really all about. He did not know that Hannah Covington was missing. He was simply trying to avoid being punished. "No, sir. Ah didn't go out."

There was an expression on Jesse's face. An expression Franklin had seen many times before. It was cause for great unrest. Franklin knew Jesse was lying to him.

"Dear God, Jesse! What have you done?"

"Nothing."

Franklin rushed to Elizabeth. She was in bed reading the Holy Bible. Franklin's entry startled her.

"How long was Jesse out of this house today?" Franklin asked, with unrestrained anger.

"He hasn't left the house today," Elizabeth answered, disturbed by Franklin's tone.

"Elizabeth, if there is one thing Ah know, it is my son. Ah know when he is lying to me."

"What's wrong?"

"Hannah Covington is missing."

Elizabeth shut her book and perked up. Her back was as straight as a board. She understood Franklin's cause for alarm. She knew Merriwhether Covington to be an unforgiving man, a vengeful man. He was a formidable foe. One that they would rather not have. Franklin turned, and headed back to Jesse's room. Elizabeth sprang from bed and followed Franklin.

"Where did you go today, boy?" Franklin barked, looking very mean from Jesse's point of view.

"You are getting upset for nothing, Franklin. He was here all day. Ah'm sure of this," Elizabeth assured.

Franklin's angry voice had Jesse on the defensive. With Elizabeth backing him, Jesse was sticking to his story. He wasn't going to admit to leaving the house for an hour or more.

"Ah haven't been outside today, father."

"Don't lie to me!"

"Om, O'm not lying, sir," Jesse said, all the more adamantly.

"You are lying to me, boy," Franklin spouted, "tell me what you've done!"

"He was here all day, Franklin. He didn't leave," Elizabeth assured.

"Was he in your sight the entire time?" Franklin asked.

"Not the entire time, but he didn't leave the house. Ah'm sure of this," Elizabeth contended.

"You know what we are facing," Franklin said, referring to Covington, "we can't afford any mistakes."

"He didn't leave, Franklin," Elizabeth said vehemently.

Franklin looked angrily at Jesse, not believing him. He turned, and went back downstairs to Farley.

"What's going on, mother?" Jesse asked.

"Nothing for you to be concerned about, dear," Elizabeth said, closing Jesse's bedroom
door, "good night."

Franklin walked into the parlor, and poured himself a wine glass filled the brim with cognac. He downed it in what seemed like one gulp. He turned to Farley. "Ah think that Ah'm going to need your help with this, Angus."

"That's why O'm here," Deputy Farley said smiling.

This was the true reason Deputy Farley came to warn Franklin. Franklin may have been cash poor at the moment, but he was still rich in land. He was still rich in knowledge and connections. With so much working for him, it would only be a matter of time before Franklin would have plenty of cash again. When that happened, Deputy Farley realized that he would be able to exploit Franklin for life. Like any good speculator, Deputy Farley was all too eager to take advantage of the situation. Franklin knew that he was about to crawl into bed with a leach, but felt that he had no choice.

"Do you understand what Ah'm asking of you?" Franklin said.

"Ah think so."

"Whom do you have in mind?"

"There is this nigger boy that Ah know. His name is Elam Haymen. He's around fifteen years, and has the mind of a small child. Ah can get him to admit to me that he took Hannah Covington. Ah can get him to admit to me, and everybody else, that he killed her."

"Are you sure the others won't question it? There can be no room for doubt."

"There won't be. As soon a he admits to killing the girl in front of everybody, Ah'll see to it that he gets strung up quickly. That'll be the end of that. Of course, they may not stop with him, but what are the lives of a few niggers?"

"Then make haste, Angus."

"Now, you know that if Ah do this, Ah'll expect certain compensations for my help?"

"Ah understand, and you will be greatly compensated."

"Good, so long as we understand each other."

Deputy Farley walked out of the parlor. He was pleased with the deal he had bartered for himself. He exited the house. He went to round up a few men so that he could locate Elam Haymen, and frame him for the murder of Hannah Covington.

As Deputy Farley walked out of the door, Elizabeth was coming down the stairs. Franklin, who had seen Farley to the door, turned and looked at her sternly, unapologetic for what he had just done. Elizabeth stopped at the base of the stairs. "What have you done, Franklin?" she asked, feeling no action on their part was necessary.

"You don't want to know," Franklin said.

"Tell me."

"Ah've made sure that Merriwhether Covington has his killer. Ah've made sure that they won't come for Jesse."

"Jesse never left this house. They have no reason to come for him to begin with."

"Ah'm just making sure, Elizabeth."

"If the child is dead, Jesse didn't do it."

"Ah wish that Ah believed as firmly as you do."

"Why can't you believe in him? He is your son. He believes in you. He speaks so highly of you."

"Make no mistake about it. Ah love my son, but he lied to me up there, and Ah know that he lied. So, Ah'm moving to protect him, to protect us."

"He doesn't need protecting, not this time."

"Especially this time, Elizabeth," Franklin contended, "Ah'm going to ride into town. Ah've gotta make sure that this thing goes the way it should. Ah'll be back in the morning."

Elizabeth looked at Franklin in a disagreeable manner, certain that he was overreacting. She was confident that Jesse was not at fault for anything that may have happened to Hannah Covington.

Several hours later, Elijah and Shelby arrived in town. There were people out everywhere looking for Hannah Covington. There were so many people out that one might have thought there was a celebration in progress. A celebration much like those commonly seen on Independence Day. People scurried about with oil lamps and torches. Elijah was the only black face in this sea of people. They looked at him curiously, wondering what he was doing there. One of the black codes in effect was that of a curfew for blacks. In Olive Branch, the curfew was ten o'clock at night.

Elijah was feeling a little nervous about being there. Even in the company of Shelby, he felt great unease. He knew that this situation had the explosive potential to get out of hand quickly. Just as Josephine pointed out, there were those who wanted to kill Elijah. This situation had the potential to give them an excuse to kill him. In relative silence, Elijah and Shelby rode to the Sheriff's office. They dismounted and went inside.

To Elijah's amazement, the sheriff was actually there, and Deputy Farley was nowhere to be seen. All the times that Elijah tried to catch up to the sheriff to petition his help, the sheriff was nowhere to be found. Now, at almost three in the morning, he was actually in the sheriff's office.

"What's he doing here?" Sheriff Hackman asked Shelby, referring to Elijah.

"He came to lend a hand," Shelby said, "Believe me, he's well versed in this sort of thing."

"No blacks are to be out after ten. It's the law," Sheriff Hackman said.

"It would behoove you to make an exception this time. He can help us," Shelby contended.

"Not if he is here to place blame on Jesse Wallace," Sheriff Hackman said, "That's earth we don't want to turn."

"I don't think you have a choice, Robert," Shelby said.

"Shelby, Ah'm not about to go accusing Franklin Wallace's son of being involved in the disappearance of Merriwhether Covington's daughter. They are the two most powerful men around. Ah'm not gonna get crushed standing between them."

"That's exactly what you had better prepare for, because all roads are probably going to lead to Jesse Wallace," Shelby brazenly advised.

"Ah don't believe Jesse Wallace would be foolish enough to do this. Ah just don't. One of them probably did this," Sheriff Hackman said, looking at Elijah.

"Why we gon' go do somethin' like dat?" Elijah said. "So, y'all kin kill us?"

"Boy, no one asked for your opinion," Sheriff Hackman said with much dismay in his voice, suggesting Elijah had best watch his step.

"You know they didn't do this, Robert," Shelby contended, "maybe, we should ride out to the Wallace plantation now."

"Ah'm not gonna do that," Sheriff Hackman said.

"I'm not going to stand by, and let you pin this on the coloreds, Robert. You are going to do your job," Shelby threatened.

"Who do you think you're talking too?" Sheriff Hackman said, offended by Shelby.

"I'm not gonna stand by, and watch you let some poor colored be murdered, because you are afraid to deal with Wallace and Covington."

"How dare you, sir," Sheriff Hackman said, feeling his integrity was being questioned.

"Dare all you like, but no innocent will be blamed," Shelby boldly stated, "not while I am around, Robert. You may rest assured of that."

"Ah don't know who you think you are, Shelby, but Ah run this town. And, Ah'll run it as Ah see fit. Ah'm not gonna go stirring up trouble until the girl is found, and if a black is at fault. He'll swing for it," Sheriff Hackman assured.

"We ain't had nothin' ta do wit' dis chil' missin'," Elijah assured.

"So, you say," Sheriff Hackman coldly said.

The sheriff's attitude had Elijah deeply concerned. It appeared to Elijah that the sheriff wasn't interested in dispensing justice fairly. It seemed the sheriff was more interested in pursuing this issue in a manner which provided the least resistance. Meaning, it was much easier to accuse a black for the abduction and possible murder of Hannah Covington. Elijah was certain that a black would be blamed for this even though the sheriff knew that in all likelihood Jesse Wallace was responsible for whatever had happened to young Hannah.

"We ain't had nothin' ta do wit' dis," Elijah reiterated.

"If y'all didn't have anything to do with this, you don't have anything to worry about, do you?"

Sheriff Hackman said in a tone not at all reassuring to Elijah.

"Mista Shelby, kin Ah talks ta ya outside?" Elijah asked.

"Sure."

They stepped outside. There was a very troubled look on Elijah's face, and rightfully so, given the state of things.

"Mista Shelby, Ah don't like dis," Elijah said, very distressed.

"Don't worry, I'm not going to let an innocent be blamed," Shelby said, understanding Elijah's concern.

"Da sheriff seem like he done made up his mind somebody black done dis."

"As I said, I won't let an innocent be blamed."

"Mista Shelby, da sheriff right. He run dis town, and da peoples gonna stand wit' 'im iffen he wanna lynch a colored fuh dis. How ya gonna stops 'em iffen it comes ta dat?"

Shelby looked at Elijah. It was a look of uncertainty. At that point, Elijah understood that there wasn't a single thing Shelby could do to stop the lynching of a black should it become necessary.

"Maybe, I could still send for soldiers," Shelby said, uncertain of what he should do.

"You do dat," Elijah said, as he began to walk up the street.

"Where are you going?" Shelby asked, as he walked briskly to catch up to Elijah.

"Ta see Mista Covington."

Shelby stopped walking. "What?"

Elijah stopped, and looked seriously at Shelby. "Iffen ya had sont fuh dem soldiers right when ya first knocked at my door, dey was still gonna habe ta rides hard all night ta git heah by mornin' from Memphis. Iffen ya sends fuh 'em now, ya can't spect 'em till afta noon or later. Mornin' less 'an three hours away. And, dat's all da time we got, Mista Shelby. Cause, dat chil' gonna be fount by den, and she gonna be fount dead. And, when dat happens, and dem soldiers ain't heah, da sheriff gonna blame and hang any colored he kin git his han's on. And, Mista Covington gon' be satisfied cause he won't know no better. O'm fixin' ta make sho he know 'bout Jesse Wallace. Dat away Mista Covington will know, and is sho ta keep da sheriff honest, which is gonna save colored lives."

Shelby walked up to Elijah and looked him in the eye. "If this thing goes the way you believe it will, and Hannah is found dead. What makes you think Covington won't believe that you brought Jesse Wallace to his attention as part of some greater conspiracy on your part to exact justice for your people? Covington may blame your people and have you killed. It could happen. You should ponder that before you go to him."

"Ah jes' gotta pray he know da truth when he hear it," Elijah replied, "Kin you thank of somethin' better we need ta do, cause Ah sho wanna hear it."

"What you propose is risky," Shelby pointed out, "it could backfire, but I think you are right. It is going to work out best, I feel, if Covington is properly apprised of what has been happening to your people. I'm going to come with you. He will be more likely to believe your story if someone white is there to back your claim."

"Ah'd say ya was right iffen ya wa'n't no union-government man. Bein' dat cha is, ya might do mo' harm 'an good. Ever' since da war ended. White folks round heah ain't got nothin' but hard feelin's fuh dem dat fought fuh da North."

"Nevertheless, I'm all you have."

"Ah reckon."

"Then, shall we go?"

The men started to walk down the street toward the edge of town to the home of Merriwhether Covington. Now with many of the southern families of wealth, they maintained a house in the country, a plantation home, during the summer months in order to raise cotton to make money. But during the winter months, they entertained and displayed their great wealth. They did this by maintaining a large home in the city limits where they would host parties.

Merriwhether Covington maintained a four-thousand square foot plantation home in the country on several hundred acres, but his in town home was nine-thousand square feet seated on seven acres. It was quite the display of wealth. The house was nothing less than splendid. There was not another house like it in the entire state of Mississippi. The house was two stories tall. The front of it was truly likened to an old world castle. It had a single gable in the center of it, which was directly over the large porch which had six large white columns. Four columns were on the front of the porch and two ran along the sides. The house extended out to two castle-style towers, one on each side.

Any man who would build such a house was sending a message. A message that he thought of himself as something more than just a man of means. He saw himself as something akin to royalty. He saw himself as a ruler. A king which sat high and looked low. Such high-mindedness was a dangerous trait in this present circumstance, particularly for a man of Merriwhether Covington's bad temperament. He wielded far more power in this community than any one man should have. With little more than just a few words, Covington could literally have every colored person down to the last child in Jago, Olive branch, and Mount Pleasant killed. This power had instilled a certain arrogance in him.

For this reason, Elijah greatly feared Covington. When this thing broke, Elijah wanted to be standing on the same side as Covington. Normally, Merriwhether Covington and his family would be on his plantation estate this time of year, but this year was different. With the war so devastating to the economy of the South (particularly to the agrarian system so dependant upon slave labor) cotton, its chief crop, was at a low point. It would be another fourteen years before cotton made a strong come back comparable to before the war. Not that Merriwhether wasn't doing his dead level best to bring cotton back immediately. He was, but it was a hard road back. It was work fit for a younger man. Merriwhether's youngest son, Christopher, was handling affairs this summer on the plantation. There were several people standing in the yard of Merriwhether Covington. Four white men, who were offended by the presence of both Elijah and Shelby. The men didn't say a word to Elijah or Shelby, but their eyes said everything that their lips did not. Elijah was determined that harsh, hate- filled looks would not keep him from seeing Covington. He walked right up to the front door, and knocked. He should have gone to the back door, as was proper protocol for blacks at the time when visiting a white persons home. But Elijah didn't feel that he had the time to waste on that, particularly since Shelby was with him. Shelby stood quietly at his side, looking back at the four white men staring at them.

"What are you doin' there, boy?" one of the men asked.

"Our business here doesn't concern you," Shelby boldly stated.

"Some damn Tory and a nigger got no business with Colonel Covington," the man said, "Now ain't the time to be botherin' him with nonsense."

Elijah knocked at the door again. The four men moved closer to Shelby and Elijah. Elijah feared that confrontation was forthcoming.

"Stop knockin," the man commanded.

"This doesn't concern you," Shelby reiterated.

"Ah beg ta differ," the man said.

"I don't want any trouble, but if you start it, know that I won't shy away from it," Shelby spouted.

"That's brave talk, Yankee. We know you, Shelby Alexander. You are a disgrace to every southerner who fought in tha war. You are a disgrace to your family, too. We know your business here. Go home."

Elijah pounded at the door again. The men moved closer, ready to enforce their order for Elijah not to knock at Covington's door. The door opened. It was Henry, a former slave of Merriwhether Covington's, who stayed on with the Covington family after the war.

"Y'all got some good news fuh us Ah hope," Henry said.

"We need to speak with Mr. Covington," Shelby said.

"You don't have to let them in, Henry," one of the men said, "besides, da boy needs ta enter from around back anyway. O'm sure Colonel Covington wouldn't want him entering through the front."

"It's about his lit' gal," Elijah said.

"Ah'm sho Massa Covington gonna wanna speak ta 'em if dey's got some word about Ms. Hannah," Henry said, looking in the direction of the four angry men. "Come on in y'all."

Shelby and Elijah entered Covington's mansion. It was like being in a palace. Henry escorted the men into the study.

"Wait heah," Henry said. "Ah'll be right back wit' Massa Covington."

Henry exited the study. The study was so nice that neither Elijah nor Shelby entertained the thought of sitting down for fear that they would somehow dirty up the chairs.

"What do you plan to say?" Shelby asked.

"O'm jes' gon' tells 'im like it is," Elijah said.

"Be wise here, Elijah. Take care to choose your words well."

"Ah will."

"I hope he will listen to reason, and not let his judgement be swayed by a war that is behind us like those four outside."

Elijah looked at Shelby somewhat distressed, as his stomach started to bother him. This was a tough situation, and there were so many things to be concerned about. "Is ya tryin' ta make me nervous?"

"No. It is just that people sometimes get lost in the little unimportant things instead of focusing on the relevant. I can't help but be concerned about that."

Henry came back and opened the study door for Merriwhether Covington. Covington entered the study followed by Henry. Merriwhether Covington was five feet ten inches, but seemed taller. He had a slender build. Fine living was apparent in the very look of him. Merriwhether was in his mid fifties. Yet, he could pass for a man ten years younger. He would appear even younger than that were it not for the gray mixed in his brown hair. His hands looked as if they might belong to a king. They were certainly not the hands and face of a man who had broken his back for long hours in the hot sun everyday just to eke out a meager living.

Merriwhether casually observed Elijah, and immediately took a dislike to him. It seemed to him that Elijah held his head too high. He did not have the look of one brought up in slavery. Elijah looked like a 'man' even to one such as Merriwhether. Merriwhether walked over to Shelby and looked at him sternly. "You have news of my daughter?"

Shelby was somewhat shocked that Merriwhether was looking to him for an answer. He seemed to have forgotten that this was the South, and that it was the order of things for Merriwhether to naturally look to him, a white man, before even acknowledging that Elijah was there.

"Well, uh, yes sir, we do," Shelby answered.

"Well, what is it?" Merriwhether said, feeling Shelby was wasting his time.

"Beggin' ya pardon, suh," Elijah said, "we's heah cause we feels like it's somethin' goin' on dat you needs ta know 'bout."

"Who is this that dares speak to me before being spoken to?" Merriwhether said, feeling Elijah was forgetting his place.

Henry, who hadn't left the room yet, spoke up. "Suh, dis heah Elijah Wright. Please, suh, jes' lissen ta 'im. It's fuh ya own good, suh."

Elijah and Shelby were off to a poor start to say the least, but Henry's endorsement helped their cause a bit. Henry had been a faithful servant of Merriwhether Covington for many years, and Merriwhether had a measure of respect for him. Henry exited the room, closing the doors behind him.

"Well, speak up, boy," Merriwhether said with a commanding tone.

"Yassuh, it's been some killin's goin' on out our way. Ah don't know iffen ya knows dat or not," Elijah said.

"Ah seem to have heard something of that," Merriwhether said.

"Well, suh, ya probably ain't heard dat we fount out who been doin' it."

"No, Ah haven't," Merriwhether answered.

"Well, suh, befo' Ah says. Ah need ta explain somethin'. Da sheriff, Ah don't know too much 'bout da man, but when he report back ta ya, whatever he tells ya, you probably gonna believe 'im. Ah believe from listenin' ta 'im dat because of who da person is dat been killin' lit' colored chil'ens, da sheriff might hand ya somebody dat ain't had nothin' ta do wit' yo' daughter missin'," Elijah explained.

"What are you saying?" Merriwhether asked with a very displeased look upon his face, "are you saying that my little girl is dead?"

Going there made Elijah nervous, and Shelby as well. It simply wasn't prudent to speculate on the child's condition. Elijah had to be very careful with what he said next. "No, suh, Ah ain't sayin' dat."

"Well, what are you saying?" Merriwhether asked.

"Da sheriff ain't done nothin' 'bout da one dat been killin' colored chil'ens. Ah 'spect, cause of who it is. Ah thank da sheriff might try ta han' ya somebody colored fuh dis, cause dat's gon' be da easiest thang fuh 'im," Elijah cautiously said.

"So, you are saying that my daughter is dead?" Merriwhether asked.

Shelby was very worried here. "That's not what he is saying, sir, but she may be. We don't mean to burden you anymore than you already are, but we have no choice. We had to come to you with this now, because later will surely be too late."

"So, you are saying that there is a strong chance my daughter is dead, and the person responsible is likely the same person that has been killing colored children in Jago. Someone the sheriff has known about, but has done nothing to stop?" Merriwhether asked.

"Yassuh," Elijah answered.

"Well, who is it?" Merriwhether asked angrily.

"Jesse Wallace," Shelby answered.

"Jesse Wallace?" Merriwhether said, shocked to hear this. "Are you certain?"

"Yassuh, when we caught up ta 'im, he was in da middle of killin' up another one of our chil'ens, had his hands round da boy's neck choking da life out of 'im," Elijah explained.

"God help him if he has done Hannah any harm," Merriwhether said.

"Ya see why we's worried. Da sheriff ain't gonna wanna do nothin' ta Mr. Jesse. He gonna wanna hand ya somebody colored. If ya don't know no better, you gonna take it at face value, and run wit' what he tells ya," Elijah said.

"I agree with Elijah here, sir. The sheriff did sound as if he were more likely to follow this course of action," Shelby said, "that way you have someone to hold responsible. Franklin Wallace gets to keep his son, and the sheriff doesn't run the risk of offending either of you."

"Only folks dat gon' lose is us colored folks," Elijah said.

"You must assert a knowledgeable presence, sir," Shelby explained, "you are going to have to force Sheriff Hackman to do his job responsibly. As he will no doubt try to hide the true facts of this matter in the darkness of your ignorance. You must not let him do so, sir. Or else, the person responsible for the injustice against your child may never be brought to justice, and I don't believe that you would have it this way."

"Ah do not know the sheriff well, but surely he knows who Ah am, and would not dare cross me so," Merriwhether said.

"With all due respect, sir," Shelby said, "it is true that you are a man of notable influence. Your wealth alone assures that Sheriff Hackman will want to do everything within his power to see that this matter is resolved to your satisfaction. The immediate problem for sheriff Hackman, however, is that you are not the only man of wealth and notable influence involved in this matter.

"Franklin Wallace also commands wealth and influence. Surely, you can see that Sheriff Hackman would also want to resolve this matter in a satisfactory manner to Mister Wallace as well. There is no way for the sheriff to satisfy you both, not without making an enemy out of one of you. Either of you could ruin him if you were so inclined. The sheriff is all too aware of this. The only safe ground for him to walk upon is to satisfy you both. The only way for the sheriff to do that is to give you an innocent."

Merriwhether began to think on what Shelby and Elijah had told him. He understood that it was very likely that Sheriff Hackman would try to deceive him. He wouldn't allow that. He had made up his mind to put pressure on Sheriff Hackman. Hackman may have been afraid of Franklin Wallace, but Merriwhether wasn't. If Jesse Wallace had killed Merriwhether's beloved Hannah, he would have the boy, and Franklin Wallace be damned if he dared stand between Merriwhether and his justice.

"Thank you for your insight, gentlemen," Merriwhether said.

"What are your intentions at point, sir?" Shelby curiously asked.

"If my daughter is indeed dead, Ah intend to see that the guilty one answers grievously for his transgression."

There was a certain relief that filled Elijah when he heard Merriwhether say this. His biggest concern during this ordeal had been to protect his people from unwarranted attack. The damning storm cloud which had loomed overhead, gathering strength, which was certain to unleash destruction upon the colored people of Jago, and the surrounding communities, was passing. Elijah felt comfortable that his people were now out of danger.

"Excuse me, now," Merriwhether said, "Ah have to make ready to see the sheriff."

"Would you like for us to wait for you?" Shelby asked.

"No, Ah'll be along shortly," Merriwhether assured.

"Thank you for your time, sir. And, we are truly saddened by the unfortunate events you are faced with," Shelby conveyed.

Without farther word, Elijah and Shelby left. Standing there alone in the study, Merriwhether was feeling something that he hadn't given much thought, fear that his daughter was dead. Having no reason to fear the worst, he thought that she was just lost. She was simply somewhere waiting for him to find her. The thought that she was dead, or that someone could have killed her, was never a thought that was front and center in his consciousness.

Twenty-Nine

The light of morning was starting to peak through. The sun did not yet shine, but nevertheless it was light enough out so that all lamps and torches could be extinguished. In the light of day, the secrets of night have nowhere to hide. Five miles from her home, the body of young Hannah Covington was about to be found.

Two brothers, who were on their way home from the search around Olive Branch, were walking through a wooded area. The two men were Tuck and Leigh Boulder. They were but humble men, and at this point weren't even looking for the child. They simply wanted to get home and have a little something to eat before taking a nap. Tuck and Leigh were twins. They were both five nine, and both had blonde hair with blue eyes. Although they were identical, it was easy to tell them apart. Tuck was heavier than Leigh. They were twenty-three years old.

As they walked along weary from being up all night, there was not much conversation between them. As Leigh, the younger of the two twins, passed a bush about fifteen feet away, he saw something which caught his attention. "What is that?" He asked.

"What?" Tuck responded.

"Right over yonder, don't cha see it?"

"No."

Leigh started to move closer to the area of bush.

"Leigh, ain't nothin' over there. Come on now, Ah'm ready to get home."

Leigh looked into the bushes. "Dear God. Tuck, come here, Tuck."

Even though there was a fearful excitement in Leigh's voice, Tuck reluctantly and slowly came to look inside the bushes. What he saw was a horrific sight. Hannah Covington was lying there dead. She had been beaten severely. It was an unbearable thing to see.

"It's her, Tuck," Leigh said, "It's Hannah Covington."

"Who would do this?" Tuck said, shocked to see the child beaten so badly.

"Let's get her, and take her, to Colonel Covington," Leigh said, ready to move in to get the child.

Tuck grabbed him by the arm. "No, Leigh, leave her be."

"Why?" Leigh asked. "Folks been lookin' for her all night."

"Just do like Ah say. Leave her be. Ah want you to go back to town and get the sheriff. Ah'll wait right here with her."

Leigh did as Tuck told him. He ran through the woods out to the road leading to Olive Branch. Amazingly, he didn't see a soul. Leigh was sure that he would see someone. He began to run toward town. He covered three miles running and walking trying to get to the Sheriff's office. Finally, in the last mile or so he ran upon a man, Edward Nash. Nash was also on his way home.

He was a tall slender man, and had a horse, a black mare. Upon seeing Edward, Leigh called out to him, running toward him.

"Ed," Leigh cried, waving his hands in the air, "we found her!"

Automatically, Ed knew that Leigh was referring to Hannah Covington.

"Where?" He asked, riding closer to Leigh.

"Back yonder a few miles in tha woods."

"She okay?"

Leigh shook his head from side to side, indicating she was not.

"Show me where she is."

"No. My brother Tuck is with her. He says for me to get tha sheriff, and bring him back. That's what Ah'm a gonna do."

Ed steadied his horse and extended a hand to Leigh. "Get on. Ah will take you."

Leigh climbed on back of the black horse, and the men raced into town. As they hit town, both of the men yelled out that Hannah Covington had been found. This news drew scores of people toward them, but they didn't stop to converse. They raced onward toward the sheriff's office.

Elijah and Shelby were both standing in front of the sheriff's office. Leigh and Ed were some distance away. At first, it was difficult for Elijah and Shelby to make out what the men were yelling, but as they drew closer, it became quite clear what they were saying. Elijah got a very sickly feeling in his stomach. The moment they had all been waiting for was at hand. Ed stopped his horse right in front of the Sheriff's office. Leigh dismounted quickly, headed inside to find the sheriff.

"The sheriff isn't there," Shelby said, "he's at the restaurant having breakfast."

"Thanx," Leigh said.

Leigh ran across and up the street headed for the restaurant. He was closely followed by Shelby, Elijah, and many more people interested in what Leigh had to tell sheriff Hackman. The sheriff was in the middle of having steak and eggs with Deputy Abner Lewis. Leigh entered the restaurant and went straight to him.

"We found her, sheriff," Leigh proclaimed, "we found Hannah Covington."

"Where?" Sheriff Hackman asked, as he pushed away from the table to stand.

"Outside of town in tha woods about five miles from here."

"She okay?"

"She is dead, Sheriff."

"Take me to her," Sheriff Hackman said, starting to feel pressured, "Abner, let Merriwhether Covington know that we've located his daughter. And, do it carefully, Abner."

Leigh began to move outside, followed by Sheriff Hackman and Deputy Lewis. As the sheriff passed Shelby, the men looked each other in the eyes. For Sheriff Hackman, it was a look of being angry with Shelby for going to Merriwhether Covington. It was a move the sheriff saw as trying to usurp his authority.

A short time later the sheriff and countless others arrived in the woods at the murder scene. Elijah and Shelby stuck close to the sheriff. The first thing that the sheriff did was enlist the help of several men to keep everyone back. Shelby had no intention of being kept away from the child's body. He got right in the thick of it, and he brought Elijah with him. The sheriff did not like Shelby's pushiness.

"You two keep out of my way, or Ah will arrest you," the sheriff threatened.

Sheriff Hackman, being lead by Leigh, continued on to the murder scene. Shelby and Elijah followed closely without saying much. Shelby would stay out of Sheriff Hackman's way so long as he was satisfied with the way the sheriff was handling the situation. As they drew near the spot where little Hannah's body lay, Tuck looked at them, happy to see them. He had felt uncomfortable being with the child's body.

"What took you so long, Leigh?" Tuck asked.

"Ah got there and back as fast as Ah could, Tuck," Leigh answered.

There were three other men standing around the area. They managed to get there before Sheriff Hackman positioned men to keep everyone away.

"Have any of you touched this child's body?" Sheriff Hackman asked.

"Ah ain't let nobody touch her since we found her, sheriff, not even me or Leigh have
touched her," Tuck assured.

The sheriff looked in the bushes, and saw young Hannah there. He stood there for a moment looking at her battered body. It was a sickening sight. Shelby nor Elijah could see the child from where they stood.

"Come on," Shelby said to Elijah, as he moved closer.

Elijah walked toward the bushes. A nervous energy filled him. He had seen more than his fair share of dead children for a life time. Yet, it was a sight he had not grown use to seeing. When first Elijah saw young Hannah, he felt sick and angry, not because the child was dead, but for what he saw. Like with all the children which had been murdered so far. Hannah too had been beaten severely, and strangled to death. However, unlike all of the children before her, she was lying on her back with her hands placed at her sides. All of those before her were found with their faces in the dirt, sprawled about like trash. No great care was shown them. There was no gentleness, as with young Hannah. In a way, Hannah almost looked as if she were asleep. It was almost as if whoever did this deed regretted having done so. Whoever did this surely felt remorse.

Elijah plainly saw this. He knew that Jesse Wallace had no hand in Hannah's murder. If Jesse had a part in this, why would he suddenly change his way of doing things? Why would he suddenly exhibit remorse and regret? No, Jesse Wallace had no hand in this. Elijah was certain of it. He was also equally certain that Micah did this, and Micah alone. Elijah wondered what madness had possessed Micah that he would so brazenly gamble with not only his own life, but with the lives of the hundreds of black families that lived around the area. How could Micah be so foolish? Elijah thought.

If the whites suspected anyone black of committing this deed, they would surely kill countless blacks without mercy. Elijah gnashed his teeth, and at his side clinched an angry fist. Had Elijah known that Micah would do this vile thing, he would have stopped Micah, even if it meant tying him down. Micah was out of control, and every black around was in danger because of it. Damn Micah for this. Damn him!

Raw and untamed emotions rippled through Elijah. His heart was pounding as he angrily wondered how Micah could be so recklessly stupid. He realized that he had to get control of himself. Elijah was afraid that his emotions would betray him. That the sheriff and Shelby would see what he was feeling, and somehow know what he knew. Elijah relaxed his clinched fist, and put on a face void of any emotion. Micah was playing a dangerous game, and Elijah had no choice but to play along with him.

Sheriff Hackman knelt down at Hannah's side, and started to examine her body. Shelby also stepped into the bushes, as he did, he saw a small piece of cloth on one of the bushes. "What is this?" he asked.

Sheriff Hackman stood and removed the cloth from the bush, and took a good hard look at it. It was a fabric which seemed to be part of a gray cotton shirt.

"Tuck," Sheriff Hackman said, "are you absolutely certain that no one has been near the girl's body?"

"Nobody, sheriff."

The sheriff visually examined the clothing of everyone there to see if the piece of fabric he held in his hand might have come from one of them. Nobody there was wearing a gray cotton shirt. The sheriff and Shelby concluded that the killer's clothes were torn while he put little Hannah's body in the bushes.

The sheriff knelt, and started to examine Hannah's body again. He lifted her right hand, which was gently closed. Between the child's fingers were strands of bright-red hair, bright-red hair like Jesse Wallace's.

"Looks as if she put up a fight and managed to pull out some of her attacker's hair in the process,"
Shelby observed.

"Looks like it," Sheriff Hackman agreed.

"You know. Jesse Wallace has red hair, sheriff. I think we need to pay him a visit," Shelby said.

Sheriff Hackman looked at Shelby with a degree of ambivalence, knowing that he should place Jesse at the top of his suspect list, but not wishing to do so. "Many people living in this community have red hair."

"But, not many that are suspected of murdering children, sheriff," Shelby pointed out, "Jesse Wallace alone holds that distinction."

Elijah stood there in silence listening to Shelby and Sheriff Hackman talk. As nervous and angry as he was, Elijah started to feel a little more secure. Maybe, Micah didn't do it. The red hair in Hannah's hands pointed directly to Jesse Wallace. Elijah was thankful to God for this, but still he was torn inside. Although it appeared so, Elijah believed Jesse Wallace didn't do this, but what could he do. If he told them that this did not look like the work of Jesse Wallace, and told them that Micah may have done this, Jesse would go free, and would most likely kill again. Micah would be killed, and there was no guarantee that an outraged white community would stop the killing with Micah, and besides, Elijah wasn't willing to turn Micah over to them.

As Elijah stood there contemplating the complexity of the situation, he heard heavy footsteps behind him. Merriwhether Covington was coming, moving with an arrogant haughty stride. Merriwhether was accompanied by Deputy Abner Lewis. Tuck saw him coming. Out of concern for seeing his daughter in a state that he was not prepared to see, Tuck stepped into Merriwhether's path. "You don't wanna see that, sir."

Merriwhether pushed the thoughtful concerned young man aside. "Out of my way, boy."

Upon seeing Hannah's dead battered body, Merriwhether was immediately grieved. He was visibly shaken. Yet, he did not cry. Both Shelby and Sheriff Hackman stood, they looked at Merriwhether, feeling sorrow for him.

Merriwhether went to his daughter, and knelt down at her side. He took her cold body into his arms, and held her tightly, as he began to weep. Everyone stood there watching Merriwhether. It was not an easy thing for them to see. They all felt sympathy for him. Some of them had children. They empathized, because it could have been be one of their children lying there. "Everybody step back," Sheriff Hackman said, wanting to give Merriwhether a moment of privacy.

Everyone complied with the sheriff's directive. They all moved a short distance away where they could not see Merriwhether in the bushes. Yet, they still heard a father's painful grief. They listened to Merriwhether weep for his child for better than ten minutes. Several times Sheriff Hackman was tempted to go to Merriwhether to comfort him, but he did not. Suddenly, the sounds of grief ceased from the bushes. Everyone wondered why Merriwhether stopped grieving. Surely, a father needed more than ten minutes to lament his child's passing. Merriwhether stood, holding sweet precious Hannah. He walked toward Sheriff Hackman.

"Who did this?" Merriwhether asked, with a look of anger in his eyes that struck fear in the heart of Sheriff Hackman.

"Ah can't say conclusively," Sheriff Hackman answered.

"And, just what does that mean?" Merriwhether asked in a restrained angry voice.

"Mr. Covington," Sheriff Hackman said in a way that suggested he was almost afraid to answer.

"Was it Wallace?" Merriwhether asked.

"Mister Covington, we've found something, but before Ah jump to any conclusions. Ah have to make some inquiries. Ah have to be certain."

"So, you have an idea of who did this? Was it Wallace?" Merriwhether asked once more.

"Sir, Ah would rather not say at this time."

"Was it someone colored?"

"No, sir, it was not," Shelby quickly answered.

"Look at my daughter, sheriff," Merriwhether said, "she was just a child. She will never blossom into womanhood. She will never marry, never have children, never grow old. Someone stole all those things from her, and there is nothing Ah can do to restore any of it to her. All Ah can do for her now is shed a tear, but that won't bring her back to me. Whoever did this will surely answer for it, do you understand? Ah will see to it."

"With all due respect, sir, law is for the lawless. It is my job to enforce the laws of the land. Ah know you are hurting, but let me do my job, don't interfere," Sheriff Hackman said.

"Sheriff, Ah won't stand in the way of you doing your job, but you had best do your job in a timely manner, and you had best make sure that Ah'm satisfied with the results, because if you can't get results, Ah'll get someone in here who can. Ah hope that Ah've made myself clear. Ah'm going to take Hannah to the undertaker so that he can make her presentable before her mother sees her. When Ah am done there, Ah will be coming to see you, and you had best have some answers for me."

Normally, Sheriff Hackman would have set anyone straight who would dare challenge his authority as the county sheriff, but there is a time for every purpose under the sun, and Sheriff Hackman perceived that this was a time for him to keep silent. He was afraid of the trouble Merriwhether could make.

It was a mistake for Sheriff Hackman to fear Merriwhether Covington. The sheriff should have asserted himself, and let Merriwhether know that he was the law. He should have made it clear to Merriwhether that no one was above the law, but he didn't. Although the sheriff was not consciously aware, his lack of assertiveness had now given Merriwhether the authority to run the show.

Merriwhether walked away with Hannah's body in his arms. Tuck took off his brown vest and covered the child's face so that the countless people waiting at the edge of the woods would not see how badly the child had been beaten. At first, Merriwhether allowed this, but as he reached the road. He uncovered Hannah's battered face. He wanted everyone to see her. He wanted the horror of it to stick in the minds of the people. He wanted their empathy and forgiveness for what he intended to do to the soul that would dare harm his child.

As Merriwhether moved through the press of people, horrified gasps were heard from everyone who saw Hannah's face. Sorrow and outrage spread throughout the crowd. Merriwhether placed Hannah's body on back of his wagon. As he did so, he noticed something that eluded him initially. He called out to Sheriff Hackman, who followed him out of the woods. Sheriff Hackman made his way to Merriwhether.

"Sheriff, there is a gold pendent with an oval locket that my daughter wears. It is missing. Have some men search that area for it."

Sheriff Hackman acknowledged that he would do so. Shelby, who was standing close by, heard what Merriwhether said to Sheriff Hackman about the pendent. Shelby's first thought was that Jesse Wallace took the pendent from Hannah's neck when he murdered her. Merriwhether left the scene with Hannah's body. Sheriff Hackman instructed Deputy Lewis to get several men and go over the area searching for Hannah's missing pendent. Sheriff Hackman got on his horse, a red dun with a white mane and tail, and rode back to town. Shelby and Elijah stuck close to the sheriff, riding back to town with him.

When they arrived back in town, Farley had also made it back. He was sitting with a look of haughty aplomb atop a magnificent appaloosa stud. He almost looked gallant sitting atop such a fine horse, but gallantry was not to be found in him. He had a prisoner with him.

During the night, Deputy Farley and several men rode into Jago. He and those assisting him invaded the home of fifteen year old Uriah Thomas and dragged him from his bed. Despite the boy's father, mother, two brothers, and sister telling them that the boy couldn't have done the deed, Deputy Farley accused him anyway, and Uriah confessed to killing Hannah Covington. Deputy Farley helped him to do so by hitting the boy in the stomach several times.

Uriah suffered from a condition in which he echoed what others said, except he had a habit of starting his statements with 'I'. Deputy Farley bound Uriah's hands and made the youngster walk all the way from Jago to Olive Branch. Uriah's entire family followed them to town. There was a sizable crowd gathered around Uriah. They cursed him, spat upon him, and hit him. Uriah was bleeding from a gash in his head and was very afraid. He didn't understand what was happening to him, or why. This was fine by Farley, as he meant to kill Uriah anyway.

Merriwhether's youngest son, Christopher, had arrived in town and had been instructed by his father to stay close to the sheriff. He too was waiting in front of the sheriff's office where Deputy Farley had Uriah. As Farley saw Sheriff Hackman approaching, he prepared to incite a riot. He wanted the good people of Olive Branch to take matters into their own hands, and lynch Uriah just as soon as he confessed.

"We got 'im, Robert," Deputy Farley called to the sheriff, "he confessed to killing Hannah Covington."

"Get control of this situation, sheriff," Shelby warned, seeing Farley had a black that he intended to kill.

"What's going on here?" Sheriff Hackman asked.

"We got him, Robert. He confessed to it," Deputy Farley insisted.

This was just as Elijah feared. Some innocent black was being accused of killing Hannah Covington. Even though Sheriff Hackman knew Uriah was not guilty, he seemed slow to Elijah to step in and stop the abuse of this poor child at the hands of this mob. The sheriff, Shelby, and Elijah dismounted.

"Sheriff," Shelby said, wanting him to step up and take charge of this situation.

"He killed her, sheriff," Farley said, "you killed her, didn't you, Uriah?"

"Kill her. Yes, Ah kill her," Uriah confessed, afraid of being hit more, not understanding what they would do to him.

Upon hearing Uriah's confession, a man from the crowd walked upon Uriah, and hit him so hard it knocked him to the ground. Another man from the crowd also started to beat Uriah. Elijah ran to the boy's aide. He jumped between the men and Uriah, shielding Uriah, taking blows in the process. Shelby also jumped in, and shoved the men back. Sheriff Hackman pulled out his .44 caliber Colt Army Revolver and shot into the air.

"god dammit, Ah will shoot the next man that starts trouble here!" Sheriff Hackman attested.

"This black bastard killed a white child, sheriff," a voice from the crowd cried, "his nigger carcass needs to swing!"

"god dammit, Ah'm the law here! When it is time for someone to swing, Ah'll let you know. Until then, you good people had best go home, cause God as my witness Ah will kill the man that tries to step outside the law here. Now, go home!"

"You siding with that nigger murderer, sheriff ?" someone from the crowd yelled.

"Listen to me, all of you! Ah have information that you don't! My deputy is mistaken here. All of you go home and let me do my job."

"We heard him say that he killed her," another voice cried from the crowd, "that's all we need to know. Let's string him up, right now."

"Ah'll say it again! Go home, because none of you know what you think you know! Don't any of you try to kill this boy, or any other colored in this county. Ah will blow the son-of-bitch's brains out that starts that kind of trouble in my county," Sheriff Hackman said, standing tall.

"Why are you stoppin' 'em, Robert? You heard him confess," Deputy Farley said.

"Did he?" Shelby yelled, looking angrily at Farley. "Did he confess of his own free will, or did you help him?"

"Shut up, Yankee! You got no business here," Farley barked.

"Like hell, I don't," Shelby countered, as he ran over to Farley's horse and yanked the bit in the animal's tender mouth, forcing the animal to fall. As soon as the horse and Farley hit the ground, Shelby grabbed Farley and dragged the big man inside the sheriff's office, shoving him into a chair.

Elijah grabbed Uriah and quickly helped him into the sheriff's office. Christopher Covington followed them inside. Sheriff Hackman also followed. The angry mob outside didn't go anywhere. Sheriff Hackman was worried that he would have to kill someone to keep the peace. Around this time, Merriwhether fought his way through the crowd into the sheriff's office. Shelby knew that Franklin Covington no doubt put Farley up to framing Uriah. With Merriwhether present, Shelby decided to make Deputy Farley tell them the straight of it.

"This boy didn't kill Hannah, and you know it, Farley," Shelby said with an intimidating gaze.

"He did it. You heard him confess," Farley said, ready to fight Shelby.

"Sit down, Angus," Sheriff Hackman commanded.

"Confessed he may have, but you forced him into it," Shelby said.

"He did it," Farley insisted.

"Farley, you are lying to us. We know that you are, because we have proof that you are. Wallace put you up to this. He told you to make it look like that poor boy there did this, so, he can protect that son of his. Well, you better listen to me, and you had best listen well. I'm only gonna give you one chance at this. Admit to us right now that Wallace put you up to this, and Ah'll look the other way where you are concerned. Otherwise, I'm gonna see that you go to state prison for your part in this. Being a lawman, you oughta know that prison ain't a place you wanna be. They work you under the hot southern sun from dawn to dusk. Then, after you've worked like a dog all day, they feed you dry stale bread, maggot-infested stew, and water. A big man like you will wither down to nothing in no time under conditions like that. They'll break you. They will break you good, but that's not all. No, that ain't the worst of it, Farley. Things that can change a man go on in places like that. Now, I don't know how true it is, but I hear that at night, when everything is quiet, and the guards are asleep, and aren't around to protect you. I hear that the prisoners get lonely.

"Their needs come out to breathe. Well, there aren't any women around.

So, I hear, they turn to each other for comfort. Well, you being an ex lawman and all, I'll make sure that they know you are. I'm sure that, like a new whore in a whore house on Independence Day, you will get plenty of attention. You had better tell us what you know. What we already know."

Farley didn't even have to think about this one. He knew what Shelby was saying was true. He wouldn't do time for anyone. "Yer right. Franklin asked me to make it look like someone else other than his son did this. He is trying to protect Jesse."

This was all Merriwhether Covington needed to hear. His anger was kindled against Jesse and Franklin Wallace. He aimed to see justice done. Elijah breathed easier, but he was still concerned. Many armed whites were just outside the sheriff's door. The sheriff did little to calm them. At some point later in the day, those people might have gotten drunk and decided to kill black people. He moved to the sheriff.

"Sheriff, suh, you gotta do somethin' bout dem folks out dere. Y'all holdin' all da proof in heah. Dem folks out dere. All they got is what dey done heard dis heah po' boy , Uriah, say. You gotta set 'em straight befo' dey start killin'."

Shelby walked over to them. "You have all the proof you need, Sheriff. You have the hair from Hannah's hand which matches the hair of Jesse Wallace, and you have your own deputy's word that Franklin Wallace put him up to placing the blame on this young boy to protect his son. Go outside and let those people know that no one colored murdered Hannah Covington."

"Do it," Merriwhether Covington commanded.

Sheriff Hackman did not like the way Covington commanded him. The sheriff had courage enough to stand up to an angry mob, but Covington's power scared him. He was afraid to stand up to him. Sheriff Hackman moved to the door followed by the Covington's and Shelby. The crowd went silent, giving ear to what the sheriff had to say.

"Earlier, Ah told you all that Ah had information that none of you did. Ah want to go into that a little deeper. Ah have certain evidence in my possession. Evidence which makes it clear that no person of color is responsible for the death of Hannah Covington. Don't take your wrath out on these people. The coloreds had nothing to do with the murder. That's all Ah can say right now. Ah know all of you are outraged by what happened, but we are handling it. All of you should go home, because you can't do any good here," Sheriff Hackman explained.

"Is that true, Mister Covington?" someone asked from the crowd.

"It's true," Merriwhether confirmed, "No one colored had anything to do with this. Now, go on home like the sheriff says."

Some people had doubts as to the truth of what the sheriff and Merriwhether were telling them. Others believed what they were told without skepticism, but all of them obeyed Merriwhether Covington.The crowd dispersed, and everyone went about his business. The sheriff, the Covingtons, and Shelby went back inside the sheriff's office. Elijah, Uriah, and Farley were there waiting in silence.

Deputy Farley knew trouble was brewing. Sheriff Hackman looked at him very displeased with him. Farley had compromised the sheriff's office. However, Sheriff Hackman couldn't be overly concerned about that at the moment. The sheriff had to turn his attention to the matter of going out to question Jesse Wallace. He would have liked to have gone alone, but that was out of the question at this juncture. The Covingtons and Shelby would insist upon being present.

Around this time, Deputy Lewis returned. "We didn't find the pendent, Robert," he said, "Ah asked a few men to keep looking for it."

"Thank you, Abner," Sheriff Hackman responded.

"I think it's high time we went out to pay the Wallace family a visit," Shelby said.

"Yes, it is," Merriwhether agreed.

"We will ride out, gentlemen." Sheriff Hackman said. "However, Ah need for all of you to respect what Ah have to do. Ah must insist that you all keep quiet and let me do my job. Abner, Angus, Ah want the two of you to come along."

Sheriff Hackman led the way as everyone followed him outside, and began to mount their horses.
Shelby stopped Elijah, who was helping Uriah out of the sheriff's office. The sheriff and the others rode off.

"There is no need for you to come along, Elijah," Shelby said, "you've done a great job keeping this situation from getting out of hand. I commend you for that, but it is probably going to work out best from here on out if you let me handle this. Your troubles are over. Wallace is done for, I promise you that. He won't plague you or your people anymore. See, that this young fellow gets home safely. I'll ride out to see you when everything is done."

Elijah didn't say anything as Shelby got on his buckskin horse, and struck out to catch up to the sheriff and the Covingtons. He was comfortable that Shelby would land Jesse Wallace in jail. Not so much for killing black children, as for the murder of Hannah Covington. It was over. It had been a long disheartening journey, but this nightmare was finally over. Elijah thought of Micah. Micah gambled, and it looked as he had won, if he indeed was the person who killed Hannah Covington. Elijah helped Uriah and his family get home, and he headed for his home.

Thirty

At the Wallace Plantation, the sheriff and those with him arrived. Franklin had been watching them approach from a window inside his home. Deputy Farley was with the sheriff. Franklin didn't know what to make of this, but the presence of the Covington's made him uncomfortable. Their presence suggested to him that Deputy Farley was not able to pull off what was agreed upon between them. "Ah want all of you except for Abner to wait here," Sheriff Hackman said.

"I'm coming with you, sheriff," Shelby insisted.

"As am Ah," Merriwhether said.

The door to the Wallace home opened, and Franklin stepped out onto the porch. "What brings you all out this way, sheriff?"

Sheriff Hackman was feeling quite pressured by Shelby and Merriwhether. He had hoped to use a degree of tact to broach this subject with Franklin. However, he knew that Covington and Shelby would insist that he approach the matter straightforward. Feeling forced to handle the matter this way, he did. "Mister Wallace," he said, "Hannah Covington was found dead this morning. Ah believe that you know of her. Ah have reason to believe your son, Jesse, may have been involved in her murder, and Ah also have cause to suspect that you have tried to cover it up. Ah would like to question you and Jesse, and Ah would like to have a look around your home. And, it is to your advantage to cooperate with us. This is a serious matter with serious consequences."

Franklin looked curiously at Deputy Farley, wondering if the sheriff and the others knew of their arrangement, but there was nothing Deputy Farley could say to guide him or help him. He assumed that Deputy Farley had betrayed his confidence.

"My son didn't kill your daughter, Covington," Franklin said, sensing inevitable conflict.

"Is that why you tried to get Deputy Farley to pass off some poor darky as the murderer?" Merriwhether confronted. "Yes, we know all about it."

Around this time, Elizabeth came to the door, venturing out onto the porch. This was a bold move. At this time in history, women assumed a very docile role in affairs deemed more suited to males, as dictated by sociological expectations. Such a matter as this was clearly the business of men. Women knew their place, and kept silent. Elizabeth wasn't about to let her son be ensnared because of Franklin's poor judgement in getting

Deputy Farley to frame a Negro. She had complete confidence that Jesse couldn't have committed Hannah's murder.

"Jesse had nothing to do with your daughter's death, Merriwhether. It was a lack of prudence on Franklin's part to try and deceive, but you have a reputation as being a hard vengeful man. And, because our son has been accused of harming several Negra children, my husband rightly moved to keep you from casting your vengeful eye toward our son. Granted, he went about it in the wrong way. Ah tried to tell Franklin there was no need for any kind of deception. My son didn't kill your daughter, but given your reputation, Franklin felt, even though Jesse is innocent, that he had to divert your need to revenge away from our son. Sheriff, you may question Jesse, and look around our home. We have nothing to hide. Our son did not kill Hannah. If searching our home will convince you of that, feel free."

"Woman," Franklin said angrily, "mind your place."

"We have to cooperate, Franklin. What you did makes Jesse look guilty of something that he is not. Whatever we can do to help put the sheriff's mind at ease, we should do. We have nothing to hide. Jesse has nothing to hide.

"Do you expect that Ah should help these men hang our son, Elizabeth," Franklin argued, "No, Ah think not."

"Don't you see, Franklin, the more we fight this, the more we protest, it only serves to heighten their belief that Jesse is guilty. He is not, and we know this. Let the sheriff speak to Jesse. Let the sheriff, and his men, search our home. Jesse is innocent. Whatever the sheriff does here will only serve to prove Jesse's innocence," Elizabeth said.

"What you fail to realize, Elizabeth, is that they didn't come here looking to prove Jesse's innocence. They came here looking to prove his guilt," Franklin looked directly at Merriwhether and drew the line, "No, they can't search my home, or speak to my son. When Ah have sent to Memphis for adequate legal representation, then, they can speak to Jesse, not before. Don't buck me on this, Elizabeth."

"Do you really think that you can hide that little monster behind some high priced lawyer from Memphis, Wallace? Ah think not. You are making his bed harder by the second," Merriwhether said, vowing vengeance against Jesse.

"You'll not touch him!" Franklin warned, pointing an angry finger at Merriwhether.

"Try to stop me," Merriwhether calmly threatened.

"This business will be conducted in a lawful manner, Mister

Covington," Sheriff Hackman intervened, trying to head off a clash between Franklin and Merriwhether, "it will be handled in a court of law by a sanctioned judge and jury."

"You'll not touch my boy, Covington. You will answer to me if you try," Franklin assured.

"He will answer for what he has done, Wallace. He will answer," Merriwhether threatened.

"Not to you," Franklin calmly asserted.

"What more proof do you need, sheriff. He has just admitted time and again that his son murdered Hannah," Christopher Covington said.

"Listen to me you little son of a whore. Don't you ever presume to twist my words, trying to make them mean what benefits you," Franklin fired back.

"Go inside and arm yourself, Wallace. We can settle this right here and now," Christopher threatened.

"If you are ready to die, boy. Ah'll be more than happy to send you on your way," Franklin countered.

"There will be none of that here today," Shelby said, "we are here to do things in the proper legal way, don't either of you forget it."

"Ah can handle the business that is my own, Alexander," Sheriff Hackman said, feeling Shelby was trying to usurp his authority.

"Then handle it!"

"Covington, against my better judgement, Ah let you and your son come along. Ah won't have you undermining my efforts here. Ah'll seize your weapons, and have my deputies escort you home if you can't control yourselves. Ah hope Ah'm clear," Sheriff Hackman said, feeling frustrated, laying down the law.

"If you try it, Ah will see to it that you are ruined, sheriff," Merriwhether threatened.

"That's your prerogative, sir, but today you will go home if you step out of line once more," the sheriff asserted. His anger fueling his courage to stand up to Merriwhether.

"Do we see them home, sheriff?" Deputy Lewis asked, ready to back the sheriff's play, as he didn't like Merriwhether's disrespectful tone toward the sheriff.

Sheriff Hackman looked Merriwhether in the eyes, staring him down. Merriwhether was livid, but was holding his tongue. He looked away from sheriff Hackman. The sheriff saw the bend in Merriwhether.

"No, Abner, Ah think Mister Covington has gotten control of himself," Sheriff Hackman said, turning his attention toward Franklin. "Mister

Wallace, you have to help me here. You are stepping away from me, away from the law. Ah'm not the enemy that you suppose me to be. Ah am not here to pass judgement. Ah'm trying to get to the truth. Ah'm trying to bring this matter to a peaceful lawful conclusion. When you fail to assist me in doing this, you diminish what the law is designed to do, and you unwittingly strengthen Mister Covington's hand. Ah'm going to be quite honest with you. Right now, the situation is not looking well for your son.

"Ah've got Deputy Farley's admission that you tried to get him to cover up for your son. Ah've got a lock of red hair found in the dead child's hand, much like your son's hair, and Ah've got several Negro's that swear that they caught Jesse trying to kill one of their children. Separately, those things may not establish guilt, but put them together, and they paint a powerful picture of condemnation against your son.

"Ah know you are probably thinking that it will be your word against Deputy Farley's word, and that many people have red hair around here, and that a Negro can't testify against a white. Well, let me assure you that Mister Covington there is going to get the powers that be to admit Negro testimony for this one time. Ah can assure you that a jury is going to believe Deputy Farley. Ah can assure you that the red hair will leave no room for doubt in the jury's mind that your son is a murderer. Ah can assure you that the fact you refused to cooperate with us will seal your son's fate with the jury.

"One of the few good things that you can do for your son, at this point, is to let me question him, and let us search your home. At least that way, you will be able to say that you did everything within your power to cooperate with us. That way, a jury won't have an opportunity to view your lack of cooperation as an admission of guilt. Hopefully, that is something that your lawyer will be able to built upon."

"Listen to him, Franklin," Elizabeth pled, "he is right."

A waivering voice inside Franklin's head wrestled with his desire not to comply with the sheriff's request. The voice told him to cooperate, because he knew that Merriwhether Covington was going to do everything he could to ensure Jesse was hung. The voice told Franklin that it was foolish to give Merriwhether another tool to work with in this effort. Yet, a gut feeling Franklin had warred intensely with this logic. Franklin was not sure what he should do, but he was leaning toward not cooperating.

Just then, Jesse stepped out of the house onto the porch. All eyes focused on him. Jesse did not know that he was suspected of murdering

Hannah Covington, but the heated argument between his father and the Covington's had enlightened him to that fact. Jesse wanted to set the record straight if he could.

"Ah didn't kill Hannah, Mister Covington," Jesse said in such a convincing way that it caused doubt of his guilt to flourish in Merriwhether's mind.

Franklin believed that Jesse had killed Hannah. He believed it whole heartedly. Looking at Jesse as he professed his innocence, Franklin realized that Jesse wasn't lying about the matter. Franklin was confused. He was certain that Jesse lied to him the night before. Franklin tried to make sense of it all. "Did you go outside yesterday, Jesse?"

"Yes, sir, Ah went out against your wishes," Jesse freely admitted, "Ah wanted to play. Ah didn't see the harm in it. Ah never left our property, and Ah didn't kill Hannah."

Instinctively, Franklin knew Jesse was being truthful. Franklin realized that had he just taken the time to talk to Jesse without a judgmental eye, this situation might have been averted. As it stood, the most damning thing that they had against Jesse was the fact that Franklin tried to get Farley to cover up for Jesse. Franklin realized the error. It made him more amenable to letting the sheriff question Jesse, and to letting them search the house.

"Sheriff," Franklin said, "If Ah let you search our home, what exactly will you be looking for?"

"A pendent for one, Ah believe that whoever killed the child took it," the sheriff said.

"Is that it?" Franklin asked.

"Anything that proves, or disproves, your son's guilt, Mister Wallace. That is what we will be looking for," the sheriff frankly answered.

Believing that he was doing the right thing, Franklin agreed to the search, certain there was nothing to find, because Jesse had no part in the murder. Franklin showed the sheriff, Deputy Lewis, and Shelby into the parlor. He would also allow the sheriff to question Jesse.

"Mister Wallace, while Ah'm questioning Jesse, would it be okay for my deputy to go ahead and begin the search," Sheriff Hackman asked.

Franklin thought on this for a moment. It was his intent to accompany the sheriff and his deputies while the search was being conducted. Franklin almost said 'no', but agreed to allow the search without his accompaniment. He instructed Elizabeth and Joselpha to show Deputy Lewis from room to room.

Sheriff Hackman looked at Jesse in a friendly, but stern, way. He started by asking Jesse several innocent questions in order to see how Jesse acted when he was telling the truth. "How old are you Jesse?" he asked.

"O'm twelve."

"How many sisters do you have?" Sheriff Hackman asked.

"Ah have five sisters."

"What are their names?"

"Joselpha, Blanch, Susie, May, and Diane."

"Did you know Hannah Covington?"

"Yes, sir, Ah knew her."

"How did you know her?"

"Well, Ah didn't know her know her, but Ah knew who she was."

"Ah see."

The sheriff now felt that he had a good feel for Jesse's body language when he was being truthful.

He felt ready to put the question to Jesse. "Did you hurt Hannah, Jesse?"

"No, sir."

"Did you kill her?"

"No, Ah didn't"

"Have you ever killed a human being, Jesse?" the sheriff asked, feeling Jesse was being truthful.

Jesse looked down at the floor, frowning. He was hesitant to answer.

"Have you ever killed Negro children, Jesse?" Sheriff Hackman asked.

"What does that have to do with the murder of Hannah Covington?" Franklin asked, wanting to skip over the Negro question.

"Ah have my reasons for asking this question, sir," Sheriff Hackman assured.

"Yes," Jesse honestly answered, with quiet pause, "Ah've killed Negro children."

The sheriff asked the question simply to see if Jesse would respond differently in some way. He was solely interested in Jesse's reaction, knowing no white jury would convict him for killing Negroes. At this point, Sheriff Hackman started to assess what Jesse had told him. Based on Jesse's body language, it was the sheriff's opinion that Jesse was being truthful with him.

Now, while the questioning was in progress, Deputy Lewis and Shelby were conducting a search of the premises accompanied by Elizabeth and Joselpha. They began the search in Jesse's room. On the closet floor of Jesse's room, lying in plain view, was a gray shirt stained with blood. It was made of the same kind of cotton clothe as the small piece of fabric that was recovered from the bushes where Hannah's body had lain. It also had a small tear in it.

Abner and Shelby examined the piece of clothe against the tear in the shirt. Sure enough, it was a match. This was proof that Jesse was involved in the murder. Shelby and Deputy Lewis stopped searching at that point. They felt absolutely certain that Jesse was the murderer of Hannah Covington.

Elizabeth and Joselpha realized that the men had found something, and were moved to great concern. Upon seeing the bloody-gray shirt, Elizabeth was shocked and horrified. She couldn't believe her eyes. Joselpha was also shocked, but was not as panicked as Elizabeth was.

"Let's go down to the sheriff," Deputy Lewis said.

Joselpha led the way, as Elizabeth had become so weak that she could barely bring herself to move. Joselpha rushed ahead and opened the parlor door. She looked at Franklin. "There was nothing I could do to stop this."

"What is it?" Franklin asked.

Deputy Lewis and Shelby entered the parlor right behind Joselpha. Elizabeth followed, as her head hung low. She believed in Jesse. Deputy Lewis handed the shirt to Sheriff Hackman.

"Is this your shirt, Jesse?" the sheriff asked.

"Yes."

Sheriff Hackman sighed, "Mister Wallace, Ah'm gonna have to arrest Jesse for the murder of Hannah Covington."

"Surely you jest," Franklin said.

"This shirt," Sheriff Hackman said.

"What about it?" Franklin interrupted. "It may have blood on it, but what does that prove."

"Hannah Covington was beaten severely. The person that killed her was wearing a gray cotton shirt. A piece of it was torn off and caught in the bushes surrounding the girl's body. This shirt has a piece torn out of it. A piece exactly like what was found at the murder sight," The sheriff explained.

Franklin had no way to defend against the proof that the sheriff held in his hand. He looked at Jesse, and shook his head in utter dismay.

"Ah didn't hurt Hannah, sheriff," Jesse insisted.

"How do you explain the shirt?" Sheriff Hackman asked.

"Yesterday, when Ah went out, Ah played down near the slave quarters. Norah Bailey was there. She picked a fight with me. She hit me in the nose, and it started to bleed. Ah wiped my nose with the sleeve of my shirt," Jesse explained.

"There is blood all over this shirt, son," Sheriff Hackman pointed out.

"While my nose was bleeding, she managed to pull my shirt over my head. Ask her!" Jesse said vehemently.

"Jesse, the bloody shirt isn't all that we have," Sheriff Hackman informed, "there is the little matter of red hair exactly like yours, which was found in Hannah's hands. How do you explain that?"

"Ah don't know. Someone put it there," Jesse insisted.

"Jesse, do you know what Ah think? Ah think you killed Hannah, killed her for reasons only you know. Ah would like to believe that one of the South's most beloved sons wouldn't have this in him to do, but far too much says you did kill Hannah. You have admitted to me that you have killed Negro children. Ah have hair like yours found in Hannah's hand. Ah have a small piece of fabric found in a bush near the her body which clearly came from this bloody shirt in my hand, which incidently you admit is yours. You did this, son. Ah know that maybe you didn't mean to harm her, but you did. Admit as much," Sheriff Hackman said.

"No, sir, Ah did not! Talk to Norah Bailey! She will tell you that we got into a fight is all! She will tell you that we got into a fight," Jesse argued.

"Come with us, son," Sheriff Hackman said.

Franklin did not want the sheriff to take Jesse from his house. He stepped between the sheriff and Jesse. Murderer or not, he was still Franklin's son. Franklin felt obligated as a father to protect his boy.

"Don't make this harder than it has to be, sir," Sheriff Hackman advised.

"Ah didn't hurt her, father. Don't let them take me away," Jesse cried bitterly, clinging all so strongly to Franklin, "Don't let them take me."

Jesse's cry was a heart-rending burden for Franklin to withstand. No matter what Jesse had done, as a father, it was a very difficult thing for Franklin to relinquish Jesse to the discipline of others. Yet, he realized that he must.

Franklin's only hope now was that a good lawyer would be able to dismantle the evidence that was so abundant against Jesse. Shelby was moved to a measure of pity for Jesse. He was, after all was said and done, just a child.

"Do you have to take him, sheriff?" Shelby interceded. "Can't you post a deputy here, and let the boy remain here until the trial."

Sheriff Hackman was somewhat shocked by Shelby's sympathy. Most of what had transpired today had been driven by Shelby.

"No, Ah think the best thing to do is to take him into town. That's the safest thing to do," Sheriff Hackman said.

"Go with them, Jesse," Franklin instructed.

"No, Ah didn't hurt Hannah," Jesse cried.

"Ah know you didn't, and we are going to prove it, but you have to go with them now," Franklin said to Jesse with fatherly lovingkindness, "Don't fear, we will be with you, your mother and Ah."

"Don't make me go with them, father, please," Jesse cried.

Franklin hugged Jesse, hating what had to be done. "Trust me, Jesse. Ah won't let anything happen to you."

"Ah don't wanna go," Jesse cried.

"Ah know, but we will be with you the entire time," Franklin tried to comfort.

"Mister Wallace, it's time to go," Sheriff Hackman said.

"We'll be with you," Franklin said to Jesse.

Franklin placed a hand on Jesse's shoulder and walked the boy outside. They were followed closely by Sheriff Hackman and everyone else.

"Ah'll need to hitch a team, sheriff," Franklin said.

"Okay," Sheriff Hackman replied, "Abner, lend him a hand."

Franklin and Jesse went to the barn to hitch a team of horses to a wagon to make the trip into Olive Branch. Deputy Lewis and Shelby went with them. A short time later they returned on the wagon. Deputy Lewis and Shelby mounted up.

"Elizabeth," Franklin said, "get the family together, and meet us in town. Ah'll get some rooms for us at the hotel in town."

"Yes, Franklin," she responded.

Merriwhether looked at Franklin and Jesse with anger in his eyes. Franklin saw it. It was unsettling.

"Sheriff, tell that one to keep his distance," Franklin said, referring to Merriwhether.

The ride into town was long and quiet. Everyone felt badly about this. Franklin felt that he had failed Jesse as a father. Shelby felt badly, because Jesse was a child. When he looked at him, a child was all that he saw. Sheriff Hackman felt ruined. Covington or Wallace, one of them was sure to bring him down. There was no doubt of that in the sheriff's mind. Deputy Farley also knew that his job and his freedom were on the line. The Covington's mourned the loss of a daughter and sister. Deputy Lewis was the only one seemingly not phased by it all.

After arriving in town, Franklin escorted Jesse into the Sheriff's office and into a cell. The next thing he did was go to the telegraph office. He sent a telegram to a well-known trail lawyer in Memphis. He sat there and waited for the reply, which came an hour later. The lawyer would be in Olive Branch by noon the next day. Franklin went back to the sheriff's office, and waited with Jesse. He would have done well to have kept an eye on the Covington's.

The Covington's had gone into the town saloon, and had begun to liquor up. Christopher began to talk to his father, but Merriwhether's mind was some place else. He did not hear a word Christopher said. Christopher realized that Merriwhether wasn't listening to him, and stopped talking. Merriwhether was very angry with Jesse and Franklin Wallace. He would not let Jesse get away with murdering his daughter.

"Murderer. Murderer," Merriwhether angrily murmured.

The murmur was so low that Christopher was unable to make out what Merriwhether said.

"What?" Christopher asked.

"Go tell everyone that you can find that I'm buying drinks for anyone who wants one," Merriwhether instructed.

Christopher looked at Merriwhether in a none supportive way, instantly knowing what his father had planned. "Are you sure?"

Merriwhether looked at Christopher in a way which signified not to question him.

"If that's the way you want it," Christopher said, rising from the table where Merriwhether and he were seated.

At the sheriff's office, Shelby was impressed with the way Franklin remained at his son's side. He knew that it was no more than any father would do. Still it was a sight which moved him to compassion for the boy and his father, considering how the relationship with his own father was suffering. Shelby approached Sheriff Hackman. "When do you plan to ride out to speak with Norah Bailey?"

Sheriff Hackman looked at Shelby with amazement and smiled. "For a man who was so all fired up to prove the boy's guilt. You sure seem double minded now."

"I prefer to think of it simply as being thorough," Shelby said, "If the girl backs his story, I'm certain you would want to know now, as opposed to during the trial, correct?"

"So, that is your reason. You wanna make sure there is no way out for him."

"Let's just say that I wanna give the boy every benefit of the doubt that he is due."

"Ah see. So, Ah assume you would like to ride along with me?"

"If it is not too much of an inconvenience."

"No, Ah don't suppose it would be."

"Should we tell Wallace?"

"Yeah, I think so."

Sheriff Hackman explained to Franklin that they were going to check out Jesse's story that he was in a fight with Norah Bailey. Franklin believed in his son. That was to say that he believed Jesse did not lie to him concerning Hannah Covington. Franklin decided that he would accompany the sheriff and Shelby to question Norah Bailey.

Norah returned to her home after her fight with Jesse. Her parents had no idea of what she was up too, and even Norah did not know the full extent of what she did, and what it meant for Jesse. As he worked in his garden, Collin Bailey saw the sheriff, Shelby, and Franklin riding toward him. He believed that perhaps Shelby had come back to try and convince him to admit that Ken was killed. He had thought of telling them many times that he had a son named Ken, and that the boy was killed. Denying Ken the way he did had rested heavily on Collin's heart. Still, he had to consider the living, as he could do nothing to help the dead. His family needed him, not his dead son. Collin walked a short distance to meet the men, as his smaller children played about the yard.

"Hello Collin," Shelby said.

"Hi, suh," Collin answered humbly.

"Collin, we came to see your daughter, Norah. Is she home?" Sheriff Hackman asked.

"Norah?" Collin asked, wondering why they wanted to see her.

"Ah need to question her, Collin," Sheriff Hackman said.

Collin became nervous. "What fuh, suh?"

"There has been some trouble in town. Norah may have some information, which may help us." Sheriff Hackman explained, "may we speak with her."

Although he was uncomfortable with this, Collin agreed. He escorted the men inside. Norah and her mother were inside preparing dinner. They were shucking corn and picking black-eyed peas. Norah looked at the men, and began to feel nervous, especially with the presence of Franklin.

"Norah da sheriff heah wanna speak ta ya," Collin said.

Norah looked at them curiously, wondering if she was in trouble, but she was warned by her accomplice that she would most likely receive a visit from the sheriff. She tried to play it calmly.

"How are you, Norah?" The sheriff asked.

"Ah's fine, suh," Norah answered.

"Ah see you and your mother are busy. So, Ah'll try not to take up too much of your time. Do you know Jesse Wallace?" the sheriff asked.

"Ah know 'im," Norah said with a loathing in her voice for the mere mention of Jesse's name. It was noticeable, and perceived as disrespectful.

There was a sort of uncomfortable silence that came over the room. Collin became even more nervous. "Mind yo' tongue, gal," he said.

Norah looked at her father, almost defiantly. She would obey Collin, but her look told Collin that she was not afraid of the sheriff, Franklin Wallace, or any white man.

"It's okay," Sheriff Hackman said, "Jesse says you and he got into a little scrap yesterday. From the looks of his shirt, it seems you got the better of him. Why were you and he fighting?"

"Sheriff, Ah ain't left our house. Ah ain't been scrappin' with Jesse Wallace or nobody else," Norah proclaimed.

Norah's parents knew she was lying. She disappeared for several days. They had no idea where she was or what she was doing. But now her whereabouts during that time were coming to light. This revelation frightened both of Norah's parents.

"Are you sure?" Sheriff Hackman asked, sensing Norah wasn't being completely truthful.

"Yassuh, Ah been heah. Ah ain't never left heah. You can ask my folks," Norah said.

"Was she here all day yesterday?" Sheriff Hackman asked.

"Yassuh, she been heah da whole time. It a lot of work runnin' this place. It take every hand jes' ta make sho food get on da table," Collin said, fearing for his daughter, wanting to protect her.

There was a certain nervousness to Collin that caught the attention of Sheriff Hackman, and particularly Franklin Wallace. The sheriff didn't know if Collin was nervous because he was lying, or simply because this was a situation in which anyone would likely feel nervous. Franklin summed it up as a man trying to protect his daughter, which he understood, but his son's life was on the line. He felt that he had to challenge Norah.

"Norah," Franklin said, moving to Norah, kneeling at her side, placing a hand on her right forearm. "Ah know you may be afraid to tell us the truth, because you are afraid that it may get you into trouble. Ah don't want you to be afraid of that. We aren't here to cause you any trouble. But if you were with Jesse yesterday, it is important that you tell us. It is very important."

"Ah ain't been nowhere near yo' son, suh," Norah continued to insist.

For a moment, Franklin forgot that he threatened Collin and his family to protect Jesse. Franklin forgot that Jesse killed Norah's brother. Franklin had forgotten that Jesse robbed her family of one of its members. He somehow expected her to forgive and forget. He lowered his head, realizing the foolishness of this belief. He knew that Jesse told him the truth about Norah, and he also sensed that Norah was lying to him now. Franklin did not know the extent of Norah's involvement in the troubles his family now faced. He simply felt that she wanted to fight Jesse for killing her brother. It was inconceivable to him that she could have been involved in a plan so ingeniously crafted as this to ensnare his son. All he saw was that Norah might have helped Jesse, but for understandable reasons, she would not, and Franklin didn't fault her for that.

"Let's go," Franklin said, as he headed for the door.

Franklin and Sheriff Hackman exited the house. As Shelby exited, he looked at Norah, He had a gut feeling that she knew considerably more than she was telling. Yet, he had no desire to pursue the matter anymore than he had. After Collin watched the men ride away, he went inside to confront Norah. "Gal, what is you done done?" he angrily asked.

"What you ain't, daddy. What you ain't," she answered in a soft submissive way.

Collin was of a mind to strike her, but couldn't bring himself to do so. He knew that Norah was trying to tell him that she took a stand for Ken. Something he was unwilling to do.

Thirty-One

As the sheriff, Shelby, and Franklin arrived back in town, the sun was setting. The men noticed that there were considerably more people in town than when they left. It was a disturbing sight for all of them, because the saloon was very busy. Far busier than it would have been on a Saturday. It was a Thursday. This massive gathering of men signaled trouble. As sheriff Hackman and the others arrived back at the sheriff's office, he was greeted by a worried Deputy Lewis.

"Sheriff, Ah'm glad you're back," Abner said, "a storm is brewing."

"How long have men been coming into town like this, Abner?" Sheriff Hackman asked.

"Right after you headed out, looks like they just started coming from everywhere," Abner answered, "Ah asked one of the men what was going on. He told me Merriwhether Covington was buying drinks for everybody."

"So, Covington has gotten everybody good and liquored up by now," Sheriff Hackman said very angrily. "Damn him, Ah should have expected he would try something like this."

"What are you going to do, sheriff?" Shelby asked.

"What Ah should have done from the beginning, put Covington in his place. Ah'm gonna break up this crowd, and place the Covington's under arrest. Locked in here they can't cause any trouble." "You are gonna need more men than you have here for that," Shelby said.

"Ah know, but where can Ah get them?" Sheriff Hackman asked. "Half the men around these parts are out there, drunk and willing to do anything Covington asks, as long as he is buying." "Ah'll stand with you," Shelby volunteered.

"You? You are full of surprises, aren't you?" the sheriff said.

"It's gonna take more than you and Abner, Robert," Shelby stated.

"Don't forget Angus, " Sheriff Hackman said.

Shelby looked in a doubtful manner at Angus. He understood the sheriff's choices were limited, but Shelby didn't trust Angus Farley. Sheriff Hackman saw the distrust on Shelby's face.

"Ah know my people, Shelby," the sheriff said, "Ah can trust Angus to do this."

"Deputize me, sheriff," Franklin said.

"Ah can't do that, Mister Wallace," Sheriff Hackman replied, "that would only heighten hostilities, make it look like the law is siding with you. That will be all Covington needs to tip the scale his way."

"You can trust him to do the right thing with his son's life, Robert," Shelby pointed out in favor of utilizing Franklin.

"Tell you what, you can stay here with Angus. If the situation doesn't go in our favor, Ah want you and Angus to get Jesse out of town. Take him to Holly Springs," Sheriff Hackman instructed.

"Agreed," Franklin responded.

"Your Mrs. is back there with your son, sir," Abner said, "have her go back to the hotel, and wait for this to be over."

Sheriff Hackman broke out a brand new .44 caliber Winchester Rifle and began to load it as Franklin went back to the jail to send Elizabeth away. Jesse was glad to see Franklin. He was certain that Norah told him the truth about the fight.

"How did it go, father," Jesse asked, "she told you the truth, didn't she?"

"That's unimportant right now, son," Franklin said, not wanting to go into it, "Elizabeth, go back to the hotel and wait there."

"Why can't Ah stay here with you and Jesse?" Elizabeth asked.

"Covington is trying to make trouble. Ah don't want you to get caught up in it," Franklin expressed.

"What kind of trouble?" Elizabeth asked.

"He's going to kill me, isn't he?" Jesse asked, having no illusions.

"If he does, it will be over my dead body," Franklin vowed.

"We have to get him out of here, Franklin. Tell the sheriff to take him out of here now," Elizabeth beseeched her husband.

"The sheriff has to put Covington down before he works this crowd into a frenzy. If it looks as if he can't, rest assured, Ah will get Jesse out of here. Now, go on over to the hotel," Franklin commanded.

Elizabeth did not like this. She feared for her son, and did not want to leave him there with danger lurking so near.

"Goodbye, mother," Jesse said sadly, as if it was the last time he would ever see her.

Elizabeth perceived it as if it were a bid of farewell. She didn't want to leave.

"Elizabeth," Franklin said, "go."

Franklin walked Elizabeth to the front of the sheriff's office and out the door.

"Franklin, tell Jesse that Ah love him," she said, realizing that she didn't say goodbye.

"Ah will," Franklin assured.

Elizabeth, filled with distress, went to the hotel. In the sheriff's office, Sheriff Hackman was ready to make his move.

"Lock this door behind us, Angus," Sheriff Hackman instructed. "Be vigilant. If it looks like we have failed, get that boy out of here."

"You can count on me," assured Angus.

Deputy Farley locked the door. Sheriff Hackman looked at Shelby and Abner earnestly. A mental toughness was shining through in him, as he handed Shelby the brass-framed Winchester Rifle.

"How do you wanna play this, Robert?" Abner asked.

"Covington is not some, redneck, peckerwood having a little fun on a Saturday night. He is a dangerous man with hostile intentions. We are gonna go in quickly, and arrest him and his son. We will do it peaceably if we can, or by force if necessary. Ah won't stand there jawing with him. Ah'm not gonna let him get this town worked up anymore than he already has. Abner, the younger Covington is yours. Shelby, it may be a bad idea to bring you along, but you are all Ah have. There will be many boys in there who love the Confederacy. Many of them know you, and won't take kindly to your presence. Be mindful of that. Stay back, let me and Abner handle this. Get in it only if things get out of control. Follow? Okay, let's go."

Sheriff Hackman started toward the saloon. Abner was to his left, and Shelby to his right.

There were many drunken men in the streets. They were not so drunken that they did not know to clear a path for the stern-faced three. Everyone knew that the sheriff meant business, deadly business. Not one dared stand in their way.

Once at the saloon, Sheriff Hackman peered inside. The saloon was a fairly large room. It was roughly forty-five feet by thirty-six feet. It was one story tall with a ten foot ceiling. A bar, which ran the length of the wall, was situated on the right side of the room. There were round tables situated through out the saloon. Near the back wall of the saloon was an upright piano. The saloon was jumping. Card games were being played. The piano music was loud. Laughter was constant, and liquor was flowing without constraint.

Sheriff Hackman spotted Merriwhether Covington at the very back of the saloon. He was moving about the room, working the drunken men, gathering support for his agenda.

"Does everyone understand what he is to do?" Sheriff Hackman asked one last time.

"Yes," Abner and Shelby responded, almost in unison.

413

Sheriff Hackman stepped brazenly through the door, moving with the swagger of a lion. He had his man in sight. Walking tall, the sheriff headed straight for Merriwhether. Christopher Covington was close at his father's side. The place went silent, and everyone stepped aside, making way for the sheriff. Many of them, smelling trouble, viewed this as an excellent time to exit the saloon. As the sheriff headed for Merriwhether, Shelby peeled off and took up position at the bar. His actions did not go without note. Several men standing around him, watched him like a hungry hawk. Abner stayed close to Sheriff Hackman. He moved to handle Christopher Covington. Abner made eye contact with Christopher, letting Christopher know that he was for him.

Abner was so sure of himself that it frightened Christopher to an almost paralyzing fault. Christopher stared back at Abner, trying to present the image of no fear, but he was sweating, and his hands trembled ever so slightly. Seeing this, Abner quickly sized him up. He knew Christopher would want no part of a fight.

Merriwhether Covington, on the other hand, had an intimidating gaze. He was ready for trouble. He would be the challenge. Merriwhether gently nudged Christopher out of the sheriff's line of fire. Christopher moved around behind them. Abner kept a wary eye on him.

"Merriwhether Covington," Sheriff Hackman said with a deep forceful tone, "come with us."

"For what? Ah'm breaking no law. Have you too perverted the law by accepting a bribe under the table from Wallace, like your deputy?" Merriwhether spouted.

"Shut your face, Covington!" Sheriff Hackman commanded. "It is you who conspires to pervert the law. Ah know what you are up to here. Let me assure you, it's not gonna happen. Now, let's go."

"Ah'm not going anywhere with you!" Merriwhether sternly vowed. "Do you see this men? The sheriff wants to arrest me for nothing, but his deputy and Franklin Wallace move about freely. They have conspired to deceive this town, and hide a murderer, by blaming some poor darky for my daughter's death!"

"All right, let's go!" Sheriff Hackman commanded, laying hands on Merriwhether to coerce him off to jail.

"Take your filthy corrupt hands off of me!" Merriwhether barked.

Merriwhether jerked away from the sheriff. The sheriff engaged him more aggressively, attempting to drag Merriwhether from the saloon. He resisted by grabbing the sheriff's throat with a forceful grip. Sheriff Hackman knocked Merriwhether's hand away from his throat. The men locked violently together. Although Merriwhether was almost twenty years the sheriff's senior, he was giving a very good account of himself.

Seeing that the sheriff was struggling hard to subdue Merriwhether, Abner leaped in to help the sheriff wrestle Merriwhether into submission. Merriwhether continued to put up a fierce struggle, but the peace officers were roughly bringing him under control.

Christopher didn't like the way the sheriff and Abner were man handling his father. He was angered by it. Whatever trepidations or fears Christopher had about conflict with Abner, he quickly overcame. "Unhand him!" Christopher cried, reaching for his pearl-handled Remington .44 pistol.

The sheriff's back was to Christopher, but Abner never took his eyes off of him. Christopher's judgement was lacking. The sheriff and Abner were simply trying to subdue Merriwhether. There was no need for a gun. Yet, Christopher was afraid to fight a man with his fist. He was afraid of being beaten. Instead, he resorted to guns to settle matters.

As Christopher made his move, Abner released Merriwhether, going for his .36 caliber New Model Navy Revolver. The sheriff and Merriwhether continued to struggle. As Abner drew his weapon, he was slightly off balance, moving backwards, trying to put a little distance between himself and Christopher. Men scattered everywhere trying to get out of harms way, knowing a fight was eminent. Shelby moved to get into it, but a man hit him across the back of the head with a whiskey bottle. He went down, and the man began to kick him.

Meanwhile, Christopher got his Remington out first. He fired on Abner. The bullet screamed past Abner's head. It scared Abner, and he lost his balance. Falling backwards, he returned fire. The shot struck Christopher in the shoulder. Christopher's second shot blazed past Abner's head. Abner's second shot missed Christopher all together. As Abner hit the floor, he felt a sharp stinging pain in his neck. Christopher's third shot caught Abner in the throat. Abner reached for his throat, realizing he had been hit.

As soon as Christopher fired the first shot, Sheriff Hackman swiftly turned to see Abner being fired upon. He quickly released Merriwhether, who fell to the floor. The sheriff whipped out his Colt Army Revolver. As soon as his weapon cleared the holster, the sheriff opened fire. He didn't even raise his arm to aim. As Christopher was delivering his third, and fatal, shot to Abner, Sheriff Hackman was shooting from the hip. He fired five times. All of his shots hit Christopher in the torso, three to the gut, two to the chest. He fell dead.

There was a bang from behind. Sheriff Hackman felt pain in his lower back. Merriwhether had blown a hole in it with his .36 Caliber New Model Colt Police Revolver. Sheriff Hackman spun around, firing on Merriwhether, falling to his knees. He only had one shot, and it missed Merriwhether. Merriwhether shot Sheriff Hackman in the chest. The sheriff fell backward onto the floor.

With the exception of Christopher, all of the gun play happened instinctively on the part of everyone involved in a few quick seconds. Abner lay dead. Christopher lay dead, and Sheriff Hackman was dying. Merriwhether rushed to his son's side. He was both grieved and angered, realizing Christopher was dead. With tear-filled eyes, Merriwhether took his weapon in hand, and walked over to Sheriff Hackman. The sheriff was almost dead. He was fighting hard for every labored breath. Merriwhether looked down on him void of sympathy.

"You killed my son," Merriwhether said, emptying the remaining three rounds in Sheriff Hackman's chest. "May God grant you no mercy."

At this point, there were only five living individuals in the saloon. The bar-keep, who was hiding behind the bar. A man who turned over a table, and took shelter behind it when the shooting started. Another who simply dived to the floor and covered his head. Shelby who lay unconscious on the floor near the bar, and Merriwhether standing over the sheriff's dead body.

Merriwhether had lost two children in a twenty-four hour period. A sorrowful rage consumed him completely. He had to lash out. He had finished off the man who killed his son, but it was not enough. It was time to turn his attentions to the one who murdered his daughter.

Make no mistake about it. It was always Merriwhether's intention to kill Jesse Wallace. Unfortunately, free liquor had unleashed the darker side of the men in this town. Were the men of this town sober minded, they would have realized that a great and horrible tragedy had just occurred. Sadly, they had lost their way. The spilling of blood had sent them into a frenzy. They had become a willing body capable of doing horrible shameless things. Merriwhether had positioned himself to become the head of this body. This great dragon of mindless destruction. Merriwhether strolled seemingly dazed out of the saloon. Forty men or more stood there in silent disbelief before him. He felt a need to justify his actions.

"Sheriff Hackman and his deputy are dead. Their deaths were not what Ah wanted, but this is what happens when a law man sells the law to the highest bidder. Life will be lost," he said, looking and feeling confused, but sounding rational. "My son, Christopher, lies dead inside as well, but he did not die in vain. Ah refuse to let his death be in vain. Many of you fought with me to obtain our liberty from the North. We were all willing to lay down our lives for that cause. Should a man be willing to do less to defend his family? Ah say to you that a man should be willing to die for his family. A man naturally has to stand when his family is threatened. He has to stand. This basic principle is why my son gave his life. This is why he sought violent means to bring about justice. He did this not as a first resort, but as a last. Many of you have a son, a daughter, a sister, or a brother. What would you do to the person who took the life of your child, your loved one? Would you let that person snicker, hiding behind a law that is for sale, or would you be willing to die in order to see that justice is done? Even if it is justice that must be carried out by your own hand."

Merriwhether's logic sounded flawless to the intoxicated ear. Even to those who were sober, Merriwhether sounded quite convincing. All of them admired his courage. His ability to do what they would want to do if it were their children. Merriwhether walked through the crowd, headed for the jail. Almost everyone there followed him, ready to help him carry out this ugly thing.

From the time the shooting started, there was discord inside the sheriff's office between Franklin and Deputy Farley. Farley knew that things must have gone badly inside the saloon. Franklin advised him that they should go, but Deputy Farley had been slow to act. He believed that Sheriff Hackman would have come out on top if gun play was involved. Franklin was not willing to make the same assumption, not with Jesse's life at stake. He wanted to get Jesse out while there was still time.

"Why are you waiting?" Franklin said, angrily questioning Deputy Farley.

"We gotta wait for the sheriff."

"The sheriff told you to get Jesse to Holly Springs if things went wrong. You heard the gun fire. We can't assume everything is fine. We have to leave now."

"We ain't gonna move until we are certain Robert and Abner ain't in control of the situation."

"By then it could be to late, we should leave now."

"We're gonna wait."

"Give me the keys to the jail cell, Angus. Ah'll take Jesse to Holly Springs. We won't run. You have my word on that."

"No, We have to wait and see," Deputy Farley foolhardily insisted.

"The sheriff may be dead for all you know. All three of them could be dead for all you know. We can't sit here waiting. If the sheriff is okay, he will understand, and he will find us. If he is dead, we are wasting valuable time."

"You considered that Covington and his men won't have trouble huntin' us down out there? Even under cover of night, our chances ain't good."

"Ah'll take my chances," Franklin brazenly spouted.

"Well, Ah won't. My neck is on the line too."

"You are a damned fool, Angus. Ah don't know how Ah could have ever trusted you to handle anything."

"Say what you want, but we ain't leavin' until we are sure the sheriff ain't coming back."

Franklin's judgement was far more superior to Farley's in this matter. His instincts told him that they had to leave now. He had to impress upon Deputy Farley how important it was that they leave now.

"Father, what's going on?" Jesse called from the jail cell in back of the office.

Franklin quickly walked back to the cell. "Everything is fine, Jesse."

"O'm scared," Jesse confided.

Hearing Jesse say that touched something in Franklin as a father. He was going to get Jesse out of there, even if he had to crack Farley's skull to do it. He boldly marched back up front.

"We are leaving, Angus. We are leaving now," Franklin said imposingly, almost daring Farley to oppose him. "Give me the key to Jesse's cell."

"We're gonna wait," Angus insisted.

"No. We are not," Franklin defiantly said, "We are leaving now. Ah won't have it any other way. Ah don't wanna go through you, but Ah will. Now, give me the god-damned key!"

"Who do you think you are?" Deputy Farley responded.

As far as Franklin was concerned, the time for talking had passed. He daringly moved to Farley, grabbing him by the collar. He spun the big man around, slinging him into the wall.

"Ah'll have that key now," Franklin said calmly, yet aggressively.

Farley was very unsure of what he should do. As he saw it, this was a complicated matter. It was not a simple black and white issue with a simple course of action. If it was complicated, it was by Deputy Farley's own judgements. Sheriff Hackman told him to get Jesse to safety if the situation turned sour. Franklin was asking him to do no more than that.

Yet, Farley was allowing precious time to burn away by factoring his own preference as to what should be done, and personal safety concerns, into the matter. Franklin was fiercely adamant in his position. He meant to get Jesse out of there now. Farley recognized that Franklin would kill him, if need be, in order to secure Jesse's safety. Reluctantly, Farley turned over the key to Franklin. Franklin let Jesse out of the cell. Farley looked outside to see a frightening sight.

"Oh my god," Farley cried.

"What is it?" Franklin asked.

"They're coming," Farley answered, almost horror-stricken.

"Father," Jesse cried, very afraid.

"Everything will be okay, son," Franklin assured.

"Come on, We can get out tha back door," Deputy Farley cried.

Angus, with an Ethan Allen double-Hammered shotgun in hand, along with Franklin rushed out the back door. Jesse was but a step behind them. For a moment, it looked as if they would barely escape, but they soon found themselves face to face with a drunken mob. There were seven of them blocking their escape. Franklin stepped in front of Jesse, shielding the boy.

"You men stand aside," Angus commanded.

"We come for tha boy," one of the mob said.

Every person in the mob facing Angus and Franklin was armed. The odds were too great. Angus knew that he would lose in a gun fight. He did not want that.

"Stand aside now. You men are interfering with the law," Angus said.

"That boy there killed Colonel Covington's daughter. He has got to answer for that," another of the mob cried out, "the sheriff and his deputy are dead. Surrender the boy or join them."

Deputy Farley started to shake. He had no intention of getting himself killed. He was seriously contemplating standing aside and letting the men have Jesse. Franklin, however, wasn't about to turn his boy over to these men. He bravely stepped out in front of Angus.

"You men had best listen to me. This is my son. He will stand trail for what he is accused of. Ah'll not see him lynched. Ah am willing to kill, and die, defending my boy. Are any of you prepared to die taking him?" Franklin boldly stated.

The men would not sway. In their drunkenness, they were also bold. They wouldn't stand down.

Deputy Farley began to back away from Franklin. This was more than he bargained for. Seeing Farley move, Jesse also started to back away, not knowing what else to do. As far as Deputy Farley was concerned, the only thing to do was to try and make it back to the sheriff's office. Afraid, Deputy Farley made a break for the sheriff's office. Jesse took off behind him.

The mob started to rush Franklin's position. One of them took aim at Franklin, firing on him. Franklin shot him dead, but the other six overwhelmed his position. Just a step or two ahead of the mob, Franklin turned to follow Angus and Jesse back into the sheriff's office.

As soon as Jesse and Deputy Farley were back inside the sheriff's office, Farley closed the door behind them. In effect, locking Franklin out. The mob was close on Franklin's tail. It was unlikely that he would have been able to get inside the sheriff's office and get the door locked before the rabble reached him. Deputy Farley didn't even give him the chance. As Franklin reached the door, so did the mob behind him. They began to beat Franklin. Deputy Farley and Jesse could hear Franklin struggling with the men. Jesse wanted to help his father. He rushed for the door, trying to unlock it. Farley pulled him away before he could.

"Stop it you little fool!" Farley barked. "We can't let 'em in!"

"But father!" Jesse cried.

"We can't help him!" Farley said in cowardly fashion.

Suddenly there was silence beyond the door.

"Father!" Jesse called.

There was no answer. Then, there was a thud at the door. The rabble was attempting to force their way inside the sheriff's office. Again, there was a hard thud at the door. The door was made of strong thick cedar wood. It would not give easily, but it would give. Against the strength of determined men, it would give. Again, there was another crash at the door.

"Do something!" Jesse screamed, knowing the men beyond the door were coming for him.

It was unfortunate for Jesse that he was depending on Farley to protect him. Farley did not know what to do. He was just as afraid as Jesse. There was another thud at the door. The door wouldn't hold much longer.

"Stop it!" Jesse cried. "Stop it!"

There was yet another crashing thud at the door. Jesse snatched the shotgun from Farley and fired into the door. The banging of the door stopped. Jesse stood there watching the door, ready to fire another round. There was a banging crash at the front of the sheriff's office. The mob was now attempting to enter through the front. Jesse rushed to the front, and fired a volley into the door. Farley followed him. There was silence at the door.

"Ammunition?" Jesse said frantically.

Farley pointed to the sheriff's desk. Jesse rushed to the desk and quickly reloaded. Just then, a voice called from outside. It was Merriwhether Covington.

"Deputy Angus Farley!" Merriwhether said. "All Ah want is Jesse Wallace. Give him to me, and you can go free. Do you hear me, deputy? You can go free, if you give him to me, or you can die with him! It is up to you."

Farley saw no way out of this mess. He looked at Jesse with the thought of betrayal visible in his eyes, carefully considering turning Jesse over to Merriwhether Covington. There was just one problem. Jesse was standing behind the sheriff's desk with a loaded shotgun. Having also heard Merriwhether's offer, Jesse was certain not to surrender the shotgun, and he would not be trusting of Farley--not now. Jesse was just a child, but the double-barreled shotgun in his hands commanded respect. Farley wouldn't try to take it from him.

"What's your answer?" Merriwhether called.

Farley didn't answer. He pondered his next move.

"Ah gave you a chance, deputy," Merriwhether said, "Ah gave you a chance!"

Jesse knew something bad was about to happen. He could feel it. Farley also sensed something bad was in the making.

"What do you think he is going to do?" Jesse asked.

"Ah don't know," Farley answered, sweat visible upon his troubled brow.

They didn't have to wait long before all was known to them. They began to smell smoke. Merriwhether was going to burn them out. It didn't take long before the sheriff's office was almost completely engulfed in flames.

From her hotel room, Elizabeth saw what Merriwhether had done. She dashed from her hotel room followed by Joselpha. With the greatest of haste, she fought her way to the forefront of the mob and stopped. Merriwhether Covington had the power here. Elizabeth ran up to him.

"Stop this!" She cried.

Merriwhether paid her no mind, as she pled with him. Inside the sheriff's office, things were getting hot. The room was filling with smoke. It made it difficult to breathe. The smoke was irritating their eyes.

"What do we do?" Jesse asked.

"We've gotta get out!" Farley answered.

"They'll kill me!" Jesse cried.

"We have to get out now!" Farley said.

Farley dashed out the front door, leaving Jesse behind. Jesse wanted to flee with Farley, but he was afraid of what Merriwhether would do to him. Seeing Farley flee from the sheriff's office, Elizabeth called to Jesse and Franklin, not knowing Franklin was not inside with the boy.

"Franklin!" Elizabeth cried. "You have to get out!"

Jesse heard his mother's voice. As afraid as he was, he was willing to go to her, but his opportunity to escape the fire had passed. The heat was unimaginable inside the sheriff's office. There was no way for Jesse to get away from the flames which now had him ensnared within. He tried to get out, but he couldn't.

"Mother!" Jesse screamed from within the flaming building. "Save me, mother!"

Hearing her son call to her from within the flame tormented Elizabeth in the very depths of her soul. She had to reach him. She dared to brave the burning flames in order to save her only son, but the flames would not allow her to pass. The punishing heat against her skin forced her to recoil.

"Mother!" Jesse cried. "Help me!"

"Jesse!" she shrilled, searching for a way into him.

"Mother! Mother! Save me!" Jesse cried.

"Someone help me!" Elizabeth screamed, desperately trying to reach her son.

Some within the crowd were moved to compassion for her, but they dared not move to help her. They greatly feared Merriwhether Covington. Franklin appeared. The men put a good beating on him, and it took him a while to regain his senses, but he was there now. He pulled Elizabeth away from the flames, and tried to break through the flames to save his son. Yet, the blistering flames would not suffer him to pass. The flames seemed to live, like a demon guarding the gates of hell.

"Mother!" Jesse cried, as though he were in pain, "Mother!"

Then, he called no more. An indescribable chill ran down Elizabeth's spine.

"Jesse!" She cried with a high pitched and piercing voice, but he could not answer. "Jesse!"

This was more than Elizabeth could stand. She trembled with dread and grief, passing into shock. At that very moment, emotionally overwhelmed, and with nowhere to run to escape this horrific reality, she collapsed.

Only now, when Jesse had surely perished, did very few people lift a finger to put the fire out. This was what they wanted. This was what Merriwhether wanted.

"The devil's got you now. You murderer." Merriwhether said, void of regret.

Franklin boiled, knowing that Merriwhether was behind what happened there. With Elizabeth still passed out on the ground being attended by Joselpha, Franklin wasted no time making his way to Merriwhether.

"You murdering bastard! Ah won't be forgetting what you've done here tonight. If Ah had a gun Ah'd kill you now." Franklin said.

"Well, Ah do have a gun, Wallace, and all these good people have heard you threaten my life. What is to keep me from killing you here and now?" Merriwhether said, not fearing Franklin. He looked down on Franklin as if he were a god holding Franklin's life in his hands. "You needn't fear. Ah'm a just man. Ah won't shoot you down in cold blood. Justice was served here tonight. We've both suffered great loss. Ah'm willing to let it go right here. Ah recommend that you do the same. I won't think twice about sending you to your murdering son."

"You no good son-of-a-whore! Ah'll see you dead!"

"Justice was served here tonight, Wallace, or are you forgetting what your murdering son did to my daughter?"

"It was for a court of law to decide his guilt! Who made you judge and jury?"

"Tonight, Ah did."

"Damn you for taking my son!"

"Ah had every right to take him!"

"You had no right!"

"Ah had a father's right!"

"Ah'll see you dead, you hear! As Ah live and breathe, Ah'll see you rotting in your grave!"

"You had best let this go, Wallace. Ah'm satisfied that justice was served, but Ah'll break you if Ah have to break you. You are barely holding on financially now. Yes, Ah know. It wouldn't take much for me to crush you."

"Do your worst, Covington, because Ah'm sure as hell gonna do mine."

"Have it your way, Wallace."

The men locked eyes. Merriwhether reconsidered shooting Franklin. Shooting Franklin would finish this here and now. Yet, Merriwhether did not. There was no tolerable reason to murder him. Merriwhether felt he had the upper hand. With patience, time, and money, he was confident that he could put an end to Franklin Wallace. He turned and ambled away from Franklin. Franklin went to his wife and daughter. He lifted his unconscious wife into his arms, and carried her, followed by Joselpha, back to their hotel room. Franklin and his house sat completely distraught. Elizabeth regained consciousness, but was in such a state of shock and grief from witnessing her son being burned alive that Doc Morteson had to give her something to help her sleep. She was resting peacefully.

As for Franklin, he sat quietly by Elizabeth's bed. He was deeply hurt, but he would not rest. Something precious had been taken from him, the life of his son. In his hurt, he longed for nothing to comfort him. Yet, there was something he craved above all else, REVENGE.

The events of this night set in motion a feud which would last ten years between Franklin and Merriwhether. Through devious craftiness, Franklin would gain the upper hand on Merriwhether and bring him to financial ruin. When he had broken Merriwhether, Franklin would kill him in a less than gentlemanly duel. Yet, this would not end his conflict with the Covington family. He would feud with Merriwhether's two remaining sons for the remainder of his life.

As for Elizabeth, despite the horrific pain and suffering that she suffered on that dreadful night. She would be the better for it. She would develop deep and responsible relationships with her remaining children. She and Franklin would grow stronger in their marriage. She would stand by Franklin, and encourage him to end his feuding with the Covingtons, but Franklin never would.

After the fire at the sheriff's office had burned out, Franklin recovered the remains of his son. In the coming days, Franklin and his house buried his fallen son.

Thirty-Two

As the next day dawned after this tragic night, the night that was could only be remembered as a very mean night, brutal and unforgiving. A night hot with madness. The kind of night that makes a man wonder if there is any sanity left in the world.

Man can be unbelievably cruel to man. This stubborn fact concerned Doc Mortenson. By all accounts, the doctor was a man of good conscience. It was his good conscience that willed him to bring a badly injured Shelby Alexander home to Anias and Katherine Alexander. The climate of the night before left Doc Mortenson fearing for Shelby. He felt the safest place for Shelby would be with Shelby's family. He was unaware that among Shelby's enemies were those of Shelby's own house.

Doc Mortenson was five feet ten inches tall. He had a slender build with blonde hair and blue eyes. He was in his fifties, and was close in age to Anias. As he pulled his wagon with Shelby unconscious on the back up to the Alexander home, Katherine Alexander came out to greet him. She was not aware that her son lay injured on the back of the good doctor's wagon.

"Good morning," she greeted, still not aware of the condition of her son.

Doc Mortenson hopped down from his wagon, and began to move around the wagon in order to lift Shelby out. "Your son has been injured, Katherine," the doctor said.

"Dear Lord," she cried, realizing that Shelby was on back of the wagon, "Anias, Justin, come quickly!"

Katherine began to care for her son, as best as she could. Soon, Anias and Justin came. They saw Shelby lying unconscious on the back of the wagon. Immediately, there was a conflict within Anias. A part of him had compassion upon his son, and wanted to help him. Yet, there was another part of him which resisted compassion's cry to feel sympathy for his son. Anias paused in his steps. He was reluctant to help Shelby.

"Help us get him inside, Anias," Katherine ordered.

Justin moved toward the wagon to help get Shelby inside, but Anias grabbed him by the arm, stopping him. "Leave him where he is, Justin."

"Anias, he is our son," Katherine said, growing angry with Anias.

"He's not welcome here," Anias proclaimed.

Katherine was deeply angered by Anias' refusal to assist Shelby in his time of need, and Doc Mortenson was shocked by Anias' behavior toward his own son.

"Anias!" Katherine yelled out in anger, not willing to suffer her husband's foolish antics.

"Are you refusing to help your own son?" Doc Mortenson asked.

"Yes," Anias replied without hesitation.

"Why? What's this all about?" Doc Mortenson asked.

"He is a traitor, a Tennessee Tory. Ah have no room for such in my house," Anias answered unwaveringly.

"Ah thought you a wiser man, Anias," Doc Mortenson said, deeply disappointed in Anias, "he is your son. You can't turn your back on that."

"Oh, yes Ah can," Anias assured.

"We are going to take him in Anias," Katherine challenged.

"No we are not. Let him turn to those he fought for to help him," Anias insisted.

"Ah can't take him back with me," Doc Mortenson informed, "It's not safe for him in town. Yesterday has to be the most shameful day in the history of Olive Branch. Six people are dead, and your son was right in the middle of it. The town burned Jesse Wallace alive last night. Merriwhether Covington and his son caused it. The sheriff tried to stop them. He and one of his deputies died trying to stop them. Shelby also tried to stop them, and this is what they did to him. Many of those same townsfolk who brought themselves to burn a child to death feel as you do, Anias, toward any southerner who fought for the North. It's not safe for your son in town. Let him stay here with you. Shelby's life may very well depend upon it."

"The war is over, Anias!" Katherine asserted.

"Ah can't forgive him," Anias countered.

"There is madness all around us, Anias, don't give in to it," Doc Mortenson said sadly, "Your boy is a fine man. He tried to stop an injustice last night, and it nearly got him killed. It takes unshakable courage to do what he did last night. Ah suspect that he got that from you, Anias; the strength to stand up and do what he believes to be right. Don't let the madness bred by this world cause you to throw away your son's life."

Anias stood there looking at Shelby.

"What shall Ah do Uncle Anias?" Justin asked.

"Help us get him inside, Justin," Katherine instructed.

Justin was slow to move. He was still looking to Anias.

"Help us get Shelby inside, Justin," Katherine directed once more.

Justin still looked to Anias for guidance. In the absence of any, Justin began to assist the doctor and Katherine in getting Shelby inside. Doc Mortenson gently began to lift Shelby's head in order to lift his body. As he did, Shelby opened his eyes and looked at Anias.

Shelby smiled a strange helpless smile. A smile which communicated everything that Shelby was unable to put into words. It was the smile of a son needing his father. The smile of a son needing his father's approval. It was the smile of a son who needed his father's forgiveness.

Without words, Anias understood this. The contempt Anias felt in his heart for Shelby began to melt away, and he had compassion for his son. Anias helped Katherine, Justin, and Doc Mortenson move Shelby inside, into Shelby's old room. Katherine understood that in order for Anias to let Shelby enter into his house: Anias had forgiven Shelby. It warmed her heart. Now, maybe, they could work at being a family once again. This pleased her greatly.

Aubrey was not so pleased. He still hated Shelby. He hated Shelby, and was not willing to forgive him. How could Aubrey forgive Shelby? How could Aubrey forgive him, when Aubrey had lost so much. Aubrey gave everything to help the South achieve its liberty from the North, to no avail. Aubrey lost too much in the war as he saw it: his face, a limb, his future. All of it was forfeited for nothing, and Shelby had a hand in it. No one should be asked to give as much as Aubrey had sacrificed in a losing effort. Where was the justice in that? The war was over, but Shelby was still winning battles. What little Shelby had lost during the war, he was now reclaiming.

Aubrey sat in his dark room as he listened to his mother, father, cousin, and Doc Mortenson take Shelby into his old bedroom, which was just next door to Aubrey's room. He heard them making such a fuss over Shelby. It seemed to make Aubrey's insides hurt to hear them so concerned for Shelby. Why should they be so concerned for Shelby? What had he lost? Aubrey listened with a hate-filled heart. He listened until there was silence. He listened until he was certain that Shelby was alone and unprotected.

From Aubrey's prospective, the penalty for Shelby's treasonable acts should be death. Why should Shelby reap forgiveness when what he had sown was worthy of death. Aubrey could find no reason why this should be so. If Katherine and Anias could forgive Shelby after all he had done, then surely they would forgive him for what he was about to do to his brother.

Aubrey quietly opened his bedroom door, and crept into Shelby's bedroom, closing the door behind him. He ambled over to Shelby, and looked down on him resting quietly. As Aubrey looked down on Shelby, he grew all the more angry with Shelby. Shelby was laying there whole, and his dreams were still within his grasp. All Shelby needed do was reach out and take them. Unfortunately, Aubrey desired to take everything that Shelby was, or ever would be, away from him. Aubrey looked around the room to see what was there that he could use to kill Shelby.

As he stood there looking about the room, Shelby opened his eyes. He saw Aubrey standing there. He had not seen Aubrey in years, and although Katherine had told him that Aubrey had been disfigured in the war. Shelby was still unprepared to see Aubrey. He smiled at Aubrey, almost in the exact same way he did at Anias, but Aubrey looked at Shelby with contempt. There were no signs of forgiveness or compassion in Aubrey.

Shelby was in a weakened state. Even someone as physically weak as Aubrey could have killed him in this vulnerable state. As weak as he was, Shelby held out his hand to Aubrey. A gesture meant to begin mending their relationship. Aubrey looked unforgivingly at Shelby. He would have no part in forgiving Shelby. Shelby was weak, and could hold out his hand no longer. He lowered it to the bed. Although, Aubrey had no forgiveness for Shelby. He was moved to compassion. He couldn't bring himself to kill Shelby, not when he was this weak, and not with Shelby looking at him. He would kill him another time. Aubrey turned and began to walk out of the room.

"Wait," Shelby weakly called.

Standing at the door, Aubrey turned and looked in an irritated manner at Shelby. "Ah can't forgive you."

"I'll say that I'm sorry anyway. I'm sorry that things turned out so wrong for you," Shelby lamented.

Aubrey laughed, finding Shelby's statement condescending. "What does that mean? Do you feel sorry for me?"

Shelby sensed that Aubrey felt he was patronizing him. He didn't want to create a larger rift than there already was between them.

"You have paid so high a price for your beliefs," Shelby tried to explain, "I regret that you suffer."

"Suffer Ah have, but Ah don't want your cursed sympathies for it. Ah believe in the South and everything the South stands for, and my beliefs are just as valid and noble as your beliefs."

"That's not what I meant," Shelby said, trying to cool Aubrey's temperament.

"Yes, it is. You think that what Ah fought for was wrong. You think the price that Ah paid for my misguided beliefs was a needless sacrifice. Ah know this is what you are thinking, be forthcoming about it," Aubrey said angrily.

"That's not what I said."

"But, It's what you meant. You always were self-righteous. Everybody else is always wrong, and you are always right, let you tell it. Well, understand this: just because your side won the war doesn't make your side right. Just because your side won, it doesn't mean you were right. The North was wrong to invade our lands, Shelby. They were wrong to force their beliefs and way of life upon us. They were wrong to leave our lands desolate and our peoples struggling just to survive. They were wrong to leave me as Ah am, because Ah stood in defense of our way of life, and constitutional rights, and freedoms. The North was wrong, and you were wrong to support them in their treacherous efforts. Your defection to the side of the South's northern enemies was an act of treason, and any man guilty of treason should be put to death."

"You want to kill me, Aubrey?"

"It's what you deserve."

The two locked eyes. It was a rather tense moment. Shelby tried to summon strength, fearing Aubrey was going to attack him. Just then, Katherine entered the room to check on Shelby. Shelby was relieved to see her. Surely, Aubrey would stay his temper with her there. Katherine was surprised to see that Aubrey had ventured from his room to greet Shelby. She also picked up on the tension between the two brothers. Inwardly, she hoped they could be reconciled. She wanted to facilitate that. It would make her happy to see her boys acting like brothers again. Yet, she realized that she could not force their reconciliation.

"Is everything okay here?" Katherine asked.

"As okay as it is going to be, mother," Aubrey answered.

"I hope not, Aubrey. I harbor no ill will for you in my heart," Shelby said almost endearingly.

"As Ah said, Ah can't forgive you, Shelby. You deserve to die for what you did," Aubrey said.

"Aubrey," Katherine said, upset Aubrey would say such a thing to Shelby.

"It's the simple truth, mother, but he needn't worry about me. The war is over, and as Ah believe Ah heard you say, mother, 'it does us no good to keep on fighting it'. Ah can't forgive Shelby for what he did, but Ah can walk beside him in peace," Aubrey said.

With that, Aubrey left Shelby's room, and returned to his own. The house of Alexander was now as restored as it could be. It was not the restoration that Katherine had hoped for, or Shelby for that matter, but it was a restoration that would allow them to move forward as a family. In the end, that was all that really mattered.

When his health got better, Shelby reported to Washington, and assumed his duties as an agent of the United States Secret Service. He served for ten years before returning home to marry and raise a family. As for Aubrey, he died in 1870, but not before reclaiming his life to a greater degree. He came out of his shell, and was not afraid to be seen by others as he was. Justin married, and lived out his days quietly. Anias and Katherine also lived out quiet lives.

Thirty-Three

As it was still early morning, Risby made his way to Elijah's house. He wanted to tell Elijah of the events that happened in Olive Branch the night before and of Solomon's passing. He did so, and Elijah was deeply grieved by what happened to Jesse Wallace, and the passing of his mentor, Solomon. Elijah never wanted Jesse to die. He was equally saddened to think that Micah may have had a hand in it all.

Elijah felt that it was time to leave Jago. A fresh start was in order, and although it was more of a mandate from Ian Everett that he was leaving. Elijah welcomed the chance to move on. However, Josephine and he were concerned for Jasmine. She had lost a great deal, and they thought that leaving Jago would do her well also. Elijah made his way to Jasmine's home. So much bad had happened in Jago. So much that he would be glad to put behind him. Elijah had come to ask Jasmine to come with them the next day, when they were planning to leave. Josephine and he wanted her to come along with them, as there was nothing left here for her. As Elijah knocked at the door, he was surprised to see that she had company. Micah was there. Elijah looked at him very disappointed in Micah's actions. He meant to have words with Micah, but not in front of Jasmine.

"How is ya been doin', Jasmine," Elijah asked, "We been worried 'bout cha."

"Ah's doin'," Jasmine responded in a tone of voice just a level above lamenting.

"Micah," Elijah said, "Ah didn't thank Ah'd find ya heah."

"I was worried about her as well, Elijah. I just stopped by to check on her. I got here maybe five minutes before you did."

"Ya comin' home today?" Elijah asked. "Ah'd like ta talk ta ya. Ah know what cha done."

"I have a little more business to take care of, but I will be home by tomorrow," Micah assured.

"We is leavin' tomorrow, probably in da mornin'," Elijah said.

"I know," Micah said, "If I am not there when you leave, I'll catch up to you."

"Dat's why O'm heah, Jasmine," Elijah began to explain, "Me and Josie thanks of ya as family. Ain't nothin' left in Jago fuh ya no mo'. We wont

431

cha ta come wit' us. Maybe, you kin start over where we goin'. Come wit' us."

"Ah can't," Jasmine said, looking at Elijah sadly.

"Why?" Elijah asked. "Rory wouldn't wont cha sittin' round heah fuh da rest of yo' life mournin' 'im. Ya know dat."

"Ah jes' can't go, not now," Jasmine said, filled with hurt.

"Ah wish ya would change yo' mind. We ain't gon' do nothin' but worry bout cha iffen ya ain't wit' us," Elijah said sincerely.

"You and yo' family been so good ta me, and O'm gon' miss y'all, but don't worry fuh me. O'm gon' be okay," Jasmine assured.

"Ah wish ya would change yo' mind," Elijah said.

"Ah can't. Ah have ta stay heah," Jasmine remained firm.

"Well, iffen ya change yo' mind. We gon' be leavin' round first light on da morrow," Elijah said.

Elijah looked at Micah. He really wanted to speak to him. Micah saw this, but he was not of a mind to deal with Elijah at this particular juncture. "I'll be home tomorrow," he assured.

"Ah's like ta speak ta ya now," Elijah countered.

"Tomorrow," Micah said, "We will talk tomorrow."

Elijah didn't want to push the issue in front of Jasmine. So, he left without confronting Micah. Once they were alone, Micah looked at Jasmine compassionately.

"Why won't you go with Elijah?" Micah asked.

"Cause Ah can't," Jasmine responded.

"Why? Is it because you don't want to stray too far from Rory's grave, or is it something more?"

Jasmine had nothing to say. Micah sensed there was another reason she would not leave.

"Byron James died last night. They say that he was seen around town so drunk that he could hardly stand. They say that he fell down some stairs and broke his neck. Is that really what happened?" He asked.

"Dat's what dey say, and dey oughta know." Jasmine responded.

"But, is it what really happened?"

She looked at Micah with deep hurt upon her face. "You remember when my Rory got his self inta trouble at Massa Drucker's place, and you and Elijah had ta help 'im out. Ah was so mad at Rory. Ah told 'im dat Drucker didn't matter none. Ah asked Rory why he had ta go riskin' every thang jes' cause dat man beat me. My Rory said, 'Can't nobody do ya harm, and not have ta answer ta me fuh what dey done.' Ah couldn't understand what my Rory was sayin' den, but Ah understands it now. Ah understands it now. And, da same go fuh me. Can't nobody do my Rory harm, and not have ta answer ta me fuh what dey done."

"Jasmine, if you are staying here to take revenge on the men that killed Rory, don't. They will get what's coming to them. I will see to that. You have my word on it."

"Ya got it all figured out, don't cha? You thank ya know me. You thank ya know what O'm up to. You is right bout one thang. Dis world ain't big enough for me, Jerad Wildman, Byron James, and Luke Galliger. Somebody gots ta go. It's gon' be dem or me."

"Believe me, I understand, but this is not your fight. It is mine."

"How you figure? My Rory was my life. Him dying don't mean nothin' ta nobody, but me."

"You are wrong, Jasmine. Rory was a man, a good man. He stood with me and my brother when not too many others would. I honor that. Besides, I told those things that call themselves men that if they started trouble, I would finish it, and that is what I aim to do. Revenge is no work for a woman. Let me handle this. I will see they get what they deserve. I promise you that."

"How?"

"You leave that to me."

With that, Micah moved to exact revenge upon Jerad and Luke, but there was a wrinkle in his plans.

It was approaching one o'clock in the afternoon as Jerad Wildman arrived home. As he prepared to go inside, he was stopped by a young-black boy. The child was no more than ten.

"Mista Jerad," the boy called, "Mista Jerad."

Jerad turned to see who was calling him. "What do you want, boy?"

"A man gibe me two bits ta wait fuh ya ta come home. He told me ta be sho ta gibe dis heah letter ta ya."

Jerad took the letter in hand. "Get on home, boy."

Jerad opened the letter. It was from Luke, written in his own hand. It read.

Jerad, we have a problem. I have learned from a Negro that I know that the Negro woman, Jasmine, is going around offering colored boys three hundred dollars to kill us. He told me that she has been going around boasting that she pushed Byron down those stairs, and broke his neck afterwards. You were right to want to kill her after we taught that lover of

hers, Rory, a lesson. We can't spend the rest of our natural days looking over our shoulders for some crazed-Negro woman out for vengeance. I will not sit idly wondering when she will come for us. I am going to finish this. By the time you get this message, I am sure to have her. I am going to take her back to the spot where we took care of her lover. Come as soon as you can.
Luke.

Jerad didn't even go inside to speak with his wife. He did not let her or anyone know what he was about to do. He understood that silence was needed in such matters. Jasmine would have done well to have remembered that simple rule, but she didn't. Now, Luke and Jerad were sure to make her pay for her loose tongue. Jerad got on his horse, and headed for Jago. He wished that he hadn't been so quick to send the little boy who gave him the note away. Maybe then, he would have learned how long ago it was that Luke gave him the note. There was no way to know how long Luke had been gone. Jerad hoped that he could catch up to Luke before he was done with Jasmine. Jerad wanted to play an intricate part in her demise. Before they beat her to death, she should be raped and sodomized. She had earned that for plotting to kill white men, Jerad thought. He would take his time and make the black wench suffer before dying.

After reaching Jago, Jerad went to Jasmine's home. He didn't see Luke's horse around. He wondered if Luke had been there already. In a straight-forward manner, Jerad rode right up to the house. He dismounted and kicked the door open with his weapon drawn. The little house was empty. That answered his question, or so he reasoned. Luke no doubt had Jasmine, and had taken her to the woods. Jerad got on his horse, and decided to ride parallel the road from the woods. Not that he was afraid of any black. He simply didn't want to be seen. Once he reached the general area of where they murdered Rory, he was not certain of the exact spot. He dismounted and began to journey deeper into the woods. It was very quiet in the woods. It had an eerie feel to it. It was a place well suited for what they had in mind for Jasmine. Had she kept her place, they would have let her live, but now she had earned certain death. Jerad was not sure that he was in the right area. "Luke!" He called, trying to get his bearings.

"Here!" Luke answered from some close yet unseen place.

"Did you get her?" Jerad asked, making his way toward the sound of Luke's voice in an almost excited manner.

"We are over here," Luke answered.

"Ah hope you've left some of her for me!" Jerad said, drawing nearer to the sound of Luke's voice. Jerad saw the clearing, but he couldn't see Jasmine or Luke. He made way into the clearing where they took Rory's life. Luke was sitting on the ground.

"You've killed her already?" Jerad asked.

Luke didn't say anything. Yet, there was a look of fear upon Luke's face, and there was a leg iron on his right ankle. It was a leg iron like those used to keep prisoners on a short leash. It took him a split second to realize something was not right. He motioned for his weapon, but it was too late. Micah had him and Jerad knew it. He slowly removed his hand from his pistol and put his hands up.

"Don't move," Micah warned.

"Damn," Jerad said.

Micah took the weapon from Jerad. He placed the pistol in the back of his own pants in the small of his back.

"Ah'm sorry, Jerad. There was nothing Ah could do," Luke said.

"You could have yelled out a warning, Luke. I would have got this black savage, but you let me walk right into a trap, and you've killed us both," Jerad said angrily.

"Sit down next to your friend," Micah commanded.

"For what?" Jerad asked defiantly.

"You have about five seconds to do as I say, or I will kill you where you stand," Micah threatened.

Jerad knew Micah would do as he said. Jerad sat on the ground next to Luke, looking at Micah with eyes filled with hate. "Now what?"

"Put on the other end of that leg iron, and lock it up," Micah instructed, "Throw me the key when you are done."

Jerad did just as Micah wanted, wondering what Micah had in mind. Jerad hoped that Micah would make a mistake. He wanted to break Micah in two.

"On your feet," Micah commanded.

Jerad and Luke stood, chained together like dogs.

"What are you gonna do?" Luke asked, very afraid of Micah.

"I understand that you two like to fight," Micah said, "I hear you beat a good man to death right here on this very spot. Rory was a friend of mine, and I ain't forgiving what you did to him."

"Ah didn't wanna kill him," Luke said, "Ah could have shot him, but Ah didn't."

"Is that right?" Micah said.

"Don't lower yourself down to this nigger trash, Luke," Jerad spouted.

Jerad had it right. He understood that Micah meant to kill them, and there was nothing that they could do to change it at this point.

"Since you things like to beat men to death, I think you should beat each other to death," Micah said looking deadly serious.

Jerad laughed. There was no way he would do that.

"What?" Luke asked, fear growing in his heart.

"I think that you heard me the first time, and is something funny, Jerad?" Micah asked.

Jerad realized the worst Micah could do was kill him, which he was sure to do anyway. So, he would not do anything that Micah wanted from that point on. He understood there was no profit in cooperating. Jerad was determined that he would die like a man, and not pleading at some nigger's feet.

"You're one great big laugh," Jerad insulted, "Yes, you are one funny stupid nigger."

"You won't think so in a minute," Micah assured, almost jokingly.

"You're gonna kill us anyway," Jerad said, "We're not gonna do the job for you."

"Really, Jerad, not even for a chance to live? I won't kill the one of you that beats the other to death," Micah assured.

"You are really one stupid-nigger fool," Jerad insulted, "You don't have a choice, but to kill both of us. Don't you think that we know that?"

"Jerad, I give you my word. I won't kill the one of you that survives this," Micah said, sounding sincere.

Jerad was laughing, but Luke wasn't. Luke knew Micah couldn't let him live, but he wanted to believe that he would. He was making himself believe that he would. Micah saw that Luke wanted to believe, and so did Jerad.

"Is this the way it's gonna be, Luke. Are you going to die, knowing that you had a chance to live. I will kill you both right here and now, or one of you can live. Tell me, Luke, which way is it going to be?"

"He can't let either one of us live, Luke," Jerad explained, "He knows that we would see him hanging from the highest tree."

"I give you my word, Luke. If you survive this, I won't kill you," Micah assured.

"Use your head, Luke," Jerad argued, "he can't let either one of us live. Don't let him sift you like wheat."

"Listening to him is what got you here in the first place, Luke. Didn't you say that you didn't want to kill Rory? If you didn't, who did? That one standing right next to you, I'll bet. With your life on the line, are you going to listen to him? Are you gonna throw away your one chance to live," Micah countered, exploiting Luke's desire to live.

"Don't listen to him, Luke. It's better to die like men, and not like swine, groveling at this black devil's feet."

"Time is winding down, Luke. You've got a choice to make, and you've got less than a minute to make it. I'm gonna kill you both then."

"Kill us, then!" Jerad barked. "That's all you can do! We aren't gonna play your game!"

Micah aimed his Remington at Luke's head.

"Ah'm sorry, Jerad," Luke said, "Ah wanna live."

"Don't do it, Luke," Jerad said, seeing Luke was going to try to kill him, "He can't let either one of us live."

"I won't kill you if you survive, Luke," Micah assured.

"Don't do it, Luke. A nigger's word ain't worth nothin'," Jerad warned, preparing mentally to defend himself.

Luke looked at Jerad. His eyes were filled with regret and confusion. With blazing speed, Luke pounced on Jerad. He landed five powerful blows that put Jerad on his back.

"Stop it, Luke!" Jerad cried, trying to turn Luke from this. "He can't let us live!"

"If you believe that, Jerad," Micah mocked, "Continue to lay there, and let him beat you to death. Climb on top of him and bash in his face, Luke."

Luke looked at Micah, not willing to comply. Micah took aim at Luke's head again. Luke knew Micah would kill him. Luke tried to kick Jerad in the face. Jerad grabbed his foot, and they were both on the ground.

"Stop it, damn you!" Jerad said stridently.

With a strong right hand, Luke pounded Jerad's face repeatedly. Jerad was not going to let Luke kill him, not if he could help it. He grabbed Luke's hand, and fired a punishing blow of his own. Luke fell over and rolled. He was dazed, but he knew that he had to fight. Luke climbed to his feet, and Jerad did as well. Luke fired into Jerad, landing head shots and gut shots. Jerad didn't want to do it, but he realized that he was going to have to kill Luke, or render him unconscious. Luke's hands were very busy. He was hitting Jerad with everything that he had. Jerad was off balance, and he did not know how to contend with what Luke was doing to him. Luke's adrenaline was flowing. He was very afraid, which caused his speed to increase. He was putting it to Jerad with unreal hand speed. Jerad wanted to cover up and wait for this pounding barrage of blows to end. He couldn't wait for Luke to tire. The blows were hurting Jerad, stealing his strength.

In desperation, Jerad reached out, and grabbed Luke by his shirt. He pulled Luke to him, and wrapped him up. Like a python, Jerad used his great strength to crush Luke. Luke could hardly breathe. The only weapon with which he had to fight is his head. With his head, Luke Pounded into Jerad's face. He did it repeatedly. Jerad let him go. Luke could hardly stand. Jerad's constricting grip took a lot out of him. He fired into Jerad's gut, but Jerad grabbed him by the throat. Jerad's powerful hands started to squeeze the life out of Luke. Luke hit him repeatedly in the stomach, but Jerad did not loosen his deadly grip.

Almost out of breath, Luke tried to pry Jerad's hands from his neck, but he couldn't. The blood vessels in Luke's eyes began to burst. He lost consciousness. Luke fell back, and Jerad fell onto him. In a fit of rage, Jerad strangled Luke until there was no life in him. Jerad realized what he had done. He didn't mean to kill Luke, only stop him from killing him.

With his hands still around Luke's throat, Jerad began to regret killing his friend. When they were teenagers, Luke pulled Jerad from a swimming hole as he was drowning. Luke was a kind, soft-hearted man; a gentle, honorable, soul. Jerad hated Micah for making him kill Luke. He didn't know how, but if he should ever get the chance. He would see Micah dead. Jerad sat on the ground next to his dead friend.

"Ah've killed him," Jerad said, "Let me go."

"You've killed him when I say you've killed him. Beat his face until I tell you to stop," Micah commanded.

"No," Jerad answered, outraged and appalled.

"I told you that I wouldn't kill you, but if you don't finish this to my satisfaction. I will blow your head off. You've gone this far. You had better go the rest of the way, if you wanna live."

Jerad wanted Micah badly, but he couldn't get to him. He had to buy time, and hope Micah made a mistake. He raised his big hand, and pounded Luke's face repeatedly. He beat Luke until his hand hurt and he was too tired to continue. Luke's face, his head, didn't look real anymore. Jerad was covered with his friends blood.

"You can stop now," Micah said.

"Let me go," Jerad said.

"I can't do that."

"Ah didn't think you would," Jerad laughed, "A nigger's word has about as much worth as fool's gold."

"I never said that I would let you go. I said that I wouldn't kill you."

At that moment, there was a sound of movement in the woods, something in the brush.

Micah didn't bother to look around. He knew what it was. Jasmine appeared from the woods. She had watched this sad spectacle, waiting for its conclusion. She knew all along that Jerad would be the winner. She strolled slowly toward Jerad, and he realized the irony of it. She stopped before Jerad, just out of his reach.

Jasmine was wearing simple grab, a gray-calico dress, almost a rag. She had on a pretty blue bonnet. It was new, and looked out of place compared to the other things she had on. She was holding in her right hand a white circular hat box, bound by thin-white string. In her right hand, she held a large machete. The blade was very sharp, and it had dried blood on it. Jasmine held the blade at an angle. She wanted Jerad to have a good look at it. She wanted his mind to wonder what she intended to do with it, but Jerad wasn't afraid of Jasmine.

"You gonna kill me with that?" Jerad snickered, looking at Jasmine as if she were nothing, and had no power over him.

"It is fitting, don't you think?" Micah answered.

"So, this is what you and this wench had in mind all along. Have Luke and me fight to tha death, and let her finish off tha one that survived. That's good, really good. Well, kill me then you black whore!"

"This is a lady. Watch your foul mouth," Micah warned.

"Or what? You're gonna kill me? She is a filthy, nigger, whore!" Jerad laughed, trying to spite them, figuring they were going to kill him anyway.

Micah began to move toward Jerad, intent on inflicting pain upon him. Jasmine held up her hand with the machete. "No Micah," she said, "Ah jes' wanna talk ta 'im."

Micah yielded, and moved to a position behind and to the left of Jasmine. To a position, where he could shoot Jerad, should Jerad try to move on Jasmine.

"Ah enjoyed killin' that nigger bastard of yours," Jerad slighted, trying to wound Jasmine, "Ah really enjoyed it, wish Ah could do it again."

"Do yo know what cha took from me?" Jasmine asked sincerely, deeply wounded by the offense. "Rory was my whole world. He really and truly was. Ah lived and breathed 'im. He da only man dat Ah ever had relations wid. He was da one and only love of my life, and dat's somethin' special. Cause, not everybody gonna find love. As much as we all wanna love, and wanna be loved, love ain't gonna know us all. It ain't even gonna know most of us. Oh, ya might find somebody dat cha kin live ya life wid. Somebody dat cha kin have a little bit of happiness wid, but most ain't gonna find dat somebody dat really and truly brangs out da best in 'em. Somebody dat dey really wanna give dey all ta. Ah don't know why dat is, it jes' seem ta be da way. So, when ya blessed wid dat somebody dat's perfect fuh ya. Somebody dat is da light of yo' eye. Ya really got yo'self somethin'. My Rory, he brung out da best in me. He was my heart. He touched my soul. He was made ta love me, and Ah was made ta love him. God brought us together, allowed us ta find each other in dis whole world. So ya see, when ya stole my Rory from me, kilt 'im. Ya done mo' 'an jes' kill a man. Ya kilt somethin' dat da world ain't got enough of ta begin wid. You kilt love, my love. Ah suffers without my Rory. Day in and day out, Ah suffers. From da day ya took 'im all da way up ta right now, Ah suffers. My flesh longs ta be in my Rory's arms. My soul aches to be wid 'im. Ah wanna be in da grave wid 'im. Ah wanna take a gun, jump off a cliff, or do somethin' ta end my life. So, Ah kin go to my Rory, but Ah ain't dat strong, dat weak. Ah gotta go on, cause Ah promised my Rory dat Ah would. Ah knows ya can't feel what O'm feelin', or understan'. O'm jes' sayin' so many empty words dat don't mean nothin' ta ya. Ya don't understand what painful and hellish misery O'm goin' through. Ya such a mean cruel hateful man dat it don't seem like ya could love, but even somebody like you must love somethin', or somebody. Ya like my bonnet, Jerad? It's jes' like da one yo' Eula wears, pretty ain't it? My Rory use ta always give me thangs, little thangs mostly. A flower picked by his hand, or jes' pretty words. It was his way of lettin' me know dat Ah was always on his mind. His way of lettin' me know dat Ah was loved. Anytime a person go to da trouble of gettin' ya a gift, it mean somethin'. Da gift of love oughta mean somethin', oughta be respected. So, you can know jes' what me and my Rory had, and respect it. So, you can feel what losin' my Rory means to me. Ah got a gift fuh ya, Jerad."

Jasmine knelt to one knee. She sat the hat box on the ground, and cut the string, and stood. With her foot, she gently slid the box close enough so that Jerad could reach it without much effort. Before opening the box, Jerad examined it closely. He noticed something that he had not observed before. Something reddish in color was leaking from the base of the hat box. He looked at the Bonnet that Jasmine was wearing. Jasmine was right. The bonnet looked like the one Eula, his bride of five months, wore. It looked exactly like the one he purchased for her birthday.

Jerad looked at the sharp bloody blade in Jasmine's hand, and at the hat box again. His heart sank to his stomach. Weakness covered his entire body. Dire weakness, weakness so powerful that he couldn't lift a finger. Every contemptible harsh word that he might have used to hurt Jasmine was stolen from his lips. Regretful fear consumed him.

"What's this?" Jerad asked, daring not to touch the box.

"All da pain, misery, and sorrow dat Ah feels. Open it," Jasmine said, smiling a half-smile, an evil smile.

"Where did you get that bonnet?"

"A white woman Ah know died. Ah took it from her. Open da box."

Tears started to swell in Jerad's eyes. He knew Micah and Jasmine would kill him, but in no way was he expecting this. "You nigger bitch!" He cried in pain. "You didn't hurt Eula."

"Oh, Ah done mo' 'an hurt her. Open da box."

"You didn't have no cause to hurt her!" Jerad cried, the tears flowing inconsolably.

"You didn't have no real cause ta hurt my Rory, but cha done it! Open da box! So, you can feel what Ah feels. Open da box. So, you can understand, and respect what love means. Open da box! So, you can always remember dat while she was dyin', wa'n't nothin' ya could do ta help her! Open it, open it now!"

"O'm gonna get you! If it's tha last thing Ah do, O'm gonna get you!"

"Open da box, Jerad! You was brave enough ta kill my Rory, but cha scared ta open a lit' box? Oh, but dat's right, ya ain't kill my Rory by yo'self! You wa'n't man enough ta do dat on ya own neither! Ya had ta have some help, didn't ya? Open dat box, or is ya jes' good at dishin' out pain, but ain't good at takin' it. You ain't no man! Open dat box, coward!"

"You go ta hell!" Jerad said, with a loud and bitter cry."

"Where ya thank Ah been livin' ever' since you kilt my man?" Jasmine revealed.

"O'm gonna kill you."

"You already did, and O'm returnin' da favor. We ain't gonna kill ya. Ah wont cha ta live, like Ah gotta live. Ah wont cha ta suffer, like Ah suffers. And, like Ah told ya befo', O'm already dead. Iffen ya wanna kill my body, come on round. You can even brang a hat box wid cha iffen ya wont. It don't make no difference no mo', not ta me."

Jasmine turned and disappeared into the woods. Jerad was distraught. Jasmine had defeated him soundly. There was no strength or defiance left in him. He was in a world of hurt. He wasn't thinking clearly. He kept looking at the box. He kept reaching out to touch it, but never did. He wanted to open it, but lacked the courage. Micah walked up to Jerad, and looked down on him, but with no real pity. Jerad was getting what he deserved in his opinion.

Truthfully, this was not what Micah was expecting. He thought that Jasmine would simply kill Jerad. He now understood that Jasmine wanted Jerad to walk a different path.

"Talk about hell hath no fury like a woman scorned," Micah said earnestly. "Look at what you've done, Jerad. So much death, and it is all because of you."

"You gonna kill me?" Jerad asked.

"Do you want me to?"

Jerad simply looked sadly at Micah. Jerad loved Eula very, very, much. The thought of losing her hurt unlike any pain that he had ever felt before. He wished that he had killed Jasmine at the same time that he killed Rory. That, in Jerad's mind, was the unforgivable thing. Had he killed Jasmine when he had the chance, Eula would still be alive.

"I imagine that if I were you, I would want to die for causing my woman to be killed," Micah said, breaking Jerad down. "Here she was depending on you to take care of her for the rest of her life, and look at what you let happen to her. What you caused to happen to her. Everyone around you, good people who trust in you. They die, but you go on living. Luke and Byron would still be alive had they not followed you, and so would your wife. Who was your wife, Jerad? Did she want children? What were her dreams? I suppose that it doesn't matter, does it? Any children that she may have wanted, all of her dreams, those things died with her, because of you. How are you going to sleep nights knowing that your beautiful young wife is dead because of you? How are you going to explain to her mother and father that you let her die. That she is dead because of you. How do you do that, Jerad? How do you look them in the eyes, and tell them that you caused their baby girl to die? Your good friends Byron and Luke are dead, because of you. Tell me, were they family men? How are you going to tell their families that you caused them to die. Are you going to even try to explain to Luke's woman that he died by your hand? Are you gonna explain to her that you killed him, because a nigger told you to? How do you suppose that she will take hearing something like that? How do you suppose white folks around here are going to see you from now on? Can you ever imagine them trusting you again? Tell me, how can they? Just look around you, all this death. See poor Luke lying there, dead by your hand. And, your poor wife, do you want me to open the hat box for you?"

"No," Jerad said sharply, lamenting. Everything Micah said pressed hard upon Jerad's mind with devastating and crushing effect.

"I don't blame you. Any man would have a hard time looking upon such a thing," Micah empathized. "You never answered my question. Do you want me to kill you? I can help you escape the pain that you must be feeling, give you a bit of peace. Do you want peace? Do you want the peace I have to offer you?"

Jerad looked distressfully down at the ground and wiped the tears away from his eyes. He nodded his head up and down, indicating he wanted Micah to kill him.

Micah took his Remington in hand and aimed it at Jerad's head. "I have to hear you say it, Jerad. From your own lips, I have to hear you say that you want me to take your life."

Jerad looked up at Micah sadly. "Yes, Ah want you to take it."

"I would like to help you out, but I can't. I told you that I wasn't going to kill you, and my word has worth. If I give you my word on something, you can count on me to do it. I tell you what I'm gonna do." Micah holstered his weapon, and took Jerad's Colt Dragoon Pistol from the back of his pants. He took all of the bullets out of it, and tossed it to Jerad. "I'm gonna leave you with your gun, and I'm gonna leave you one bullet. You'll have to drag Luke's body a few small steps to get to it, but it'll be right here on the ground for you. All you will have to do is load your weapon, and then you can give yourself some peace. I recommend a shot to the head, it's quick. You don't have to listen to me, however. Just about anywhere you shoot yourself is gonna get the job done, but it will take some time to die. If it were me, I wouldn't want that."

Micah turned and ambled away, dropping the bullet five steps from Jerad, disappearing into the woods. But unlike Jasmine, he stopped in an obscure place, and watched to see what Jerad would do. If Jerad did not have the strength to kill himself, Micah would do it, as he could not let Jerad live.

Jerad sat there for some thirty minutes holding the gun, distraught beyond measure. He climbed to his feet, and dragged Luke's body over to the place where the bullet lay. He sat on the ground and loaded the weapon. He sat there another thirty minutes with the gun in hand.

Micah wondered if he would really do it. It was hard for Micah to sit patiently through this. He wanted Jerad to do it, and be done with it. Micah believed that Jerad was going to do it, but if Jerad should lay the weapon down. Micah would take Jerad's life.

Finally, Jerad put the Dragoon in his mouth. This was a very brave and masculine way to take your own life, Micah thought. Jerad couldn't do it. He removed the weapon from his mouth. Jerad placed the barrel of the pistol upon his chest, directly over his heart. He pulled the trigger, and within minutes, he was dead.

Micah emerged from his hiding place, and walked over to check that Jerad was dead. He was. Micah looked curiously at the hat box. He thought of Jasmine. It took something to do what she did. Something that he didn't think she had in her. Micah strode over to the hat box, looking down on it. He picked it up, and bravely looked inside. He was both shocked and amazed by what he saw. No, he would never have thought Jasmine had this in her. He placed the lid back on it, and sat the box on the ground.

All of this had to be hidden. He found a soft patch of earth in the densely wooded area. There he dug a deep hole. It had to be deep. He didn't want any wild animals to dig up what would be hidden there. Micah took the irons from Luke and Jerad's legs, and put their bodies into the hole he had dug. He also took the hat box, and put it inside the hole with the bodies. He buried everything, but the memories of what happened, inside the hidden grave within the dark woods. By the time he finished, it was well past dark. He rode to Jasmine's home to check on her. He knocked at her door, and she let him inside.

"You wont some coffee?" she asked.

"Yeah."

Jasmine poured Micah a cup of coffee, and sat across the table from him with her fingers interlocked.

"That was a rough piece of business out there today," Micah commented, almost casually.

"Jerad dead?" Jasmine asked, knowing he was.

"Yeah, he took his own life. That's what you had in mind, is it not?"

Jasmine looked at Micah sadly, almost regretful, but did not answer.

"I looked inside the hat box," Micah added.

"Did ya?"

"Yeah, I was shocked to see what was in it. A large black rabbit, tied in a ball with it's throat cut."

"Why dat shock ya?"

"I thought that you killed Eula, and placed her head in the hat box."

"Why should Ah kill her? She ain't never done nothin' ta me. Da sins of her husband ain't hers."

"I'm curious about a few things. How did you get Eula's bonnet?"

"Ah didn't. When Rory first got back, he took me ta town, and bought me up a few dresses, and that same fabric that her bonnet made from. Ah remembered dat bonnet, cause Jerad was there buyin' it fuh Ms. Eula. It was so fine and pretty to me. Ah knowed Mrs. Bush wa'n't gon' never sell dat bonnet ta me; bein' she done sold one ta a white woman; but Ah thought she might sell me da fabric; and Ah could make my own; and dat's what Ah done."

"One more thing, what were you gonna do had Jerad opened that box."

"Ah knowed what he was gonna do. But iffen he had opened it, Ah was gonna take a heavy stick, and beat 'im ta death."

"You are really something, Jasmine, something good. Rory did a good thing by himself when he took you to wife. I hope you come with Elijah and me."

There was a knock at the door. Micah and Jasmine looked at each other wondering who it might be. Jasmine rose from the table and answered the door. It was Naomi. Naomi was surprised to see Micah there.

"Hello, Naomi," Micah said.

"Hey," Naomi answered, feeling Micah wanted to make Jasmine his woman.

"Well, I'll be on my way," Micah said, "If I never see you again, I want you to know it has been my honor to know you, Jasmine. Bye Miss Naomi."

"Bye."

Jasmine and Naomi watched Micah get on his horse and ride into the night.

"He ain't wastin' no time makin' his move on ya, is he?" Naomi said.

"Naomi, it ain't dat way."

"Oh, yes it is. Ah kin tell when a man like a woman."

"Naomi, it ain't like dat."

"If you say so," Naomi said, certain Jasmine was to Micah's liking.

Thirty-Four

Riding alone in the night, Micah decided to camp in a little spot just off the road not too far from home. He didn't want to face Elijah this night, and he had to think over if he wanted to tell Elijah what he had done concerning Jerad Wildman and Luke Galliger. In the end, he decided not to tell Elijah. There was no need for him to know. Such things rest heavy on the conscious. Such things rest heavy on the soul. Micah would not have Elijah burdened by the killings. It was bad enough that the memories of what happened there in the woods tugged at his own conscience. The guilt of it was quite a burden, even if Jerad and Luke were deserving of it. Micah sat there, and took out the pendant that he took from Hannah Covington, regretting what he did to her. He sat there thinking the entire night. He didn't allow himself to fall asleep. Nightmares were sure to haunt him for what he did to Hannah Covington.

Morning finally came, it was sunny and beautiful. It was a soft pleasant day filled with promise, filled with peace from Micah's perspective. Even so, Micah was still reluctant to face his brother. Several hours went by, and the momentary peace that he felt was gone. It had been replaced by the dread of facing Elijah, and the knowledge of what he had done to little Hannah Covington. Before long, he gathered enough nerve to return home. When he got there, he found himself wishing that Elijah had left early in the morning, as he said he would. That way it would have taken Micah a little more time to catch up, but Elijah and the rest of the family, were still there.

Also, to Micah's surprise, Jasmine was there, holding Caleb in her arms, with Naomi along side her. The ladies were standing next to a small wagon, hooked to Rory's gray mare. The wagon had limited cargo space, but even so, there wasn't much that Jasmine was taking with her. There wasn't much at all that she wanted to take from this place. All worth taking, in her opinion, rested in a warm bit of earth in a lonely cemetery.

"It's good to see you, Jasmine," Micah said.

"Yeah, Ah reckon, O'm gon' come on wid y'all," Jasmine said smiling at Micah.

"Uh, hello, Micah. Ah guess you ain't seed me standing heah," Naomi said jokingly, feeling Micah wanted Jasmine.

"Hello, Naomi," Micah replied.

"Ah's comin' along too. Me and Jasmine gots ta take care of each other," Naomi said.

"That's a good thing," Micah responded, "We will talk later."

"Okay," Jasmine said.

Micah walked toward the house.

"Told ya he wont cha," Naomi said, like a giggly teenager almost.

"And, Ah told you. It ain't like dat," Jasmine responded, "and, you probably wonts 'im anyway."

"Well, he all right," Naomi said.

Truthfully, Micah was very attracted to Jasmine, and she to him in a way. Nevertheless, there are some pains that never heal. Pains that keep you tied to the past in a way that you are content to let be. Jasmine would never take another husband, and upon her death in 1918 as a result of the great flu pandemic of that year, Caleb would return her to Jago to be interred next to her beloved Rory. Naomi would be for Micah.

As Micah walked to the front porch, Mama Julia exited the house. She wrapped her arms around Micah, glad to see him. "We missed ya, boy. It's good ya done come home," she said.

Just beyond the door, Micah saw Josephine, Risby, Ran, and Elijah. They all smiled at Micah. All but Elijah that is.

"Y'all, would ya give me and Micah a lit' time ta talk, please," Elijah said.

Micah stepped into the house as everyone else stepped out. The door closed behind them. Finally, the two brothers were face to face. Micah knew that Elijah felt what he did was deeply irresponsible and offensive.

"What was you thankin?" Elijah said with anger. "Don't you know dat cha could've got every black round heah fuh miles killed? And, dat lit' girl, Micah, did ya do dat? How could ya ta dat do her? Dat was jes' wrong, ain't no excuse fuh dat!"

Micah wanted to defend himself forcefully by getting loud with Elijah, but he remained calm. "You are right. It was regrettable, not excusable, but it was time to bring this injustice to an end. That's what I did. If there was some other way, I would have pursued it. I did not want to kill that child, but they left me no choice. I live in a world that denies me justice for no other reason than the color of my skin. I live in a world that despises me for no other reason than I look different than it. I live in a world of reckless hate. A world that won't allow me to hold my head up with pride in who I am. I am seen and not seen, treated like nothing. It is not a disgrace to be black. I am somebody. I will not be disrespected by them just because they feel that they have the right to disrespect me. I won't stand for it. I am not less than the whites are, and if they won't give me justice of their own accord. I will have it in spite of them," Micah said with great conviction.

Elijah looked at Micah, feeling sadly for him. It seemed to Elijah that it would do no good to tell Micah that he did not have a right to kill Hannah Covington. That he didn't have a right to place the lives of the black people of this community in jeopardy. Sadly, Micah didn't see his wrongs, not clearly anyway. There was so much anger and pain in Micah. The world of callous men had driven him into a place of deep hurting. Micah was lost. Elijah felt pity for him.

"At da end of harvest, durin' da winter and early spring months, when thangs was slow, and we didn't habe ta work in da fields from sun-up to sun-down, momma use ta always take us ta worship da Lawd Sundays. Ya remember? It would be cold out, and sometimes it would be rainin' kinda light like. Still, she got us on ta church. It was four miles goin' and four miles coimin' back, but still she got us on ta church. We was lit' boys, and she would carry you on her hip when you got tired, remember? Sundays was da only days slaves had ta rest, but momma would get us on ta church. Wa'n't no easy life fuh her, she could habe used her rest, but she got us on ta church. Why ya reckon she done dat? Why ya reckon she went through so much trouble ta git us ta da house of da Lawd? Ah'll tell ya why. She done it cause they's hope in da Lawd, and peace ta dem dat keeps God's commandments. Momma wonted us, wonted you, ta habe hope. She wonted you ta habe peace. Ya see, dat's da whole duty of man, ta keep God's commandments. So, ya kin know God's peace. Ah kin tell by da way ya lookin' at me dat cha thank O'm a fool. Ya thankin' dat dems dat keeps ya on ya knees prayin' ta God ain't worried bout keepin' God's commandments. Dey ain't worried bout knowin' God's peace. Ya thankin' dat iffen dey ain't worried bout it, you can't be worried bout it, cause you gotta guard yo'self against dem. Ah guess dat's da test, whether ya gon' trust in yo'self, or trust in God who made ya. Ah know you done seen thangs, done thangs. Thangs dat won't let cha sleep in peace nights. Ya done dem thangs thankin' dat ya did it fuh good. Ya thank dat iffen a man visits strife upon ya, ya visit mo' strife upon him. Ya thank iffen a man hits ya, you gotta hit him harder. Ya thank dat iffen a man hates ya, you gotta hate 'im back. Dat's yo' way, and O'm heah ta tell ya dat yo' way injures yo' own soul, and robs ya of peace. Is dat what cha wont fuh yo'self? Ah kin scarcely read, but what Ah reads is God's word. It look like it take me all day jes' ta read a page, and git some understandin' from it, but Ah keeps at it. Ah wont ta know God's commandments. So, Ah kin know his peace. See, when ya keep da commandments of God, not only do ya habe God's peace, you habe God in yo' life. When you habe God in yo' life, it don't matter if ya a slave, or a free man. It don't matter if ya rich or poor. It don't matter iffen men despise and hate you fuh no good reason. So long as you habe God, he will make your burdens lighter to bear. He'll make it so you kin git through life without feelin' like ya lost and alone wit' nowhere ta turn. Dat's God's peace. Dat's da peace momma wonted us ta habe. The peace God wonts us ta habe. Read God's word. So, you kin keep God's commandments. So, you kin know God's peace."

Elijah's words reached Micah. As if awakening from some deep sleep, Micah came to himself, and realized what he had done. Feelings of contrition swelled within him. Micah clearly saw the things he had done as iniquity. Micah looked down at the floor as a frown blanketed his face. He was moved to sorrow for his wrongs. Micah realized Elijah was right. He did not know peace. Micah finally realized that peace was what he had been in search of all this time. He ran away from home, searching for peace. He wondered to Canada, Mexico, and every place in between searching for peace. He fought a war, searching for peace. He returned home, searching for the peace he could not find. He killed Hannah Covington, thinking he did it for the greater good, thinking it would restore the peace. He caused the deaths of Jesse Wallace, Jerad Wildman and Luke Galliger, thinking he did it for good, for right, because these individuals threatened the peace.

Micah pondered how strange it was that he needed only look no farther than God's inspired word for peace. A calm over took him. It was a brief calm, a brief peace. Micah found it difficult to let go of his sense of judgement. It was hard for him not to be obedient to his own will.

"What would you have me do? Let them walk all over me, and smile about it," Micah said, trying to justify his actions, battling the conflict inside of him.

"No. Even Christ boldly stood again' what he knowed to be wrong, but he never defiled hisself. Da man who follows afta God must stand again' evil, but he remembers at all times dat he a son of God, and don't devise wickedness, and don't inflict evil," Elijah said sincerely.

"Somehow, that seems unfair to me," Micah said, looking earnestly at Elijah, "When I know, they will devise wickedness, and inflict evil upon me."

"It ain't 'bout dem. It's 'bout you, and who you gonna be. Is you gon' be a son of God, or is you gon' walk in yo' own way. It ain't in man ta direct his own steps. You can't go on denyin' yo'self peace, because of what somebody else might do. Ain't no profit in dat."

"Maybe, but I've gotta survive in this world. It's a harsh world, cold and uncaring. And, if the world brings the fight to you hard and cold, you had better stand up, and fight it back hard and cold."

"Ah never said da world wa'n't harsh and cold, but you kin make it a lit' less harsh," Elijah said in a comforting kind of way. "You kin make it a lit' less cold and uncarin'. All ya habe ta do is turn from da way of dis world, and walk in da way of God."

"You make it sound as though it were an easy thing to do. Maybe, it is for you, but I'm not as noble-minded as you. Nothing in life is easy. I'm struggling every day just trying to make it. *My* way, the way of this *world*, is what I know, and it has gotten me this far."

"Well, Micah, Ah done said all Ah kin say. Ah pray ya find yo' way to God. Ah really do, cause da road you travelin' is gon' see ya troubled and unhappy all da days of yo' life, or see ya dead. Ah don't wonts dat fuh ya. God's road is a better one 'an ya travelin'. Ah hope ya see dat some day. Come on, and let's finish loadin' da wagon. Ah wanna be on our way by noon."

Elijah opened the door, and everybody helped to finish loading the wagon. A little before one in the afternoon. They were ready to leave. Jasmine and Naomi climbed into their wagon. Mama Julia, Josephine, and little Caleb climbed into Elijah's wagon. Ran and Risby stood there looking all teary eyed.

"Ah hate ta see ya go," Ran said.

"It sho ain't gon' be da same without y'all," Risby said.

"Ah's gon' miss y'all too," Elijah said emotionally, " O'm gon' miss dis land. Ah was born 'round heah. Ah growed up 'round heah. Always figured Ah was gon' return to da ground heah, but Ah guess God got somethin' better up da road fuh me."

"Where y'all gon' go?" Ran asked.

"Oh, Ah don't know," Elijah said, "We'll jes' get on da road, and see where it takes us.

"Ah hear Tennessee is nice. You can own farmland there," Risby said.

"Out west is better. Ah hear all kinds of oppurtunity is out dere," Ran said.

"Well, we'll see," Elijah said, "We best be movin' on now. Ain't a whole lot of daylight ahead of us."

"Ah's gon' truly miss ya," Ran said one last time.

Elijah hugged Ran and Risby. They had been through a great deal together. It was an emotional moment. Elijah climbed onto his wagon. He raised the reigns and struck down. The team of mules began to move. Everyone said bye, as they started to move out. Ran and Risby watched them ride out of sight. Both of them would live quiet and peaceful lives there on out. They would never cross paths with Elijah again.

On his horse, Micah moved up along side Elijah on the wagon. As they journeyed onward, they came upon a fork in the road. They halted there for a moment. Micah looked out at the fork in the road. For some reason that he did not know, Micah began to reflect on what Elijah said to him earlier, about trusting in himself, or trusting in God.

Elijah looked at Micah serenely. "Which road, Micah?"

Strange Elijah should ask him that, Micah thought. He slowly turned his head to look at Elijah, feeling Elijah was asking him much more than simply which road they should travel. Whether it was true or not, Micah felt Elijah was asking him if he intended to continue trusting in himself, or was he going to trust in the wisdom of God. Micah looked down the two roads once more in deep thought on the matter. Again, Micah heard the meek voice of his brother call to him.

"Which road?"